Of Our Own Device

M. K. South

Hope you'll enjoy my book.

MK South

For Teddy for whom love is all that matters.

Acknowledgements.

I'd like to express my deepest gratitude to Kim and Julie for their generosity, to my sister An for her straightforward critique and encouragements when I had doubts, and to Teddy for his loving support of me in all I do.

I would also like to thank all the readers of the 'beta version' of this novel and their unfailingly enthusiastic comments which carried me through while it was in the making.

This undertaking wouldn't have been possible without you all!

Contents

"Love is a striking example of how little reality means to us."

Marcel Proust, *In Search Of Lost Time*

PART I - A RELUCTANT SPY

Chapter 1

The second act of *Evgenii Onegin* was nearing the end. Without turning his head, Jack skewed his eyes at his company for tonight, a visiting jazz diva from Chicago. She looked mesmerized, probably as much by the handsome Russian tenor who played Lensky as by the aria he was singing.

Nine minutes.

From his seat at the end of the second row in the amphitheater, Jack could see half of the stalls, but most importantly, the courier in row fifteen, the last seat on the right. He was doing good: unremarkable in his dark-framed glasses and camel-colored blazer, motionless, eyes glued to the stage. Like everybody else in the audience, much of whom were foreigners. The rest were from all over the Soviet Union and for them, attending a performance at the Bolshoi was as sacrosanct as a visit to the White House was for an American on a trip to Washington. Especially when the show was Tchaikovsky's *Evgenii Onegin*. And never mind that it was performed by a guest ensemble from Leningrad— Bolshoi Theater was the place one had to visit while in Moscow.

Jack cut a glance to the other side of the amphitheater. William and his wife were in the first row, both looking engrossed in the opera. But Jack knew he didn't need to worry. He was covered.

Seven and a half minutes.

The courier rose from his chair and tiptoed to the nearest side exit.

Five.

The stalls, the amphitheater and dress circles in front were still, no one else seemed to be following the courier out. William leaned in and whispered something in his wife's ear. She nodded. All clear on Jack's side of the audience too.

Two.

On the stage, Onegin arrived at the duel scene and would soon start his haunting duet with Lensky.

Jack leaned in to whisper in his date's ear. "Connie, I need to go out... to the gents." He grinned sheepishly at her arched eyebrows. "Sorry. I'll be back... Or will wait for you by the door."

She glared at him, shrugged and turned back to the stage. The Lensky-Onegin duet wasn't something keen musicians like her wished to miss.

Just as Jack had thought. He threw a last glance at William, stood up quietly, bending forward to mask his height, and slipped through the side exit.

The narrow, curving corridor with antique brass-and-crystal lamps on the wall was empty. And so was the hall, exquisitely decorated with bas-reliefs, frescoes on the vaulted ceiling and brightly lit by three majestic chandeliers.

However, when Jack stepped onto the marble U-shaped double staircase, he caught a glimpse of a man walking down the last flight of stairs—tall, lean and blond; dark slacks and pullover.

Shit. He could swear no one else had left the audience after the courier. William had given him an "all clear" signal too. So either this person had sat in one of the few seats outside of Jack's and William's lines of vision—the one percent chance they had resolved to take—or he hadn't been in the auditorium at all.

Which meant he might not be a spectator.

Which meant he might be one of the KGB surveillance squad.

Dammit! What now?

Think, Smith. Think!

He couldn't turn back to the auditorium, shouldn't: doubtless there were many eyes here, watching him, watching all foreigners who might behave suspiciously. Usually, he wouldn't hesitate to behave oddly, as if acting on the spur of the moment. It was part of his elaborate alternative cover. But not today, not on a collection operation. Even if it was a dry run. Today he must stick to the plan, to the minute, as though this were a real op.

OK, so... If he'd just go into the toilet and take a leak, there was no way the tails could link him with the courier, right? Worse came to worst, he wouldn't be able to collect the dead drop. But then they would know for sure whether the KGB had singled him out, or that his deep cover had held so far. It was a win-win, one way or the other. Jack hoped he would be able to collect though.

He swiftly descended the carpeted stairs, heading to the men's rooms on the ground floor—just someone desperate to relieve himself. As he reached the bottom of the staircase, the courier emerged from the corridor leading to the toilets and started ascending on the other side. His eyes skimmed over Jack, a polite but blank expression on his face. He didn't know Jack; for him the deaddrop op was for real.

When Jack opened the door to the men's room, the tall blond man was standing at one of the urinals. He was young, no more than twenty-one, twenty-two, judging the profile of his face. A bit young for a KGB operative. And his neatly combed hair was too long. Nah, not KGB... Too eye-catching with that body—lean, muscled and lithe at the same time. Especially in that close-fitting navy blue pullover and the dark gray slacks, snug around the narrow hips.

As if he had heard Jack's thoughts, the youth whipped his head around and glared at him. Then just as abruptly, he turned away and zipped up.

Jack walked quickly into the furthest stall, locked the door and started noisily undoing his belt. He heard the steps, then the water running into the washstand. Then the men's room door opened, then closed softly and silence fell. He waited for five minutes, walked out of the stall and lingered by the washstand for another two. Still nothing. He slipped into the stall where the deaddrop was and locked the door. Another three uneventful minutes passed before Jack stepped onto the toilet bowl and collected the item left by the courier—a matchbox in a clear plastic bag glued to the inside of the cistern high on the wall. He flushed the plastic bag in the toilet, slipped the matchbox into the inside pocket of his jacket and exhaled sharply. Done.

And he was still in the clear.

It had been four months since Jack was transferred to Moscow to replace one of the junior staffers in the office of the Cultural Affairs Officer at the Embassy. The position was a clean slot that had never been used by the CIA before, and the Soviet/East European—or SE—Division had worked hard to secure it for someone like him, a rookie without a track record *and* with an alternative cover.

Unlike other case officers who could easily blend into any environment, any crowd, Jack's whole appearance went against the fundamental rule of anonymity imperative for field officers: six feet tall and brawny, with a shock of chestnut hair, striking, bright blue eyes and a broad, goofy grin that lit up his whole face, he was a man people noticed immediately. Only his name was ordinary. In fact, it sounded like too obvious an alias: Jack Smith. His classmates and even a few instructors at the Farm, the training facility at Camp Peary, Virginia, used to joke about it. Some of them hadn't even tried to hide their skepticism about his suitability for the job.

However, high and continual visibility was the main idea behind the new tactic to be tested: those placed under this alternative deep cover were supposed to attract attention to themselves from the get go and maintain it with their behavior at all times. The objective was to be categorized by the enemy's counter intelligence services as someone not to be taken seriously and therefore not worth wasting resources on. This was how Joe Coburn, SE Division's chief of clandestine operations, planned to beat the suffocating, around the clock surveillance the KGB put on his case officers with known or suspected covers. This was how he had decided to plant two of his staffers behind the Iron Curtain, and one of the two rookies selected to test the new approach had happened to be Jack.

Thus, a year into his overt job as an assistant cultural affairs officer at the US Mission in Frankfurt, Jack was summoned to HQ and instructed to pack his bags to be shipped to Moscow.

On March 1st, 1985, Jack landed at Sheremetyevo Airport.

* * *

It started drizzling again, and the traffic was infuriating. It always was in downtown Moscow when it rained; or worse, snowed. He should have taken the Metro and left his car at the diplomatic compound where he lived. But Jack enjoyed driving his blue and white Mustang convertible. A lot! Even secondhand, acquired and transported from West Berlin, the car was way above Jack's personal budget and aspiration—had it not been for the Agency's special allowance he could have never afforded it. But it was part of his meticulously crafted identity (a spy in a flashy car? Surely not, unless he was James Bond!), together with his job, his hobbies, his pursuits. Everything that made up his life, for as long as he was on this deep cover posting. And that was okay with Jack. Especially the Mustang. So he drove it whenever he could, even if it meant that he had to fight his way through erratically merging and parting flow of sturdy, mostly old and dirty Soviet-made cars, driven by hurried and frustrated drivers, mostly men.

The Russians.

They turned out to be not entirely what Jack had been taught about them. Even after the month-long, twenty-four/seven, immersion course at the Army's Russian Institute in Garmisch, Germany, he still hadn't quite deciphered them. There was something about them that he couldn't put a finger on.

But hey, he'd just been here for four months, right? What he could do was make more friends with locals. Part of his job anyway, and the part that had always come easy to Jack. Sometimes it surprised him how easy it was for him to make quick friends with people — something to do with his smile, he figured, his easy banter and his willingness to make a fool of himself to make them laugh. More often than not, they would soon conclude that Jack was their best friend. He never dissuaded any of them.

It took him a while to find an empty spot amongst the non-Russian made vehicles with red diplomatic plates on the narrow street behind the Embassy. He locked the car and hurried towards the back gate, navigating around the puddles on the potholed sidewalk, keeping clear of the rainwater that poured from the roofs in long silver strings.

"Hey, Jack. Have a late night? How was she?" The marine at the gate winked at Jack as he waved him through.

Jack grinned, zipped his thumb and forefinger across his mouth and walked through the full-height turnstile.

A mile and a half from Red Square, the US Embassy was a Stalinist neoclassical building clad in yellow stucco and generously adorned with obelisks, pedestals and thick cornices. Jack thought it was not entirely different from the massive nineteenth-century buildings of downtown Washington D.C. Made him feel like home… Well, sort of.

And even more so inside the compound, with all Americans milling around — diplomats, secretaries, security and support personnel, contractors, engineers and Seabees from the Navy's construction corps who were renovating the old chancery building. Lately, there had also been a steady flow of visitors of various designations, from different government agencies. Jack found his way through the busy courtyard, smiling broadly, tossing off heys, and what's-ups and catch-up-laters left and right.

As he entered the central, office part of the building, Jack stopped to chat with a girl from the visa office whom he had taken out for a ride in his Mustang a couple of times. She wanted to know if he was free the coming Saturday. When Jack pleaded guilty that he wouldn't, Katia was upset. But she quickly came around when he offered to bring her goodies from Helsinki where he was planning ongoing this weekend.

"Oh, Jack, you're so sweet!" She was all smiles again. "I'll give you a small list, alright? It won't be very long, I promise!"

"Alright… Listen, Katiusha, I need to run. I'm sooo late."

"Of course, Jack, go. See you later in the canteen?"

Jack gave her a wave and another toothy grin and hurried towards the elevators.

The tiny office he shared with one of the other six USIA staffers was located on the sixth floor. It was one of the Embassy's "top floors" where all sensitive reporting was generated and transmitted — political, economic, military, consular, analysis and assumptions, rumors and hearsay; the State Department's, Pentagon's, CIA's, FBI's, NSA's and God only knew who else. These floors were accessible only via a bulletproof metal door located on the last, ninth floor. No Russian had ever set foot through this door, Jack was told by the security officer who had given him the mandatory briefing on his first day of arrival in Moscow.

Jack stepped out of the plywood-paneled elevator, fumbled inside his shoulder bag, looking for his ID badge.

"It's okay, Jack. Come on in." One of the marines at the door, a youngster fresh out of school, waved him in. "You are late today."

"No problem, Frank, I got it. Don't want you guys getting in trouble." Jack flashed the badge and a grin at the kid and complained, "Bloody traffic! I hate it when it's raining here."

"Better than no traffic whatsoever." The other marine swore under his breath. He was sitting behind a tiny station tucked in the corner on the side of the metal door and didn't even raise his head from whatever he was scrutinizing on the three monitors in front of him.

Jack nodded sympathetically and walked through the heavy door.

Their job was no fun: the thirty marines who guarded the chancery building and the Ambassador's residence, Spaso House, lived on the Embassy grounds. They were allowed to venture out in the city only a few times during their assignment, and only in groups of at least three. *And* they were not allowed to socialize with the locals, not even with the Embassy's local staff. No wonder they partied like there was no tomorrow every weekend at their little bar in the northern wing of the building where they were quartered.

Jack bounded down the internal staircase and hurried along the narrow, carpeted corridor to his office. He stopped at the door and fished the office key out of the bag. As a rule, the offices were locked at all times from either inside or outside, even the ones on the secured floors.

"Hey, Jack." His co-worker poked his head out from his tiny cubicle across when Jack walked into his own and sat down. "Thought you wouldn't be able to get up this morning."

"Morning, Glenn. The traffic's hellish today. Thought I'd never get here."

When Jack didn't elaborate, Glenn grunted skeptically, then said in a more serious tone, "William was looking for you twenty minutes ago. You'd better go see him. Like *now*. I suspect he isn't in a good mood today."

By virtue of his position as Jack's direct boss along both the overt and the covert lines, William Osbourne was one of the two people at the Embassy who knew Jack's real occupation; the other was the CIA's Chief of Moscow Station, the COS. During their very first meeting, William had told Jack bluntly that he had opposed Jack's selection for this posting and the only reason he was here been that the chief of ops had insisted on his candidacy. Jack had thought he caught a fleeting shadow of unhealthy curiosity in his new boss's eyes when William asked if he knew Joe Coburn well. Jack suppressed the urge to snap "what the fuck does *that* mean?" and said neutrally, "like everybody else?"

Thus, his association with William Osbourne had a peculiar dimension that went unnoticed by others, but made some people think that Jack was William Osbourne's protégé. Ha-di-ha!

Jack was still trying to find his way around the heavy-duty politics he had been plunged into since he joined the Company. It was different from what he'd been told about the job when he was recruited. It had started with the spy craft training, alright: on intel gathering and analysis, paramilitary and clandestine activities like surveillance detection and agent recruitment. However, since he actually began working, he had been spending most of his time writing reports—on whom he had met that day, what they had said, and how many times he had been followed. Not to mention trying to figure out the intricacies of relationships, positions, interests and priorities of his superiors and peers. It felt like everybody spent more time on the fringes of the job than actually doing it.

Granted he had participated in a couple of clandestine operations—one in West Berlin about a year ago and one in Moscow, a month after his arrival. Plus, he had ID'ed and assessed a candidate for recruitment, a diplomat from the Czechoslovak consulate in Leningrad. It was after this latter achievement that William's opinion about him seemed to have marginally improved—he had started cutting Jack some slack.

Jack stopped in front of the door with the nameplate saying "William L. Osbourne III, CAO" on it and knocked cautiously.

"Come in. It's unlocked," a voice from within called.

Mr. Osbourne obviously had his own rules. Or maybe he had just been waiting for Jack to report.

"Why, Jack, good of you to drop by this morning."

William didn't look up from whatever he was reading when Jack stepped into the room. The CAO was indeed not in the right mood, Jack knew it the moment he walked into his office.

"I'm sorry. The traffic was atrocious, and I stupidly took the car, instead of the Metro." Jack had figured out early on that his boss liked it when people admitted their foolishness rather than blamed it on circumstances, especially when Jack was doing the confessing.

William looked up from his papers, grunted and held his eyes over his black-rimmed glasses. "No problems with the singer, whatshername?"

Doh! Is this a diplomatic office or a fraternity dorm, for Christ's sake?

"Everything is fine. I delivered her to her hotel after the late dinner last night. Tim will pick her up at eleven and take her to Spaso House to meet with Mrs. Hart."

"Good... I hear she's already called the office this morning, asking for you. Said she needed an escort who spoke Russian."

Jack rolled his eyes and smiled apologetically.

"All right, sit down, Jack. I need you to take care of two things for me. First, the Foreign Minister's office called. Unfortunately, neither the Minister nor any of his deputies will be attending the July 4th reception tomorrow."

"Oh. Anything happened?"

"Probably... We've been told that Deputy Minister of *Culture* will attend instead."

"Deputy Minister of *Culture*?" Jack arched his eyebrows.

"Yep. Leonid Dmitrievich Novikov." William's upper lip curled slightly as he read the name on a document on his desk. "The man was appointed two months ago, out of nowhere. Probably another of Gorbachev's cronies. Ambassador Hart has asked me to take care of him at the reception… Now, we've also been informed that the Deputy Minister will be attending with his daughter."

"His *daughter*? Is this a new *glasnost*-themed protocol?"

"Maybe, who knows? So, I'd like you to *take care* of Miss Novikova at the reception. I know it's short notice and you won't have time to run her background. But I'm sure you'll be just fine playing it by ear."

"Are we sure she's the right material?" Jack said the last word under his breath.

"Don't worry. You won't have to baby-sit her, if that is your concern. According to the spokesperson, she's seventeen or eighteen. All right?… Good. Now the second thing. The upcoming Youth and Students Festival. I want you to attend all events with the American delegation. Especially those sponsored by the Sovs. Glenn and Steve will take care of the press. You and Bruce will take care of the delegates. There'll be around three hundred of them. Most with leftish inclinations. So start reading up," William said and mouthed "the files". "You know the drill."

"I'm on it."

"Good. Let me know if you need anything."

"I'd like to go to Helsinki next week, William. I'm running short on personal supplies. And if that's alright, I'd like to stay over the weekend… If there's nothing pressing, of course."

The CAO looked sternly at him, and for a moment Jack thought he would say no. His heart fell. But then William's face relaxed, and he nodded.

"All right, you can go and stay for a weekend… But first make sure that our guests are taken good care of tomorrow."

"Yes, of course, William. Thank you."

Jack was already turning the doorknob when the CAO asked, "By the way, how's the preparation for the physicists exchange program going? Anything of interest on the Berkeley team?"

Jack returned to the desk. "Nothing worth mentioning for now. But I'll need your help to get the materials on the Russian team. So far, we've been given only one name—Professor Volkonsky, Mikhail Alexandrovich, academician. The father of the nuclear winter theory, according to the Soviet textbooks."

"Volkonsky? I know the name. Well, besides the fact that it's the name of an old Russian patrician family." William Osbourne prided himself on being an expert on Russian history. "All right, I'll see what I can get." Jack was half way to the door when his boss added as an afterthought, "Oh, and by the way, good job last night."

Chapter 2

Awareness came to Jack in waves before his regular 7 a.m. alarm. He groaned inwardly, kept his eyes tightly shut, mentally trying to pull back the slipping away shreds of sleep. His hand was already on his morning glory, not yet in action, but soon to be.

His horniness had been a nuisance lately. He had thought that a bit of action with Connie the other night would give him some relief, buy him some time. It wasn't exactly what he needed, but had to be enough for a while. At least until his next trip out of the country. In the meantime, his hand was all he had. His hand and his phantom.

At some point in his futile struggle with himself, Jack's mind had taken pity on him and created a phantom. The only constant inhabitant of his secret world, the phantom accepted happily anything Jack wanted to do to it—took on any appearance he fancied, any name, any coloration. Once in a while, Jack would give it a face. Of someone he had come across, in real life or in a movie, whose chiseled face or hard, muscled body had stuck in his mind. However, those images were always transient: the face would eventually fade away; the contours of the body might stay a while longer. For over a year now, that had been all to indulge Jack's secret desire, the one he had never been able to will away, no matter how hard and how long he had tried.

Jack had had his first taste of the forbidden fruit at nineteen during his first year of station at the U.S. air base in Ramstein, Germany. He didn't like to remember his first... well, you couldn't call it a relationship even though it had lasted for three years—not when for the other party it was all about getting together for a couple of fucks once in a blue moon. Nonetheless, Jack had learned a lot from the man. Who had also helped him with the jobs, the ones Jack had now. But when Jack started thinking that his lover and mentor was his best friend, and maybe more, he told Jack that "men like them" should never have best friends. In fact, if Jack wanted to succeed the way he was, he had to learn to rely on himself alone. Be his own best friend if need be. Everything else—*everybody* else—was transient. Replaceable.

"Always think of yourself first, Jack. And by the way, get yourself a wife, boy. The sooner the better."

Jack picked up his stupid, broken heart and returned to his phantom. Like a true friend, it took him back without a word of reproach.

After the army, Jack tried to date girls. However, the dates never lasted, as they required more heterosexual sex than he could force himself to give. Finally, during his third year at Cal State University, he met a girl he liked and thought he could live with. Traditional and always impeccably attired, Carmen was kind to Jack, almost maternal. She took charge of his Spartan studio apartment and most of his needs, spending most of her time at his place, even though she lived with a cousin in a brand new three-bedroom house by the beach.

Dating Carmen was easy, mostly thanks to her old-fashioned ways. However, their formal engagement didn't survive the planned twelve months: the morning after the graduation party, half-asleep and still hazy from gallons of booze consumed the night before, Jack tried to have sex with her... the wrong way. By breakfast, Carmen had gathered up her belongings, handed Jack back his spare key and asked him not to call her again, ever. Because she wanted a proper, decent husband and father for her children, "not a... a deviant". Her tone was cold, her demeanor prim and composed: little Carmen knew exactly what she wanted. Jack could neither blame her nor hate her for that—he didn't know exactly what he wanted back then. Maybe not even now...

Jack sighed and started stroking himself, the friction bringing relief but not much in the way of true pleasure. He was glad he had asked for a trip to Helsinki. He was going to stay there over the weekend and get what he desperately needed. Two days in Helsinki would keep him going for another few months until his home leave was due. Then he would find a way to make it up for himself, preparing to return to Moscow in winter. December was the time when most of the Embassy staff and their families headed back home for holidays. Jack didn't need to go home for Christmas, didn't have a "home". Ever since his Ma had passed away and his father... Never mind his father...

The more Jack thought about it, the more a weekend in Helsinki sounded like the best plan ever: besides getting laid, he would be able to watch the much advertised LiveAid concert for Africa on Finnish television too—uncensored, unlike everything here in this goddamn country. He would hole up with whoever it would be in a hotel room where they'd have sex, drink beer and watch the concert. Sex, beer and rock'n'roll.

Lots of sex and *lots* of rock'n rockers.

Rockers?? Where the hell is *that* coming from?

Whatever...

Jack gave himself a few hard pulls and came without a sound.

Once in a while, he wished he could also do something about the empty spot in the middle of his chest. But the next moment, he'd start berating himself.

You selfish bastard, nothing is enough for you, huh? Look how far you've come in nine years! You were nothing, just another clueless, penniless redneck, with no life nor prospects. And look at you now!

A junior officer with the USIA (okay, so that was who he was to most people around him, including his USIA colleagues), stationed at the American Embassy in Moscow; a job, with a salary he had never dared dream of having; a life, the type he had only seen in movies. An American Dream kind of life—well, sort of. Not exactly like those you read about in books or see in movies, but one nonetheless. Jack's very own.

What more do you want, Smith? Get a grip and make the best of it, whatever comes your way. It's all been good, hasn't it? It's all been good...

Jack opened his eyes, swung his feet off the bed and trudged barefoot to the bathroom.

* * *

As he was one of the diplomatic staff who spoke Russian, and because he was entrusted with taking care of Ms. Connie Love, the visiting jazz singer, Jack had been asked to be at Ambassador Hart's residence an hour before others. Thank God, Spaso House was only a brisk ten-minute walk from the Embassy. It was even luckier that it had stopped raining at noon, so Jack didn't have to worry about parking and getting his brand new tuxedo wet.

His next worry, as soon as he arrived, was how to divert Connie's attention to other people, including Mrs. Hart, who happened to be the singer's big fan. That was what occupied Jack until the first guests started arriving. With an apologetic smile, he asked her to excuse him to attend to his other, far less enjoyable responsibilities that he was not in a position to ignore. Reluctantly, she let him go. But not before making him promise to come see her after the reception.

Jack was halfway down the marble staircase when he noticed Amanda in the hall below, a few steps ahead of her husband. Twenty-five years his junior, svelte, British-born Amanda Plante was Mike Demidoff's third wife and a freelance columnist on the Soviet art and music scenes. The couple had a rather unconventional marriage: Mike, the resident correspondent for the US News and World Report, chose not to notice his wife's barely veiled flirting with Jack. Or with other men, for that matter.

Jack had happened to sit next to her during his first visit to the Bolshoi Theater two months earlier. She had invited him for lunch the next day and they had been seeing each other often since—for drinks, lunches and a couple of dinners at her and Mike's place.

Despite their quick and easy friendship, Amanda remained a bit of an enigma. In public, she flirted with Jack shamelessly, like she was on mission. However, twice when they found themselves in circumstances where sex was inevitable, both were drunk—or pretended to be—enough to end up sleeping it off at the opposite sides of the bed. They didn't talk about it afterwards, but continued their flirty escapades. It suited Jack just fine: a fling with somebody else's wife was a fine touch to his cover that his bosses endorsed.

However, parading his "relationship" with Amanda for the benefit of his KGB observers was one thing. Having Amanda around while working on a wild card assignment *and* having an aging diva after a piece of his ass was a different thing altogether. Jack put on his best smile and descended the stairs towards her.

"Good evening, Amanda. You look absolutely stunning today."

She was indeed, in a little sleeveless black dress. She gave him an once-over, smiled sweetly and said, her voice low, "I can say the same thing about you, sunshine."

"Mandy, I'm working tonight, okay?" Jack whispered, his eyes already on her husband, who was coming up behind her. "So, please... Hey, Mike. How are you?" He thrust his hand out to Mike. "I'm telling Amanda here that I envy you. Why is that that you, the old guard, gotta have the best of deals—women, jobs, houses?"

"Jack. Wait until you are my age and you will get your share. With jobs and houses, that is. I wouldn't complain about women if I were you." The good humor of Mike's smile didn't reach his eyes.

Amanda slapped her husband's arm playfully. "Tsk-tsk, boys, I'm still here. If you're going to continue down this path, I shall leave you to it and go to say hello to Mrs. Hart." She took three quick steps up, then whirled around. "By the way, Jack, did I mention that you looked absolutely delicious in a tux?" She flashed a juicy-red-lipped smile and sashayed up the stairs.

"She can be a handful, can't she?" Jack said, smiling sheepishly. "But I still envy you, Mike."

"You said it, Jack." Mike was gazing after his young wife, still holding up the smile, but suddenly he looked tired and resigned.

They gossiped on the latest in the local politics for a couple of minutes before Mike excused himself and followed his wife to the ballroom upstairs.

Jack continued downstairs. He was heading to the men's room when someone called out to him, "Jack, the Russians have arrived."

"Be right there," he said over the shoulder, quickly walked in to the toilet and closed the door.

He hoped he would survive tonight, baby-sitting an ageing American jazz diva *and* a Russian teenage *nomenklatura* girl, at the same time trying not to be too obvious with his tasks to a sharp-tongued British columnist. This sounded worse than trying to break out from heavy surveillance on an operational run. Was it in his job description and he had missed it?

Lara Novikova turned out to be not what Jack had expected. For starters, she looked older than seventeen; more like nineteen or even twenty. And pretty: high cheekbones, translucent skin, large gray-green eyes, full-lipped sensual mouth. Stately, with her sandy hair swept up in a formal coiffure, attired in a high-collared blouse and floor length skirt. And she had an air of entitlement about her that Jack hadn't seen in other Russians so far.

After accepting Lara's profuse compliments about his Russian, he showed her around the grand ballroom, introduced her to senior Embassy officers and some guests he knew, including Mike and Amanda. Then he took her to the long buffet lined with a battery of bottles of Coca-Cola, American whiskey, Finnish vodka and cartons of Marlboros. Only after they sat down in the corner, sipping on their Cokes, did Jack learn that Lara was a fourth year student at GITIS, the State Institute of Theater Arts, and already acting in an experimental theater. She offered to invite Jack to a musical they were staging. He then learned that she loved American movies and her current favorite actor was—

"Robert Redford," Jack offered helpfully, recalling the rerun of The Great Gatsby in Moscow cinemas last month.

"The Great Gatsby? Him, too. But I meant another one. I saw an old film with him last week at the Actor's House. Rock Hudson. You know him, *da*? Isn't he so absolutely manly?"

Jack's grin never faltered but his heart skipped a beat at the mention of Rock Hudson. He knew the actor alright, thought he was gorgeous, too. But he had also heard rumors about Mr. Hudson's unconventional choice of sex partners. Why had this Russian girl brought him up with Jack?

"I see. So you like the old school. Anyone younger than Rock Hudson and Robert Redford that you like?" He flashed his dimples at her.

"Are you fishing for compliments?" She smiled indulgently, touched his sleeve briefly with her fingers. "*Nu kharasho*, alright, I like you too, Jack. You have beautiful eyes. I've never seen anyone with the eyes of such an amazing blue." She peered squarely into his eyes and continued on one breath, "As for American actresses, the one I absolutely adore is Liza Minnelli. You know the film Cabaret, *da*? Do you like it? We're staging the musical at my Institute and I'm playing the part of Sally Bowles."

Shit, what is this?

Or maybe he is being paranoid?

"Is *this* kind of show permitted here now?" Jack acted up surprise. "With characters of, um, non-standard orientation?"

"You mean the role of Brian Roberts? That he is *goluboy*... uh, homosexual?" she whispered.

"I thought he was bi-sexual," Jack whispered back.

Christ, it was his first engagement that could lead to potential information sources and where was this all going? He was being framed. Wasn't he? It looked like it: a Russian beauty, who shared his interests, alluding to his other, secret interests. A classic entrapment scenario, exactly what they had taught him at the Farm.

"What difference does it make?" Lara shrugged. "It's not acceptable here, anyway. So, unfortunately, we had to modify it: Brian Roberts is normal. I mean a regular man in our show... A shame!" She sounded genuinely disappointed.

But then, she was an actress. A Russian on top of it all.

* * *

"You can't trust the Sovs. Can't befriend them. If they are not working directly for the KGB, then they are informers. Or they will be forced to inform the moment the KGB finds out about your association with them. They always—I repeat, always—find a way to make your Ruskie friends and contacts report on you."

Their Chief Instructor at the Farm, a retired field operative, was adamant about the KGB, informers and entrapments. Rumors were that he had been burnt and kicked out of the USSR back in early sixties. The story Jack had heard involved a Russian woman, so the man's experience was obviously firsthand. But what about Soviet dissidents and defectors? Jack didn't ask—you don't gain anything arguing with old birds. They didn't even encourage academic debates. And it was just fine by Jack: he preferred proponents to opponents, especially those who supported him and helped him to move forward, toward his ultimate goal. Which he kept to himself, too.

* * *

Ms. Love's performance was a mixed success. The Western block guests were raving and wouldn't let her go; the third-world diplomats, led by the Soviets, clapped half-heartedly with dutiful smiles on their bored faces, surreptitiously cutting longing glances towards the door to the ballroom. There, on long tables along one wall, draped in the Union Jacks, a buffet was laid out, with all the booze acquired for the occasion from Finland and West Germany. Introduced by Comrade Gorbachev in May, the Soviet "Prohibition" was having the same effect in Russia as the one half a century ago in America: people just drank more whenever they had a chance and looked for those chances with the resolve of people about to die of thirst, determined to find a spring.

"Have you enjoyed it, Lara?" asked Jack, clapping enthusiastically.

Sitting with her in the second row, he avoided looking at the stage, from where Connie had been shooting poisonous glares at him. As for Amanda, he had given up dodging her sarcastic remarks every time she brushed by.

"She is fabulous!" Lara exhaled as if she had been holding her breath for the entire performance. "Jack, introduce me to her."

Oh, no! You won't like it, girl.

"I don't know, Lara. Your father's entourage—how to put it?—did not make her feel appreciated. She may feel a little let down, you know."

"They're a bunch of *derevenstchina*, peasants. My father included." She threw a quick, "whatever" glance to where her father sat in the first row. "Besides, who in their right mind would put a concert right before *zastolie*—vodka and good food? What do you expect?"

"That's the protocol, Lara," Jack said apologetically.

"What a nonsense! Your ambassador should have let her perform after at least the first case of whiskey. *Then* she'd have been their favorite American singer."

"But—"

"She could have even been invited to sing at the Palace of Congress in Kremlin. Try it next time. Seriously."

"Alright, I'll tell Ambassador and Mrs. Hart."

"Please do." A know-it-all smile was curling her pretty lips. Then her expression changed, and she tugged at his arm. "Nu, Jack, could you introduce me to Ms. Love? *Pozhalusta*, please!" Now her eyes were like those of a child begging for a new toy in a shop window.

"Alright. But you should be prepared for a less than warm welcome."

He led her to the small sitting room along the corridor set up as the singer's dressing room, knocked cautiously on the door, steeling himself for a potentially grouchy reception.

"Come in." Connie's voice sounded guarded.

She was alone in the dressing room. Great, he could do without witnesses for what he suspected awaited them. Jack put on The Smile—eyes, teeth, dimples and all. Back at the Farm, Ms. Hall, their profiling instructor, had told him that women would kill for that smile.

"Connie, I'd like to introduce Miss Lara Novi—"

"What d'you want, Jack?" Connie twisted from the dressing table to face him, the deep purple, embroidered robe slipping from her shoulders. "To impress your Russian pussy? Not at my expense, pretty boy."

Ouch!

Jack toned down his smile. "Connie, I'm just doing my job... I mean now," he added quickly, catching a glint of wrath in her heavily kohled eyes. He dropped his voice half an octave. "C'mon, Connie, it was different with you, the other day. Honest to God! It was something... wasn't it? Haven't had that for a long while." That much was true. At least there was one thing he didn't have to lie to her about.

Connie glared at him for what seemed like an eternity, then her scrunched mouth softened. "Alright, Jack, we'll talk about it later… So, whatshername, you sayin'—"

"My name is Lara Novikova," Lara declared in thickly accented English from the doorway where she had been standing, watching the exchange, her expression impassive. She stepped up, inserting herself between them. "Verry khappy to meet you. You are grreht sin-gherr." She grinned at the oh-shit looks on Jack and Connie's faces and switched to Russian. "Don't worry. My English isn't good enough to understand everything you said." She bobbed her head at Connie, still smiling, then turned to Jack. "Please tell her I'm the sharing type. I believe everybody deserves to get the best they can. Anything they want badly enough."

Jack translated it dutifully, mentally kicking himself—he had spent two hours with her and hadn't asked if she spoke English. Dimwit! He was so fucked if someone knew.

Connie had nothing to say in response to the girl's thinly veiled allusion and the ensuing short conversation ended on a friendly note. She, however, turned down Lara's invitation to come see her performing in a student concert at the Moscow State University, MGU.

Lara wasn't upset, instead made Jack promise to come. "*After* sorting things out with Ms. Love, of course," she murmured, looking like a cat that had just had a bowl of cream.

The rest of the evening was rather uneventful in comparison. Jack and Lara spent most of it drinking the sweet Soviet champagne that locals favored, eating canapés and chatting about movies and music and the cultural life in Moscow. Lara offered to introduce him to the famous Soviet actors and writers she knew—she would invite him to one of the Sunday gatherings her mother loved to organize at their *dacha*. If Jack was interested that is.

Jack was interested, of course. He hoped William would be pleased with the leads generated from this last minute assignment.

By the time he saw Lara and her father off, most of the guests, from both Eastern and Western blocs, were in a state where foreign diplomacy consisted of hearty slaps on the backs and slightly slurred, almost sincere toasts to friendship and the prosperity of the other camp.

Chapter 3

They learned what had happened at the Ministry of Foreign Affairs the next day.

After twenty-eight years as the Minister of Foreign Affairs of the USSR, Andrey Gromyko, nicknamed "Mr. Nyet" by the West, had been replaced by a little-known functionary from the Georgian Soviet Socialist Republic, Eduard Shevardnadze. Since Gorbachev was elected in March to lead the Communist Party of the Soviet Union, Gromyko's dismissal was the third bombshell he had dropped, following the nationwide anti-alcohol campaign and his speech in Leningrad, where he had admitted that the Soviet economy was slowing down.

The news raised eyebrows on the top floors of the Embassy and generated a whirlwind of activity: urgent meetings, quick analysis—of how the news had been worded and the reactions to it, both officially and from people on the street—followed by a flood of cables to HQ. Officers who spoke Russian were encouraged to spend most of their time reading local newspapers, observing and meeting with their local friends and contacts.

It suited Jack just fine. In fact, mingling with people was the part of the job that he enjoyed the most. Including *these* people, most of them stern at first, uncompromising and in your face. Okay, so they were unsmiling and rude at times. But so were most of the cowboys Jack had known back on the barren plains of Wyoming. It was just life—their life. The one he had been lucky to escape.

The truth was, under their rough veneer Jack recognized the stamp of resignation. Then, once in a while, in some younger eyes, he would see a glimmer of hope and defiance. It struck too close to his heart, left him wanting to make allowances. Even to the grim faced *militsia* guards in gray uniforms outside the Embassy and in front of his apartment block—they were just trying their best to do their jobs, to live their live, maybe the only way they knew how.

Lara called that night. She instructed him to meet her the next day at the MGU's main entrance, and explained where he should leave his car—he would drive his car, *da?* They could go out after the concert. "We'll find something interesting to do afterwards," she promised before bidding him sweet dreams.

That night the phantom didn't visit Jack. He felt restless, but the edginess also subdued his yearning, leaving it smoldering somewhere deep inside, its warmth almost soothing.

However, the next morning the restlessness returned with vengeance, but now there was a new shade to it—anticipation. He didn't know for what, just felt that something was about to happen. Something big. Life changing.

Gorbachev is going to declare the end of Cold War.

Yeah, right!

He plodded to the kitchen, had his morning mug of coffee without sitting down, left his ham sandwich untouched on the plate. Then he dived head on into his weekend chores. As a haunting tune by the Eagles streamed from the cassette player, a wave of anxiousness rushed over him again.

Are you falling for a girl, Smith? That would be the first.

Nah, it couldn't be, he knew it so well by now. It was probably this song that he had been playing over and over again.

"You know the Queen of Hearts is always your best bet. But you only want the ones that you can't get…"

He turned off the player and switched the TV on, upped the volume, trying to drown his restlessness in the sounds of the language, whose rolling and shushing consonants were oddly soothing to his ear.

The weekend traffic was light and Jack arrived at MGU's main building on Lenin Hills earlier than planned. He lingered at the parking area on the side street, gazing up at the dark silhouette of the giant Stalinist building against the deep blue sky, its gilded, star-topped spire straining to poke cotton-candy clouds that floated idly by.

Even on a Saturday afternoon, the place was bustling. Jack paused on the top of the vast staircase and lit up a cigarette, taking in the panorama of the architectural complex around the University Square.

The Soviets had surely mastered the concept of "grand". But then, while the skyscrapers in Los Angeles and New York, which Jack had briefly visited once, had made him feel small and insignificant, this massive compound somehow, inexplicably made you feel inspired to be part of its universe. A ploy of the Soviet propaganda? May well be…

"Jack, there you are! Why aren't you coming in? Come, I need to go back to start preparing for the concert."

Lara's admonition shook him out of his reverie. He turned around to meet her, a ready smile on his face. "Sorry, I was just having a smoke. How are you, Lara? You look different today… Lovely!"

She did look different: younger and eager, hair pulled back in a ponytail, dressed in a short, stonewashed denim jacket over a flowery dress that ended way above her knees, and a pair of high-heel sandals. Sexy, that was how she looked. Jack appreciated women's beauty, even if it did nothing more to him than that.

"You like it?" Lara beamed, gestured at her trendy outfit, the sign of status in this country of mostly drab colors and unstylish clothing. "This is more me, not how I was the day we first met. That was how I'm *supposed* to be. According to my father. My father and I have a deal: if he lets me be who *I* want, I can be what *he* wants me to be from time to time. Good deal, *da*? But let's go in now. We will talk about me later."

She took him to the checkpoint inside the row of four gigantic doors. A uniformed militiaman checked their guest passes, gave Jack a hard stare before waving them through. He followed Lara along a series of corridors, tall stairs leading up and then down, connecting hallways with alabaster columns and cathedral-like ceilings. The Russians called MGU "the Temple of Sciences". Now he understood what they meant, could even feel it—in awe and enlightened at the same time.

After the fifth turn and another marble staircase, Lara stopped in front of a small crowd of people waiting to get through the doors of what looked like a concert-hall size auditorium.

"I'll leave you here for now. I have to go backstage to prepare." She put a hand on his arm. "Here's your invitation. Your seat is on the right side, at the end of the second row. I'll join you when I'm done with my numbers, *kharasho?*"

A nimble man in his late thirties with a haggard face framed by uncombed dark hair flew up the stairs and passed by in haste. "Larachka, are you coming?" he called out. "You aren't even dressed up. Hurry up, dear! Your suitors will wait for you, don't you worry!"

"I'm coming, coming, Viktor Viktorovich!" She beamed after the man, then turned to Jack. "That's our director, from my institute. He's amazing! I will introduce you to him... See you later, Jack?" She gazed into his eyes, a hint of promise in her smile, and flitted away after her director.

Jack followed the last spectators into the auditorium, slipped into his place and steeled himself for a hearty dose of Soviet propaganda.

Contrary to his expectations, the student concert wasn't half bad. The program had obviously been prepared with a foreign audience in mind because a third of it was comprised of mostly old American and British hits. Lara sang two Russian songs Jack had heard before and two of Liza Minnelli's numbers—Cabaret and New York New York. She was good, even though her voice was nowhere near Liza's.

However, what arrested Jack's attention halfway through the concert and never let go was a student band called *Krylia*, Wings. When its five members came out on the stage, Jack's eyes zeroed in on the guitarist in the center who later turned out to be the band's lead singer.

It was the tall guy from the men's room in the Bolshoi.

Except today, he looked like a rocker: uncombed blond curls hiding half of his face, leather bands on the wrists, black t-shirt and stonewashed jeans, frayed at the edges, snug on the hips and thighs. Jack couldn't tear his gaze away from him for the entire performance.

The band's repertoire consisted of vaguely familiar Russian and French songs, and covers of English ones he knew well. When he wasn't singing, only playing his guitar, the front man kept his lips pressed tightly together, his mouth a straight line. But when he sang... Hell, the guy had some voice, there was no two ways about it. What struck Jack most was his perfect English, with virtually no trace of an accent.

Jack's first thought was it was too much of a coincidence to run into someone twice in four days in a city as large as Moscow—someone he didn't know, someone like *this*. But the boy looked even younger than at the theater and there was this air about him... Defiance maybe?

Nah, not KGB.

Lara joined him in the audience during the intermission. She waved and exchanged a few words with young people sitting on the row behind them, said thanks and smiled politely to the compliments of their neighbors, before settling down next to Jack.

"So, did you like it?"

"Oh yes, Lara. You were great! And I love the Liza Minnelli's numbers. Excellent choice!"

She waved a dismissive hand. "I wish my English was better. I should be able to learn to speak it well. I'm an actress after all. Have you noticed how good Eton's English is?"

"Ethan?" Most Russians struggled to pronounce the diphthong "th".

"*Ee-tohn. Krylia*'s lead singer. He's so good, *da*? He could be a professional singer, you know. Instead, he's a physicist. You see, *our* physicists are multi-talented. They are geniuses! Eton definitely is," she said dreamily, like a smitten fan girl.

"Eton? What an interesting name... Is he Russian?" Jack asked casually.

"Of course he's Russian. Alright, *half* Russian. His father was American. That's why he has this name: a cross between your Ethan and our Anton. His full name is Eton May Volkonsky. But everybody calls him Eton Volkonsky."

Jack's radar pinged at the familiar surname.

Volkonsky? A physicist? He can't be Professor Volkonsky's son, can he? A little too young—what, twenty maybe? Twenty-one max. Unless Mikhail Alexandrovich Volkonsky married late. But hasn't Lara just said that his father's American. *Was* American? He would ask William to get him the Volkonsky file A-S-A-P.

"Volkonsky? Isn't that an old, aristocratic family name, as in Prince Volkonsky? One of the Decembrists?"

"Jack, you really know our history well, don't you?" Lara was smitten. "Yes, he is indeed from the house of the Princes Volkonsky, not that it matters much nowadays. But his grandfather is a prominent scientist. An academician. Eton has taken after him. And his mother is a well-known translator of English language literature."

"What about his father? You said he was an American."

"Oh yes, but he died when Eton was little. Eton doesn't talk about his father, so I don't know much about him. Except that he was a scientist. Maybe a physicist, too."

"So, is Eton one of your suitors, too?" Jack asked tersely, overplaying it a little to get her going on the topic.

"Jack! I didn't know you were a jealous type." She giggled. "He's a good friend of mine, not a suitor. And he has tons of admirers himself. Did you see the reaction of the audience? He's popular, our Eton."

The lights dimmed at that point and the band took the stage again, Eton in the center, barely looking at the audience.

Lara leaned in and whispered, "Do you want me to introduce you to him?"

Yes!!

"Why not? You're going to introduce me to all your friends anyway, aren't you?"

"*Kharasho*, Jack. I will. After the concert." She turned back to the stage, obviously pleased.

Jack didn't remember much of the rest of the concert. Except for the songs performed by *Krylia*. Well, by that boy, Eton, if he was to be completely honest: most of the songs were poignant, haunting and every time the guy sang, his delivery was so raw that it would leave Jack's insides tied in knots. He stole a glance at Lara, then at his neighbors on the other side. Their eyes were transfixed on the stage, faces emotional.

The concert was drawing to a close when Lara asked, out of the blue, "Do you like the *Eagles*?"

"Excuse me?"

"Eagles, the American band. Do you like them?"

What is this, for God's sake? How could she know what he listened to at home?

"Yes, I like the Eagles. Why?" he asked cautiously.

Lara smiled at him mysteriously. When the song ended, she stood up and breezed towards the side of the tall stage. Eton stepped out to kneel at the edge of the stage, leaning his long-limbed body forward. As she talked to him animatedly, he threw a quick glance in Jack's direction and nodded, his expression inscrutable.

He probably didn't recognize Jack. But then why should he? Jack was just someone he had run into in the gents at a theater a few days ago and briefly exchanged glances with. Today, Jack was someone in the audience, could easily have been one of the admirers, couldn't he?

Of that body? Yeah. And the voice... And overall, he doesn't look that bad: blond with dark eyes. In fact, he looks—

Lara sat down next to him, looking triumphant.

"What is it?" The effort it took him to keep his tone light surprised Jack.

"You'll see. You will *hear* shortly."

On the stage, after a short exchange with the other band members, Eton stepped up to the microphone.

"Our last song for tonight is at the request of lovely Lara Novikova, our future movie star." The young man's voice was unexpectedly deeper than when he sang, and throaty. "For her American guest, Jack. An Eagles' song... Hotel California."

Jack shivered. The audience erupted in a wave of happy cheers and applause. It was obviously a song they had heard before from this band and loved. Eton threw another quick glance in their general direction, poker-faced, and turned back to his band.

Arrogant bastard!

Oh, c'mon, the kid is just playing cool. Give him a break!

Fine.

But why had they chosen this song? There was absolutely no way they could know about *his* California, right? Nobody knew. Only his Ma, with whom he had shared his secret dream once, when he was ten. Only once. Because it only brought more sadness into her tired eyes. More than Jack could bear. So he never mentioned it again, not to her and not to anyone else. Nobody cared about Jack Smith's foolish dreams anyway, and his father even tried to beat them out of him. But Jack had stubbornly nurtured his dream, like a delicate potted flower hidden in a dark, cluttered attic, away from people's eyes. His own ranch. In California...

The three guitarists had started the intro when Lara turned to him again. "This is one of their best songs. Eton's best. You will like it," she said in a loud whisper, beaming.

"Thank you, Lara. It's very sweet of you," Jack said, dutifully tearing his eyes from the singer on the stage to smile at her.

He had already figured that the band was good, but *this*—this was almost as good as the Eagles themselves. When Eton started his solo, Jack's breath caught in his throat. The Russian singer's rendition was so intense that it left Jack motionless for its entire duration, gaping at the stage, letting out a shuddering breath only after the last guitar chords had died.

Christ, how in hell does he do *that*?

Jack stood up along with Lara and the students, applauding heartily, trying to hold his quivery smile steady. The younger crowd was ecstatic, jumping to their feet and cheering boisterously. The few older ones stood up cautiously, started creeping out of their places towards the aisles, clapping and smiling politely.

"Did you like it?"

Jack jumped a little and turned to Lara. She was watching him closely, trying to read his reaction. Her eyes were shining.

"Oh, yes. Thank you, Lara. It was amazing! Almost like the Eagles themselves."

"I think they are better. I've heard the record—we all have. Many times. And *we* think that even though *Krylia* will never be as good as the Eagles, our Eton sings this song better than *your* Don Henley. Don't you think so too?" she stated rather than asked.

"Yes, he's terrific, *your* Eton. I agree." Jack nodded, acceding readily.

He was rewarded with a benevolent smile. Then Lara pulled at his arm, motioning him to sit down. "Wait for me here. I need to catch them before they disappear." She pointed at the stage. "Let's go out for dinner tonight. All of us."

Jack nodded after her and sat down, watching as she made her swift progress towards the stage. The band was wrapping up instruments, still throwing smiles and acknowledgments to their friends in the audience as it thinned out. All except Eton. Absorbed in what he was doing, he looked like he lived in his own world. He stopped moving when Lara came up to him, listened to her with a shadow of a smile. He glanced at Jack, then his eyes lingered on the other side of the auditorium, nodding faintly while Lara spoke.

Jack inhaled deeply. He didn't realize he had been holding his breath since the beginning of Lara's conversation with her friend. He shifted his gaze in the direction Eton had just looked.

There was a group of seven young people, two girls and five boys, sitting and standing at the other end of the first three rows, chatting and laughing amongst themselves while watching the band pack up. Jack noticed that one of the girls, a round-faced brunette, was watching the stage more intently than the others, barely talking. She beamed with delight when she caught the singer's gaze lingering on her little group.

Lara returned and pulled at his arm. "We are going to a restaurant with Eton and his band. Let's go, Jack. We will wait for them in the hall. Meanwhile, I will introduce you to Viktor Viktorovich. He teaches acting at our institute. He is the director of that musical I told you we are staging. Cabaret, remember?"

Jack did. He was sure it would be interesting, maybe even useful, to meet a Soviet director who was staging an American musical that Jack thought rather sensitive for these people's mores. It should be interesting, shouldn't it? If only he could concentrate on it a little.

What is the matter with you today, Smith?

"Of course, Lara, I'd love to. Let's go."

If Jack had thought he'd been fully prepped for all possible situations he could ever run into in the Soviet Union, he was wrong.

Chapter 4

Viktor Viktorovich Karelin set off Jack's alarm bells from the first hello.

The way he shook hands with Jack, the way the scraggy Russian quickly checked him out, head to toe, with that appreciative look Jack had seen directed at him many times before, everything about the man flashed "queer" in bright neon lights. What confused Jack and immediately put him on the defensive was that Karelin didn't even try to be discreet about it.

Thanks to an extra, and furtive, effort he took in preparing himself for this assignment, Jack knew that male homosexuality was a criminal offense in the Soviet Union. Those prosecuted for *muzhelozhstvo*—"man sharing bed with man"—could get up to five years in a gulag. And here was this man, in your face and unapologetic.

Shit! What do they know? And if they do, then she must be KGB. Is it possible? The only daughter of a Deputy Minister?

Why not? Haven't you been told that they all are KGB informers?

Jack recalled how the gay topic had first surfaced. Around twenty minutes into their acquaintance, Lara had casually dropped that her new favorite American actor was Rock Hudson. Then she mentioned that they were staging "Cabaret" and regretted that they couldn't do Brian Roberts part the "right way". She had called him *goluboy*—gay. Although, as far as Jack remembered, that character's orientation in the musical was somewhat ambiguous.

Next, she had insisted on introducing Jack to her director and here they were. Did she know that the man was as queer as a three-dollar bill? How could she not? Yet, it looked like she was coming on to Jack, too. What was this if not a very cunning setup?

"So, how did you like the concert, Jack?" Karelin's voice snapped Jack back to the present. "I suppose Larachka has told you that we are preparing for the Youth and Students Festival. We hope our foreign guests will appreciate it."

"It was an excellent performance," Jack said. "I enjoyed it quite a lot. In fact, it was my first live concert in the Soviet Union and now I regret that I didn't make an effort to see local performances sooner." He actually meant it and was glad he didn't have to fake his enthusiasm.

Jack turned to Lara, hoping she would say something and rescue him from Karelin's deep-set, pale-gray eyes that were roaming over his face, his shoulders and chest. She smiled at him, nodding encouragingly, but didn't say anything.

Karelin did instead. "You are right, Jack. Our students sometimes are better than professional singers and actors. They are not censored like professionals, thus they can afford to be themselves. As long as they don't aspire to become People's Artists. That is when they have to start playing by the rules." He smiled fondly at Lara. "Except for our Larachka here. She dares to be what she is *and* plans to become a people's actress."

"I'm just following your example, Viktor Viktorovich!" Lara was clearly pleased, gazing at her director with adoring eyes. "Jack, you *must* come to the show we are staging. I mean Cabaret. You will never see anything like this in our theaters. Maybe even in yours." She threw another smitten glance at Karelin. "Viktor Viktorovich is going to stage another one, a rock opera. He's trying to persuade Eton and his band to play in it."

The last piece of information piqued Jack's attention. "Didn't you say he's a physics student?"

"Eton Volkonsky is an exceptionally gifted young man," Karelin answered instead. His eyes lit up, a peculiar smile warped the corners of his thin lips. "He could do anything—be a physicist, an engineer, a singer-composer, an actor. Or even a professional boxer. It's a pity that he can't make up his mind as to what he really wants."

Jack stared at the Russians as the two of them continued discussing Eton—how good he would be in Karelin's next show, how he was just the right "material" for the opera, how silly of him to refuse such an offer. Lara couldn't agree more, begged her director to give her some time—she was confident she would be able to persuade Eton.

"Eton will be perfect in this role," Karelin said, when he had finally noticed Jack's baffled gaze. "He has this exquisite, suppressed intensity about him. Passion boiling just below the cool surface. Imagine him in ballet tights, bare-chested, wet-haired, with his guitar. He won't even need to act much, being himself will be enough... It's a Russian thing, Jack. You may not understand."

Suddenly, an irrational urge to punch the scrawny director in the face swept over Jack. "With due respect," he said, "but maybe Eton doesn't *want* to act. Maybe he wants to be a scientist."

Karelin snorted. "That boy doesn't know what he wants. Otherwise, he wouldn't have been scattering his talents and energy on so many things. He can be great in anything he puts his mind to—if he graces it with his heart *and* mind! One thing at a time. Not everything at the same time."

Jack opened his mouth to retort, but Karelin's eyes drifted over his shoulder and settled on something behind Jack. "Eton, you're just in time! We are talking about you. I am telling our American guest here that you are born to be an excellent actor. If you choose to be one... In addition to other things, of course."

Jack spun around, all of a sudden nervous.

Eton Volkonsky was coming up to them, carrying his guitar in a soft black case. On his right, touching shoulders with him, was the round-faced brunet Jack had noticed earlier in the auditorium. A tall, skinny youth with a beaked nose and a head full of rampant auburn curls was trailing a step behind on Eton's left.

"Eton, Anya, come here!" Lara waved at them. "This is Jack. He works at the American Embassy, in the cultural section. Jack speaks perfect Russian and knows Russian history and literature so well, it's amazing! Jack, this is Eton. And this is Anya and Gosha."

Jack offered his hand to the girl first. "Jack Smith. Pleased to meet you".

"Very pleased." Anya's handshake was lukewarm, her weak smile stopping a mile short of her eyes.

Jack turned to Eton and looked straight in his eyes. "Jack Smith. Pleased to meet you,

Eton. And thank you, and Lara, very much for the song. It was amazing."

Eton's gaze was fixed somewhere just below Jack's left ear while Jack was speaking. When Jack offered his hand, he looked down at it and his eyes widened, as if he had been offered a toad. Then he took Jack's hand and finally raised his eyes.

They were rich brown, like melted chocolate. And impenetrable.

"Very pleased... Eton Volkonsky."

The young man didn't smile but his handshake was firm. His narrow palm was warm against Jack's, but the fingers were cold and they gripped around Jack's hand with the strength Jack hadn't expected from the singer's lanky figure.

He shook off the moment of weirdness, pulled his hand back and offered it to the other boy, the youngest of the three. "Jack Smith, pleased to meet you."

"My name is Yegor, but you can call me Gosha. I'm so glad to meet you, Jack. Can I call you Jack? You're from America, *da*? From whereabouts in America?" The kid was genuinely delighted, almost bouncing with eagerness.

"From California. And yes, you can call me Jack, that's my name." Jack smiled at him and stole a quick glance at Eton.

California was part of his "legend", his meticulously crafted identity *and* he was planning to settle there for the rest of his life, after this stint with the Agency. So, yeah, he was from California.

Eton eyes were fixed on an invisible spot between Jack's shoulder and Lara's, as if he was tuned out of the conversation. But Jack noticed that his Adam's apple bobbed as he swallowed, his lips pressed together even tighter.

"*Pravda*?! You're not joking, are you? Like in Hotel California? Have you been to that hotel?" Gosha took a step closer, his eyes full of awe.

"C'mon, Gosha!" Anya and Lara objected. Anya stopped short, but Lara continued in a reproaching tone, "Don't be such a child. You'll have time to torture Jack with all your questions later. Now we need to get ourselves to the restaurant." She turned to Karelin. "Viktor Viktorovich, please, come with us."

There was a moment of silence while Karelin's eyes trailed from Lara to Jack, rested for a second longer on Eton, then back to Lara. "Thank you for inviting me, Larachka, but I'm engaged tonight. I'm leaving you, young people—enjoy yourselves... Jack, I'm sure Larachka will take a good care of you around here."

Jack bowed his head in a formal gesture of acknowledgement. He wasn't sure what the Russian director meant, but he didn't like it, anyway. He liked it even less when the man's eyes went back to Eton and lingered for another moment before he bid his goodbyes and walked away.

What was that all about?

Lara's voice jerked him out of his bewilderment. "Let's go, guys. Eton, are you driving?"

"Yes, I am, and so is Grisha. We will take everybody with us. Are you going with your guest?" Eton looked pointedly at Lara, as if Jack wasn't there.

"Yes, I'm going with Jack." She took hold of Jack's arm.

"Alright, see you at the restaurant... Let's go, Anya." Eton turned around and walked away without even a glance in Jack's direction.

Jack looked after the departing singer and his friends, stumped.

"Don't mind him," Lara said, pulling at his arm. "Sometimes Eton can be a little awkward around strangers. But he's real nice. And a great friend. Honest! You'll see." She laughed quietly at the doubtful expression on Jack's face.

Whatever. As if he cared. To hell with him that rude and arrogant bastard.

Except that this rude and arrogant bastard was the grandson of Prof. Volkonsky, the man with whom Jack would apparently be interacting as part of his USIA assignment very soon.

They pulled out of the parking lot, turned right and joined the light traffic heading northeast toward the city center. It was a beautiful afternoon, and it felt like the summer had finally and fully set in. They talked about the weather and how great it should be out of town at the *dachas*. Or at one of Moscow's numerous parks.

"So, what is the story between Karelin and your friend Eton?" Jack asked when there was nothing else to say about the weather, *dachas* and parks.

"What do you mean?" She whipped her head to frown at him.

Ah-oh. So there *is* a story then, huh?

"I mean, it seems like Viktor Viktorovich thinks Eton is a genius of a sort. Wasn't it what he said? Or did I get it all wrong?"

Lara's face relaxed. "No, you've got it right. Eton is very talented indeed. But it's true too that he is a little... undecided. Not very focused maybe... Not very stable."

"How so?" Lara hesitated with the answer and he decided not to push it. "That's alright, Lara. Don't worry. You don't have to tell anything you don't want to. I just thought that your friend was an interesting character. So naturally I was curious."

But she was her usual self again. "Yes, of course he is... *Kharasho*, I'll tell you. But promise you won't tell Eton that I've told you about him. He hates it when people talk about him. But it's inevitable, *da*?"

By the time they reached downtown, Jack thought he knew everything about Eton that Lara did.

That at twenty-one Eton was the youngest *aspirant*, postgrad student, at Prof. Volkonsky's lab at the MGU, which did some research related to atmosphere or astrophysics or "something like that" — Lara didn't know exactly what.

That whatever research they did at this lab wasn't the subject Eton majored — he'd actually majored nuclear physics and graduated in April, having completed his last two years of studies in just one.

That his graduation dissertation was based on a research project he'd been doing with Anya and Gosha from the Faculty of Mathematics and Grisha, an *aspirant* from the Faculty of Physics. Lara couldn't tell what the project was about, but apparently it was a "very serious" piece of work, because right after the graduation Eton had been offered a position as a researcher at the nuclear research institute in Dubna. But guess what, Eton had turned down the offer and joined his grandfather's lab instead. To the great disappointment of his faculty and big shots from Dubna.

Jack also understood what Karelin had meant when he alluded to Eton's vacillations. Apparently, the boy had been a promising talent on the MGU's boxing team. Then, during his second year at the University he had started drinking and ended up in a detention center for drunkards at a *militsia* station once. His coach had forgiven him that time. However, shortly after, Eton had beaten up someone else and left him flat on his back with a broken nose. He'd sobered up real fast after that incident, but it was too late: they had thrown him off the team. Eton then had formed *Krylia* with his childhood friend Seva, the drummer. The band had shot to fame overnight. Nowadays Eton didn't touch a drop most of the times. Except a *zapoy*, drinking bout, once in a blue moon.

"It's a deeply Russian thing, Jack, nearly spiritual. All Russian men, peasants and aristocracy alike, used to succumb to drinking bouts once in a while. Till these days." Lara leaned forward, watching Jack's face, as if making sure that he understood this little quirk of her menfolk correctly.

These days, however, Eton stayed home, behind closed doors, and wouldn't let anyone in till he was good and sober again. But she'd never told Jack any of *that* of course! *Da?* She glared at him sternly.

Jack also got an earful about Eton's friends. Eton, Anya and Seva were childhood friends, from the same apartment block in the downtown district of Chistye Prudy. The three had played in that same courtyard, gone to the same school and now they were at the same university—Eton was a physicist, Seva a fifth year biology student and Anya was a fourth year math student. Same as Gosha. Who was from a small town in Siberia, near Lake Baikal. And by the way, it was Gosha who was the true wunderkind of them all: at nineteen, the kid was the youngest researcher in some math field that, from what Lara had heard, was even more complex that nuclear physics.

They reached the central Arbat Street and parked the car on a side alley. A five minute walk along a narrow street lined with century old neo-classical buildings and they were at the Central House of Actor.

They were warmly greeted by the doorman, then by the head waiter. Both of them asked after Lara's parents and looked at Jack pryingly. It was obvious that Lara and her parents were regulars here and Jack figured he might not be the first man to have escorted the girl to this exclusive, by local standards, establishment.

The dining hall was small, simply decorated, but clean and cozy. The headwaiter took the two of them to the reserved long table in the far most corner and left them to wait for their friends. By the time the others arrived, Lara had ordered a four-course dinner for the whole company of ten.

There was a slight commotion when Jack was introduced to those he hadn't met, followed by Lara and Anya fussing over the seating arrangement. When finally everybody settled down, Jack found himself between Lara and Gosha. Sitting across the table from them were Grisha the *aspirant* and all members of *Krylia*. Except their front man.

Eton was sitting at the other end, on Jack's side of the table, and all Jack could see of him, whenever he turned to talk to Lara, was the young man's hands. They were never still, moving around, rolling things between long, slender fingers—a paper napkin, a piece of white bread, the stem of a tall goblet of water, a cigarette.

Jack brushed aside the sting of disappointment, tried to focus on his conversation with Gosha. The boy dived head on into questioning him about America and California. He wanted to know everything Jack cared to tell him and only slowed down when food arrived.

The chatter around the table resumed as they were waiting for the mains to be served. The conversation switched from the concert at the MGU to the Youth Festival at the end of the month. Jack had already learnt from Lara that she and *Krylia* were all members of the large team representing Soviet students at the event. Apparently so was Anya.

"Anya, please! Help to get me on the team! I'll do anything—cleaning up, manning the curtains!" Gosha leaned forward, looking pleadingly at Anya. "Oh, I know what I can do! I'll do the lights for the performance. Yes, I know Eton can do it too. But please, let me!"

"Gosha, I told you. Don't be a child." Anya pressed her lips together.

"Oh, come on, Anya, surely you can put in a good word for him. It would cost you nothing," Grisha said. He was older that the others and sounded more grounded, mature.

"Anya? Please!... Eton?" Gosha called, leaning further forward, trying to catch Eton's eyes.

Everybody turned to Eton. Jack bent his head a little, following their gazes.

The bandleader turned to the pleading boy and, for a split second, his eyes locked with Jack's. He quickly shifted his gaze to Gosha, then on Anya on his left. "Don't worry, Gosha. We will get you into the team."

"But Eton—"

"It's alright, Anya. We will get him in the club, will we not?" he asked quietly, but his tone was firm.

"Alright, we will try," Anya conceded and everybody relaxed, most of all Gosha. He immediately launched into a discussion with the band members across the table about what he could do for them in terms of lighting, craning his neck from time to time to grin happily at his savior.

By the end of the dinner Jack knew in minute details what kind of light and sound system the Soviet Students Club would feature at the Festival—if they let Gosha do it—and the Soviet program prepared for guests from other countries, including the guests from America. They all looked at Jack expectantly and he assured them that the guests from America would most certainly like it.

At around nine o'clock the chubby waitress who'd been serving them came up to their table, smiled sweetly at Lara and without hesitation put a narrow white folder on the table in front of Jack. "Your bill," she said, staring at him with a bored expression on her face.

"No, please pass it to me," Grisha and Eton interjected in unison.

Jack nodded at Grisha, smiling, then turned to Eton. "Please, let me pay for this."

"No, you're our guest today. I will take it." The young man's tone was staid, and he didn't return Jack's grin.

What the heck is the matter with you, man?

Jack swallowed, tried to keep his voice amiable. "Please allow me to do it this time, Eton. For the sake of our acquaintance. I hope we'll have other occasions." He wasn't too sure about other occasions though.

Lara came to his rescue. "It's alright, Eton. Let Jack pay this time. He wants to do it for the sake of our friendship. We can always invite him to our *dachas* for lunch in return, *da?*" She beamed, thrilled at her own idea. "Yes, let's do that! Let's invite Jack to your *dacha* next weekend and all of us will host him. Treat him to a true Russian lunch. What do you all say, guys?"

The boys made approving noises, Gosha even clapped. Jack and the girls watched Eton expectantly, waiting for the verdict. The bandleader didn't break eye contact, but Jack noticed that his chest heaved, like he'd taken a deep breath. Or maybe sighed in resignation.

"*Kharasho*, alright. We invite you to our *dacha* for lunch next weekend."

I'll be on leave in Helsinki next weekend. I've been waiting for this leave for three fucking months!

"Next weekend," Jack said. Please, say Sunday, please!

"Yes, next Saturday. At our *dacha*... We'll be glad." Eton dipped his chin and first his lips, then his whole face softened visibly.

"Next Saturday..." No, I want to watch LiveAid next Saturday!

"Yes... Will you come?" Suddenly, Eton looked so young and vulnerable that Jack's heart sank.

"Yes, of course, Eton, with pleasure. Thank you for inviting me." Jack smiled weakly.

The name's Jack by the way, shithead.

The blood was rushing in his ears, but Jack couldn't tell if it was frustration or excitement. Whatever! He had to do what he had to do. He would make sure he made up for himself later. *And* he could always get the videotapes of the concert afterwards, right? Someone would have recorded them for sure.

But why, Smith? Why??

'Cause it's your fucking job, that's why!

Chapter 5

The next morning, the very first thought that unfurled in Jack's mind, even before he opened his eyes, was whether William had managed to get him the Volkonsky file yet.

Oh, c'mon, it's Sunday, for Christ's sake!

Even with his eyes closed, Jack knew that it was still early. But he also knew he wouldn't be able to get back to sleep. Not with the annoying restlessness that seemed to be turning into a permanent feature in his life. He sighed. Right, might as well do some jogging this morning. If only to freak the hell out of the guard who, Jack had no doubt, would immediately alert his minders.

Back at Cal State, then later on the East coast and during his study at the Army's Russian Institute in Germany, Jack had been a regular jogger. But here on this posting he had to cultivate an image of a loud and overly friendly American of rather unpredictable behavior. As a result, nowadays Jack would jog off and on, at odd times. Would take Metro instead of his flashy Mustang on a whim, strike up quick friendships with locals and chat boisterously with people on the street. He was also never shy to show off his language skills and his familiarity with local customs, history and culture, checked out local hangouts—provided they were public. He also frequented a handful of bars catering to foreigners—the places he knew were infested with the KGB or its informers at any time of the day. In short, he went out of his way to get noticed. Because when you were too obviously curious, too spontaneous and a blatant show-off, you could hardly be an intelligence officer. So far, the tactic seemed to have worked well: Jack was pretty sure that the KGB didn't suspect him, and that was why his personal tails hadn't been shadowing him regularly of late.

Besides the routine analysis of local news, one of Jack's main tasks was to identify, assess, develop and recruit local agents. He was supposed to get close to them, find out about their likes and dislikes, their strengths and most importantly their weaknesses. He was to become their friend and then to convince them to work for the Company—either by persuasion, bribery or blackmail. Jack hoped his persuasion skills, which had gotten him a few praises from the recruitment instructors at the Farm, would suffice and he wouldn't need to resort to the latter. Well, at least not any time soon.

Anyway, recruitment was what he would eventually do on this posting—when his bosses decided he was ready. In the meantime, he didn't have to do the recruiting. Others did it, he didn't know who—everything in their trade was strictly compartmentalized. All he had to do was to identify and assess the potential target and report to William Osbourne. Since he was the least shadowed, Jack was also tasked with prospecting for potential sites for dead-drops, then loading and unloading them for other case officers who ran agents. Not that others at Moscow Station knew it was Jack who was helping them to connect with their agents. Only William and the COS knew, and only William worked with him on the details of the ops; the rest only knew that there was another deep cover intelligence officer at the Embassy. And that was alright, just a peculiarity of the job...

It was fine as long as in the end he would get what he wanted. A hotel—

What?? No, a ranch! A ranch in Cali-fucking-fornia!

By eight, Jack was back at his twelve-story, chain-link fenced compound. He nodded amiably at the *militsia* man in the guard box and got a dirty look in return. After a shower, he decided he had plenty of time to go out for a quick breakfast of *bliny*, pancakes, at the tiny shop near the Metro station.

By ten, he was back in his apartment.

By eleven thirty, he had restlessly moved from the kitchen to the sitting room, then to the bedroom and back, for the tenth time, trying to keep himself and his mind busy with any chore and distraction he could think of.

He answered the phone when it was still on the second ring. It was Lara. Of course— who else would it be? She was apologetic: her father wanted her to be home because they were having his boss, the minister, and some of his other colleagues over for lunch at their *dacha*. But the boys were performing this afternoon on the open stage in Gorky Park and the rest of the crowd should be there too. Jack could meet them there—if he wanted.

He said he couldn't as he would be busy too. What else could he say? Surely not that he was disappointed as hell. Because, he wasn't. Why should he be? To hell with them, those Russian kids. They were just students, not much potential there anyway. Except the little Lara Novikova. And maybe Eton Volkonsky? Maybe...

After the call, Jack decided he'd have lunch at Uncle Sam's, the diner with a bar on the Embassy's grounds that served hot American breakfasts, lunches and dinners seven days a week. Someone from the singles crowd would surely be there. Later on, he would hang out with his Marines buddies at their bar.

It seemed like a good plan and in fifteen minutes, Jack was driving out of his compound. However, when he reached Sadovoe Koltso, Park Ring avenue that circled the central part of Moscow, instead of going north towards the Embassy, he made a left turn and headed south-west. Twenty minutes later he left his Mustang in the vast car park in front of Gorky Park, bought a ticket at the gates and strolled in, trying to enjoy the beautiful summer day and not to think about what he was doing here.

He spent the afternoon wandering around the park. Struck up a conversation with an elderly couple, was invited to share a picnic lunch by a group of Czechoslovak students on a language exchange program. Then he hooked up with three high-school girls whom he had smitten in five minutes flat. They took Jack to the open stage where the concert was at its height and spent another hour telling him all about the bands and singers who were performing, most of them non-professional.

And none of them were *Krylia*.

By six o'clock, Jack decided that he had had enough of Gorky Park for one day. He bid goodbye to the girls and in less than an hour was ordering a cheeseburger at Uncle's Sam. By the time it arrived, he had downed a double shot of Jack Daniels and was chasing it down with a pint of beer.

He got loaded and uncharacteristically rowdy that night at the Marine's Bar, raised a few eyebrows, and Grant asked him quietly if he was okay. He wasn't too sure, but laughed and said, "Of course I am. Why the fuck wouldn't I be?"

By eleven, he called a taxi to take him back to his place. At home, he stood under the hot shower for a long time, leaning forward, arms stretched out, palms flat on the tiled wall, watching as water streamed down his legs, formed a swirling and gurgling cone over the drain hole.

What the fuck is wrong with you today?

He didn't know exactly what was wrong. It just was.

The next day Jack had just started typing a report about his interactions with the Sovs over the weekend when William called on the internal line.

"Jack, do you mind coming over? I have something for you."

The Volkonsky file!

"Yes, coming."

He nearly knocked the chair down as he stood up. In the corridor, he tried to pace his steps to the one minute it normally took him to stroll over to his boss's office. He took a shuddering breath and knocked on the door softly. There was a loud click, and it swung opened, as though William had been standing by it, waiting for Jack.

"Come on in. And lock the door."

The CAO went back to his desk, turned around and looked at Jack intently with a curious expression on his face, as though he was seeing Jack for the first time. Or like Jack had just done something out of the ordinary.

Jack noticed that the door to a room at the back of his boss's office was ajar. He had never seen it open before. Something extraordinary must have happened.

"Got the Volkonsky file for you."

Yeesss!!

"Oh, right. That was quick. Thank you... Anything of interest?"

"Have a look for yourself. It's a microfilm... You can read it in there." William tipped his chin at the door. "Take as few notes as possible."

Jack walked over and opened the door to the back room. It was tiny, no larger than a closet, and brightly lit. There were the microfilm developing equipment at one end of the long, narrow desk along the wall, a compact microfilm reader at the other end and a few other tradecraft tools in between them. Jack shut the door and sat down on the straight-back chair in front of the reader.

William must have been reading the file: the microfilm was loaded and the frames showing on the screen didn't look like the cover page. It was also obvious that they were intentionally left at that particular section.

Jack's eyes were glued to the illuminated glass screen as he devoured the text.

"Wife, Anastasia Andreyevna Volkonskaya, nee Rezanova, 1922... Housewife. Deceased 1980. Descendant of the Rezanov's house (Count Nicolai Rezanov, Russian American Company, 1799-184?)."

"Son, Sergei Mikhailovich Volkonsky. DOB February 27, 1939... Graduate of MGU, 1960, chemical engineer. Colonel of the Soviet Army, Turkistan Military District... Divorced. KIA 1980, Afghanistan."

"Daughter, Vera Mikhailovna Volkonskaya, DOB May 8, 1944. Divorced. English-language literature translator, writer. Member of the Union of Soviet Writers... From 1963 to 1968 was married to Emil Jonathan May, DOB November 30, 1929. American. Mathematician... Cryptologist at the NSA."

What?! I'll be damned!

Jack's heart accelerated to a sprint, sweat broke out around his hairline and under his arms.

"Defected to the USSR in August 1960 together with an NSA colleague and allegedly lover (unconfirmed) Martin Hamilton (Hamilton - May Defection, 1960)."

Holy shit! The NSA? Defector... Lover?? His father was...

Jack was stunned, lost his focus for a moment.

Eton May Volkonsky, son of an American defector. Son of a queer American defector. And the grandson of the acclaimed Soviet academician hailed in the Soviet Union as the Father of the Nuclear Winter Theory.

Un-fucking-believable!

"So, what do you reckon?" William asked as Jack sat down in the chair in front of his desk.

"We need to talk," Jack pointed at the ceiling with his eyes, implying the Tank.

Placed within a large, windowless room on the ninth floor, the meeting space they called the Tank was a giant transparent bubble made of double-layer Plexiglas and raised five inches off the floor. It was the only place in Moscow believed to be one hundred percent safe from any kind of eavesdropping by the KGB. The Ambassador held his weekly country-team meetings here, and it was used regularly for confidential meetings and discussions by all agencies' reps at the Embassy.

"That serious?" William was mildly surprised, which didn't happen very often.

"We need to brainstorm about this. They haven't done the sweeping this week, have they?"

All offices at the Embassy were routinely swept for listening devices. It used to be a once-a-month job Jack had heard, but with the increasing number of bugs of various sorts discovered lately, the security office had been sweeping the offices section of the chancery building twice a month. They didn't bother "cleaning" the living quarters anymore.

"Let me see if it's available." William picked up one of the two phones on his desk and dialed an internal number. "Osbourne speaking. I need to use the Tank... Right away, if it's available... An hour max?" He raised his eyebrows.

Jack nodded.

"Fine. Thanks. We're on our way." The CAO put the receiver down. "Let's take this upstairs."

In the space of time it took William to lock his back room, then his office, for them to walk up to the ninth floor, get into the Tank and close the door behind them, Jack mentally went through the last two days, decided on what he was going to give William and what not just yet. He would eventually. But not all... And maybe not to William.

The room was bare, except for a long, light color laminate desk with twenty aluminum chairs around it, a blackboard at the far end and a small table at the door with a battery of plastic bottles of water and stacks of paper cups.

They sat down opposite one another at the end closest to the door and Jack laid out in detail his interaction with the Soviet students—well, almost all details. About Lara and the signs of her hitting on him, her introducing him to her friends, her director. About Eton Volkonsky, his music band and his group of whiz kids from Moscow State University. He then told William about Eton's invitation to his *dacha* next weekend. But before that, he'd run into the man at the collection site in the Bolshoi, on the night of the dry run.

"What's your take on it?" William asked when Jack had finished. "Volkonsky's assignment as the main counterpart in the exchange program. This story with his grandson, what's-his-name? Eton? Hmm, strange name." William rubbed his chin.

"It is strange. On the other hand, it looks like an uncanny coincidence to me. The joint program has been commissioned by the WMO and the USIA offered to sponsor it, correct? Professor Volkonsky is considered the author of the nuclear winter theory, at least here in the Soviet Union. So who else would they put forward? Then this girl, Lara Novikova. It was you who asked me to baby-sit her at the reception, remember?"

"So I did. It was a last minute change on the guest list. It could have been arranged."

"It could have, but she's too... unstructured. For a KGB recruiter, I mean. Even for an informer."

That drew a barking laugh out of William. "Look who's talking?"

"Too young, too." Jack ignored the jibe. "I think she's just a spoilt little daddy's girl. She's smart, though."

"A honey trap?"

"Maybe. Although it doesn't feel that way." The truth was he couldn't formulate yet how it felt.

"All right. What about the others? Anyone who looked like an informer? Or a recruiter?"

"The Anya girl. She's an obvious type—a Komsomol leader, serious, brainy. The political commissar type. She'll go far. But she steered clear of me." The feeling was mutual, but William didn't need to know that, either. "Then there was a Jewish guy, Grisha. He is a likely candidate for the KGB. The oldest of the lot—twenty three, twenty four maybe. An MGU *aspirant*, postgrad student. Quite an achievement if you are not from the *nomenklatura* stock and he didn't look like it. Then again, he seemed to have cash. Offered to pay for our dinner at the restaurant. Didn't seem to be singing the party line though. Didn't even try to suck up to Anya, who was the obvious party material. In short, he'd be the one who I think can be persuaded to trade information on his classmates and professors for a seat at MGU and a stipend."

"What about Professor Volkonsky's grandson? You said he's a genius or something?"

"They all seemed to think so. He is a tricky case. Theoretically, he should have the KGB all over him, given his background: American father, even if he was a defector, grandfather is an internationally acclaimed academician. But from what Lara and her director say, Eton Volkonsky is a rather unstable character. The KGB would stay clear of such a character—

too unpredictable to manage… What you think?"

"Maybe."

"I also suspect that Professor Volkonsky has enough connections 'upstairs' to step in for his grandson, if need be."

"Possibly." William studied him for a few seconds. "So you don't think he's KGB then?"

"I think they're too young. Except maybe the Jewish guy, Gri—"

"The Sovs are never too young to be informers. Communism is their faith. Thought you took the Soviet history course at Cal State."

"Maybe it is their faith." Jack sighed mentally. "And then maybe it isn't. Things might have changed. Especially since Gorbachev has announced his *glasnost*… Don't you think so?"

"You're reading too much into it. It doesn't mean a thing. They're still the main enemy and we're still in the arms race. That hasn't been called off, the last I've heard. And even if I see a little slacking on their side, it's a bluff, as far as I'm concerned." William's tone was as hard as his eyes.

"Maybe… Do you think we can get the Hamilton - May file? See what we can get out of the Volkonsky pair. Just a note though: the boy doesn't come across as a social type." Jack frowned in concentration, said slowly, "On the other hand, he seems to have an awful lot of friends for an antisocial type. So it's possible that he just dislikes Americans."

"Are you saying you won't be able to crack him? Thought Joe Coburn said you could do anyone." William's lips twitched, pale eyes boring into Jack's.

What the fuck did that mean? He couldn't know, could he?

No, he couldn't. No way!

"I just met this guy once, last Saturday. You can't expect him to fall in bed with me from the first hello, can you?" Jack held his boss's gaze steady, allowed himself to shrug. "But given his parentage, *and* assuming that he's not KGB, I'm not at all surprised that he shuns Americans. Especially those from the Embassy… C'mon, hasn't Eton May Volkonsky just become an object of keen interest to the CIA? Right after we went through that file. These people aren't stupid, you know."

William mulled over it. "Fine. So what's the plan? Besides me getting the Hamilton - May file. You think you've got a target?"

"I need more time. But what I'm pretty sure is that the KGB will be all over them, especially young Volkonsky, the moment they realize that I'm hanging out with them. And they will probably start shadowing me again."

"All right, let's do it. With a bunch of scientists and physicists, things might turn out… interesting. I'll brief Joe on this. He may have ideas. What about the Novikova girl? Are you planning to take her up on her advances?"

"I think I should take any invitations or introductions that come my way. At the end of the day, if she isn't the right target, she can still open lots of doors. She does it quite happily, it seems. I think she's taken Comrade Gorbachev's notion of openness quite literally."

"All right. You do that. I'll cover your bases internally."

"Thank you, William. I'll be waiting for the file."

"Fine. But I also want you to probe that Volkonsky offspring sooner rather than later. A nuclear physicist whiz kid with family connections? Why did he turn down a Dubna job? Supposed to be the top job for nuclear physicists in this country, isn't it? Curious."

"I'm hoping to find out this Saturday. Or shortly after." Jack was curious too, so no hardship at all. "Most of these kids will be part of the Soviet delegation at the Youth Festival. So I expect to see plenty of them during the event, too. Hopefully, afterwards too. *And* I'll be meeting with Professor Volkonsky when the Berkeley team arrives in August."

"All right. Keep me in the loop." William stood up, ready to leave. "By the way, are you canceling your trip to Helsinki?"

Dammit! He had completely forgotten about the trip with all this agitation. But he couldn't bear not to go—he needed it, even if it was just a day or two.

"No, I'm going. I'll take the train on Wednesday night and be home by nine Saturday morning. Lunch at the *dacha* won't start before noon anyway. I need to get them some presents, too. So I'll be running an expense account."

"Approved. But you still owe me a full written report on your dealings with the Ruskies. By the end of today."

Jack sighed. Friggin' reports! One part of the job he absolutely hated.

Chapter 6

Jack passed the next few days in a state of anxious anticipation he couldn't shake off. Not even with an extra shot or two of whiskey at the Marine's Bar after work and then again before turning in.

On Wednesday evening, before boarding his train to Helsinki, he called Lara from the station. He told her he would be back on Saturday morning and asked if she wanted anything from Finland. Finnish salami, smoked salmon and a bottle or two of Smirnoff vodka, for the lunch at the *dacha*, she said, calling him *daragusha*, a sweetie, and hung up.

When he and his companions on the trip—two staffers from the commissary, along with their wives—all settled into their first class coach, Jack turned down the invitation for a nightcap, citing a headache, and retreated to his compartment. He quickly undressed and sprawled in between cool, starched sheets. He hoped that the steady rocking of the train and its tuck-a-tong refrain would put his mind to rest, at least for a while.

It did. That night Jack dreamt of California, and of a magnificent wooden ship with great crimson sails and heavy, iron-wrought cannons, heading towards the sunlit California. His California.

Jack's plans in Helsinki didn't quite turn out as he'd intended: on Thursday night he was invited to dinner at the house of the American Consul General and couldn't say no, and on Friday, when he got to the only place he knew he could get what he needed he found it closed. There was an announcement in Finnish stuck on the door, but Jack couldn't read what it said. By that time, it was too late to scout for another place or to cruise the bars—aside from the fact that he also didn't know where. In the end, he picked a joint within walking distance of his hotel, one that looked most likely he might get lucky in some way—any way!

By the time Jack boarded the train to Moscow, all he had managed to get to keep him going was a blowjob in the restroom delivered by the stocky, bleached blond waitress who had also served him a salami sandwich and a cup of watery coffee. The combo left Jack thirty dollars short, frustrated and totally disgusted with himself.

He felt restless again that night and neither the rhythmic rocking of the train, nor his friendly phantom could do much to help. What shocked him was that for the whole time he was in Helsinki he had thought about the LiveAid concert only twice!

* * *

On Saturday morning, Jack was barely out of the shower when Lara called.

"Good morning, Jack! Are you ready? I want to get to *dacha* early. The weather is gorgeous, but they say it may start raining in the afternoon. We'd better hurry up."

"Good morning, Lara." He wouldn't normally identify callers by name on a phone he knew was tapped. But even if Lara wasn't with the KGB, she was of a high enough stature to be friends with foreign diplomats without serious consequences. "I just got in. I should be ready in half an hour."

"Oh, a whole hour before you get here!… Alright, fine. You're going to pick me up, *da*?"

Jack hadn't made up his mind about that yet.

There were only two places outside Moscow where foreigners could go without permits from the Ministry of Interior—Tarasovka, twenty kilometers northeast of Moscow, and Peredelkino, twenty kilometers southwest. The first was where the Embassy had its two *dachas*; the second was where the local elite—writers, scientists, and some politicians— had theirs. Peredelkino was also the place where Boris Pasternak had written his Doctor Zhivago and later buried in the local cemetery, both frequently visited by foreigner tourists. And Peredelkino was the place where he'd been invited today.

It meant that Jack could safely drive his flashy car with diplomatic plates to the *dacha*. But then, even without his car, the security would eventually know that he'd been there. On the other hand, he wanted to see Lara's reaction to his attempt at being discreet. If little Ms. Novikova was in any way associated with the KGB, like William thought she was, this would probably be the opening of an out-and-out spy game.

He had hesitated for too long, and Lara was on the line again, impatient, "Jack, are you still there? Are you coming to pick me up?"

"Lara, I'm not sure if I should drive my car to Peredelkino."

"Why not?"

"You've seen it haven't you? It doesn't exactly blend in here. Besides, it's with diplomatic plates."

"What's wrong with that?" She sounded genuinely confused. She was either a truly clueless, spoilt girl or a great actress.

"Lara, I'm a foreign diplomat. Maybe you don't realize it, but the hosts might have nepriyatnosti, unpleasant issues, with the authorities after my visit." She was quiet, obviously digesting it. "I'm sure you know that we foreigners are followed and informed on all the time. I do not wish to cause any trouble to… your friend and his family… To be honest, I'm not even sure if my visit is welcomed by—"

"But of course you're welcome, Jack! He's invited you himself, hasn't he?"

"If I remember correctly, you invited us all to his place. He had no choice."

Lara chortled. "Oh, don't you worry about that. I don't know anyone who can make Eton do something he doesn't want to."

Jack winced, kicking himself for having this conversation on the phone. Now the eavesdroppers had another name. But then maybe they already knew if this girl was with them. He tuned in to Lara's chatter.

"…shy to say no. Even to people he shouldn't… It's alright, Jack. He meant it when he invited you to his place."

"Alright. You know your friends better than me. I just hope that there won't be any nepriyatnosti afterwards. For any of you."

"Oh, Jack, you're so attentive! I wish we had more men like you."

He could hear her smiling, smitten. No, sweetie, I'll bet you don't.

"Thank you, Lara… So where should we meet to take a taxi to Peredelkino?"

The Volkonskys' *dacha* was a standard Soviet affair: a wooden structure on a six-hundred square meter plot overrun with fruit trees, flowering bushes and a small vegetable garden. Painted teal green, with white windows and door frames, the house was adorned with a beautifully carved fascia under a steeply pitched, reddish-brown roof. The narrow path from the gates to the house was paved with coarse concrete tiles.

It was Gosha who rushed out to greet them as soon as Lara pushed the gate open, an ear-to-ear grin on his flushed face.

"*Privet*, Lara," he threw over his shoulder, heading straight for Jack. "Jack! Welcome to a Russian *dacha*! Is this your first time at a *dacha*? Hope you will like it. Maybe it's not as big as your ranch in California, but it's very nice out here too. There's a forest and a lake. We will show you." He finally noticed Jack's outstretched hand, grabbed it with both of his. "It's so good that you could come, Jack. Everybody will be so glad to meet with you again."

"I'm glad too. Thank you all for inviting me." Jack grinned back at the boy.

He was still shaking hands with Gosha when his gaze drifted over the boy's shoulder, toward the cottage where Eton had emerged in the doorway and was walking slowly down the steps.

"*Privet* Eton," Lara said. "Hope we're not late. Jack has just returned from Helsinki this morning. He brought presents for Vera Mikhailovna. Is she on the veranda?" She breezed by Eton and disappeared into the house without pausing.

Gosha mumbled something about Vera Mikhailovna that Jack didn't catch—his eyes and attention were fixed on the tall, lanky figure clad in faded jeans and white, loose t-shirt, strolling towards them.

Something was different about Eton today that Jack couldn't put a finger on. Until their hands were clasped in a mighty handshake and Eton said quietly, "Hello and welcome to our house," his deep voice rumbled and his face creased in a shy little smile.

Damn! The boy could actually smile and be friendly.

And the freckles across the bridge of his nose and over his cheekbones made him look… younger, maybe?

Not so damn hard-assed.

Jack felt his face splitting in a huge, toothy grin. "Thank you, Eton. It's very kind of you to invite me to your house. I hope your family doesn't mind having an… a foreigner as a guest in their home."

Eton's smile waned a little. "No. It's not a problem. They don't mind. But, um, my mother is unwell today. She had stayed at home, in the city. Grandpa is busy today, too." His ears flushed pink, and he broke eye contact, suddenly interested in something over Jack's shoulder.

Okay, so the older Volkonskys did mind after all. And Eton was a bad liar. But there was nothing Jack could do about it now. On the positive side, it looked less and less likely that this boy was with the KGB: he was sure the Soviet security organs wouldn't employ people who couldn't tell a lie without blinking an eye… Same as the Company, wasn't it?

"I hope it's nothing serious. I've brought a little something for her. And for everybody."

Jack held out the large plastic bag of goodies he was carrying.

The young man hesitated, eyes fixed on the bag, and for a moment Jack thought he was going to turn down the presents. Finally, he accepted the bag, taking it by the sides with both hands. He met Jack's eyes, and the color started spreading slowly from his ears onto his cheeks, bringing out his freckles, the crooked smile creeping back onto his lips.

"You shouldn't have. But thank you very much."

"Just a token of appreciation for inviting me here."

There was an awkward moment of silence, like Eton was not sure what he was supposed to do, then he stepped aside. "Please come in." He motioned a hand toward the house, holding the bag to his chest with the other.

Stepping out of the bright sunlight into the house, it took a few moments for Jack's vision to adjust to the darker interior. When he could see again, he quickly scanned the place, his practiced mind effortlessly registering all little details.

The front room was about the same size as the sitting room at the Embassy's *dachas*, not more than three hundred square feet. It was crammed with heavy antique furniture—a round table with six chairs, two sofas, one large and one smaller, with embroidered, well-used cushions on them, a cupboard with tableware and a tall bookcase overflowing with old books and magazines. There were two closed doors on the right and one open door to the left, which Jack guessed was a kitchen. Two female voices could be heard from that direction, arguing, one of them was Lara's. She sounded upset and a little whiney.

"But how could I know that Vera Mikhailovna would—"

"Girls, stop quarreling. Our guest is here," Eton announced, his deep voice carrying through the sitting room into the kitchen, then turned to Jack again. "Please feel at home."

Lara, then Anya emerged from the kitchen, followed by a heavy-set, matronly woman in her fifties—graying hair pulled back in a heavy bun, a large, bright green apron over her flowery dress. Turned out, Varvara Petrovna was the Volkonskys house help. She wasn't the type of invisible-in-the-background help you'd normally see in movies, or like old Lin and his wife Amy the at the Ambassador's house. She was well-read ("Same name as Jack London's? Very good. He is my favorite American writer. And all of us Russians, in fact."), and in charge. Equal. More like a family member. But she was help, nevertheless, and it said volumes about her Soviet employers.

The woman chatted affably with Jack for a few minutes, then told the young people to take him to the river and show him the forest while she was preparing the lunch. Anya said she would stay to help and told Lara, her tone imposing, to do the same.

Lara pouted her pretty lips, but surrendered. "Alright." She flitted up and hooked her arm through Jack's. "You're in good hands with the boys. Gosha is a Siberian and knows a lot about nature. He'll tell you all about it." She smiled at him reassuringly, like a mother sending her child to school for the very first time.

Gosha bounced up to Jack, beaming. "Anything you'd like to know about our nature. Just ask! Don't worry, Lara, we'll take good care of Jack. *da*, Eton?" He pulled on Jack's arm. "Let's go. We will show you the forest."

In five minutes, they were walking along a grassy path in a mixed forest, with Gosha in the lead and Eton closing the ranks. The boy chatted on, telling Jack the names of the trees and bushes and flowers, asking if they had similar ones in California, and what other kinds of trees and flowers they had in California, and what people did in California on a sunny summer day.

Eton hardly said a word for most of the walk, but Jack was strangely aware of his silent presence behind him. A few times, he got a strange feeling, like he was being watched. But he fought the urge to turn around. Soon, they reached a clearing in the woods and stopped, gazing in wonderment at the sight in front of them.

The meadow was covered in a thick, lush carpet of overgrown grass, densely peppered with white and yellow flowers. Slightly off the center, drenched in golden sunlight, a dozen silver birches huddled up in a tight, almost perfect ring—tall, shimmering, proud. Ten yards to the left stood a single birch tree, nearly as tall, but not entirely the same: unlike the others, its long, willowy branches cascaded down, like a silver-green waterfall, nearly touching the ground, hiding most of its bright white trunk.

"Beautiful, isn't it?" Gosha breathed out, grinning happily. He pointed at the solitary tree. "It's a weeping birch. This type isn't very common around here. Nobody knows how she got here. Just sprung out on one perfect day. That's why she's excluded from the ring by her sisters. You have to be like everybody else here to be part of the group—trees, or people, or everything... It's different in America, *da*? I've read that you Americans put individualism above all and it's acceptable to be different in America. *Da*?"

I wish, friend.

"Yes, more often than not it's alright. But not always," Jack said, eyeing the trees. "And yes, they're gorgeous. I've never seen anything like this in California." He couldn't stop himself from stealing a glance at Eton and winced mentally at the double meaning his words might have carried across. "But our birch trees are different," he hurried on, turning to Gosha. "Not as tall and not as straight. And they don't cluster in the same way too. Not as... exclusive."

And I do mean birch trees!

Eton kept his gaze on the birches for another moment, as if mesmerized, then turned to Jack, his eyes squinted from the bright sunlight, a faint smile playing at the corners of his mouth. Or maybe it was a smirk, for all Jack knew. He looked at Jack like he was seeing through him. It unsettled Jack a little, and he decided that talking about something neutral should diffuse the tension—in case any was brewing.

"It's beautiful here. The vegetation is more vibrant than where I'm coming from. Colors are richer, smells are stronger. Everything is more... intense."

Christ, and you call this "neutral"? He's seeing through you like you're made of glass. Look at that little smirk of his, moron!

He can think whatever he wants. I'm talking about plants, ok?

Eton finally nodded, his smile widened a fraction. "Maybe you're right. The flora here has a rather short window of opportunity to come out and shine like this." He turned to gaze at the meadow again. "It will all be gone by October—withered, brown and gray... Not sunny all year round like in your California."

Jack tried to discern any hint of mocking, but the Russian sounded sincere and, if anything, a tiny bit wistful. But maybe Jack just imagined it—why would he be? And what was it with these people and California, anyway?

"You know a lot about California?" He didn't mean it, but somehow the question came out as a challenge.

Eton's smile dropped a notch, but Gosha let out a chortle. "Oh, Eton knows an awful lot about Calif—"

"Gosha!" Eton didn't smile any more, his face a stony mask Jack had seen on him the very first time they had met.

"What? Isn't it true?" the boy asked innocently. "Jack would be interested to know that you know so much about California."

"Come on, what's so interesting about it?... Anyway, let's go back now." He was talking to Jack now, but his eyes were elsewhere.

"Alright... But I don't mind talking about California, if you like. Anything you want to know," Jack added, addressing Eton's straight back as they headed to the *dacha* in the reverse order.

He thought he heard a muffled grunt and saw the blond head bobbed. But it could also just be the walking on the uneven ground.

Fine. Whatever. To hell with you, Eton Volkonsky!

But he still had a job to do and for now this infuriatingly unapproachable guy was his job. It meant that he had to find a way. But most importantly, he shouldn't take his unsuccessful attempts so far to heart. One couldn't always win, could he? Besides, it was just a job.

That night Jack's thoughts kept wandering to the report he would write about his visit to the Volkonskys' *dacha*. He contemplated including things like what they had had for lunch and the songs they had sung after the two and a half hour meal. But William would probably tell him to cut down on irrelevant details and stick to the point.

And the point was that Grisha, who they'd thought was the likeliest informer, didn't show and Anya, the next on the list, continued to keep her distance, and tried to keep Lara away from Jack, too. That somewhat undermined their assumptions about who out of this group of Soviet students could be with the KGB. Secondly, most of the conversation revolved around Russian and American plants, food and weekend pastimes. At first. Then, somehow, it veered off onto LiveAid, which Soviet TV hadn't broadcast. Jack didn't know how the young people knew about it when the local newspapers hadn't carried any news about the concert. They just did. They also knew most of the American and English bands and singers, whose performances were aired across the globe while they sat in the summer garden in Peredelkino and talked about them, and then sang some of their songs—Led Zeppelin and the Rolling Stones, Status Quo and Dire Straits, Mick Jagger and Bruce Springsteen, Eric Clapton, Madonna and the Police. That was what they had been talking about most of the afternoon and into early evening.

As for the Volkonsky kid, he had turned out to be a hard nut to crack. So Jack needed more time.

What Jack was sure he should keep out of the report was the topic of California, the strange, almost hostile reaction it had stirred up in Eton and his stubborn refusal to talk about it. Nor should he mention the baffled look on Eton's face when the young man realized that Jack could have stayed to watch LiveAid in Helsinki, but had come back instead to spend part of his weekend with a bunch of Soviet students he barely knew. Jack couldn't explain to himself why he thought he should hold back those details. He just felt in his gut that they'd better go unreported. For now.

That and the fact that the little shithead hadn't called him by name. Not once!

Chapter 7

Next morning, Jack had to make an effort to keep his mind from wandering to what he would write in his report on Monday and focus on what he was going to do today. A brunch at Uncle Sam's? He hadn't had it for two weekends in a row. Maybe he would take Grant and Frank or any one of the marines who were not on duty today for a cramped ride around town in his Mustang—treat the guys to some local sights they hardly ever had during their posting in this country.

Jack was making himself a cup of instant coffee when the phone rang. He looked at his wristwatch. 9:37 a.m.

Lara?

He reached for the kitchen extension of the phone. "Hello?" he said in English.

Nothing.

He switched to Russian, "*Alyo*, I'm listening."

There was a faint exhale, as if the person at the other end was forced to start a conversation, then a deep voice rumbled, "Good morning. This is Et—"

"Hey, how are you? Great that you're calling." Jack kept his banter vague. "I wanted to thank you again for the invitation. I enjoyed it a lot."

"Oh... Alright. I'm... I'm glad," Eton stammered, apparently baffled at being interrupted unceremoniously. "I got your phone number from Lara. Hope you don't mind."

Jack cringed at the mention of Lara's name, but went on reassuring him, "Not at all. Glad that you're calling." He wondered what this was all about.

"My mother's asked me to pass her thanks for the presents..." Eton sounded awkward, like he wasn't sure himself why he was calling. "She asked me to tell you that she was sorry for not being able to host you. So I thought I'd call... to say thanks. And apologize. Like she asked..."

Jack could visualize the color creeping over the young man's cheeks and ears. "Please don't mention it. I hope your mother is feeling better today."

He was still not sure where this was all going and wondered if he should try to cut the call short to minimize the amount of information the eavesdroppers could glean from it. He didn't want to, didn't know when he would next receive a call from Eton May Volkonsky.

"She's better, thanks. It was a bout of migraine." He hesitated, sounding uncertain again. "Listen, we're playing in Gorky Park this afternoon. I mean the band. On the open stage, near the fountain... If you have time, of course... And if you would like to come."

"Yes, of course!" Jack grinned into the mouthpiece. "I would love to see you guys performing again. Do you play there every weekend?"

"Yes, usually during summer. But last week Alexei, our bass guitarist, got sick. So we didn't play."

That explained why he hadn't seen them at Gorky Park last week.

"So, if you're free this afternoon..."

"I am free. I will come. And may even bring friends. They've never been to such a performance here and will love it, I'm sure."

"You think? Alright, I'll see you later. Around three o'clock?"

"Of course. Thanks for letting me know." The young man's name was swirling on the tip of Jack's tongue, but he bit it back. "I'll see you later."

"And Jack, thank you for the cigarettes," the young man said quickly and rang off.

Jack gaped at the handset, then placed it carefully in its cradle on the wall.

Did he say "Jack"? He actually called me Jack.

Of course, he called you Jack, it's your name, stupid.

Yeah, but... Damn, yeah!

"You're welcome, Eton," he mouthed, grinning like a fool. Then he looked down at the mug of coffee in his hand and poured it all down into the sink. It was going to be a great day and Jack wanted something better that a mug of lukewarm instant coffee.

He knew something had happened the moment he reached the narrow street behind the Embassy and started looking for a spot to park his car. There were too many cars with diplomatic plates parked around and they all belonged to the Embassy staff who didn't live in the compound and had no business being in the office on a Sunday morning. Unless there was an emergency.

He noted William's silver Volkswagen Rabbit and two identical steel blue, four-wheel-drive Toyotas that belonged to two case officers with "known" covers of second secretaries of the Embassy.

Jack locked his car and hastened to the gate. "Hey, Charlie." He pushed through the heavy-duty turnstile. "Are we having an after July 4th party today or something? I had a hard time finding a parking spot."

The young marine at the gate didn't smile back. "Hey, Jack. You don't know yet, do you?"

"Know what?" Something was definitely wrong.

"Peter Strauss from the political section was detained by the Sovs last night."

"*What?!*"

Peter Strauss was one of Moscow Station's case officers. Based on what Jack had been able to pick up from William in the past few weeks, the Station had been preparing for an operational run. Jack had figured it was a bren, a brief encounter, with an agent whom Peter had run. That was probably what had happened: Peter had been rolled up on the op run. Because there was no other way a diplomat would be detained—only if he'd been caught red handed. Spying.

Jesus Christ!

And what about the agent he had been meeting with?

Shit!

Jack refocused his attention on Charlie.

"...and he was only released around five this morning. From Lubianka." He paused, looked at Jack pointedly.

"You must be joking!"

Lubianka was the nickname of the gray granite building that housed the KGB and the notorious prison within its bowels.

"I'm not. That's why everybody's in today. Including Ambassador Hart... Your boss is in, too, by the way. You guys hunting for hot news or somethin'?" He tried to give Jack a taunting smile, but it was obvious that he was shaken.

Even so, Jack didn't think the young marine understood the implication of the event: that Peter Strauss had been caught spying.

"Christ, no! I had no idea until you told me. Beats me what William is doing here today." He shook his head. "Maybe I should go find out. Thanks for giving me a heads-up, Charlie. Later?"

"Sure, Jack. See you at the bar."

Jack hurried across the compound's courtyard to Uncle Sam's, his mind working a mile a minute. It was the second busted operation in under three months since he'd arrived in Moscow.

The first one was a cable tapping setup, code name GTTAW.

Planted by the CIA in the early eighties, it was a listening device with a recorder on underground communication lines between Moscow and a nuclear weapons research institute in a small town southwest of the city. Ever since, Moscow Station's officers had been making regular runs to the manhole to retrieve the tapes and place clean ones.

Unloading TAW was Jack's first op in Moscow, barely a month after his arrival. He didn't manage to get down the manhole: his tiny receiver picked up the alarm pulsing from the widget when he was two hundred meters from it. It could mean that the device had been tampered with. Jack aborted the run and returned empty handed. It then took the SE Division's chiefs and Moscow Station a month of debates to decide to send Sam Pattingson to retrieve the tapes. Sam was at the end of his tour and having him ambushed by the KGB and expelled from the Soviet Union was a more palatable risk than losing a deep-cover officer. The tapes Sam brought back turned out to be blank. The HQ tech team couldn't determine whether they had been faulty or had indeed been tampered with. In the end, it was decided that the risk was too high and the site was abandoned.

So first TAW and now this.

Jack didn't know which asset the KGB had busted this time along with Peter. He hoped it was not VANQUISH, EASTBOUND or MEDIAN. He knew that it wasn't right to feel more protective of some agents over others—they were all supposed to be friends of America. But he couldn't help it.

From the Soviet operations files he had read in at HQ, GTVANQUISH, GTEASTBOUND and GTMEDIAN were the only three Soviet agents who were not KGB officers: two were scientists at classified research institutes and the third was a disarmament specialist at the Soviet think-tank, the Institute of USA and Canada. All three were volunteers who had approached the CIA and offered to work for them. In fact, it had taken VANQUISH nearly a year and a healthy dose of recklessness, shoving copies of classified documents into Embassy staff's cars before the then COS had persuaded the SE Division chiefs to allow him to respond to the Russian scientist's desperate measures.

Jack didn't learn anything at Uncle Sam's he hadn't heard from Charlie. Most people who were there for Sunday brunch—several contractors, a group of Seabees and a handful of Marines—were expecting to hear more at the country briefing the following morning. In the meantime, the consensus was that since the consular officer had brought Peter back from Lubianka, it had probably been a KGB setup. And since he'd been detained by the KGB, Peter Strauss would be declared *persona non grata* and given the usual forty-eight hours to get out, together with his wife. People speculated whether there was something behind the detention, or it was just a tit-for-tat for the highly publicized arrest of the Soviet spy ring in Virginia nicknamed "the Walkers and friends" a few months back. A bespectacled Seabee argued that the Soviets were typically quick with settling scores and a few months was too long for them. So it probably meant that Pete had been up to something.

"Maybe he is with the CIA," said the burly engineer-contractor who sat to Jack's left at the bar.

"You think so?" Jack asked innocently. "He doesn't look the type… Or does he?"

By noon, Jack had finished his brunch of grilled burger, took his beer and moved from the bar to the table at the far end of the room where six Marines, including Grant and Frank, were congregated. The topic of Peter Strauss' detention had been exhausted and the general conversation at Uncle Sam's revolved around LiveAid. Everybody was moaning and cursing the Sovs for not transmitting at least part of the event, envying those who had managed to escape to Helsinki or West Berlin to watch the concert on television. Jack didn't mention his trip to Helsinki and his early return for the lunch at a Russian *dacha* the day before.

It was nearly 2:00 p.m. when Grant, Frank and Kevin had finally got all their clearances for a trip into town with Jack. The four of them packed themselves like sardines into his two-plus-two convertible and headed off for a city tour. An hour later, they rolled into Gorky Park's vast parking lot, bought four tickets at the massive columned entrance and strolled inside. Jack had to make a conscious effort to slow his pace.

It was another beautiful, sunny day, and the place was swarming with people of all ages and nationalities.

"Those are not Russians, are they?" Kevin asked and pointed his chin at a group of Latin looking young people striding in front of them, chatting and laughing.

It was the first overseas posting for twenty-year-old Kevin from Montana and sometimes he reminded Jack of himself so many years ago on his posting in Germany.

Frank coughed out a laugh. "Christ, Kev, can't you tell Latinos apart from Sovs? Don't you have Mexicans or Peruvians in your Montana?"

"Fuck you! It's my first outing since I've arrived, okay? How do I know that they aren't Georgians? Or Uzbeks… Or what-the-fuck-ever."

"C'mon, Kev, take a close look at them: do they dress like the rest of the people around here?"

"Guys, stop bitching," Jack intervened. "They're foreign students, Kev. There're lots of them here from developing countries—Africans, Arabs, Asians."

Kevin smiled at him, shamefaced. "Yeah, we been briefed about foreign students. I just wasn't sure."

They continued chatting about foreign students while they walked, but Jack lost all interest in the conversation the moment they reached the central fountain and saw a large, elevated stage to its far left.

There was a band of four on the stage, singing an unfamiliar Russian tune. The crowd in front of the stage was young, consisting mostly of Russians, but with some foreign students too, as far as Jack could tell, including the group of Latin Americans they had followed from the gate.

Jack scanned the area around the stage, looking for the blond... the band—Seva, Alexei the bassist who presented himself as Alex, Yura the lead guitarist and Vadim on keyboards. And Eton, of course, their front man. Eton May Volkonsky, a nuclear physics wiz-kid.

He couldn't see them anywhere.

When the performing foursome finished their last number and left the stage, the young long-haired, bearded presenter strolled out and declared with mock boredom, "And now let us welcome to the stage... Who do you think?... Yes, it is Eton Volkonsky and his band, *Krylia*. Meet them, friends!" His last words were drowned in the wave of girlie shrieks and guys' cat calls, whistles and applause, and the announcer was bouncing with them too.

The cheering continued as the band walked out on the stage, Eton closing their ranks, and started plugging in and tuning their instruments. It was only when they were all set to perform that they turned to the audience and smiled a little. All except Eton.

"Do all their bands look so... unfriendly? They're students, you said?" Frank asked, his tone skeptical.

"Yep, they're students. I don't know, maybe it's the Russian take on how rockers should behave," Jack shrugged, caring not at all what Frank thought of Russian bands—he was too busy watching the stage.

He saw Eton skimming the gathering in front of him from under his eyebrows and fought an impulse to wave at him and shout "right here". The guy might be looking for his friends in the audience, for all Jack knew. His girlfriend, maybe. Or maybe not—Jack had noticed neither Anya nor Gosha when he was trying to spot his new Russian friends in the crowd.

Right then Eton turned his head and their eyes locked. Both froze for the briefest of moments and the singer's face relaxed a little, while his lips pressed together even tighter. But it could also be a hint of a smile, right? Jack exhaled sharply, grinned back and waved at the stage.

"D'you know them?" Kevin looked at him with surprise.

Frank belched a laugh again. "Kid, you'd better ask who Jack *doesn't* know."

This time the usually quiet Grant spoke up, "What's the problem with you today, Frank? Give him a break, man."

"I was invited to their concert last Saturday. And then we had a few drinks afterwards," Jack explained. That was all these guys needed to know.

"Really? That's cool, man." This time Frank was impressed. "Were they good?"

"Think so. You'll see," Jack said, not ready to share what he really thought of the band. Especially of their front man.

They were good. Good enough for the crowd of a hundred or so of usually rather dour Muscovites to go a little wild and sing along, together with a few dozen foreigners, Kevin and Frank amongst them. The band's repertoire that balmy afternoon consisted mostly of covers of old and some new top of the charts English language songs. Most of them were soft rock ballads, like Led Zeppelin's The Stairway to Heaven and Going to California, and Bryan Adams' Straight from the Heart. But when they began playing a harder rock piece called Runaway that Jack vaguely remembered hearing before, the audience got so excited that it attracted a group of four militiamen. Then a man, obviously a militiaman in plain-clothes, stalked out on stage and started an animated exchange with Seva and Alex, while Yura and Vadim tried to position themselves between Eton and the intruder.

It was time to leave. Jack didn't want to go, but he couldn't stay either, in case the situation got out of hand. Especially not with the three Marines with him.

When they were out of the crowd and leaving, he turned to look back at the stage. The wide alley leading to the exit was in the range of vision of those on the stage and Eton must have caught the commotion in the crowd out of the corner of his eye because he shifted his gaze to look at them. At Jack.

Jack smiled apologetically and pointed his head at militiamen, who were working the excited fans. Then he raised his hand, opened palm forward, and quickly curled the fingers into a fist at his shoulder—salute!

Eton nodded, but didn't return the smile. Then he turned away and started talking to his band members.

Fine. Whatever.

Jack walked briskly away, the three Marines in tow. But as they were nearing Gorky Park's monumental gateway, the faint sounds of music starting up at the central fountain reached them and Jack almost stumbled.

It was Hotel California.

Chapter 8

On Monday morning, Jack didn't have to wait for the country briefing to learn why Peter Strauss had been detained. As he sat down with his morning coffee and turned on the local radio, it declared to him in a menacingly dispassionate tone that at 20:53 hours on Saturday, July 13th, 1985, the special unit of the State Committee for Security of the USSR, a.k.a. the KGB, had caught an officer of the CIA, Peter Strauss, in the act of spying; that the said Peter Strauss had worked at the U.S. Embassy in Moscow under the cover of a second secretary; that the Ministry of Foreign Affairs of the USSR had issued an official protest to the Ambassador of the USA and that Peter Strauss and his family had been given forty-eight hours to leave the country.

The one thing it didn't mention was what act of spying Pete had been caught doing and if anyone else was involved. But Jack had little doubt that he had been arrested during a bren, a brief meeting with his agent, that had gone terribly wrong.

And the agent? Jack grimaced. Please, let it not be one of the civilian agents. Sure, he felt sorry for Pete, but that was part of their job. They were soldiers in this special war and had been drilled to exhaustion to fight it right. Those guys were amateurs, with only a few of hours of instructions and no practice to talk of.

Come to think of it, with Peter ousted, the Station would be shorthanded and, until HQ arranged a replacement, the assets Pete had run would probably be reassigned to the remaining case officers. And that should include Jack. Shouldn't it? Maybe he'd get to handle one of the civilian assets. Maybe he would hear about it from William this morning.

He didn't hear from William until a few minutes to 2:00 p.m., when Glenn returned from the lunch break.

"Jack, the boss wants to see you."

Jack was finishing his report on his visit to the Volkonsky's *dacha*, together with a ham sandwich and Coke. "What, now? You know what it's about?" He took the last bite of the sandwich.

"Yep. Todd and I just had lunch with him down the cafeteria." Glenn flopped on the chair at his desk. "Now he wants to see you. Just a briefing before he takes off. He's leaving for Munich tonight. Something has turned up and HQ wants him over there."

William's unscheduled trip to Munich was news. Jack had been hoping that the Hamilton—May file would arrive this week and he would be able to read it in his boss's little back office. Apparently, that case had gone down the priority list and Jack was sure the thing that had moved up to the top wasn't what Glenn was thinking.

"Okay. Coming." Jack took the last swig of Coke, tossed the can into the dustbin under his desk and started collecting his papers. "Any news on Pete?" he dropped casually, putting the documents away in his desk drawer and locking it.

"Not really. Except that they've been debriefing him in the Tank the whole morning... Who'd have thought," Glenn mumbled, then popped his head out from his cubicle. "Have you?"

"Have I what?" Jack leaned out of his and cocked an eyebrow.

"Ever suspected that Pete was with the CIA?"

"Hell, no! I'd have never guessed. He looks too, um, a little overweight for a CIA agent… Don't you think?" He eyed Glenn innocently.

That touched a nerve in Jack's portly co-worker. "Whatcha mean?"

"Well, aren't they all supposed to be in tip-top shape?… Like Robert Redford in 'Three Days of the Condor' at least?"

Glenn chortled. "You're hilarious, Smith… And by the way, he's a case officer. Agents are the Ruskies he ran. Till last night."

"You're probably right." Jack shrugged and closed the door behind him.

William looked bleary-eyed and uncharacteristically crumpled. Jack noticed a bottle of Black Label Johnny Walker with the cap broken and an empty tumbler by the pile of files on the narrow, side desk.

"Come in." The CAO let him in and locked the door. "You can take a seat, but we're moving upstairs in a minute."

"Right."

It was happening: Jack would be briefed too after all. He sat down on the chair in front of the desk, watching his boss expectantly.

William parked himself behind the desk. "How are the preps for the Berkeley team's visit going?" He moved some papers around on his desk, distracted.

"Nothing new since we spoke last. I'm still waiting for the list of their Russian counterparts… And the HM file."

William looked up. "What?"

"H-M file," Jack repeated, accentuating each letter.

"Oh, yes. Well, it's not coming this way."

"It wasn't? Why?"

"Our *friends* don't want it here. Just in case… You'll have to *go out* to read it," the CAO said tentatively, then added, "When I get back."

"At HQ?"

"Possibly closer. We'll see… How was *the lunch*?" William tilted his head toward the window to indicate the world outside. "Have you met the senior Volkonskys?"

"Nope." Jack shook his head. "They didn't show. And neither did the Jewish guy."

"Hmm. Interesting."

"I've finished the report, but thought it might not be a priority right now… But I can bring it over now, in case you'd like to read it before you leave," Jack offered.

"No, it can wait. *If* there's nothing of significance."

"Nothing so far."

"Fine." William reached for the phone and dialed an internal number. "Yes, it's me. We're on our way… All right." He put the receiver down and stood up. "Let's go."

The chief of the CIA Moscow Station was already in the Tank when they walked in, sitting at the far end of the long, conference table. The confined space stank of cigarette smoke as if a roomful of people had been chain-smoking here for the last twenty-four hours. Which was probably what had happened here in reality. The tall dustbin near the service table in the front corner was overflowing with paper cups, some with coffee stains, empty Coke cans and water bottles. There was a thin paper file in front of Nurimbekoff, a pencil, an empty glass and a half empty bottle of water.

"Mr. Nurimbekoff, sir." Jack watched the COS warily, without his usual smile.

"Jack. Come on in. And Marat is fine." His voice was gravelly. Tired. He poured himself a half glass of water and gulped it down.

Of medium height and slender built, Marat Nurimbekoff was the first generation American-born Kazakh from Boston. He was deceptively soft mannered and even-tempered, but Jack didn't believe it for a moment: for a non-Caucasian in his forties to get where he was, he must have mastered a few things at the Company and internal politics was undoubtedly one of them.

"I suppose I don't have to explain the reason for this unscheduled briefing."

"No, sir. I suppose we can skip that part. Unless you can share anything in addition to the country briefing this morning."

Nurimbekoff exchanged quick glances with William, then nodded. "Yes, I think I can. We're planning to break your cover with the team shortly, anyway. I need everybody fully on board from now on."

That was unexpected. Jack had been prepared to keep his deep cover for as long as possible if not for most of his posting. But four and a half months into it? Was it that dire?

"So soon? When are you planning on doing it?" Jack asked, his tone neutral.

"As soon as William returns with full details."

Nurimbekoff was not forthcoming, but that was enough for Jack to figure that William was going back to HQ. He cut a glance at his direct boss and nodded. "Right."

"In the meanwhile, you'll be checking in with Marat," William said.

"Okay." Jack bobbed his head again, watching the COS expectantly.

Nurimbekoff sighed. "Pete was ambushed."

"On a bren?"

"Yes." Nurimbekoff looked at William. His expression didn't change, but his jaw clenched.

"I just figured," Jack hastened to explain. "There was too much prep going on."

Now both men gazed at him with interest.

"And the agent—was he rolled up with Pete or before?" Jack pretended he hadn't noticed the stares.

"Possibly before. The whole set-up of the ambush was too elaborate, Pete thinks. And no, we don't know yet how long it's been since he was compromised," Nurimbekoff added. "In case you're wondering about the quality of the intel."

There was a moment of awkward silence, then Jack asked cautiously, "May I know which agent?"

Nurimbekoff threw a glance at William again, rubbed his chin and sighed. "VANQUISH."

Shit!

"No!" Jack hoped his disappointment didn't show.

"Unfortunately… Anything else you want to know?"

"Is there anything I can do?"

The COS's face relaxed. "Yes, Jack. For starters, you can help to read a deaddrop signal for William, in about…" He looked down at his watch. "Three hours from now."

"I'm off to the airport in two hours," William explained.

"Of course. I'll do that."

"Were you shadowed this morning?" Nurimbekoff asked.

"No… I did a quick SDR this morning. I'm still clear."

"Good. I'm afraid you're the only one who isn't shadowed. For now. Don't expect it to last though. Alright, let's have a look at the site."

The COS pulled out a large, folded sheet of paper from the file in front of him and spread it out. It was a detailed map of the location of the signal, not far from the center of the city.

For the next thirty minutes, they discussed the op. It was one of the easy ones and did not require special prep in addition to a standard briefing. Jack only needed to drive by a certain building along Kutuzov Avenue, one of Moscow's prestigious parts of the town, and see if a blue circle was chalked on its right end. It would mean that the agent had successfully collected from a deaddrop at a different location. No circle, no collection. They agreed that Jack would do a two-hour surveillance detection routine before the operation, driving around town. If the signal at the site was affirmative, and the agent had unloaded the drop, Jack was to call Nurimbekoff's apartment from within the Embassy's grounds to say the code word "Blue". If it was negative, the code was "White". For emergencies, the code was "Red". *And* he was to be on standby 24/7, in case the COS needed his help. In which case Jack would receive a message with the emergency code and he was to come up to the Tank at the indicated time.

It had started raining around four in the afternoon and by five all potholes and cracks on the battered streets of Moscow were filled up with rainwater. The rain slowed down enough after the rush hour for Jack to be able to read the surroundings comfortably while negotiating the incessantly diverging lines of traffic. Which was handy as he hadn't worked on this particular site before and hadn't had time for a test drive. He was still clear of surveillance.

After an hour and a half of driving around in the downtown, Jack finally headed to the large duty free shop on the far end of Kutuzov Avenue that catered for diplomats and top government officials—five miles from the Embassy and about a mile further down the road from the signal site. He took his time cruising the abundantly stocked aisles, watching for faces he could have seen elsewhere in the last few hours. Thirty minutes later, he left the shop with a bag-full of imported foodstuffs he didn't really need.

On his way back, Jack picked up the signal—a blue circle the size of a soccer ball on the wall of an old apartment building. Drawn at about waist height, the sign looked like the deed of a naughty youngster. Thus, the collection had been successful. Now Jack had to return to the Embassy and call the COS. Maybe he could do it from the public phone at Uncle Sam's *and* have his dinner there... As for the groceries he'd just purchased, perhaps he could give them to young Gosha and his friends—*if* he saw him and his friends any time soon. Maybe he should call them, too... Eton... No, Lara. Right, he would call Lara and invite all of them for...

Jack noticed the man at the edge of the pavement from a distance, even from the third lane where he was driving. He was tall, wearing a gray mackintosh-type raincoat. He was standing still like a statue amidst the steady flow of pedestrian hurrying toward the nearest metro station, staring fixedly straight ahead. But that was not what had caught Jack's eye. It was his odd, peaked leather cap. It look... foreign. In his left hand, the man was holding a white plastic bag stuffed with newspapers and something else heavy. A bag with WOOLWORTHS printed on it in big block letters.

If Jack hadn't known any better, he would have thought that it was some sort of signal. But it couldn't be, could it? Two signal sites less than a mile from each other? With the reading scheduled on the same day of the week? Nah, not possible. He stepped on the brake and switched to the second lane, watching the man out of the corner of his eye.

His Mustang must have caught the tall man's eye because he turned his head and stared straight at Jack. When his car came opposite the man, Jack looked through the side window at him. Their eyes locked for a brief moment before the car passed by. The man's lips moved and a cold weight settled in the pit of Jack's stomach.

Was it what he thought it was? Had the man said "Help"? Jack checked the rear mirror.

Something had happened in the split second he was watching the road: one moment the man was looking after his car and the next he was turning abruptly and hurrying away in the opposite direction. Or maybe he thought that his signal had been read and left? So it meant it was a signal... didn't it? But was it possible that... Neither Marat nor William had mentioned... How in the hell could it be?

Jack switched back to the third lane and sped toward the Embassy. He parked on a side street, locked the car and walked briskly to the iron gates. He noticed a militiaman hovering at one corner of the building where usually there was none, and a couple of plain-clothes men lurking at the other end.

"Hey, Jack." Grant waved at the other marine inside the check point and the gate buzzed open. "Back for dinner? Or it is work today?"

"Forgot to close the safe in the office." He made a face. "Then dinner."

"Okay, man. Catch you up at the bar?"

"Sure. Later." He waved a hand and hurried across the compound to the diner.

It was still early and half of the tables at Uncle Sam's were unoccupied. The bar area was busy though, and Jack headed toward it. He ordered a beer, chatted for a few minutes with the bartender and some contractors who worked on the Embassy's new building, then excused himself and sauntered to the public phone in the corner near the restroom.

Nurimbekoff picked up the phone on the third ring. "Hello?"

Jack pitched his voice low and said slowly, "Good evening, sir. This is *Redford*. I've got a package for you that has to be delivered right away."

There was only a fleeting hesitation on the other side, then the Station Chief said, "Right. I'll be in my office in ten minutes, Redford." The line went dead.

Jack hung up, took his beer back to the bar and rejoined the conversation. Ten minutes later he suddenly remembered leaving the door of his office unlocked—he thought so, he wasn't sure, couldn't recall exactly, but maybe it was a good idea to go up and check lest he got in trouble tomorrow morning. He ordered a hamburger and fries, said, "I'll be back", mimicking Arnold's Terminator, and left the diner in a hurry.

Jack gave the same story to the two marines at the metal door on the ninth floor who logged him in, and added, as he was passing through, that he might take fifteen minutes or so to check the incoming cables for his meeting in the morning. Inside the bulletproof door, Jack took two flights of stairs down, and walked along the darkened corridor. He had been on this floor only once before, but knew the set-up of Moscow Station's offices like the back of his hand. He stopped at the farthest office and knocked softly.

The door opened instantly. Right inside of it, there was another door.

"We need to talk?" Nurimbekoff asked quietly, indicating upstairs with his eyes.

"Yes." Jack nodded.

"Okay. Let's take it up then."

The COS locked both doors to his office and strolled briskly to the staircase, with Jack close on his heels. When they reached the room where the Tank was, Nurimbekoff produced a set of two keys from his pants pocket and opened the door with one of them. Of course, he was the Chief of Moscow Station; why shouldn't he have unlimited access to the facility?

Nurimbekoff waved Jack in, locked the door behind them and only then turned the lights on. After opening the door to the Tank with the second key, he walked in and switched on the lights in the see-through room.

"Sit down, Jack," he instructed and sat down. "What happened?"

Suddenly, Jack wasn't sure if the incident with the man on Kutuzov Avenue had actually been something or it was just a figment of his imagination, inflamed with the events of the last two days.

"Sir... Marat, may I ask if we have another signal site one mile from the one I went to read this afternoon?"

"Not that I know of." The COS peered at Jack thoughtfully. "What did you see?"

Jack recounted the incident, leaving out the part about the strange man mouthing "Help!" to him. Now he wasn't sure if it was indeed what he'd seen. Maybe the man had just exhaled.

Nurimbekoff listened to him without a word, watching him closely, his slit-narrow black eyes boring into Jack's, almost unblinking. When Jack finished, he was silent for a minute. "So what made you think it was a signal?"

That took Jack aback a little. "Well, he looked... out of place: a foreign hat, a foreign plastic bag, standing on the curb of the busy street, on a spot visible from all angles. If you ask me, I'd say it looked like a distress signal. Someone asking for exfiltration." He faltered, still uncertain if he should mention what he thought the man had said.

The COS didn't miss a beat. "What else, Jack?"

"I think he said 'help' when I passed by him."

"He did or you *think* he did?"

"He said something, and I think 'help' is what he said," Jack insisted.

"But you're not sure."

"No, I'm not a hundred percent sure what he said. But he looked... desperate."

Nurimbekoff nodded, his eyes still boring into Jack's. "Describe him again."

"Five-eight, five-nine. Well-built, judging by the shoulders. He was wearing a loose gray raincoat, so I couldn't tell if he was heavy. Either dark blond or light brown hair—I couldn't see much because of the cap. The cap. It was unusual: black, peaked. Could be leather. Like a military hat but the peak was lower. And it looked soft. The bag. White... ish. Used. Woolworth's' in large capital letters. It was filled with newspapers and..." Suddenly a thought struck him.

"What is it?" Nurimbekoff asked, his tone insistent.

"Something about the bag. Something was not right..." He tried to visualize the plastic shopping bag in the man's left hand. "Woolworth's, the logo... It's supposed to be in red letters against white background, right? You know the store, don't you?" Or maybe not— you wouldn't be one shopping at a discount store, would you, Mr. Nurimbekoff?

"Yeeaah, I think it *is* in red caps," the COS conceded slowly.

"Well, it was not on the bag. It was white cap letters on a red rectangular background. And..." Jack closed his eyes, trying to recall the logo on the shopping bag, "There was no apostrophe before the 'S'," he concluded, opened his eyes and exhaled deeply.

"Are you sure?" Nurimbekoff was looking at him pensively.

"Yes, I am."

"Does it mean anything to you?"

"White caps on a *red* background? Like in code 'Red'?" Jack made quotation marks with his fingers, then asked quietly, "Do we use specially made Woolworth's bags for signaling?"

"No, we don't." Marat rubbed his chin. "But maybe others do."

"You mean the FBI folks?"

"Nay. And these people might not need to make *special* Woolworth's bags for... any purpose. Have you ever been to England, Jack?"

"I haven't... You mean it could be an MI5 asset?" What is this? What's happening, for Christ's sake? "What's going on, Marat?"

"I don't know, Jack. But it's good that you've called me right away. Very good." He stood up. "I'm assuming that your main reading this afternoon was positive."

"It *was*, sir… Marat."

"Good. Let's go."

In the corridor, he was turning the corner when the COS called softly behind him, "Jack."

Jack turned around.

Nurimbekoff's tone was almost gentle when he spoke up again, but Jack could see his face clearly in the dim light of the corridor—he was not smiling. "No need to tell William about the man with the bag."

Chapter 9

The next day, agitation over Peter Strauss' arrest continued to simmer beneath the busy purposefulness the Embassy staff tried to project. Theories and speculations floated around, but no more facts. Except one: that the Strauss family had packed their bags and left the country.

Jack busied himself with preparations for the Youth and Students Festival and other USIA projects he was handling. He put aside the physicists exchange program though, as it kept his mind sidetracked to the Hamilton - May file and... No, it was just about the file.

He went home early, made himself a sandwich and sat down in the kitchen to the sounds of Desperado. His apartment was on the twelfth floor and from the kitchen window he could see the roofs and chimneys of old factories. At the turn of the century, the Proletarsky District used to be an industrial outskirt; now it was just two metro stations away from the central Boulevard Ring. The sun was going down and the clear blue sky was stained with deep pinks and oranges, and suddenly Jack felt frustrated that the only Eagles' cassette he owned didn't feature Hotel California. He used to buy everything that had a mention of California. What the hell had happened to Hotel California? He'd make it damn sure he bought that album next time he was back in America... Or maybe these Russian kids had their own record of the song. He'd love to have it. Lara had said "our Eton is better than your Don Henley" and she might be right, the boy was something...

Just before 10:00 p.m., Amanda called to ask if he wanted to have lunch at Hotel Peking the following day. They had had lunches at that restaurant twice before and Jack vividly remembered that both times she hadn't enjoyed the food. He offered to take her to the more expensive restaurant at Hotel Nationale instead, but Amanda insisted on her choice.

"It's quieter there. Okie-dokie? See you tomorrow then, handsome", she said in a sing-song voice and hung up. She sounded as if she was high.

Before he fell asleep, Jack's thoughts wandered back to his new Russian friends. William had cleared him to develop these leads, so he could, *should* invite Lara and her friends to his place for dinner. One of these days... Maybe he could get video tapes of the LiveAid concert for them... When he was out to read the Hamilton - May file... Maybe next week?

* * *

Amanda had left most of her *Stolichni* potato and egg salad, and finished only half of her beetroot soup, yet again. She was distracted.

"You don't like the food here, do you? Why do you keep coming here then?" Jack asked when the grim-faced waiter had cleared their soup plates.

"I like the place." She gave the room a look over. "Don't you?"

"I do, too. It's always quiet here. Right?" Jack cocked an eyebrow, gave her a teasing grin.

She smiled back. "Right. And I've noticed that *you* like the food. Works for me... By the way, why didn't you tell me that Bob Dylan is performing here next week? Thought we had a deal—you tell me about the inbound American celebs?"

"Bob Dylan? I didn't know." Jack was surprised. He'd thought at least the consular section, if not his outfit, had the most updated list of visitors. "How do *you* know?"

"Mike and I were at a Russian friend's over the weekend and there was this guy, a poet, couldn't stop talking about how he'd arranged for Bob Dylan to sing at their concert on the eve of the Youth Festival."

"No, I heard nothing about it. But how come the Russians don't advertise the event? I haven't seen any posters anywhere either."

Amanda shrugged. "It's the way things are done here. Anybody who needs to know will know; the rest don't need to know."

A thought struck Jack. "Do you know if they are selling tickets?"

"I can get you an invitation."

"Can you get me ten?"

Amanda burst out a quick laugh. "Jack, you aren't planning on black-marketing them, are you?"

"Nah! I want to invite a group of Russian kids... A student rock band," he explained to Amanda's raised eyebrows. "And their friends. I met them a couple of weeks ago."

"Is little Miss Novikova part of the group?" She narrowed her eyes, smirking faintly.

"Maybe, don't know yet." Jack grinned sheepishly. "The others are science students, from the MGU... Thought the boys from the band would love it."

"No problem, handsome. I'll see what I can do for your friends." She stood up and reached for her handbag. "I'm going to powder my nose. Could you order a tea for me in the meanwhile? With milk, please."

"Sure." He nodded, smiling at her, his mind quickly changing gear.

It suddenly dawned on him that there was a pattern to their lunches at this place. He couldn't immediately recall if they were all on Wednesdays, but was pretty sure that they were neither on Fridays nor Mondays. Amanda would take a seat from where she could see the staircase while Jack would be sitting with his back to it. She would excuse herself before dessert and go to the ladies' coming back ten minutes later, a little breathless, like she had been doing something strenuous. And she had always been a little distracted in this place.

Mandy, oh, Mandy. What are you up to, girl?

His eyes followed her as she disappeared behind the door, his mind working a mile a minute. He didn't think she was a KGB agent—as a columnist, she didn't have access to intel that could be of interest the the KGB. Or, she could be a link in a daisy chain—one of a string of people who would leave or collect signals, sometimes messages, pass them to the next person in the exchange, never knowing the identity and sometimes even the face of their fleeting contacts. Possible? If not for a little detail: except the case officer, all others in a chain were usually locals. And that would leave just one possibility: an intelligence officer. In which case, she wasn't with the CIA: as far as Jack knew, the Company hadn't used civilians without diplomatic immunity as case officers for some time now. That left him with "someone else's intel officer".

Amanda Plante, a British-born columnist, married to a well-established, reputable American reporter of an influential international magazine.

Married for three, four years maybe?

The image of the man on the curb of the wide avenue flashed through Jack's mind. A man with a plastic shopping bag with Woolworth's logo on a red background…

* * *

Marat is saying, looking thoughtful, "And they might not need to make special Woolworth's bags for… any purpose. Have you ever been to England, Jack?"

* * *

Christ, Amanda, being here without a diplomatic cover? You're suicidal, girl!

Jack recalled Mike's face at the reception, looking after his departing young wife—tired, resigned. Did he know?

Amanda was a little breathless when she returned to the table.

"Everything alright?" Jack's concern was genuine.

"Yes." She smiled weakly. "Just a bit of a headache. I've taken a pill… They haven't brought the tea yet, have they?"

"Not yet. Maybe they're waiting for you to come out."

He turned around and waved to the two waiters who were talking quietly in a far corner of the virtually empty restaurant. One of them detached himself from the wall he had been leaning against and sauntered toward their table.

"Can we have our tea and coffee now, please?"

The waiter glared at Jack and said, his tone bored, "Your tea and coffee will be here in a minute." He turned his back on them and walked away unhurriedly.

"What's wrong with these people?" Jack exclaimed, acting exasperated.

"Equality. Or the socialist interpretation of it: 'I'm equal to you, hence I'm not your servant. The only ones I'll serve are those who are *more equal* than me'. You don't look 'more equal', handsome… Not without your tux on," she added with a fond smirk.

"You're a snob, Mandy. You probably shop exclusively at Harrods, too, with your little black dresses and hats. Don't you?" Jack threw the bait and held his breath.

"Nah, I shop at TJ Hughes, sweetie. I'm from around Liverpool, remember?" she said, turning on her Scouse accent. "You know TJ Hughes? It's like your Wal-Mart."

"Dude, we don't have, like, TJ Hughes in Sacramento," Jack retorted jokingly. "*But I know Woolworth's. I think you have it in England, too… Don't you?*" He grinned innocently at her.

Amanda didn't drop her gaze and held her half smile. But for the briefest of moments her eyes lost their glimmer as if the light was switched off in them. Then, with a blink of her eyes, it was on again. She knew the signal.

"We do indeed," she said, stretching her smile. "But I don't shop there personally. Don't ask me why. I just don't."

"I don't shop there either. Prefer The Broadway if you know which one I mean. So maybe I'm a snob just like you, swee'pea." He flashed his dimples at her. "So, tell me, Mandy, what do you know about Russian rock? And rock bands?"

It turned out she knew lots, including major names and bands of the Soviet rock scene, having attended two semiofficial rock festivals in Leningrad and Tallinn. She hadn't heard about either *Krylia* or any rocker named Volkonsky though. But she could always ask her local friend, a journalist and the ultimate authority on the Soviet rock. She could even introduce him if Jack was interested.

Jack was interested alright. In fact, he was interested in anything to do with... his potential target. She promised to invite her friend and Jack to her place.

The mention of Woolworth's in the conversation with Amanda Plante didn't make it into Jack's report the next day. It took him some internal debate to decide against it. It had been just a hunch, the type Nurimbekoff didn't seem to favor. William had a soft spot for speculations, theories and suspicions, but he was away and Jack's reports went straight to the COS in the meantime, and the man, Jack figured, preferred facts. The ones Jack didn't have just yet.

* * *

Jack was finishing his routine read of a heap of local newspapers when Todd the intern called from downstairs. "Jack, a package for you. From MGU. I think it's the Russian scientists list you've been waiting for."

Finally!

"Thanks, man. I'm on my way."

Ten minutes later, back at his desk and slightly out of breath, Jack opened the large, white envelope and pulled out two sheets of typewritten paper. The first was the cover letter with standard formal greetings and references to various previous correspondences. The other was the list with names, titles and specializations. Jack gave the cover page a brief scan and focused on the name list.

1. Volkonsky, Sergei Mikhailovich, Prof., Faculty of Physics, Dept. of Atmospheric Physics, Head of Laboratory of Nuclear Winter, MGU.

2. Arceniev, Dimitri Alexandrovich, Doctor of Science, Faculty of Mathematics, Dept. of Applied Mathematics, MGU.

3. Gradsky, Pavel Borisovich, Candidate of Science, Faculty of Environmental Studies and Policy, MGU.

4. Gussman, Semion Abramovich, *aspirant*, Faculty of Physics, Dept. of Atmospheric Physics, MGU.

5. Volkonsky, Eton Emilievich, *aspirant*, Faculty of Physics, Dept. of Nuclear Physics, MGU...

5. Volkonsky, Eton Emilievich, *aspirant* — postgraduate student—, Faculty of Physics, MGU...

5. Volkonsky, Eton... Department of Nuclear Physics... MGU...

Eton Emilievich... Eton, son of Emil...

Volkonsky, not May, just Volkonsky...

Eton Volkonsky...

Eton...

It took Jack a concerted effort to stop reading the name over and over again and continue with the rest of the list.

6. Tepman, Grigori Izmailovich, *aspirant*, Faculty of Physics, Dept. of Nuclear Physics, MGU.

7. Shubin, Yegor Ivanovich, student, Faculty of Applied Mathematics, MGU.

Grigori Tepman and Yegor Shubin. Grisha the *aspirant* and Gosha the wunderkind.

The one name that was expected to be on the list wasn't there. Dr. Vladlen Alexin, according to Jack's papers, was the MGU's leading specialist on computational modeling. His participation in the joint project had been requested by the American side and endorsed by the WMO. According to Alexin's file, he had spent three months at Berkeley the previous year, working with his American counterparts on a mathematical model for the nuclear winter project.

Now, instead of Alexin, the Russians had put forward a Dmitri Arceniev, Doctor of Science, from the Dept. of Applied Mathematics. Two weeks before the American team was to arrive.

Jack sighed. Complications. Now they'd have to contact the MGU to find out why the composition of the Soviet exchange team had been changed. Maybe he'd better call himself and try his persuasion skills on them. Or maybe he could ask Eton and his friends, Gosha and Grisha... Or Eton...

Damn, who would have thought that the boy would be on the team?

For Christ's sake! Can't you just focus on the job?

Okay, okay. I'm on it.

Forget about that boy. He's not the type. And this is no place for it either.

Right. It's not the place, nor the type...

Jack exhaled sharply and reached for the name cardholder.

He was about to hang up the phone when a young female voice finally answered, "Allo?" The unfriendly tone immediately reminded Jack why they usually asked the local staff to deal with official establishments.

"Good day. I'm calling from the American Embassy," he said, laying on a thick American accent that was usually very light in his fluent Russian.

That caught her attention—thank God, most Russians treated Westerners, especially Americans, with awe and a little fascination thrown in. "Good day," she said more amiably. "This is the office of Professor Volkonsky."

"My name is Jack Smith. I'm from the US Information Agency. Who am I talking to, please?"

"Elena... You can call me Lena." She was young: not only had she left off her patronym, she even offered her informal first name.

"Very well, Lena. I'm calling to ask about Professor Volkonsky's team who will work with our scientists from Berkeley. We received the names of the specialists on your team. I believe it is not altogether correct. Who I can talk to about it, please?"

"You can to talk to Deputy Dean Lykova. She's in charge of all the personnel matters. I can give you her phone number."

Jack didn't want to talk to the personnel department—their team assistant Tanya had spent enough time on bureaucratic procedures with them already. Now he wanted to talk to someone who could spare him the official bullshit and give him a plausible explanation instead, and maybe even solve his problem.

"Thank you, Lenochka," he crooned, going for a little sweet talk, calling her by a diminutive name. "But maybe I can talk to Professor Volkonsky first? I will come to your office. Today or tomorrow? Please help me, Lenochka," he cajoled, adding even more American twang. "I'm in so much trouble because of this last minute change."

That seemed to work: the girl said with a smile in her voice, "Oh, I don't know... Mikhail Alexandrovich is not here yet and I'm not sure what time he will show up."

"You will save my life, Leno—."

"Wait a minute, please," she said into the phone, then turned to someone else on her side of the line, "Hello, Eton. Mikhail Alexandrovich hasn't arrived yet. Do you want to wait for him?"

Eton!

Jack's fingers jerked. The pencil that he had been toying with during the exchange with the girl flicked, made a somersault in midair, hit the back of a guest chair with a loud click and landed on the floor. He heard a deep voice saying something but couldn't make it out.

No, don't go!!

Then Lena said, "Give me a minute. Let me finish with this American from the embassy." Eton had probably asked her about the American from the embassy, because she went on explaining, "He wants to meet with Mikhail Alexandrovich. Today... His name? *Djehck Smeet*... You know him? *Kharasho*, alright." She spoke into the phone again, "*Djehck*? Eton Volkonsky wants to talk to you. He's professor Volkonsky's... from professor Volkonsky's lab."

Jack cleared his throat. "Yes, of course."

There was a pause, some muffled noise as the receiver changed hands, then Eton's voice said tentatively, "*Allo*? Good day, this is Eton."

He sounded formal again, like that morning when Jack had come to his *dacha* with Lara. But at least the boy had volunteered to talk to him and that should count for something, right?

"Hello, Eton. It's great that I can talk to you..." Jack knew exactly what he had to say, had even prepared a little speech—I'm calling on the account of the Soviet team's composition—but instead blurted out, "I didn't know you were on professor Volkonsky's team." He stopped short, and started over, "I've received the list of names of your exchange team and found out about you. I'm glad… I mean, it's great…"

Christ, what are you babbling, dimwit? You're calling because…

"Yes, it's been decided only recently. I'm glad too. I mean, it's an honor for us to work on an international project. Together with American scientists…" Eton trailed off, probably also realizing that it sounded too formal. He took a deep breath and said quietly, "I didn't know you were the coordinator of the exchange program."

He sounded shy, not accusing, but Jack blinked at the fleeting nip of guilt, anyway.

"I'm sorry. I should have mentioned it. Just didn't seem to have a chance." It was not entirely true, but that was alright—that was business. The unusual thing was that Jack was strangely aware of it and somehow it unsettled him. "Listen, Eton, I'm actually calling about Doctor Alexin. You may not know, but the WMO's office specifically asked for his participation from your side… Eton? You still there?" he prompted when there was only silence in response to his explanation.

"Yes, I'm here. And yes, I know about the request for Doctor Alexin's participation."

"So what happened? Why isn't he on your team?"

"He cannot." Eton sounded cornered and ill at ease.

"Why not? He's one of your leading specialists on the Nuclear Winter Theory, isn't he? Isn't an international research program sponsored by the WMO important enough for him to participate?"

"It is. But he's… away."

Eton wasn't telling something, but not hiding it very well either.

"And you can't tell me more."

"I cannot. Sorry."

Lara had said nobody could force Eton do anything he didn't want to. If so, there was probably no point in pushing him.

"Alright, Eton. Can I meet with Professor Volkonsky, anyway? Today maybe?"

"*That* I think is possible. Lena will fix the time for you."

"Good. Thank you, Eton."

"But it will not make Doctor Alexin join the team. If that's what you want to talk to Professor Volkonsky about."

"You sure?"

C'mon, Eton, give me some more.

There was a moment of silence, then Jack heard a sigh and Eton said, "He's not in Moscow."

"Can Professor Volkonsky talk him into coming back? Perhaps we can help, too? We can ask our Ambassador to assist, or even engage the WMO's office, if necessary."

"No one can help."

"Why not?" Jack insisted. He sensed that something had happened and nobody could help, but he had to continue playing his role of a thick-skinned embassy functionary.

There was a pause, then Eton said quietly, sounding resigned, "We don't know where he is."

Lena's voice immediately objected in the background, "But Eton, we were told not to tell them!"

"Wait a minute, please," Eton said into the phone, then off the phone to Lena, "They'll know, anyway. If they haven't already. We can't hide it forever. It's fine, Lena."

Lena's sulky voice said, "as you wish", and Jack could visualize her shrugging and turning away.

"So what happened?" Jack was aware that he was putting the boy on the spot by getting him to talk on the phone about something apparently he'd been told not to let the Americans know. But it was too late to worry about it now—Eton had already spilled it.

There came another sigh, followed by the softly rumbling voice that was beginning to give Jack odd flutters in his stomach, "As I said, we don't know. He just disappeared two months ago."

"Two months ago? But didn't he speak at the Nuclear Winter Conference in Madrid in May?"

"Yes, he did. Then disappeared... Look, Jack, that's all the facts I know. The rest is speculation, alright?" His voice was firm, putting a full stop to the conversation on the topic.

"Alright, I understand... So it means that a meeting with Professor Volkonsky will not help, right?"

"No... But you can come visit the lab anytime."

"Thank you, Eton. I will come for a visit one day... Hey listen, do you guys want to go to a Bob Dylan concert? He'll be here for the Youth Festival."

"Is it true? I've heard nothing about it."

"He'll perform on the 26th, at Lenin Stadium. I'm trying to get tickets for you and your friends."

"Thank you very much, Jack. It would be great."

"No problem," Jack breezed, pushing away the thought that Amanda might not be able to get ten invitations. "How do I get hold of you?"

"Call me." Eton read the phone number twice, then added, "You can call me as late as midnight." His voice was unsure again and Jack found himself grinning.

"Alright, I'll call you when I get the tickets."

"*Kharasho*, alright."

"And Eton?"

"Da?"

"Thanks for letting me know about Doctor Alexin. It is very helpful." He knew he owed it to Eton and the invitations to the Bob Dylan show were not enough.

"No problem."

"Goodbye, Eton. Talk to you later."

"Goodbye... Jack."

There was a loud click, and the line went dead.

Three days later a cable from HQ informed Jack about Dr. Alexin's disappearance in Madrid, the day after the International Conference on Nuclear Winter. The Soviet Embassy had filed an official statement with the *Policia Nacional*, which had immediately launched an investigation. All it had been able to gather was that on May 8th, 1985, at around 18:00, Dr. Alexin had walked out of his hotel in the central part of Madrid with no luggage and never came back. No one had seen or heard from him since. The case remained open, but with neither evidence nor leads, the investigation was going nowhere. One view was that Dr. Alexin, a prominent Soviet physicist, a pioneer in global climate modeling and the creator of the mathematical model for the nuclear winter theory, had defected to the West. The alternative one was that he had been kidnapped, or even assassinated by the KGB.

Amanda called on Friday to ask if Jack wanted to come over for dinner on Sunday. She had invited some of hers and Mike's friends, including Artyom "Art" Tomsky, who knew everything there was to know about the local rock scene. Oh, and by the way, Jack would get his ten tickets to Bob Dylan's show as he wanted at their Wednesday lunch—he still liked the food at Hotel Peking's restaurant, didn't he?

Jack put down the phone and let out a deep breath. Now all he had to do was wait. Till Wednesday. Then he would call Eton, as late as midnight, and ask where they could meet.

Chapter 10

On Saturday, Jack woke up earlier than his usual weekday alarm, anxious and flustered again. He didn't remember his last dream, only that it had something to do with someone blond and that it was impossibly erotic. His raging boner was an aching testimony to that. He walked barefoot to the bathroom, turned on the cold shower and stood under the freezing spray until he was shaking. That and an hour of jogging should wear his body off sufficiently to keep him going for a while, Jack decided, heading back to the bedroom to put on his tracksuit. Until he figured out a better way to deal with his growing friskiness.

Maybe another trip to Helsinki.

Or maybe he'd chance it wherever the Hamilton—May file would be delivered for his perusal.

The morning was wonderfully crisp and sunny and an hour of jogging around the block settled down his disquieted mood. By the time Jack was riding in the lift up to his apartment, he knew what he wanted to do today: he would call Lara and invite her out. He hadn't talked to her for over a week, so it was high time to make an effort to keep up with this potential contact. Maybe he would take her to the movies. He had been frequenting movie theaters around Moscow, with girls from the Embassy's local staff or sometimes alone, to maintain his image as a movie buff. In truth, he didn't mind it at all, even enjoyed some of the Soviet pictures.

He was opening the door when he heard the phone ringing. He kicked the door shut behind him, stole a quick glance at the clock on the wall as he was walking briskly into the sitting room.

8:27 a.m. On a Saturday.

Eton.

Don't be stupid! It's most probably Lara. Hasn't called for a week now, has she?

It was neither. Instead, it was the communications officer on duty in the Embassy's general com-room. After an apology for an early call, he informed Jack that there was an urgent cable for him and he should come to pick it up. Jack feigned exasperation, bitching about a ruined Saturday, then conceded to come collect it the soonest.

Jack showered and changed, gulped down a cup of instant coffee and by 9:30 a.m. was in his office, opening his urgent cable message.

It was from William. Jack was to take the Sunday afternoon flight to Frankfurt, hire a car to drive to Munich where he was to report to the CAO office on Monday morning. The U.S. mission's phone numbers, the travel itinerary, the details of the air and hotel bookings were enclosed.

The Hamilton—May file. Finally!

Jack reread the cable. The instruction for him to leave on Sunday now struck him as a little odd. The Company was usually pretty good at keeping business for weekdays. Unless it was the type of business that couldn't wait. Which was not infrequent, truth be told. But in this particular case, he couldn't see what was so pressing. The Hamilton—May file could wait another twelve hours, couldn't it?

Secondly, his flight back to Moscow was scheduled for the following Sunday. It meant that he was going to spend a week in Munich. Was the dossier so big that he needed a whole week to go through it? Jack couldn't imagine it was.

Or maybe Munich was just another transit stop, like Frankfurt, to cover up his final destination, Washington? All just for reading the files on a couple of NSA staffers who had defected to the Soviet Union some twenty years back? It was all a bit overplayed if Jack was asked. But orders were orders, and he'd be on his way to Munich in just over thirty six hours.

However, it also meant that he wasn't going to dinner at Amanda and Mike's on Sunday.

Jack sighed and reached for the phone.

Amanda was out and Jack chatted with Mike for a few minutes, apologized that he wouldn't be able to come to dinner. Mike said oh well, his tone neutral, then said Amanda would be upset: she had invited a couple of other friends who also shared keen interest in everything Russian—an attaché from the British embassy and his wife. Apparently, Amanda had been raving to them about Jack and the couple looked forward to meeting with him.

Yeah, right, an attaché from the British embassy is dying to meet me three days after I mentioned "Woolworth's" to Amanda.

Before ringing off, Jack asked Mike to tell Amanda that a friend of his would call her to pick up the invitations for the Bob Dylan show.

Jack put down the phone and glared at it for a minute. Now he needed to call Eton and instruct him how to collect the invitations. But he couldn't call him from the Embassy, knowing that all outgoing calls to local phone numbers were tracked. Therefore, it would have to wait. Until he could call from a pay phone, at a time Eton was most certainly home. "As late as midnight".

Twenty past eleven was as late as Jack could hold off. It bothered him that he felt anxious, couldn't wait to make the call, and kept telling himself that it was part of his job. It was a flimsy excuse, he knew it, and the attempt to justify his actions to himself frustrated Jack even more.

He stopped on the way home from the Marine's Bar and called Eton from a *taxaphone* on the street.

Eton answered on the fourth ring. "*Allo?*" He sounded snappish, like he was interrupted from something important.

Jack ignored the tone and offered a lively greeting in Russian, "Good evening, Eton. This is Jack. Hope I'm not interrupting you in the middle of anything important."

He probably was: there was muted clatter, like something much heavier than a pen landed on the floor, Eton saying "damn", then "oh sorry, that's not for you", then there was the sound of a deep intake of breath and Eton finally said, "Good evening... Um, yes, I'm repairing this audio system for my friends."

"Oh. You're working late," Jack noted.

"I've promised to repair it by tomorrow afternoon. For her birthday gathering." He sounded apologetic, and it made Jack smile for no obvious reason.

"I see… Listen, I'm calling about the invitations to Bob Dylan's concert. I won't be able to bring them to you."

"Don't worry about that. Some other time."

"Oh, no, it's not what I meant. You'll get then. But not from me."

"From who then?"

"You'll need to call my friend Amanda. She's a journalist. Very knowledgeable about the Soviet cultural scene," he added, as if it would somehow persuade Eton to call her.

"What about you? Are you going?" Eton asked, sounding suspicious.

"Yes, I am. I hope so… You see, I have to go out of town, on business. But I should be back in time for the concert… Listen, I'll try my best to be back in time, alright?"

"*Kharasho*. I'll see you at the concert then." Eton sounded relieved. He took down Amanda's phone number as Jack read it to him, then said, "You can leave me a message, if I'm not home when you call. I mean, in case you need to call… for anything… When you're back from your trip…"

"Can I?" Jack tried to keep the grin out of his voice, not wanting to add to the young man's obvious unease.

"I have a message recording machine on my phone."

"I see." As far as Jack knew answering machines weren't prolific in the Soviet Union.

"It's convenient. And simple to make."

"You mean you've made it yourself?"

"Yes. It's very easy to make."

Jack heard a shrug in his tone and recalled Gosha going on and on about the audio and light system Eton was supposed to do for the Soviet Students Club at the Youth Festival.

"I can make one for you, if you want," Eton offered.

Jack's grin faded. They had been advised by the security office against using answering machines and to bring all their electronics to the workshop at the Embassy if they needed to be repaired. Now a Russian was offering to make him an appliance considered the best place to plant a bug. So it hadn't been a coincidence after all, had it? God, he was such a sucker!

"Sorry, you probably have one from America," Eton said, sounding embarrassed.

"Thank you, Eton. But I don't use an answering machine here. We've been told not to."

"Why?"

Jack opened his mouth to retort "because they're too easy to bug", but changed his mind—he wasn't ready yet to confront this guy. Needed to sleep on it. "I'm sorry, Eton, I have to go now. I'll try my best to be back for the concert, alright?"

There was a pause, then Eton said quietly, "Alright. Thank you, Jack… And I'm sorry if I said something stupid that offended you. I didn't mean it."

There was a loud click, followed by a jarring beeping tone.

Jack lingered in the booth, clutching at the phone handle, a hot wave of disappointment swelling in him.

So you're so good at making people believe you're their best of friends, huh? Get real, Smith!

* * *

When Jack arrived at English Garden Guesthouse, an elegant boutique hotel inside Munich's largest park, he found himself already checked in. The man at the front desk handed him his room key without asking for Jack's identification documents. In the room, a large, brown envelope was waiting for him on the king-size bed. There were car keys and papers inside, and a printed note with his itinerary for the day. The note read, "12:00— Lunch with Mr. Derek Malone at English Garden Hotel's restaurant (reserved). 13:30— Dep. to Garmisch (car keys, papers enclosed; ask the front desk for the car park). 16:00— Arr. USAG Garmisch. Contact Maj. Harrison for further instructions."

Like in a spy movie.

Jack rolled his eyes at himself.

You *are* a spy, shithead! Christ, when are you going to take it seriously? It's not a game!

Right...

At noon sharp, Jack was sitting at the back of the cozy restaurant—shirt, tie and all. This Mr. Malone could be some big shot from the NSA, he'd figured, and thought he should make an effort to look presentable—after all, he'd be the face of the Company in this inter-agency information exchange.

Through the French window on the left, he could see a lush private garden that overran into the grounds of the city park, Englischer Garten, the namesake of the exclusive little hotel.

Back in his army days, as a pool driver at Ramstein Air Base, Jack used to take big shots and their guests to upscale restaurants and bars. But never, in his wildest dreams, had he imagined that one day he'd be wining and dining in such places, as if he'd had been born into this kind of life. But things kept happening to him, good things, handy, and here he was, Jack Smith from Dry Creek, Wyoming, in a classy little restaurant in Munich, suit and tie and all. Sometimes he had a hard time believing that it wasn't just a dream.

He had been lucky, truly lucky, for most of his life, given his circumstances, meeting the right people at the right time. People who somehow thought that he was good at something, worth helping, God only knew why.

The first of those people was Ms. Linda, his English teacher from grades seven through ten.

Plain and young, fresh out of teachers college, she was passionate about American literature, a subject that nobody in his class or his school thought much of, maybe not even in the whole state of Wyoming. One day, when she couldn't get one goddamn word from his class of nineteen redneck kids, not for the first time either, Jack raised his hand and asked what else Jack London had written, besides The Call Of The Wild which was their reading assignment that month. It was intended as a diversion for his class, to get *her* talking instead of asking them questions. Jack got a thumbs up from his pals, a few pats on his back and a free Coke afterwards. But what he didn't care to admit, even to himself, was that he couldn't stand the hopelessness in Ms. Linda's eyes anymore. Why? Well, it annoyed the shit out of him and he thought he'd had enough, that's why.

That day, Ms. Linda decided Jack was the one who could share her passion for books. To Jack's own surprise, he got hooked and by ninth grade had devoured her personal book collection. Plus the books she borrowed for him from the tiny public library in Rawlins.

Ms. Linda's books, and before that his Ma, were the only things that helped Jack stand the place and life of privation he'd been born into, when all he wanted, as long as he could remember, was to grow up and run away to California. Or anywhere. Because *anywhere* was a hundred times better than Nowhere, Wyoming. And even more so after his Ma died—hadn't been able to shake off her deep chest cough, after an exceptionally cold winter, and was gone one day, leaving Jack behind with his constantly drunk father and no one else within a ten mile radius. Books were what got Jack through back then. Books and Ms. Linda.

At first.

Once in a while, she would invite him to come by her place to pick up a new book. She lived in a tiny apartment over the Laundromat, five miles from the school, so dropping by for fifteen minutes was no hardship at all. Especially when, more often than not, she would offer Jack a sandwich or a bowl of soup or a slice of cake. However, in the tenth grade, Jack noticed that Ms. Linda was looking at him somewhat differently: more like staring, sometimes with an odd little smile on her flushed face. Other times she would stand too close, leaning into him, or putting her hand on his shoulder for a bit longer than necessary.

In the end, he bedded her. Or she him. Either way, it didn't really matter. What bewildered Jack was that he felt neither good nor proud about it. Nothing like what other boys raved about scoring with a girl, the older she was the more glory to the winner. So he kept quiet about it.

Truth was, he didn't have the heart to turn her down after everything she'd done for him, and then gazed at him with that hungry, pleading and at the same time deeply shamed look on her face. So Jack just closed his eyes and gave her what she seemed to be wanting. However, he couldn't do it anymore after the fourth or fifth time, when Ms. Linda began to feel more confident and vocal. Because then even the image of bare-chested Butch Cassidy behind his closed eyes couldn't distract Jack from the whiny, little girl voice and oversized, squashy breasts she kept pressing his hands onto.

Jack dropped out of school. Got an approving grunt from his old man for the first time. He never saw Ms. Linda again. Heard she moved back to her hometown in Nebraska.

Unfortunately, it meant that Jack had to drive fifty odd miles to Rawlins in his barely breathing truck, if he wanted to read books. The alternative was to give up reading altogether. Because he didn't want anybody knowing about this odd pastime of his, thought it was kind of weak, girly. He held out for two months before caving in: cut back on what little he earned for cigarettes and beer to be able to spend on a trip a month to Rawlins.

Until he fell asleep over a book one night, bone-deep tired after a hard calving day. And found himself on the floor in the morning, kicked out of bed by his father. Jack ended up with a shiner and bruised ribs that kept him wincing for three days. The book fared worse: thrown out of the window into the dust, it barely survived. And his father's parting words were that he'd burn any shit like that next time he found it and knock those stupid ideas out of the lazy sonavabitch he wished weren't his son.

Defeated, Jack resolved to take the book back to the library. And start figuring out how and where to flee from the goddamn place he hated.

That was when he found himself sitting in his dead truck on the side of the road, on his way back from Rawlins, planning on packing up his two shirts and pair of old jeans and taking off. Well, when he'd recovered a little from another bashing tonight, because sure as hell he was going to get one, if he wouldn't get his piece-a-shit of a truck started, like in another five minutes!

It didn't. Instead, an old Buick stopped by and its driver asked if Jack needed help.

Mr. Jennings, a recruiter, did help Jack and not only with his truck. It turned out he was from poor ranch stock himself, way up in Montana, and knew first-hand the kind of life Jack had been trapped in. And he knew just the way out for Jack. The long and short of it, a month later Jack enlisted, was assigned to be a truck driver and on his way to Travis Air Force Base, California.

The deal with Mr. Jennings had cost Jack sixty dollars he hadn't had, but managed to scrape up by sneaking out and selling his old man's precious rifle and Whiskey Gurl, the young bay mare, the best of the four horses on the ranch. It had almost broken Jack's heart to let go of her, but he hoped that she would be better off at any other, proper ranch. Then, for another ten bucks, leaving Jack with the last ten and change, Mr. Jennings had told him about the Montgomery GI Bill: if Jack didn't mind getting less cash every month for his cigarettes and beer—"And girls," the recruiter winked at him knowingly—by the end of his service, he would get an education benefit and could enroll in a college.

The GI Bill was the most incredible thing Jack had come across. All he had to do was catch up on the stuff he missed after dropping out of school. So he worked his ass off whenever he had a spare minute, plodding through textbooks he borrowed at the air base's library, in between military drill, mechanical training, physical training, and more drills and driving, routine vehicle maintenance, and God knows what else.

He had more time for study at Ramstein Air Base where he was reassigned a few months after enlisting. It was there that he discovered that learning languages was easy. Within a year, he was chatting up local girls in fluent German, picking up French and even some Polish from the airbase's local and foreign personnel with whom he'd become quick friends.

Then he met Joe.

The older man gave Jack his first taste of things he craved but had little idea of how to go about getting them. He also taught Jack many things, first in Germany, then, over the years, in America. Some of the things Jack learned the hard way. But to be fair, Joe had been a good mentor to him, maybe even the best, and Jack was indebted to the man for where he was now—half way to his dream ranch in California.

Anyway, that was all that Joe was to him now—his mentor. Jack was over with—

"Well, well, well. Look who we have here. You sure have cleaned up nicely, haven't you, boy?"

Guh! He should have guessed. His itinerary had been so well orchestrated, so controlled. So Joe Coburn.

Jack stood up and turned around to face the Soviet and Eastern European Division's Head of Clandestine Operations. If Joe had come out himself to meet with Jack, it had to be something more than the Hamilton—May file.

Of medium height and average built, with sandy graying hair, Joe Coburn was a perfect specimen of what the Company wanted its field officers to look like: inconspicuous, forgettable, easily transformable into someone else. Today he seemed to be himself though, dressed casually in a cardigan of deep burgundy color and charcoal gray slacks. He looked tired.

"Good afternoon, Mr. Malone." Jack wasn't too sure what the rules of engagement on this occasion were and decided to play it safe by using the name given in the instruction.

"Call me Derek, for now," said Joe as they shook hands.

He gave Jack an appreciative look over, motioned him to return to his seat and sat down on the opposite chair. A barely noticeable taunting smile played at the corners of his thin lips.

"Alright, Derek," Jack said formally and sat down.

The last time he had talked to Joe Coburn was over fourteen months ago before his departure for his first posting in Frankfurt. It had been all business, like it had always been in DC. In fact, Joe had never let it slip, not even when they were alone in his office, that he had ever known Jack other than as one of his junior staffers. But as he was leaving after the individual briefing in Joe's office, the chief of ops had shown him to the door, said under his breath, "Be very careful, boy."

"I told you, Jack, you'd go far. Didn't I?" Joe stretched his shoulders and neck, all his movements deliberate and feline. "With your skills, your looks and your luck. A combination you don't come by every day."

Joe Coburn had a way of putting his interlocutors ill at ease with his blunt remarks. That was what he was doing to Jack now. He was one of the very few people who could stifle Jack's ready supply of words. And his tone was one he had used talking to Jack back in California, and in Germany before that, but never in Washington DC.

"Thank you," Jack mumbled, self-conscious and edgy.

"You're in luck again, boy."

"Am I?" Jack brushed aside Joe's appreciative smirk and the word "boy" that rubbed him the wrong way.

"You are. With the two high profile cases you've landed… The Nuclear Winter exchange project and this May-Volkonsky case. The fact they are related plays nicely into your hands."

"Since when has May Volkonsky become a case?" Jack wasn't sure how he felt about Eton May Volkonsky becoming a "high profile case" in the Company's books.

Joe watched him closely as though weighing whether Jack could be trusted with what he was going to say. "When we approached them for the H-M files, the NSA folks jumped at your connection… They want us to develop this contact and jointly run it," he explained. "In exchange for information."

"Oh. So they have information that the boy has potential?"

"What they currently have is what we've provided them with, as the background for our request for the files. They've decided the target has potential… What's *your* assessment, Jack? Has he?"

"Well, the guy is a nuclear physics scientist in the making. Reportedly gifted. So yes, he is promising. But at this point, there's no indication as to where he's going. In fact, he is said to have turned down a rare offer of a position at the International Research Institute in Dubna—a dream job for any scientist in the Soviet Union. This seems to corroborate his friends' view of him as being rather unpredictable." Jack's tone was matter-of-fact, his gut clenched in a tight ball.

"That's what I thought too." Joe looked pleased. "Nevertheless, they insist the target has good potential for *their* coverage of the Soviet nuclear research."

"But they want *us* to run him."

Joe tilted his head.

"And what if he's not suitable?"

"Why don't you develop him first? Then we'll see how it goes. Assignments like this don't come round often, Jack. You do this and consider the next progression is yours. Maybe even this year. Now, didn't I tell you that you were one lucky bastard?"

"Thank you." He tried to ignore Joe's playfulness and the heaviness that was settling at the bottom of in his stomach. "What about the Nuclear Winter project? You said it's one of the two."

Joe waved his fingers at the waitress who was hovering in the far corner of the dining room in their line of sight, then turned to Jack again. "Let's have lunch first. We can talk about it later, on our way to Garmisch."

Jack nodded.

Right. It meant he was to drive Joe Coburn from Munich to the US Army Garrison in Garmisch-Partenkirchen. Two hours in the closed confines of a car with Joe Coburn. Who was obviously in a playful mood today. Jack didn't like the thought, but as it stood, there was little he could do about it.

Chapter 11

They picked up the car at the hotel parking lot, loaded their suitcases and headed south, along miles of forests that run up to the suburbs of Munich. And for the whole while, Jack's mind was preoccupied with a stub of a boarding pass that had fallen out of Joe's wallet as they were paying for their hotel rooms. Joe had instantly snatched up the little square of paper and stuffed it back into his wallet. But not before Jack caught "British Airways", "London" and "Munich" printed on it.

"By the way, the Brits have expressed their appreciation for the service rendered by Moscow Station last week," Joe dropped casually when they left behind the suburbs.

So he'd noticed Jack catching a glimpse of the boarding stub. "The Brits," Jack mumbled.

"Yes, the Brits... They would have missed the distress signal if not for you. But it also was because of you that their agent nearly screwed up his own exfiltration."

"What happened?"

"Apparently he took you for the signal reader and left the site. *Before* his reader turned up."

Jesus!

"But my car carries American dip plates. How could he... Unless we..." He threw a quizzical glance Joe's way.

"No, we don't team up with the Brits in Moscow. The poor bastard was probably fazed. His KGB colleagues had been on his ass for some time."

"Was that what the Brits said?"

Joe barked out a laugh, looked at him in mocking disbelief. "Jack, in our trade nobody tells anyone things like this. You haven't heard anything from me either... Except for their appreciation. That will go in your records. As well as Marat's. He's happy with your performance, by the way."

"Thank you. I'm glad... So, what happened to the agent?"

"Exfiltrated."

Joe's answer was clipped but Jack caught a hint of bitterness in his tone. It suddenly occurred to him that this incident with the MI6 agent could be associated with the recent roll-ups of their own assets and officers.

"He was the third asset busted by the KGB in the last few months, wasn't he? Including GTTAW?" he asked quietly.

Joe lit a cigarette, took a long draw, rolled down his window and blew the smoke out. "Fifth," he dropped, his face grim.

"*What*?!" Jack stared at him.

"The others were all ours, including an FBI." Joe took another deep drag on his cigarette and sighed heavily.

Holy shit!

"Anyone managed to come in?"

"One. At the Russian embassy in Greece. He was spooked and called for help. Exfiltrated two months ago. You know about VANQUISH. The FBI's agent has missed three contact slots so far. They think they've lost him."

"Jesus. What's going on, Joe?" he asked, incredulous, dropping his official tone.

"I don't know, Jack. Something obviously isn't right."

Joe didn't tell him anything about the Nuclear Winter project, said that Jack was not cleared for that information. Neither had he anything to say on the disappearance of Dr. Alexin, when Jack asked, except that the culprits might as well be the Sovs as the Americans, their interests were that entangled. The only thing he was sure about was that it wasn't one of *his* ops, but God knew what else the bosses had in their books.

Joe sounded frustrated as he rambled on. Jack had never seen him in such a mood before, neither had he heard him bitching about the thriving factional squabbles at HQ. He guessed his chief of ops found himself on the wrong side of the fence and felt a tinge of sympathy for the man. Despite his shortcomings, Joe Coburn was known for a nearly religious belief that they were indebted to the agents he and his case officers ran and did all he could to protect them. That was why the SE Division's field officers forgave their chief of ops for pushing them a little too hard a little too often.

However, Jack's sympathy and forgiveness didn't extend to physical comfort. He braced himself when Joe told him he needed a pit stop. It was an unwelcome *déjà vu*: which was exactly how he and Joe had become lovers over eight years ago, on the forest floor, off the two-lane road that ran from K-Town to Jack's airbase.

He slowed down, drove off the road and stopped in front of an opening in the thick wall of firs they were passing by. He cut off the engine, took out a cigarette and rolled down his window.

"Aren't you going to stretch your legs?" Joe asked.

"No, I'm good, Joe. I'll wait here." He puffed out a cloud of smoke, kept his eyes firmly on the road in front.

Joe was silent for a moment, watching his profile, then put his hand high on Jack's thigh, squeezed it lightly. "You sure? I know you want it too."

Jack closed his eyes. Fuck. Fuck his horniness! It had been a nuisance for months now and he didn't know how much longer he could go without. He was so over Joe, but even just thinking of sex—of *not* having sex with him—had left Jack half hard.

It's only sex. The same sex you get at any bar in Frankfurt. Or Munich. Or San Francisco.

No, it's not.

You need it, right? It's like taking an aspirin and a Coke when you've got a headache.

Anyone but Joe Coburn!

C'mon, just a quick fuck. Close your eyes and think of someone else.

Eton...

What?!! You're out of your fucking mind, Smith!

He exhaled sharply, opened his eyes and turned to Joe.

Who was still looking at him, waiting for an answer, his eyes slightly squinted, his hand hot and heavy on Jack's thigh.

"I don't think it's a good idea," Jack said quietly.

"Why?" Joe's tone wasn't challenging, not even irritated. Just curious.

"I don't think I need more baggage to try to slip through the polygraph. And neither do you, Joe. It isn't worth it… Is it?" Jack threw the ball at the older man. Then, realizing that it might have come across as bitter, he added, "You told me to be very careful. I'm doing just that."

Polygraph tests were something that all Agency's staff had to go through: nobody was hired without passing the lie detector, codenamed LCFLUTTER, first. Once inside, everybody had to be "fluttered" routinely, field officers more frequently than others. As a result, passing the polygraph when you had something you wanted to keep to yourself was a bit of an issue. It required nerve and skill. Joe had taught him a few tricks about that too and Jack had turned out to be a good student.

However, the polygraph was only part of the reason. The other, major part, which Jack didn't have the heart to tell his mentor, was that he was so done fucking around with him. He wanted Joe to take his itch elsewhere. He wished the man got the message and leave him alone.

Joe looked at him for a long moment, his expression neutral, then he nodded and withdrew his hand. "Fair enough… Alright, I'll take a leak, anyway." He opened the door and put a foot on the ground. "You can stretch your legs if you want, Jack." He closed the door carefully and strode quickly into the pine forest.

It was nearly 4:00 p.m. when they reached Garmisch. After dropping the chief of ops off at Edelweiss Lodge where visiting VIPs usually stayed, Jack checked in at the Russian Institute's boarding house. Everything was the same as when he'd been here six months ago, taking the pre-posting course of Russian and Soviet studies. Jack had dinner with two of his old instructors who'd welcomed him back like a prodigal son, then had a beer with a group of off-duty officers in a village pub a mile from the garrison. He stayed back when they left, ordered a double scotch and downed it in one shot.

His sleep was dreamless that night.

The Hamilton - May dossier was a curious collation of facts and speculations split into three sections. The first was the personnel files of the two men when they were employed by the National Security Agency, notoriously known as the most secretive agency the American government ran. The second section contained reports and findings of several independent investigations into the defection, and the last comprised various briefs from the FBI, CIA and State Department, as well as a collection of news clips, records of private conversations and even rumors about the case.

The gist of the case was one day in June 1960, after four years as code-breakers at the NSA, Richard "Rich" Hamilton, 29, and Emil Jonathan "EJ" May, 31, defected to the Soviet Union via Mexico and Cuba. Their disappearance was discovered a week after; however, only when the two appeared in an elaborately staged press conference in Moscow a month later that their defection was confirmed. In their statement, the men expressed their deep disillusionment with the U.S. government's drive to build up first-strike nuclear capabilities, which they called "suicidal". Furthermore, they accused the U.S. of deliberately violating the airspace of other nations and then lying about them and misleading public opinion.

The defection had left both politicians and intelligence officials dumbfounded and Jack could see why. What unsettled him was that, based on someone's off the wall remark, overnight, it had snowballed into a "queer traitors" case that rocked the country. The two men were labeled "sexual deviates" and the NSA began screening their staff in search of other queers. In the course of the following year, the NSA fired twenty-six employees claimed to be a "security risk" because of their alleged "sexual perversions". Over the next decade, the NSA and Pentagon carried out a number of investigations into the Hamilton— May defection, none of them producing any evidence to support the claims that the pair's primary motive for defection had been their sexual orientation. In fact, no hard evidence was ever found that the two were indeed homosexual. Nevertheless, the Pentagon continued portraying them as a couple of queers in all its public statements.

In the meantime, a year after their highly publicized press conference in Moscow, Rich Hamilton moved to Leningrad. EJ May remained in Moscow where he was accepted by the MGU as a mathematician in one of Prof. Volkonsky's research programs. Shortly after, he married the professor's daughter, eighteen-year-old Vera, fathered a son with her the following year, divorced her five years later. That same year Rich Hamilton drowned in a fishing accident. He had never married.

The last, short brief on EJ May was by the CIA, dated December 1976. It reported, in terse, cable-like language, the death of E.J.M., the cause being "alcoholic intoxication". In other words, Emil Jonathan May had drunk himself into oblivion, at the age of forty-seven.

Damn! What is their problem, old bastards? Why couldn't they be like... like other fathers? Hope he didn't... was kind to his son. Emil Jonathan May from Eureka, California... California, huh? He'd better have been good to the boy.

Jack scrolled the microfilm to the section where the last picture of EJ May was included. A strong featured, handsome face. A little haggard and tense, but determined.

A good face. Not mean like my old man's. He couldn't be too bad as a father... Blond, pale gray eyes. Not warm brown. The boy must have the mother's eyes...

For Christ's sake! Would you focus on the job?

Fine. Done with the file anyway.

He pulled the cassette out of the microfilm reader, switched it off and looked at his watch. It was nearly 6:00 p.m. It had taken him the whole day to plow through the dossier after all. Tomorrow morning he would go through the much thinner CIA file and then he would be ready to discuss it with Joe.

Joe Coburn who could read Jack no worse than a lie detector.

When Jack returned to his room in the evening, there was a note on his desk inviting him for breakfast with Mr. Malone at Edelweiss Lodge, followed by a hike in the mountains.

Next morning, when Jack came to the restaurant, the chief of ops was already there, reading a newspaper with his coffee. They talked shop while eating their breakfast, with Joe sharing news from home—local politics and football. If the man harbored any ill feelings about the unpleasant incident the day before, he hid them well: Jack couldn't detect anything out of the ordinary in Joe's tone or conduct.

After breakfast, they took the trail outside the village and headed towards the mountains. They walked briskly for ten minutes, barely exchanging a word, then Joe slowed down.

"So, how is he, this EM junior? Is he queer like his old man?" Joe asked, not trying to hide his sarcasm.

Jack almost stumbled. "What? I don't think so. And it's clear from the files that there's no evidence to support that allegation... is there?" He hoped Joe wouldn't pick up on the defensiveness he felt.

"The NSA folks want him to be queer. So that they can go back to their original 'queer traitors' theory."

"They want *What*?? Is this some kind of a joke?"

"Part of the reason they never made the findings public. It gives them an avenue to revisit the case. When opportune."

"But even if the father *was* gay, it doesn't necessarily mean that the son is too, does it?" Jack stopped. It was ridiculous, and Joe should understand this more than anybody else, shouldn't he?

Joe turned to him, motioned his head for Jack to continue walking. "You're right, it doesn't. Their thesis is that if the son happens to be gay, then it doesn't matter if the father wasn't. It can be used as circumstantial evidence that the father was, too."

"But it's like twenty five years ago. Who even cares about this crap anymore?" Jack was aware that he was beginning to sound contrary, but couldn't get past the absurdity of the premise. He stopped again, staring down Joe's back, incredulous.

"You'd be surprised. There're still people at the NSA and Pentagon who do. Sometimes other people's treason can get personal, Jack... Especially when the defectors were from the shop you used to run at the beginning of your glorious career." Joe finally noticed that Jack was no longer at his back and turned around. "You don't look convinced. Alright, let me make it easy for you. He doesn't need to be queer. He just needs to be *persuaded* to work for us and, if possible, *that* way."

"You mean they want him to be honey-potted into working for us," Jack said flatly.

Joe didn't respond, not even with a nod. He stared at Jack with an odd smile that didn't reach his eyes.

"And I'm the one who's supposed to do it," Jack concluded gravely, a chill running down his back. The morning sun lavished its warmth on them, flushing a wave of heat on to Jack's face and ears, leaving a cold, slippery feeling inside.

"You got it, boy." Joe exhaled, like he had just done some weightlifting, suddenly looking older and tired. He set off walking again.

Reluctantly, Jack followed him. "Why me?" he wanted to ask, but the answer was obvious—who else if not him? He was probably the only queer case officer in the SE Division, besides the chief of ops himself. And the man had probably recruited him for assignments like this in the first place.

Damn you, Joe, you conniving bastard!

Alright, so he was screwed anyway, from the day he had stupidly agreed to join the Company. But the boy? It wasn't his fault that his daddy had deserted his almighty employer a quarter of a century ago.

"Why him?" he asked quietly. "He's not even out of the university yet. And he doesn't have access to any meaningful information. The kid will be ruined once we're done spinning him. All for nothing."

Joe stopped walking. "*Not* 'for nothing', Jack. You forget that he's part of the Nuclear Winter research program. Now, we don't know at this point what we'll get from *this* connection, but this is the second assignment you'll be running. This one at the request of the State Department." He set off again, gesturing Jack to follow him. "Besides, you have reported that he's a genius and has great potential. If that is true, you'll steer him to join some top secret research facility. And there you are: you'll have cultivated another VANQUISH. From scratch. He'll be your star agent, Jack... Besides, this kid was ruined for an ordinary life the day he was born."

Jack stared at the back of Joe's head for a long moment, then asked quietly, "What about me, Joe? Wouldn't this op mark me as queer, too?"

Joe swirled around. "No, it wouldn't. Don't you worry about it. It will be a Director's case op, classified as top secret. I'll run it myself. If it works, it will only mean that he's gay, or with queer inclinations, and you have mastered the seduction skills. If it doesn't, nobody'll be the wiser... Besides, you'll be exempted from polygraph on that part of the op." He paused, watching Jack closely for his reaction. "But that's only Part A of the op."

"There's a Part B?"

Of course, he should have known. The operation couldn't possibly be plain vanilla if the SE Division's head of clandestine operations had come out to the field himself to brief Jack.

"Yes. And Part B is this: if this boy happens to be an informer, or is being run by the KGB, like Marat and William think, they'll try to turn the tables and pitch *you*. And that will be the perfect entry for you as a dangle. You can't think of a better one."

"A dangle... Right."

At least it was inspiring that Joe Coburn trusted him enough to select him to be a dangle—a spy who posed as a traitor and through whom disinformation was fed to the other side. It was considered the most cunning elements of spy wars, the others being "collection", or simply spying, and "denial", or hiding the information the enemy wanted. Denial also included uncovering and arresting the enemy's agents, something the KGB had been doing quite successfully lately. Now it looked like the SE Division's chief of clandestine ops was planning to insert a dangle, as a counter measure. The key was to select someone who was reliable enough to be fed to the KGB because there was always a risk that the opposition could triple the dangle up.

But this also meant that his deep cover in Moscow would be pierced as he must be identified as a CIA officer to be attractive enough a target for the KGB.

"... So if Part B comes into play, Part A will naturally fall away. As I said, the direct benefit for you is that you won't be polygraphed in relation to the seduction part of the op. As a Director's case operations officer, you'll have a special status." Joe peered at him. "Any questions so far?"

"Yes. I was under impression that the Sovs didn't recognize, um, homosexuals as a matter of principle. Now you're saying they may pitch me with *that*?"

"C'mon Jack, you should have figured by now that what they preach isn't exactly what they do. F.Y.I., they tried that previously, and in Moscow too."

"What? When?"

"Some thirty years ago. Two marines were compromised. That was when they got the floor plan of the Embassy. They also tried to pull that off with a case officer."

"Are you serious?" Jesus Christ, why hadn't they been told about this, neither at the Farm, nor at the SE Division's internal ops training? Weren't they supposed to know about *everything* they would be up against?

"It only happened three times in the last thirty years. All unsuccessful."

"And now it's our turn to use it on them."

"We've never used it on the Sovs before. Besides, they know our internal security policy since the McCarthy's times. They won't see this coming, not from us... Being the first mover is always an honor, Jack. Hope you know that. You can become a legend if you—if *we*—succeed. You understand?" He stopped to face Jack, smiling at him encouragingly.

Sure he did: Joe was trying to turn him into the Company's unique, controversial asset and institutionalize it—*him*. Jack had heard stories about Joe Coburn's intricate special ops in East Asia, most of them successful, according to the grapevine. He had never thought that Joe would put him smack in the middle of one such scheme.

He didn't return Joe's smile. "Yes, I understand. It's all been decided, hasn't it?"

Joe headed off up the hillside, motioning Jack to follow him. "You can still say no. But I wouldn't advise it... Besides, this case guarantees a fast track career progression. Not to mention the perks that go with the job. You know it, don't you?" He cut an emphatic glance at Jack.

"I do. And I appreciate you offering this case to me, Joe... Can I ask something? What will happen to the NSA and the Nuclear Winter agendas if Part A falls away and I become a dangle?"

"Ah. Now, that is a good question, Jack. Then you'll sell both of them to the KGB. Your main story line will be our keen interest in the Nuclear Winter program. That will also explain why the May kid has been chosen for access. But that will only happen if they pitch you. And *that* will happen if the kid turns you in. Until such time, you'll keep your current cover."

"I see." He didn't, it was all so convoluted. "Let me get this straight. Does this mean that both the NSA's and Nuclear Winter agendas have been designed to be fed to the KGB?"

"No, they're a real deal. But we can always *adjust* them at a later stage if the need arises. Especially the Nuclear Winter part... But don't you worry about that now. It is Part B—*if* and *when* we get to that point."

The mill was right about Joe's ploys—they were intricate and with many moving parts, making it hard even for the players to get the full picture. Except maybe for the controllers of the game. The one thing Jack thought he figured right was that his chief of ops was fully prepared to sacrifice the NSA's and the State Department's agendas if that helped the Company to pull off its own game plan.

"Right." What else was there to say?

"Agreed? There's a good boy." Joe patted him on the back. "Now, let's have a quick trek on this loop. I want to be back by lunchtime. We'll go through the details of the op in the afternoon. Shouldn't take more than a couple of hours."

Is that it?

"And tomorrow?"

"No plans for tomorrow. You can take a couple of days off and spend some time in Munich. Just don't go wild." He looked at Jack sideways, a faintest of smirks playing a corner of his mouth.

Yes!

"I need to go back to Moscow. Friday morning the latest," Jack said after a moment of hesitation.

What?! You need to spend some time in Munich, moron!

"I got invites for a Bob Dylan concert. He's coming for the Youth Festival, apparently. I'm taking young Volkonsky and his friends to see it. And Deputy Minister Novikov's daughter."

"Good job. But with this new op up and running, maybe you should back pedal with her a little. We don't need complications with her. For now."

"I understand. So, shall I move my flight up?"

"Aren't you going to stay in Munich?" There was a hint of surprise in Joe's tone.

"Yes, tonight, if we'll be done by mid-afternoon, and tomorrow. I'll take the morning flight on Friday."

You stupid sucker, you've been offered a four-day stay in Munich. Four fuckin' days!

I have a job to do. Just been assigned a special op to run.

Yeah, right. That's the reason, huh?

That is the reason. And he is the target. Getting to him is what Joe wants me to do.

"Will that be alright?" Jack forced a smile at his chief of ops.

Joe Coburn stared at him for a few seconds, unsmiling, then he shrugged. "If you must. Just be careful, boy."

Chapter 12

The project Joe Coburn had brought with him was codenamed GTTALION. It was drafted by someone at HQ, with input from Moscow Station's chief, and preapproved by the DCI. As Joe was obsessed with minute detail and Jack determined to leave as little ambiguity as possible to avoid dealing with it in Moscow, it took them almost four hours to plow through the details of the project outline—activities, expected outcomes, target agents, technical support, covers, and various options in case the planned activities got botched up. According to the plan, Jack could take his time building a friendship with young Volkonsky, sharing his hobbies, whatever they were, gradually steering him in the direction the Company wanted. He was to go to the young man's shows, student parties and discotheques, or fishing, drinking, womanizing, if that was what the target was into. Jack's USIA assignment as a coordinator of the Berkley Nuclear Winter team's visit and work at the MGU gave him four months to get close to the target on "justifiable" grounds. By the time the Americans left, his relationship with Eton and his friends was expected to be established enough not to give grounds for questions and suspicion. Then, in a year or two, depending on the situation, Jack would make a move on Eton May Volkonsky, code name GTSALT. In short, he had all the time he needed to cultivate a new GTVANQUISH.

It was agreed that during the first stage of the op Jack would keep his deep cover and stay clear of other case officers at the Embassy, most of whom were known to or suspected by the KGB. The exception was William Osbourne, conveniently placed as his USIA boss. However, Jack's reports in relation to TALION that went through William and the COS would not include the seduction part of the op, codenamed GTSEABROOK. On this part, Jack was to report directly to the chief of ops—in person, at their meetings that would take place once every few months. In cases of emergency, he was to dispatch an innocuous cable from the general communication room to a special mailbox at the headquarters of the USIA with either or both of the words "water" or "sea" embedded in the text. The cable would be collected on the hour and Jack would be instructed on the next steps within the following twelve hours.

Except for SEABROOK, Jack's other tasks and reporting lines remained the same. And he didn't have to worry about Nurimbekoff wanting his deep cover to be lifted because the COS felt short-handed. It had been agreed with Nurimbekoff that Jack's cover would stay intact and HQ would look into the Station's staffing issue.

"Anything you need?" Joe closed the file in front of him. "For the new op?... For yourself?"

"A recording of the LiveAid concert would be great. To share with the Russians. I'm sure that'll score me a few brownie points with young Volkonsky and his band."

"You mean of the entire concert?"

"Yes... A homemade recording off the live television program, if possible."

"You got it." Joe nodded with a faint approving smile.

Jack left Garmisch after 6:00 p.m. He took the highway and was at the southern outskirt of Munich by half past seven. The rush hour traffic had already subsided, and he got to the English Garden Hotel in no time, parked the car and checked in. He showered and changed quickly and shortly after eight was flagging down a cab three blocks from the hotel. He headed straight to the red light district behind the main train station. To hell with the SDR, he'd just have dinner, hang around for a while and would take surveillance detection precautions later, *if* he decided to go for some action.

He didn't. By 10:00 p.m. and his fourth beer Jack felt exhausted. Mostly by the agitation that had been nibbling at him since the moment Joe Coburn let him in the Director's case ops. Maybe he should go to bed early and sleep it off. Then maybe tomorrow he would be in a better mood for some action he needed. He wandered back, feeling oddly cocooned in his own world in the midst of the bubbling nightlife of downtown Munich. Back at the hotel, he had a double shot of whiskey at the bar downstairs and went to bed.

The next morning Jack woke up feeling rested and at ease. A thin ray of sunlight came through the narrow gap in the heavy velvet curtains and he decided to laze in bed for a change. It was his day off, he was in a classy hotel, back from behind the Iron Curtain and there was nothing waiting to be taken care of—well, at least nothing urgent. Not even the morning wood! He chuckled, stretching like a cat. Come to think of it, he couldn't recall the last time he'd had such a peaceful moment.

It was almost ten o'clock when Jack came down for breakfast. The restaurant was empty, except for an elderly couple at the table by the French window. He ordered a big breakfast and sauntered to the newspaper stand in the corner near the door. The hotel obviously catered for English and French speaking clientele, as besides local newspapers, there were copies of today's The Times, Financial Times, Le Figaro, and a yesterday's copy of the New York Times.

Jack picked up a copy each of the Times and Suddeutsche Zeitung and returned to his table. He opened the English newspaper first and... froze, eyes glued to the title in big block letters on the front page: "ROCK HUDSON: AIDS DIAGNOSIS CONFIRMED."

"Mr. Rock Hudson, an American movie star... Pasteur Institute, Paris... press release... being evaluated and treated... complications of acquired immunodeficiency syndrome..."

Jack stared at the newspaper for what seemed like an eternity.

How could it be? Jesus Christ, how could it be?

* * *

The first time he read about AIDS, then called GRID for "gay-related immunodeficiency", was in the spring of 1982, early into his dating days with Carmen. One evening she came rushing into his tiny studio, an expression of disgust on her pretty face, and handed him a copy of the New York Times. It was opened on the page with a long, feature article about the outbreak of a "new homosexual disorder". She insisted that Jack read it at once. He did, dread and bile rising, clogging his throat. By that time, rumors had reached him about a strange cancer spreading in the gay community. He hadn't paid much attention to it since he'd been trying to change—to date girls and stick by them. But this... Holy fuckin' shit!

When he put down the newspaper, Carmen demanded that he had to stop hanging out with Tommy and Cruz, who, as she'd heard, were a couple of queers. The nerdy Tommy Horvitz was Jack's classmate and his friend Cruz was a second year art student. One couldn't imagine a more dissimilar pair than completely closeted Tommy and gregarious Cruz, who kept up appearances only for his friend's sake. Jack would have a drink with them occasionally and was always left feeling sorry for Cruz. So he told Carmen he wasn't going to ditch his friends because of some stupid rumors. And that she shouldn't take for granted everything people said, for that matter. Would she believe it if someone had told her that he, Jack Smith, was gay?

Carmen gaped at him, then burst out laughing. "Don't be silly, Jack. If you're gay, then I'm a footballer."

They left it at that.

A year after that incident, and by that time it was after little Carmen, too, Jack caved in and drove three hours across the border to Tijuana to get what he craved.

By that time, AIDS had claimed over four thousand lives in America and Europe—gay and straight, young, old and children—and was spreading across the world with frightening speed. Jack didn't learn about it until much later.

* * *

Jack left half his breakfast and returned to his room, the copy of the Times tucked under his arm. He locked the door, sat down on his bed and re-read the article three more time, shaken to the core by the actor's brutally honest admission.

"I am not happy that I am sick. I am not happy that I have AIDS. But if that is helping others, I can at least know that my own misfortune has had some positive worth."

Jack wanted to talk to someone, to share his thoughts and fears, to get some comfort, if nothing else. But the only person who knew about him was Joe—well, besides a string of one night stands and quick fucks at the back of some dubious bars over the years. He didn't want to talk to Joe, even if he knew Joe could offer good advice. But it was not advice that he needed. What he needed was—

Oh, for Christ's sake, stop moping around and go do something about it!

Fine!... I will, alright?

Just go and do it already.

He didn't go out until late in the afternoon, and in the end settled for "regular" sex.

The woman who took him home was a nurse, tall, athletic and blonde, refreshingly straightforward and open-minded about experiments in bed. And she didn't mind the time it took her to get Jack up and going, and the fact that he couldn't climax until he took her from behind. Afterwards, she gossiped about her co-workers while they drank coffee in her tiny, spotless kitchen. Around 10:00 p.m., Jack thanked her and excused himself, citing an early morning flight. She made him promise that he'd call her when he was in town again. He gave her a friendly peck on the lips and left.

He felt relieved, if only a tad drained. Emptied.

Empty.

Jack arrived at the airport two and a half hours before his Lufthansa flight to Moscow. Only to learn that it was delayed for technical reasons and that the new time of departure was 9:00 a.m. It was a hassle, but what could he do? At least he would be back by 2:00 p.m. Moscow time. One hour to get home from the airport. Still plenty of time to prepare for the concert. And to call Eton... And Lara, of course.

However, by 9:30 a.m. it was obvious that the flight was further delayed. An hour later, they were told that "for technical reasons and passengers' safety" the carrier had decided to change the aircraft. The new time of departure was 12:30 p.m. It meant that he wouldn't get to Moscow till 5:30 p.m. and home till 6:30 p.m. and that was only if he was lucky with the Friday night traffic. What's more, it meant that he wasn't going to see *him—them*—for a week: both they and he would be tied up with the Festival activities, they at the Soviet Students' Club and he with the American delegates.

They boarded at 12:30 p.m. as announced, but the aircraft didn't actually take off for another hour. By that time, Jack had lost any hope of making it to the concert. He wanted to tell the stewardesses to get lost when they kept offering him drinks, then newspapers, then a blanket, snacks and whatever else they had, every five fricking minutes. But he smiled politely, accepted everything they gave him, then left them untouched on the vacant seat next to him.

It was almost eight o'clock when Jack got home. He changed quickly and went out. For a walk, he told himself.

He walked the empty streets until dark before calling Eton from a *taxaphone*. The phone rang three times before the unhurried rumble came on: "*Privet*, hi. If you'd like to leave me a message, please do it after the tone."

"Hey, Eton, this is... eh, me. Sorry I'm calling only now. There were some unexpected complications with my trip and I got back late. Hope you guys liked the concert. Talk to you later, alright? You can call me anytime... if you wish. Bye."

When Jack returned to his place, he poured himself half a tumbler of whiskey and took it to the bedroom. He laid on top of his bed for a long time, nursing his drink, thinking about Rock Hudson and whether he should tell Lara about him.

On Saturday morning the 12th International Festival of Youth and Students was opening at Lenin Stadium. Jack was supposed to meet the American delegates at 8:45 a.m. at the mammoth Hotel Rossiya that flanked the Red Square. From there they were to take buses to the stadium.

He was having his coffee in the kitchen, listening to the local morning news, when the phone rang. He leaped to answer it.

"Hello?"

"Good morning... Jack. Apologies for calling so early," the familiar, warm baritone said tentatively.

"Hey, good morning. No problem at all. I was hoping you'd call... I left you a message," he said redundantly and made a face at himself.

"Yes, I got it. Sorry I didn't call back. It was too late when I got home..." He trailed off, as if unsure what else to say. Then, as Jack opened his mouth to explain why he hadn't shown last night, Eton asked tersely, "What happened?"

"My flight was delayed, and I only got home by eight. Sorry, I couldn't call to warn you… all. It was, um, *inconvenient.*" He hoped Eton understood what he meant.

"I understand."

"So how was the concert? Did you like it?"

"Yes. It was good." There was a smile in his tone of voice. "Bob Dylan sang four songs."

"That's all?" Hadn't Amanda said it was a Bob Dylan concert?

"It was an international poetry night, not a concert. Your Allen Ginsberg was a guest, too."

"Allen Ginsberg?" Christ, how were all these folks getting here with no one at the Embassy knowing anything about, not even the Company?

"Yes. He's popular with intellectuals here. You know, don't you?"

"I've heard." As well as of the beatnik poet's openly gay lifestyle. Didn't the Soviets know about it? Either way, he wasn't going there with this young man. "Hope you enjoyed it, too."

"It was alright."

Right. Maybe not so much.

"Are you guys going to be busy during the festival?" Jack asked when no further elaboration seemed to be coming from the other end.

"Yes. At the Soviet club… And you?"

"I'll be accompanying our delegates during the festival. Will be tied up for the whole week, too."

"Hope you'll come visit our club. With your delegation."

Was he inviting Jack to come to his club?

"I will, if we are invited."

"You are. I've seen the visiting schedule. You, your delegation has been invited for the gala night."

Jack wasn't sure how he felt about it. Part of him was delighted that Eton wanted to see him again, but the other part was wary about the young man's obviously keen interest in his visit to the Soviet club. Why was he so insistent?

"Will you come?" Eton prompted quietly, and Jack recalled the first time they met and Eton asking if Jack would come to his *dacha*—his expression and his tone so vulnerable, it had melted Jack's insides.

"Of course I will."

"Alright, then."

Did he sound relieved or Jack had imagined it?

"Listen, I have to go. We're going to the Festival opening. See you later?"

"Yes, see you."

"*Poka*, Jack, till then."

Jack put down the phone and sat staring at it, re-winding all his interactions with Eton May Volkonsky from the start. The Russian had been unfriendly at the first meeting, almost hostile, then warmed up when Jack came for lunch at his *dacha*, even smiled a little. The next time they talked, he had told Jack about Dr. Alexin's disappearance that he'd apparently been told not to share with American counterparts. And just now he had practically insisted that Jack came to the Soviet Students' Club. Wasn't it a bit too fast?

Haven't you been trying to get close to him, too? Got him invitations to the Dylan show. Brought him cigarettes from Finland.

Yeah, but that's my job.

So? Maybe it's his job, too.

Jack sighed. He didn't want it to be "his job too". Even if the man was officially Jack's job now.

* * *

The opening ceremony of the 12th World Festival of Youth and Students was awe-inspiring. The hundred-thousand-seat stadium was packed with young people of various ethnicities, in national costume or uniforms specially tailored for the occasion. The central section of the audience, opposite the dignitaries guest box, used different colored sheets to create waves and multicolored patterns, animated images of earth, Red Square, historical events or anti-war slogans. Hundreds of schoolchildren danced in the arena in total cohesion, athletes formed dozens of towering human structures, thousands of white doves soared into the bright blue sky as a massive children's choir sang about peace and happy childhood. In closing, representatives of a hundred and fifty countries, dressed in national costume and holding national flags, circled the stadium track. Jack had never seen anything like it in his life. But then, apparently neither had the rest of the audience, maybe even the performers themselves.

However, it wasn't the magnificent performance that dazed everyone—those at the stadium, the Soviet TV audience watching the event live, and soon the rest of world. It was Comrade Gorbachev's opening speech that beat it by miles.

It began as usual, asserting that the Kremlin's goal was a world without wars and weapons, alluding to reactionary forces and their relentless efforts to hang on to power they derived from the arms race. He recalled the atomic bombs dropped on Hiroshima and Nagasaki and declared that the Soviet Union favored the complete banning and elimination of nuclear weapons. Then, stunning everybody, he announced a five-month unilateral moratorium on nuclear tests in the Soviet Union, starting August 6th, the 40th anniversary of Hiroshima.

The man was a master of the game: his timing was perfect, the choice of place and audience impeccable, the announcement dramatic. This was a move the Americans didn't see coming from the new Leader of the Soviet Communist Party, only five months into his appointment. It caught them completely off guard.

Jack knew better than to accept the statement at face value. But he had to admit, it was a daring move. He suspected there was an ulterior motive to the Soviet unilateral moratorium. Bah, for all he knew, the Sovs might be running out of money because of this spiraling, never-ending arms race with America. Could be possible, couldn't it? The state supplied *everything* to its people here and Jack saw how poorly shops were stocked in Moscow and Leningrad. He suspected they were even emptier in more distant corners of the Soviet empire.

Anyway, he held his breath waiting for Washington's response to Moscow's declaration.

And the answer was a resounding "no". The White House rejected the proposition off-hand, claiming that it was not in the United States' interest—unless and until such a ban could be verified.

Jack wasn't too surprised at his Government's hardcore response. It was a shame as it handed the Soviets the advantage in the propaganda war if nothing else. So now, what he and his colleagues attending the Festival's events would face were endless, oftentimes sarcastic, remarks and questions about America missing this unique opportunity to cut back the arms race. He didn't look forward to it.

The first two days of the Festival were heavy on seminars, political debates and philosophical discussions that took place at several major universities around Moscow. Gorbachev's unilateral freeze of nuclear testing and the White House's refusal to do the same were the main underlying theme of meetings, marches and rallies around town. The Soviet and leftist press sought out leaders of delegations for comments that praised Moscow and condemned Washington. Even some of the Western mainstream journalists were impressed by the Soviet leader's move.

By the third day, Jack was getting weary of Soviet propaganda he'd been enduring at various functions he had to attend with his delegation. The only relief from this during the day was the unreserved fraternizing of young people of various nationalities at multiple venues around the city. Parties raged every night into the early hours, and the mood was as if the party would never end.

The following afternoon, his delegates were taken to yet another political discussion, this time with the representatives of the Soviet students at the Moscow State University, the MGU. Jack would have skipped it, had the forum been held at another place, with another audience. But the MGU was different: *some* MGU students were part of his job—if *they* were going to participate in this forum. No, he was certain that *they* would.

Chapter 13

When Jack arrived at the MGU's main entrance with a bus full of his casually dressed compatriots, they were greeted by a group of official-looking young people wearing formal smiles. After ceremonious welcome and introductions, the American guests were escorted through the labyrinth of corridors with vaulted ceilings and marble staircases to one of MGU's vast auditoriums. Jack recalled the last time day he'd been here, invited by Lara for the rehearsal of their concert. It hadn't been a month, but felt like a lifetime ago.

Jack couldn't spot any familiar faces amongst the Russians, so after a while, he decided to sneak out of the forum, feeling he'd reached his limit of undiluted Soviet propaganda. He empathized with these people's hopes and beliefs, but his understanding could endure only so much.

The auditorium's only door was located at the same level as the blackboard, presided over by staid Soviet characters and informal-looking Americans. Jack tiptoed down the steps along the wall, smiling apologetically in response to disapproving glares, carefully pulled the heavy door ajar and slipped out.

Once outside, he sighed with relief and headed down the long corridor to a small niche at its far end. He'd spotted it when he was looking for a place for a quiet smoke prior to the meeting. It cradled a tall window and a narrow, sealed door that lead into a tiny back yard. He perched himself on the windowsill, the corridor leading to the auditorium at his back, pulled out his pack of Lucky Strikes and fired a cigarette.

It was gray and drizzling outside as if it hadn't been sunny and warm just yesterday. And last weekend. And the weekend two weeks ago, at the *dacha* in Peredelkino. Jack hoped it hadn't been his last sunny weekend at a *dacha*... at *that dacha*, with the pine forest, the birches, the river and a long, leisurely lunch in the garden. He wondered if they had horses somewhere around those country houses. Would be nice to ride a horse in the forest. He hadn't ridden a horse for ages and missed it so...

He heard the sound of approaching footsteps behind him, but didn't turn to look. Russians rarely socialized with strangers, so maybe they would just pass him by if he didn't make an eye contact, didn't smile at them.

The footsteps died behind his back and Jack resisted the impulse to turn around. He needed a moment of solitude, just a few minutes, to finish his smoke at least.

"Hello, Jack," a deep voice said.

Jack jumped, almost dropped his cigarette. He turned around in his seat, an ear-to-ear grin on his face.

"Sorry. Hope I'm not disturbing you. I saw you walking this way, so I thought..." Eton smiled awkwardly and shuffled his feet.

"*Privet*, Eton!" Jack slid off the windowsill and thrust his hand to the young man. "No, not at all. It's good to see you! I'm glad you've decided to come by and say hi."

This time the youth didn't hesitate to grasp Jack's hand in a cordial handshake, blushing a little. Then he hoisted himself onto the sill, three feet away, and Jack returned to his perch, inspecting him with interest.

Eton was wearing a formal white shirt tucked into dark gray trousers with a black leather belt, and black lace-up shoes. His blond hair was combed down neatly and he looked every bit the academic type he was supposed to be, completely different from the cool, unruffled rocker Jack had seen before.

Eton reached into his trouser pocket and produced a pack of cigarettes. Marlboro red. He noticed Jack glancing at the pack and smiled shyly. "Your present. Thank you again."

"Nah, don't mention it." Jack shook his head, feeling absurdly pleased.

"The discussion in there nearly short-circuited my brain. Thought I needed a smoke too," Eton mumbled, lighting his cigarette.

"I didn't see you in there." Good work, huh, Smith?

"I saw you."

"So... what do you think about all this serious stuff they are discussing in there?"

Eton was silent for a few moments, peering at him as if assessing whether Jack could be trusted with the answer, then shrugged. "It's all rhetoric. I hope they will start doing what they are saying they should do. Before long."

Coming from a Soviet, it could only be a provocation, or an attempt to buy the trust of a Westerner, to get close to him. Jack peered at the young man, trying to discern any sign of pretense. Eton fidgeted under his gaze, but didn't drop his eyes and Jack noticed color creeping up onto his ears.

"Are *you* doing anything?" He realized that it sounded like a challenge and added, "Or you prefer to just skip the talking part?"

"I do what I can," Eton said and there was no defensiveness in his quiet answer, only sincerity. "What about you?"

"Me? Well, strange as it may sound, coming from an Embassy official, I'm not really into politics. I prefer to stick to my neck of the woods — culture, history... People. I like meeting with people. Different kinds of people. Like you, for example. I find you, how to say it, fascinating." Jack shook his head reassuringly, seeing Eton's face turning ten shades of red. "No, I'm serious. You're unique here. Different, *da*? Back home, I knew some Russian Americans, offspring of mixed American and Russian couples. In America, they're just like everybody else. But here, you're the first. I mean a Soviet citizen of American heritage. And that's... that's great! And please don't kill your friends for telling me about you. I am the culprit. I was curious about your excellent English when I heard you singing the first time." He laughed softly. "Sorry, I've embarrassed you. I just wanted you to know that... well, it's good to know you, Eton."

"Thank you... I'd rather you treat me like, um, other common folks." Eton gazed out of the window and said quietly, "Sometimes it's tiring to be different here." He dragged his eyes back to meet Jack's, gave him a crooked little smile.

"I see. Alright, I'll try... So, I assume you speak English as well as you sing in English. Do you?"

Eton hesitated for a moment. "Yes, I can speak English. Haven't spoken for a while though. So it might be a bit rusty."

"You know what? Let's speak English. You and I." Jack lowered his voice conspiratorially. "I rarely have a chance to speak English with Russians here. It will be... different, *da?*"

Eton dropped his eyes to inspect the remains of the cigarette in his fingers, chewing on the inside of his bottom lip. As Jack was beginning to think that maybe it wasn't such a good idea after all, the Russian looked up and nodded. "Okay, let's," he said in English. "It will help me to practice it."

His English didn't need any practice as far as Jack could tell from the two clipped sentences Eton had uttered. He had the faintest, soft rolling accent that could barely be traced back to Russian, but he spoke noticeably slower than when he did in Russian, like he was watching himself choosing correct words.

"Your English is very good. But some more practice never hurts, does it?" Jack nodded encouragingly and carried on in English. "So tell me, Eton, in layman's terms, what exactly is this nuclear winter thing all about and what it is that you guys are trying to achieve. I'm coordinating the exchange program on behalf of the sponsoring side, but to be honest, I only have a general idea about this theory of yours. That the world will be plunged into a long winter if there is a large-scale nuclear war. Is it true, or it's just a... like the worst case scenario?"

He was down playing his understanding of the program to be true to his "character", and to get the boy talking about it. Additionally, he thought it wasn't a bad idea to get the other side's perspective. A firmer grasp of the subject wouldn't hurt either for the sake of his *other* assignment. Especially if it could help him understand why the State Department had requested CIA coverage of a scientific exchange program. Joe hadn't elaborated on this matter, and Jack thought he could try to figure it out himself.

That was all work of course. But leaving aside all the hassle of the dual jobs, deep inside Jack felt that he'd believe whatever this reserved Soviet post-grad student had to say. And that Eton wouldn't think less of Jack because of his shortcomings, real or acted up, and would tell him as it was.

He was right. In the next twenty minutes, Eton explained to him what nuclear winter theory was all about, and the consequences the scientists were predicting after a major nuclear exchange. His explanation was simple and brutally precise, and at times oddly poetic.

"An explosion from a typical two-megaton nuclear bomb is like a piece of the sun dropped on the earth. Even if it is for a moment, the outcome is, ugh, unimaginable... Remember Hiroshima? *That* bomb's power was only a fraction of the standard warheads we have today. In fact, less than one thousandth. Can you imagine it?"

He told Jack about the history of nuclear winter theory, also known as nuclear twilight theory, that was only a few years old. He described the controversy generated by the conclusions arrived at by several groups of scientists. The two polarized views were based on different assumptions and mathematical models used to project the outcome of total nuclear war in Europe. Surprisingly, this time the division line cut across American and Russian scientific echelons. At the front line of the Western radical view was a group of scientists called RAPTT, named after the initials of the five leading scientists from several universities across America. Prof. Ackerman was the "A" in RAPTT. In the Soviet Union, the leading authorities were Prof. Volkonsky, Dr. Alexin and Dr. Ivashin. Eton also explained what the joint Soviet - American mission was expected to achieve during the four-month program.

It was a revelation to Jack, and he felt annoyed with himself that he hadn't done his homework for this overt assignment, like he normally did for his covert ones. For him, it had just been a scientific exchange program between two universities, one with a flashy name, and it hadn't sounded that important at the time.

"So you're saying that the program's mission is to review all studies done so far and to come to a conclusion: how likely it is that we'll end up in a months-long winter — *if* there's a major nuclear war in Europe."

"Correct."

"And you guys will have to determine how many bombs it would take to push us over the edge."

"That's right. And if a major nuclear war can be contained."

"And half of you think that it's all greatly exaggerated, while the other half believes that, between America and Russia, only a fraction of our arms would suffice to blow up the daylight."

The corners of Eton's lips twitched as he nodded.

"And you're saying that no more than a thousand bombs is all that's needed," Jack insisted, eyeing the young man suspiciously.

"Possibly less."

That sounded scary. Jack recalled reading that America had about twenty-five thousands nuclear bombs and warheads. The Soviets had probably even more. And what about other countries — France, Great Britain, China? That *was* scary!

"It means that the rest of the world's arsenal is just one huge, friggin' waste of money?" he concluded.

"That's politics. You said you weren't interested in it." Eton pointed out with a straight face, but his squinted eyes were gleaming.

Jack felt heat rising to his ears and forced a quick, goofy laugh. How in the hell had it happened that this youth was telling him about nuclear wars and global politics like he was Jack's older brother and Jack was a twelve-year-old kid? And the weird thing was that Jack didn't feel belittled by it. On the contrary, he felt oddly pleased. And proud. Of Eton Volkonsky. Who was Jack's—

Nobody. He's nobody to you.

He's my target. And will become my star agent one day as Joe said.

Target - yes. Star agent - maybe. But that's pretty much it.

Of course that's it. Who's saying it isn't? But he needs to believe that I'm his friend.

He does, not you, dickhead.

Jack pulled out his Lucky Strikes, flicked out a couple and offered one to Eton.

"So which side are you on in this debate? And how many bombs do you think each of our sides need?"

The amused expression slid off Eton's face like a mask and suddenly he looked older. "None. We need none," he said quietly.

"Oh, like Gorbachev said at the Festival opening? The world without weapons and wars. Do you believe him?" Jack felt a twinge of guilt at having to do this to the young man, who had been so open and sincere with him so far.

Once again, Eton refused to pick up the challenge. He looked Jack in the eye and shrugged. "You know that's all politics."

"Okay, I agree. It's all politics. And your Gorbachev is a great politician. Even I can tell... Anyway, coming back to nuclear winter models. You haven't said which side you're on. Or should I ask which side Professor Volkonsky and you are on?"

Eton looked through the window, on which the mist from fine drizzle was amassing into thin, winding rivulets. When he turned to Jack, a sad smile was shadowing his lips. "We are on the opposing sides," he said with a sigh.

"Oh." Jack was taken aback by such a straightforward answer. "So are you on Professor Ackerman's side, then?"

"No. Professor Ackerman is on the same side as my grandfather. And I suspect his whole team is, too."

Was this guy for real? He didn't even try embellishing the story, not even a little bit. It didn't sound like a setup either, Jack was almost confident about that. What would the KGB benefit from Jack knowing about the rift between all these scientists? *If* the boy was with the KGB. More and more, Jack was inclined to think that he wasn't. He decided to push Eton a little further.

"What about Dr. Alexin?"

Eton looked at him from under his eyelashes, head bowed. "He was... I am on the same side with him. Basically, he and I are on the American side, minus Professor Ackerman's group," he clarified, watching Jack intently.

"I thought Dr. Alexin worked at Professor Ackerman's lab at Berkeley last year? Wasn't it the same project? How come they now have different views?"

Eton shrugged. "That's how scientific research works. One day we agree, then the next day we completely disagree. On details of what we agreed before."

Jack pondered on it for a few seconds. "Could it be the reason why he disappeared?" he asked cautiously. "Because he disagreed... with something you guys are doing?"

"Maybe. I guess so... I don't know, Jack. I'm not supposed to discuss his disappearance with you Americans."

"You're told not to by...?"

"What difference does it make? He's gone, okay?" Eton exhaled sharply. It looked like his patience with Jack's questioning was running thin. "And I don't believe he will come back... I wouldn't either, if I were him," he finished under his breath and turned away to look through the window again.

Oh. So this wasn't what Jack had thought it was, then? A defection? But Joe Coburn had said—

"Eton! Volkonsky!" A young female voice called from the end of the corridor where the auditorium was. "Where have you disappeared to? Come help us to explain your nuclear winter thing to these Americans, will you? They don't understand!" She sounded exasperated, apparently with the thick American delegates.

"Coming," Eton called out to the girl and slid down from the windowsill. "We'll be having a gala concert at our club on Thursday, with a discothèque afterwards. We—I mean *Krylia*—will be playing. The American delegation is invited too... Will you come?"

He sounded bashful again and hopeful, and it made Jack feel all warm and light. "I wouldn't miss it for love or money." He grinned at the young man—teeth, eyes, dimples and all.

Eton smiled back, blushing slightly. "Okay, I will see you then?"

"You will."

They didn't shake hands as Eton took his leave, and Jack turned around on the windowsill, eyeing the tall, lithe figure. The young man never looked back, but Jack knew he was aware of him watching: as he was about to turn the corner, Eton raised his right hand to the level of his shoulder, palm facing forward, then quickly curled his fingers into a fist. Salute!

That night Jack dreamed he was explaining the nuclear winter theory to Joe, William, Marat and his cohort of intelligence officers, in the large auditorium at HQ called the Bubble. In fact, it looked like the entire headquarters was packed into the room. Jack was on the podium at the front, telling them in Eton's voice:

"The explosion from your typical two-megaton bomb is like a piece of the sun dropped on the surface of the earth. Remember Hiroshima? *That* bomb carried the yield of only one-thousandths of our standard warheads today. One. Thousandth. Think about it... Now imagine us dropping a thousand such bombs on a thousand major cities worldwide. Besides their complete obliteration, the bombing will produce a gigantic amount of dust and soot. It's like putting a giant match to a straw mountain. That is not to mention the oil fields and forest fires. So, it is the dust, the soot and smoke from burning cities, forests and oil fields that would forever change the world we know today. Once the sides exchange a few thousand megatons worth of bombs that will be it. The irreversible, global climatic change will be triggered. The raging fires will produce a colossal amount of smoke, which together with dust aerosols will be lofted into the high atmosphere. Once there, the sunlight will further heat the smoke, lifting it even higher. In the stratosphere, where there is no rain to wash it out, the smoke will persist for years, shielding the earth from the sun. With no sunlight, the temperature in the entire northern hemisphere will plunge thirty degrees Celsius, even during summertime, and will remain below zero for months. Maybe even for years. The world's agriculture will be dead, the food supply chain destroyed."

Jack paused, looking into his colleagues and compatriots' faces, some of them impassive, some disapproving, then he asked quietly, in his own, shaky voice, "But even before the nuclear winter sets in, what will happen to the people of the thousand cities that are targets of the nuclear strikes? What will happen to them? And to those who will be unlucky to survive?"

He was jolted out of his strange dream, covered in cold sweat, and couldn't get back to sleep for a long time.

Chapter 14

Lara called early on Wednesday morning. She was running late for her Soviet Students' Club, but wanted to make sure Jack was coming to the gala concert and discotheque they were throwing the next day. Everybody would be there—*Krylia*, Viktor Viktorovich of course, the MGU crowd and lots more. Besides Americans, the club had also invited the Cuban, Nicaraguan and Vietnamese delegations. Lara and her friends had met with all of them a few days back and they had all been tons of fun, especially the Latin Americans. But most importantly, there would be a surprise waiting for Jack—without revealing all, *Krylia* would be playing in a special show staged by Viktor Viktorovich. She was sure Jack would love it.

Krylia in Karelin's show? Jack didn't like the idea of Eton and Karelin working together on a musical, but said he would be there, no matter what, not in the least because he hadn't seen her for ages. She said, "see you tomorrow, *daragusha*," blew him a kiss and hung up.

After the call with Lara, Jack contemplated phoning Amanda to ask if she cared for lunch. He hadn't talked to her since their last lunch at Hotel Peking and wondered if anything would change in their flirty relationship after the exfiltration of the MI6's agent Joe had told him about in Germany.

He called her office from the Embassy. She was on her way out—to a forum sponsored by the East German delegation. She already had a lunch date and Jack would never guess with whom—Dean Reed, did Jack know him?

Jack had heard about the American-born singer-actor who lived in East Germany and was a big star on this side of the Iron Curtain. He said no, he didn't, but would love to meet him if Amanda thought he should.

She thought so indeed. They agreed to meet at the Soviet Students Club's gala concert as Dean was invited too and would be singing there.

After releasing the call, Jack sat at his desk a long while, staring at the gray partition in front of him. How strange life was that women who were after his ass always tried to impress Jack by introducing him to other men, some of them talented, some intriguing, some drop-dead gorgeous. And some all of the above...

The following afternoon they met in the foyer of Hotel Cosmos, a twenty-five story, semi-circular building of steel-and-glass, which catered primarily for guests from Western countries.

Dean Reed turned out to be mild mannered and soft-spoken, unlike Hollywood movie stars one saw on American TV. There was also a touch of sadness, or maybe resignation, beneath his friendly façade, the type that melted women's hearts on the spot, and maybe even some men's, even though most would never admit it. Having spent a late night at the Embassy reading up on "Red Elvis", by now, Jack already knew that the actor was a heartthrob of two generations of Soviet moviegoers who loved East German-made westerns: Dean Reed's typical role in those movies was of a good white colonist, friend to Indian chiefs and their people.

They were met at the door by the whole committee that was led by Anya who turned out to be the Soviet Club's vice chair. Jack didn't hesitate to make use of his status as the official representative of the American delegation and present the American-born actor to Anya. She was all smitten in a minute and looked at Jack with a breathless, grateful smile. Finally, he'd managed to get to her, too.

There was another person who was thrilled by Dean Reed's presence and didn't try to hide it—Karelin. The scraggy Russian all but devoured the handsome singer with his eyes and it made Jack want to gag. He prayed others didn't see through the little spectacle Karelin was giving. But it wasn't meant to be: turned out Amanda knew Karelin.

She kissed with him three times the traditional Russian style, and launched into a quiet, animated conversation, as if resuming it from where they'd just left off a short while ago. In a few minutes, Karelin clapped his hands and ordered all performers, including Dean, to the dressing rooms at the back of the stage to prepare for the concert. Amanda, Jack and Dean's media-security escort were told to come back in an hour.

"Care for a quick snack?" Jack asked when he and Amanda found themselves on their own.

"With you, anytime, handsome."

She winked at him and took his arm. They headed towards the staircase.

"Looks like you know *him* well." Jack said.

"Who you mean?" Amanda arched her shapely eyebrows.

"The Russian. Karelin," he mouthed. "Interesting character."

"Ah, *him*." Amanda picked up on his effort to be discreet within the walls of a hotel they both knew wired. "I met him at an *experimental* theater."

She narrowed her eyes, peering at him and Jack figured it meant something not officially permitted. Underground, maybe?

"He's very talented and quite well known, actually," she continued. "*Outside*, too. I attempted to introduce him to some of *our* experts. It didn't go down very well. For *him*." She sighed.

"Why?" Jack thought he knew why.

"The organs don't like him."

"Because he's... *different?*"

She turned to him at that. "Did you pick up on *that?*"

Jack rolled his eyes. "C'mon, Mandy! He doesn't even try to be discreet about it. Checks up every moving body with a..." He waved his hand in the direction below his waist and made a face.

The corners of her mouth twitched in a little rueful smile. "You're right. He doesn't want to be discreet about it. To his own detriment. Stubborn as an ass, this man. Insists that it is his right to be what he was born to be. And if they acknowledge that he's brilliant in something, he wants them to accept the rest of him."

"That's hard, man... I thought it was a criminal offense here. How does he *cope?*"

"Apparently, he's got protectors high up," she whispered as they reached the restaurant door and stopped, waiting to be seated.

When they had placed their order of *bliny* pancakes with minced meat and coffees, Amanda gave him a thoughtful look, as if debating whether she should mention it, then said, "Your little friend L. is an interesting case too."

"You think so?" He cocked his brows, copying her.

"Very open... In fact, maybe too open?"

"Why is it bad? I thought Gorbachev had announced the season of openness recently. Maybe she's taken it literally."

"Maybe... So who has she introduced you to so far? Besides her *favorite* director, obviously."

"To her student friends, mostly. The band. You met them last week. At the concert."

Not that he was going to tell her that some of those students were involved in an international project, which had suddenly become a special joint project of the CIA and NSA, with the State Department spicing up the combo.

"That's right, the band. By the way, I've asked *my* friend about them. The rock pundit I told you about, remember? You asked me a few weeks ago if I knew them."

Of course, he remembered: he had intended it as a spur of a moment question, an idle chat most folks may or may not recall afterwards. But of course if she'd been trained like him, she would remember even inconsequential things like this.

"I did?" Jack furrowed his brows. "Can't recall now. So, what did your friend say about them?" About him.

"He didn't say much about the band. They're just a good student band, popular at discotheques around universities in town. But apparently, their front man is known in *other* places," she said, watching him closely.

"Other places? Like what?"

"My friend says he's a talented musician. He heard the boy singing his own piece once, at a... ah, *private function*. My friend was impressed. He tried to invite him to participate in a festival afterwards. But the guy turned him down flat."

"Rock festival?"

"Yep. They are semi-official, organized twice a year, in Leningrad and Tallinn."

"Oh, yeah," Jack intoned, as if he had just recalled it. "I remember now. You said you'd been to one of those. Leningrad, wasn't it?"

"Yes. They're not bad at all, if you ask me."

"Why did the boy turn it down then?"

"My friend figures the boy wants to stay clear of things not fully endorsed."

"I see."

Curious. Did it mean the boy played by the rules? What about him letting Jack in on Dr. Alexin's disappearance? Was it a dangle? For him? Somehow, it didn't feel so.

"You know that he's from a prominent family, don't you?" Amanda asked suddenly, watching Jack from under her eyelashes.

"Yes. From an old aristocratic family. The patriarch of the family is a prominent scientist... I'm actually coordinating a joint project where he represents the Soviet side."

"Seriously? Interesting." She sounded surprised. "What's the project about? Come to think of it, Jack, you've never told me what exactly you do at the USIA."

"C'mon, Mandy, of course I told you! Mostly student exchanges, study tours from America and Soviet Union. And escorting 'somebodies' on cultural exchange visits. Like Ms. Love who you met at the Fourth of July bash, remember?" He made a face.

She laughed quietly, reached across the table and patted his hand. "Poor Jackie... So I take it that little Ms. N. is your job too?" She didn't even try to be subtle.

And what do you really mean by that, Mandy?

"Yes, initially. I was asked to host her at the Ambassador's reception. But as you've said yourself, she's very friendly and knows a lot of interesting people. Don't you agree?" Jack held her gaze, just a touch of challenge in his smile.

The waiter brought their food and drinks at that point and the conversation moved to other things. Amanda promised to organize another gathering at her place for Jack to meet with her rock guru friend. Maybe she would even invite the young rocker that her friend was so enthusiastic about, she added like an afterthought.

Yeah, right, because he's such a hugely potential Soviet rock material, huh? And no relation to Prof. Volkonsky, obviously.

The gala concert started promptly at seven. The program comprised three distinct parts. The first, formal section featured standard anti-war, "for international solidarity" songs and dance pieces. A professional, Soviet style pop group accompanied several singers who performed the songs Jack heard frequently on the local TV. When it was Dean Reed's turn, he did Beethoven's Ode to Joy, then *Venceremos*, which fired up the Latin Americans guests: they highjacked the song and chanted it for nearly ten minutes. American delegates clapped politely, even tried to sing along, but it was obvious that they were neither very familiar with it, nor felt particularly inspired. Thank God the first section was only ten songs long and the second part started with the surprise Lara had mentioned enigmatically on the phone the day before—a mini rock opera featuring musical arrangements from a famous Russian rock opera called "Juno and Avos" and several classical compositions by Beethoven, Mozart and Carl Orff arranged as rock pieces.

Karelin's show was very bold, considering the State censors' tolerance threshold. How it had got past them for showing at the Festival beat Jack. All twenty dancers and singers, including four girls, wore black, high-waist ballet tights and suspenders on top of white undershirts, their hair wet and gelled down. Jack wondered if the audience had picked up on the Russian director's allusion—that people were all the same, irrespective of gender, race... or anything.

He cut a glance at Amanda and caught her eye. She mouthed "wow" and shook her head. Obviously, she too hadn't expected this.

On the stage, the show was in full swing and Eton and Lara were singing a duet. Jack hadn't recognized them until they started singing, because during most of the performance all the singers and actors covered their faces with black and white masks on sticks, all of them smiling and serene. And it was only during the grand finale, when the whole group sang Hallelujah to Love from Juno and Avos, that the masks were removed to reveal color paintings on the actors faces, displaying other emotions—anger, despair, bewilderment, but also hope.

Eton sang the lead part of the entire show and ended the last song on a knee, with the entire cast and the rest of *Krylia* lined up behind him. His delivery was so raw and intense that Jack thought he would black out if it lasted for a minute longer.

The audience was ecstatic and wouldn't let the troupe go. So they repeated the closing song, with the audience singing along the refrain—"hallelujah to love, hallelujah to love, halleluuu-jah". Dean, who had been sitting on Amanda's other side, joined them on the stage, lending his powerful voice to the Russian student choir. Karelin had to come up the stage and promise that the singers would return in the next part of the concert for the audience to let them go.

The last part featured *Krylia* and a Cuban band called *Marianao* from the University of People's Friendship. It didn't take long for the two bands to join ranks and accompany each other's performance, cheering and challenging the other to improvise. Toward the end, when Eton muttered into the microphone that his next song was Hotel California, for American guests from California, the Cuban band insisted on accompanying him. After a quick consultation, Eton did their version of the song, following the Latin beat which left the Cubans so thrilled they couldn't stop hugging him and clapping his back afterwards. And during the entire performance of the song Jack hoped that nobody, especially not Amanda, would notice how stupid he looked with an ear-to-ear grin that he could barely contain.

The concert finally finished at around 9:30p.m. The MC, aided by two translators, announced a break in the program and invited everybody back in an hour for the discotheque. In the meantime, the guests were invited to enjoy traditional Russian refreshments and snacks in dining room on the ground floor.

"You staying?" Jack asked Amanda.

"Maybe not. I've had enough for one day. You?"

"I'll stay for a while." He smiled sheepishly at her. "But I'll take you home first."

"No worries. It's just a short ride on the Metro. I'll be home in half an hour."

"You sure?"

"I'm a big girl, Jack. And Moscow is a safe place. Especially with enhanced security for the Festival." She patted his arm and winked. "Besides, I'm pretty sure little Miss N will be unhappy if I steal her date."

"Her *date*? Where is *that* coming from?" Jack acted up his surprise.

"Ah, Jack, you shouldn't leave your friends and *friends* on their own, if you want to keep things under wraps. She's now *my* friend too."

"Did she tell you that? That's ah…" He was about to say that it wasn't true, but changed his mind. "Very kind of her. I wasn't sure if she was getting the drift."

"So it's true then?" Amanda narrowed her eyes.

Ok, so maybe Lara hadn't told her anything of the sort.

"She's a nice girl, isn't she?" He grinned at her innocently.

"Well connected too... Anyway, I have to go, Jack."

At the exit door, Jack made another attempt at being chivalrous. "Let me walk you to the Metro station at least, Mandy."

"Don't worry. I'll find my way." She tiptoed to give him a peck on the cheek and said quietly, "Try not to get yourself in trouble, handsome."

He watched her hurrying toward the Metro through the glass wall, then ventured to the restaurant room where snacks and soft drinks were arranged for the guests of the Soviet Students' Club. None of the performers was there, so Jack hooked up with a group of his Americans delegates, mostly girls, who decided to stay on for the discotheque.

When they headed upstairs for the dancing, Jack excused himself, promising to join them shortly. In the men's room, he locked himself in the cubicle at the far end, sat down on the toilet and closed his eyes.

He felt drained. Tired of the constant need to play something or other with everybody. There was a time when the only thing he had to hide was his sexuality. Now he couldn't even tell what he was doing, let alone who he was.

Get a grip, for Christ's sake!

But why? Why am I doing this?

'Cause you're good at it.

Because Joe says so?

Yes, because Joe says so and because you damn well know it, too. It's a sure shot at getting what you want. A ranch in California. Remember?

Oh yeah, a ranch... And this is the only way, huh?

Why are you whining? It has all been good so far, hasn't it? You're one ungrateful bastard, Smith!

It was true, it had all been good. So far.

Jack washed his hands at the sink and marched upstairs, determined to charm the pants off whoever he'd meet on his way to the Soviet discotheque. However, his resolve started to wane when sounds of disco music reached him on the second floor. He faltered for a moment on the landing and headed toward the end of the gallery where he noticed a secluded corner behind a large, marble pillar. He parked himself in the narrow gap behind it, lit a cigarette and leaned on the balustrade, watching people coming and going on the ground level.

He was half way through his smoke when he heard approaching voices, first a girl's and then... Eton's. They stopped on the other side of the pillar, just within Jack's earshot, and Eton started talking again.

"Sorry, I couldn't get out earlier. Thanks for waiting up. I just wanted to tell you that—"

"I know what you want to tell me, Eton. It's about Max, isn't it?"

It was one of the interpreters at the concert, the petite girl with big, dark frame glasses who had been translating from Russian to English and Vietnamese. Jack hadn't been able to place her: she had looked both Asian and Caucasian, spoken flawless Russian and

Vietnamese, *and* fluent English. She *was* probably mixed.

"... but not only," Eton was saying. "It's about you, too. You know, Max is devastated. That's bad enough. But what about you, Lina? Have you thought everything through? About what you're doing."

"I know I've hurt Max, and I am awfully sorry for that. But I can't help it. I love another person and I have to be with him." The girl's tone of voice was firm, uncompromising.

"Are you sure this... *thing* with the other man will last?"

"You're Max's friend and I know you want what's best for him. Unfortunately, it's not good for me."

"How can *it* be good for you? The guy's married, for God's sake!" Eton exclaimed, sounding incredulous.

The girl made a exhaled sharply, as if exasperated, then started talking, softly at first, her voice strengthening as she went on. "Eton, one day, when you meet someone who's... exactly like you've always imagined them, you'll understand. Nothing will matter then. That they're married, or ugly as sin, and not prepared to... to change anything for you. Even if you know it won't last and it'll hurt you in the end. But in your heart of hearts, you'll know what you have to do: to be with that person, no matter what. For as long as it lasts. It's not just love, Eton. It's fate." She sighed again. "I know it doesn't make a lot of sense to you. Neither does it for Max. Because you two are physicists. Too rational. Sorry, I don't mean to be demeaning. I'm just not sure you understand." There was pity in her last words, like she was sorry for Eton for not knowing what love and fate was.

"I understand more than you think, Lina. But Max is my friend and I'm trying not to be judgmental here. I hope you've thought it all through."

The girl let out a short, sad laugh. "But that's the point, Eton. You don't *need* to 'think it through'. You just know what you have to do... I'm sorry, I have to go now. He's waiting for me downstairs. And thank you for worrying about me. I truly appreciate it. You're a very good friend, Eton. *Poka*."

Eton lingered back after the girl had gone. Jack heard him fumbling, dropping his lighter, muttering, "Damn", then clicking the lighter and sighing heavily.

Jack was still deliberating whether he should step out of his hiding place and apologize for accidental eavesdropping when Anya's voice called out to Eton from the other end of the walkway. Eton called back, "Coming", blew out forcefully like after a deep drag, and walked away.

Jack stood behind the pillar for a few minutes, his cigarette stub long dead between his fingers. Then he took off, walked quickly down the staircase and out of the hotel.

He didn't believe in fate. He wasn't some silly, lovesick teenage girl who hadn't the slightest fucking idea about the rough side of life. What he believed in was hard work and perseverance. And he knew what he wanted. Or right now, what he didn't want: he didn't want to smile, he didn't want to run his mouth doing small talk, he didn't want to be everybody's kind of guy. And he didn't want to think why.

And there was one other thing Jack didn't believe in—love. Because he knew that love was not for the likes of him. Like Joe had said.

Right?

Chapter 15

Jack woke up with a splitting headache and a gutter taste in his mouth. His throat was parched and his stomach was making angry, protesting noises. Which reminded him that he'd only had few snacks since lunch yesterday. He carefully turned his throbbing head to look at the alarm clock on the bedside stand and saw a tumbler and the almost empty bottle of Jack Daniels. If his memory wasn't failing him now, the bottle had been half full last night. He sighed. So much for a couple of shots as a nightcap.

Jack focused his watering eyes on the clock. It was nearly eight o'clock.

Shit. He'd be late for... for anything he was supposed to do today. He couldn't recall right now what and where.

He inched his feet out from under the light blanket, gingerly put them on the floor and pulled himself up into a sitting position. What felt like a bolt of lightning shot through his head and he moaned softly. He sat still for a minute, waiting for the throbbing in his head to subside, then slowly stood up and staggered to the bathroom.

Once there, he fished out a bottle of aspirin from the small medicine cabinet on the wall and took two tablets, washing them down with a gulp of tap water. Now all he had to do was to wait until the pills kicked in and he could think straight again. In the meanwhile, maybe he could try a cool shower and brush his—

The telephone shrieked in the sitting room and Jack winced. A temptation to ignore it skirted his hazy mind, but he pushed it away—it could be William, or someone with a message from him. Jack sighed, wobbled into the front room and picked up the phone.

"Yeah," he breathed into the mouthpiece and didn't recognize his own voice.

"Jack, it that you? What happened to your voice?" It was Lara, and she sounded suspicious.

"Good morning, Lara. I'm afraid I'm sick." He must be, with this killer headache.

"You're sick? Have you called a doctor yet? Anything serious?"

It took him a few minutes to persuade Lara that it was nothing too serious, just food poisoning maybe, and that he needed neither a visit to the doctor just yet, nor the chicken soup she had offered to bring over.

"Thank you very much, sweetie, but no need, really. I'll be fine by noon." He hoped sooner, like in half hour maybe, after a cool shower and a glass of cold milk.

"Alright then. Take lots of water. You sound awful, Jack... So that was why you disappeared without saying goodbye yesterday, *da*?"

"Sorry about that, but discotheque isn't a good place to be sick."

"Everybody was wondering where you'd gone. And whether you liked our concert."

Jack wanted to ask who everybody was, but Lara clearly expected him to comment on *her* performance, so he obliged. "I liked it very much, Lara. It was terrific! And quite *innovative*, too."

"That's our Viktor for you. Eton was so good too, *da*? Even better than we all expected.

Viktor was so pleased." She didn't call Karelin deferentially Viktor Viktorovich anymore. Something had changed. "Anyway, Jack, I have to run now. I will call you later to see how you're doing and if you can come to the Festival closing. They say it will be grand. Better than the opening."

"If I feel better in the afternoon... Please give my regards and congratulations to *everybody*. And apologies for leaving without saying goodbye. *Poka*, Lara."

Go, girl, just go! You've said too much already.

"Get well soon, Jack." She blew him a kiss and hung up.

Jack put the receiver down and stood motionless for a few moments, his eyes closed, then took off to the bath room, where he doubled over and threw up into the sink.

He felt human again, after two glasses of cold milk and a mug of steaming coffee, and promised himself next time to remind Jack Smith's stupid self why he shouldn't drink more than a shot or two of whiskey on an empty stomach.

He didn't get to the office till after ten o'clock. Glenn was out, and he felt relieved that he didn't have to make conversation any longer this morning. He dropped his shoulder bag on the floor by the chair, sat down and only then noticed a yellow note stuck in the middle of his desk. "Call me when you're in. W.", it said in William's handwriting.

So now what? William had a key to his office and could come and check up on him anytime? Ridiculous.

Jack sighed, picked up the phone and dialed his boss's extension.

The CAO answered immediately as if he had been waiting for Jack's call.

"Good morning, William. This is Jack. You wanted me—"

"Morning, Jack. Could you come over, please?"

Something had happened.

"On my way."

Jack steeled himself, hoping he didn't look too worn out on close inspection. He dropped a few mints in his mouth and headed out, locking the door behind him.

William's door flew open before he even knocked, his raised hand left hanging in the air. "Come in and sit down."

That didn't sound very promising. And William was talking a fraction louder than necessary. "How's your car? Are you driving today?"

Shit, he did look like crap then.

"No, I took the Metro today. I—"

"Alright. You can bring it in and leave it with the Embassy's garage tomorrow morning. They will check up the electrics. You said it was malfunctioning, didn't you?" William asked emphatically in response to Jack's blank stare, then nodded, prompting an answer.

"Yes..."

Tomorrow's Saturday. What's going on?

"So I've arranged a checkup for you."

"Oh, okay. Appreciate that... But may I—"

"I take it that you were writing your report when I called." William looked at him pointedly and nodded emphatically again.

"Yes, in fact I was." Jack was still lost, but tried to sound firmer this time. Not that he could ask for an explanation right here right now anyway as it sounded like something serious had happened, something that required a briefing in the Tank. Later.

"Could you please include these details in it?" The CAO pushed a sheet of paper laying in front of him toward Jack. In William's spidery handwriting, the note said, "1) Make a list of all locals (excluding the Embassy's staff) you have come in physical contact in the last month. Esp. on the job. 2) Try to recall all IOs you knew or briefly met in '82 - '83 at the Farm and esp. at HQ (no need to write down). 3) 1900h in the Tank w/ MN."

Jack raised his eyes to stare at William, then re-read the note.

Physical contact? What the fuck did *that* mean? And to recall all intelligence officers he had known and met? What was this—an alternative polygraph test?

William smirked, obviously getting Jack's drift. "Don't worry, Jack. It isn't about your personal life."

Jack looked straight in William's eyes, trying to keep his expression blank.

No, he couldn't know... Could he? Joe had said that neither Marat Nurimbekoff nor William Osbourne would know about the "seabrook" part of operation GTTALION. It must be something different altogether.

"Right. But can I have some background to this, um, task, please?"

"You'll get all the background you need." William indicated upstairs with his eyes.

Okay, so that probably meant he would get information on "need to know" basis only. He hoped at least they would tell him what the heck this "physical contact with locals" really meant... Geez, how had Joe survived all this shit for, what, twenty years, maybe?

"Alright. I'll prepare the required information... Is that all?" He wanted to get back to his office and start figuring what potential implications of his interactions with locals as well as his colleagues back in America could be.

"That's all for now. And please leave this here." William pointed at his note that Jack had picked up to take away with him.

"I take it that I am to bring the required info to the meeting this afternoon... In writing?"

"Yes, item one is in writing. Try to recollect as much as possible."

Jack nodded.

"I'll come by your office to pick you up for the meeting."

Jack muttered okay, stood up and headed for the door, the little wheels in his head already spinning at full steam.

It took him an hour and a half to compile the two lists. He did the Soviet list first, since his memory was fresher, and in forty minutes, he had a list of a hundred and thirteen people, of whom forty-three were related to his covert job in one way or another. The Volkonsky group was already a quarter of those forty-three. And he'd had "physical contact" with all of them at least once: a hearty handshake and a friendly grin were Jack Smith's signature gestures. Even with those who he had no intention of being friends with.

The mental list of his colleagues took him longer. Firstly, 1982 was the time when Jack had just been interviewed for the job, so he didn't remember *all* the people he had met at Langley, with most of them only once. He did remember his course-mates and trainers at the Farm, though, where he took the eighteen weeks training in 1983. And a fair number of operations officers and managers at HQ. So this list would have been longer, had Jack had to write down all the names.

By the time William shepherded him upstairs, Jack still hadn't come up with any likely explanation for the odd tasks he'd been asked to perform. The only thing he'd figured was that something had happened, and he prayed that it wasn't another screw up with their Soviet assets.

Marat Nurimbekoff didn't look half as bad as the last time Jack saw him here in the Tank when the Station chief had briefed him about Peter Strauss's entrapment. In fact, he looked upbeat, like a man who had gained back his control.

"Come on in, Jack," he said, smiling a little as he stood up from behind the conference table. "I haven't seen you since your return from Munich, have I? Congratulations with your new assignment." He offered Jack his hand.

"Thank you, sir. Marat." Jack shook the man's hand, smiling back politely. "It's an honor and I'm really excited about this project... I'm hoping that we have some good news this time," he said after a pause, searching Nurimbekoff's eyes for clues.

"Well, I'd say we have more balanced news this time. I believe William has asked you to recall your interactions with all your Soviet contacts recently and also all colleagues you knew at HQ."

Jack mentally noted that he didn't say "physical contact" nor mentioned the Farm.

"Yes, I've put together a list of the Russians with whom I shook hands or brushed by in the last few months. And I've also tried to recall the colleagues I met back in '82 - '83 at HQ and the Farm."

"Very good. Let's start with the latter."

Nurimbekoff returned to his seat at the meeting table and gestured Jack to sit down across from him. He studied Jack's face for a few seconds before asking, "Have you come across anyone named Ed Howard at HQ at any time? I don't think your paths crossed at the Farm."

So Nurimbekoff had read both Jack's and this guy Howard's files recently and already knew they hadn't met at the Farm. The name didn't bring to mind anyone and Jack wished they'd told him what was going on.

"Should I know him?" he asked guardedly, then conceded when the COS didn't respond to his question, "No, it doesn't ring a bell."

Apparently, his answer didn't fully satisfy Nurimbekoff. "Let me give you more details," he said. "Edward Lee Howard, early thirties, chestnut hair, brown eyes, five eight, five nine, hundred and fifty five to hundred and sixty. Originally from New Mexico. Has a light southern accent. He was with the SE Division until May '83... Take your time, Jack. It's important."

Jack was sure he had never met the man, but tried to reflect on the time when he had joined the Agency. He had probably missed Edward Lee Howard by a few weeks or even days. As he recalled, May 12th was the day he and twenty four other new recruits had been sworn in at the domed auditorium at Langley everybody called the Bubble and then introduced to relevant people in the Directorate of Operations. He was pretty sure Howard wasn't one of them.

"No, sir. I've never met with nor heard about Mr. Howard." He hesitated, then asked anyway, "May I ask who is he and why is it important if I met with him or not?"

Now Nurimbekoff seemed visibly pleased with Jack's answer. He nodded, exchanged glances with William, then turned to Jack again. "Ed Howard was a case officer who was to be placed in Moscow under a deep cover—similar to yours, Jack—in June of '83. In May, just before his departure to Moscow, he failed three or four repeat polygraph tests and was asked to resign. It has just been uncovered that he was selling information to the KGB. No need to worry," he added, noting Jack's startled expression. "Apparently, he knew only two officers who are currently on duty here... Or rather *were* as Peter Strauss has gone back already. And Sam is supposed to be repatriating in a month or so."

He said "supposed to be repatriating". Which meant that things might have changed. Maybe because of Pete's premature return from the field.

"Does it mean that this Howard is responsible for the roll up of VANQUISH and TAW?" And two other fouled up cases he'd heard about from Joe?

"We believe so."

Christ, this Edward Howard had no doubt read all forty-two files on the Company's Soviet assets—as Jack had before the Moscow posting. How much else had he already sold to the KGB? And what about the FBI's and the British assets? What had happened to them? He couldn't know about them, could he? Jack couldn't recall reading anything on them. Must be something else.

"Have we got him?" Jack asked eagerly.

"The FBI is on him now."

It sounded rather evasive and Jack figured the turncoat was still on the loose. "May I ask how we got this information on Howard if we haven't brought him in yet?"

The Station chief's face eased a fraction. "We've got a high-level walk-in source."

"We did? When?" Jack was surprised. Another volunteer? Aren't we a lucky bunch?

"Yesterday." Nurimbekoff stated, obviously pleased with the speed the source had been debriefed, the information processed and actions taken.

"You don't mean here in Moscow, do you?"

Nah, it couldn't be Moscow. It would have been suicide for a KGB officer. Because it must be a KGB officer—who else could have information on the KGB's American assets, except their officers?

"Nope. And this is only the preliminary information from the first debriefing."

Jack was impressed. He wished the FBI had moved as fast with Edward Howard to minimize the damage he could potentially make to the Company's agents and their case officers.

"I'm assuming the list of my Soviet contacts is also related to the preliminary information."

"Correct. We've received the information that the Sovs are using the spy dust again."

"Pardon me?"

"Spy dust," William cut in. "Haven't you been briefed before your posting?" He sounded like it was Jack's failing that he didn't know about this dust, whatever it was.

"No, we weren't briefed about spy dust. Not sure why." Jack kept his tone level, gazing straight in his boss's eyes.

Nurimbekoff threw a quick side-glance at William. "It's a kind of microscopic chemical agent," he explained to Jack. "The KGB used it in the past to track who the Embassy's staff were meeting. They sprayed it on the floor mats and door handles of the cars."

"You mean *targeted* personnel? Like those they suspected to be... intel officers?" Jack almost said "spies".

"We believe so," the COS tilted his head. "The security office has never done an overall assessment of the situation, so the extent of the application of the substance is uncertain as of now. This may change soon, though... In any case, for now we need to make sure that you're still clear and so are the agents you help the team to run. I understand that William has asked you to bring your car to the garage. We'll get Don Steward to take samples off it himself. And maybe to visit your apartment too. So you can invite old Don home for a drink one of these days. William will let you know when."

Don Steward was the Regional Security Officer at the Embassy and normally wouldn't be doing these kinds of jobs. If he did, it would be at the COS's special request. Which meant that Jack's deep cover was being gradually pierced and more people would be learning about his real occupation.

Jack sighed mentally. Like he could do anything about it.

"Alright. Let's have a look what you've got here." Nurimbekoff pointed at the thin folder Jack had brought with him.

Jack picked it up from the desk and handed it across the wide desk to the COS. Inside, there was a four-page list of Russians he'd had some sort of contact with in the last two months. "These contacts include the two brush passes I did last month. I don't know who they were—you do... You know, my gut feeling is I haven't been targeted... so far." Seeing quizzical looks on Nurimbekoff's and William's faces, he explained, "I've barely been covered during the last two months, sometimes clear of surveillance for a week at a time, up until I returned from Munich."

The two men studied Jack with obvious interest and he wondered if they read all those reports he wrote, every friggin' day. Since neither of them said anything, Jack continued, "I understand that the Sovs have increased security and coverage of all Western embassies during my trip. I've noticed that too, albeit it's still rather casual."

They looked pleased about the news, but the station chief wanted preemptive measures to be taken, anyway. As a result, Jack was instructed not to get in physical contact with any of the potential targets, especially in relation to operation GTTALION. At least until the Berkeley team arrived. Then Jack would have a legitimate reason to deepen his relationship with the Soviet team.

It meant that Jack couldn't see *any* of them till at least next Monday when the first official introductions were going to take place at the MGU. And he'd thought of inviting them home for an American burger and rib dinner—as an apology for disappearing without goodbyes the night before. Some other Saturday maybe. He hoped they would forgive him. And he would then be able to tell Eton what a terrific singer he was.

Chapter 16

Lara called again on Saturday morning to check up on Jack and to tell him that he'd missed a lot by not coming to the Festival closing—it had been outstanding, she'd never seen anything like that in her life, she said, sounding breathless. Jack conceded, but there wasn't anything he could do: work had gotten in the way and it looked like he'd be tied up through the entire weekend. Lara was upset. In fact, she was calling to invite him for a lunch at her *dacha*. Eton and his band would come as would Viktor and some classmates of hers. Jack said he was sorry as hell he'd miss it, but hoped there would be a next time. He also wanted to invite them to his place for an American dinner of burgers and ribs, he said. That cheered her up a little and she made him promise that he would do it soon.

Jack dropped his Mustang off at the Embassy's garage before noon and then spent the entire day in the compound, first at Uncle Sam's, watching the rerun of Dodgers games, then at the Marines Club, ending the day at the Seabees' hangout.

On Sunday, Jack went out for his non-routine jogging. He came back two hours later, showered, put on his weekend wear, denims and boots, and took the Metro to the Embassy. He spent the rest of the morning in the office, writing his routine report and going through the Berkeley team file once again.

The chancery building was empty and quiet and not having to talk to anyone while watching his every word helped him to forget for a moment the suffocating surveillance and eavesdropping wherever he went. He hoped the KGB folks in the building across the ten-lane Tchaikovsky Street, whose job was to "microwave" the Embassy building, were having a Sunday off with their families.

Around 1:00 p.m. he came down to Uncle Sam's for lunch. He spent two and a half hours there, eating his lunch, then sipping beer and talking sports and politics with his new Seabee friends. Until it was time to go to the airport to meet the Berkeley team.

Actually, he was not required to do the airport pickup. It would have been perfectly okay to let their team assistant to do it. But Jack thought he could at least try to make his compatriots feel welcome, to guide them through their first hours here, until they were settled enough to recognize that, underneath the abrasive surface the Russians were kind and generous to a fault. Jack hoped that at least the three of them with the Russian roots would be more understanding. He wasn't sure why it was so important to him that his countrymen did not judge these people too quickly. It just was.

If they were understanding, Prof. Ackerman, Sara Gallagan and Val Sitkoff weren't showing it. In fact, right from the beginning Jack felt that they were here to confirm some preconceived ideas they had about the land of their ancestors. Val and especially Sarah looked at Jack with barely hidden skepticism every time he tried to explain the peculiarities of the Soviet life and ways. The other three members of Prof. Ackerman's team—Mike, Howard and Kyle—were more sympathetic and chuckled good-naturedly at the survival tips Jack shared with the group as they rode in an old minivan from the airport to the hotel.

Universitetskaya Hotel belonged to the MGU and was the place where students from

Western countries on short-term exchange programs were usually accommodated. It was a standard Brezhnev period edifice—gray fifteen-story building that resembled a massive flattened concrete cage. Good thing Jack had warned his charges to brace themselves for Soviet reality *before* they saw the place: dark and dingy lobby and corridors, a militiaman guarding the passage to the floors, and smelly elevators. And the place was probably bugged, he cautioned them for good measure.

Jack pulled his usual trick, coaxed the sullen woman at the reception to smile at him, then at the rest of the group. She even took it upon herself to show them to the fourteenth floor where their rooms were—neat and clean, albeit very Spartan, except Prof. Ackerman's, which was slightly larger and featured a tiny couch tucked in between a desk and the windowsill. With beds that reminded Jack of military bunks, it could have been rather depressing, if not for the view from the wall-length windows: with no other skyscrapers in sight, the only ones floating over a sea of lush green below were the MGU's main tower and Kremlin's spires and stars further beyond.

On Monday, Jack escorted the Berkeley team to MGU for their first meeting with their Soviet counterparts. They were brought to an auditorium at the Faculty of Physics where the Soviet scientists with half a dozen support staff were waiting.

A tall man in his mid-sixties with a mane of gray-white hair and black-rimmed glasses rose from his chair at the front of the lecture hall and hurried to meet them with open arms. "Leon, my friend, welcome to Moscow!" he exclaimed in slightly accented English.

Jack spotted Eton as he entered the room, tagging behind the Berkeley scientist. Out of the corner of his eye, he saw the young man watching him somberly, as he scanned the group of Russians, trying to determine who was who. When Jack finally turned to him, Eton looked away and started talking quietly with one of his team. On Eton's left, young Gosha was all smiles. He waved enthusiastically at Jack, then pulled at Eton's shirtsleeve and said something to him. Eton nodded, but didn't look in Jack's direction.

Fine. Whatever. Maybe he was offended that Jack had left after the concert without saying goodbye and hadn't called to apologize for his abrupt departure either. Jack had been hoping that Lara would tell her friends that he'd been sick. It looked like she hadn't after all.

He dragged his attention back to Prof. Ackerman who was introducing his team to his Soviet counterpart, starting with diminutive Sarah.

"Ms. Gallagan, pleased to meet you." Volkonsky took Sarah's hand in his and patted it with his other hand. "I've read your paper on the effects of volcanic ashes and gases on climate in Icelandic region with great interest."

Sarah beamed, the severe expression that had clouded her pretty face since arrival slowly evaporating. "Thank you very much, Professor. I'm honored that you're familiar with my work."

Prof. Volkonsky chuckled affably. "Young lady, I make it a rule to learn as much as I can about people I work with. *If* I can," he added and turned to shake hands with Kyle.

It looked like the professor had access to international research materials, down to the level of individual universities, if he knew about a paper written by a post grad student from Berkeley. As far as Jack knew, only people associated with the State's priority projects and those with special clearances had this level of privileged access to information.

When the two scientists reached the end of the line where Jack stood, slightly apart from the rest of the Americans, he stepped forward, smiling wide and stretching his hand out to the Russian scientist. "Jack Smith, sir. I'm the coordinator for your exchange program from the USIA side. Glad to meet you, Professor. I've heard so much about you."

Volkonsky studied him with interest, smiling amiably. "So you're the famous Jack, then," he said, shaking hands with Jack. "I've heard a lot about you too, young man, from my students. They say you're an enthusiast of Russian history and culture. I'd love to have a chat with you about Russian history one of these days."

Jack's grin never faltered, but his stomach flipped when he heard that some students had been talking about him. "I'll be most happy to. It's one of my favorite topics, sir."

"Very good, Jack. We'll do it soon." Volkonsky patted Jack's arm, then turned to his counterpart. "Now let me introduce my colleagues and students to you and your team."

He beckoned the Russian team members to come closer and began introducing them one by one, starting with Dr. Arceniev.

It turned out all Russians assigned to the exchange program spoke some English. All except Gosha. He didn't leave Eton's side, looked at him like Eton was his savior, and then grinned at the Americans as he shook hands with them, saying "*khello*" over and over, looking thrilled to bits and embarrassed at the same time. By the time Eton and Gosha reached Jack at the end of the line, the members from American and Soviet teams had broken into small groups, trying to get acquainted closer.

Gosha rushed to Jack's side. "Jack! So great that you could come." He offered his hand to Jack. "Will you be with us *all* the time? This program will be so cool, I just know it!" He was almost bouncing with excitement.

Jack gave him a pat on his shoulder. "No, Gosha. I don't think I should. I'll only be in your way once you start your research and tests... But I do hope I can join some of the lighter events," he said, watching Eton out of the corner of his eye.

Eton was talking to Val quietly, his demeanor calm and confident, like the two of them had known each other for a long time. Jack felt a sting of resentment. Why couldn't he talk to Jack like that? Why did he always seem so wound up with Jack while he was obviously at ease with others?

Gosha pulled at his sleeve and said something, and he snapped back to reality. "Sorry, you were saying, Gosha?"

"I said Mikhail Alexandrovich is asking for me. I'm going, *kharasho*?"

"Oh, alright. We'll talk later."

Gosha bounced away to the other side of the room where the two professors were discussing something animatedly with Sarah and Dr. Arceniev.

Jack looked at Eton who was still talking to Val. He was the only person in the room who hadn't shaken hands with Jack yet. As if feeling Jack's eyes on him, Eton turned around and gave him a slightly startled look. He said something to Val, smiling weakly, then headed toward Jack. A tight expression was clouding his face again.

It suddenly occurred to Jack that the Russian might know about him and his secrets.

Don't be ridiculous. He's coming to talk to you, isn't he?

Exactly. He has to if he is with the KGB. Right?

Maybe... Nah, can't be. Not him.

Eton stopped in front of him, smiled his awkward little smile and offered Jack his hand. "Hello, Jack," he said in English, the color creeping slowly over the tips of his ears.

"Hey, Eton. What's up?" Jack squeezed his hand in a hearty handshake, grinning. "Hey, listen," he added hurriedly. "About last Friday. I meant to call you—"

"Don't worry about it. Lara told me that you were sick. You okay now?" He sounded genuinely concerned.

"I'm fine. Thank you. I'm fine." He puffed out a deep satisfying breath. Yeah, that was how he felt—fine, real fine. "But I'm sorry, anyway, that I didn't call you over the weekend. Had some urgent work," he explained. "I wanted to tell you that you were awesome at the concert." Seeing Eton's face flushed red, he said quickly, "Didn't mean to embarrass you, but it's true. I've never met anyone who could do *that*! I think you should do more singing. You're *really* good at it."

What the heck? You're supposed to steer him in the other direction. He's a nuclear physicist and your potential star agent, remember?

I will. Need to win over him first that's all.

You sure?

Yes, goddamn it!

The smile slipped off Eton's face and he stared at Jack, suddenly ill at ease. "But I'm a physicist, not a singer," he said quietly.

"You can be whatever you want to be, Eton." Jack wasn't sure why the boy was bent out of shape all of a sudden, hastened to reassure him, "If nuclear physics is what you want to do, you go right ahead and do it... I just thought you liked singing."

Eton tipped his chin, but the anxiousness didn't fully ease off his face, so Jack changed the subject. "You know, I told Lara that I'd like to invite you guys to my place for an American dinner. Burgers and ribs. How about this weekend? Are you guys free?" The Berkeley team had arrived, so bringing their Russian counterparts to his place was legit, right?

However, Jack's new subject didn't put the young man at ease at all. If anything, it stressed him even more. "This weekend? Um, we're going out of town." Now he looked anxious. "There's a heatwave forecasted for this weekend. Everybody will be going out to their *dachas*. Or to the countryside."

"Oh. I didn't know about the heat wave... So where you guys going?" Jack asked lightly, steamrolling over a wave of disappointment.

"To a place in the countryside, not far from Moscow. It is an old village on Istra River. We go there sometimes..." Eton looked pained, like he had committed a faux pas and was hoping that Jack would forgive him.

"Sounds like a nice place. I'm sure you guys will have a great time there." Jack smiled reassuringly at him. What else could he say? Surely not that he wished he could go with them too because he—

"Would you like to come with us?" Eton asked, wide-eyed, as if he had just startled himself with his own question. "I mean if you're interested…"

Of course, Jack was interested. Damn, it would be totally… nice. There was just a tiny inconvenience: he needed a travel permit. From the Service of Diplomatic Corp under the Ministry of Foreign Affairs, which everybody knew was run by the KGB. So travel permits application was a painfully lengthy process.

"I'd love it, Eton. Only thing is I'll need to apply for a travel permit. Peredelkino and Tarasovka are the only two places outside of Moscow we can go to without a permit."

"Oh."

"I can apply for it tomorrow," Jack said quickly, hoping that the young man wouldn't change his mind in the face of such complications. "But I'll need details about this place—the address of a hotel or any place I can stay. We can't stay in a private house," he explained, smiling apologetically.

"There's no hotels there," Eton said quietly.

"Nothing at all in the vicinity?" Jack's hopes were slowly evaporating.

Eton stared at a spot over Jack's right shoulder for a moment, then met Jack's eyes, his own thoughtful. "There *is* a place nearby. A vacation home, *dom otdykha*… I need to check. I'll let you know tomorrow. Is that alright?" His face creased in a shy little smile, setting off a flight of butterflies in Jack's stomach.

"Tomorrow it is then. Thank you so much for inviting me…" He nearly said "out again" but bit his tongue in time. There was no need to embarrass the reserved youth more that he'd already had with his enthusiastic American ways.

However, by the time he saw Eton again on Tuesday evening, the young man didn't have any news for Jack. They met at the restaurant at Moskva Hotel, at the edge of Red Square, where William hosted a dinner for the joint Soviet-American project. As its coordinator, Jack was tasked with entertaining twenty or so guests, introducing people and facilitating conversations between the Americans and Russians who were not part of the joint project. And so he only managed to exchange a few words with Eton when he caught him in the doorway, coming back from the gents.

Eton looked upset, kept apologizing that he couldn't tell Jack anything concrete as he'd promised. Except that he had asked Lara to help with reservations at the vacation home. Jack was disappointed, but smiled at him and said, "That's alright, Eton. Next time maybe."

By Wednesday noon, it was clear that he wasn't going anywhere. It was too late to book a room at one of the Embassy's *dachas* too, so Jack braced himself for a muggy weekend in Moscow. He vowed that he would get off his butt and take his Marine friends to Gorky Park again. Or maybe for a ride on Moskva River, and he would not think of… other places outside of this goddamn city that was beginning to feel like a prison.

Jack was locking his desk, ready to leave the office, when his phone rang. It was nearly six o'clock and Glenn had already left. He glared at the phone, then sighed: if it was more work coming his way, so be it; he wasn't in the mood for socializing, anyway.

"Jack Smith speaking."

"Hello, Jack. This is Sarah. Sarah Gallagan."

"Hello, Sarah. How are you?" It was work after all.

Unless she was calling to ask him out for a drink. He didn't think she was though—little Sarah's world seemed to be ruled by Prof. Ackerman's needs... Or maybe the hunky professor wanted to have a drink with Jack?

Yeah, right. That's all you can think of, huh?

"... Listen, the Russians have arranged a trip out of town for us this weekend. To some place called, uh, *Dom Ot'dykha Lesnoye Ozero*." She was obviously reading the name off the written text. "It's a vacation house in the forest, forty clicks from Moscow, they say."

Jack's heart skipped a beat. "I see."

"Leaving Friday afternoon, coming back Sunday afternoon."

Wow, wow, hold your horses, girl.

"Sarah, I don't know if we'll be able to arrange travel permits for you in two days. I'll try tomorrow morning, but—"

"Jack," she interjected, impatient. "You don't need to do *anything*. They say they have arranged everything for us all. Including travel permits."

"Have they?"

Did she say "us all"?

"That's what they say. For all of us, Jack. Including you. You're coming, aren't you?"

Chapter 17

The out-of-town trip arranged for the American scientists triggered a series of urgent meetings in the Tank, followed by a flurry of encrypted communications with HQ. That it had been arranged at short notice and included an American diplomatic staff made the whole affair rather suspect. Both Osbourne and Nurimbekoff decided that the KGB was finally making their move—either through Eton or Lara, or anyone else of the Russians on the trip. And the light surveillance on Jack so far was probably part of the ploy.

They were probably right. Jack swallowed down his disappointment, primarily with himself, that he had so stupidly let himself be duped by the seeming friendliness and openness of a bunch of Soviet students.

Serves you, right, Smith. You're too fucking naïve. You're behind the Iron Curtain, remember?

He was instructed to call Eton Volkonsky and try to find out more about the trip before an op planning session the following day. Since it all looked like an open move from the Sovs, Jack could made his call from his apartment or even from the Embassy. But he couldn't: deep down, an ember of hope was still smoldering in him, refusing to die—that they were all wrong and it had nothing to do with the KGB.

He called Eton from a *taxaphone* shortly after 10:00 p.m., twelve streets away from his apartment block. He was half way through his late night jog and was sure he wasn't being followed.

"*Allo?*" Eton answered instantly, sounding out of breath.

"*Privet*, Eton. This is Jack," he said in Russian, trying to keep his tone neutral. It sounded flat to him.

"*Privet*, Jack. Good that you're calling." He seemed to be smiling, too. "I called you earlier this evening, but you weren't home."

And he was chatty today, too.

"Sorry, I was out. I'm actually calling from the street."

"Ah, alright... So, um, listen, we've arranged travel permits for you and the Berkeley team to go to the countryside. We've also booked rooms for you... At the vacation house I told you about," Eton added, sounding less certain when Jack didn't say anything. "Jack, do you hear me?"

"Yes. Sarah told me. She was very excited about the trip." Jack winced at the resentment he could hear in his own tone. "Thank you for arranging it. I'm sure everybody will love it."

Oh, c'mon! You're a professional, aren't you?

There was a pause, then Eton asked quietly, "Has anything happened?"

You're pathetic, Smith!

Jack sighed, rubbed his face with his free hand, and forced himself to smile into the phone. "Nothing happened. I'm just catching my breath here. I've been jogging. Stopped for a break... and to call you. I wanted thank you for arranging this trip for m-uh... for us. I look forward to it." This time he almost meant it.

"No problem." Eton sounded relieved. "But you should thank Lara, not me. She's pulled it off."

So it was Lara after all, not *him*.

Jack's grin widened. "How did she do that? Never seen anything done *that* fast since I came here."

"Her father helped."

"I thought so. But how?"

Eton sighed, reluctantly giving in to Jack's persistence. "We thought it was a good idea to take, um, the guests to the countryside. So our department made a group application. And Leonid Dmitriyevich, Lara's father, helped to expedite the travel permits."

"I see. So it was your... department's initiative then."

"Uhmm."

Jack could visualize the color creeping on the young man's forehead and ears. Would the KGB be using someone like him? On the other hand, he didn't think Deputy Minister Novikov's was the only office that had made this trip happen. But what the heck? As long as he could—

"There's a small problem," Eton was saying apologetically. "It was too short of a notice. As a result, there were only five rooms left at the vacation house. Hope you don't mind sharing rooms."

"Not a problem. But what about you? Where are you guys going to stay?"

"We'll stay in the village. About five kilometers away."

"I see..." In truth, he didn't see yet what they were trying to pull off—*if* they were indeed going to.

"So who's coming with us?"

"Same crowd: Lara, Anya, Gosha, Seva, Grisha and me... And Dmitri Alexandrovich. I mean Dr. Arceniev. He's hosting Professor Ackerman and his team... And you, of course."

Curious. Did it mean he was Eton's guest? Or maybe Lara's and Eton's? That was fine by him too. He just wished it had been only *that*—a trip to the countryside with a group of Russian friends. But he knew he could never be sure.

"Sounds great. I look forward to it... Listen, do you want me to bring anything with me?"

"Like what?"

"Tape recorder, music, games... Something to read..."

There was a momentary pause and Jack held his breath.

"We plan to have a lunch in the village. We will bring food and drinks with us."

"So what should *I* bring?"

"The usual?" Eton sounded like he wasn't sure himself what one should bring to a lunch in a Russian village. "It's up to you, Jack. Anything you want."

"Alright," Jack said with a quiet chuckle, relieved. "The usual it is then."

"The bus will be at the hotel at three o'clock."

"I'll be there at three. With 'the usual'... Right?"

That drew a quiet laugh at the other end. "Yes, 'the usual' is good."

So that was that, he'd got as much as he could and there was nothing else to discuss with the man. And it was high time to move, too—he'd been standing on the street, talking on the phone longer than advisable.

"Anyway. Thanks again, for all your trouble. See you on Friday."

"Don't mention it. It's nothing. *Poka*, Jack, I'll be seeing you."

Jack lingered for a moment in the smelly aluminum-and-glass booth, staring at the heavy phone set in its cast iron casing, then stepped out and set off jogging again—in the opposite direction from his apartment block. He wanted to be totally worn out by the time he got back, so that he would crash out the moment his head hit the pillow.

The operational planning on Thursday night took two and a half hours. As a result, it was nearly 10:00 p.m. when Jack finally left the office. He dropped by Uncle Sam's for a late night snack, sat alone in the far corner of the diner and left in under twenty minutes. During that time and then again as he was riding the nearly empty Metro, Jack replayed the scenarios he and his bosses had brainstormed in the Tank. In each of them, one of the Russians probed or even attempted to recruit him. Jack thought most of the scenarios seemed unlikely, except two—one with Lara Novikova, the other with Eton Volkonsky. His bosses had agreed, but insisted on going over all potential setups. In short, Jack was to take the bait, if that was what they were going throw at him. Or to yield very subtly, letting himself be recruited by whoever it was that would pitch him.

At home, Jack threw a few things in his duffel bag, took a quick shower, and headed to the sitting room, the wet towel wrapped loosely around his waist. He broke the cap of a new bottle of whiskey, poured himself a quarter of a tumbler and plodded back to the bedroom. He sat down on the edge of the bed and stared down at the amber liquid as he swirled it in the glass, forcing himself to tune in to the night sounds around him and not think about the op briefing.

Muffled explosions and shouts of what sounded like an action movie from the adjacent apartment where Sam, an intern from the visa section, lived. More distinct shrieks and yowls of a child from below where a young couple from the Angolan Embassy resided with their three children, the youngest of whom cried almost every night. Muted rumbles of an occasional heavy trucks from the street below, reminding him that his place was a stones-throw away from the old manufacturing district of Moscow.

So they had been grooming him as a dangle, hadn't they? Could have told him... Or maybe that was what Joe had done, in Garmisch? He had come out to brief Jack himself, hadn't he? Maybe it was Jack who hadn't got it. Maybe Joe had recruited him for this type of tactic in the first place. "It would only prove that you're a perfect honey trap" he'd said...

Christ, Smith, you're such a stupid sucker!

Too late to worry about it now. Like he had a choice...

Jack raised the tumbler to his lips and downed the fiery liquid in two big gulps.

Being late for the trip was as much a part of the op plan as his cover. Jack lingered at an exclusive duty free shop on Kalinin Avenue choosing the "usual stuff" for the trip. By the time he got to the hotel, nearly everybody was standing with their bags on the side of the entrance, waiting. Two guitars in soft battered cases were leaning against the wall near the door.

Jack scanned the gathering as he walked up to them from the taxi drop off. Lara in a bright flowery dress, laughing, surrounded by Val, Kyle, Mike and Grisha; Anya in a pale flowery dress, talking quietly to Seva and Gosha; Howard and Eton discussing something serious, judging by their furrowed brows and thoughtful expressions. And no sight of Prof. Ackerman, Sarah and Dr. Arceniev.

Gosha noticed Jack first, broke away from his group and hurried to greet him with his usual ear-to-ear grin. Seva and Anya followed the boy, and they met half way. Jack shook hands with the boy, offered The Smile to Anya who smiled back shyly and said that she was glad he could join them. When the men finished shaking hands, Lara announced that they were good to go.

It turned out that Prof. Ackerman had decided to stay back in Moscow over the weekend — "to take care of a couple of personal matters". So had Sarah, without explanations. Since the group now was comprised of young people, there was no longer a necessity for Dr. Arceniev to formally host the Americans. The role of the Department of Physics as the sponsor of the out of town trip had dwindled down even further when Lara and Anya unilaterally took command over the men.

The seating arrangement on the bus fanned out along the same lines as on the ground: Lara with Val and Kyle with Mike took the first two rows on the left; Anya, Eton, Grisha and Howard took the seats across the aisle. And so Jack found himself in the company of young Gosha and the soft spoken Seva the drummer — the two people whose names were at the bottom of Moscow Station's list of suspects. It was as if the prime suspects knew all about it and decided to leave Jack dangling. So for most of the way all he did was stare at Lara in an exaggerated display of jealousy, trying to figure if this was a KGB ploy to make him lower his guard before their real move.

At the hotel, Lara had greeted him by explaining that she was practicing her English, and Val and Kyle had volunteered to coach her. Jack affected hurt feelings, countered that he could tutor her, too. She patted his arm, giggling and looking very pleased, and said that she preferred to speak Russian with him. So she had been laughing and flirting with the Americans all the way to the vacation house, throwing mischievous glances at Jack from time to time.

Anya, who didn't speak English, was engrossed in a thick book she had produced from her bag as soon as they hit the road. Eton, Grisha and Howard discussed in hushed tones an experimental mathematical model, as far as Jack could tell with two rows of seats between them. Eton sat half turned, talking over the back of the seat to his interlocutors in the row behind, his face serious most of the time. Jack tried not to look that way. But once in a while, when their eyes met, for the briefest of a moment, the young man's expression would soften and the corners of his mouth would curl up in a shy little smile.

The vacation house Forest Lake was hidden deep in a forest, on the inside shore of a big, sharply bent lake, which fed into the Istra River. The L shaped complex consisted of two buildings, each facing one side of the bend of the lake: the smaller one was a Germanic style mansion, the larger, two-storey structure looked like a poor replica of a neo-classical estate house. On their ride here Jack had learned from Seva that the place belonged to the Ministry of Culture and catered to its civil servants, their families and guests—the mansion for senior officials, the other building for mid-level bureaucrats, people's artists, local movie stars and the like.

It was nearly five o'clock when the bus rolled into the driveway. The sun was still ablaze and the heat haze distorted the thick, humid air, permeated with the spicy scent of pine trees. As soon as they pulled up to the door of the larger building, Lara announced that they were all going to stay together at the holiday home—they had five rooms after all and that should accommodate the whole group. *And* they could all go swimming on the lake in fifteen minutes. Anya tried to object, but Lara was adamant, and with Grisha and Gosha supporting her, Anya finally gave in.

Without waiting for others, Lara breezed through the door to the reception. Anya quickly joined her and the two launched into an animated discussion with the plump, kindly looking woman about room allocations. The men, having left the bags by the door, sauntered out again, some pulled out their cigarettes, others inspecting the surroundings.

In under ten minutes, Lara flitted out and pronounced triumphantly in her heavily accented English, "Listen, people!" She waited until the men turned to her, then continued. "Vee khave five room. Grisha, Seva and Gosha. You stay in big room. Val and Kyle, you stay in one room. You don't mind, yes?" She looked at Val sternly, then turned to Mike and commanded, "Mike, you stay veeth Khovard... And Jack." She turned to him and asked softly in Russian, "Would you mind sharing a room with Eton? Otherwise he'll be the fourth in the room, with Grisha, Seva and Gosha."

All the eyes turned to Jack, even those who hadn't understood what Lara had just said.

So there it is, Lara and Eton teaming up on him. That being the case, they must know that foreigners, especially the embassy staff, could not share accommodation with locals. But that aside, Jack did actually mind sharing a room with Eton—he knew he mustn't.

He was acutely aware that everybody was looking at him expectantly, like he was some spoilt brat. He couldn't see Eton, who was outside of his field of vision, but was pretty sure that was what he was thinking, too.

Fine! He was supposed to let them recruit him anyway, wasn't he? His bosses would just have to deal with it since they had put him in this position in the first place.

"It's fine, Lara," Eton said quietly, stepping up to her. "Perhaps Jack is not supposed to share rooms with us locals. I'll stay with the guys... Or I can go to the village."

Jack finally broke out of his trance. "No! No need, Eton. We can share the room." He grinned reassuringly, seeing a look of concern on the young man's face. "It'll be fine. Seriously."

"No problem, Jack, I'll be—"

"No, I insist... Please?"

"So, it's agreed, then!" Lara quickly concluded before Eton could object again. "And Anya and I will share the last room. Perfect!" She darted back into the building, calling out to the administrator as she went, "We're all set, Nina Ivanovna. You can give us the keys now."

Except Val, the rest of the Americans, who'd been watching the exchange with interest, turned to Jack, asking what it had been all about. He had to explain it to them that he wasn't supposed to share accommodation with local folks. They nodded understandingly, but nobody offered to switch places with him. He was on his own.

His and Eton's room on the ground floor was more spacious than he had expected. In fact, it was at least twice as large as any hotel room Jack had stayed so far in in this country. There was a good seven feet between the two single beds against opposite walls, complete with two bedside tables instead of one shared that regular hotel rooms usually featured. There was also a sofa with a low, glass top coffee table and a Panasonic TV set on a stand. The large window was opened and a light breeze caressed floor-length cream curtains, half drawn to reveal neat rows of birches and pine trees outside.

Jack stopped in the middle of the room and turned around to face Eton. "Which bed do you choose?" he asked in Russian, smiling weakly, trying to shake off the strange awkwardness that had descended on him since the moment the administrator had handed him the key. This hadn't happened to him often and he couldn't understand what it was that flustered him. Maybe it was the anticipation of a move by the other side, sometime on this trip.

"You choose." Eton's expression was gloomy, and he didn't meet Jack's eyes.

Okay, so maybe he was offended after all.

Jack sighed. "I'm sorry I sounded like a spoilt brat. But it was not a reflection on you. You were right. We're not supposed to share accommodation with Russians. But what the heck." He smiled and tried to catch the young man's eyes. "Eton? It's fine, really."

Eton stopped inspecting the room and looked at him. "I don't want you getting into trouble because of me," he said quietly, his tone sincere. "I can stay in the village. It's only—"

"You don't have to go anywhere. Stay. Please? And don't you worry about me. I'll live." He offered Eton his full, toothy grin. "So. How about you taking the one near the window? So you can escape when you can't stand my snoring anymore."

He knew he didn't snore, but figured he might need to lock himself in the bathroom that was within a few strides from the other bed—in case he had a hard… time falling asleep.

Eton chuckled in response and nodded. He walked past Jack, dropped his bag on the floor and carefully laid his guitar on top of the bed by the window. And just like that the weirdness Jack had been wrestling with evaporated and everything suddenly felt just right.

Chapter 18

Jack was not ready for a swim in the lake. He was afraid that after months of deprivation his body would react inappropriately to the sight of hot, scantily dressed young bodies. He needed to spend some time in the bathroom to make sure he wouldn't be parading around with wood in his swim trunks. He set his shaving kit on the plastic shelf under the mirror in the bathroom, walked out and leaned against the wall.

Eton was fiddling with something in his bag on the bed, his back to Jack.

Jack cleared his throat. "Hey, Eton, why don't you change and go to the lake with the crowd?"

Eton whipped around, startled, stared at him with a question in his eyes.

Jack smiled sheepishly. "I need a minute in the bathroom. I'll catch up with you guys."

The young man's expression was a curious mixture of doubt and anxiety. And something else, Jack wasn't sure what. He gazed through the window, then turned to Jack. "Do you want to go swimming now?"

It looked like Jack wasn't the only one who had reservations about swimming and he wondered what Eton's problem was. "Not really," he shrugged. "I don't mind exploring around the lake though. It looked beautiful from the bus. Maybe I'll take a dip later. How about you?"

"I agree." Eton looked relieved. "We have two more days here. Lots of time."

"Okay. Maybe you can show me the place, then. You've been here before, right?"

"Yes. Not right here, but not far away. In the village… It is a unique place."

"Unique? How so?"

Eton furrowed his brows, choosing his words carefully. "It is part of one complex, together with this vacation house. An old village in Russian traditional style. For, um, VIP guests."

"For VIP? How interesting." The system must be changing if they let a bunch of foreigners visit such an exclusive place.

Or was it part of the plan to get to him?

"The houses are log cabins," Eton continued. "There're hunting places… And it is also used by film studios. To make historical movies."

"I see." Jack nodded, thoughtful. "Do they have horses in the village?"

The enthusiasm slipped from Eton's face and suddenly he looked ill at ease again. "Yes. They have a small… herd."

"Can we ride them?" Jack asked, wondering what he had said to cause this mood swing in the guy again.

"Perhaps… If you want."

He didn't sound at all eager, but Jack decided to press on. "Great! Let's go to the village then." He pushed off the wall, all set to go. Riding horses, that was what he wanted to do today, even if the idea seemed to bother Eton for some reason.

Eton chewed on the inside of his lips, thoughtful, then nodded. "Okay. I'll go tell the guys. Will wait for you at the front door."

Jack watched as Eton walked quickly past him, keeping plenty of space between them, and out. As the door closed behind him, Jack leaned back against the wall and closed his eyes.

So this was probably it. Eton would be making a move on him after all. Today. But how could it be? How could it be him? *So* not the type.

However, when Jack emerged from the building, he found Eton waiting for him with Gosha. It turned out the boy had pleaded to tag along the moment he learnt Eton was going to take Jack to the village to see horses.

The forest trail they walked was only wide enough for two side by side. As a result, Gosha and Jack marched in front, rubbing shoulders, and did most of the talking. Eton behind them only spoke up when Gosha turned around to ask him a question. The conversation circled around life on a ranch in America compared to life in rural Russia that Gosha knew well. The boy obviously missed it—he couldn't tell Jack enough about his last summer vacation at his grandparents who lived a small village near Lake Baikal.

It took them forty-five minutes to get to the village, and during the whole time Jack was intensely aware of being watched. He even caught Eton's eye on him when they stopped abruptly as Gosha swirled around yet again to ask a question. Eton quickly looked away, biting on his lip. Had he known better, Jack would have thought the man had been checking him out... Had he?

Nah, he was just the clumsiest informer the KGB had ever employed.

The picturesque village snuggled into the curve of the meandering river that fed into Forest Lake. On its other side, the settlement was surrounded by expanses of mixed forest. It looked like a traditional Russian village from some historical movie indeed. The two dozen houses along the unpaved main street were old but well kept, all with elaborately carved fascia and chest-high wooden fences and tall gates. They could see the bright blue and gold cupolas of a small wooden church at the end of the road.

The stable was at the far end of a long, low-rise building that also contained a barn. The cattle were inside the barn, but a couple of dozen of horses were grazing within a fenced off area of a meadow between the village and the birch grove. Jack inhaled deeply, taking in the familiar yet oddly foreign smells of cut grass, manure and horses. Gosha went to look for the headman while Jack and Eton strolled to the paddock.

The horses were taller than the American breeds Jack knew, with long arched necks, powerful chests and long, slender legs. Most of them were grays, with only a couple of blacks and a handful of bays.

As they leaned against the wooden railing, Jack pulled out his pack of Lucky Strikes and offered one to Eton. "Aren't they magnificent?" Jack breathed out. "Do you know what breed they are?" he asked just to make a conversation, not expecting a knowledgeable answer from the man he thought of as a city dude.

"Orlov trotters." Eton said, his eyes also glued to the graceful animals. "Used to be popular as racing horses before the revolution."

"You know about horses?" Jack turned to him, surprised.

"A little." Eton shrugged, his eyes still averted. "My uncle used to take me to a place where they bred them."

"He used to? Not anymore?" From the file Jack had read, Eton's only Russian uncle had died in action in Afghanistan around five years ago.

"He died."

"I'm sorry." He was and in no small part because he had to play a clueless foreigner with this young man.

"That's alright. It was some time ago." Eton turned to face him and smiled his crooked little smile. "Nearly five years."

"Can you ride a horse?"

Eton resumed his scrutiny of the herd at the far end of the pasture, took a drag on his cigarette. "I used to... could... I have not ridden for a long time."

Jack gave him a sideways glance, waiting for him to elaborate. He didn't. He was obviously uncomfortable with their conversation and Jack couldn't figure why.

"Whereabouts in California did you live when you were little?" Eton asked out of the blue and shot a quick glance at him.

Jack's insides clenched. Here we go.

"Well, actually, I'm from Wyoming."

What the fuck, Smith? It's California according to the legend, remember?

"I mean *originally*. I moved to California to live with my uncle when I was ten," he breezed, eyes firmly fixed on the horses in the pasture. "He had a small ranch a hundred miles north of Sacramento. Cows and horses..."

Eton turned to him, all eyes. "What about your parents?"

"They died in an accident." Jack took the last pull on his cigarette, dropped the butt and crushed it with the sole of his boot.

"I am very sorry for your loss, Jack," the Russian said very quietly, his expression solemn.

Jack bit on the inside of his cheek. "It's alright... Uncle Ben, my Ma's brother, he lived alone on his ranch and took me in. The two of us... we managed."

Shit, why was this so difficult all of a sudden? It wasn't like he was spinning a legend for the first time.

"My father died when I was twelve. He was from Eureka, California. Have you been there?" Eton's tone was so hopeful, it made Jack's guts squeeze.

"No. But I know where it is. And I'm sorry about your Dad, too... So, did he tell you a lot about California?"

"He did... I guess he missed it."

Jack was about to ask how his parents had met when Gosha's voice cut in from afar, announcing his arrival with the headman. They brought only two sets of tack since Eton had said he would just watch. But in the end Jack persuaded him to join them, insisting that he'd much rather ride bareback—he'd done it so many times back in California and missed the experience.

The horses were even more magnificent up close, with unusually big, soulful eyes. Kuzmich, the headman, chose a gentle dappled mare for Eton and a young bay mare for Gosha. Jack chose a spirited, black stallion called Ikarus. It took him a while to get the horse to come to him, but once they took off, Ikarus turned out to be one of best mounts Jack had ever ridden, sensitive to all his moves and vibes, and exceptionally responsive.

With Gosha leading the way, they started off at an easy pace along the river. Eton rode his mount carefully, the same way he spoke English, but it was obvious from his gait that he'd been taught at least the basics of dressage. Jack rode behind him and couldn't take his eyes off the arresting sight the young man made.

Ikarus sensed his excitement about the "sight". He started dancing around restlessly, snorting and whinnying a little. Jack broke into a gallop, yelling "heehaw" and laughing like a teenager. When he dashed back and nudged his horse between the two mares the Russians were riding, Gosha showered him with compliments. Eton gazed at him with his usual tight-lipped smile, and a shine in his eyes that looked to Jack like approval. He laughed, feeling free-spirited and a little giddy.

When they brought the horses back to the stables, Jack insisted on brushing his mount down. Afterwards, Kuzmich took them on a tour around the stables and the barn where a group of women were milking cows. Jack cajoled the chore from one of them and a few minutes later presented her with a jug full of milk. When he turned around to look for his companions, he caught Eton gaping at him with a strange expression on his face. But he spun around and walked out quickly the moment he realized he'd been caught staring.

Jack completely charmed the villagers when he told them that he used to be a cowboy on a ranch. The women made him promise to come back again, said he could stay in any of the village houses he wanted—anyone in the village would be honored to host a true cowboy from America.

They didn't get back to the vacation house till after nine o'clock. And got told off by Lara. Jack pleaded guilty and promised to do anything she wanted during the rest of the weekend. That pacified her somewhat. She snaked her arm through Jack's and proposed in her usual, not-accepting-no-for-an-answer manner, that they made a bonfire by the lake— after Jack, Eton and Gosha had eaten their dinner—and then Eton and Seva took their guitars out.

And so they did. And it was the best night Jack could remember having. It turned out Val was a decent guitarist and a singer, too, so they borrowed another guitar from the recreation room and two tambourines, and then sat in a circle by the fire, singing Russian and American tunes late into the night. They were joined by two young couples vacationing at the holiday house. One of them brought a bottle of Stolichnaya and a glass, and they passed shots of vodka around the group. They closed the night with Hotel California and everybody joined in, singing their hearts out. Eton's rendition of the song was different this time—still poignant, but softer, not so intense. He smiled demurely and deliberately avoided looking at Jack while he sang. But when on the last note he finally met Jack's eyes, Jack knew that it had been for him.

After nearly three hours, the "authentic Russian lunch" in the shade of apple and cherry trees was finally coming to a close. It had started at noon in the garden of the village's guesthouse, the large wooden dwelling nearest to the forest. The hosts were the caretaker of the guest accommodations and the headman Kuzmich, with their wives serving. Jack had never seen such an abundance of food at public eateries in Moscow, not even the high-end ones. The foreign fare he'd brought hadn't even made it to the table. Except his bottle of vodka that joined the company of the other two, brought by Eton and Grisha. Now, the last one was almost empty, because the village men had kept saying that true Russians couldn't leave the table before finishing the *good* stuff.

Half an hour earlier, the girls, followed by the American guests, had excused themselves and headed into the house for an after-lunch nap. Then Eton had got up, said, "I will be back", and left. He hadn't returned.

Finally, Jack got up, his head wooly, and excused himself, too. However, instead of going into the house, he sneaked out through the back gate and sauntered into the forest, finding his way along the river's bend.

The afternoon sun was blazing in the sky of the deepest blue, fluffed up by scraps of pearly clouds. The air was heavy with moisture, and heady-sweet scents of chamomile, ripe apples and pears. Jack wouldn't mind crashing for half an hour, but didn't want to go to the room in the house allocated to him and Eton. The boy had looked unsteady when he left the table and Jack suspected that he was sleeping it off in their room. He wasn't ready to face him yet, not in his horny-as-hell state and not here. No, definitely not a good idea.

Eton had sat right across from him during lunch, a wide expanse of snow-white tablecloth between them, covered with rough, peasant style plates with hearty Russian food. And during the whole three hours he had stubbornly avoided looking at Jack, saying only a few words to him. He'd hardly talked to anyone else, for that matter.

What was wrong with that boy? Jack had thought they were becoming friends after all the talking they had done.

The night before, after the bonfire, Eton had been fine. A little pensive maybe, but otherwise sociable. They had lain in their single beds and talked about California. The bright moonlight poured through the open window near Eton's bed and the trees outside cast dancing shadows on the walls. As usual, Jack was the one doing most of the talking, as Eton wanted to hear everything he cared to tell about his university days. Jack was only too happy to oblige—as long as it wasn't about his time at "his uncle's ranch in California". They must have fallen asleep while talking, for Jack couldn't recall what they'd talked about last.

The next thing he knew he was waking up alone in the room. Eton's bed was empty, the bedding was all scrunched up, like it had been a wrestling pad. He didn't show for the bus ride to the village either, so they left without him. Finally, Eton turned up just before lunchtime and offered no explanation for his absence. And then, he would neither talk to Jack nor meet his eyes, loosening up a bit only after a few of shots of chilled vodka.

Shit, why did it—why did *he*—bother Jack so much, getting him all bent out of shape?

Why couldn't he just take it easy? Damn you, Eton, you little bastard! He wished he could do something—

A moan to his right jolted Jack out of his restless thoughts. He stumbled to an abrupt stop, then diverted furtively into the birch-and-willow grove on his right. He could see the river a dozen yards in front of him, its gilded ripples shimmering through cascading veil of weeping willows along the shore. A figure was sitting on the ground, leaning against an old willow tree, head thrown back against its trunk, knees up and parted.

Eton.

When Jack's eyes adjusted to the deep shade under the thick foliage, he saw something else that sent waves of searing heat rushing through his body.

Goddamn!

Eton's jeans were open and pushed down to let his erection free. He was stroking himself gingerly as if his engorged cock was too sensitive to his own touch. His eyes were closed, lips swollen and parted. He looked drunk. And completely oblivious to the world.

Eton whimpered again and Jack found it hard to breathe, suddenly dizzy. He reached his hand out to steady himself against the nearest birch tree. But as he made a sidestep closer to it, a twig snapped under his foot. He froze with his hand inches from the intended support, for a moment forgetting to breathe.

The young man turned his head slowly, his eyes flew open, but it took a few beats for him to realize that he had an audience. Then a flurry of emotions flashed across his face in a quick succession—panic, embarrassment, then defiance. He stared back at Jack with that dark, what-the-fuck-are-you-looking-at expression that Jack knew meant trouble.

"Sorry, I was walking down to the river... Didn't mean to..."

The silence that followed was charged with unease, but Jack could think of nothing to explain why his eyes were still glued to Eton's right hand. Which hadn't moved an iota since its owner discovered he was being spied on.

Eton followed Jack's gaze. His fingers flexed and a challenging smirk curled up one side of his mouth. "Want to help or what...," he said in English, his voice low and gruff.

"Yeah!" Jack's instant response surprised himself.

You're a moron. It's a trap!

So what? I'm supposed to seduce him, anyway. So it'll be a reverse SEABROOK, big deal.

Since when isn't a big deal?

Since today. Now!

As he covered the short distance to the willow tree on unsteady feet, tiny voices in his head chanted "it's a trap, it's a trap", getting more frenzied with each step closer to the Russian. When he finally reached Eton, he dropped to his knees beside him, not entirely sure what he was doing. His mouth was dry, his jeans too tight and uncomfortable, and he was afraid he would come right then if tried to adjust himself. He spat what little he could muster up into his trembling hand and whispered, "Lemme."

Eton let go of himself and Jack's fingers closed around him. The young man hissed and

Jack gulped, two pairs of eyes fixed on Jack's hand wrapped around Eton's erection, both breathing heavily, too far gone to speak. Then Eton clasped both of his hands firmly over Jack's and started pumping, his eyes shut, head thrown back, biting on his bottom lip, trying to swallow back the moans that were rumbling deep in his throat.

He came hard, with a choked groan, after only a few strokes, clamping his palm down on the spurting milky fluid that quickly spread over their joined hands. It was the hottest thing Jack had ever seen, and the sight sent him over the edge. He yanked one of Eton's hands, slippery and smelling of pure sex, pressed it hard between his legs, pumped twice and came in his jeans like a goddamn teenager.

When Jack came down from his height and opened his eyes, the first thing he saw was Eton's eyes on him—huge, dark and molten. The young man immediately dropped his gaze and his whole face slammed shut. But not before Jack had caught the expression Eton clearly tried to cover up. Amazement. The young man fumbled in a pocket of his jeans, pulled out a large handkerchief and hastily cleaned himself. Then he pulled his jeans up and zipped them. All in complete silence, his face gloomy, eyes firmly fixed on his hands.

"Eton?"

Jack's first impulse was to comfort the youth, to tell him it was alright. But he wasn't sure himself if it was alright. In fact, he wasn't sure of anything at that moment.

Eton didn't look up. If anything, his lips squeezed even tighter, his whole face looked pinched. He stood up, unsteady, staring at the ground.

"Eton, you don't have to—"

A peal of female laughter somewhere nearby cut him short, followed by a flirtatious voice chirping in heavily accented English, "Oh, Khovard, you are bad boy, yes? I know you, physicists—you secret, how to say, dangerous, yes?"

It was Lara, still high after the lunch. Howard mumbled something inaudible, and she giggled again.

"Not vorry about Jack. He is good man. But, how to say *staramodny*? Ah, old style? Old fashion, yes. I like Jack, but I am for free love. Like your American flower child, yes, children... Yes?" Howard said something in respond to that. "Yes, we swim there and nobody find us. It is not far. We go?" she asked impatiently, sounding closer.

Seeing Eton's startled expression, Jack sprung up and took a step toward him. "You can walk back along the shore," he whispered. "They won't see you under the willows." He pushed Eton lightly on the arm. "Go."

His answer was the faintest of nods and the next moment Eton was gone.

Jack undressed quickly, left his clothes under the willow tree and tiptoed into the river.

The water was warm on top, cold a few feet below the surface. It cleared his mind and set the wheels in his head spinning.

So, what the heck had just happened?

Joe had said the KGB had used this kind of honey trap on Americans before, so for a moment there Jack had been convinced that was it. But if it was a trap why hadn't the guy acted upon it when Jack had stepped into it? They'd been taught that the KGB always used specially trained officers or agents for their honey traps. And Eton Volkonsky? Okay, so he was an excellent performer, too. On stage. But the way he'd acted just now... It could go into the Farm's book of case studies as the worst executed honey trap ever. Jack recalled how Eton had fled, without even a glance at him.

Nah, he looked like one very confused kid.... The way Jack had probably looked when he finally figured out at the age of fourteen why the image of bare chested Butch Cassidy had done it for him every time while even the prettiest of the girls hadn't.

So. Did it mean that Eton May Volkonsky was...?

Holy shit! But how could it be? He looked *so* not the type that Jack wouldn't have guessed in million years.

Oh, c'mon! When was the last time you looked in the mirror, Smith? Why do you think women are after your ass all the time and hardly any men?

Alright, alright... But does it mean that his father was—

You told Joe yourself that it didn't mean shit, did you not? Why this crap now?

But how on earth do the NSA folks know that the May offspring was—

They don't. They just resolved to throw the bait and pray to God that something would turn up. And *you* are the one who is going to deliver that "something" to them. And to Joe... Aren't you?

He recalled Eton's eyes on him yesterday in the village—full of warmth and admiration, then startled and something else... There had been something else in those dark eyes...

He took two lung fulls of air and dived, propelling himself down into the river's cold, still layer, until he touched its silky, silt-covered bottom.

Lust. That was what he'd seen in Eton's eyes and hadn't got it.

Chapter 19

The night breeze stroked the curtains, making the moonlight dance with deep shadows on varnished floorboards between the beds, filling the room with spicy-fresh scent of the pine forest outside. It took Jack all his willpower to keep his breath steady and not toss and turn in his bed. How on earth could Eton sleep so peacefully, so nonchalantly, after their encounter by the river? He had been fast asleep when Jack emerged from the bathroom, aroused and ridiculously nervous. That had been an hour ago and, Christ, he was so hot and bothered he could barely keep still.

Eton had been completely poker-faced afterwards, acting like nothing out of the ordinary had happened between them—throughout the long walk back to the vacation house with the rest of the group, during the dinner, and then through the movie all of them had watched in the recreation room—a video-tape of Romancing the Stone dubbed in Russian. Eton sat at one end of the row, Anya clinging to his arm, while Jack at the other end vied to win Lara's attention back from Val and Howard.

Okay, that was all fine, just how it should be, all things considered. Although at one point, little alarm bells went off in Jack's head: Eton's behavior seemed too skilled, like he had been trained, perhaps? His suspicions, however, had quickly evaporated when he caught Eton alone in the restroom before the movie. He nodded at Jack as though he were a stranger and walked out on him. Then after the movie, he disappeared without a word.

Now, what was Jack supposed to make of all *that*? Could it be that the guy had just been drunk and didn't remember anything?

But Jack hadn't been drunk, not to the extent of not remembering their little action by the river. Jesus Christ, it had been so hot that it had left him half hard ever since. So much so, he desperately needed relief. Like now, or he wouldn't last till morning.

Fine. To hell with you, Eton, you little bastard.

He turned his head a fraction, ever so slightly, to look at the bed against the opposite wall. Eton was lying on his back, his hands folded neatly on his stomach, breathing evenly, blond curls in disarray.

Okay, so he couldn't actually see the color of Eton's hair in the dark, but he knew. He even knew how they would feel between his fingers, against his skin—soft, silky. Sensual...

Great! Now you need to go to the bathroom to wring it out, dumbass.

Just then, Eton chest heaved, as if he's heard Jack's thoughts, and his head turned a fraction in the direction of Jack's bed. Both kept still, Jack becoming more conscious of his own uneven breathing with every passing second.

Finally, Jack caved in. "Eton? You sleeping?" he called softly.

Eton didn't respond right away, and when he did, the clipped answer came out on a deep exhale, like he had been holding his breath. "No."

"Can't sleep?"

"Yes... Um, no."

Jack held his breath. "Need help?" he offered and winced, his joking tone sounded lame even to his own ears. The silence lasted longer this time and Jack wanted to kick himself under the bed sheet. So the boy had probably been drunk after all. "Sorry. Don't mind me, Et—"

"Yeah."

It was faint as a breath and at first Jack thought he'd imagined it. He raised himself on an elbow, staring at Eton's dark, still silhouette. "What didjah say?"

"Yes. I need help," Eton said quietly but clearly. He sounded tired. Or resigned. Like he'd given in to an internal battle with himself.

Jack felt a pinch in his chest. He threw his sheet aside and sat up in his bed. Now what? They couldn't really do anything in the room—Jack wasn't sure these walls didn't have ears.

"Wanna go for a night swim?"

"What?... Oh, okay." Eton sat up too.

"Let's go out separately." Jack was all business in a heartbeat. "I'll go first. You wait here for five minutes, then follow me. I'll be waiting at the head of the forest trail. Okay?"

"Okay."

Jack quickly dressed up, grabbed a large towel from the bathroom. "See you in a few minutes?" he asked from the door, not caring if he sounded too eager.

"Yes. Five minutes." There was no hesitation in Eton's voice this time.

"Okay. Don't forget to bring your towel." Jack let out a quiet laugh that sounded nervous even to himself and slipped out.

The moon was bright like a floodlight, radiating a vast circle in the cloudless sky, bathing the world beneath in its milky glow. Jack walked straight into the shadow of the tall pines at the trailhead and leaned against the closest tree. He had counted to three hundred and sixty eight when he saw Eton strolling towards the woods. He moved with the grace of a panther, deceptively unhurried, but Jack could tell by the deliberateness of each step that he could strike without warning.

As Eton reached the trailhead, Jack detached himself from the tree trunk. "This way," he called in a loud whisper, and the young man's face creased in a shy smile as he saw Jack. "Let's go swimming." He grinned back and puffed out a deep breath when Eton dipped his head.

Within a few minutes, they reached the stretch of the shore lined by a range of old weeping willows. Jack dropped his towel under a big tree and started undressing.

He was down to his boxers when he noticed that Eton was standing there motionless. "Have you never skinny-dipped?" he asked lightly, trying to shake off the awkwardness that had descended on him again.

"I'm sorry?"

"Swimming naked. Have you never swum naked with your friends?" Suddenly Jack felt like a complete idiot.

You're not his friend, Smith. Not yet. Besides, didn't they tell you at the Institute that proper Russians don't undress on the first date?

He let me give him a hand job today. Why playing coy now? Not like he's some little virgin girl.

He was drunk... Probably.

Drunk my ass!

"Yes, I have. A long time ago. Sorry, I wasn't sure," Eton finally responded, sounding self-conscious, but Jack could hear a smile in his voice. He started peeling off his clothes hastily.

Jack turned away to give him some privacy. Besides, for some reason he didn't want Eton to see that he was hard and ready. Not just yet. So as soon as he had shed his boxers, Jack darted toward the lake and plunged in. Even though the water was warmer than the air, it felt like cool satin against his hot skin. When he could no longer feel the silkiness of the silt under his feet, he turned around. Eton was pushing himself hard against the water, quickly closing in on him, his face looking both startled and determined. Jack smiled encouragingly at him, took a deep breath and dived under.

The moonlight was like liquid silver poured over the surface of the lake, but from underneath it looked more like a light beam shining through a layer of dark silk. Jack made another hard stroke, propelling himself down deeper, and broke into the cold layer of lake water. He stopped and twisted his body around. He could see the dark shape of Eton's body moving slowly toward him, still tiptoeing on the lakebed. Then he stopped, sprang off the ground and dived under too.

He reached Jack in a few strokes and rotated to position himself vertically. Now both of them were at the same level in the water, within an arm reach, their eyes open, huge and unblinking. Then, like in a slow motion movie sequence, Eton raised his hand, reaching toward Jack. When his fingers just about to touch Jack's chest, something clenched in Jack's stomach and suddenly he was out of air. He pushed himself up abruptly, out of the water.

He didn't see, but could feel that Eton was close behind him. He catapulted out of the water right after Jack, both of them panting, water streaming down their startled faces and bare shoulders.

Eton started talking quickly, sounding distressed, "I'm sorry! So sorry! I didn't mean—"

"It's okay." Jack got his breath and composure back. He smiled reassuringly at the distraught youth. "It's alright. I just needed to take a breath. That's all." He caught Eton's hand, pulled under the water and pressed the palm to his chest, just above his solar flex. "You can touch me, Eton... If you want."

"Yeah?" Eton breathed out, eyes glued to his hand on Jack's body.

"Yeah... Anytime..." Jack whispered, short of breath again and a little dizzy.

Focus, Smith, you loser. Get a grip. This is it, the start of operation TALION. The "seabrook" part.

Eton's gaze traveled slowly up, roamed Jack's shoulders above the water's surface, then moved further up, to his mouth. His lips popped open, like the breath he had been holding finally broke through, and he sucked in a new, shaky breath. When Eton's eyes finally met his, Jack knew he had won this round.

The expression on the young man's face was a mixture of amazement, awe and lust. He pulled back his hand, raised it above the water and reached it out to Jack's face. However, instead of touching him, Eton's fingers only shadowed his jaw, then traced down to Jack's neck and shoulder. His lips moved as though he was saying something, but no sound came out.

Jack closed his eyes, feeling faint from the anticipation.

He wasn't exactly a timid type whenever sex was involved, not at all. In fact, he was normally the one who took the initiative, telling his sex partner in no uncertain terms what it was that Jack Smith wanted. In any circumstance like this, he would quickly make the next move and take control of the situation. Somehow, this time Jack didn't. He let Eton take his time exploring him and he had absolutely no fricking idea why…

That's enough. Move it, Smith!

Jack opened his eyes, gripped Eton's wrist and pulled the hand down under the water again. The cool water had eased his erection, but he was still aroused, he hoped enough for Eton to get an idea of what he wanted.

Eton's eyes flew shut, and he leaned into Jack, as if his legs were buckling under him. Except they were suspended in the water. Jack circled his arm around Eton's waist, pressed him briefly against his body, Eton's hand still between them.

"Let's move to the shore, okay?" Jack whispered, pulling away, smiling softly at the young man's startled eyes. "We may drown, if we continue *this* right here."

Eton nodded, looking dazed. He was a goner.

They got out of the water, with Jack leading the way, and hurried into the deep shadow under the willows. Jack reached their belongings and bent down to pick up the towels. He straightened up, about to turn around to hand one of them to Eton and… found himself clasped in an iron grip. Two strong arms wrapped tight around his waist and chest, palms flat on his abdomen and over his heart. A lean, hard body pressed flush against him, ragged breath heated his neck, a throbbing hardness pressed into his backside. Jack sucked in a breath. Oh yeah, he wanted sex with Eton, he had no doubt about it anymore. But *this* was not exactly what he had had in mind.

However, that wasn't what dazed him: in that single moment, Jack suddenly realized that he wouldn't be able to say no to this man, whatever he might want to do with him.

"Jaack…" Eton let out an odd little sound, half sob half laughter, then whispered fervently into Jack's neck, right behind his ear, "Never wanted anything like *thisss*!"

He loosened his grip, repositioned himself deftly to Jack's front, took Jack's face in between his hands and covered his lips with his mouth, his tongue forcefully seeking entrance. And Jack opened up to him, something he never did on a "first date".

The attack on his mouth didn't last very long. Too soon, Eton pulled back, leaving Jack with a startlingly cold and empty feeling. He dropped to his knees and buried his face in Jack's stomach, arms around his waist, his breath hot over the tip of Jack's aching cock. Jack threaded his fingers through Eton's curls and closed his eyes. Even soaking wet they felt more sensual than he had imagined. He sensed rather that heard the rumbling moan, somewhere deep in Eton's throat as he pressed his cheek into Jack's erection.

"Lemme?" Eton croaked, raising his head.

Jack gulped and nodded, for once his voice failing him. He was not sure what was happening to him, everything was so different, so—

Oh God!

A scorching yet achingly sweet sensations pulsed through him the second Eton's lips closed tightly around him. His legs began buckling.

He grabbed at Eton' shoulders. "Wait!"

Eton stopped and carefully let go of Jack. "Sorry. Did I hurt you?" he rasped, sounding worried.

"Christ, no!" Jack choked out a breathless laugh, shook his head. "But I won't last long."

He lowered himself onto his knees, wrapped his arms around Eton, dropped his head onto his shoulder and held very still, trying to wind down a little, the night chill his ally. He didn't want it to end quickly, didn't know when would be the next time that he would have *this*, whatever it was that was happening to him, with this man. He wanted it to last like forever, it was so fucking good.

"You like it?"

Eton's voice was still laced with concern and Jack hastened to reassure him, "Hell, yeah!"

You have no idea!

"Then let me? Please?"

And he let him Eton take over, worship his body, his manhood, his whole being.

Afterwards, when he could think straight again, Jack couldn't explain to himself why he let Eton have his way with him. Normally, he was the one in control, giving pleasure the way *he* wanted. Somehow, this time he had just given himself over to this man and the strangest thing of all was that it actually felt alright.

No, fuck it! It felt like nothing he had ever experienced before—Eton's hard, muscled body against his, his taste in Jack's mouth, his scent so heady, his hungry caresses intoxicating. Everything he did was so... Jesus, how could someone make you feel like this? It was as if sex had always been in black and white for Jack, and suddenly, for the first time, he was seeing it, feeling it in a kaleidoscope of luminous colors he hadn't known existed.

They hadn't lasted long, never got down to fucking, Eton in a frenzy pushing him quickly over the edge. And as he'd exploded in thousands brilliant little suns, a thought flitted through Jack's rapidly fading consciousness, and he tried to push it away right there, right then. Because it was pure nonsense and there was absolutely no reason for him to be imagining that when this was all over and he was out of here, Eton would remember him sometimes as his... as someone he had wanted so very much... once...

Chapter 20

Consciousness came to Jack all at once and he immediately knew he was being watched. He held very still for a few moments, trying to keep his breath even and deep, then opened his eyes without warning. And saw Eton.

The young man was squatting by the bed, watching Jack with a strange soft expression on his face. It vanished the instant he realized he was staring right into Jack's eyes. He rocked back on his heels but didn't stand up. "Good morning," he said, smiling self-consciously.

"Hey. Whatchadoing on the floor?" It came out a little gruff and Jack cleared his throat.

Eton's smile widened a fraction. "Waiting for you to wake up."

Oh.

"What time is it?"

Eton looked down at his watch. "Um, eight minutes past six."

"Christ, Eton, did you sleep at all?"

The previous night, after their "night swim", Eton had insisted that Jack return first. Back in the room, Jack undressed quickly, brushed his teeth and jumped into bed, fully prepared to wait for his roomie. After fifteen minutes, he got up and walked barefoot to the window. The moon was raging in the velvet sky peppered with brilliant specks of stars. The night chill had dried the air, leaving it crisp, infused with delicate nocturnal smells. Jack stood by the window for a few minutes, then returned to bed. He didn't remember when sleep had knocked him out.

"I did... a little. Have you woken up now?"

"Yes." Jack grinned, feeling unreasonably pleased. "Why?"

"Come. I want to show you something."

"What, now?" Eton looked so fine this morning that Jack didn't want him to move away just yet.

Apparently, the young man had other plans. "Yes. We'll be back before the others come down for breakfast."

Oh well, he'd better get up then. "Okay." Jack threw his sheet aside.

As he put his feet on the floor, his shin rubbed against Eton's jeans-clad thigh. Eton swallowed, grabbed the denim jacket from the floor and sprang to his feet.

"I'll wait for you at the back entrance, by the garage." His eyes darted at Jack's thighs and he swallowed again, before turning away and walking quickly out of the room.

Jack was done with his bathroom routine in under three minutes. He got dressed quickly, gave his unruly hair a raking with his fingers and was out the door. The vacation house was deserted. He crept stealthily along the dark corridor to the back door, praying that he didn't run into anyone he knew—or didn't know, for that matter.

Eton was waiting for him by the garage with his jacket on. Next to him skulked a military green motorcycle with a sidecar, the type Jack had only seen in World War II movies.

"Are we riding this?" he asked skeptically. It looked old, and the sidecar was too close to the ground. "Where did you get it?"

"Borrowed in the village," Eton said. Then, probably noticing Jack's doubtful expression, he added, "Don't worry. It is strong enough. I've tested it." He kick-started the bike, mounted it and turned to Jack, indicating the passenger seat with his head and eyes.

"Are you going to tell me where we're going?" Jack asked sternly, climbing into the sidecar.

"Nope." Eton's tone was deadpan at first, but his face softened at Jack's baffled expression. A hint of a smile crept up to his eyes. "You'll see."

The sturdy motorcycle, an Ural M-72, turned out to be faster that Jack had thought, and they had to shout to hear each other, the wind blowing in their faces was so strong. In the end, Jack resolve to sit back and enjoy the bumpy ride, as the dirt road rushed by, just a dozen inches below. They bustled through the woodlands, then across a vast field of wilting, purplish-brownish flowers and Eton shouted over his shoulder that it was buckwheat. Then they entered another forest, and Jack figured it was the same mixed forest that ran from their vacation house, for miles and miles southwest. Finally, they stopped at the end of the narrow forest road and Eton cut the engine.

"Now we walk. It is only five, six minutes from here."

"*What* is?" Jack demanded, feigning impatience.

Eton gave him a closed-lipped grin, a mischievous glint in his eyes. "We're almost there. Let's go." He swirled around and set off into the forest.

What was it with these Russians? Didn't they know how to ask at all?

But all Jack could do was to roll his eyes and follow him. However, he quickly forgot his gripe about commandeering Russians as he ogled the fine man walking in front of him. He wanted to jump him, pull him into his arms, inhale his scent and then... But Eton was so eager to show him something, whatever it was, that Jack thought he could wait for another five, six minutes and maybe *then*...

He noticed the gap in the trees when they were still a few hundred yards away. From afar, it looked like a small forest pond of unusual color, the water changing from deep green to bright blue the closer they got. As they approached the opening, he realized that it wasn't a pond, but a lush, grassy meadow, densely carpeted with flowers of intensely blue color. It took him a few moments to identify them. Cornflowers. He hadn't known cornflowers could be *that* blue.

Okay, so he'd never thought much about cornflowers in the first place—for him they were just weeds. But *this*... this was like a watercolor painting, the type you see in art galleries. Or like a fairytale, if he was asked to describe one.

Jack stood rooted next to his Russian friend, gaping at the vision in front of them, their shoulders and arms touching. "Wow... It's beautiful," he murmured.

"It is," Eton breathed.

"How did you find this place?"

"A villager told us about it last year."

He could hear a shrug in Eton's tone. "*last* year? But how did you know that they're in bloom *now*?"

"I checked it out," Eton dropped casually, not looking at Jack, and headed into the meadow.

A thought struck Jack. "When?" Jack asked, following him. Eton mumbled something in response that he didn't catch. "Eton, *when* did you check it out?" he insisted, addressing Eton's back.

"Yesterday... You like it?"

Jack stumbled to a halt.

Of course. That was why Eton had been missing yesterday morning—he'd been scouting out this place. Then had borrowed the motorcycle in the village.

But then, it meant that he'd planned this side trip *before* their afternoon encounter by the river, didn't it? And if he wasn't KGB—and Jack was almost sure now that he wasn't— then didn't it mean that he...?

Finally realizing that he was getting no answer, Eton stopped and turned around.

"Yes, Eton, I do like it. Thank you." It was all Jack could think of saying: the realization that this man had gone to all the trouble of finding this place, of bringing him here just to show him *this*, had robbed Jack of words.

Eton said nothing, just gazed at him with an odd little smile on his face. An expectant smile.

Now it seemed like he wanted something from Jack. "What?" He cocked an eyebrow.

"The color," Eton prompted.

"Yes, it's a striking color. In fact, I've never seen any..." And it suddenly dawned on him what the young man meant and what the visit to this amazing place was all about.

Eton's smile grew beyond its usual proportions, creasing his whole face. He sighed contentedly, shook his head softly, gazing straight into Jack's eyes. "Neither have I." He wasn't talking about the cornflowers.

Okay, so Jack was used to people commenting on his big blue eyes and long, thick lashes. His Ma had told him once, when he was a clueless kid, that the color was true blue. Later Jack had figured that his father probably hated him partly because of his eyes— the old man's eyes were light brown and his mother's dark brown, almost black. Girls, though, never failed to mention them, and swoon over them; and so occasionally did men, especially those he fucked. But no one had ever offered their compliments to him in such an extravagant yet incredibly sweet way.

A sudden hot wave washed over Jack, leaving him with a huge lump in his throat. He took two large steps toward Eton, grabbed him by his biceps and yanked him into his arms. "Come 'ere... You," he whispered brokenly and pressed his nose and mouth into Eton's neck, just below his ear.

Eton froze for a second, then his arms closed firmly around Jack's waist and back, and he pressed his whole body into Jack's, from head to toe, aroused already. Then he took hold of Jack's head and attacked him with his mouth, his tongue, his hands.

The next thing Jack knew they were on the ground, trying to rip the clothes off one another like they'd gone mad. When they were all but naked, Eton stopped abruptly and held very still, his expression changing quickly from lust to determination, to anxiety and then... pleading?

"Eton? What you want?" Jack was ready for anything, since everything this man had done to him last night felt so unbelievably good. *Almost* anything.

Eton swallowed. "I want you to...," he started confidently, but his voice broke and he finished in whisper, "Take me... Please?"

It took Jack all his patience and stamina, all his skills to loosen Eton up and ready him for what he wanted. He had never done this for anyone before, never needed to, but now, for some reason, he felt compelled to do it.

Oh, c'mon, whom was he kidding? He *wanted* to, like never before. And he wanted Eton to feel at least half as good as he made Jack feel.

So he traced every line of Eton's body with his tongue, from his sweet, greedy mouth down to his ankles. He took his time over each of the hardened nipples, his cock the deep color of lust, his chiseled thighs and prominent muscles at the back of his legs, coated in silky, light blond hair, the maddening curves of his taut buttocks and the opening into the abyss of joy at their heart. He drove Eton to a state of delirium, chanting Jack's name like a prayer, then flipped him over and entered him, Jack himself barely holding onto shreds of his willpower. As soon as he felt Eton's body going rigid beneath him and heard his choked-up groan, Jack let himself go. His climax was so powerful that it left him momentarily blind and deaf, unable to move.

When he came back to his senses, he collapsed on top of Eton, nuzzled his cheek in an awkward, sexless gesture, then rolled off to one side. They lay there for a long time, hands and legs touching, saying nothing, feeling like they were floating with the clouds in the bottomless blue sky, sated and completely free. Wild grass and blue cornflowers were thick and pliant under their backs, dancing in waves around them, gentle morning sun caressed their hot exposed skin and Jack thought that it was probably *he* who would be remembering *Eton* as his best... *special* friend, KGB informer or not. And that was alright.

After a while, Eton sat up and began putting on his clothes. Jack suppressed a sigh: he didn't want to get up just yet. He wiggled into his boxers and jeans and stretched out on the grass again, hoping that Eton would settle back next to him.

But instead, the young man rested his head against Jack's side, just below his heart. Jack froze.

He wasn't into after sex cuddling. He had been turned down the very first time he tried it and, being a fast learner, Jack had never made the same mistake again. After that time, with all his casual fucks over the years, he'd never felt the urge. Even with little Carmen it hadn't been completely effortless, despite the fact that he had genuinely liked her. So now, Eton's move caught him off guard. On top of that, he hadn't expected it from this reserved man.

For a moment, Jack wasn't quite sure what to do. But it felt so... so right! Jeez, everything about Eton felt so right, he couldn't begin to wrap his head around it. He exhaled carefully, counted to ten and draped his arm over Eton's midsection in a deliberately casual move.

Eton puffed out a deep breath, reached for his jacket and started fumbling in the pockets. He pulled out a pack of Marlboros and lit a cigarette. After taking a quick puff on it, he offered it to Jack without looking at him.

There definitely was something wrong with him today. How else to explain his retarded reaction to everything Eton did or said? Jack wrestled out of his trance, took the cigarette, brushing the tips of his fingers against Eton's wrist in the process, and brought it to his lips.

The filter was slightly damp and tasted like Eton, and he wondered idly how a smoke could taste so perfect. Maybe it was the sun and the bottomless sky, and this special place with its tall grass and flowers. Cornflowers. From now on, they wouldn't be a weed in Jack's book anymore—how could they be when someone like Eton seemed to think that they were something special?

"What was the name of your dog... when you lived on the ranch?" Eton asked out of the blue.

"'Scuse me?"

"You must have had a dog when you were little... Did you?" The youth looked at Jack sideways, worrying his bottom lip, eyes wide with anticipation.

"Yeah, I did," Jack said tentatively, unsure where it was all going. "I called him Ace." It was the name of the mongrel puppy Jack's Ma had given him for his sixth birthday and his old man had taken it away a week later. Jack didn't like to remember that time. "Why?"

Eton let out a short, soft laugh, his face visibly relaxed. "Nothing... You'll think it's stupid."

Jack noticed the color creeping onto the young man's ears. "I won't," he promised.

Eton inhaled deeply on his cigarette and puffed out a big cloud of smoke. "I used to know—" He stopped, swallowed and started over. "My father used to tell me about, um, the son of his neighbor rancher. When he still lived in California... His name was Jack, too. And he had a dog, named Buddy... Told you it was silly." Eton shrugged and chortled, obviously trying to make the whole thing sound inconsequential. He averted his eyes to gaze at the sky, a picture perfect of nonchalance, but Jack could feel Eton's heart racing under his hand.

Okay, so Eton was lying. And not very convincingly too. What Jack couldn't make out was which part of it was a fib. There was something in it—the innocence of the story, the way the young man confessed it—that made it sound like it might be genuine. But then, he'd started by saying "I used to know". How could he have known anyone in California when he had never been there in the first place?

Jack reached for Eton's wrist, brought the rest of the cigarette in his fingers to his lips and took a last, deep drag. "How about you? Did *you* have a dog when you were little?"

Eton crushed the cigarette butt into the grass. His head moved softly against Jack's side. "No. My mother and I lived with my grandparents. My grandmother had asthma. So we couldn't keep dogs or cats at home."

"What about your father? Didn't he live with you, too?" According to the files, they had divorced when young Eton was five.

"No. My parents divorced when I was little."

"I'm sorry… But he taught you English, right?"

"Yes. And mathematics… And about California," Eton added like an afterthought.

But Jack knew better: according to Lara, California was Eton's old flame.

Wasn't it? Or was it a KGB ploy after all?

"So you know a lot about California then?"

Jack had asked him this question before, in another forest, near his *dacha*, but the young man had bluntly brushed it aside that time. Now, he plucked a blade of grass and stuck it in one corner of his mouth and just when Jack was beginning to think there would be another push back, Eton said, "I do. But mainly its history. I have read a lot about it… One of my grandmother's ancestors was… um, visited California in the eighteenth century. To establish trade relations on behalf of the Emperor. "

"Count Nicolai Rezanov?" Jack was pleased he'd done his homework on Prof. Volkonsky's family.

"You know about him?" Eton's head rolled against Jack's side again. He looked surprised, but then his shoulder jerked in a shrug. "But then why not? You know a lot about us and our history, don't you?"

Now, what do you really mean by *that*, huh?

"I do. And not only the history," Jack said, echoing Eton's answer. "I may even have learned about it the same way you have about California." He held his gaze, not trying to soften the challenge in his tone.

Eton didn't react to it. He smiled a little, seeming satisfied. "Perhaps you had access to more research materials than me. My grandfather told me about all the resources you had at your universities."

"He's been to America?"

"Twice. He visited California, too."

There was a hint of wistfulness in Eton's tone and it reminded Jack of his days back in Wyoming. He knew the feeling so well.

"Do *you* want to visit California?"

It was callous of him to ask that question, knowing what he knew about Eton and his Californian dreams. But Jack had to continue playing his role of an overly friendly and a bit thick-skinned American. Because it was his goddamn job after all.

Eton was silent for a long while, watching the clouds floating in the sky through his eyelashes, and Jack thought he wouldn't get an answer to this question. But after a long while, Eton looked straight in his eyes and said simply, "It is the second thing I've always wanted."

He smiled shyly and Jack recalled him whispering in his ear the night before "I never wanted anything like *this*". He had to close his eyes for a second as he realized when California had become "the second thing" for this unbelievable man.

It was time to head back. Jack wrapped his arm tighter around Eton's chest and shook him up a little. "Time to go, friend." He didn't want to, but it was getting late and he thought he could live without people's questions later on.

Eton sighed and sat up. "I know." He stared at the ground, then looked up and said quietly, "Thank you, Jack."

"For what? It's me who should thank you. For bringing me here." Jack sat up and tugged on his undershirt. "This place is amazing." He pressed his hand onto Eton's back, brushed away two blades of grass that were clinging to his t-shirt.

"No, you don't understand. I…" Eton glanced away, gnawing on his lips, then looked at Jack. "I never felt so free… So… just *me*."

His tone was so passionate that it got Jack worried. "That's alright, Eton. But you know, you should be *very* careful back there." He whipped his head, indicating the vacation house, Moscow, the rest of the world. "You know that, don't you?"

The smile slipped from Eton's face and he suddenly looked tired and older than his twenty-one years of age. "I know." He looked down at his hands, his long fingers rolling a long stem with two cornflowers at the end. "Don't worry. Nobody will know about it… About you."

Eton raised his head and Jack saw a world of loneliness in the brown, soulful eyes. His gut clenched. "It's not only about me, Eton. It's about you, too."

Is that so, asshole? Isn't it a bit late to worry about him now?

He made a move on me first! Could still be a honey trap, couldn't it?

What if it isn't? What then, huh?

How the fuck would I know "what then"? It just happened, okay? He'll just have to deal with it.

"Don't worry about me. I'll be fine." Eton smiled reassuringly at him, the smile not quite reaching his eyes. He sprang up and offered Jack his hand. "Let's go back? To the real world."

Jack grasped his hand, picked up his denim shirt with his other hand and pulled himself to his feet. He drew Eton into his arms, gave him a quick hug, a nuzzle and let go. "Yeah. Let's do it."

And we'll deal with it somehow. We will, friend, I promise!

Chapter 21

The real world that waited for them was not a friendly place. In fact, it conspired to crowd the wondrous weekend out of Jack's mind, cramming it with other incidents and issues, some pressing, some unnerving and some both.

On Monday, it took Jack much longer to write his weekend activities report. He took pains over each word, phrasing it so that Moscow Station's bosses wouldn't pick up on the "seabrook" part of the op—as instructed by Joe Coburn. He put off figuring out how to deliver the news of progress with their potential star agent to the chief of ops. In the evening, he stole himself for the debriefings with the station chief and William in the Tank.

If they were surprised that nobody had made a move on Jack during the trip, they didn't show it. Spy games were waiting games and the first thing you were taught as a new intelligence officer was to be patient. Nurimbekoff nodded approvingly when Jack was done with his analysis of the situation with the potential targets.

When Jack finished, William informed him that the security office had found only secondary traces of spy dust, official name NPPD, on his car and the door of his apartment. The conclusion was that Jack wasn't targeted by the KGB, but had picked it up from Embassy staffers who were and with whom he had had physical contact lately. When Jack asked who were the targets, he was told that the substance had been found on cars, apartment door handles and floor mats of all Moscow Station's officers. And the list didn't end there. In fact, it included nearly a half of the Embassy's diplomatic staff, and it was only a matter of hours before the State Department made an announcement and the findings would be out in the open.

The announcement didn't come until late on Friday. Then on Monday, first the Embassy's staff, then the rest of the American community in Moscow were invited for official briefings. They took place at the Ambassador's residence, Spaso House, as the Embassy premises couldn't accommodate such a large congregation. It took two days and six rounds of briefings for the Security Office to advise around five hundred concerned Americans that the KGB had been using a potentially cancerous substance on some of them in order to identify Soviet citizens they were meeting with. Within hours, the spy dust account hit international press and raised an uproar in America.

Following the exposé, the flow of enquiries and paperwork for departing American nationals doubled overnight. As a result, Jack, a Russian language speaker, was asked to assist the overwhelmed consular section in handling their compatriots' dealings with the local authorities. He welcomed this little diversion from his daily routine, especially the reporting, which had become rather limited since he didn't interact with a lot of Russians during that time. The drawback was that he had to postpone his burger and ribs dinner for his Russian friends.

As a result, by the end of the third week, Jack had only managed to exchange a few words on the phone with Lara on her way out, and leave an innocuous message for Eton on his answering machine. He wasn't sure if his young friend had called back, maybe he had when Jack was out. Which was most of the time, from early in the morning till very late at night, every day during those three weeks.

On the second Monday of September, after weeks of silence, Amanda called, just before lunchtime. Only to tell him that she was leaving Moscow. And Mike. And since Jack was her best friend in Moscow, she felt compelled to call to let him know. She would miss him, she said, but hoped they would meet again sometime, somewhere.

Jack was dumbstruck. He insisted that they get together for lunch or coffee, or at least a brief farewell meet so she could tell him what had happened. Amanda said it wasn't possible that she was leaving the next morning. Her tone of voice was strained, and she seemed unwilling to talk about anything. The only other thing she wanted to tell Jack was that she had given his phone number to her rock guru friend Artyom and that he would call Jack when he got invites for local rock festival in Leningrad or Tallinn—Jack was still interested, wasn't he?

She hung up shortly after. Jack sat there staring at the angrily beeping handset, wondering what had happened between Amanda and Mike since the last time he had seen them together. It had been only two months ago, at the Fourth of July reception at Ambassador Hart's residence.

A week later, headlines in the New York Times and then the Times provided Jack with a clue of what might have caused Amanda to leave Moscow and her American husband of only four years, unexpectedly and in a great hurry.

On September 12th, accused of spying against Britain, twenty-five Soviet diplomats and journalists were expelled from the country. The Times also carried an article, apparently leaked by the British authorities, about a Soviet diplomat and senior KGB official, Oleg Gordievsky, who had defected to the West. It described Gordievsky as a KGB Colonel and the head of the KGB station, *rezidentura*, in London, who had also been working for the British intelligence service since mid-sixties.

Two days later, Moscow retaliated with an expulsion of twenty-five Britons from Moscow and Leningrad. The British immediately responded by ordering deportation of another six Soviet officials and the Russians followed suit by throwing out a similar number of Brits. At which point Margaret Thatcher put her food down and announced a halt to the series of tit-for-tat expulsions.

Amongst the thirty-one expelled Britons, three were journalists and two businessmen, people without diplomatic immunity. The fact that they were deported, not arrested, could only mean that the Soviet security organs did not have anything incriminating against them, and used them only to keep the scores even with the Britons.

Against this background, Amanda's sudden departure just before the spate of expulsions was more than suspicious, and Moscow Station deduced that MI6 had probably decided to play it safe. The fact that they had been using Mike Demidoff, an American citizen and a high profile journalist, as a cover for their intelligence officer on the inside of the Iron Curtain made the Americans uneasy, yet unable to do anything about what had already transpired. Jack felt sorry for old Mike and wondered if he knew or maybe even suspected that he had been used.

On the other hand, Jack now knew the name of the man with the Woolworths shopping bag on the curb of a Moscow avenue—Colonel Oleg Gordievsky, MI6's star agent according to Joe Coburn. Jack suspected Amanda had been acting as the courier for Gordievsky and the rather conspicuous fling with Jack had been her additional cover. But, hey, he couldn't really hold a grudge against her, could he, when he'd been covering up his own secret with their sweet, playful friendship?

However, spy wars were not the only thing that preoccupied Jack toward the end of the summer of '85. A calamity that had been roiling under the surface of the public's attention for several years erupted in August onto the front cover of TIME magazine, titled "AIDS - The Growing Threat". And just like that, overnight, Acquired Immunodeficiency Syndrome had turned from a "gay men's plague" into a disaster of global proportions.

On September 17th, President Reagan talked about AIDS in a nationally televised press conference and about the budget his government was allocating for a research program on AIDS. In Moscow, for a month it was a subject of undertone conversations at Uncle Sam's, the Marines and the Seabees clubs. Very few of the gossipers were worried and sympathetic; most were disgusted and scared.

It took Jack nearly three weeks to get hold of one of the three copies of TIME magazines in the Embassy's library. He didn't want to ask the librarian to reserve it for him and as a result, had to make several visits to the library, every time pretending to have come for something else. He got lucky only on the fourth time: found a copy in the newspapers section, a bit tattered by this time, with a stain from a coffee cup on the back cover.

The stories it carried were bone chilling. The magazine quoted experts saying that the disease was spreading exponentially, doubling every ten months; that it was claiming not only gays and drug-addicts, but also a growing number of heterosexuals, those who had been living in the fast lane. Furthermore, amongst victims were children and senior citizens infected through contaminated blood transfusions at some hospitals. The worse news, however, was that the virus was spreading so fast, mutating in the process, that finding a cure resembled shooting at a constantly and rapidly moving target.

The most shocking thing to Jack was widespread, at times downright heartless, discrimination of those considered at risk. One of the articles quoted a morbid joke which was going around, reflecting the sense of desperation in the gay community: A young man comes home and says, "Mom, I have good news and bad news. The bad news is that I'm gay." The mother is distraught and asks for the good news, in hopes that it would cheer her up a little, and the son answers, "The good news is I'm also dying."

But the story that broke Jack's heart was about a young man in Los Angeles, dying of AIDS, shunned by his family and friends. A woman from a volunteer support group assigned to help him told TIME's correspondent that when she had helped him with his will and funeral arrangements, he broke down crying. She hugged him, trying to comfort the poor soul, but it only made him cry harder. When he finally calmed down, he looked up at her and said, "No one's touched me in so long."

Jack put down the magazine and closed his eyes. He thought he knew the feeling. He had never thought a simple human touch, an artless embrace could mean so much, could make one feel like he had felt that day at the head of the forest trail, on the way back from the cornflower field.

He had been standing by the motorcycle waiting for Eton, his eyes closed, breathing in the summery scents of the forest, tuning in to the distant call of an owl, feeling oddly at peace. Eton came up quietly and wrapped his arms around Jack, rocked him a little, murmuring Hotel California's refrain softly into his ear. Then he brushed his lips on Jack's temple and let go, taking away with him the warmth and something else Jack didn't have a name for...

He jolted awake from his day dreaming, eyes flying open, staggered to the cupboard and poured himself a generous shot of whiskey.

He re-read the articles three times and by the end had practically memorized them. His thoughts kept circling back to Eton and their enchanted weekend in the country; to what they had together, did together, something so different that he was still trying to wrap his head around it. Under different circumstances, he would be horny as hell just thinking about it, playing it over and over again in his head, which would eventually lead to giving himself the sweet relief he otherwise couldn't get in this country. However, this time the gravity of what he had read had now morphed into a dark, menacing feeling at the pit of his stomach.

He wasn't worried too much about Eton: he was pretty sure that he was Eton's first man. Besides, he hoped that AIDS hadn't crossed over to this side of the world—nothing in the articles seemed to indicate that it was the case. What had raised worrisome questions, however, was Jack himself.

He had always used protection whenever he ventured out for the sex he'd needed in the last few years. But the articles said that one could be infected for years without developing the full-blown disease. The truth was, for a short while after Joe, he had had unprotected sex with God knows who. He had never tested himself for anything, never felt the need. What if he had contracted it somehow? What then? And now Eton... No, he didn't want to think about it. It was impossible... Right? All he needed to do was to get himself tested. One of the articles said that nowadays all donor blood centers tested volunteers for AIDS and the results as well as the identity of the donors were kept confidential. That was where he would get himself tested, at a donor blood center.

In Helsinki maybe, or in Germany, wherever Joe Coburn summoned him to for their next meeting. Yeah, that was what he was going to do, send Joe a coded cable in regards of SEABROOK. As soon as he had come up with a story to tell Joe about its progress.

It had been over a month since that long weekend in the countryside and he had neither made up his mind about it, nor notified the chief of ops about the progress. Maybe prior to sending the cable, he should set up a meeting with Eton and check out where things stood between them. He hadn't talked to his friend since the trip, had left only one message on his answering machine.

You're a lousy friend, Smith.

It's not like he's my girlfriend or something. He's a big guy. He knows guys disappear when they're busy... Doesn't he?

After what he did for you?

He hasn't called me either!

You sure?

He wasn't. Shit. He was a lousy friend after all. And the fact that he had never had someone he considered his best friend or special friend, or even a star agent, didn't sound like any kind of excuse to him.

So that was that: he would call Eton tomorrow, as late as midnight, to ask if *Krylia* were playing anywhere. And then he would try to get hold of the guy while he was alone—Jack only needed a minute—to ask if he wanted to… to catch up. Somewhere. Jack didn't know where they could 'catch up', just the two of them, but thought maybe Eton would know—it was his hometown after all, he should know, right? And then he would find a way to tell Eton about AIDS and that he had to be careful—with anyone, regardless, even with Jack. Until he knew for sure that he was good and clean.

If they could find a way of having sex again somewhere.

Sex with Eton…

He moaned soundlessly, stretched out on the couch, unbuttoned his jeans, closed his eyes and started stroking himself.

He didn't know when sleep took over, vaguely remembered moving during the night from the couch to the bed. But in the morning, he knew why his sheets were damp and he was feeling so light and contented. There had been one never-ending cornflower field in his dream and a blond man in the sun, gazing into his eyes, smiling demurely and saying, "I've never felt so free".

Jack stayed late in the office, came down to Uncle Sam's for a quick dinner, then hung out at the Marine's Bar till past eleven. He left his car parked outside the Embassy and took the longer route to the second closest Metro station, trying to gauge the status of the surveillance. Since the bout of expulsions between the British and the Russians, the KGB had intensified the coverage of the known Moscow Station's officers, or so William had told him. However, it seemed they didn't put Jack in that category and his minders continued tailing him only half-heartedly, once in a while. Still, it never hurt to be extra vigilant, as their counter-surveillance instructor at the Farm used to hammer into their heads. So when he emerged from the Metro, Jack took a roundabout route back to his apartment block.

He was clear of surveillance. And it was seven minutes past midnight already. Jack took a last, surreptitious glance around and behind him and headed toward the *taxaphone* at the corner of a Stalin era building, which he had noticed from a block away. He prayed that it was working as half of the time Soviet payphones didn't.

This one worked though. Jack dialed the number from memory, smiling already and tapping the heavy, iron-cast handset with the tip of his fingers.

The phone rang three times, clicked and a laughing, obviously drunk female voice squealed in his ear, "Let go! Let go of me! Let me answer the phone first! Eetohnn!!!"

Jack blinked, the grin slipping off his face like a melting wax mask.

It was Lara.

He hesitated for half a second, hung up and walked out into the night.

PART II - A PHYSICIST A LYRICIST

Chapter 22

Journal 5, 1985

July 6, Saturday. Midnight. Almost.

A busy day today: rehearsals for the Festival, concert in MGU. Dinner at the House of Actor: Anya, Lara, Gosha, Grisha, Seva and Krylia boys. And him. Jack from California.

Is it a joke? Must be. Because it could not be real. This kind of thing happens in fairytales, not in real life.

What am I doing anyway? I am NOT going to write another Dear Jack journal. Because he is NOT "Jack from California".

All right, he is. But not that Jack. And I'm NOT going to write to HIM.

What I am going to do is I will go to bed and forget about this foolishness in the morning.

1:05 a.m.

How can anyone's eyes be that blue??

The color of winter sky on a sunny day. Clear and bottomless. Dizzying.

The color of the cornflower field we were taken to last summer. Mesmerizing.

July 7, Sunday. 11 p.m.

Dear Jack,

Don't know why I am writing this.

Yes, I know. Because I wrote a similar diary when I was a kid. What I don't know is why I am addressing this to you. You are not Jack I used to write to. That person didn't exist. He was a boy dreamt up by me when I was nine.

That was when I told my father I didn't want to write my English diary to him anymore.

Writing a diary was how Father taught me English. He spoke to me strictly in English. When I went to school, he gave me an expensive-looking notebook and asked me to write to him every day. About my friends, my days and what I learned at school. He then read it on Saturdays when I came to stay with him. On Sundays, Grandma came to take me home. Father gave me a new notebook every year.

When I was nine, I told Father I wanted to write my journal to someone else. To a friend. He said fair enough, told me to pick up someone I wanted to write to. Tom Sawyer, for example, he said. But I didn't want Tom: he had Huck as his best friend. I didn't want to be the odd one out.

I spent several days thinking about a name. Johnny, Bobby or Jim, I could not decide which one to choose. I decided to ask Mother for help.

One day, I went to see her in our study room. I found her making notes in a book, several others lying open around her typewriter. She was doing her postgraduate dissertation at that time, on contemporary American literature. The book she was reading was covered in little white paper markers sticking out from between the pages. There was a name printed in big letters on its cover over a portrait of a handsome man. Jack Kerouac. Other books on the desk were also either about him or by him. I asked her if Jack was her favorite American name nowadays.

I remember her staring at me and me thinking that perhaps I should not have asked her that question. But she smiled at me and said yes, it was her second favorite American name after Eton. Her smile was sad, and I decided that my friend's name would be Jack. I thought if I had a friend named Jack, it would cheer her up a little. Silly, I know. But I was only nine.

The following Saturday, I told Father I wanted to write my diary to Jack from Calif. That was where Father was from. I wanted my friend to be from there, too. Like he and his friend Martin Hamilton that he kept telling me about. Father did not say anything, only nodded. So I started writing to Jack.

My parents divorced when I was five. One day, Mother picked me up from the kindergarten and we went to live with my grandparents.

I never understood why she did it. She continued loving him, even after he died. She cried often that year, at night. In the morning, she would try to hide her swollen eyes and we would pretend that we did not notice. I think she was heartbroken because he did not love her as much as she loved him. She said he drank a lot.

He never drank when I visited him. Not until after his friend Martin who lived in Leningrad drowned. Something broke in him and he was not the same ever again. He started drinking hard. I think he missed Calif. Talked about it often. About the time he and Martin used to go camping in the forest, riding horses in the mountains or fishing in a forest lake. His stories were like fairytales. I still remember names of the places he talked about: Six Rivers, Marble Mountain, Aspen Lake, Sun Pass.

About you. If not Lara, I would have never thought of inviting you to our dacha. My brain was on vacation yesterday. All I could think about for the whole evening was how one's eyes could be that blue. On top of the fact that they belonged to a Jack from Calif. Surreal!

I have to tell Mother and Grandfather that I have invited an Am. to our dacha. Grandfather will be fine: he likes foreigners. Not Mother. I don't look forward to when she learns that you are from Calif. She has been avoiding Americans as long as I remember. She even turned down a trip to Am. once. She will find an excuse to be absent this Saturday, too.

I wish Gosha would stop asking you about Calif. I do not want to hear about it anymore. Do not want to hear you talking about it!

E.

12:37 a.m.

That last thing was not true. But, God, please help me not to make a fool of myself in front of him!

July 9, Tuesday. Midnight.

Told Mother today. As expected, the moment she heard about you, she suddenly recalled that she had promised her friend Valya to come help with her dissertation. I give up.

I will not tell Lara that Mother is not coming to the dacha. She will be upset. Sometimes Lara acts as if she is in love with Mother. Lara is like that with virtually anyone she likes. Last Saturday she behaved as if you were her boyfriend. As far as I know, she was seeing you for the second time. Please don't get me wrong: Lara is a good person, a good friend. But she is too expansive with her feelings.

E.

July 12, Friday. Midnight.

Grandfather is not joining us tomorrow after all: he is invited to the dacha of someone from the Academy of Sciences.

Lara says the authorities have decided not to broadcast LiveAid on TV tomorrow. It is so stupid! I wish they showed at least a few songs, something! It is for the people of Africa, for heaven's sake!

You said you liked our concert. I am glad. Friends say Hotel California is the best song in my repertoire. Perhaps because it is about California? Don't know. Hope you were not just being polite when you said you loved it.

Love is too strong a word.

E.

July 14, Sunday. 11:15 p.m.

Dear Jack,

I don't know where to start. These last two days, seeing you, talking to you... You are like him! Like I imagined him - Jack from Calif., the little cowboy. How can it be?

I have found the old journals I wrote as a kid. In one of the boxes in the attic at the dacha. I took the journals home and read them last night. Until 3am. I found the postcard and sat staring at it. Don't know how long. I could not believe my eyes: it was you, Jack S. from Calif. It must be how you looked when you were eleven or twelve. The only difference was the color of the eyes: they are brown in the postcard, not the incredible blue like in reality.

I still remember the first time I saw the postcard. It was the year I started writing to Jack from Calif.

A colleague of Grandfather's came back from an exchange trip in Am. and brought Grandma a small present — a pamphlet and a collection of postcards from an art exhibition. I remember him telling us about the artist — Nikolai Feshin, a

Russian living in America. Grandfather's friend lamented that we, his compatriots, didn't know much about him and his work. That was when I noticed the postcard.

It was a reproduction of a Feshin's painting of a dark-haired boy. He was wearing a white shirt and blue jeans, a straw hat and a red kerchief around his neck. "Little Cowboy" it was called. And I told myself that it was the portrait of my friend Jack.

God, this is so silly! I am a grown-up man and talk like a nine-year-old about someone who does not exist. Never existed! This is ridiculous.

But what about you, Jack? YOU exist: I have seen you. Talked to you. I shook hands with you. You brought cigarettes for me. Marlboro red. My favorite. From now.

You do exist. In the form that exceeds my imagination.

I want to be friends with you. I want you to tell me about Calif.

E.

July 15, Monday. 11:30 p.m.

Newspapers carried news today about a diplomat from the Am. embassy who were caught spying. Do you know him? Did you know he was with CIA?

You must have many friends. Gregarious, easygoing. As if you are sparkling when you smile. All my friends are still talking about you. Lara is in love with you and does not even hide it. Anya is the only person who is still cautious about you. She warned us today to be careful with you as you might also be a spy. Seva laughed and told her to relax: it is hard to believe that an Am. spy would be spending his time with a bunch of Soviet students. He is right.

Told Karelin today that we would sing in his rock-opera at the festival. It is about Calif. Hope you will like it.

Will you come?

E.

July 18, Thursday. 11:00 p.m.

Dear Jack,

I have been sitting here for ten minutes already, trying to come up with something meaningful to write. My brain keeps replaying our conversation on the telephone this morning. Mostly two things:

1) you are the coordinator of our NW exchange program - what kind of strange coincidence is this?? and

2) we are going to see Bob D's concert. Together.

It means I will see you again. Soon.

About Alexin and the way I talked to you this morning. Please don't be offended. We have been told by the dean's office not to talk about his disappearance, esp. with the Berkeley team. But how? He worked at Prof. Ackerman's laboratory last year. Of course they will ask about him! I don't see how we are going to NOT talk to them about it. It is stupid even trying.

I think he has defected to the West. I don't blame him. I think his NW model was the last straw: it didn't produce the results expected from him. That is only half of the matter. The other half is that he truly believed that his model was correct. I, too, think he is right.

E.

July 20, Saturday. 5min. to midnight.

You just called.

I didn't expect you to call so soon, only 2 days after I had given you my number. I was caught by surprise: dropped the soldering iron on the floor, sounded rude. Don't know why you make me feel awkward.

That is not true. I know why: I want to see you again. To talk to you. To find out if you are the Jack who I imagined was my friend. I know it is childish and doesn't make any sense. But I can't help it.

E.

July 27, Saturday. 0:25 a.m.

You didn't show up. It upset me so much that I almost didn't enjoy Bob Dylan's performance. But when I came home and found your message on my auto-response, it was like I could breathe again.

Things affect me in a strange way these days: even the smallest of the details are blown out of proportion, like through a magnifying glass — things, sounds, colors, words, senses, feelings...

I will call you in the morning before I leave for the Festival opening.

E.

July 30, Tuesday. 11:47 p.m.

Dear Jack,

So glad you came to our forum. I saw you right away. You looked around, but did not notice me. I thought you were avoiding me. You looked - I don't know - distracted, perhaps? It took me a while to make up my mind to follow you out.

You were sitting on the windowsill, smoking. The moment I saw you smiling at me, I knew I had been an idiot. Don't know why I thought you didn't want to see me. Never seen anyone smiling like you.

Russians don't know how to smile, I in particular. I wish I could express what I feel. Like you. Never been good at that. So I try to express myself through actions. Through music. Through poetry. That I don't show anyone. Ironic, isn't it?

We talked for nearly an hour. In English.

I lost my speech when you suggested speaking in English, just you and I, because it is different. How did you know?? Hope you didn't think I didn't want to. Because it's the opposite. Jack, I have been talking in English to you since I was nine. Of course, I would, cowboy, just you and me!

Then you asked me about the NW theory. I told you briefly. What I didn't mention is that it's not one of my favorite topics. I don't agree with the version of the model we are running. But for once, Grandfather doesn't allow any debate. He tells us to do it that way and no questions. Don't remember another time he was so dictatorial.

Perhaps I shouldn't have joined his laboratory. But this is the only prospect for me to be on a research program that may include a trip to America. Besides, what other justifiable reason did I have to refuse the offer to work in Dubna? I don't want to work there. I will never be able to travel to Am. if I work there. Not with my family background.

Jack, I want to visit Calif. one day.

I wish you could show me your Calif. One day.

E.

July 31, Wednesday. Midnight.

Tomorrow is the gala concert at the Soviet Club. I am so nervous. It is not like I never performed on stage. It is the same singing, with a little more acting involved, that's all. So what is the problem?

Perhaps it is because of Karelin's costumes. They are different. And his staging is unusual. They make me feel as if I am exposing the side of me that people don't know. Shouldn't know.

But his direction is extraordinary. I will be lying if I don't admit that he is a great director. His shows make you think differently. He defies standards, tradition, beliefs. The norm. Doesn't it make him a genius?

The only thing I wish is that he keep his allusions to himself. Or I will punch him in the face one day. I will, honestly.

To hell with Karelin.

Hope you will like the show. It is about a love story between one of my ancestors, Count Rezanov, and a Californian girl. She waited for him for 33 years.

Mother continued loving Father long after he died, even if she denies it.

I wonder how long I would love a someone if I meet that one person who is right for me.

E.

August 3, Saturday. After midnight.

Just returned from the closing of the Festival.

I have never seen anything like that! So grandiose, so inspiring and uplifting that by the final chords everybody was hugging and kissing those standing next to them. Many people were crying.

I wish you were there with us.

All right, I will say it: I wish you were there with me and I could hug you, too. A friendly hug.

That is not true, either. It's not just a friendly hug that I want. To hold you, that's what I want. I close my eyes and I can feel how your body fills my arms, all hard muscles and strength. I feel your hair against my cheek, your breath warming my face, your heartbeat against mine. And I know in that moment I will lose myself. To you. Even if I know, I am not someone you will ever want.

Lara said yesterday that you were not well after our concert. I had been disappointed that you had left. Now I understand. Hope you have recovered.

2:15 a.m.

How could it come to this? From you being someone I met only 4 weeks ago, to you being my friend Jack from Calif., my cowboy, without you even suspecting it. And now this: I'm thinking about you every minute I'm awake, I dream about you at night. And I want to touch you so much my fingers ache and I can't get enough air in my lungs.

I want to touch your beautiful face, your smiling lips, your powerful neck; to put my hands on your shoulders, your chest, over your heart.

I know it will never happen. Because you are not like me.

Why am I like this? Flawed. Perhaps I was born with various little skills and talents to compensate for the fact that I am flawed. In one key aspect that defines my being as a man. I am still a man, just not the kind this society accepts. But then this society doesn't accept many things. Heavy metal rockers, for example.

I realized I was this way when I was eighteen. It was when I started having dreams about someone I met at a boxing championship. Before that, men in my dreams were not real people from my everyday life. One was a cowboy on a cigarettes ad in a foreign magazine. Yes, a cowboy again. Another one was Timothy S. of the Eagles (by the way, he is from Sacramento, Calif.). They were always men from some faraway lands and I thought nothing of it - they were just childish dreams in which I wanted to be like them. So I thought.

Then I met Timur. He was nineteen, on the junior boxing team from Leningrad Univ. I ended up against him in the semi-finals. And I started thinking about him and having "that" kind of dreams about him. It scared me so much I floored the guy in the second round. Despite him being heavier than me, maybe even more technically skillful. After that, I took to drinking. Because then dreams stopped haunting me. They kicked me out of the boxing team after I broke someone's nose in a drunken fight. I deserved it.

This "issue" with me, they call it a mental sickness. I don't believe it. I know I am sane and my mind is sharp enough to work on complex applied nuclear physics models. I spent two years on the last one, partly to prove to myself that I was mentally sound. But this craving is perhaps some sort of physiological flaw, nevertheless. Perhaps that is why some of the men who are rumored to have this "sickness" are so brilliant (Karelin is one of them): nature has given them that genius to compensate for the inherent flaw of the flesh.

After T., I understood that my dreams were not childish dreams about the kind of man I wanted to be. I dreamed of men I wanted to be with. And I realized it was not something I could share with anyone I knew. Perhaps not with anyone ever.

Hiding it is not hard - I have plenty of practice. It is similar to not telling anyone about my friend Jack from Calif. Or that I knew English better than any English teacher at school. Father told me that being different was not a good idea in this country and I should try to be like everybody else. I think he had learned the hard way and tried to make it easier for me. I thought the "different" part of me was related to him, because he did not fit. Until I realized what my difference was. Sometimes I wonder if Father knew.

So no, it is not particularly hard. Just lonely sometimes.

Sometimes I wish I could talk about it with someone. But who? Grandfather would not want to hear about it, I am certain. Mother will probably disown me, like she did Father, for the reasons I will never know.

And you. I don't even know if you would still want to be my friend Jack and if I should write to you after my admission. What I know for sure is that I am not going to tell you in reality. Like I will never tell any of my other friends.

Except it is so hard with you. It is almost painful to have you standing close, to see your smile, to bask in your friendliness and not being able to stretch my hand out and touch you. But if I touch you, I think I will go insane with wanting more.

I better stay away from you.

Please, don't be offended if I behave rudely with you. I don't mean it. I just can't help it. Especially with you. Because I want to hold you so much.

E.

August 4, Sunday. 10:10 p.m.

Dear Jack,

Tomorrow is our first meeting with the Berkeley team. Hope you will be there too. Hope you will not notice how awkward I feel in your company. I will try my best to be "sociable".

Lara has just called. There will be a heatwave toward the end of the week and we are all going to the countryside. She said she wants to invite you to come with us, but Anya is against it.

Perhaps Anya is right: you may have more interesting things to do than spend your weekend with us. Our wise Anya.

I wish you could come with us to Istra. It is a beautiful place. Authentically Russian. You would like it.

E.

August 5, Monday. 8:30 p.m.

I invited you to come with us.

I did it on impulse. You wanted to invite us to your place this weekend and looked disappointed when I told you we had other plans. So I blurted it out. And only started breathing again when you said you would love to join us.

However, there is a problem now: travel permit. I forgot that foreigners need permits to be able travel to other cities. And I don't know how diplomats get theirs.

Another thing: will it look strange if I ask someone (who??) to help with a travel permit for you alone? A diplomat spending a weekend with a bunch of students in the countryside. It will look strange, will it not? Damn!

10:07 p.m.

I have a solution: we shall invite the Berkeley group and you to the countryside. It is in the plan anyway, for September. Why not earlier?

Called Grandfather. He said it was a good idea. He had thought of inviting them to our dacha this weekend, but I convinced him that Istra was better. The girls at the lab will apply for travel permits tomorrow morning.

Then called Lara, asked if her mother could help booking rooms at the vacation home. It belongs to the Min. of Culture. And I asked if her father's office could help with the travel permits. She was very pleased when she learned you are coming with us and promised to help. You can rely on Lara to get what she wants. Great thing about Lara is that she always helps friends in need.

She was thrilled when I told her about the guys in the Berkeley group. She loves it when there are men surrounding her - she reigns them like Cleopatra. I think Seva, Gosha and I are the only men she likes that she has not tried to subjugate.

Hope she will like Val and leave you alone.

Don't go after her, Jack, she will break your heart. She is a good friend, but she also has a major flaw: she must have all men she likes. (Even Karelin! I'm sure she knows about his "flaw"). And I know she likes you. A lot.

Don't know what I will do to her if she breaks your heart!

Don't even want to think that she will get to you. Don't let her, Jack!

E.

11:55 p.m.

Don't know what it is with me - I feel so restless. Pray to God we'll get the permits and you will come with us. It is a beautiful place, truly Russian. The villagers are permitted to keep old traditions alive. So that a few can enjoy them. Sad, isn't it?

Last year a villager took us to an amazing place in the forest. A cornflower field. The wild grass and flowers grew so thick that it looked like a carpet. And the color of the flowers was so strikingly blue that we stood with our mouths open for a long time.

They were the same color as your eyes.

E.

August 7, Wednesday. After midnight.

Dear Jack,

I am sorry I didn't have any news for you. Please believe me, I am more anxious to get them than you are. For you, it is just a weekend trip to the countryside with a group of ~~friends~~ acquaintances; for me, ~~it is it feels like something so important that~~ I want it more than anything.

I called Lara. She was certain the permits would be ready by tomorrow afternoon. She made her father call someone at the Min. of Interior for help. Sometimes Lara can go overboard with getting what she wants. But this time, I am deeply thankful that she is like she is.

This makes me a hypocrite, doesn't it?

So I am. I don't care. Just want you to come with us.

E.

August 7, Wednesday. 10:05 p.m.

Got the permits! You are coming with us!!

Jack, I am so

10:20p.m.

You just called.

It was a short call. Something wasn't right. You sounded tired. Or like you gave up. You said you were jogging and stopped to catch your breath. But you sounded as if you were... Doubtful, perhaps?

Maybe it is because of the travel permits. You said you never seen anything being done here that fast. Is it what has made you suspicious? What exactly do you think happened here?

I think I know: you think our security organs are involved. Perhaps you think we work for the organs - who else can get travel permits that fast? After all, you are an Am. I am certain you have been told to be vigilant about our security organs. Even we have to be.

Jack, please do not be concerned about us working for the organs. We don't. I believe my friends don't work for them.

I have to believe it.

E.

Midnight.

36 hours before we meet. I wish I could do something to relax.

I wish I kept vodka at home. I don't anymore, I have learnt my lesson. But sometimes I wish I did. Like now. To stop thinking about you, about how I will see you for 3 whole days, everyday; how I will sit next to you, talk to you, walk in the forest and swim in the lake with you.

No, swimming is a bad idea. I will go crazy and do something stupid if I see you unclothed. The way I see you when I close my eyes: smooth, sun-caressed skin under my hands, broad chest and shoulders against mine, powerful arms and legs encircling me. And above me, two lakes of astonishing blue. Like the color of those cornflowers, pieces of the bluest of the skies.

I know you are not like that. I know it is just a fantasy, never to happen, except in my dreams. Always in my hopeless dreams.

Have to find a way to take you to the cornflower field. It will be my present to you, cowboy.

Yours always,

E.

Chapter 23

August 11, Sunday. 10 minutes to midnight.

Dear Jack,

I will not be able to sleep tonight. Hardly slept for the last 3 nights.

The 3 days and 2 nights that I will hold in my memory forever, like a precious gift: the 3 days and 2 nights when you unraveled and set me free. You showed me how it feels to be true to my true self. I never knew it could feel like that. I never thought I could feel like that! I would have never known if it were not for you. For this, I am grateful.

And you: I never imagined, not even in my wildest dreams, that you were would want me. All I had to do was ask, and you gave it yourself to me. The way I had painted only in the roughest of brush strokes in my imagination. I had never thought I would ask something like that. But I felt feel I can tell you anything, and you will accept it. Let me be myself, without judging.

It must be Fate. How else to explain the fact that you have been in my thoughts, in my dreams for so many years, and now come to be with me in person. For me to give myself to you and to hold you in my arms. For me to love you. There, I have said it.

I love you, my blue cornflower, moy vasil'yok.

E.

August 12, Monday. 2:00 a.m.

Can't stop thinking about the things we did. There was a moment I thought I was going to die — of all the sensations and feelings that kept swelling in me, to the heart breaking point. How can someone do that to you???

I hope I gave you back a fraction of what you gifted me with.

But there is also this thought that won't let me be. It is poisoning all my memories about what we had together. That you were so skillful and confident in what you were doing. "Practiced" is the word. You have done it before. With someone else. Perhaps not even one.

Stop it, you stupid! Don't want to think about it anymore! Because if I keep going like this, I will break something. Hit someone.

I am sorry.

August 12, Monday. 10:27p.m.

Dear Jack,

I still cannot believe what happened between us. That you are like me. No, not flawed. Different, like me. And that you were with me! That you gave me what I thought I could never have. Not here, where I don't know if I can trust strangers with my secret. Ha! I cannot even trust my childhood friends with my secret, let alone strangers!

Yet, I trust you. You, the real you, are still a stranger. Yet, it feels like I have known you for ages. Everything about you is how I imagined it, sometimes even more: you lived on a ranch in Calif.; you love horses and can ride without a saddle; you know about Russian history, literature and culture, and we can talk about anything. Like we did in the past. And you continue telling me that I should sing more because I am good at it. You always told me that whenever I had doubts. When Mother would say she wanted me to be a scientist, not a long-haired rocker. She does not like them (as if she knows them!), thinks they will ruin me and my career. A career I do not want.

I shall sing more. I shall sing my own songs. For you, cowboy.

And I shall be the physicist that my family wants me to be. I can do both.

E.

P.S.: Tomorrow I am leaving with Grisha, Seva and two other guys for shabashka, to do some construction work in a sovkhoz not far from Tula. We will be away for a month. Last summer we worked there for a month and the sovkhoz paid us 800 rubles each, in addition to lodging in a hay shack and food. Not bad, isn't it? That is 3 times what Grandfather makes and more than 4 times what Mother makes in a month. I will buy a new guitar and give mine to Sashka, the boy at Gosha's dorm. The kid will starve to death trying to save most of his meager stipend for an old professional guitar.

I will call you tomorrow evening before I leave to the train station.

E.

August 13, Tuesday. 9:05 p.m.

Dear Jack,

I understand now what Lina meant when she said that what she had with that other man was greater than love. She was right when she said I would only understand it when I met the one for me.

I am surprised I didn't realize it earlier - everything about you is so obvious that you are the one. I should have recognized it earlier, even before I discovered that you ~~like things~~ were like me. But you have always been my best friend and I would have loved you even if you were not. Even if I know we can never be together. Even if I know you will leave this country one day. Even if you do not share my feelings. I know you don't. For you I am just someone you met a month ago. A student in a group of students you coordinate.

Does it make me weak? Pathetic?

I don't care. I will take with gratitude whatever you can give—your friendship, your hand, your smile. Maybe your body and your lips sometimes? And that soft light I saw in your eyes that day in the cornflower field.

You friend forever,

E.

10:05p.m.

Called you twice, but you were not home. I feel bad leaving for a month without letting you know. I regret that I did not tell you over the weekend. What if you call me when I am away? You may think that I am avoiding you after what happened. Please don't! I want to see you, to be with you more than you will ever know.

I should have called you yesterday. I regret I didn't.

Have to go now. I will call again from the train station. I won't be able to call from the place we are going. Sorry.

Yours always,

E.

September 12, Thursday. 10 a.m.

Dear Jack,

Just returned from Tula about an hour ago and got your message on my auto-response. Have listened to it ten times. You did not say much, but at least I heard your voice. I thought my heart would burst out of my chest. I have never felt like this before! How does one deal with this without doing something stupid?

We have done very well this time: each got 1,000 rubles. Had not expected to get that much. On the downside, I will not be able to play guitar for some time: I have rubbed my fingers raw mixing cement and laying bricks a month long. But I have some ideas about the music I am going to write. A short rock-opera. About nuclear war. Or what would happen if it happens.

I have been thinking about the question you asked when we talked about NW at the MGU: climatic effects of nuclear winter aside, what about all the people at the bombing sites in the nuclear exchange that we are modeling? What will happen to them?

I am deeply shamed that I had never paused to ask myself this question. I focused only on the details of the mathematical models, the assumptions, the temperature distribution, the climatic and environmental consequences of such a nuclear exchange. These are the key components of our research. I know, this is not a worthy excuse. You are a thousand times right - people, human lives should be the focus of any research related to the use of nuclear arms.

It only proves that I am a callous, superficial person. And you, cowboy, you are a humanitarian.

I will call you in the evening. Perhaps we can meet somewhere. Perhaps we can...

E.

Midnight.

Called you twice. You were not at home. Perhaps you are out of the country on a business trip again. Called Lara. She hadn't talked to you in a while, too, and didn't know if you were in town.

I didn't expect that I would want to see you this much. It caught me by surprise, even scared me. Somehow, it has become not enough just thinking about you during the day and dreaming about you at night. I want to see you. To talk to you in person. To hold you. To drink your breath from your lips. To listen to your heartbeat. To drown in the blue of your eyes. To give my body to your hands, to your desire.

And I want it all the damned time!

Don't know what to do about this. I have never felt like this before.

E.

September 14, Saturday. 9:45 p.m.

TASS has reported on TV just now that 25 British diplomats and businessmen are being deported for activities not "compatible with their status". They mean spying, of course. Twenty five people. That's a lot. Somehow, I suspect not all of them are spies; some of them might have been added just for extra "spice".

I wonder what Amanda thinks about all this. I like her: she is sharp, notices the tiniest of details, asks pointed questions. When we met at Bob D. concert, she asked me how I had got to know you. I think she looked relieved when I told her that Lara had introduced us. I wonder what she had thought before.

We should all meet up when you get back from your trip. I will mention it to Lara. She is good with arranging meetings and events.

My rock-opera is going well. I should play it to someone. Artyom T.? He is a recognized authority on rock music in this country. He told me some time ago that I should join one of the rock-lab festivals in Leningrad. But with a different band. He didn't think some of my guys were good enough. I said no that time. Perhaps I should reconsider. Will need to rearrange the band though: don't think all of my crew would want to play at an unauthorized rock festival. Taking part in those may attract attention from the organs. But Sevka will be in the seventh heaven—he has always dreamed of playing at a rock festival.

Will you come to see us play if we pull it off?

E.

September 16, Monday. 9:00 p.m.

Dear Jack,

I had a quarrel with Grandfather today.

We had a work session with the Berkeley team this morning to discuss the final version of the model and data input. I wanted to share my reservations about the model but Grandfather cut me short. It blew me away: it was so not like him. I did not force the issue and shut up. After the meeting, he called me in his office and started telling me off. For what? I had only tried to express my point of view, for heaven's sake! Isn't it what scientific debate all about?

Don't know what has got into him lately. He seems so defensive about the NW model that Dimitri Alexandrovich has developed. In truth, D.A. took over Alexin's model since his disappearance and "expanded" it. I have questions about this "expansion", but they do not want to open a discussion. And Prof. Ackerman supports them. All right, Prof. Ack. is not a mathematician. But what about Val? He is a doctoral student in mathematics. He should be able to recognize the deficiencies, shouldn't he?

Or maybe it's me who is not getting it? I am not a mathematician after all. But Alexin had some reservations about it too, didn't he? About the results of his own model.

Will try to find out from Gosha - he has done all the groundwork for D.A. anyway.

Good thing that Anya is not part of the exchange program. Otherwise, it could all have ended with her and me fighting over this damned model with Grandfather and her father (don't remember if you know that D.A. Arceniev is Anya's father). She does not need this controversy, especially when Americans are involved. Not good for her future work at MGU. She will go far, our Anya, our clever girl.

Anyway, I told Grandfather what I thought. He told me to listen to him and not to argue just this one time. Because it is "crucial for the mutual success of this international project that we all are coordinated". Doesn't sound like science to me. More like politics.

Maybe I should quit the project.

But if I do, how am I going to see you?

No, I shall stick with it. And will keep my mouth shut.

I shall see you again. Soon.

E.

September 18, Wednesday. 11:05 p.m.

What is going on? Another 6 Englishmen have been deported from the S.U. today. We definitely need to meet with Amanda one of these days. When you are back.

It is Gosha's 18th birthday next Tuesday. He will finally be considered a grown-up by everybody. We are planning a surprise party for him at my place. The guys will get him drunk within an hour, but I am sure he will be in the seventh heaven. I should try not to get drunk though. Not with this heavy feeling, like lead weight in my chest. Not with this maddening feeling of wanting something I know I can never have.

It seems everything I want badly is unattainable. Why? Is it because I want too much? I already have more than many people around me do. Yet, I always want things that seem out of my reach.

Like being your best friend. And more.

Like visiting Calif.

I have dreamed about it since I was five or six, inspired by my Father's stories—like fairytales they were. It was his longing for the place that infected me with

- 166 -

the need to reach it. He never told me why he had decided to come to live in the SU, though.

Sometimes I feel like Ostap Bender from Twelve Chairs (I'm sure you have read it) — he and his silly dream about Rio de Janeiro. He never gets there in the end. That story ends sadly. What about mine?

Mother says I am a hopeless dreamer. That I should grow up and be a physicist like I have been taught to be. She may be right. Perhaps I should.

I will call you over the weekend to see if you are back. Maybe we can meet somewhere. If not, I will see you at Lara's birthday next Saturday. She is going to invite you. If she has not yet done so.

I shall see you soon, cowboy.

Yours always,

E.

September 20, Friday. Midnight.

Lara called Amanda at her office and was told she had left Moscow. For good. Family affairs, they said. She said she had also called you and you were not home either.

What is going on? Where are you, Jack? You have not left unexpectedly, like Amanda, have you? No. Please, no! I have just found you in person. I have just had one little taste of you. I cannot lose you just yet!

I will go crazy if I don't hear from you soon.

E.

22/9. Don't know what time it is.

I am drunk. Couldn't even wait until I had a decent reason for it —Gosha's birthday. I am sorry.

I miss you.

I never understood love songs and poems in which someone loves someone else so much it hurts. I thought: how could love hurt? It was supposed to be a happy feeling, was it not? Now I know. It is dark and painful and lonely. It is like acid — eating away your insides, bit by bit, until there is nothing left, only a hollow shell of you. Makes you want to do something vicious. To someone. To yourself.

The worst part is I also know that one day you will leave and I will never see you again. Just like Count Rezanov and Conchita. The difference is he loved her back, a little. I will not even have that.

September 25, Wednesday. 11:00 a.m.

Dear Jack,

Finally managed to put the guys out of my door an hour ago. The apartment looks like a hurricane has gone through it. Even after me trying to tidy it up. I will have to ask Varvara Petrovna to come earlier this week and help me with cleaning.

Hope Gosha won't get into too much trouble for missing his classes today. I told him to go back to his dorm and sleep it off. I should have let him sleep here, instead of sending him off with the guys. But I needed some time alone so much that I was happy when he said he would go with the guys. I am the worst friend.

I shall make it up to him later.

Cannot take my mind off the telephone call last night. Lara and Sevka, both drunk, fought to answer it. By the time I wrestled the telephone from them, there was nobody there. Whoever called, they hang up.

Was it you, Jack? Were you back at last and called me? I want it to be you.

I will call you tonight.

E.

Chapter 24

Next morning Jack woke up feeling weary and with the familiar emptiness in the middle of his chest. Except that now it was almost overwhelming.

After returning to his apartment the previous night, he had sat on the couch in the sitting room for a long time, trying to stare down the half-empty bottle of Jack Daniels, wishing he could gulp it all at once, go to sleep and not think about Lara's laughing voice on the phone. He would have, had it not been for the operational run in two days' time—he was expected to pick up a package left by one of the agents in a park on the west side of the town. A pre-op dry run with Marat and William had been scheduled for the next day. In the end, he had settled for one single shot and put the whiskey bottle back in the cupboard, berating himself for calling Eton on the eve of an operation. He hadn't been able to fall asleep for a long time, and when he finally had, his slumber was ragged and fitful.

In the morning, the bout of self-criticism resumed the moment his mind focused and started functioning again.

You're a moron, Smith. You shouldn't have called him last night. Not before an op run.

He's my job, too. I'm supposed to cultivate him. Haven't got in touch with him for a while.

Your job? That was what you were thinking about when you called him, huh?

I thought I needed to get in touch with him before I send a message to Joe.

Yeah, right. And look at you now. You're distracted and sure as hell will make some stupid mistake. What did you think, idiot? Or rather, what did you think *with*? Hmm, rather obvious, huh?

Fuck you!

Exactly! That is all you think of nowadays.

Jack slammed his hand down on the alarm clock that had started shrieking on the bedside table, swept out of bed in one fierce move and stomped morosely into the bathroom.

The briefing in the Tank didn't finish until 9:00 p.m. and by the time Jack got back to his apartment it was close to midnight.

He had managed to block the previous night's call and all its implications from his mind for most of the day—people around him, daily tasks and the nitty-gritty of the upcoming covert operation helped to keep them at bay. But now, when he was alone again, unwelcome thoughts and suspicions started crawling out of nowhere again, invading his mind with their accusations, tearing to pieces the delicate fabric of the strange warmth that had begun weaving around his heart.

Jack heard the phone ringing while unlocking the door, but for once didn't hurry inside to answer it. He felt exhausted and didn't want to talk to anyone. Least of all to Lara or Eton if it was either one of them. Anybody else from the Embassy could wait until morning, too. He dropped his shoulder bag by the door, took off his jacket and shoes and walked in his socks straight to the bedroom. There he stripped quickly down to his boxers and went to the bathroom. He felt like he would kill someone if he didn't have a hot shower right then.

He was getting into in the bathtub when the phone rang again, kick-starting his heart into a sprint. He jerked the shower curtain behind him and turned the hot water on full force. No, he wasn't going to answer it. He must have his head clear and focused for his run the next day. *Then* he would figure how to deliver to his bosses the confirmation that Lara Novikova and Eton May Volkonsky were with the KGB after all.

They *were* with the KGB, weren't they? How else to explain why they had been pretending that they were "just friends" all this while? Jack didn't give a flying fuck that they were screwing each other, no he didn't, but why hide it? There had to be a reason and the only reason he could come up with was that they were with the KGB.

And suddenly it came home why he had been keeping himself busy, staying out as late as he could for the last month and a half, why it had taken him a month to make those first phone calls to Eton and Lara. He had been in hiding, trying to keep himself out of touch, subconsciously hoping he wouldn't be pitched by anyone after what he and Eton had done during that long weekend in the countryside. Because if nobody made a move on him, it would have meant that the guy wasn't with the KGB. Right? Jack had wished so much that he wasn't.

Now, finally, had come the moment of truth, the proof that they were with the organs after all. That Jack had been compromised. Acquired. And should expect their next move on him any time.

And Eton? God, the boy had been good, Jack had to give him that. So good that for a moment there he had believed that Eton had genuinely liked him. The way he liked Eton. Yeah, okay, so he liked Eton, so what? Big deal. Actually, it was even *better* that he liked Eton—made it easier to seduce him, in accordance with SEABROOK. And the fact that the guy had turned out to be the greatest fuck he'd ever had was like a bonus. He just had to make sure that it didn't become addictive before he was out of here. Once home, he would find someone just like him. There were hundreds of them back home—blond and singing and the rest of the fun.

But that would be in the future when he was out of here. For now, the tables were turned, and it wasn't Eton who was going to be Jack's star agent. In fact, it looked like it was going to be the complete opposite—Jack Smith, the star agent of the KGB. He didn't think Eton was a KGB officer, though—an informer at best, if not just a willing bait. Same thing with Lara. Both of them were too young to be operatives.

Or not, like William insisted?

In any case, the KGB would pitch him, eventually. Maybe that was why the surveillance on him had been rather sporadic all the while; they'd targeted him already and had been lulling his guards by keeping a very light tap on him. But how did they know that he was a case officer? They had to know, right? They wouldn't have set up such an elaborate honey trap had they not been positive about Jack's affiliation. And since they hadn't caught him red-handed, they must have been tipped off.

Yeah, that was probably it, if his own shop had been grooming him as a dangle. And operation GTTALION had been set up exclusively for Jack to sell it to the Sovs, despite Joe's assurances that that wasn't the intention. What about SEABROOK? Had Joe and

Co. intentionally leaked it to the KGB, too? Wasn't that why they had recruited Eton in a preemptive move against the CIA's op?

Jesus Christ, this is so fucking twisted! So Joe-esque. I wish I wasn't—

Yeah? You wish? You should have thought about it *before* you let Joe get to you. But no, you wanted a "friend". With benefits. Someone who cared, huh? Ha! That's what you get when you jump at the first one who comes along. So now deal with it, pal. And with Joe, too.

Right. Joe. He had to deliver the "sea-water" message to Joe as soon as possible, before the Sovs made their next move. And he'd better find a plausible explanation for why it had taken him so long to notify the chief of ops of his "progress" with the target.

Shit.

Yeah, right. You've fucked it up, haven't you, Smith?

He wrenched the taps shut, shoved the shower curtain out of his way, climbed out and snatched the towel that was draped over the barely warm radiator. He had just pulled his pajama bottoms on when the phone rang again, making him jump.

For Christ's sake! Get a fucking grip!

Jack closed his eyes for two seconds, took a deep breath and walked quickly out into the sitting room. He sat down on the edge of the sofa, took another deep breath and picked up the phone.

"Hello?" he said in English.

"Jack! Good evening! Finally, I've got hold of you! Where have you been?!" Lara sounded breathless and genuinely pleased. Real good actress.

"Good evening, Lara. How have you been?" he breezed, switching to Russian.

"I've been busy. The academic year has started, you know. Besides, Viktor is staging a new musical. And I'm singing the leading part in it. So, yes, we've been quite busy. How about you? Have you been away again?"

"No, I've been here." He didn't need to be diplomatic with them, did he? They'd got what they needed—his ass.

"Really? I've been trying to get hold of you, but you were never home."

"You did? I was probably busy, too. Or out late... When did you call?"

"Last week. I called you twice. You weren't home. I called Amanda, too, but her secretary said she'd left for good. It was so unexpected. Why has she left?"

"I don't know. She didn't care to tell. I only learned about it just before her departure."

"She didn't tell you? I thought you were... close *friends*."

Right, of course *they* knew it, since the little act with Amanda had been staged primarily for *them*. "What do you mean by *that*?"

"Just that you were close friends. *Da?* At least I'm pretty sure Amanda liked you *a lot*." She lowered her voice conspiratorially.

"Where did you get it from, Lara? She was married, for heaven's sake."

"So what?" There was an indignant shrug in her tone of voice. "Marriage can't prevent people from liking each other… Even when you're only dating someone, you can still be attracted to somebody else. Happens all the time."

"It does?" Jack asked skeptically, not sure where it was all going.

There was a slight pause, then Lara asked cautiously, "Jack, are you mad at me?"

Was he? No he wasn't—why should he be? They were just doing their jobs, like he was doing his, nothing personal. "Should I be?"

There was a sigh at the other end of the line. "So you are. Because I've been going out with Val, *da*? Is it why you have been avoiding me? Avoiding us?"

Val?? He didn't give the slightest damn about Val. Or Howard. Or anyone else she chose to screw around with. "No, I'm not avoiding you, Lara. I've just been very busy lately. Really. That's all." He sighed.

"So, are we still friends?"

"Yes, we're still friends." If that is all you're calling to ask me.

"Wonderful! So you'll come to my birthday this Saturday, *da*?"

"Your birthday? Of course I will come, Lara. Thanks for inviting me… Would you mind if I ask how old you will be?"

"Not at all! I'll be twenty." She sounded very pleased with herself.

"Ah, a round number, huh? My warmest congratulations."

"Thank you, Jack. So, it's 7:00 o'clock at Restaurant Aragvi on Gorky Avenue. You know it, *da*?"

"Yes, I do. It's a great place." It was one of the oldest and best restaurants downtown Moscow, featuring Georgian and Caucasian cuisines.

"Excellent! I'll see you on Saturday then."

It sounded like she was ready to bid him goodbye. However, now Jack wasn't ready to let her go just yet.

"Yes, thank you again, Lara. By the way, did you call me earlier this evening, half an hour before this call? I was in the shower and couldn't pick up the phone."

"No, I didn't. Must be *someone else* calling you late," she said mischievously.

Right. And you know who that was, girl?

"Must be. I've been wondering who…"

"You must have plenty of people calling you home late, no? I'm pretty sure I'm not the only one." She giggled again. "But that's alright. As long as I'm the first in line," she declared, then added when nothing came from Jack's end, "I told you from the beginning that I liked you, didn't I?"

"Yes, you did. Thank you, Lara. I'll keep it in mind." He shook his head, mystified.

"Very good. I'm leaving you in peace now. And will expect you on Saturday."

"I'll be there. Good night, Lara."

"Good night, *daragusha*," she said in a sing-song voice and hung up.

Jack stared at the phone in his hand, shook his head again and dropped it in the cradle with a loud clunk. Whatever game *they* were playing with him, it was absurdly juvenile.

So juvenile that it was almost ingenious.

Moscow Station's operation to unload the deaddrop in Fili Park started at 1:00 p.m. on Thursday. Due to the heightened surveillance after the expulsion of 31 British citizens, Nurimbekoff had decided to use the Station's entire contingent of "professional staff" to create a smoke screen for Jack. Except for the COS and William, none of the officers knew whom they were covering for.

Starting 1:00 p.m., at intervals of fifteen to thirty minutes, six other case officers and William left the Embassy in their cars and commenced what looked like surveillance detection runs, the type employed on clandestine operations—elaborate and meticulous many-hour drive around the city, with stops at innocuous and sometimes random places.

Jack left the Embassy on foot at 4:40 p.m., ten minutes after William, and headed towards his Mustang parked on a side street nearby. According to the plan, the car wouldn't start and after five minutes of trying Jack got out, bitching out loud, slammed its door shut, locked it and stomped to the nearest Metro station. He was pretty sure he was clear of surveillance. Nevertheless, he carried on with his SDR, using Metro and random taxis, with the objective of reaching his final destination by 8:00 p.m., just before dark. Once the drop was unloaded, he was to head toward the side entrance of the park where a red Lada with specific plate numbers would pick him up and deliver him to a large duty free shop on Kutuzov Avenue, four kilometers from the park. William would be there and would give Jack a lift back to the Embassy.

The operation went without the slightest hiccup.

At 8:04 p.m., Jack picked up a plastic bag with documents, rapped in dirty rags to look like trash, behind the back of a bench at the far end of the park, near the river. It was unseasonably cold and, although it hadn't been raining for the last two days, there weren't many people in the park. Three drunkards on a bench near the entrance bitching at each other; a group of schoolchildren running around playing some sort of war game; two old women hobbling towards the exit, each carrying a loaf of dark bread and a carton of milk in their fishnet *avoska* sacks. Jack sat on the bench for a few minutes, watching the sky behind fluffy blankets of clouds turning deep purple and dark blue, then stood up and strolled casually to the side exit.

At 8:28 p.m. he got into the back seat of the red Lada parked on the street fifty meters from the gates, nodded a silent greeting to the driver who gave him one single sullen glance through the rear view mirror.

At 9:05 p.m. Jack "ran into" William and his wife Marie-Ann at the duty free shop and at 10 p.m. was having a late dinner with a couple of contractors at Uncle Sam's, feeling drained and high at the same time.

He left the Embassy's grounds at half past eleven and flagged down a taxi, then, still high on adrenalin, ran his mouth non-stop all the way home. He generously overpaid the taxi driver, figuring the man was probably a KGB informant—weren't they all? He had beaten them all today, he could afford to be charitable.

He didn't get back to his apartment until midnight, nursing the tiredness deep in his bones. After a scalding shower, he fetched his bottle of whiskey out of the cupboard, poured half a tumbler and sat down on the sofa.

It was *not* looking good. He was starting to rely on alcohol a bit too much nowadays, to unwind and get to sleep...

Lara had said that her "friend" Eton had drinking bouts sometimes, behind the closed doors... How had that kid got so low? He was only twenty-one...

He wouldn't let himself fall to that point. No, he wouldn't. Shouldn't...

He gulped down the amber liquid in two big mouthfuls, the heat unfurling from his throat to his stomach, then he put the tumbler down carefully on the coffee table, stashed the bottle back into the cupboard and staggered into the bedroom.

Sleep took hold of him shortly after his head hit the pillow, but sometime during the night, he jerked violently and sat up, disoriented. He wobbled to the bathroom, took a leak, washed his hands and looked into the mirror.

So they had played him, so what? Wasn't it exactly what he was doing to them? It was just their jobs—he was doing his, and they were doing theirs, right? So what was his fucking problem?

And the problem was that—

No, he didn't even want to go there.

Chapter 25

The cramped little office he shared with Glenn was empty when Jack arrived to work the next morning. Jack dropped his shoulder bag on the floor under his desk, took off his jacket and glanced at his watch. Eight minutes past nine. For once Glenn was later than him.

He wasn't alone for long though. In five minutes, there was a sound of a key in the lock and Glenn rushed in, a little out of breath. "Hey, Jack!" His stocky co-worker locked the door and turned around. "We missed you yesterday. It was Thirsty Thursday, remember? Where were you?" He put his briefcase on his desk, sat down.

"Morning, Glenn. What's up? Don't tell me the Dodger's lost to the Astros! Not after their winning streak this summer."

"They lost—"

"No shit!"

"Indeed. But that's not *the* news." Glenn rolled his chair back so he could see Jack.

"What is it, then?"

"Don't you read newspapers anymore, dude? Where've you been?"

"Herding the Berkeley folks. I need at least two double shots after each of their meetings, my brain hurts so much. So what's the news? C'mon, Glenn, just spill it!"

"Looks like our security services are having a winning streak, too. Remember the arrest of the Walker family in June? They were spying for the Sovs. And then that Sharon Something-or-other woman, caught in July? Well, now they say they have a walk in case. A high-ranking KGB officer."

"No shit!" Jack's eyes went wide.

Jesus Christ, how could *this* be in the news?

"You've said that already." Glenn was obviously pleased with Jack's reaction.

"I'll say it again, man: no shit. Isn't this kind of news supposed to be top secret or something? Where did you read it?"

"Maybe it should. Nevertheless, it's all over the news. On the front pages of the Washington Post and New York Times yesterday. I'm sure it'll be on the NBC tonight."

"Geez! I want to see it with my own eyes." Jack stood up. "Hope the library has a spare copy of the Washington Post left."

"You'd be lucky. If they don't, I'm sure you can borrow it from William." Glenn smirked amiably.

Year, right. He hoped he would be able to get more than that from William. Later maybe, if not right now.

The breaking news article in the Washington Post was not particularly big, but its headline was disparaging: "Soviet Union Has Agents In CIA, Defector Says". If that weren't enough, it went on to spill the name of the "high-ranking officer in the KGB", identifying him as Vitaly Yurchenko and revealing that he had defected while in Italy in early August.

Jack recalled his conversation with Nurimbekoff and William in the Tank, when he had been asked if he had known Edward Lee Howard, an ex-CIA officer who might have turned renegade. That seemed to tie in neatly with what the articles were saying now—if Yurchenko's information was true, it confirmed the suspicions that the Agency had been compromised by its own. The article went further, stating that the defector was in the hands of the CIA and was being debriefed at a safe house not far from Langley. Approached by the newspaper, the CIA spokesperson had refused to provide comments.

Jack was shocked. This was wrong, so wrong. This wasn't how defections were supposed to be handled, was it? According to the procedure, defectors' identities were kept confidential; then after debriefings, which could take months, they were usually given new identities under the Agency's defector resettlement program. And there was no way the information about the defector could have leaked out had the Agency been determined to keep it from the public. So what kind of game was this now? For once, he thought it wasn't Joe Coburn's handiwork...

Was it? No, Joe would never do this to an agent, even if it was a defector. Poor bastard, what was he going to do after his debriefings were over?

When Jack got back to his office, Glenn told him that William wanted to see him—with or without the report on the meetings between the Soviet and American scientists. Jack rolled his eyes, grumbled, "It's not even ten yet, ferchristsake", and headed back out the door. Maybe William would tell him what was going on.

William didn't tell him anything. He scribbled on a sheet of paper that they were going to have a meeting in the Tank at 6:30 p.m. The debriefing after the previous day's operation, Jack figured. Should be a short one this time, so he would be able to catch up with the crowd at the diner later on, have a few beers and exchange notes about this bizarre Yurchenko affair.

He spent the rest of the morning writing his full report on the op run, figuring he would have to file it anyway, debriefing or not. In truth, he spent half of that time trying to decide how to reveal to his bosses his suspicions—and his reasons for having them—about Lara Novikova and Eton Volkonsky, and most importantly whether it was time for him to cable the "sea-water" message to Joe. And if not now, then when?

By lunchtime, he had resolved to delay making his revelations until after Lara's party. Maybe he would have some hard proof by then. He would probably get some prep' talk tonight after he let the COS and William know that Ms. Novikova had invited him to her birthday party. He didn't think the KGB would make a move on him before then—they hadn't been in a hurry so far, right? He hoped that would remain the case for as long as possible.

When they got up to the Tank, the Station Chief was already there reading a document in a thin file in front of him. He stood up, shook hands with Jack, smiling, said, "Great job", and waved him to sit down. As Jack had expected, the post-op debriefing took less than twenty minutes. However, just when he thought that they were done for the day and opened his mouth to ask about the Yurchenko defection case, Marat said, "Now, about your other project."

"Yes, sir." He nodded, looking at Nurimbekoff eagerly, hoping the recoil he felt in his stomach didn't show.

"How's your relationship with the Soviet nuclear winter team going? Where are you with Eton Volkonsky?"

"I'm sorry, I've nothing new to report. I've been so swamped for the last month or so, I haven't had a chance to meet with any of them again. Had only a phone call with Novikova. I mentioned it in my report... By the way, last night she called to invite me to her birthday celebration. Tomorrow at seven, restaurant Aragvi on Gorky Avenue."

"That's good." Nurimbekoff's tone was neutral. "I'm assuming that the whole crew will be there."

"I'm hoping so, too."

"We need you to step up the development of Eton Volkonsky, Jack. This is now your priority. He and his grandfather, Professor Volkonsky."

"Has anything happened?"

"Yes, there've been some developments. We now need additional information on Professor Volkonsky and his nuclear winter work. To be precise: on his *original* nuclear winter work. It's needed to corroborate other information we've recently acquired."

"Is it related to the debriefing of this guy Yurchenko?" Jack asked cautiously.

The COS hesitated with his answer. "It is... William will work you through the details. In a nutshell, the entire nuclear winter program might be a major disinformation campaign cooked up by the KGB. To discredit our government's nuclear arms strategy."

"But it's a joint Soviet-American program, is it not? Sponsored by the World Meteorological Organization."

"It is now. But apparently the *original* Soviet project dates back to 1980. According to the source, Volkonsky led a group of scientists who were supposed to produce a study on the effects of a nuclear exchange over Germany... Nineteen eighty was when we first announced the deployment of the Pershing missile systems in Europe," Nurimbekoff explained, as if reading Jack's mind. "We need to get hold of this study. Or information about it at the very least. Two of our people at HQ are already working on leads in the scientific circles in the US and Europe. But the key originator is here and, as it happens, you have access to him. And to his family members."

"Yes, sir." Jack nodded, looking inquisitively from the COS to William. He was still not clear about the significance of Prof. Volkonsky's study, how it was linked with the KGB and what other information it was supposed to help to corroborate.

Once again, Nurimbekoff had divined Jack's silent question. "The study might have been ordered by the KGB. We need to verify this information."

"Together with its assumptions and conclusions," William chimed in. "Would be good to know that, too."

His bosses were not forthcoming about the whys and wherefores of the assignment, but hey, his job was just to get the information, not to analyze why and how it would be used. He was sure the Company or the State Department, or both, would find a good use for it.

"William will brief you on the details of this assignment. Later... Questions?" It looked like Nurimbekoff was ready to adjourn the briefing.

"May I ask about the status of Edward Howard? Has he been taken in?"

The Station Chief exchanged quick glances with William, then turned to Jack again. "The FBI's working on it. Don't worry, Jack, it's under control." His tone was soft, almost like he was trying to sound soothing.

It meant this Howard guy was still on the loose. Jack didn't know how the FBI operated, but felt it had been too long now—nearly two months had passed since the day the Company first learned about Howard. And now this odd Yurchenko case.

"May I ask a question about this defection case that's all over the news? Vitaly Yurchenko." Jack pretended he didn't notice William's glare.

"You want to know why his defection and identity have been leaked to the press."

"Yes, sir."

"You're right. It's an unusual case." The COS sighed, but held Jack's gaze. "A high profile one. Well, due to the necessity of sharing the source with other agencies from the very beginning, it's been decided to handle it this way. Nevertheless, his security is guaranteed. He'll continue to enjoy our *full* protection until his debriefing is deemed complete, and he's been resettled."

It sounded like a party line to Jack and he thought the COS didn't fully believe his own answer either. "I'm assuming that this is just an exception, not a change in the rules," he said quietly.

William leaned forward abruptly as if to make a sharp reply, but Nurimbekoff raised his hand. "There's no change in the rules," the COS said calmly. "This is indeed an exception. We'll see how it goes... Now, coming back to your assignment. I want you to make this new angle to GTTALION your priority. The code-name is FOX. We need the information about the *original* Soviet nuclear winter project, the sooner the better. Call on all sources you have or can get access to: Prof. Volkonsky, Eton Volkonsky, the MGU Nuclear Winter team, the Berkeley team, the Lenin Library. Anything else you can come up with. William will work with you on the details. All clear? Great." He stood up and picked up his file from the conference table. "That's all from me. I'll leave you two to work out the logistics."

After Nurimbekoff left, Jack spent another twenty minutes with William discussing the line he should take the next day with his Soviet "friends". They agreed that Jack would invite them to his place for dinner the following weekend and henceforth would try to keep in close contact with them, especially with the Volkonsky family, whether the KGB made a move on Jack or not. They would reconvene to discuss a concrete plan of action for FOX the following Wednesday when William returned from Leningrad.

They were at the Tank's door when William suddenly recalled that he had received five video cassettes for Jack with the diplomatic pouch from the USIA. "I've had a quick look at them," the CAO said. "They were recordings of the LiveAid concert from the BBC live broadcast. They're in my office, if you wanted to collect them right away".

A quick look? The weekly pouch from the USIA normally arrived on Monday night and today was Friday.

"Yes, I'll pick them up now," Jack nodded, all enthusiastic. "Great timing. I'll check them out, before sharing with our Soviet *friends*."

Jack spent half of the evening with the diplomatic crowd at Uncle Sam's, discussing the unfolding story about the KGB defector. When they left, he joined Grant, Frank and two other Marines at the bar, then followed them to the Marines Club. He tried to keep his fraternizing compartmentalized, since most of the diplomatic staff didn't mingle with the Marines. In fact, the Marine guards occupied the lowest rung of the Embassy hierarchy and many, especially the diplomats, looked down on them.

But not everyone. Some female staffers of the State Department and even a few diplomatic wives frequented the Friday and Saturday night discotheques at the Marines Club where they openly went after the young Marines' asses. The most notorious amongst them was Stella Ricci, a junior officer from the consular section. It was as if her New Year's resolution was to get into the pants of all Marine guards at the Embassy. And not only theirs: once she had all but raped Jack in the men's room, but having encountered his halfhearted response, she let him be ever since.

Jack leaned against the bar with his warm beer, watching two dozen hot bodies shaking to the disco beat in the middle of the small and dimly lit clubbing room. He wondered idly whether local discotheques were different from this lusty show by sex-and-recreation-deprived young men and a handful of accommodating women. He thought they were different—after all, local men could get all the sex they wanted at home, couldn't they? At home, where they could drive their women wild, shrieking into the phones "let go of me" when someone called. Nah, probably they just danced at their discotheques. He wondered if Eton went to discotheques. Well, ok, so maybe he and his band *played* at discotheques, but did he dance?

"Jack!"

Frank rolled up to him, a lewd grin on his sweaty face, obviously tipsy and horny. Jack rocked back slightly when the marine leaned into him and shouted in his ear over the blaring music, "We're going to my room. Wanna join?" He indicated with his head at four other marines dancing with Stella and two tall, blond girls Jack didn't know.

"With the girls?" Jack shouted back, arching his eyebrows.

Was he serious? It would be a security breach, wouldn't it?

"With the girls." Frank nodded happily.

"You'll get yourselves in trouble, Frank."

"Nah! We'll be back before the Club closes. You joining us? C'mon, man. It'll be fun."

"Who are the blondes?" Jack had no interest in joining, but he didn't want to say no outright either. "Never seen them here before."

"Rita and Anna? They're from the German embassy."

"You sure? They don't look German to me." If anything, Jack would say they looked like Russians. Who were not allowed in the Embassy's grounds except the designated office area, and definitely not after the office hours.

"You worry too much, man. Sarge brought them from the bar at Cosmos Hotel. Said they're Germans. Maybe he checked their passport too." Frank guffawed. "So, you coming with us or what?"

"Nah, I'll pass. Thanks, man. I'm gonna head back soon. But you guys, don't get yourselves in trouble. Know what I mean?" He sincerely hoped Sergeant McMahon, if not his Marines, knew what they were doing.

Jack left the Marine's den soon and drove home, all the while unable to stop thinking about the strange events of the day. His thoughts bounced from one incident to another as he struggled to understand each of them and their implications: the leak of Yurchenko's identity to the press; the continuously evolving agendas in relation to the nuclear winter project; what looked like a serious security breach at the Embassy, instigated by the Marines. Who were there to prevent such breaches in the first place.

All those events were worrying and didn't inspire a lot of confidence in the prudent practices of his job and his work place, but at least they kept Jack from dwelling on one fact that annoyed him no end: that Eton May Volkonsky had gotten to him so easily.

That for a moment he had foolishly imagined that what they had had together during those two days in the Russian countryside was real.

Chapter 26

Located in one of Moscow's prime settings, Restaurant Aragvi was housed in the basement of an art-nouveau style building facing the town hall, a towering crimson edifice with a golden crest, across Gorky Avenue. Since the tsarist times, the restaurant had been famous for its Georgian cuisine. Legend had it that it had been Stalin's favorite restaurant and that he had had a private tunnel built between his office in the Kremlin and the restaurant's basement.

The main dining hall was a long chamber, with a vaulted ceiling supported by four arches. The ceiling and the walls were beautifully decorated with Caucasian style frescoes and floral ornaments. A long table under a starched white cloth was laid out in the center, overlaid with flowers, crystal bowls full of black and red caviar, gilded fine china plates with smoked red and white fish, a selection of cold meats and cheeses, several types of breads and bottles of Georgian wines.

Lara was reigning over her guests from the seat at the head of the table, facing the door, and saw Jack the moment he emerged at the door. "Jack!" she called out, waving at him. "Come on in. We're waiting for only you now!"

Jack headed toward her end of the table, smiling at her broadly, stealthily scanning the congregation.

There were about thirty guests around the table, all of them young and most of them trendy, even by western standards. It looked like a no-parents night. Which was a shame as Jack had been all set to meet with Deputy Minister Novikov and Mrs. Novikova. He had even brought an additional present for her, courtesy of the Company. He noted Gosha, Anya and... the rest of the crowd at the end of the table near the door, Val and Howard amongst them.

He gave them all a quick nod and turned to Lara, who had stood up and was waiting for him to approach. "Dear Lara, my warmest congratulations on your birthday! You look ravishing." She did indeed, in her cream-colored, tight fitting pantsuit, her hair dyed strawberry blond. "I wish you... anything you can think of. May all your wishes and dreams come true."

"Jack! I'm so glad you could come." Lara launched herself at him.

He held her gingerly as she pressed her body against his, circling her arms around his neck. He lifted her up briefly, then carefully put her down and distanced himself from her more than enthusiastic embrace. "A little something for you." He handed her his present. "Hope you'll like it... And I love the hair."

"Thank you, Jack. I'm glad." She opened the plastic bag and pulled out a pink box, then another, dark green one. "French perfume!" She squealed, looking up at him, all smiles and a little breathless. "Is this is all for me?"

"One is for your mother. I thought she would be here, too."

"Oh, Jack! Thank you so much! You're so attentive. She will love it!"

Sensing that Lara was about to launch herself at him again, he said quickly, "I'm very glad. So let's not keep your other guests waiting. Where should I sit?"

The table had been filling up as the guests arrived, starting at the end where the hostess of the event presided, so he found himself at the other end where Eton and friends together with his compatriots were clustered. Jack greeted them again and sat down next to Gosha.

"Jack! How are you? We haven't seen you for a while." Gosha was as breathless as Lara had just been.

"I'm sorry, I meant to drop by the university, but have been so busy this past month. I hope everything is fine with you and the Berkeley team?" He nodded at Val and Howard who were sitting across Eton.

"Things are great! You know that we're more or less done with the program, don't you? A month earlier than planned. So they plan to leave earlier now."

Jack had heard about the progress of the joint program, but not about the American team's plans to return home earlier than originally scheduled. "Yes," he said vaguely, annoyed with himself for not being up to date with his charges' plans. "Sorry I couldn't spend more time with you all."

"We were trying to find you, Jack," Anya said, leaning forward to see him, her eyes warm.

He didn't realize that he was so popular with these young people—first Lara telling him off for disappearing, then Gosha, and now Anya. "I have been completely swamped at work, coming home very late for the entire month."

"And you missed another birthday," she noted with a friendly reproach.

"Whose birthday?"

"Gosha's. Our Gosha turned eighteen this week. He's a grownup man now." Anya put her arm around the boy's shoulders affectionately.

"Come on, Anya." Gosha shrugged her arm off. "You're like my mama, really."

"Belated happy birthday." Jack shook the boy's hand and punched him lightly on his shoulder. "I owe you a birthday present."

"Thank you so much! I will look forward to it. But let's start eating. Lara will be very upset if we just sit here and talk." He turned his attention to the food on the table.

"Jack, try this *satsivi* chicken," Anya said, leaning forward and holding out a large plate in his direction. "It's delicious."

"Oh, Jack, you're in trouble now," Seva, who sat across him, said with a friendly smirk. "She thinks you're under-fed."

"Oh, stop it, Seva!" Anya scolded, but her eyes were smiling.

"It's true." Gosha shoveled the starter onto his plate. "She makes sure that we're all well-fed at all times."

"Gosha!" Anya wrestled the appetizer plate from him and passed it to Eton on her other side.

"But isn't it true? We ate so much on my birthday that we couldn't eat anything the next day! She cooked for my birthday," Gosha explained to Jack, who was listening to the exchange with an amused smile.

"Did she? Good for you."

"They made a surprise party for me at Eton's place." Gosha beamed at his friends. "Anya baked a bunch of pies, *pirozhki*, made three kinds of salads and aspic. Lara brought a huge cake and imported cold cuts, and the guys bought drinks. It was awesome! Such a pity you couldn't come."

A few days ago. Eton's place. Lara's drunken voice on the phone. Tuesday?

"I'm so sorry I missed it. Last Sunday, wasn't it? I was actually free. What a shame!"

Say Tuesday! Please!!

"No, it was on Tuesday. Anya and Lara skipped their classes to prepare the food. Eton told me to come to his place after the classes. And there they were, all waiting for me!"

So it *was* Tuesday... Still, it did not necessarily mean that the two of them weren't with the KGB.

Jack felt his face splitting in an ear-to-ear grin. "Sounds like you guys had one hell of a party. I bet everybody was happily drunk by the end."

Anya clucked and shoved lightly on Gosha's shoulder.

The boy laughed. "We were, most of us. Except Anya. And maybe Eton. He didn't look that drunk, right, Anya? Lara and Seva, on the other hand, almost killed each other, fighting over... Everything!"

"Don't exaggerate it," Seva objected, feigning exasperation. "We only fought once during the entire evening. Bitching doesn't count."

"Right, I forgot. It was Eton who nearly killed you two with his telephone." The boy snickered, clearly very pleased by the memory of the party his friends had thrown for him.

"He did?" Jack leaned forward, trying to get a glimpse of the man in question.

Eton was talking to Howard, or rather listening to the American who was telling him about his plans to visit Leningrad, nodding occasionally. He looked different again: a deep, golden tan, the sun-bleached hair trimmed shorter, the charcoal gray crew-neck pullover giving him a solemn air. Like he had matured during the last couple of months, no longer the boyish-looking youth Jack had seen the first time at the Bolshoi, but a fully grown man. A very fine one at that.

Eton must have felt Jack's gaze on him. He turned his head and met Jack's eyes. When he saw Jack smiling at him, his lips pressed together tighter and he quickly looked away, like a person caught staring inappropriately.

Fine, Eton. You don't have to look at me. In fact, you don't have to do anything about me... Yeah, don't do anything, please. Just be like... like you were back *then*...

The birthday party was soon in full swing. At eight o'clock, a band started playing and the guests quickly spilled out to the small dancing area in front of it.

Karelin made a grand entrance around nine with a huge bouquet of crimson roses. He presented his regards, stopped to exchange a few words with Eton and his band, nodded to Jack, and left after barely fifteen minutes.

Deputy Minister Novikov and his stately wife arrived just before ten o'clock. They had been at a recital at the Philharmonic Chamber Hall down Gorky Avenue and popped in after the show to see if Lara needed anything. Jack was quickly presented to the bosomy Mrs. Novikova who was instantly charmed by Jack's present—a bottle of Dior which Lara rushed to hand over to her mother—, then by his small talk. After a few minutes, Jack excused himself and switched his attention to the Deputy Minister. Soon they were talking about the extension of the cultural exchange program between the Soviet Union and the U.S.

Jack had heard from Glenn, who was coordinating the project, that the negotiations hadn't been easy. Both sides stuck to their guns on details, most of them related to the rise of unofficial visits of American singers and musicians to the Soviet Union. The Russians were frustrated that the Americans couldn't "coordinate" their "cultural workers", and the Americans couldn't make their counterparts understand that they didn't "coordinate" the private sector. The Deputy Minister looked at him with interest when Jack suggested that the two countries' cultural exchange might already have resumed—through his and his gorgeous daughter's attendance of the American Independence Day reception. And that maybe something simple but extraordinary, such as the the Bolshoi's prima-donna Maya Plisetskaya coming to a reception at the Ambassador Hart's residence, would be yet another step forward. The Russian studied Jack thoughtfully for a second or two, then changed the subject.

Lara's parents retreated after a couple of rounds of toasts, leaving their daughter and her young friends to continue their party. As soon as they disappeared, the band struck up ABBA's Dancing Queen and Lara was swept away by her classmates to the dance floor again.

Jack grinned and shook his head in response to her enthusiastic gesturing, mouthing, "Sorry, I don't dance", and returned to his end of the festive table. It was deserted as all his neighbors had joined Lara. He turned around in his seat to watch young people enjoying themselves. He had been wondering the other day if Eton danced, so here was his opportunity to—

"You don't dance?" asked a deep voice behind Jack's back and his heart leaped in his chest.

He made an effort to turn around slowly, to restrain his smile. "Hey Eton. No, I don't. I like to watch people dancing though. How about yourself?"

Eton sat down on the chair next to Jack. "I do. Sometimes." He was having problems with small talk again.

"But not today, huh?" Jack decided he wasn't going to make it easy for him today.

"No, not today." Eton looked at him intently, like Jack was some nuclear physics problem he was trying to figure out.

"Having a good time though, aren't you?"

"Um, yes." His lips crinkled in a shy little smile.

"Good. Haven't seen you in a while. How have you been, Eton?"

"Not bad. I was away. Got back last week."

He pulled out a pack of Marlboros from a pocket of his pants, flicked out a couple and offered them to Jack who held the fire for Eton before lighting his smoke.

"So where—"

"I called you," Eton blurted out at the same time with Jack.

Both stopped, watching each other expectantly, waiting for the other to continue.

"So you called me?" Jack exhaled, feeling ridiculously pleased.

"Yes." Eton smile grew an inch wider. "A few times. But you weren't home."

A few times, huh? And why was that, Eton? What did you call me for?

For heaven's sake! You had you dick up his ass, remember?

Alright! So I'm a jerk. Are we happy now?

"I'm sorry. I have been completely swamped with work the last couple of months... So where did you go? Some sort of vacation? Got yourself a nice tan."

"No." Eton shook his head, still smiling, but now looking a little self-conscious. "We were... uh, doing some construction work. Built a house of culture for a *sovkhoz* near Tula. For money."

"Seriously? Did it pay well?"

Construction work? Was this guy for real?

"We got a thousand rubles each this time." Eton shrugged, took a drag on his cigarette.

Jack swallowed, suddenly overcome by the desire to feel the tip of *that* cigarette between his lips, like *then*, in the cornflower field. "I didn't know construction work here pays that well." He wondered how much their work for the *organs* fetched. "You do that often?"

"Every year, since I started in the university. It pays for the instruments in the band."

Right. And he had thought that they were just a bunch of spoilt *nomenklatura* kids.

The music changed to a slow tune and some of the dancers returned to their seats around the table.

Gosha plopped down into his seat on the other side of Jack. "And why don't *you* dance, Jack? Eton, why are you keeping him here? Lara will be mad at you for monopolizing her guests." Gosha seemed genuinely worried at the prospect of Lara being mad at his friend.

"Don't worry. He's not monopolizing me. He's keeping me company as I don't dance... I was actually about to tell Eton that I'd like to invite you guys to my place next week. For an American dinner. What do you say? I've got copies of the LiveAid concert from a friend of mine."

"Awesome! Everybody would love it, right, Eton?"

Eton didn't look convinced and Jack's heart fell. Why was it so difficult with this man? He didn't seem to be able to get to him. Except that one time in the countryside... But he shouldn't think about it, not now, should focus instead on what Eton was saying.

"... if everybody could come, though."

"Will *you* come?" Jack insisted.

"Of course. Absolutely." Eton tipped his chin, smiling weakly, then turned to Gosha. "We can't miss LiveAid, can we, Gosha?"

Okay, so the LiveAid tapes worked, then. At least he'd got this right. He would try to figure out the rest later.

Jack didn't get another chance to talk to Eton one on one. Shortly after, Lara breezed up and dragged him to the dance floor for a slow dance. She clung tightly to him, giving Jack no chance of distancing her from his body, even for a hair-width of space. He held her around her waist carefully, trying to avoid moving around too much, not letting her rub against him. He cut a quick a glance at the end of the table where he had sat with Eton and his friends.

Seva and Val were watching him dancing with Lara—Seva with a very amused expression on his face while Val's eyes were shooting daggers at them. Eton sat with his back to the dance floor, his head held high, his body rigid. Then as Seva said something, laughing, he stood up, moved his chair back carefully and walked out of the dining room.

Aw, c'mon! What the heck did that boy expect him to do? It wasn't like they were a number or something. They weren't even friends! They'd just shared one great tumble, that was all. So why should he feel bad about flirting a little with one of the boy's female friends?

Jack stopped moving and tried to peel Lara's arms off his shoulders. "Lara, I think maybe we should—"

"Yes, I agree! Let's go, *daragusha*." She grabbed hold of his hand and pulled him after her, heading towards the door.

"Lara, where are you going?" Jack tried to hold her back, the realization that she had gotten it all wrong descending on him like a heavy, damp blanket.

Or maybe it was part of their plan?

"Come on, Jack. Nobody will find us."

"Lara, can you hold on for a moment, please?" Jack pulled her to a stop when they were out of the door and everybody's sight. "I don't think it's a good idea."

She looked at him expectantly, arching her eyebrows.

"I'm not supposed to—"

"You want me, *da*?" She threw a suggestive glance at his crotch. "I know you do. I want you, too, darling. So why aren't we supposed to?"

"I'm a diplomat, Lara. We're not supposed to, eh, have relationships with the local people." He wished he sounded more confident for his own good.

"Oh, what nonsense, Jack. We're all human beings, irrespective of our convictions, yes?" She snaked her arms around his waist, rocked into him, then murmured, smiling seductively, "If this place is what worries you, don't be. It's safe. I know for sure."

So it *was* a setup. She was making a move on him after all, like William had always thought she would. But then why had Eton acted like he was…? No, it was just himself, who was being stupid: it was part of their act, quite an elaborate one. He should have figured by now.

"Lara, I can't. I'm sorry." He wasn't ready for this, even if it was his job. Not today. Not with *him* around. Joe had said he could take his time to develop the leads, right? So there was no hurry.

Lara stopped rubbing against him and stepped back, but didn't take her arms from around his waist. "Why?" There was surprise written all over her face, impatience too, but no anger.

"This is just not right. You deserve more than a quick bang in the toilet." He smiled at her softly and touched her cheek with his fingertips. "You're a special girl."

Lara studied his face thoughtfully, then shrugged. "I do anything I want, Jack. Even if it's a quick bang in the toilet." She chuckled, but her eyes weren't smiling. "But if it's not working for you, that's fine. I'll wait." She reached up and cupped the side of Jack's face with her palm. "*You* are a special man, Jack. Worth waiting for. As I already told you." She smiled at him, her smile confident and a little taunting. "Alright then. Let's go back. And promise me you won't be upset if I disappear with Val in a few minutes. We'll still be friends, *da*? And remember, I must be the first in line!" She shoved Jack playfully in the middle of his chest, swirled around on her heels and flitted back into the dining hall.

Jack exhaled sharply, hesitated for a second then walked quickly to the men's room in the corner of the short hallway. He prayed it was empty. He prayed he would find Eton there. Shit, he didn't even know what he prayed for...

It was empty.

Jack locked himself in one of the two cubicles, leaned against the cold tile wall and closed his eyes.

He could do this. It was his goddamn job. He would let them frame him, recruit him and then run him. Both sides. Case officer Smith would be a dangle, a double fucking agent, if that was what everybody wanted.

There was just one little thing *he* wanted—that one Eton May Volkonsky wasn't part of this convoluted equation.

Chapter 27

Jack woke up to the sound of rain bombarding the window of his bedroom. He rolled his head, facing the monotonous sound, and peeked through his eyelashes. It was still dark. He pulled the blanket over his head and went back to sleep. When he opened his eyes again, the gray morning light was seeping through the curtains and there was no sound of rain anymore. The alarm clock on the bedside table showed twelve minutes past seven.

The previous night, when he had returned to the dining room after the incident with Lara, she had already disappeared with Val. Nobody seemed to take any special notice—they were all been busy dancing, drinking and eating, and generally enjoying themselves. Jack scanned the room, searching for Eton, but did not see him—he'd gone, and so had Anya. So after a short while Jack took his leave. He felt like a bastard for no rational reason and tried to tell himself that it was all part of the ruse to get to him. By the time he got home, he managed to convince himself that it was all a KGB ploy and that there could not really be any hurt feelings between any of them. Hadn't Lara acted completely cool? She had been very professional. Therefore, he should be too.

Jack got up and peered out of the window. The world outside was cold and gray and soaking wet. It did not look too windy, though, and he decided he was going to piss his minders off by jogging in this ungodly weather.

It started drizzling again half an hour into his run. The streets were deserted, with most of the shops still closed. Jack noticed a phone booth at the corner of the brick building from afar and trotted across the street toward it. He shut the door of the booth tight and looked at his Swatch. 8:13 a.m.

Still early. But then, *he* would be home for sure. Jack owed it to him, right? The guy had said he had called him a few times. Jack owed him at least one call in return. Especially after the way they had parted the day before.

Oh, ferchristsakes, just make the damn call already!

Jack fumbled in his belt bag for a two-kopek coin and quickly dialed the number. He closed his eyes, manning up for whatever conversation it would turn out to be. He hadn't the vaguest idea what to expect or what he should be saying, and which hat he should put on with the guy now.

"*Allo?*"

Eton's voice sounded tired and Jack's gut clenched. "Good morning, Eton. Hope I'm not too early." He didn't say his name, but hoped he would recognize him.

There was a slight pause, then Eton said cautiously, "Good morning. No problem. I've been up for some time."

"How are things?"

"Good. Thank you. Yourself?" It sounded like Eton was as uncertain about this conversation as Jack was.

"I'm fine. Just fine, thanks... Listen, I'm calling because yesterday, you know, we didn't manage to, um, I didn't..." Oh, fuck it! "I should have called you earlier, Eton. Like a month and a half ago. I am sorry. I don't have any good excuse for why I didn't." He was getting himself straight into the trap, but that was alright. In case there was no trap, and it was all just his and his bosses' sick imagination.

There was a sigh on the other end and Eton voice rumbled in, low and soothing. "You did call. I got your message."

"Right, a month after, um, later."

"It's alright. I was away for a month. Glad you're calling now... You calling from the street?"

The alarm bells erupted in Jack's head. "Yes... How do you know?" he asked cautiously. The phone booth's door was closed and there was virtually no noise coming in from the light traffic on the street. He heard Eton's low chuckle.

"Just guessing. The three times you called me, you always did so from the street. I guess you don't trust your phone at home."

Have you figured that out, too, smarty-pants?

"You're right. I have a problem with most of the equipment and places when they are *predesigned* for my use. If you know what I mean."

"I do. That is also why you don't call by name those who call *your* telephone... Right?"

God, the boy was quick!... *If* he wasn't with the *organs*.

"Right. How about you? Do *you* trust *your* telephone?"

There was a slight hesitation. "Never thought about it... Never had anything, um, *special* that I couldn't say openly on the phone... To *someone*," he added quietly.

"Welcome to my world."

There was a moment of silence, then Eton said quietly, "I understand."

Do you, really?

"Listen, Eton. About yesterday, with Lara—"

"It's alright. I understand *that*, too. Maybe more than you think." He sounded sad. Resigned.

"Are you sure?"

"Yes... Besides, knowing Lara, I would be surprised if she didn't have a go at you... I also understand that what we, um, what happened in August was just a onetime thing. It happens. So don't worry. You don't owe—"

"Eton, stop! Listen to me... Eton?"

"I'm here."

"It's not like *that*, alright? And I do owe you... But we have to be *very* careful. You understand? You know what can happen if we aren't, don't you?"

I'll be pitched if you're with the KGB, or you'll be sent to a gulag if you aren't. That's what'll happen, Eton. Hope you know it, friend.

"I know. I will be careful... Can we meet, um, sometime?" Eton asked tentatively, then quickly added, "Just to talk."

A warm feeling spilled over in Jack's chest and he laughed quietly into the phone. "Sure we can. Just to talk."

"When? I mean, let me know when you will have time."

Jack hesitated for only a second. "Do you want to see a movie or something?"

"Alright."

It should be fine for two young men to see a movie together here, shouldn't it? Even if one was a student, and the other was a diplomat from the American Embassy.... Fuck it, he didn't care. He was assigned to develop this young man, so he could go about the task as he saw fit.

"I'll have a look at a movies announcement board and will call you in an hour."

"Alright. Talk later, then."

He could tell Eton was smiling.

"*See* you later, Eton."

Jack hung up, peeled the grin slowly off his face and tucked it away. For later.

He called Eton an hour later and told him he would meet him at 2:00 p.m., at the movie theater Vityaz, a short walk from Metro Station Belyaevo. He had picked this cinema because he recalled Lara mentioning that Eton lived in this district, on the southern fringe of Moscow. Besides, it was a part of the city that he thought westerners didn't venture into very often, so the likelihood that the place was wired was lower than places down town. *And* he wanted to get a feel for the area where Eton lived in case he needed to come here again... sometime...

By two o'clock Jack was smoking outside of the cinema theater's entrance, two tickets to a re-run of an old movie in his pocket. The place was not particularly busy, partly because of the time of the day, partly because of the weather. It suited Jack just fine. He hoped Eton did not mind seeing an oldie, though—he had said he just wanted to talk, right? They had one and a half hours to kill before the movie started and they could always hang out some more afterwards if the guy had more to say. He chuckled to himself, imagining Eton filling the one and a half hours they had with small talk.

Yeah, right, he'd better have all his ammunition ready, and today he didn't mind it at all.

He caught sight of Eton when the young man emerged at the far end of the small square in front of the movie theater, still a few hundred meters away. Eton saw him too and quickened his pace, his lips slowly easing into the crooked little smile that Jack could visualize with his eyes closed. "*Privet*, Eton. How are you?" he greeted him in Russian, thrusting his hand out, smiling broadly.

Eton's long fingers wrapped around Jack's hand and he wondered again at their strength.

"*Privet*. Sorry, I'm late."

"Nah, it's only five minutes... I've bought tickets to 'Moscow Doesn't Believe In Tears'. Is it alright?"

"Sure. It's fine."

"Good. It starts at three-thirty. Hope you don't mind waiting."

"No. I can handle an hour and a half." The corners of Eton's mouth twitched, his eyes warm as they searched Jack's face.

"Alright, then. Let's go inside and find a bite at the cafeteria. I haven't had my lunch yet, so I'm starving."

The cafeteria upstairs featured a glass cabinet with a selection of three varieties of two-bite size *butterbrods*—barely buttered bread topped with paper-thin slices of salami or cheese. The shelves behind the counter were virtually empty, and only a few of the dozen aluminum tables with matching chairs were occupied.

Jack carefully sat a plate stacked high with *butterbrods* on the plastic top of the table at the furthest end of the hall. Eton set two bottles of Pepsi and two glasses down and looked skeptically at Jack's lunch.

"Will that be enough for you?"

Jack plopped down on the chair and smiled reassuringly at the younger man. He found he shared an affinity with the Russians for a proper meal taken in due time. "Don't worry. I will get myself another helping if that's not enough." He took one *butterbrod* and bit off half of it. "So, Eton. You wanted 'just to talk', right? Tell me."

Eton's ears pinked, but he didn't drop his gaze. "It's my turn, right?" he asked, like he was picking up from where they had left off the last time, nearly two months ago. "What do you want me to tell you about?"

About your grandfather's original nuclear winter project. About what it is that you and Dr. Alexin disagree about with your grandfather and Prof. Ackerman. About what are you gonna do now that you know what I'm like. What you gonna do about it, Eton?

"Tell me what you like more, researching nuclear physics or singing in a band. And why." It was his day off, goddamn it, and he wanted to pretend for a moment that he wasn't behind the Iron Curtain and could be pitched anytime; that he was just hanging out with his best friend on a rainy Sunday afternoon, talking about things he had never done in earnest with anyone before.

And Eton told him. About how he had first touched a guitar at the age of seven and never looked back. About his constant battle with his family and his teachers, and later on with himself, over who he should be, a scientist or a rocker. About how in the end he had negotiated a deal with them—that he would do what they wanted in exchange for them letting him be and do what he wanted. Math, physics and later nuclear physics came easy to Eton, and he never lost any sleep over them. Music, on the other hand, was a different story. Firstly, he had only taken guitar and basic music theory classes at the district's Palace of Young Pioneers. Then he taught himself by playing back Jimmy Hendrix's, the Eagles' and Cream's songs which he copied from pirated records he borrowed from friends. When Eton started writing his own songs, they came about with heartbreak—his father died that year. He was the only person through whom Eton felt a strange connection with California, a place he had always dreamed of visiting one day. With his father gone, it was as if the dream had died, too. Maybe that was why his songs were so sad, and that was why he did not play them to others often, except to his closest friends.

When he finished his story, Eton asked Jack about his ranch in California and it was Jack's turn to describe his ranch to his friend, down to the smallest details. He knew exactly what it looked like—how it *would* look like, one day.

They did not notice the time passing and very nearly missed the beginning of the film, one of the Soviet all-time favorite movies about love found and love lost. They sat on the last row of the half empty theater, their knees touching, sometimes their arms, and occasionally their fingers, and Jack thought he had never felt so close to anyone, so intimate, a feeling both frightening and exhilarating. And he told himself that when the time came to move ahead with his operation, it wouldn't be, shouldn't be much of a problem for him to snap out of this dream world where he and this amazing young man were the best of friends.

Chapter 28

On Monday, Jack spent two hours writing a three-page report on his dealings with locals over the weekend. Lara and her father featured prominently in it as did Eton Volkonsky. What he didn't include was Lara's attempt to seduce him.

Running into Frank on guard on the ninth floor caused Jack to mull over his dilemma of whether to mention to William that the Marines had been taking girls to their rooms. Girls who had claimed to be German but hadn't looked it, in his opinion.

Before their departure, Moscow-bound case officers had been instructed that one of their duties was to counter any attempt by the Sovs to penetrate the Embassy. The Station was supposed to cooperate with the State Department's Regional Security Officer in all matters related to the Embassy and its staff. By now, however, Jack had come to realize that his bosses were more interested in running agents and collecting information than in the tedious work of protecting the Embassy, and cooperation with the RSO was not high on their priority list. So he doubted William would do much if he told him about the Marines incident. Maybe he would tell Jack to go talk to Don Steward himself. Besides, Jack empathized with the young, sex-deprived marines who were severely limited in recreational activities they could engage in this country. Not to mention that he hung out with some of them and they considered him a friend. So he decided to let it pass and mention it to the RSO the next time he noticed any such irregularities.

For a couple of days, conversations at lunchtime and after hours circled around two headline stories: Gorbachev's letter to Reagan proposing a fifty percent cutback in offensive nuclear weapons and the new $27 million aid package to the Nicaraguan *contras* administered by the State Department. Then on Thursday, two new topics emerged to dominate small talk at Uncle Sam's and in the American community in general—the FBI's nationwide search for Edward Lee Howard, an ex-CIA officer suspected of selling information to the KGB, and the death of Rock Hudson.

Both stories unsettled Jack, albeit in different ways.

The fact that Howard was still at large meant that he might continue providing information to the KGB, thus compromising more assets. That is, if he had indeed been responsible for the recent disastrous roll-ups of the CIA case officers and their agents. Four so far this year, according to Joe, excluding the British agent that Jack had accidentally helped exfiltrate in July.

Rock Hudson's untimely death reminded Jack of his resolution to test himself for AIDS, somewhere outside the country, the sooner the better. Which reminded him that he'd had unprotected sex with his friend Eton. Which further reminded him that he had yet to send Joe a message with "sea-water" code. In the meanwhile, his friendship with Eton Volkonsky seemed to have progressed to a new stage. *And* Jack was going to see him again in two days—for an American burger and ribs dinner at his place. This, in turn, might progress their "relationship" even further, one way or another.

When Glenn left for the day, Jack spent nearly an hour trying to formulate in his mind the message he was going to transmit to the chief of ops. By 6:30 p.m. an innocuous communication had gone out to a mail stop address at headquarters of the USIA, with code words "sea" and "yellow" for low emergency status embedded in the text. Two hours later, the communication was picked up by a clerk dispatched from the general services at Langley. Next morning, Jack received a coded response confirming that his message had been read and instructing him to wait until further notice.

He put down the cable and sighed in relief. He had been nervous what his "sea-water" message would bring down on him—a face-to-face meeting with Joe where he would have to report about his progress of SEABROOK. He hadn't made up his mind yet if the Russian was a KGB informant or an innocent victim of their elaborate honey trap, a clueless target chosen by the Company and the NSA for their joint operation for his father's sins. What Jack had no doubt about was that Eton May Volkonsky was queer as a three-dollar bill.

So now, with the meeting delayed "till further notice"—and God only knew what would happen in the meantime—Jack had plenty of time to reflect and figure how to go about this whole affair. Including the fact that he got hard just thinking about the guy. Which was pretty much most of his free time nowadays. *And* he still needed to get himself tested for AIDS, if he was to continue to "develop" his star agent along the lines of SEABROOK.

You sure it's because of the job alone?

Okay, so he had to have himself tested because he was planning on hanging out with Eton and couldn't wait to find a place where he could get another taste of the mind-blowing sex he'd had with him once.

On Saturday morning, after Mariya Ivanovna, who came once a week to do the cleaning and washing, had left, Jack's place was all set for entertaining his Russian friends. The Panasonic TV set had come back from the repair shop at the Embassy the previous day. Five VHS tapes with LiveAid recordings stacked neatly on top of the VCR. The fridge fully stocked with imported canned beer, ham, sausages, cheese, fruits and a carton of Marlboros from a duty free shop. A couple of bottles of Stolichnaya and loaves of brown bread from a local store, all lined up on top of the fridge.

His bedroom looked tidy and fresh, too, almost homely. It was a shame that he would never be able to use it for anything more than sleeping in. And jerking off sometimes. Unless he decided to bring a girl home. Some foreign girl, not local, someone from the contractor crowd. Maybe Stella—that girl seemed always to be on the lookout for a fresh piece of ass and wouldn't insist on a relationship. Now that Amanda was gone, he should seriously think about it. It would be good for his legend, would add another layer of safety so that he could spend more time with...

He spun around and walked quickly to the door.

Jack spent three hours at Uncle Sam's, had his lunch at the bar, shared a beer with the Embassy's courier-in-residence, waiting for his order of burgers and ribs to take home and grill. He returned home just after 4:00p.m., feeling strangely anxious.

It was the first "reception" he was throwing at his apartment here in Moscow *and* for the type of guests he had never entertained before. Shouldn't be too different from the kind of blowouts he used to have at his place when he was at Cal State, should it? They were students, too. The difference was that their visit to his place might implicate them with the omnipresent Soviet security organs. Unless they worked for these organs in the first place. The question was who amongst them did?

The day before, he and William had gone over the list of Jack's guests, focusing on those at the top of Moscow Station's list of suspects: Lara, Eton, Grisha, Anya. However, when Jack called Lara to fix the time he would meet them on the street to escort them past the *militsia* men, she said she wouldn't be able to come: her father was invited to his boss's place for dinner and wanted her to go with him. She told him to call Eton and arrange the time with him.

He did. Only to find out that only five of them would be coming to his place—the *Krylia* crew, minus Alex the bass guitarist, and Gosha. Eton apologized for the last minute dropouts, but instead of making up some story about his friends' busy social schedule, he went on explaining, in a pained voice, that visiting the house of an American diplomat was not something every Soviet student was comfortable doing. He hoped Jack understood.

Of course, he did and couldn't blame them. But it meant that Moscow Station might need to revisit the list of its suspects. Could it be that they were completely off the mark about this group of young people?

He met them on the street at half past six, ushered them past the *militsia* guard and into his apartment building. As they waited for the geriatric elevator, a group of five African children aged six to twelve ran down the stairs and past them out into the courtyard, squealing and waving toy swords and guns. Seeing the baffled looks on his guests' faces, Jack explained that they were the children of Angolan diplomats who lived on the first three floors.

Up in Jack's apartment, the young people crowded for a minute in the corridor, taking off their jackets and inspecting his dwelling with unhidden interest mixed with poorly concealed surprise. Jack wasn't sure what exactly they had expected to see at his place, but obviously not a standard, Soviet type accommodation, furnished with imported but well-used fixtures.

"Have you been living here long?" Seva the drummer asked, trying to sound casual. He took off his shoes and proceeded into the sitting room in his socks, followed by others.

"Since March. I inherited this apartment as well as my job from the guy who lived here before me. He had to return home unexpectedly, for health reasons. The place was fully furnished, so I thought, why bother re-furnishing it?" Jack explained and stole a quick glance at Eton.

He was taciturn as usual, but looked more relaxed and smiled more easily, as if he had left a layer or two of his invisible armor at home. He was the only one who didn't look surprised, just curious. Jack also noticed that Eton quickly checked him out as he was taking off his jacket.

"Please make yourself at home," Jack said when they were all crowded into his sitting room. "That's the LiveAid tapes on the VCR. Feel free to put them on," he added, seeing the boys' furtive glances towards the TV and tape recorder.

They thanked him in unison and Seva quickly proceeded to turn on the TV and the VCR, while Vadim and Yura picked up the tapes and started reading the covers on which the names of bands and performers were scribbled in tiny, neat handwriting.

Jack left them playing with the tapes and went to the kitchen. Soon, Eton appeared at the kitchen door. He shuffled his feet, hands stuck deep in his jeans' pockets, then asking shyly, "Can I help… with anything?"

"What, you don't care to watch the concert with your friends?" Jack teased, feeling exuberant.

"Hope you'll lend me the tapes." Eton sounded like he was certain that Jack would. "I'll make copies. For everybody."

Jack opened fridge and pulled out two trays with burgers and marinated ribs. "Alright then. You can help by washing the tomatoes, cucumbers and spring onions. They're in the plastic bag on the windowsill." He pulled a big glass bowl from the cupboard and handed it to Eton. "Here, take this."

The young man took the bowl from Jack's hands, his fingers covering Jack's for the briefest of moments. He gazed at Jack with the expression Jack remembered seeing on his face when he was telling Jack about his childhood. The corners of his lips were curling up in the familiar shy little smile. "Jack, I—"

"I'll only lend you the tapes if you promise to return them in a couple of weeks," Jack said a fraction louder, shaking his head emphatically. He tapped lightly on his ear with his forefinger and pointed at the ceiling.

The lost look on Eton's face eased, and he nodded. "I promise to return them in two weeks," he said in the same tone as Jack, chuckled quietly and sauntered to the window, brushing shoulders with him as he passed.

Jack rolled his eyes. He would need to talk to the boy, tell him that he really should be more discreet in public. Even with his friends, whom Eton obviously trusted. Even when they all accepted Jack as their new friend. Even if one's personal space here was considerably tighter than in America and casual touching and even hugging between male friends was nothing out of the ordinary. He just needed to be very careful, that boy.

… Well, provided he wasn't doing it for a purpose.

The evening was a hit. By the second tape, they had finished their third helping with three rounds of beer and the boys moved to the sofa to have an unobstructed view of the TV screen. Seva, Vadim and Yura lounged on the three-seater, their arms and legs touching, with Gosha on the carpeted floor, leaning back against the couch, his head almost resting on Seva's lap. Eton sprawled out on a chair next to Yura, who slapped him on his leg excitedly from time to time, commenting on a passage from a song or a riff. They were completely at home, sometimes ignoring Jack and sometimes talking to him as if he was part of their tight-knit group, asking for his opinion, then booing him down when Jack said with a straight face he liked Sabrina and Modern Talking.

Jack sat next to Eton, his chair turned back to front, positioned slightly further back to better see his friend out of the corner of his eye. After a while, he stood up, dropping his hand casually on Eton's shoulder, and asked if everyone would like tea or coffee. He was rewarded with happy cheers, nods and grins, including one from the person for whom he did it.

They hadn't had another chance to be alone before the third video tape was finished and the gang suddenly realized that it was close to midnight and time to leave. While his guests were putting on their shoes and jackets at the door, Jack dashed into the kitchen. He scribbled a few words on the edge of a local newspaper, tore it off and rolled it into a small ball. Then he turned to take a plastic bag with salami and canned ham out of the fridge and hurried back to his guests. He gave Gosha the bag, saying that it was a belated birthday present from him. It provoked a torrent of thanks from the very pleased boy and approving nods from the rest of the crowd.

Jack saw his guests out to the street and accompanied them for a block toward the Metro station to make sure that they were not harassed by the *militsia* men. When he noticed that he and Eton were walking side-by-side behind the rest of the group, Jack pretended to stumble, bumped into Eton and stealthily deposited the tiny paper ball into his jeans' back pocket.

"You alright?" Eton stopped walking.

Jack winked at him and mouthed, "Back pocket. Read at home".

The corners of Eton's lips curled up as he nodded.

Back in his apartment, Jack quickly cleaned up the sitting room, grinning like a fool. For once, he was pleased with what he had been taught at the Farm—the brush-pass skills once again proving to be useful. He hoped Eton would be pleased too when he got home and read the note, which said, "Will call tomorrow 4 o'clock".

Chapter 29

The weather had been just short of perfect since Thursday: warm, sunny and radiant, and even the bare trees looked frugally elegant, like in a Chinese aquarelle, against the cloudless blue sky. It was as if the autumn had decided to make a final statement before giving in to months of miserable cold.

It was just after two o'clock when Jack got home from a softball game, between American and English-Australian teams this time. He quickly showered, put on a pair of dark, nondescript slacks, a plaid shirt and old tennis shoes, took his jean jacket and left again. He flagged down a taxi four blocks from his apartment, alighted near the Revolution Square downtown, and took the Metro to Izmailovsky Park.

There was an informal art and flea market at the northern end of the vast park that the authorities let the locals run. One could find just about anything here, from decent paintings and sculptures by little known artist to broken brick-a-brack sold by their owners as antique, from goat-fur socks, shawls and gloves, to dry and pickled mushrooms sold by kindly *babushkas*. Besides this semi-official entrepreneurial outlet and the formal "recreational and cultural park", Izmailovo boasted one of the largest urban forests within the boundaries of Moscow. It was the perfect place to get oneself lost, be it alone amongst the multitude of people milling around the marketplace, or with a friend in the miles and miles of woods.

At four o'clock, he called Eton from a *taxaphone*.

Eton answered on the second ring, sounding rushed. "Da."

"*Privet*. It's me."

"*Privet*."

He didn't say anything else but Jack knew he was waiting for Jack to tell where he wanted them to meet.

"I'm at Izmailovsky Park."

"You want me to come out there?"

"Can you?"

"Will be on my way in five minutes."

"You'll be taking the Metro?"

The Metro was usually the fastest way to get anywhere in town—*if* you lived near a Metro station. Jack didn't know how far from the Metro Eton lived. It could be an hour and a half or even more if he didn't live anywhere near it.

"I'll drive. It will be faster. I will be there in forty-five, fifty minutes. Where shall I meet you?"

"I'll be waiting at the exit of the Metro station. Say, at five?"

"Will be there at five."

Jack strolled towards the flea market, feeling jubilant and edgy at the same time, occasionally snatching stealthy glances behind to see if he had any followers today. He didn't. And that left him with mixed feelings, yet again. He tried to push out of his mind the implications of not being shadowed and instead focus on enjoying the beautiful, sunny afternoon. Which he would soon be spending with his friend Eton Volkonsky... In thirty-five minutes.

Thirty-five? He thought at least an hour had passed since he'd talked to him...

At 5:00 p.m., Jack was leaning against the front wall of the bulky, square-columned structure that was the exit of the Metro Station Izmailovky Park. He was halfway through his cigarette when Eton appeared from behind the corner of the building.

He was wearing a pair of stonewashed jeans and a purplish-gray long sleeved jersey, the rolled up jeans jacket in his left hand. He looked more foreign than Jack today. More American, if Jack was asked for an opinion, someone you could easily run into anywhere in San Francisco or Washington.

"Sorry. I'm late again," he said in Russian as they shook hands and smiled apologetically. "Had to look for a place to park."

"No worries. I'm just having a smoke here." Jack grinned back, feeling ridiculously pleased.

Eton gave him a look over. "You look different today."

"I do?"

"Thought you always wore denim clothes," he noted shyly.

The guy was observant, too. Good spy material.

Jack shrugged. "Yes, I normally do. But sometimes you want to look like everybody else around you... Right?"

The smile slipped off Eton's face. "Right. I understand."

"Great... So, what would you say we take a walk in the park? We can talk and... maybe go to a movie later on..." Jack wasn't sure yet how far he wanted to go with the young man today.

Yeah, right...

Alright, so he hadn't figured out a place yet for what he really had in mind. With Eton. He was struggling to come up with a place where he could take the operation to the next level. But there was nobody here with whom he could brainstorm about this part of the op, so he had to scramble on his own.

Apparently, Eton noticed his hesitation. He said nothing, just nodding a faint smile, but Jack thought he'd heard a stifled sigh as he turned away.

They strolled in silence at first, then, as they entered the park's grounds, Jack turned to his friend. "You know what? I've decided that I should learn more about the nuclear winter theory."

Eton looked at him in surprise, but didn't say anything, waiting for him to continue.

"I mean, I want to know everything about it: how it started, why, where, by whom. Well, you've told me bits and pieces about it already, but I want to do my own little research project. And I'd also like to understand why you guys disagree on… On whatever you disagree."

"Are you serious?"

"I am. You see, I have handled quite a number of projects so far, but have never taken time to get to the heart of any of them. In my line of business, you don't really need to get to the heart of the matter to be able to coordinate a project. Understanding the gist of it usually suffices. The most important thing is knowing what's required of you." Actually, this was as true of his covert job as of his overt one.

They turned left from the central alley onto a small lane leading deep into the park.

"Why the nuclear winter theory? It is not the only project you're in charge of, is it?" Eton asked, sounding skeptical.

And Jack had thought that the guy would be pleased that he was interested in his project. What was his problem, anyway? Or was it Jack who wasn't getting something about his future agent?

"True, I have others. But I thought maybe you'd help me with this one?"

Eton stopped in his tracks. "You want *me* to help you?"

"Yes. If you don't mind, of course."

"No, I don't! Sorry, I thought you were going to…" Eton looked relieved. "Never mind. Yes, of course I'll help you." He set off walking again. "Although, I must admit, it's not one of my favorite subjects."

"Is it not? Why so?" Jack was surprised. "I thought since your grandfather was the author of this theory, it would be only natural for you to… No?"

Eton shrugged. "He is *one* of the original authors. So was Alexin. Who interpreted the modeling results differently… Somehow people keep forgetting that."

"How different is this different?"

Eton cut a glance at Jack, the corners of his mouth inching up. "You want all technical details or a figurative explanation?"

"A figurative version will do for now… Until you've taught me the technical aspects." Jack arched his eyebrows at him.

"Alright. Let me ask you first. Have you ever been to London?"

"No. Why?"

"Neither have I." Eton tilted his head, poker-faced. "But I've read that they have heavy smog there often… Don't suppose you've been to Mars, either." He turned to check on Jack's reaction and grinned when he saw Jack's face. "Just preparing the background for the picture."

Jack shot him a glare. Smartass!

"So, in very rough strokes, here's a snapshot. Grandfather's model projects that the area where all nuclear bombs have been dropped will resemble Mars. Alexin's model, on the other hand, projects that it will resemble London in seriously heavy smog."

"I see…"

"Admittedly, those climatic conditions, whatever they are, will last for a long time."

"For how long?"

"For a month. Several months. Maybe a year... We don't know."

"What do you mean you don't know? What do the models show?"

Eton let out a long sigh. He stopped, fumbled for his cigarettes and offered them to Jack.

"The key problem of both models is that the consequences of the type of nuclear exchanges we're modeling are unpredictable. Incalculable."

"What does *that* mean?" Jack was completely lost now.

Eton sighed again and took a couple of hard pulls on his cigarette. "It's difficult to explain without technical details... Jack, do you mind if we drop this topic for now? Until you have read up on it? I'll give you some materials... Is that alright?"

"Alright. I'll have a read. And I'll be interested to read the very first study on the subject. If you got one."

"I'll see what I can find... Do you want to carry on along this path?"

They were standing near the end of the asphalted alley, which continued as a dirt path deep into the forest. Jack threw a quick glance behind them, then at the path, and finally at the young man standing next to him. The park alley behind them was deserted and Eton was waiting for his answer, his glance flicking from Jack's eyes to his mouth and back.

Damn! Jack knew the need so well. "Yeah, let's continue." He smiled weakly and swallowed, conscious of the heat that had ignited below his waist and started spreading.

They sat off along the pathway carpeted with fallen leaves and framed by groves of birches, aspens, ashes and maple trees. Some of the trees were bare, some still trying to hold onto their pale green, yellow and russet foliage, tinted with shimmering golden hue by the late afternoon sun. They walked side by side, the silence becoming more charged with each passing second, the yearning almost palpable. Then Eton veered off the trail and, without looking to see if Jack was following him, headed into the birch grove. Jack didn't need prompting.

When the trail disappeared from the sight, Eton halted abruptly and swirled around. He took a quick step back as Jack was still walking forward and they collided in a full-bodied embrace, hands flying everywhere, trying to grab and pull the other as close as humanly possible, mouths hungrily fumbling for a place to land, lips to devour, taste to savor.

"Jaack..." Eton moaned into his neck, just below his ear, the sound sending an electrical current through Jack's body.

"Yeah," he rasped, grinding against Eton, trying to catch his mouth again.

Jack wasn't big on kissing, but this, Jesus, this was just... No, he couldn't find the words for *this* right now. But he didn't need words, all he needed was *this*.

Eton propelled him backwards and pushed against the nearest tree, his shaking hands struggling to unbutton Jack's shirt in an attempt to get closer to his chest and shoulders. Jack held Eton's head fast between his hands, his tongue deep in Eton's eager mouth.

A young voice suddenly called out somewhere nearby, "Come on, Grandma. That's enough. The basket is almost full of mushrooms already. Can we go home now?"

An elderly voice grumbled something in response, further away.

Eton wrenched out of Jack's hands and jerked back two steps, looking past Jack, wide-eyed, breathing heavily.

Jack snapped back to reality. "Eton," he hissed, buttoning up his shirt with swift fingers, the part of his mind that was trained for hostile situations immediately in control. "Eton, look at me." He smiled reassuringly at him. "They haven't seen us, alright? Your clothes."

Eton looked down, adjusted himself and let out a shaky breath. "I'm sorry," he whispered in English, avoiding Jack's eyes.

"It's alright."

It was *not* alright. In fact, it was a bitch of a situation, but what could he do? What could *they* do?

"Let's get ourselves out of here," Jack said. Eton nodded gloomily and his heart sank a little. "We'll figure something out. Don't worry." He didn't have a solution, but felt compelled to say something to cheer his friend up a little.

They headed back towards the forest trail and in a minute caught up with the mushroom hunters, a young teenage girl and her grandma with a basketful of mushrooms and a bouquet of pretty golden leaves in their hands. Eton only nodded to them, but Jack greeted the two cheerfully, asked them about their trophies, then they parted ways, the womenfolk marching back to the park's main alley, they in the opposite direction.

They trudged in silence for a few minutes, hands deep in their pockets, each watching his own feet, half a meter of empty space between them.

Finally, Jack heaved a sigh and said, "There must be a place, right? I just don't trust any place that I know here... I wish we were back home. In California."

"What about my place?"

Jack peered into his face. He didn't know that he could trust Eton's place either. But then, if this was part of the ploy to get him, then he might as well take advantage of the situation. Right? He would get another taste of this great lay and let them frame him. He wasn't going to make it easy for them though.

"You sure you want to bring a foreigner home?"

"We can wait till it is dark. There will not be many people out and around... And if someone asks, we will tell them that you are an *aspirant*. A Russian language post-grad student... From Yugoslavia."

"From Yugoslavia?" Jack studied him with interest.

"Yes. Nobody will know you're not... Maybe we won't even meet anyone."

Oh, fuck it, he would think of how to report about this unplanned visit to Eton's place later. It just so happened that in the course of his assignment Eton invited him and he decided that it was a perfect follow-up to the Russians' visit to his place the day before. A great opportunity for building up rapport with his target, right?

"Okay, Eton. Let's do it. Your place, then." He was all business again, suddenly feeling such an uplift that he laughed quietly. "After dark, right? OK, let's go back in the park and find something to eat. Before it gets dark."

When they got back to the market area, the place was winding down for the day and was virtually empty, most of the buyers and peddlers gone. They found the last *shashlyk* stall still open, bought the remaining three skewers of grilled pork and two bottles of warm Baltika beer for three rubles, and ate their dinner standing up at a high table near the stall. They chatted to the elderly Armenian couple who ran the stall as they were closing down for the night, mostly Jack did: told them that he was from Yugoslavia, his name was Aton Voykovich and he was doing his post-grad dissertation on the Decembrists at MGU. He stole a quick glance Eton's way as he was spinning his story and laughed when he saw a poorly hidden baffled look on his friend's face.

After their dinner, they picked up Eton's car and drove to Belyaevo. They took a roundabout route, staying out until close to 9:00 p.m., the time when the Soviet families gathered around their TV sets for the evening news, some with their dinners. They didn't talk much, comfortable in their companionable silence, sharing a cigarette, then another one, listening to Soviet pop and oldies on Radio Moskva. As they were nearing Eton's place, they agreed that Jack would get out on the main road, wait for fifteen minutes, before walking up to Eton's apartment on the tenth floor.

It was dark when Eton parked at the curb, a block away from his apartment building. He repeated the entrance and apartment numbers twice, eyeing Jack intently, like he was trying to make sure that Jack wasn't going to change his mind.

Jack smiled and patted him reassuringly on his knee. "I'll see you in fifteen minutes or so." He didn't feel as confident as he knew he appeared.

When the car rolled off, Jack lingered on the corner of the street, lit a cigarette, covertly scanning the surroundings. Aside from the light traffic on the road, the sidewalks were virtually empty. Satisfied with his inspection, he walked in the direction the car had gone, towards the inner courtyards and multiple entrances of the mammoth hulk of the apartment block. He only ran into one young couple, scurrying toward the entrance to the right of Eton's. He rode the elevator to the sixth floor, then took the stairs the rest of the way up, just in case.

As he was standing in front of Eton's apartment, Jack could hear the opening lines of the national news program *Vremya*, The Time, from behind the three neighbors' doors; the smell of sour cabbage soup *stchi* was seeping out of the apartment on the far right. He took a deep breath, unsure what was making him so nervous, the prospect of being framed by the KGB here, tonight, or... No, that was it. He was nervous because he might be framed by the KGB — a normal reaction, right?

The door opened almost as soon as he pressed on the bell, as if Eton had been standing right behind it, waiting. His face creased into a relieved smile. "Come in." He let Jack in and closed the door quickly behind him. "Come in, please," he repeated, in English this time. "Please make yourself at home."

"Thanks, Eton. I'll try."

The apartment was a standard Soviet affair: a short corridor leading to two rooms to the left of the door and, to the right, a toilet, a bathroom and a kitchen, in that order. Not too different from the one Jack lived in, with two small bedrooms along a narrow corridor and a sitting room at the end. It had a familiar smoky smell about it too, a masculine smell, and also of burnt solder wire and coffee and pine-fresh scent of soap. From where he stood near the door, Jack could see only a small part of the furnishing in the sitting room—mahogany-colored wall cabinets, a corner of a table and a chair of the same color, a thin woven carpet on the floor.

There was a metallic click at the door, the sound of the chain lock falling into place. Jack let out a quiet exhale: there would be no staged break-in today then, the type he had been told about at the Farm, when they caught a foreigner red-handed at the place of his local "friend's" place in the act of something illegal—like making out with him, for instance—and blackmailed into working for them.

"Are you hungry?" Eton asked behind his back.

Jack turned around.

"Or maybe tea… or coffee…"

The young man stood close behind him, hands deep in his pockets, biting his lip, looking like he wasn't sure what he was supposed to do next. His eyes were dark and smoldering. And he was staring at Jack's mouth again, with that hungry look that was becoming so familiar so quickly.

Jack reached out, caught him by the front of his jersey and pulled him close. "Yes, I'll have some… later," he whispered and covered Eton's mouth with his.

Eton's arms wrapped around him immediately and he pressed his whole body into Jack's, aroused and breathless. He went straight back to unbuttoning Jack's shirt. When he was done with the buttons, he pushed the shirt off Jack's shoulders, peeled his undershirt off his body, pulled back a little and rasped, "Let me look at you."

"What?" Jack opened his eyes, disoriented, struggling to understand why the exquisite pressure had gone from his body.

"I want to see you." He raised both of his hands, touched Jack's face, then shoulders, traced them down his chest, his sides, his back, the caresses feather-light, as if Jack's body was some precious object that should be handled with the utmost care. "I'll be done just by looking at you," he murmured, breathing heavily, his eyes hazed over, like he was going to shoot any second now.

"No, wait!" Jack shook him by his biceps. "Not yet." He started unfastening Eton's belt quickly with one hand, working on his own with the other. "Have to lose these… C'mon, Eton!"

Eton snapped out of his near gone state and started feverishly pulling off his jersey, together with his t-shirt.

"Bedroom?"

"Yes."

They fought their way to the bedroom, leaving pieces of clothing scattered on the floor, unable to keep their hands off each other for even a moment. They fell on the bed, still not fully unclothed, arms and legs around each other, rutting against each other like they were trying to crawl into one another's skin.

It didn't take long for them to reach the place where nothing else mattered but them, both were so far gone. And when they came, one after the other, each stifled his joy against the other's body, the last shreds of awareness reminding them to keep it down, even within the confines of their own little private space. Then both drifted off, stunned and washed-out by the explosive power of their releases, still tangled up, like they were never going to let go. And in the fleeting moment before slumber overtook him, Jack wished that the intensity of these sensations, this inexplicable ecstasy would lessen the next time round. Because he knew he couldn't let himself get addicted to *this*, whatever "this" was that this man gave him.

Chapter 30

The first thing that registered with Jack when he came around was the feeling of wholeness and peace he didn't remember having recently. Or maybe ever. Like he belonged here, wherever it was that he was now, with someone lying next to him, their bare leg touching his, their breath on the side of his face. He then recalled that he was at Eton's place. That he had just had sex with him. In his bed.

Jack opened his eyes.

The room was full of shadows that skirted around a single source of light, a lamp under a gold and brown shade on the bedside table to Jack's left. It looked cluttered with books and also some electronic equipment, but Jack couldn't make out yet what it was, because his eyes went immediately to the man next to him.

Eton was lying on his right side, folded arm under his head, watching Jack's face with a strange soft look in his eyes that Jack had caught on him twice before. Both times, Eton had dropped his gaze and his whole face had slammed shut. This time, though, he didn't take his eyes away, and the expression stayed.

"Hey," Jack smiled at him, stretching a little. "You alright?"

"It was, um..." Eton knitted his eyebrows, looking a little pained, then blurted out, "Astounding. No... I have no right word for it."

"Mind-blowing," Jack offered, his smile growing. As was the pressure below his waist. He wasn't sure how long they had been dozing, but apparently, it was enough for the sated feeling to wear off and the long-neglected yearning to start building up again.

"Right. And we haven't even done anything yet... Have we?" Eton's expression was both shy and hopeful.

"No, we haven't." Jack was aware that he was now grinning like a fool, but he didn't care. He really liked this man—he could read Jack's mind where it mattered. He rolled onto his side to face Eton and pushed a knee between his legs, pulling him close by his waist. "C'mere."

Eton's breath hitched as he pressed himself against Jack's thigh. He extended his right arm under Jack's neck and wrapped it around his shoulders, his left arm grabbing and pulling at Jack's waist at the same time. "I want you," he whispered, running his hand over Jack's erection. "Like last time."

"Okay... But not so fast," Jack sucked in a breath, trying not to give in to the overwhelming pleasure. "We need to do this right this time."

"Okay..." He pulled at Jack's hand and pressed his fingers onto himself.

Jack tried to unwrap himself from Eton's embrace. "I need a condom."

"A what?" Eton pulled back and stared at Jack, his expression blank. He didn't let go of Jack's hand though.

He was right: Eton knew nothing about the safe sex rules between men. Which meant he probably didn't know about AIDS either. Jack sighed mentally. He wished he'd told

Eton about AIDS while they were on their way here. Somehow it had felt too forward, too clinical, to talk about it at the time.

"I need to use a condom, Eton. For *your* protection."

Shit, why was it so hard? So he'd been with God knows who, so what? Why should he feel awkward telling a new guy about it?

"Why? Are you alright?" Eton demanded, but there was only concern in his voice, not fear, nor repulsion.

"I think I am... I don't know. I haven't got myself tested yet. We should have used it the first time, too. I just didn't have... Never mind. I'm sorry." He pulled his hand from Eton's and rolled onto his back. Now he could forget about sex with Eton.

"But what is it? For what haven't you been tested?"

"You know anything about AIDS? Acquired immune deficiency syndrome? No? I'll tell you all about it later. For right now, all you need to know is this, Eton: you can contract it through unprotected sex... with men. Once you get it, it'll kill you, sooner or later. 'Cause there's no cure for *it*."

There was something like fear now in Eton's eyes. But instead of moving away from Jack, he rocked forward onto him, put his palm flat on Jack's chest and peered deep into his eyes. "What about you?"

"No, I don't think I have it! Don't have any symptoms. And I've been, um, careful... But, still, I don't know for sure. And I want to be sure." He brushed the back of his fingers along Eton's jaw. "Don't want any chance of you being exposed to shit like this, bud... Or anyone else, for that matter," he added and shrugged, faking nonchalance, startled by the searing wave of anxiety that unfurled at the pit of his stomach.

Eton's expression relaxed, the corners of his lips arched up and he exhaled slowly. "You scared me... Thank you. For worrying about me." He leaned forward and nuzzled Jack's cheek.

"I'm sorry, Eton. I should have thought about it—"

"Don't worry about it. I will be fine. I'm sure you're fine, too." He sat up by Jack's side. "But if you think we should use a... eh, condom, okay, let's do that."

"You sure you still want me to—"

Eton bent down and placed a quick, bruising kiss on his lips. "Yes, I want you. Told you, Jack. I never wanted anything like this," he whispered fiercely in Jack face and let out a sad chuckle. "You don't understand."

No, he didn't. Maybe it was a Russian thing. He would try to figure it out later. For now, all he knew was that Eton still wanted to fuck.

"Alright. Gimme a minute."

He sprang up from the bed, picked up his slacks near the door of the bedroom and fumbled for his wallet. He sensed rather than saw Eton watching him intently as he pulled a pack of two condoms out of the wallet which he stuffed back into the pocket and dropped the slacks on the floor. He set the condoms on the bedside table and laid back down next to Eton. "Tell me what you want," Jack whispered huskily in the young man's ear, reaching down to fondle him.

"I want to look at you when you… take me." He caught Jack's fingers and pushed them between his parted legs. "Now, Jack… Please."

"Okay. Now it is."

And Jack gave it to him, what Eton wanted, the way he wanted. He rocked into him slowly at first, Eton's legs over his shoulders, pumping his silky-hard shaft in the same rhythm, then he picked up pace when Eton closed his eyes, his head thrashing on the pillow, biting on the edge of one palm to stifle the moans. When Eton erupted in his hand, Jack let himself fall over the edge, too, once again caught by surprise by the explosion of pure, undiluted pleasure. And by a tangle of emotions he didn't understand. Didn't want to think about them right then. And about the peculiar look in Eton's eyes that he didn't hide anymore. Bah, he was Russian; they said nobody could understand the Russian soul, so Jack shouldn't even pretend he did. Just let him be… Let it be…

Jack woke up with a start, a thought that he was late for something immediately springing to mind. He opened his eyes and tried to roll onto his back, but couldn't. Only then did he register an arm wrapped around his waist, a warm body pressed against his back, hot breath at the back of his head and the musky smell of sex.

Eton.

The young man stirred behind him and pulled Jack closer into his front. Jack's eyes darted to the alarm clock on the bedside table. 11:42 p.m.

"Eton." He tugged at the arm wrapped around his waist.

"Mmm." Eton inhaled deeply, pressing his nose and mouth into the nape of Jack's neck.

"It's almost midnight… I have to go."

He had never felt bothered—in fact, he hadn't felt anything at all—when he used this line so many times before. Somehow, this time it scraped his insides like sandpaper. Jack wiggled slowly around in Eton's arms, draped his arm over his waist and pressed his forehead against his.

Eton's eyes were closed, his face a blank mask. But he didn't move away either, which was good, considering the circumstances.

"I'm sorry, Eton. I can't stay… You know that, right?" Jack dragged the tip of his forefinger along Eton's lips and they parted, letting out a breath. A sigh.

He finally opened his eyes and forced a little smile. "I understand… I will drive you home." He sat up quickly, then got up, leaving Jack startlingly lonely in his bed.

"I'll take the Metro." Jack sprung up too and started collecting his clothes from the floor. "Do you mind if I take a quick shower in your bathroom?"

"Of course, please. I will get you a fresh towel… Then I will drive you to your Metro station," he added under his breath.

Eton was heading out of the bedroom when Jack caught him by his arm. "Eton, I'm sorry." Jack sighed, feeling like an asshole. "But it would be better if you are not seen taking me home after midnight."

"I understand *that*. But if you think it would be better for *me*, then don't worry about it. Tell me what works, or doesn't work, for *you*." He smiled weakly and dragged a fingertip from Jack's shoulder to the middle of his chest. "Let me get you a towel."

They agreed that Jack would leave first and walk along Profsoyuznaya Street, which ran in front of Eton's apartment block all the way to the city center. Eton would pick him up in his car in about ten minutes and take him downtown where Jack would take the Metro back to his place. They clenched in a bear hug in front of the door, Eton said, "See you in ten minutes", and closed the door quickly as Jack sneaked out onto the landing.

The sound of an action movie was coming from behind of the door next to Eton's, nothing from the other two. Jack walked stealthily down the stairs, all the way to the ground floor, and closed the entrance door quietly behind him. He strode to the main street and headed toward the city center along the wide tree-lined footpath that ran parallel to the main road.

Eton caught up with him when he was close to the nearest Metro station. He stopped the car at the curb, a few meters ahead of Jack, keeping the engine running. Jack quickly cut across the lawn that separated the pavement from the road, got into the car.

Eton took off the moment the door was closed. "You're fast," he said and handed a cigarette he was smoking to Jack.

"Didn't think sauntering around on the street after midnight was a good idea... for a foreigner."

Eton stole a quick glance his way. "You don't look too out of place dressed like that. Besides, there're lots of foreign students living around this area."

Jack took a few deep drags on the cigarette and passed it back to Eton. He didn't like what he was going to say, but he had no choice, if he was to continue his friendship with this young man, the way he was hoping it could be. The way he needed it to be.

"Eton, I need you to *fully* understand what we've got ourselves into. I'm not sure you do," he said, looking straight ahead of him, and only when he finished speaking did he turn to Eton.

"I *do* understand. But please go ahead if you think we need to go by your rules."

Jack sighed. "They're not *my* rules. They are precautions we must take if we are going to be friends and to... see each other. Do you want it?"

Eton cut a quick glance at him, his face solemn. "Yes, I want it. I will do what you think we must, Jack."

"Great. Because if we aren't careful, you'll end up somewhere in Siberia and I'll be thrown out of here in a heartbeat." Well, not exactly: it was the last thing that would happen, once the KGB was done with them both.

"I could also be blackmailed by the KGB into... um, reporting to them." He passed the cigarette to Jack. "Not sure about you. You're a diplomat. They might just throw you out of the country."

Jack took the last draw on their cigarette, rolled the side window down a fraction and threw it outside. "I'd be blackmailed before you, actually. I'm an American, remember?"

Eton's head jerked around at that. "But you're a cultural officer..."

"A diplomat. From the American Embassy." Jack arched his brows emphatically.

There was an oh-shit kind of silence, then Eton said, "I'm sorry. I hadn't thought about *that*."

"Now you know… Sometimes they even attempt to trap us with this kind of ploy. I mean with sex. Because we are not supposed to have… um, *relationships* with locals."

Shit, he absolutely hated playing cat and mouse with this man.

There was a long moment of loaded silence, before Eton asking quietly, "You think I am… such a trap?"

Fuck it! He didn't want to believe it and he wanted Eton to know it.

"I don't want to think you are, Eton. I just want us to be… friends."

Friends? You're such a fucking sham, Smith!

I do want to be friends with him! The best of friends. And fuck the Company, fuck Joe, fuck the KGB!

They were nearing a big crossroad where the avenue split into two parallel roads. Eton took the right lane and turned into the smaller inner road lined with two neat rows of trees, almost bare of their leaves. He stopped the car at the curb and cut off the engine. Except for very light traffic on the main road, the street was deserted.

Eton stared into the night for a long moment, took a deep breath and turned to Jack. "Jack. I know what I'm going to say will not make any sense to you. You may even think that I am a fool. That's alright. If it can stop you thinking that I am a KGB trap."

"I don't—"

"No, let me say it, please… So… Um, when I was nine, I had an imaginary friend. His name was Jack. He lived in California, on a ranch. And I wrote a diary to him for many years. Then two months ago, I met you. And you turned out to be, um, like I had always imagined *him*. So, Jack from California, you *are* my best friend. Whether you want it or not. And if you can't reciprocate, that is fine, too. I understand. After all, you have known me only for two months. For *you*, I am just a student in your exchange program."

"Eton, that's not—"

"Please, let me finish… Yes, I know the consequences of being a homosexual here. And you have just made me realize what can happen to an American diplomat like you if… if *they* know. Jack, if you think that being associated with me will cause you trouble, I shall not seek meetings with you anymore. I shall disappear. The only thing I am asking is for you to believe me. I am *not* with the *organs*. I shall never work for them! Even if I may end up in Siberia for who I am… Do you believe me? Jack?" He tilted his head a little, peering into Jack's face, a jumble of emotions flickering on his own.

Jack bit on the inside of his cheek, his stomach in knots. He felt like he would suffocate if he didn't say what was on his mind, right here right now. But he couldn't, not without jeopardizing the whole operation, not without admitting that…

No, you can't do that!

Shit, he was in such a mess! *He* was such a mess…

"Yes, Eton. I believe you." He forced a pained smile and swallowed hard. "And it means the world to me that you think of me as you friend. Thank you, bud." He twisted in his seat and leaned over. He gripped Eton by the neck, pulled him closer and rested his forehead against Eton's.

Eton surged toward him, cupped the side of his face with one hand, seeking his mouth. "Jack…"

"Oh, Christ, Eton! You'll be the death of me, I swear," he mumbled, laughing helplessly, touched Eton's lips softly with his own and pushed him back in his seat. "C'mon, now. Take me home, friend."

* * *

On Monday, the snowballing spy and defection scandal reached the Embassy in the form of feature articles carried by all major American newspapers. Not only did they provide sensitive details about Vitaly Yurchenko's background, they chronicled the saga of Edward Lee Howard, a CIA-created traitor who had been selling the Agency's assets to the KGB. The articles quoted affidavits by Howard's ex-colleagues, showing that he had turned up on the FBI's radar screen a year before Yurchenko's defection.

Apparently, fired by the Agency on the eve of his Moscow assignment, Howard had confided to two of his friends, both CIA employees, that he had been contemplating going to the Soviet Embassy in Washington DC to offer information. Yet, he had continued working as a government employee in Santa Fe, New Mexico. Until the CIA had shared the information on Howard obtained from Yurchenko with the FBI and the bureau had finally issued a warrant for his arrest. The following day, Howard had disappeared from under the FBI's 24/7 surveillance, simply vanished. That was a week ago, and the FBI was still looking for the man.

As if that was not enough, The Washington Post carried a feature article about the CIA assets that Howard had sold to the KGB. In particular, the newspaper recounted the story of Adolf Tolkachev, an engineer at a closed research facility in Moscow, who had been the Agency's most valuable asset in the Soviet Union for many years. Quoting affidavits in Howard's case, the article wrote that Tolkachev had been providing the CIA with information on Soviet avionics, cruise missiles, and other technologies, and that he had been arrested by the KGB in July. Thus, the fate of GTVANQUISH was exposed to the public.

It was a complete nightmare and Jack was sure that other officers, including senior staff, were as baffled by the unprecedented leakage. The difference was that he couldn't share his worries with anyone here, except maybe the chief of Station.

The only positive side of the scandal, as far as Jack was concerned, was that it kept the management's attention focused on the progress of Yurchenko and Howard cases as they evolved, holding back the development of new assets and projects. As a result, Jack didn't feel much pressure to move aggressively ahead with his assignments. And he still hadn't heard back from Joe about their next briefing on SEABROOK. Jack suspected that other new and existing Soviet operations had been put on the back burner, too, with the priority given to the damage control activities that he wasn't part of.

Which was just fine by him. It gave him time to come up with a solid story for his next meeting with his Division's head of ops, when he would have to report on his progress in building up the friendship with his future agent, Eton May Volkonsky, codename GTSALT.

Chapter 31

October 7, Monday. 1:37 a.m.

Dear Jack,

Glad you let me take you at least to your metro station. It was night, Jack. Nobody saw us.

Can't believe I told you about Jack the Little Cowboy. Not only that, I hinted that I think of you as him. You must think now that I am an idiot. A romantic fool who failed to grow up.

Doesn't matter. As long as you stop thinking that I'm with the organs. That I might be a trap.

I am not offended. I understand why you would think that. You must think that ANY Soviet person who likes you and wants to be friends with you potentially is an informer. Is that it? It must be lonely not to be able to trust anyone. Hope you have friends amongst your own people that you can trust. I wish I could do something for you. So no, I am not offended. Just cannot bear you not trusting me. I would do anything for you, Jack. Anything! But of course you don't know that.

Maybe you don't think I am a fool: you said it means the world to you that I think of you as a friend. You called me "friend". And before that, you wanted to protect me. From yourself, just in case. You didn't want any chance of me being exposed to it. Acquired immunity deficit syndrome, or whatever you called it. Only someone who cares would do that for you, deprive themselves of the pleasure they could get. I know, you liked being with me. I saw it on your eyes. Perhaps you got almost as much pleasure from being with me as I being with you.

"Almost" because it means much more to me than it does to you. I know it, too. And that is okay. I love you, Jack.

E.

October 9, Wednesday. 11:08 p.m.

Dear Jack,

I have put together a list of articles and research materials on NWT for you. Need to find a way to give them to you. Maybe you will call me this week.

I have been thinking: why are you interested in NWT? I tried to look at it through your eyes. You are right: it is not the theoretical, scientific premise that is important whenever nuclear weapons are involved. It is the idea of us, both our sides, using nature's intrinsic powers to destroy nature itself. And ourselves. We, humans, are self-destructive. And we, nuclear physicists, feed this self-destructive trait with our work. Is this what you think too?

E.

October 10, Thursday. Nearly midnight.

Dear Jack,

Gosha told me today that Deputy Dean Smetannik had asked him about our visit to your place, what we had done and who else had been there. Gosha has been telling everybody about the visit and LiveAid concert tapes since weekend. And about you. He likes you. A lot. Problem is he talks too much. I told him to watch his mouth.

I have made copies of your tapes for everyone. Now I have to give them back to you. Together with the list of the reading materials on NWT. It actually contains some materials that can only be read at Lenin Library. If you have a pass, perhaps we should go there together. I will show you how to find them.

I will call you tomorrow.

Or not: You said I should only call you about "social events", like movies, concerts, discotheques. You would call me about the rest. I will have to wait until you call me.

Good night, Jack.

Long after midnight. Don't even know what time it is.

Does sex qualify as a "social event"?

Sorry, I am being stupid. ~~It is just~~ I miss you.

My bed feels so cold and empty I can barely stand to sleep in it.

Maybe I should not have brought you home.

Never thought it is possible to miss something or someone this much. It drives me crazy. What will I do when you are gone?

I am a romantic fool, Jack, but I am not stupid. And I try to be honest at least to myself: I know you will leave this country one day and I will not see you ever again.

E.

October 11, Friday. 9:47 p.m.

Dear Jack,

I was summoned to DD Smetannik's office this afternoon. He started with some nonsense about some Komsomol activities that I had missed, etc. Then he gave a long-winded speech about special interests of the country, that everybody with connections to westerners should help the motherland, that I am well positioned to do this and it is good for my career prospects etc. etc. Told him if he wanted me to be a stuckach, a rat, he should go talk to Grandfather.

I don't know what kind arrangement Grandfather has with them. He told me on my first day at the University that I might be called up and they might try to recruit me as a stukach. He told me that I should tell him about it immediately. And send them to talk to him. This is actually the third time they tried this with me. It worked the previous times. Should work this time, too.

But this brings up a question I have tried not to think about: why Grandfather can pull this trick over and over again? And once again, I do not want to think about it. I am a coward.

I won't mention this incident to you. You don't need to worry about such things. Yours always,

E.

October 13, Sunday. 0:35 a.m.

You didn't call yesterday. Hope you will today. And we will meet somewhere. I just want to talk to you.

Not true. I want more than just to talk to you. I want you all to myself. In my bed. In my arms. Does it make me selfish?

No, it makes me one big, utterly in love fool.

Talked to Artyom T. today. He said if I want to participate in the rock lab in Leningrad, I have to register by the end of January. Said if I want to change some members of my band, he would help and introduce me to good musicians. He didn't say directly, but I know he thinks that for rock-labs we need a more technical drummer than Sevka. A professional.

I can't do this to Sevka — he has been dreaming of playing at a rock festival for years. Have to come up with something, so he can play with us.

I also must prepare for the festival. Need to write at least three good pieces by January. Not worth entering otherwise.

This is it, what I have always wanted. I know you are with me on this, cowboy. You told me I should play more because I am good at it. So I will.

Midnight.

Just finished reading the articles about AIDS in the magazine you gave me. Don't know what to say. Never heard about anything so horrifying before.

Now I am worried. You can't have it, Jack. You cannot! You said you had been careful. Did you mean you used protection?

It means that you had sex with others. One? Two? Many? Did you meet them at "gay bars" they write about in the articles? Sounds like there are a lot of them in San Francisco. Sounds like there are many gay people there.

I never asked if you ~~have~~ had "someone" in Calif. Someone like you must have many suitors, both men and women. Gregarious and friendly, admired by everybody. So beautiful that sometimes it hurts to look at you. How can you not have crowds of suitors? I know you have them here, too.

Maybe you are friends with me because you don't feel you can trust anyone else here. Why else someone like you would choose to be with a twenty-one-year-old like me? Who knew nothing about being with a man before you and may not even have another after you. It does not make much sense.

It means you trust me? You have chosen me to be your friend. Your special friend.

I'm sorry, I'm confused. And scared.

And I love you. Jack, I will hold you in my arms even if you have this gruesome illness. I will never let go.

No, I don't believe you have it.

Your friend always,

E.

October 14, Monday. 11:25 p.m.

Dear Jack,

I hope you didn't mind me calling you. I need to talk to you. Can't stop thinking about AIDS. About you. I could not say that on the phone.

Hope we can talk about it at Lenin Library. See you on Wednesday.

E.

October 16, Wednesday. 10:08 p.m.

Dear Jack,

Feeling better after talking to you. I'm sure you don't have "it". But I agree: you need to take the test to be 100% sure. And doing it in Helsinki is perhaps a good idea. Even though it means that I won't see you for a few weeks.

I will miss you. Can't wait for you to come to my place again.

Talking about my place. Last time we met, you asked how come I have it. And a car. You are right, it is unusual here for a young person like me to have an apartment and a car of my own. Most people don't. Hope you believe me and don't think that I have all this because I'm working for KGB.

It is sad, but I got my major possessions through my family's misfortune.

The apartment used to belong to my father. It was given to him by the government when he first came to the SU. Mother and I lived there too, until we moved to Grandparents' place. Father lived there until he died. Mother never got down to selling it. I think she feared even going there. So it remained unoccupied for many years. Grandma used to rent it out before she passed away. She had a heart attack a month after my uncle Seriozha died in Afghanistan in 1980.

When I was eighteen, I told my family I wanted to live there. On my own. It was when I realized I was gay. Mother and Grandfather were against it, but in the end, they gave in. All right, it was not that simple, but you got the gist.

Same thing with the car. I inherited it from uncle Seriozha. He taught me how to repair it and how to drive it the year Father died. He taught me to ride horses, too. Then in 1980, he was transferred to Turkmenistan, then Afghanistan. Three months later, he was killed in action. He was one of the first few officially killed on the Afghan soil, the first senior officer. He was a colonel. Awarded an order of the Hero of the Soviet Union. Posthumously.

That's the story of my family.

E.

October 17, Thursday. 11:25 p.m.

There is this thing that has been bothering me for the last 2 days: you seem too keen to learn all about the NWT. Seems right for someone who is coordinating a NW project. And the fact that you asked me to help also seems fair: you want us to be friends, right? Special friends. So this part is fine, too. But what is this about the "original NW project"? You have mentioned it three times. You said you wanted to read it. You implied that Grandfather was the author of this "original research" work. I'm not sure what work you meant and why it is so important for you. Maybe I should ask you next time we meet.

Maybe you will have your blood test results by then and would like to come to my place again.

God, I am pathetic! All I think about most of the time nowadays is sex. About "mind-blowing" sex — your words.

Does it feel like that for you too?

I have slept with 3 girls; one of them was very "experienced". But it was nothing like this. Not even close. So my question is: is it mind-blowing because it is with a man or because it is with you?

I have no proof, but suspect it is because it is with you.

E.

October 20, Sunday. 11:45 p.m.

Talked to my guys today about participating in the rock festival in Leningrad. They are all for it. I'm so glad. I'm sure we will make it. We have also come up with a solution for Sevka. He and I will take special classes at the conservatory from now until February—he for drums, I for guitar and instrumental composition. I need it too.

That will take all our free time and the time that is not free. Grandfather will be unhappy. But c'est la vie. He has been telling me for years that I am not focused on what I want to do. Now I am. It is a shame he and I want different things for me.

I want to ask Karelin to advise us on the staging of my rock composition. I know he will be happy to help. Just hope he is not too much in my face.

I wonder if he knows about me. He is not very discriminate about who he likes.

Or maybe he knows exactly who he likes, and it is those he likes who are hiding it ("closeted" is the word they used in your magazine). Like me. Like you.

He did not show any special interest in you though. A good thing too. Because I would have knocked him out flat in 2 seconds if he did. Maybe he can't tell about you. I never thought you could be like me. Not in thousand years!

I look at people differently now. Less judgmental perhaps. Thanks to you, my friend.

E.

October 23, Wednesday. 11:59 p.m. Not midnight yet!!

Dear Jack,

I am so glad! So relieved that I want to howl. I knew you didn't have that dreadful disease. Don't know how, but I knew in my heart that you didn't. Couldn't have it. Not you, cowboy.

About this "original" NW study: you said you had heard about it from Prof. Ackerman and now are interested to know about its origin. Then you gave a long-winded monolog, like you do sometimes. You almost lost me there, my friend. Mainly because I was too busy looking at you. But I got the message: that had you not been assigned to the NW project, you would not have met me. That is why this project is important to you.

I want to stretch it into thinking that meeting with me is important to you. I want to be important to you, Jack. I wish I could give you a fraction of what you have given me already. So if the NWT is important to you, so be it.

It is a shame that Prof. Ackerman left for home already. I could have asked him. Don't know if anyone else in his team knows anything about this "original" study.

How stupid I can be! Wouldn't asking Grandfather directly be the best? Don't know what is wrong with me today—I have been behaving, reasoning like a child since I saw you at Lenin Library this morning.

Ha, you have this strange effect on me: you reduce me to a breathless, mumbling, trembling, sex-starved mess. And the strangest thing, I am not ashamed of you learning about what you do to me.

Somehow, I feel you don't want to know. And that is okay, my friend. Moi vasil'yok. My blue cornflower.

E.

October 27, Sunday. 10:52 p.m.

Lara called this morning to ask if we want to use Karelin's studio for practicing. No doubt Karelin's idea. Doesn't matter. We will take him up on the offer. Don't want folks at MGU to know we are practicing for a rock festival.

Lara also said that she is going to the movies with you in the afternoon. And that you two might go to dinner afterwards. She said Anya and I should join you two next weekend. Told her I would think about it.

I am trying to look at it objectively:

A. We have met 12 times in around four months. Talked around twice as many times on the phone.

B. You have your life in which you are a "regular" ladies' man. I have mine in which I am "regular", too.

C. We had sex 4 times. According to you, it was mind-blowing. I have no words to even start describing it.

D. You said it means the world to you that I consider you my friend.

E. You implied that meeting me is important to you.

F. You have never said or implied that you will not go out with others, men or women, strangers or my friends.

Hence, there is absolutely no reason for me to want to kill someone. Or get completely drunk. For a week. For a month. So that I can finally stop wondering what works better for you on a Sunday afternoon - to be with Lara or with me.

I am sorry, Jack. You have given me no ground to think about it in these terms. It is just me. I just do. Because I ~~to~~ miss you.

E.

October 31, Thursday. 10:17 p.m.

Dear Jack,

I have read a very disturbing article in Literaturnaya Gazeta today, called "Panic in The West or What is Hiding Behind the Sensation Surrounding AIDS". It is written by someone who sounds like he knows what he is talking about. He quotes published sources, mostly American, including publicly available statistical evidence etc. Essentially, it says that AIDS was developed by the US military as a biological weapon and accidentally spread out as the result of the experiments on unsuspecting civilians. It lists other similar US covert biological warfare programs. The ones conducted in third-nations countries; the experiments currently conducted at Fort Detrick, Maryland, the place where AIDS has allegedly been created. According to this article, the US military has been testing it on people in Haiti and on drug addicts, homosexuals and homeless people in Calif. All unbeknownst to them.

This is very daunting. I don't want to believe it.

But what unsettles me most is that if I had not learned about AIDS from you before I read this article, I might have bought the story on the spot. Now I look at it with different eyes.

I have re-read the article 3 times. The evidences it gives are mostly circumstantial. The quoted statistical data is from a popular source, not from a scientific publication. I don't know, maybe I am grasping at straws here. I don't want to believe it. And I know most people here will.

I need to talk to you about it.

11:27 p.m.

Sorry, Jack, I had to call. I am glad I did because now I will see you on Sunday. And I am sorry I lied: I don't have tickets to the conservatory. Mother mentioned it the other day - she has been invited to a Shostakovich evening at the conservatory. It was the first "social" thing that came to my mind. But I will get the tickets if you want to go.

Or we can go to Artyom's place. He is hosting a rock band from Sverdlovsk. They are very good. They will be giving a small concert. Of course, it is all unofficial. That is the reality of the Soviet rock scene. Hope you don't mind. They will be thrilled to have you as a guest. Our rockers love Americans.

E.

November 2, Saturday. 0:05 a.m.

Jack,

I had dinner at Grandfather's this evening. After dinner, I asked him about his original NW study. He looked at me with surprise and asked where I had heard it from. I said from Prof. Ackerman. I didn't mention it was you who had heard it from Prof. Ackerman, not me. Don't even know why. Grandfather was surprised again, said that it had never been printed in any widely available publication. Then he said that maybe Alexin had told him about it. Then, Grandfather thought about it again and finally said that if it is not absolutely necessary for my research, maybe I don't need to read it. At that point, someone called him on the phone and we left it at that.

Jack, Grandfather has never before told me that I didn't need to read something if that something was related to scientific research. Why he doesn't want me to read one of his studies? What is there in that study that is not already known and controversial?

I am mystified.

E.

0:42 a.m.

Why do you want to read it, Jack?

Chapter 32

Jack was dazed. There seemed to be no end to the unfolding of the story of Yurchenko's defection. Since it first hit the news in late September, American newspapers and news channels had been carrying stories and opinions about the developments on a regular basis, including information obtained during "top-secret" debriefings of the Russian by the CIA and the FBI. Within days of the defection, The Washington Times published the first piece of classified information about Edward Lee Howard.

The Howard story immediately turned into a front-page news in its own right, complete with the coverage of the FBI's futile search for the man. In early October, the State Department confirmed that Yurchenko had defected in Rome. In the third week of October, The Wall Street Journal carried an editorial on Vitaly Yurchenko. He had revealed "a wealth of Soviet spy information", the paper said, noting that some of it had been made available by sources within the CIA. One of the leaked documents involved Adolf Tolkachev, the CIA's most valuable human assets in the Soviet Union. The article called his exposure by Howard "gross mismanagement and ineptitude" reaching to the highest levels at the Agency.

During the last week of October, NBC Nightly News and The Washington Post featured another story revealed by Yurchenko, this time about the fate of yet another defector and CIA's agent. Nicholas Shadrin, born Nicolai Artamonov, had defected to the US in late 60s when he was a torpedo destroyer commander in the Soviet Baltic Fleet, and had been working as a double agent for the CIA ever since. In the end, the Agency had failed to protect him: in 1975, the KGB had attempted to abduct Shadrin in Vienna, but the operation had been fouled up and he died in the process.

With all the bat crazy shit going on, everything the Company had taught Jack—how to handle agents, how to ensure that their identities and their lives were protected by all means—now looked rather rhetorical, to say the least. If any Soviet, who had been nurturing an idea of changing sides, read one of these stories, they would most probably kill the thought right away. And Jack wouldn't blame them. Besides, how useful is a defector's information, if it keeps ending up in the news before the CIA and FBI can do anything with it? Jesus!

Since the bizarre Yurchenko story started unfolding, Jack had only managed to exchange a few words about it with Nurimbekoff. Both times the Station chief had assured him that the Company was doing everything to identify and manage the leak, and that everything was under control. The hell it was! Now both Nurimbekoff and William had been recalled to HQ for two weeks and Jack had nobody to share his concerns with, or to get some insight on what was really going on, and it had left him both unsettled and irked.

One welcome disruption to his stalling undercover routine was Secretary of State Schultz's visit to Moscow in preparation for the summit scheduled for early November. Once again, Jack's Russian language skills were called into use: Ambassador Hart asked him to help the organizing committee. And Mrs. Hart, if he didn't mind.

Of course, Jack didn't mind. But as a result, he was asked to come in to work on Sunday, the eve of Schultz's arrival.

Working on Sunday was a letdown, though: he had agreed to meet with Eton on Sunday and go somewhere with him—a Shostakovich night at the conservatory, or anything else his friend could think of for them to do. He preferred "anything else" and suspected that Eton might want to as well. Now their plans would have to be put on hold.

He called Eton on Saturday morning on his way to work.

He had been thoroughly covered every day for the last eight or nine days—ever since he'd been asked to help with preparations for Shultz's visit. So Jack had decided to leave early and make the call somewhere on the way to the Embassy before his minders caught up with him. He figured they wouldn't expect him to leave the apartment before 8:00 a.m. on a Saturday and would scramble a little when the *militsia* guard alerted them that Jack had left on foot.

He was right: he was clear of surveillance all the way to the Metro Station Proletarskaya, the further one of the two stations within a walking distance of his compound.

Eton picked up the phone in three seconds. "*Allo?*"

Jack could hear a hint of a smile in his voice and bit on the inside of his cheek. No matter how much he was disappointed that they couldn't meet, he hated disappointing Eton even more. "Hey, Eton. It's me."

"*Privet.* Listen, I lied to you when I said I had tickets to the conservatory. I don't have them. But I can get them if you're interested. Or we can go to see a rock performance if you like. I need to talk to you... Jack?"

Jack let him do his surprise speech, smiling to himself faintly, reveling in the sound of the low, soothing voice, until Eton called his name, sounding worried at the lack of response.

"Yes, I'm here. It's fine, Eton, don't worry about it. I want to catch up, too. But it looks like I can't make it. I've been asked to come in for work today and tomorrow."

"On a weekend?"

"Yes. We're preparing for... a VIP visit. I'm sorry."

Eton didn't respond right away and when he did, Jack could tell that he was trying not to sound upset. "Alright. Maybe next Sunday then? Or..."

"Yes?"

"My grandfather has invited the Berkeley team to his place next Saturday. They're leaving soon as you know. So it's a kind of farewell lunch... Will you come?"

"Yes, I'd be delighted to join—if I am invited."

"Great. I will tell him... But I still need to talk to you, separately. About, um, the *original study*."

Jack pricked up his ears and tried not to sound too eager. "Yes? Have you found it?"

"No, not yet. But I want to ask you... Why do you want to read it?"

Jack froze. This didn't sound good. Maybe he had pushed a bit too hard and made Eton suspicious. He had to come up with a plausible explanation, like right now. But the guy was smart as a whip and Jack didn't think he could feed him more stories about Prof.

Ackerman telling him about it without Eton figuring out that Jack was bullshitting. He was out of his depth facing these scientists and now regretted that he had agreed to William's suggestion to point to Prof. Ackerman as the source of his information about this goddamn "original study".

"Why? Has anything happened?" he asked slowly, trying to buy more time.

"I asked grandfather about it."

"And? What did he say?"

"He said I didn't need to read it, if it's not important for my research."

"Oh."

So the information that this nuclear winter theory was a KGB's "active measure" against the US government's policy might be correct after all. In which case the Company would want the study, anyway.

"Jack, what did Professor Ackerman say about it? That's what I want to talk to you about... I didn't tell Grandfather that it was *you* who was interested in the study," he added and sighed.

Fuck William and his recommendations!

"Eton, I'm so sorry. I haven't been very straightforward with you about it. It's rather complicated... As a matter of fact, I didn't hear it from Professor Ackerman directly... I've heard it from my *boss*... Remember him?"

"Yes, I remember him." Jack could visualize Eton knitting him eyebrows in concentration.

"So, *he* heard about it from Professor Ackerman... You're right, Eton, we need to meet. Let's meet next Sunday."

"Alright... But you're still coming to the lunch on Saturday, aren't you?"

Eton's tone was hopeful, and it set off a cloud of butterflies in Jack's stomach. "I wouldn't miss it for anything!" He grinned into the phone. "But it will be better if you or someone would call my office on Monday. With an official invite. Know what I mean?"

There was a slight hesitation, then Eton said firmly, "I understand. Lena will call you on Monday... I will think of where we can meet next Sunday. It's my turn."

"Great! Thanks, friend... Listen, I have to run now. See you later?"

"Yes. *Poka*."

Jack hung up, turned around slowly and unobtrusively scanned his surroundings before heading down the escalator to the trains. He was still in the clear.

And he had a week to come up with a real good story of how he'd learned about the original nuclear winter study and why he was dying to read it. He hoped Nurimbekoff would be back next week, or at least William, so that he could get the story cleared by his bosses.

Both of them returned on Monday. However, on Tuesday, the briefing Jack had requested was canceled due to yet another development in the Yurchenko defection saga.

In the late afternoon on Monday in Washington DC, around midnight in Moscow, Colonel Vitaly Yurchenko, the highest-ranking defector in the history of the CIA, gave a press conference from the newly built Soviet Embassy, announcing that he had returned to the Soviet side.

He claimed that he had been abducted by the CIA and brought to the U.S., where he had been kept in isolation, forced to take drugs and denied the possibility to get in touch with Soviet representatives. Furthermore, Yurchenko stated that he had not divulged any secret information when he was not drugged and in control, and that he had first heard of Edward Lee Howard when his handlers had brought him newspapers with stories about him. Then three months into the captivity, thanks to a momentary lapse in security, he had been able to break out to freedom and come to the Soviet Embassy.

It was the most bizarre story Jack had ever heard, and he had little doubt that most of the Agency's staff shared his incredulity. He didn't believe Yurchenko's account, and a ten-minute briefing with William on Wednesday night confirmed his suspicion.

But then the whole affair meant either that the Agency had handled the man so appallingly that he had decided to re-defect, or that he had been a dangle. Either way, all information obtained from him during the debriefings would now require additional layers of verification. And that included the lead on the origins of the nuclear winter theory that Yurchenko claimed to be one of the KGB's "active measures", or in layman language disinformation.

That was pretty much what Nurimbekoff told Jack in the Tank on Thursday evening. Besides, if the info on Prof. Volkonsky's original study was corroborated, it would act as an extra layer of assurance that other information gleaned from Yurchenko might also be true. On the flip side, it would point to the cause of his re-defection, implying that the Company had screwed up in handling the most important KGB spy that ever defected to the US.

When Nurimbekoff had finished with his briefing, Jack outlined what he wanted to tell Eton about his knowledge of the original nuclear winter study: William had first overheard drunken Alexin ranting about it to Ackerman during the cocktail party at the Conference on Nuclear Winter in Madrid in May. Alexin insisted that it was the KGB's handiwork and Prof. Volkonsky had been told to put together a team to produce a study on the effects of a total nuclear exchange over Germany. Later on, when William asked Ackerman if it is true, the scientist shrugged it off, saying that Alexin had always been paranoid about the KGB. This story then tied in nicely to Alexin's disappearance in Madrid after the conference, putting the blame squarely at the KGB's door. Next, William mentioned this incident to Jack as a joke at one of the Embassy's BBQ events. Jack was intrigued by the story, decided to do a little research of his own and asked Eton to help him in his research. And the reason he hadn't mentioned all this to Eton earlier was because the existence of such a study implied Eton's grandfather's association with the KGB, and he had thought that Eton wouldn't have liked it.

"That's what I propose to tell him," Jack concluded and took a deep breath, watching Nurimbekoff's face closely for reaction.

William spoke up first. "Are you proposing that we let them know that we know about the original study? Why would we do that, Jack?" he asked with exaggerated disbelief.

"Well, they will only know that the Company knows if, one, *they know* that I'm a case officer, and, two, Eton Volkonsky is working for them. At the moment, we have no indication that either one is a fact. Besides, I'm more inclined to think that the boy is *not* with the KGB."

"That's *not* a foregone conclusion. *And* I still don't see the rationale for giving away information about what we know."

"I may not see the whole picture, but from what I know, it looks like it won't do any harm if they know about it." Jack was tempted to add that with all the information that had already been leaked to the press, what harm could a little morsel of info like this realistically do to them. But he bit his tongue.

"He may be right, William," the COS finally said. "Giving *this* piece of information away may in return get us more of what we need... Good thinking, Jack."

"Thank you, sir."

However, William was not through questioning Jack's proposal. "Explain why me. And why bring Alexin into the story?"

"I thought it would be best if the source was twice or even three times removed from me. Gives me an opportunity to speculate openly about the information without stressing about its accuracy. On the other hand, it has to be a source that young Volkonsky thinks of as reliable. Alexin is a perfect source in this instance. One, nobody can verify now what he said or didn't say, and two, Eton seems to side with him on the model they've been running... I can't claim that I knew the man and that he told me about this study. So I thought you, William, would be the best conduit. You know Ackerman, you are senior enough with the USIA to attend an international conference, you could have met with all of them there... Also, I think it will be a great test to determine whether the boy is with the KGB and whether the study is a KGB plot. It would create quite a stir if they found out that we know about it... Don't you think?" Jack looked at the two men across the desk, waiting for their reaction. When he saw that no response was forthcoming, he continued, looking at William apologetically. "Besides, I've already mentioned to the boy that I'd heard it from you, William. I'm sorry. He put me on the spot with his question. I had to tell him something."

"Alright, Jack. I think it makes sense," Nurimbekoff nodded and looked at William expectantly until the CAO nodded his silent agreement. "But we'll need to run your story by HQ, before you start spinning it to the Russians. I don't expect there'll be any major change to it. Maybe some fine-tuning here and there. Should be all set by the time you talk to him on Sunday. Try to avoid talking about it at his grandfather's, though. Unless you get a green light from William *before* your visit to Volkonsky's place."

"Yes, sir... Marat. I understand."

"We're all set then... And I'll find time to chat to you about this Yurchenko affair soon," the COS added quickly when Jack opened his mouth to ask a question. "Are we good?"

Jack nodded, mumbling, "Yes, sir", and the meeting was adjourned.

That night he couldn't fall asleep for a long time.

He got up at half past one, went to the sitting room to get himself a drink, took it back to the bedroom and sat down on the edge of the bed. "I'm sorry, Eton, but it's my job," he

- 224 -

whispered, staring down at the tumbler with a triple shot of whiskey, and heaved a sigh.

Joe had said that the kid had been ruined for a normal life the moment he was born. He was probably right. And it also meant that if Jack didn't do the job, Joe Coburn would assign someone else to do it. So it was better Jack than somebody else. That way he could at least try to make sure that the boy wasn't harmed... for nothing.

Yeah, it was definitely better.

No, fuck it! It *couldn't* be anyone else but him. Because he was Jack, and he was from California, even if it was an impossibly childish idea.

Chapter 33

It had been raining for over a week. Except for a short spell on Thursday when the entire country had watched the military parade on Red Square on the occasion of the 68th anniversary of the Great October Revolution, in person or via live broadcast on TV. The rumor was that the clouds had been sprayed with chemicals to temporarily seal the moisture in. It had not brought out the sunshine, but at least the morning stayed dry. It had been pouring with a vengeance ever since.

The patience draining rain had eased to a drizzle when Jack parked on a narrow side street, fetched the umbrella and the bouquet of pink roses from the front passenger seat and hurried to the building where the Volkonsky family lived. The turn of the century, art nouveau building featured a large and airy foyer. It also looked notably better maintained that the Brezhnev era nondescript apartment block where Jack lived. He took the old, but clean and brightly lit elevator to the sixth floor. There were only two doors on the spacious landing with well-worn, but still beautiful tiled floor. He pressed the bell on the door on the left.

The heavy wooden door opened immediately, as if the woman in her early forties who opened it had been standing behind it, waiting. She was petite and attractive, with dyed, sandy blond hair and big, dark eyes. Now Jack knew for certain where Eton got his soulful brown eyes. Except the woman's eyes were sad, as if she had seen all the sorrow of the world. She was wearing an elegant dark purple knitted dress and street shoes.

"Good day. I'm afraid I'm a little early. Hope you don't mind." Jack flashed his teeth and dimples at the woman and offered her the roses. "This is for you. You must be Vera Mikhailovna."

"Good day. For me?" She wasn't at all surprised, accepted the flowers gracefully. "Thank you very much. Please come in."

Jack stepped inside and quickly looked around. The cabinet for overcoats and street shoes was on the left; on the right was an old-fashioned hall table and a bookcase overflowing with books. There were three doors to the right of the hallway; the center one was half-glass.

Jack turned to the woman. "My name is Jack Smith. I'm coordinating the Soviet - American project Mikhail Alexandrovich is running. I've heard a lot about you."

"You have? You can hang up your jacket here." Vera Mikhailovna pointed at the cabinet.

"Yes. From Lara. You're her role model."

"Oh, that girl! I've heard a lot from her about you, too. Let me see… A very polite and handsome American who speaks excellent Russian and knows all about our culture and history. It must be you." She smiled faintly and motioned her hand towards the glass door, "This way, please."

The door on the far left swung open and Eton emerged in the doorway. "Good day, Jack. I heard your voice." He sounded out of breath and looked ill at ease.

"Eton. How are you?"

"I see you have met with my mother," Eton said as they shook hands, his expression skeptical.

"I have. And hope I'll have a chance to talk more to Vera Mikhailovna today," Jack turned to her, all smiles.

Vera stood motionless, staring at the two of them, and Jack saw her expression change from surprise to uncertainty to something like… fear, maybe?

Nah, he was just imagining it. She couldn't possibly know about Eton… Could she?

"I apologize. I have a meeting today that I couldn't reschedule. I was actually on my way out," she said, suddenly in a hurry, and walked past Jack into the main room. Then as if recalling her manners, Vera turned around. "I'm sure Eton and my father will do a great job in hosting you today. Please forgive me." She offered them a weak smile that didn't reach her eyes and disappeared in the guest room.

"Did I say something wrong?" Jack looked at Eton, confused. "I'm sorry if I did."

Eton rolled his eyes. "Don't worry about it. She's like that with, um, Americans. Don't mind her, please." He motioned toward the glass door. "Please, come in."

But Jack was not yet ready to come in. "Does she know," he asked, keeping his voice low and mouthed, "About you", pointing his finger at the young man's chest.

"No! No one knows." Eton shook his head vigorously. "Except you," he whispered. "It's alright, Jack. Don't worry about her."

Jack opened his mouth to say that he hoped he would have another chance when the doorbell rang again and Eton went to answer it. It was Pavel and Liova from the Soviet exchange team. The professor, in a tie and vest and soft house shoes, came out to greet Jack and his students. After a round of handshakes, he ushered them into the sitting room, instructed them to make themselves at home and retreated.

There were four doors around the perimeter of the guest room, all of them closed. Through the one on the right, one could see a kitchen through its glass panes and hear faint sounds of chopping. The sitting room was large and cozy, furnished with old-fashioned cabinets with china, couches with embroidered cushions, and a big standing clock. The dominant colors were brown, gold and cream, and there were a couple of dozen paintings in heavy frames on the walls. A large dinner table was set up in the middle of the room with curved legged chairs around it. Fine blue and cream tableware, silver cutlery and crystal glasses were laid out on a pristine white, starched tablecloth.

Eton's mother hurried out of one of the doors, apologized again for not staying for lunch and bid her goodbyes. She was polite, but distant, not smiling. Well, at least not to Jack. Soon after she had left, Anya and Gosha arrived. After an exchange of greetings, Anya said her father sent his apologies that he wasn't able to join, but would drop by after lunch. She then excused herself and disappeared in the kitchen. When Eton caught Jack's quizzical glance, he explained that Dmitri Alexandrovich, Anya's father, had warned beforehand that he couldn't join.

Okay, so Dr. Arceniev was Anya's father. No wonder she studied at MGU and lived in this prestigious area. He should have worked it out earlier. Still, it didn't explain why she acted as if this was her home. Jack hated to admit it, but he didn't like it at all.

When the Berkeley team arrived, yet another round of handshakes and greetings ensued before everybody sat down: Sarah and Kyle on both sides of Prof. Volkonsky at the head of the table, with the rest of the Berkeley team next to them, and the Soviet team at the other end. Jack found himself seated among the Russians, next to Eton at the end of the table and Gosha on the other side.

After helping the Volkonsky's housekeeper to lay out the starters, Anya took her place on Eton's right and launched into small talk, like a dutiful hostess. She asked whether Jack watched Soviet movies and which one he liked. "Moscow Doesn't Believe in Tears", Jack said and it made Anya beam with delight and glare triumphantly at the boys. He was also rewarded with a quick brush of a leg against his under the table, as Eton leaned back in his chair, looking pleased.

As the conversation about Soviet cinematography continued amongst the Russians, Jack tuned into the conversation at the other end. Mike was telling Prof. Volkonsky and Grisha how he, Howard and Kyle had attended the military parade on Red Square two days before. They thought it was "impressive and stimulating", as red-headed, enthusiastic Mike put it, and Jack thought it was probably just as well that the trio didn't speak a word of Russian and missed the heavy-duty propaganda speeches at the parade.

"Do you think if Gorbachev had delivered the opening speech at the parade instead of the Defense Minister, he would have extended the moratorium on nuclear tests?" Sarah asked, addressing her question at no one in particular.

"Why not?" Val shrugged. "He seems quite enterprising with his first year initiatives."

Sarah was about to retort, but Pavel was faster. "Do you think your government will agree to Gorbachev's proposal of a joint moratorium?"

Jack fought the impulse to sigh. He didn't like political debates between Americans and Soviets. He had his own views about it, which he seldom shared. So he tried to avoid these discussions whenever possible. Maybe if he just kept his mouth shut, nobody would ask him a direct question.

"Hard to tell," said Val thoughtfully. "I'd like to say yes, but it really depends. My understanding is that both sides agree on the big picture, but disagree on technical details."

"Maybe results of our program can help make decisions." Liova suggested in heavily accented English and looked around the table. "Of course, if they are made known to our leaders. For the summit in Geneva, for example. You think so?" he asked Val.

"Possibly. Who knows?" Val shrugged again.

Grisha stood up and excused himself. He bumped at Eton's chair as he was heading out and indicated the door with his eyes. Eton nodded faintly, but he remained seated. Nobody seemed to notice the little exchange, except Jack. And Anya. Her eyes followed Grisha, then she excused herself a minute later and went to the kitchen, taking Gosha with her.

"Maybe that is why our project is... eh, we are in a hurry at the end? Mikhail Alexandrovich, do you know the reason?" Pavel asked.

Volkonsky smiled enigmatically and took a sip from his glass of fortified wine. "It's entirely possible. Perhaps we should ask Jack about it. He's the coordinator of the project, isn't he?"

Ok, so he was put on the spot after all. The problem was Jack had learnt about the early completion of the project from Gosha, over a month ago. Since then he hadn't been able to pinpoint exactly who had made the decision to rush the program and release the results earlier than originally planned. The Soviets had been pointing to their American counterparts, and vice versa. The only thing he was certain about was that it wasn't the USIA.

"I agree," he said, trying to keep it vague. "I, too, hope that the results of this project will help our leaders reach a positive agreement at the summit."

"Irrespective of the results of our project, I don't believe nuclear weapons would actually be used in a modern war," Mike said suddenly. "Their main purpose is deterrence. To discourage the enemy... um, the opposite side from attacking you using nuclear weapons."

"What about Hiroshima and Nagasaki?" Liova challenged.

"That was the only time they were used, wasn't it?" Mike insisted. "Exactly because we were the only country that had the nuclear weapons. They've never been used since. And the reason we've been able to maintain stability is exactly because of this: their use assures mutual destruction."

"There's no evidence that nuclear weapons have *ever* worked as an effective deterrence mechanism," Sarah butted in. "In fact, there *is* actually evidence that they are pretty useless for that purpose."

Jack noticed Val rolling his eyes and mouthing, "Here we go". Everyone at the table now turned their attention to Sarah and Mike.

"What do you mean 'useless'?" Mike asked, obviously making an effort to keep his tone light. "What evidence are we talking about?"

"I'm talking about *historical* evidence. Like the Yom Kippur War. Or the most recent Falklands conflict, for example. Neither the Arab coalition nor the Argentineans had nuclear weapons, and they knew perfectly well that the Israelis and the Britons had them. Yet they attacked them first, anyway. And what good did their nukes do for the Israelis and the Brits?" She paused, waiting for objections, but nobody said anything. "They never got down to using them any way... So I actually agree with you, Mike: nuclear weapons aren't used in modern wars, irrespective of whether the opposition has them or not... The Korean and Vietnam wars are two other examples: we had nuclear weapons, the other side didn't. We never used them and in the end lost the war. So my question is: why bother having them?" She looked at the men around the table and concluded, "They're useless. Total waste of time and money!"

"Ah! That's where you might be wrong, Sarah," Val said, his tone slightly taunting. "This is where the economics come into play. For some, they mean *lots* of money. And who cares if it's coming from the taxpayers' pockets."

"Are many Americans thinking like you?" Pavel asked with a shocked expression.

"America is a free country." Val shrugged, but his smile was amiable. "Anyone can think whatever they want. What matters is whom you know to promote your thinking... But I agree with Mike. Maybe we haven't had a major war since World War II *because* of the nuclear arsenals we've accumulated."

"Maybe we haven't had such a war because nobody wants it in the first place?" Jack asked tentatively. "Who wants its population annihilated in a nuclear exchange? Nobody wins." He looked around the table, seeking support.

"That's not technically correct," Kyle said, leaning forward to see Jack from the other end of the table. "Nuclear weapons are not designed to annihilate the population."

"No?" Jack smiled sheepishly. "Sorry, I'm not a nuclear weapons specialist. But that's the impression one gets from listening to depictions of what, um, 'the other side' is gonna do to you."

Kyle, a nuclear engineer, shook his head. "It's all propaganda, Jack. Nuclear weapons are designed to destroy the other side's nuclear and conventional arsenal with very high accuracy."

"What about Hiroshima and Nagasaki?" Liova challenged again. "They were not military targets."

"You're right they weren't," Kyle agreed. "But in that particular case, it was a test of a new weapon America had developed. Nobody knew what the consequences would be. Everybody was just hoping that it would finally draw an end to the war."

"It doesn't matter that nobody knew about the consequences," Sarah said. "It worked and Japan surrendered."

"Japan surrendered because we declared war on them," objected Liova.

Sarah tilted her head to one side. "That's one way of looking at it. I believe that the use of nuclear weapons in this particular case was a critical factor in ending the war. Maybe not for the right reasons, but it *was* decisive. Unfortunately, this single instance when it was used against the civilian targets now defines the deterrent aspect of our nuclear strategy."

"It's an interesting point of view, dear Sarah," Volkonsky said. "I have to say, I may agree with you on the American nuclear strategy. In a way… But would you mind terribly if I say that destruction of civilian targets has never been a serious deterrent factor in military actions? And the reason is quite simple: generals and politicians never hesitate to sacrifice civilian population to achieve their goals in a war." The professor ignored the shocked expressions on Liova and Pavel's faces. "That is why the claim that Hiroshima and Nagasaki played a *decisive* role in ending World War II is debatable. If my memory doesn't fail me, Americans started bombing Japanese cities in March of 1945. In six months, more than sixty cities were bombed and destroyed. All civilian targets. Yet, the Japanese didn't surrender till August."

"You're absolutely right, professor: not until we dropped the nukes," Sarah said pleasantly.

"I agree," Volkonsky smiled at her amiably. "It's so easy to see them as playing a decisive role, because the surrender came shortly after the bombings. What I'm saying is that it is disputable that they played a decisive role *because* they were dropped on civilian targets. Allow me to be a little controversial and present a hypothetical scenario… Imagine for a moment that Hitler had developed nuclear bombs *before* Americans and by 1945 had a few dozen bombs. What would be the immediate assumption about what he would use the bombs for?"

"To destroy the Soviet Union and the allies?" said Pavel.

"To conquer the world," stated Sarah.

"Indeed." Volkonsky nodded. "Now assume he used his bombs against the allies and dropped them on civilian targets. What difference do you think it would have made? By that time, Britain and the Soviet Union had already suffered blanket bombing of their cities by Germans. Some cities had been obliterated. Like Stalingrad. Or had millions starved to death, like Leningrad. Yet, that didn't deter either the British or the Soviets from fighting till the bitter end. If anything, it actually made people more united, more determined to win. Don't you agree?... Now, had Hitler developed nuclear bombs first, London and Moscow might have shared the similar fate with Hiroshima and Nagasaki. Parts of New York and Washington might have been destroyed, perhaps. More people might have been killed. But would it have prevented the defeat of Germany and Japan? I don't think the outcome of the war would have been different. What do *you* think?" He ran his eyes around the table. "Now. What it *would* have changed, is *our perception* of nuclear weapons. Instead of being a symbol of the victor's military might, they would have been regarded as the weapons of an evil man used for evil purposes. Instead of being a decisive instrument that secures victory in a war and uphold peace, they would have been looked upon with contempt, as a symbol of failure... Don't you agree?"

The young people around the table gaped at Volkonsky in silence, trying to process the idea he had just suggested and the message behind it. Jack stole a glance at Eton. He looked stunned, too, gazing at his grandfather as if he was seeing him for the first time. He hadn't participated in the conversation, looked mostly at his plate, occasionally nibbling at the food, but Jack was sure he hadn't missed a word.

"Mikhail Alexandrovich, what are you saying?" Pavel exclaimed.

"What Mikhail Alexandrovich is so diplomatically saying is that America's nuclear policy is flawed because it relies on two *false*, in his view, assumptions," Sarah said, watching Volkonsky closely. "The first is that nuclear weapons are militarily decisive. Because we take for granted that they won the World War Two. And the second is that nuclear weapons are historically justified. Because we believe that if Hitler had had them, he would have used them to conquer the world. Am I correct, Professor?"

"It's always a pleasure to talk about history with you, my dear." Volkonsky smiled at her and took another sip of his wine. "You have a rare ability to also see things from a *different* perspective."

Sarah beamed. "So do you, Mikhail Alexandrovich. And the pleasure is all mine."

Apparently, Mike was not done with the topic just yet. "Okay, if the American policy is flawed, what about the Soviet Union's?" he asked, furrowing his ginger eyebrows. "You are part of this equation. The buildup of nuclear arms has been on both sides and as far as I know the Soviet arsenals at times exceeded ours."

Ilyia and Liova stared at him, not even trying to hide their alarm. Everybody turned to Volkonsky.

"Ah, yes, Mike. The Soviet Union developed its first nuclear bomb several years after America," the professor said, choosing his words carefully. "As a result, our nuclear policy has been shaped as a reaction to the way America implemented its policy. Admittedly, it has also been built upon the tenets of Marxism Leninism teachings about the class conflict.

Which I know you do not share. As such, I think we shouldn't delve further into this subject, lest we wage a new debate about capitalism and class conflict. May I suggest we proceed to our main course? Liova, could you kindly ask Varvara Petrovna to serve the main course now? And ask An'echka and the boys to return, please."

They stayed clear of other loaded topics for the rest of the lunch and it ended amiably with Val and Mike's account of their trip to Leningrad a few weeks earlier.

Afterward, Jack's thoughts kept returning to Eton's stunned face as he listened to his grandfather's nuclear weapons theory. It looked like neither he nor others at the table had ever heard the professor talking on the subject. Could it mean that Volkonsky's theory was directed at Jack, the only American official in the room? If so, what had he been trying to convey? The two things that had stuck with Jack were the professor's statement that Americans' belief about the role of nuclear weapons in a war was erroneous, and his veiled allusion that Americans could also be wrong in believing that nuclear weapons would be used by "an evil empire" to conquer the world.

And then there was another thing that bothered Jack, and he spent more time pondering over it that night: whether Vera Volkonskaya knew that her son was gay.

Eton seemed to believe that she didn't. Somehow, Jack felt that she did. Or maybe she denied even to herself that she knew. Especially if she knew that her husband had been queer, too. Wasn't it why she had left him with her five-year-old son? Wasn't it why she had been so adamant, according to Eton, that he had to become a scientist, not a long-haired rocker, the type who was always into misdeeds? If that were the case, wouldn't she be suspicious of Jack when she learnt of his friendship with Eton? She might even confront him if she was any kind of Russian. Especially because Jack was an American, like her husband... About whom she looked so wounded even now... Or did she?

Christ, this was so frigging complicated. He wished he hadn't accepted Joe Coburn's "special assignment". But then, he wouldn't have known Eton, would have never known how it felt to be in his arms, with Eton gazing at him with that mysterious look in his eyes that made Jack go all weak inside. Made him feel like he would do anything for Eton... Of course he wouldn't, it was just a feeling, a momentary weakness, one he shouldn't let stick if he was to do what he needed to do. It was his job after all, goddamn it!

Chapter 34

Jack called Eton early next morning as they had agreed. The phone rang three times and Eton's voice kicked in, asking him to leave a message. Jack called again an hour later and got the same message. This time, it left him worried. He didn't think Eton was avoiding him, so it meant that something had happened. Maybe yesterday, after the lunch at his grandfather's place. Or maybe he'd just stayed there overnight and hadn't managed to return early this morning.

Jack called again at ten. Again, Eton wasn't home, but the message on the answering machine had changed. "Sorry, I'm not home. My mother has been hospitalized. Please call me again late in the evening."

He puffed out a breath of relief, suddenly realizing that he had been more worried than he had thought. And immediately felt guilty: there must have been an accident after all, albeit not with Eton, but it was his mother and the boy must be worried sick.

He dialed Lara's number. It turned out that while they were having lunch at her father's, Vera Mikhailovna had had a dizzy spell in the street, had fallen and broken her ankle, and Eton had taken his grandfather to see her in the hospital this morning, and Lara and Anya were planning to go visit her this afternoon too.

They chatted for a few minutes more, then, just as Jack was about to bid her goodbye, Lara said, "I'm free today after the hospital. Let's go to the movies." When he failed to respond right away, she admonished him, "Oh, come on, Jack! You spent the whole afternoon with Eton, Anya and the crowd yesterday. Don't say you can't go to the movies with me today!" There was little he could say to that which wouldn't go down the wrong way with Lara, so he agreed to take her out.

He spent the rest of the morning at Uncle Sam's, shooting the breeze with the contractors and marines who drifted in for their Sunday brunch, beer and gossip. At around noon, Stella Ricci turned up in her quest for lunch and company. Jack was sitting at the bar, giving survival tips to a newbie contractor in exchange for a beer. Normally he would have pretended not to notice her, in the hope that she would find herself another, more willing target. However, it had been a while since Amanda left and he hadn't been seen out with a woman, so Jack thought he should make an effort. He waved at her and invited her to join. When the contractor left, they moved to the table in the far corner and Jack endured an hour of handholding and her rubbing her legs against his under the table, and her gossips about her colleagues, her boss's wife who frequented the Marine and Seabees dens with her, then about some girls the marines had taken to their rooms, who she thought might not be Germans like they claimed they were.

At two, Jack excused himself, saying he had to visit an acquaintance at the hospital. She let him go, but only after giving him her phone number and making him promise that they would catch up soon. "For a dinner date *and all*", she said, smiling at him emphatically. Jack had to make an effort to look thrilled when he said he looked forward to it.

He picked Lara up outside of her house and spent the rest of the day with her: they watched an old French action flick, starring Jean-Pierre Belmondo, then had dinner at the restaurant on the second floor of Hotel Rossiya, with a spectacular view of the multicolored onion domes of St. Basil Cathedral. It was nearly eleven when he brought Lara home. He tried to give her a goodbye peck on her cheek, but she turned her face up and snaked her arms around his neck and they ended up kissing. He peeled her off his body, saying apologetically that it was better that they were not seen "doing this" on the street. She peered at him skeptically, said goodbye and flitted through the entrance of the building where she lived.

On his way home, Jack left his car on a side street and walked a couple of blocks until he found a phone booth tucked away in a corner of a building, out of reach of the dim streetlight.

"*Allo*?" Eton sounded tired.

"*Privet*, Eton. It's me."

"*Privet*... I'm sorry I wasn't—"

"It's alright. I know about your mother... How is she now?"

"She's better, thanks."

That's all?

"Good to hear. Hope she'll be out of the hospital soon... What are the doctors saying?" Jack asked when there was no response forthcoming from the other end.

"Two weeks in the hospital. Until her ankle is set."

Had he sounded annoyed? Or just tired and sad?

"Take it easy, friend. Her foot will recover soon, I'm sure." Still nothing. "Eton? Are you there?"

He heard a sigh, then Eton's voice came in, low and testy, "Mother said you and Lara are dating."

Gah! Women.

"I'm *not* dating her. She insisted that I took her to the movies and I couldn't say no." When no response came again, he said quietly, "Eton, I think your mother knows."

"Knows what?"

"About you."

"*What*?... No. She doesn't know." Now Eton's tone was calm and confident. "Nobody knows... Except you."

Jack leaned back on the glass wall of the phone booth and closed his eyes. He couldn't tell Eton that his mother might know because she had also known or at least suspected about his father. He wasn't supposed to know anything about Eton's father.

"I think she does. Trust me." I saw it in her eyes yesterday. "That is why we need her to think, um, the way she's thinking about me and Lara... And she needs to think the same way about you and Anya. Or any other girl you know. Do you understand?... Eton? Are you still there?"

"Yes." Eton sighed heavily. "I don't like it. But I understand what you're trying to do."

He didn't say he was going to do it too, but at least now he knew what had to be done. And that was good enough. For now.

"We'll talk more about it when we meet. But it's important that people think what they're thinking now. Do you understand?"

"When can we meet? We need to talk about the *study*."

He wasn't going to make it easy for Jack, was he?

"I'll call you on Tuesday."

"This time?"

"Yes… And Eton? I wish I could change how things are in this world. But I can't. So I try to manage them somehow… I'm sorry. I just don't know what else I can do about it."

"Alright. Talk to you on Tuesday. *Poka*," Eton mumbled and hung up.

Jack lingered in the booth, the heavy handset in his hand, contemplating calling Eton again and telling him that—

Tell him what? What else could he say on the phone that would make Eton feel better? There was nothing he could do and the boy would just have to deal with it.

He hooked the handset up in its cradle, returned to his car and drove home.

He felt like an asshole and couldn't understand why. He *had* to tell Eton what he should do to take care of himself, right? Who else would if not him? The boy was completely oblivious and had no self-preservation skills whatsoever, was set to expose himself at the drop of a hat. It was a miracle that he had survived so far without anyone figuring him out, probably thanks to his cool, intensely masculine appearance—all edges, nothing soft. The one that would bring Jack Smith down one day—*if* he wasn't careful and got carried away. Christ, he wished he could have taken the boy back to California, to his ranch—his *future* ranch. The two of them could just dig in and let the world implode.

"The two of us"? You're out of your fucking mind! You're emotionally compromised. God, you're in such deep shit, Smith!

So I am. Big deal! I'll shake it off. I will… Will ask Joe for a short break and get out of here for a while.

Yeah, and what are you gonna tell him, dimwit? You've just started this assignment, you're nowhere with it yet and already asking for a break? They'll fire you, like they fired that Howard guy.

Fine. I will just move on with my ranch.

Is that right? How convenient. And what about Eton? What will happen to him after you quit? Are you going to leave his ass high and dry, just like that? What kind of friend are you? He thinks of you as his best friend, and you? God, you're such a fucking sham! No wonder you don't have anyone you can call your best friend.

Except Eton. *If* he still wanted to know Jack, should he happen to learn about Jack's cowardly thoughts.

Right. He wasn't going anywhere. He'd stay right here and see to it that Eton May Volkonsky was safe and knew how to deal with being who he was. Until it was time for Jack Smith to leave the country. He knew he'd have to leave one day, but that day hadn't come yet. In the meantime, he had a job to do. And he had to try to find a way of dealing with his temporary infatuation with his friend Eton. Somehow. Before it was too late.

* * *

The preparations for the Geneva summit dominated the life at the Embassy, and as a result William couldn't book the Tank for a weekly debrief with Jack. The only thing the CAO told him was that Jack was being seconded to Munich and was to leave on Wednesday. It meant that he was finally set for his debrief with Joe Coburn.

He spent nearly two hours writing a three-page report on his lunch at Prof. Volkonsky, his analysis of the conversation about nuclear weapons, and what he thought the professor had tried to convey, then the rest of the morning and early afternoon trying to formulate in his head what he was going to tell Joe.

He hadn't made up his mind yet on what he was going to tell his chief of ops about the "development" of Eton May Volkonsky and if he should tell Joe about what he'd learned about him. Well, that is if Joe hadn't deduced that Jack was *temporarily* emotionally involved with his target. Jack needed to come up with a good story to explain that too.

Late in the afternoon, when he brought his report to William, Jack told his boss about the women he had seen hanging out at the Marines Club. Perhaps the Station could take a closer look at the situation. Or maybe Nurimbekoff could have a word with the security officer. William shrugged and said that Jack could report the incident himself since *he* was a frequenter of the "establishment" and *he* had witnessed it.

Jack went back to his office to mull over William's suggestion. He didn't want to lodge an official report. Besides the fact that he hung out with Frank and the crowd and they considered him a friend who wanted be a whistle-blower in a closed-knit community in the heart of the Soviet Russia? So he resolved to catch old Don at Uncle Sam's and talk to him informally.

Stella called just as he was about to leave the office and to ask if he wanted to have drinks, or dinner, or both. Jack wasn't particularly thrilled about the prospect, but thought he should make an effort. So he said he could only do a quick dinner, then he had to get back to the office to finish a report he was working on—he was leaving on a business trip and had to clean up a pile of documents before that.

They had their dinner at the bar of the Hotel Intourist on the edge of Red Square, flirting and laughing noisily to the annoyance of a prim-looking, obviously foreign couple two tables away. Stella tried to persuade him to take her to the ladies, or to the gents, whichever suited him better. Jack said in a loud whisper that he wasn't keen on starring in KGB-produced porn videos and it made her giggle uncontrollably. He drove her home, necked with her in the dark entrance of her apartment building and promised to come up next time when he was back from his business trip. When he returned to his car, he lit a cigarette and sat smoking for a long while, trying to get rid of the sweetish scent of Stella's perfume that made him want to puke.

On the way home, he stopped to call Eton. He was ready to hang up when his friend finally picked up the phone.

"It's me. *Privet.*"

"*Privet...* Anything happened?" His tone was worried—Jack wasn't supposed to call till the next day.

"Everything is fine. It just... A business trip has cropped up unexpectedly and I'm leaving on Wednesday. For a week. Can we meet tomorrow afternoon?... Eton? You there?"

"Yes. But I can't do tomorrow. I'm sorry."

"Oh..." Jack bit back his disappointment.

"Can we meet now?"

"Now?" He looked at his watch. 10:17 p.m.

"Yes. Where are you?"

"I'm on my way home... Calling from the street, near Metro Station Avtozavodskaya."

"I can get there in thirty five - forty minutes... Jack?"

Oh, screw it!

"Alright. I'll meet you half way, at the head of Pushkin Embankment, off the Third Ring Road."

"Will be there in thirty minutes max."

"Park at the beginning of the street. I'll find you."

"On my way," Eton said, clearly smiling, and hung up.

Jack got to the place in less than twenty minutes. He found an empty parking lot that belonged to an old office building nearby, tucked his car in the far corner, and walked under the bridge to the other side.

It started drizzling, the fine spray smearing the murky glow of the streetlights, turning it into orange haze. The road was empty, except for an occasional truck or car. Jack turned up the collar of his jacket, strolled over to the other side, walked a few hundred meters up, then crossed the street and headed back. He crossed over again, ready for another purposeful walk down the road when he saw Eton's car. He stepped forward to the curb, into the headlights.

Eton rolled to a stop right next to him and Jack got in quickly.

"Geez, didn't expect it'd be so cold!" He puffed out a shuddering breath, scooping the raindrops from his face.

"I'm sorry. I should have thought about that." Eton turned on the heater, pulled out a pack of Marlboros and offered them to Jack.

"I'll live." Jack grinned at him and took the pack. "So, let's take a drive then, friend." As they took off, Jack lit a cigarette and took a hard pull on it. "Yeah, I needed that," he said with a long, satisfied exhale and handed the cigarette over to Eton.

"Tastes better when you share, right?" Eton mumbled, the corners of his lips curling up in a knowing half-smile. He took a couple of deep drags and returned cigarette to Jack.

Damn! Since when had this man started reading his mind? Maybe he *had* known Jack since he was nine, like he claimed. Jack chuckled. "Damn right."

They drove in easy silence, taking turns puffing on their smoke. When they had finished it, Jack flicked it out of the window and turned to Eton.

"Alright. I have an unpleasant story and unpleasant news that we need to talk about. Which one you want to hear first?"

"The story... Is it about my grandfather's *original* nuclear winter study?"

"It is. I wasn't sure how to tell you."

And, looking straight ahead of him, he gave Eton the story vetted by his bosses. He tried to soften the indication that his grandfather might have worked on the project at the KGB's order. Eton listened to him without interruptions, like he wasn't listening at all, but Jack knew better. When he finished, Eton was silent for a long while, worrying his lower lip.

"It means Grandfather has been cooperating with the *organs*, doesn't it?" he finally asked, his eyes fixed firmly on the road. When Jack didn't respond, he sighed. "It makes sense."

"It does?" Jack had expected disbelief, denial, even anger, but not this.

"Yes... He has always been able to, um, protect me from them. When they *approached* me." He glanced at Jack sideways. "A few times. I didn't want to think how he did that."

"Did what?"

"When I entered the university, Grandfather told me that I would be approached by the organs. That they would try to make me report on others. He told me to tell him immediately if that happened. And to tell the person who approached me to go talk to him. It worked. They never came back... At least not the same people."

"And you don't know how he did it."

"I didn't want, tried not to think about it."

Jack mused over it. "So, knowing what you know now, do you think this original study was, could have been done at their behest?"

Eton didn't answer right away, but when he did, he sounded resigned. "Possible."

"Right."

Jack put his hand on his friend's thigh and squeezed it lightly. Eton immediately took hold of his hand, his long fingers wrapping around Jack's. Jack wanted to reach out and pull him into a hug. Instead, he lit a cigarette and gave it to Eton.

As they reached the end of Lenin Avenue, Eton turned left on Krymsky Val, drove across the bridge over Moskva River and along the second ring road that circled the wider downtown part of Moscow.

"I need to think it over," Eton finally said. "Can we talk about it later, when you get back?"

"Sure. Whenever you're ready."

"Okay, thanks. I appreciate it... Now about the news."

"Right, the news."

God, he hated telling Eton this, but who else would do it, if not him? He was supposed to be his friend, right? He had to try to live up to Eton's expectations of him as his best friend.

"Eton, I really hate having to say what I'm gonna say. And I don't know how to say it to make it easier."

"Don't worry. Just say it as it is. I'll live." Eton gave him a weak smile that stopped short of his eyes.

- 238 -

"Okay. I know that you know what would happen if either you or I, or both of us are ousted. I know you understand that you, we need to be *exceptionally* discreet. More discreet than you've ever been. Because I am a foreigner and I am being watched continuously. You know that, right?"

"Yes. I know."

"Okay, good. But it's not only that, Eton. You said yourself that this, um, thing between us was short term." Eton's jaw muscles flexed and Jack hastened to add, "Okay, maybe as long as I'm here. And since I have been through *this*, um, *being* like this longer, I need to make sure that we're good. You'll just have to trust me, Eton... On this account." He looked expectantly at Eton until the young man nodded. "Good. Now. You know that eventually I'll leave, right? I'm sorry. I need us to be very clear about it."

"Don't worry. I know." Eton's voice was calm and steady.

Jack sighed and pinched the bridge of his nose. "Okay. So, let's talk about how we should deal with it, both now and, um, later... Goddamn it, Eton, I just need to know that you'll be *safe* when I'm gone!" he exclaimed, caught by surprise by his own outburst.

Eton turned to him, startled. "I'll be fine, Jack. Don't worry about me."

"No you won't! If you don't try to behave, to live a life like... others. You know what I mean?"

There was a loaded pause, then Eton asked quietly, "You want me to go out with girls?"

"I think you mother knows or at least suspects about you, Eton."

Again, Eton didn't respond right away. "She does, but not what you think."

"What d'you mean? What *does* she know then?"

Christ, how many more surprises was this man going to throw at him tonight?

Eton chewed on his lip, then sighed. "Remember I told you about my imaginary friend, Jack from California? My mother knew about *that* Jack." He shrugged awkwardly. "Gosha told her that you are from California."

"So... she knows that you think of me as your, um, imaginary friend in the flesh."

"No!" Eton shook his head and sighed again, "Maybe she suspects it... I'm sorry. This is so silly."

It was, but somehow it didn't bother Jack. On the contrary: that Eton seemed to think of him as his imaginary friend come to life made Jack feel oddly warm and fuzzy inside.

"It's alright. Stranger things happen in life... I guess it may even play into our hands. Hopefully, that's the only thing she thinks when she sees us, um, hanging out. We can't have her thinking anything else."

"She mustn't know. She can't deal with that... Alright, I'll try to be like others. I'll date girls and maybe even marry one later. When you're gone." His tone was resigned, and it cut at Jack's insides like broken glass.

"Eton, I wish—"

"Is that why you date Lara? So that she tells my mother about... you and her?"

"I have to, if you and I are going to hang out."

"I understand."

"I'm sorry, Eton. I just want you to make an effort and keep yourself out of harm's way... I wish there was another way." He lit a cigarette and rolled the window down a fraction.

"But there is another way for *you*, isn't there?" Eton asked after a long pause.

"What way?"

"I've read that gay men can live openly in America. That there are many of them in California. You can live like them. If you want... Right?"

God, this man was incorrigible!

"It's not as simple as you think."

"Why not?"

Now it was Jack's turn to sigh. "For starters, I can't in my line of work. I'll be thrown out of my job in a heartbeat." Besides, he had never thought about that possibility—being closeted was the only way he knew how to deal with being queer. "And it only sounds like there are many openly gay folks in America. In reality, they are a small minority. And they are all discriminated against."

"But at least you have a choice... Maybe when you leave your job and buy a ranch."

"Yeah, maybe I will... one day," Jack said thoughtfully, watching his friend with wonder. "But that day hasn't come yet. I can't quit my job now... I don't *want* to."

Eton turned to him, solemn, then his face eased into his usual crooked little smile. "I don't want it either. I shall do as you say. Don't worry, Jack. I shall keep myself safe. I promise."

It was raining heavily now and the streets they cruised along were deserted, but they felt warm and safe in their confined rolling world. Eton told Jack about *Krylia*'s plans to participate in the rock festival in Leningrad, about his decision to drop his other interests and focus on playing and writing music. Jack said he should, if it was something he truly wanted, and tried not to think that it wasn't the direction he was to guide his friend to and that he'd be in big trouble should his bosses find out about it. Then they just sat in companionable silence, sharing a cigarette and listening to the muted sounds of the tires on the rain-drenched asphalt, the sloshing and creaking of the windshield wiper, the sulky rumble of the engine. As they were nearing the starting point of the drive, Jack directed Eton to the empty parking lot where he had left his Mustang in a dark corner. When Eton parked next to Jack's car and turned off the headlights, they reached for each other and embraced, their mouths coming together naturally in a slow, tender kiss, and Jack's heart broke a little when Eton whispered against his lips, "Thank you, cowboy... For everything".

Chapter 35

Jack checked in at English Garden Guesthouse in the early afternoon. On the desk, he found a note telling him to meet Mr. Derek Malone at 7:00 p.m. at the bar of Restaurant Pfistermühle, near Marienplatz, a short taxi ride from his hotel. He unpacked and sat down on the bed.

He had over five hours to kill before the meeting with his chief of ops. He could visit a bar in the red light district behind the main train station or he could spend all five hours honing the story he had prepared for Joe about how he had been "developing" his potential agent.

He settled for the former, picked up a taxi in front of the hotel and told the driver to take him to the red light district. Should anybody be interested, it would be super easy to check out where he had headed immediately upon arrival.

As Jack expected, half the bars in the area were still closed. He chose the first open one, sat down at a table near the bar and ordered a beer. By the time he left, an hour and a half later, he'd had two beers and a quick fuck in the back room with a petite and curvy Caribbean looking woman who hadn't batted an eye when he said he wanted anal sex.

It started snowing, but he decided to walk back, nevertheless. It was close to 6:00 p.m. by the time he got to the hotel. He took a scorching hot shower, put on casual clothes, lay down across the bed and closed his eyes.

He could do this. If he considered it just another covert operation, with a bit of a polygraph test thrown in. It was a good idea to have got laid too: he felt more relaxed now. Maybe another drink would put him further at ease. He got up, went to the mini-bar where he picked a miniature bottle of whiskey, unscrewed the cap and took a mouthful of the warm, amber liquid. Then he went to the bathroom, brushed his teeth and looked at himself in the mirror.

Big blue eyes that everybody seemed to notice first. Good, strong nose. Mouth a little soft. All in all, an easy-on-the-eyes, friendly face.

Still tense, though. Relax! And where is that goddamn Jack Smith's signature smile?... Yeah, that's better. You're good to go.

He exhaled sharply, returned to the room, put on the coat and walked out.

At the restaurant, Jack ordered himself a beer and sat down at the bar to wait for Joe. Derek Malone. Maybe he shouldn't have been drinking that much on an empty stomach, but it made him feel warm and good, diluting the adrenaline that had kept him high-strung since his arrival in Munich.

He had finished two thirds of the stein when the familiar voice said behind his back, "Good evening, Jack. I see you've started without me."

Jack turned around and smiled sheepishly. "Good evening, Mr. Malone. Um, Derek. I was early, so I thought—"

"No worries. I'll join you in a minute." Joe smirked, not unkindly, and gave Jack a quick appreciative look over. Then he turned around and waved for the maître d'. They were taken into a small dining room with vaulted ceiling, wood-paneled walls and arched, medieval style windows. When they had been seated at the table in the far corner, the maître d', a rotund, balding man in his fifties, asked if *Herr* Malone wanted to try the chef's special. Apparently, the establishment knew Joe well.

They ordered the daily special, the boiled prime beef from the copper pot, and a bottle of Gewürztraminer. They talked about international politics and the upcoming summit while drinking their wine, waiting for their food to arrive, then about domestic news, sports and arts through the meal. And not once during the course of the dinner did Joe mention anything related to work. It all looked more like a date, rather than an informal, pre-debrief meeting with the chief of ops, and Jack didn't like it at all.

"I hope you enjoyed the food," said Joe when they finished their coffees, offering Jack his lazy, out-of-the-office smile.

"Thank you. I did. You can hardly find anything like this in Moscow," Jack said, hoping that the mention of Moscow would pull his boss back to business. "Unless you're invited home by *nomenklatura* friends."

It worked: Joe's eyes lost most of their playful glimmer. He turned to a waiter hovering nearby and gestured for the bill.

"I'm sure you're going to tell me all about it... Care for a brandy in my room?"

No, I don't.

"Wouldn't it be better with a fresh head tomorrow morning? I mean the debrief." Jack tried to project an air of all-business eagerness.

"It would. But we should briefly discuss the agenda for the next few days. I won't hold you up for too long... In case you want to go out again." The corner of Joe's mouth twitched.

Jack's smile faded.

"Don't worry. You're not under surveillance." Joe smirked. "I called you this afternoon to see if you wanted to meet up earlier. I was told that you were out. I trust you were careful."

"I always am. Don't worry about *me*."

The waiter came up and handed Joe the bill which he signed without looking. When the waiter had left, he turned his attention to Jack again. "So, a quick chat and a brandy in my room? I'm staying in the hotel in this building."

Jack nodded. Joe wasn't exactly asking if he wanted to.

Up in his suite, Joe poured them two glasses of brandy from the bottles in the mini-bar, handed one to Jack and sat down in the second armchair on the other side of the coffee table.

"Alright. We have two choices. We can stay in Munich and do the briefings *here*. In this hotel room." He pointed a finger at the floor. "Then drive to Garmisch on Monday where you'll have a read-in on a new assignment at the garrison. You'll have a weekend free with a place to stay that is paid for... Alternatively, we drive to Garmisch tomorrow morning and stay there for five days... Of course you can always return to Munich for the weekend and pay for your own stay, if you wish."

A weekend in Munich would probably cost Jack a half of his pay, if not more, taking into account the "recreational activities" Joe suspected he would be seeking here. The alternative was that Jack would have to spend two days in a hotel room working with Joe Coburn.

Who was studying him expectantly, with no hint of the earlier smirk.

"I'd rather go to Garmisch tomorrow."

"You sure?"

"I think it's better that way," Jack said quietly but firmly.

"Alright. We're leaving tomorrow morning then." Joe took a sip of his brandy. "I'll pick you up at your hotel at nine sharp."

"Okay. I'll be ready."

Is that it?

Joe took another sip of the brandy, looking at Jack thoughtfully. "Are you dating anyone?"

Jack's heart skipped a beat, but he held the eye contact. "Yes, I am." He tried to relax his face, not letting the challenge he felt seep through.

Joe continued inspecting him without a word, his face impassive.

"With a woman from the consular section." He was glad he'd made an effort to go out with Stella. He had no doubt it was a hot gossip at the Embassy by now.

"Good. I was worried about you a little when that English woman left... Is this serious? I'm assuming this one is single." There was a hint of curiosity in Joe's voice now.

"She is. We've just started dating. So I don't know yet... Maybe."

Jack didn't like the conversation, but his personal life was part of his job, too, in this line of business. Especially considering his personal "circumstances" that Joe was aware of, close and personal.

"You should get married, Jack. I told you this before. I don't think we'll be able to place you on your next posting if you remain single. It will be difficult to use the State Department jobs as cover for you."

"I know, Joe. I'm trying."

"The best would be if it's someone internal. From the department. Or at least from the Company... But of course it's your choice. It's your life after all." Joe shrugged. "Let me know if you need help."

Jack didn't need Joe's help with *this*, but said, "Thanks, Joe. I'll keep that in mind."

Apparently, the half-heartedness of his response didn't escape the chief of ops. He examined Jack pensively for a few seconds, then asked, his tone almost gentle, "Do you have *someone*, Jack?"

Jack slammed down on the impulse to shoot a bristled response. He cocked his eyebrows and said with fake surprise, "Yes, Joe. As I said, I'm dating a—"

"You *know* what I mean," Joe said flatly.

Jack held his eyes, willing himself not to flinch, nor swallow, nor lick his lips, and say in the same flat tone, "No, I don't have anyone... Who would I have in Russia, anyway?" He allowed himself to shrug.

Joe scrutinized him for a moment, then nodded. "Good. Please don't do anything stupid, boy. You have a promising career. Don't go and screw it up. Just pick a pussy and marry her. You could even hit the jackpot with your looks and... other charms." His face relaxed, and he smirked. "And no need to bristle. I mean you well. You know that, don't you?" He leaned forward and patted Jack on his knee, his expression almost affectionate.

"Yeah. 'Preciate that," Jack mumbled and gulped down the rest of his drink. "I think I'd better go. If there's nothing else we need to discuss."

He needed to get out of there as soon as possible and start figuring out how to tell his boss about his "progress" with Eton, without Joe figuring out what was going on.

Joe glanced down at his watch. "No, that's all for now... Are you planning to go *out* again?"

Jack put his glass down on the coffee table and stood up. "Maybe... Yeah. For a while."

"Be careful." Joe stood up and followed him to the door.

"Okay. I will... Good night, Joe." He nodded, not looking back.

"Jack."

Jack stopped rooted at the door and slowly turned around, his heart sinking.

Joe stood within an arm reach, a mask of nonchalance on his face. "I think it's better for you if you stay *here*. Safer... You'll get the same thing. For free. And no need to waste time on an SDR."

"I don't think it's a good—"

"And don't give me that crap about polygraph. You're exempt from it... For now," Joe added emphatically, his gaze heavy on Jack's face.

Jack opened his mouth to say that as far as he was concerned, they were *so* through, but the words stuck in his throat. He had never been a "relationship" to Joe, had he? He was just someone who gave the man what he needed. In return, Joe made sure that Jack had what *he* thought Jack needed. It was a fair play, as far as Joe Coburn was concerned, so why should there be any resentment or hurt feelings? Relationships only complicated things unnecessarily and Jack was supposed to have adopted his mentor's view by now.

"What is it that you get *there* that you can't get from *me*?" Joe challenged. "You want me to give you head? Huh? Fine, I can do that, too." He took a step closer, put his hands flat on the door on both sides of Jack's head, trapping him, and hissed through his teeth, "If you can still give it to me hard and fast afterwards. That's all *I* need... I know you need it, too."

"It's not *that*." Jack pushed him by the shoulders and stepped aside.

"Then what? What is it, Jack?"

Shit... Fuck! How was he supposed to report his progress with SEABROOK now? The man would know immediately that Jack was emotionally involved. There was no way Joe Coburn would believe that he would have sex with a virtual stranger because it was his job and wouldn't have it with the only person, as far as *Joe* knew, who took care of him. It didn't make sense. Unless there was something else going on.

"I think William suspects something... About you. And me," Jack said, uneasy.

The chief of ops took a step back. "William? What makes you think so? What did he say?"

"Nothing specific. But he keeps making allusions. Insinuations... I meant to ask you." Jack took another step away from Joe and raked all ten fingers through his hair.

"He does?" Joe was thoughtful for a moment, then said reassuringly. "Don't worry about William. I'll take care of that." He reached out and put a hand on Jack's arm.

"What do you mean? So he knows?" Jack pushed his hand away, suddenly anxious.

"He doesn't know anything you need to worry about. As I said, I'll take care of William."

"And how you gonna do that?"

"That's none of your concern, Jack. Just leave it to me."

"You must be joking! How is it *not* of my concern if he *knows* about me?" Jack was losing his cool together with his formal tone.

"He doesn't."

"How in the hell can you be so sure?"

"Because I know where *that* is coming from," Joe said evasively, stepping away from him.

Jack exploded. "Dammit, Joe! I want to know *what* William knows and *how*."

Joe's brows went up, his eyes widened. He had never known that Jack Smith had a temper, too. "Okay, Jack, okay... Well, William was part of a small team that originally designed the strategy for, um, the SEABROOK type of ops. It had been conceived a few years before you joined, but only recently approved for implementation. On an experimental basis, in conjunction with this joint project with the NSA. As I told you, only five people know the details. And since you report directly to me on a part of the op that has a queer link, with May Senior, William may suspect that something's going on. But he doesn't know shit about *you*, Jack. You shouldn't—"

"Are you kidding me? If he suspects that I'm a fucking 'honey trap', what do you suppose he'll make of it, Joe? Why didn't you warn me about him?"

"You don't *have* to be—"

"And why the fuck didn't you tell me about... all *this*?" Jack threw his hands up in exasperation, for a moment at a loss for words. "That you've been cultivating me for *this* fucking *operation*, all the while? Maybe right from the beginning..." He hated himself for sounding bitter, but couldn't help it.

"I didn't plan on it in the beginning. I took a bet on you, Jack, and you've proven to be the best, out of the whole pack."

It was the highest compliment in Joe Coburn's books, but Jack took it like a slap in his face. "Proven with my dick, huh?" He stormed up to Joe and spat out in his face, "That's *all* you want from me, Joe? My dick? For yourself and your grand fucking intelligence schemes?" He grabbed Joe by the front of his cardigan and pushed him backwards. "Is that all you want from me? My fucking dick? You'll get it, right fucking now!"

Jack gripped at his shoulders and forced him down on his knees. Joe didn't fight back, let Jack shove him around. And it only made Jack madder because he knew it was exactly what Joe wanted from him. But by now, he was out of control and couldn't stop himself. He undid his slacks in two seconds, pulled his dick out, half hard with all adrenaline going, and thrust it in Joe's face.

Joe had never gone down on Jack, never asked Jack to do it either, hard and fast fucking had been all he ever needed. Now he looked at Jack wide-eyed, breathing hard, as if he was unsure of what he was supposed to do about it.

"You wanted to give me head, didn't you? This is your chance," Jack grated out and thrust his penis against Joe's lips.

Joe gulped, opened his mouth tentatively and licked the tip of Jack's cock. Jack grabbed himself at the base and pushed into the man's mouth. He winced, sucked in a breath as Joe's teeth scrapped his shaft, and pressed his free hand down hard on Joe's shoulder.

"Goddamn it! You don't have a fucking clue how to give head, do you? What kind of queer are you?"

Joe let go. He gazed at Jack wide-eyed, a shadow of awe in his eyes that Jack had never seen before. Jack hauled him up, undid his belt with a couple of forceful pulls, pushed Joe's pants down, then him too, on all fours.

"Jack, wait!" Joe sprung up. "Condom... You need a condom. I have it here..." He reached for his trousers pocket and started fumbling in it.

"Oh, fuck it! Fuck you, Joe!" Suddenly Jack's aggression was seeping out of him quickly and with it his erection.

"No, wait! I'll do it, Jack. I'll suck you... Come 'ere." He grabbed Jack's hand and knee-walked up to him deftly. He then wrapped his other hand around Jack's now half flaccid penis, bent his head down and took him in his mouth, his teeth covered this time.

Jack hissed and made a weak attempt to push the older man away, but his other head was winning the battle. So he just closed his eyes and gave in to the sweet sensation he craved, but couldn't hardly get in the place he was sentenced to. He kept his eyes closed, trying not to flex his hips. And only when Joe's mouth was gone, replaced by a tight feeling of a thin layer of rubber being rolled on his shaft, that he opened his eyes.

Joe was already on all fours, his pale and a little saggy ass on display and at Jack's mercy. "Jack?" he called weakly, looking at Jack over his shoulder, his eyes swimming with lust.

Jack spit on his palm, gave himself a few close-fisted pumps, stepped up and propelled himself into Joe in one hard stroke that caused them both to grunt in pain and guilty pleasure. He held still for a moment, trying to reign in his breath, then closed his eyes again and started thrusting, hard and fast.

It was all over in under a minute. And as he leaned forward, his hands on the older man's back, post coital shudders fading, Jack whispered brokenly under his breath, "I'm sorry", and bit hard on his lip to keep a name from slipping out.

* * *

Joe came to pick him up at 9:00 a.m. sharp. They mumbled their good-mornings and Jack followed the chief of ops to his car parked near the hotel entrance. When Jack deposited his suitcase into the trunk, Joe waved him to the passenger seat.

They rode in silence while Joe navigated through the traffic on the narrow streets of the downtown. Once they rolled out onto a wide road, Joe glanced over at Jack and asked with an amiable smirk, "You sleep well?" The man was in his usual after-fucking mood—mellow and a tiny bit distracted, as if he was still savoring the memory of the sex he had had.

"Yeah... A couple of shots helped." Jack forced a thin smile.

"You're not relying on alcohol too much, are you, Jack?" He looked briefly at Jack again.

"No. Just a shot or two. Now and then."

"Good. Try to keep it that way, boy."

Jack nodded. He tried to look and sound normal, like nothing out of the ordinary had happened between them yesterday. Like Joe wasn't driving him now, for the first time ever.

Like he hadn't noticed the awe in Joe's eyes when he had shouted at him and shoved the man around the previous night. Jack hadn't liked that look and wasn't proud of himself, remembering it now. He wanted to hate the man for pulling him into all this shit, but deep down he knew he had himself to blame in equal measure. Joe hadn't exactly twisted his arm when he invited Jack for interviews with the Agency's recruiters. And hadn't Jack enjoyed and even been proud of his job in the beginning, even if that positive feeling had been short-lived? No, he couldn't hang all the blame on Joe Coburn. The man had done what in his mind was "mutually beneficial" for all concerned. He even tried to take care of Jack, in his own quirky way.

"About William. Like I said, don't worry about him." Joe threw a quick encouraging half-smile at him. "He knows *nothing* about you, Jack. He just... resents you."

"Resents *me*? Why on earth would he resent me?"

The patrician William Osbourne III? Nah, not possible.

Joe wavered before responding. "He wanted to be *the* first in the scheme. You get extra brownies points for running a successful pilot—a bonus, even an early promotion. Told you this, didn't I?"

"He wanted to be a raven?" Jack stared at his chief of ops, incredulous—William wanted to play a honey trap in *this* kind of op? "Are you saying that William Osbourne is queer?"

"No, he isn't. He just wanted to do the pilot. But we didn't get a green light till this case. And you've landed it, you lucky bastard." He smirked fondly at Jack.

"And how does William know that this is *that* kind of op?"

"I don't think he knows. I'd say, he suspects. He's read the Hamilton - May file. It has a queer angle. You have been assigned to develop May junior. You report directly to me on SEABROOK which neither he nor Nurimbekoff are cleared for. It all adds up, doesn't it?"

Maybe it did, but Jack didn't like it all the same. "Maybe," he muttered.

"Just ignore it. There's nothing he can do about it... Alright? Are we good?"

Jack bit on his lip, unsatisfied, but nodded all the same.

"Do you want to tell me about the May kid while we're driving?" Joe asked when they bulleted out on the highway. "Save you time for other things."

Jack's guts rolled into a tight ball and he willed himself not to respond right away, hesitating for a second or two, as if thinking. "Alright."

"Good. Where are you with him?"

"I've made a move on him." Jack looked straight ahead as he spoke, his tone impassive, and only after he'd said it, did he turn to meet Joe's eyes.

"You have? Ahead of plan, aren't we?" Joe looked surprised, and a little guarded.

Jack held his eyes and nodded.

"Oh-kay… Are you going to tell me more? Did you fuck him?"

Jack fought the impulse to clench his jaw and throw "it's none of your fucking business" at his boss. "Christ, Joe, d'you need to know this shit?… Okay. No, I didn't. Alright?"

"No, it *isn't* alright." Joe shook his head but his laid-back mood stayed. "The fact that you don't need to write it up and don't get to be asked about it under polygraph doesn't mean you don't have to tell me about it… C'mon, Jack, you know the drill." He gave Jack an encouraging half-smile. "When, where and how."

Jack sighed and bit on the inside of his cheeks. He shouldn't have agreed to be drawn into this shit in the first place. Now it was way too late. And given the circumstances, he should consider himself lucky that Joe was at ease and a little distracted right now.

"The weekend in the countryside. I'm sure you've seen the report. Everything was there. Except… the move." Joe kept silent, but Jack knew he was expecting more. "He was drunk. Everybody was. I went for a walk to clear my head and ran into him. He was chilling it off by the river. So I joined him and… He was caught off guard, but didn't resist. So, we, um, jerked each other off." He shrugged, trying to brush away the startling sense of disgust. With himself.

"What happened afterwards? The next day?"

"Nothing." Jack shrugged again, made sure he kept a steady eye contact. "He acted like nothing had happened and I didn't push him."

The lie came out smooth and easy, surprising Jack himself. He hadn't planned to lie, he just hadn't thought through what he was going to give Joe after the previous night. Turned out this was it and he didn't feel the slightest reservation about it. Ha, they'd been drilling him to lie most naturally, most convincingly. He had turned out to be an excellent student.

"But he didn't shun me either," Jack breezed. "We met a few times since—at the library, at my place, with his gang. Went to see a movie once… It's all in my reports."

Joe's expression was relaxed and easy. "Alright, Jack. Well, I don't see how we can put this incident to use, anyhow. Sounds like he was drunk… Keep it that way and I'm sure you'll have another chance. Don't hold back then and don't let him forget. See if they pitch you after *that*." He finally noticed Jack's clenched jaw, reached out and patted Jack's knee. "You've done well, boy. Keep it up."

When Jack was done with his updates, the chief of ops briefed him about a new project he was assigned to. Jack would be seconded to East Berlin where he would "accidentally" run into a Stasi officer targeted by East Berlin Station. Jack was to observe him, engage him if possible, and assess him for vulnerabilities. Joe's eyes were not easy and smiling any more when Jack asked suspiciously why him—he simply stated he considered Jack the most suitable candidate. It seemed that Joe had put their little extracurricular activity firmly in the past and was back in this chair as the chief of clandestine operations.

Jack spent the rest of the day reading the microfilmed file in one of the garrison's briefing rooms. He got his answer to why him: the chief of East Berlin station, who'd identified the target, indicated that the man was either a homosexual or had some sort of "other unorthodox sexual interests".

He had suspected as much. It looked like SEABROOK wasn't the only op Joe had been planning on using him in this role. He should have known when he accepted to run SEABROOK that the chief of ops didn't waste his resources on one-shot things, never did anything without long term planning. But knowing Joe, it had already been too late even by then. Fucking Joe Coburn! And worst of all, not only couldn't he quit now, he didn't know when he would be able to. Not with Eton waiting for him to come back and... He didn't know what Eton expected from him, either. He just knew he had to come back.

They finished the briefings by Monday noon. The new op in East Berlin wasn't expected till sometime in February, and Jack was to spend a couple of weeks at the consulate in Frankfurt prior to that. In the meantime, he was to continue with his assignments in Moscow, but shouldn't aggressively pursue his friendship with the Russians. Instead, he was to let them do the pulling.

Jack spent the three days at the American consulate in Munich helping the local USIA team. The assignment wasn't particularly time consuming and, as a result, Jack spent half of his time reading and watching news on the Geneva summit.

The only agreement reached at the summit was for the leaders of the two superpowers to visit each other's country. It was an outcome that had been expected by most diplomats, agents, politicians and everybody else, since the preparatory meetings hadn't yielded even one meaningful concession on either side.

Jack never mentioned to anyone that he preferred the Soviet proposal—for the two superpowers to cut their nuclear arsenals by half. Knowing what he knew now about the nuclear winter theory, he thought the proposal made sense. He was disappointed when the White House rebuffed Moscow's invitation to join their unilateral moratorium on nuclear tests. And even more so when the Reagan administration announced the first successful test of the new Strategic Defense Initiative.

However, following the news and discussing world politics weren't the only things Jack did in Munich. Every evening he had dinner with his colleagues, or some random people he'd met at the consulate. At the end of the dinner, he would tell them, laughing and joking, that he was going to check out local nightlife. Then he would cruise bars and clubs downtown and, except for a quick, surreptitious fuck with a tall, blond man at the back of a nondescript bar one night, would spend the night out with a woman.

And all that time he tried not to think about what he had advised Eton to do to keep himself safe. Because Joe had given him exactly the same counsel on how he should live his own life, for safety's sake. He wished he could tell Eton something different, something better, but what could he say if he hadn't yet figured out how to live his own life in a different, if not better way.

Some encouraging news caught up with Jack when he returned to Moscow. Within two days of each other, American newspapers front-paged stories about three arrests:

of Jonathan Pollard, a former U.S. Navy intelligence analyst, who had been spying for Israel, of Larry Wu-Tai Chin, a retired CIA analyst who had been spying for China, and finally of Ronald Pelton, a former NSA employee, who had been selling information to the KGB. Jack had heard about the latter case from Joe. The chief of ops had told him that information on Ronald Pelton had come from Yurchenko, together with the tip off on Edward Lee Howard, whom the FBI had lost track of back in September.

It was a strange year, with all these intel assets being busted and rolled up on both sides. Jack prayed that this disastrous wave would go over his head and leave him unscathed in this harsh and unforgiving place. He had to stay here for another year or two to ensure that his future agent Eton May Volkonsky, code name GTSALT, was ready for recruitment.

And more importantly that he knew how to keep himself safe.

His friend Eton... Okay, maybe he was more than just a *friend*. Maybe even more that his *best friend*. For now...

Chapter 36

November 12, Tuesday. 11:37 p.m.

Dear Jack,

I have been thinking about what you told me about Grandfather and his NW research. The more I think about it, the more I'm convinced you are right — he has been working on this project for KGB. Is that why he has been so defensive about Alexin's mathematical model? Has he been "influencing" Anya's father and the American team so that the model they are running shows the desired results? Exaggerated results and conclusions. But why? Why would the organs want the results to be exaggerated? And why would Prof. Ack. and his team go along with it? What's in it for them?

Cannot believe Grandfather has been working for the organs all this while. How could he?? It is so not like him. But taking into account how he has been able to shield all of us from them, it must be true.

Yes, that must be why — to protect us, his family. They haven't touched us so far, have they? Poor Grandpa. Knowing him, it must be hard for him to sell his soul to the devil.

What does all this tell about me, then? I have been aware that I am shielded (by Grandfather) from troubles. But subconsciously I have refused to recognize what it really meant. Because it is convenient. And safe. It gives you a false sense of freedom. At the expense of Grandfather's freedom. It makes me a hypocrite, does it not? A selfish bastard. But what should I do? What can I do?

I wish I could talk to you about this. Maybe someday.

And I want to know about Grandfather's original study, too. I will look for it myself. It is easier for me anyway: I can use the MGU's library and the specialized sections at Lenin Library that you may not get a pass for.

Grandfather said I shouldn't read it. Is he afraid that I will challenge its conclusions? But he already knows that I have a problem with this study — so what's new?

Perhaps he is afraid that I will challenge it openly and will attract the attention of the organs. Yes, that must be it. And if they pay attention to me, it may lead them to you. You don't need this. Not you, cowboy. I don't want it.

Grandfather is right — I should be very careful about this original study.

November 14, Thursday. 10:45 p.m.

Dear Jack,

They have just showed a strange press conference on TV, given by a Soviet diplomat named Yurchenko. He claimed he had been kidnapped by the CIA in Rome, taken to the USA and kept there drugged for 3 months while they tried to get sensitive information out of him. Then he managed to escape from his guards and come to the Soviet Embassy in Washington. His story sounded like a cheap spy movie to me. What I find curious is that it is the third spy incident in the last 5 months: first, our organs arrest a CIA agent in the act of spying; then we expel thirty-one English diplomats and businessmen for spying; and now this.

He said he is just a diplomat. What would the CIA want from "just a diplomat"?

You said the organs would blackmail you if they had a chance (if they "know") because you are an Am. diplomat.

What would KGB want from a cultural affairs officer? Maybe access to the information at your embassy? Possibly.

What would you do if this happened? If they knew about you? (and me)? Will you tell your bosses that you are blackmailed (and what with) or will you give away the information they want?

I would admit it.

But what if I were in your position and you were in mine? What if I knew that once I admitted it, I would be thrown out of the job, sent home and would never see you again? What would I do?

I have no answer to this question.

I am a fool: you are not me. You are not haunted by these kinds of questions and self-doubts. Are you?

E.

November 17, Sunday. 3 minutes to midnight.

Dear Jack,

I have been thinking about what you said about dating girls.

I know I have been untruthful with everybody about who I truly am. For a long time. But choosing someone and lying purposefully to them? I don't know. I have promised you that I will do it; I just don't know how I am going to live with it.

E.

November 18, Monday. 10:30p.m.

This is about girls again.

You mentioned Anya when you said I need to date girls. I want to tell you about her. I will tell you in person some time later when we have enough time.

So, Anya. She has been my friend since we were kids. She and Sevka. We called ourselves the Three Musketeers when we were young teens. We used to tell each other everything. I told them everything, too, except about my imaginary friend Jack, don't know why; but in hindsight, it is good that I didn't tell them.

Then one day, things changed: we grew up. We continued being best friends, but we stopped telling each other everything.

I know Sevka likes Anya more than he puts on. I think he loves her. But he wouldn't tell her. Because we are best friends.

All right, so that is not entirely true. He stays away because ~~he thinks Anya and~~ ~~I~~ Anya likes me. More than I want to admit. I have been trying to ignore this for a long time.

And this is not all. It is more complicated than that.

Anya's father, Dmitri Alexandrovich, was once in love with my mother. Mother used to go out with him when he was doing his post-graduate research at Grandfather's dept. Then one day Father appeared in the dept. and Mother fell in love with him. People say it was love from the first sight. They got married soon after. She was only nineteen, younger than me now. A few months later D.A. married Anya's mother. She was Grandfather's assistant.

Tamara Tikhonovna does not like Mother. I remember when my parents divorced and Mother and I came to live with my grandparents, T.T. caught Mother in the courtyard a few times and confronted her. I didn't understand why she behaved like that. Not until much later. I didn't even get it when Anya told me once that her parents quarreled because of Mother. We were eleven. Anya understood it even back then, but I didn't. Not until one day when I came home and overheard D.A. telling Mother that he would always wait for her; that she only needed to tell him one word and he would leave everything and be with her.

I guess he is still harboring hopes. He has always encouraged Anya to be friends with me. And so she has been, against her mother's will. T.T. does not like me either. That is why Anya feels at home at our place; but I hardly go to hers, even though her family lives in the next building.

It's complicated. Anya thinks it is fateful that both her father and she are "tied" to our family. She confided about it to Lara once. Lara told Sevka; he told me. He tried to look glad, for me, but I knew he was sad. Perhaps even heartbroken.

And so, my friend, here we are, in a classic love triangle. Except that I love someone I can never tell my friends about. Like I never told them about my pen pal, the Little Cowboy.

Hope I will not hurt my best friends. At least, not more than I may already have.

Yours always,

E.

November 21, Thursday. 11:30 p.m.

Dear Jack,

The summit between Gorbachev and Reagan was concluded in Geneva today. TASS reported that they didn't reach an agreement to reduce nuclear arms by 50% as proposed by our side. I wouldn't be surprised if there were more conditions to our proposal than simply that. But why couldn't the Am. side take this opportunity to find a solution to reduce the redundant nuclear arsenal? Even if our NW model is hugely exaggerated, neither of our sides needs the existing stockpile of nuclear arms. It doesn't make any sense to me. I'm certain it doesn't make sense to you, either. I wonder if you know why your gov. didn't go along with Gorbachev's proposal.

I keep recalling the conversation about the nuclear policies and history lessons at our place 2 weeks ago. I had never heard Grandfather expressing such views on this topic before. In fact, he doesn't like to talk about politics. Why did he talk about it that day? Somehow, I think it was because of your presence. Because you are from the Am. embassy. I wonder if he wanted to provoke you to talk about politics. Or maybe he wanted to convey some message.

I do not believe Grandfather would inform on anyone. Not even on you, cowboy. Not him, I'm sure. Maybe that's why he has sacrificed his work and his scientific integrity to them instead. That's what we do in our family for the ones we love.

E.

November 23, Saturday. 00: 20 a.m.

Dear Jack,

I played the piece I composed to my guys yesterday. I call it "Atomic Twilight". They like it. We have agreed to practice it for the Leningrad rock fest. I am thinking of asking Karelin to stage it for us.

I have also written a song that I want to play at the rock fest, too. Don't know if they will like it. Don't even know if my guys will want to play it with me. It's a love song. Russian rockers don't usually do love songs, esp. not ones written in the first person like mine. We Russians are not good at telling the ones we love how we feel about them. How much we love them. We do "things" for them instead, without words.

I wish I could play my song to you one day. It is for you.

E.

8: 38 p.m.

Izvestia published Gorbachev's interview with western journalists today. Something he had said caught my eye. "For, despite all our differences, in perception and approach, we do have something in common - our understanding that nuclear war is inadmissible, that it cannot be waged and that there will be no winner in a nuclear war." And then he said "the world has become a safer place" because of the summit.

I wonder if he referred to the NW theory. I wonder if the report on our work had indeed been delivered to him before the summit. If so, did he share it with Reagan? A report based on inaccurate results.

I have been thinking: does it matter if the scientific results are inaccurate, if they help to achieve global results desired by millions? As a physicist, I don't have an answer.

E.

November 24, Sunday. 11:45 p.m.

Dear Jack,

There was nothing wrong with me. Honest! I was just so glad to hear your voice that I did not know what to say.

You said your trip was okay, but you sounded tired. Or maybe I imagined it. Hope everything is really okay.

I didn't about the plans for Grandfather and Dmitri Alexandrovich to go to America. Didn't realize that there must be the last meeting between our team, Prof. Ack's team, your organization and the WMO to agree on the final report. I wish I could join. Even if I know I am the last person you all need there. Especially when I am not in complete agreement with it. I wish I could go, anyway.

Perhaps one day.

See you at Grandfather's lab on Wednesday.

Yours always,

E.

November 27, Wednesday. 9:43 p.m.

Jack,

There was something not quite right with you this morning. You looked worn-out, with deep shadows under your eyes. It was very subtle, but I think you avoided me. You tried to keep some distance between us. What is wrong, cowboy?

You know what? Let's go to the movies - Anya, Lara, you and I. Like you said we should. I will call Lara.

11:25p.m.

We are going to the movies on Sat. Lara will get the tickets. She will call you tomorrow.

E.

December 1, Sunday. 1:00 a.m.

Jack,

I deeply regret for ruining the evening for everybody. Only Lara did not notice; or maybe she just ignored it as usual. Anya felt there was something wrong, too: she tried to brighten the mood up in her awkward, serious girl way. Poor, kind Anya.

And you. I spoiled the evening for you, didn't I? I am so sorry.

The truth was I could not just sit there, watching Lara flirting with you, throwing herself at you. Touching you. Like you belong to her. I should have thought twice before asking Lara to get movie tickets for the four of us. I was stupid to think I would be able to control it. How wrong one can be! I cannot do it, Jack. I would rather not knowing about it. Not seeing it at least.

I wish I could at least tell you how sorry and ashamed I was. That was what I thought about when I drove you home. As usual, I could not make myself open

- 255 -

my damned mouth. But I think you knew. Even if both of us acted as if nothing had happened, didn't even talk much at all. Just sat there smoking, listening to the radio.

I don't know how this is possible: a simple act like sharing a cigarette fills me with such intense connection with you that I feel like I can close my eyes and never open them again. I feel complete. How can this be?

How can one live after this, knowing that you will never feel this ever again?
E.

December 8, Sunday. 11:12 p.m.

Dear Jack,

Thanks for letting me know you will be tied up this weekend. I would have spent most of the day home yesterday, waiting to hear from you. (God, I sound like a love-sick little girl! And the strangest thing, I am not ashamed. I know you will not laugh at me, should you know. Will not judge me. How do I know? No idea. I just do.)

I went to visit Mother and Grandfather and stayed overnight. Haven't slept over there for ages. It felt strange sleeping in the bed that I used to sleep when I was little, then a teenager, dreaming about what we (Jack the Little Cowboy and I) would do in the forest near Eureka, Calif.—hunting, fishing, swimming in the lakes. Father said there are many lakes in that region. I remember one—Fallen Leaf Lake. Don't even know where it is located exactly. And it felt surreal to be thinking of the little Jack from Calif. when you, Jack, are out there somewhere, in Moscow.

There is another thing: while I was reading Mother's magazines last night, I came across an article in Sovetskaya Kultura, about AIDS in the Soviet Union. It said that there are only "less than 10" cases of AIDS in the entire S.U. It also said that this disease affects mostly homosexuals and drug addicts. That is not what the articles in TIME magazine you gave me said. Also, if this disease spreads at the speed they say it does in a country where people are aware of it, how can it be contained to only 10 people in a country where most people don't even know what AIDS is??

You may not believe it, but this is the first time that I have read a mention of Sov. homosexuals in a Sov. newspaper. Maybe I should subscribe to this newspaper.
E.

December 15, Sunday. 1:30 a.m.

Dear Jack,

I am tired, but don't want to fall asleep. Don't want to stop running through my head the vivid images of you, of us, right here in my bed, around an hour ago. The scent of you still on my pillow, even if you have taken all your warmth away with you. But I know when I close my eye, I will see your face again—above me, within reach, looking down at me. Your lips, swollen by my kisses, smiling. A drop of moisture rolling down your cheek. Brows like two powerful wings, spread wide above the dizzyingly blue eyes. I can swear I saw happiness in your eyes. For a brief moment the troubled look that has taken root in them recently went away and suddenly I feel lightheaded. Just by looking into those eyes and seeing that strange soft light shining down on me.

Afterwards, I asked "does it always feel like this?" The question startled you. Perhaps you thought I was asking if sex with others makes you feel like ~~with me.~~ I made you feel. Of course I would never ask you such a question. It is weak. It reeks of jealousy. But I admit, I want to know. I keep telling myself that I don't care. But I care: I wish I was the only one who could make you feel like that.

You gave me a long-winded answer. In short, you said "it depends". Of course it does, I know that. For me, it depends on whether it is you or not. Never mind. I think you knew what I meant. And you will never know how happy I was that I could make you feel that way. Even for a fleeting moment.

Yours for always,

E.

9:12 a.m.

About the sex. I still can't find a right word for it, for mind-blowing now seems getting old. Somehow, it is losing to the feeling of completeness that possesses me when I hold you in my arms. I can live, or die, for it alone, if there is nothing else.

I love you.

E.

December 18, Wednesday. 9:48p.m.

-25C tonight. The weather forecast says it will stay this cold till the end of the week. A perfect weather to curl up in bed with someone. You.

This is for you:

> I want to ask the stars
> how to shine
> for you alone
> through the glare
> of the city lights.
> I want to ask the trees
> how to green
> into your dreams
> about a different land
> where I have never been.
> I want to ask the desert
> and every grain of sand
> how to erase
> and how to mend
> the hate,

intolerance
and pain,
to help us stumble not
on each step
over our prejudiced
differences.
I want to ask the truth
how to make
my stupid self believe
that
even the faintest ray of hope
might be not
between us...
I want to ask you:
Why?
But then I look away
every time
wordlessly
you gaze at me,
willing me
to silence my question...
 E.

December 20, Friday. 11:55 p.m.

Dear Jack,

This is about me and girls again.

I know I have been hiding behind Grandfather's back for a long time, pretending that I could do everything my way because I am special. (Different, yes; but special?? It is such a joke!) So hiding behind someone's back is not something entirely new for me, is it? Why should I feel offended by the idea?

So I will do what you said I should. I will choose a girl and hide my true self behind her back. Because it is convenient. Because it is safe. Because it gives you a false sense of freedom to do what you want most - to be with the one you truly want. The only one.

I will do it, Jack. I will be a bastard and do it. For you, moy vasil'yok, my blue cornflower. To keep you safe while you are here. With me. I will think of what to do "after you" later, when you are gone from this place. From my world, but not from my heart.

Never from my heart.

 E.

Chapter 37

Back in Moscow, Jack discovered that the Geneva summit was a preoccupation of not just the entire Embassy staff but of the whole of the Moscow populace—and seemingly of the rest of the vast country.

The news of the Reagan-Gorbachev meetings had been on the front pages of the international and local press for several days running. All major Soviet newspapers printed the full text of the Soviet - U.S. agreement, and even some of the transcript of Gorbachev's one-hour-forty-minute long interview with journalists before he had left Geneva. For once the news was printed free of political commentary. But that wasn't all: during those few days, the Soviet news media dropped its standard anti-American invectives and even ran lengthy quotes from Reagan's report on the summit to the Congress—all this without a single negative comment.

On Friday, the day Gorbachev returned to Moscow, the country's leading newspaper Izvestia took another unprecedented step: the front page of the evening edition carried interviews with common people whom correspondents had stopped on Red Square to ask their views on the Geneva summit. Most of them were positive. Most pointed out the joint declaration that "a nuclear war cannot be won and must never be fought". It was obviously a novelty to Soviets to hear that America did not want war—the same America that was always depicted as warmongering and dictatorial.

These extraordinary events prompted speculation and interpretation by western political analysts about the emerging trend in Soviet policies. The most frequent comment was that it all looked like Gorbachev's *glasnost* was finally becoming real.

For a few days after his return, Jack tried to stick to Joe Coburn's recommendation not to be aggressive with his Russian friends and let them do the pulling. But on Sunday he gave in and called Eton. They chatted on the phone for fifteen minutes and Eton told Jack that *he* was going to do the "review" of his grandfather's work because it was easy for him.

He saw Eton again when he went to the MGU to debrief with the Soviet nuclear winter team and to discuss Prof. Volkonsky's and Dr. Arceniev's trip to America. He was uneasy, but forced himself to sound natural as he talked about the travel itinerary which included a two-day visit to Berkeley. He felt Eton's eyes on him, burning holes in the side of his face, but when Jack turned his head to look at him, Eton immediately dropped his gaze. His face was the usual impassive mask, only his long, nervous fingers seemed to live a life of their own.

The following day Lara called and announced to Jack that he was going to the movies with her, along with Anya and Eton, to see a rerun of "Kramer vs. Kramer".

"This Saturday, at the House of Actors," she said, referring to the exclusive cinema in the extravaganza of a building on Arbat Street that housed the Soviet actors' association.

Of course he said yes—they were doing the pulling as Joe wanted, weren't they?

The double date turned out to be rather awkward. Jack and Lara ended up making most of the small talk, with Anya responding with exaggerated enthusiasm to compensate for

Eton's sullen silence. He was edgy and distracted and hardly looked in Jack's direction all evening and Jack had little doubt why: Lara clung to him like they were joined at the hip, first touching his arm every so often, and then holding his hand through the movie. By the end of the evening, Jack regretted that he had agreed to this stupid outing.

But after they'd dropped the girls off, Eton drove him home and somehow everything eased back into place. They spoke little as they rode through deserted Moscow streets, letting their fingers brush and linger as they shared a cigarette, listening to Vysotsky's coarse yet balmy voice singing about stealing his love away from the enchanted forest to make their Eden together in a shed.

As Eton parked the car two blocks away from Jack's apartment building, Jack reached for his hand to say goodbye. Eton held on to it and awkwardly pressed their clasped hands against his stomach. He gave Jack his crooked little smile, a pained expression in his eyes. Jack cupped his other hand to the nape of his neck and shook him lightly.

"It'll be alright, bud," he said with a smile, trying to exude the confidence he didn't feel.

December started on a disconcerted note for most at the Embassy: the process of moving all Soviet employees from the central wing to the outer buildings on the Embassy grounds had begun. The move had been announced while Jack was on his mission in Germany, so when he returned, it was constantly the subject of office chatter.

When Nurimbekoff returned from the headquarters the first week of December, he confirmed the rumor that had been circulating since the outbreak of the spy dust scandal in August: the State Department was planning to replace the Embassy's two hundred or so Soviet employees with Americans and the recruitment of the first batch had already started.

The State Department did not issue its official announcement until mid-December. By that time, a sense of anxiety and disgruntlement had descended on the local staff, most of whom had been working at the Embassy for many years, some for over a decade. As a result, the Soviet employees spent a great deal of their time whispering and speculating quietly in corners. Some tried to secure their future with the Embassy by lobbying the American staff members with whom they felt most comfortable discussing their plight. Jack seemed to fall into this category for many of them, because he found himself spending all his free time, and sometimes even working hours, chatting with the local folks. He felt for them, but knew that there was nothing really he could do for them except give them his time, his sympathy and occasionally a useful tip.

On the second Friday of December, having exhausted his reserve of excuses, Jack gave in to Stella's insistent invitations to go out—for a "date *and all*". They had their drinks then dinner at the bar of Hotel Intourist again, then took a taxi to her place on Lenin Avenue at around midnight. She would have raped him right in the cab, had Jack been drunker than he was. As it was, he managed to fend off her attacks until they were in her apartment and the door slammed shut. When he left her place early in the morning, Jack silently thanked God that it was winter and his shirt with most of its buttons ripped off was well hidden under his heavy overcoat.

He took the Metro back home and called Eton from the street for a chat and to let him know that he would be tied up that weekend. Which wasn't exactly true. He just couldn't face Eton after the night with Stella. Of course, he had explained to Eton that they must date women, if they were to continue to see each other sometimes. Still, he didn't want him to know it for a fact. At least, not immediately *after* the fact. He was sure that Eton would be able to smell on his skin that he'd just had sex with someone else.

He managed not to talk to Eton for the whole week, but then on Saturday he gave up fighting with himself. Early in the morning, he called him to make sure Eton would be home in the evening.

When Eton drove him to a Metro station downtown after midnight, Jack was subdued and pensive. In his apartment, he brushed his teeth, gulped a triple shot of whiskey and went straight to bed, reveling in Eton's scent that was clinging to his skin.

After his first visit to Eton's place, Jack had stopped kidding himself about the guy. About the reason he wanted to see him most of the time, and why he thought about him most of the time. And he had finally admitted to himself that it had nothing to do with his assignment—he had become emotionally involved with his target. *Temporarily*, he had stubbornly insisted to himself.

But now, after Joe and Stella and half dozen other fucks in the last few weeks, it was dawning on Jack that he might not get that "thing" with anyone else that he'd felt with Eton tonight. And *every* time they were together. And it wasn't the sex that made him realize that, even though it had been no less mind-blowing than the first time. It was Eton holding him afterwards: their bodies fitting together like puzzle pieces, his back to Eton's front, Eton's lips occasionally pressing into the back of Jack's head, Eton's fingers softly drawing little circles in the middle of Jack's chest. Everything felt so goddamn right that he thought he could just close his eyes and die, right there, right then in Eton's arms. How would he ever be able to find *that* with anyone else wherever else he ended up after... after Moscow? How was he supposed to *live* with the knowledge that someone could make him feel that way, but that he would never be with that "someone"? Ever! How the fuck... How??

It took Jack three days to stop feeling as if he had lost direction and to regain his balance.

Eton called him a few days later to say that his family invited Jack "to meet the New Year in the Russian tradition" at their place—if Jack didn't have any other plans for that night, of course. His grandfather and mother would be in and out, and Lara, Anya, Seva and some other friends of Eton's would drop by between 7:00 p.m. and midnight.

Jack didn't have any particular plan for New Year's Eve. Most of the Embassy's American staff—including both his bosses, Stella, and others with whom Jack hung out—had either left or would be leaving shortly to spend the Christmas holidays with their families in the U.S. Jack was amongst the few who were staying behind. He didn't have a home or a family to go back to.

He was touched, knowing that for Russians, New Year celebrations at home were for family and close friends only. He had little doubt that the invitation came primarily from Eton, but the fact that his family had agreed to have him at their place on this night meant that they had accepted him as a family friend. Still, he wanted to be absolutely sure that he was not imposing, or rather, being imposed upon the family by his friend. So he kept asking Eton if he was sure it was alright for him to come until finally Eton said impatiently that he would ask his mother to call him. Jack laughed sheepishly and said there was no need and that he was extremely honored.

They talked on the phone two more times before New Year's Eve, but didn't see each other.

At seven sharp on December 31st, Jack was pressing the doorbell of the Volkonskys' apartment, a bag of presents and a bouquet of white chrysanthemums in his hands.

The door swung open and Eton smiled at him, wide and eager. "Jack, hello! Come in, please," he said in English, stepping aside to let Jack in.

He was wearing a cobalt blue, vee neck cashmere sweater and black dress trousers. His combed back hair looked damp, like he was just out of the shower. Jack noted that he had never seen Eton wearing a turtleneck, a garment favored by Russian men. He *was* different, this boy.

Jack walked past him into the entry hall, put the bag down on the floor. "Thanks so much again for inviting me," he said and extended his hand.

"I told you, we're glad to host you for the New Year's Eve." He looked a little flustered, and didn't break the handshake, just stood smiling, gazing into Jack's eyes. Then he yanked at Jack's hand and pulled him into hug.

Jack had barely managed to move the flowers out of the way before he found himself wrapped tightly in Eton's arms, cheek to cheek, the young man's long, lean body pressed against his own. He tensed up immediately. "Whatchadoin?" he hissed, trying to extract himself from the embrace.

Eton chuckled softly, tilted his head back to gaze into Jack's eyes, but didn't let go. "Nobody's home." His eyes were fixated on Jack's mouth.

"Ah... Let me put down the flowers at least."

As soon as the flowers were out of his hands, he found himself in Eton's arms again, his mouth on Jack's.

"Christ, Eton... you'll be... the death of me..." Jack mumbled, laughing quietly through the soft, open-mouth kisses.

"I will die with you... Don't worry." Eton pulled back for a moment, his face deadpan, his eyes sparkling with tease, then went right back to Jack's mouth, pushing his tongue between Jack's lips.

After a minute or two, Jack gently pushed on his shoulders. "Eton, we shouldn't, bud... Not now." He smiled apologetically and traced the tip of his finger across Eton's moist and already slightly raw lips. "You don't wanna look like you've just been kissing. Not without Varvara Petrovna home, at the very least. Right?" He winked at Eton wickedly and let out a quiet laugh at his friend's expression.

"That's disgusting!" He gave Jack a light shove in the middle of his chest.

"Guess what your folks would think if they came home now and saw that there's no one here but me. And you with this I've-just-been-kissed look on your face."

Eton's expression sobered. "Sorry. I didn't think about that."

Jack's heart squeezed. He pulled the young man into his arms, planted a gentle kiss on his temple and whispered, "It's okay, bud. Just be a tiny bit more careful. At all times. Alright?" He let go of him and picked up his presents. "For you. And everybody."

"Thank you so much. You really shouldn't have... Mother will love the flowers, I'm sure."

He walked past Jack into the sitting room and set the presents on the carved side table in the corner by a live fir tree. Voluminous and of ceiling height, it was generously decorated with multicolored glass balls, paper chains and lights. The light in the room was dimmed to let the lights on the New Year fir tree shine. The dining table was laid out in the middle of the room again, with eight place settings this time.

"So, where's everybody?" Jack stood in the doorway, looking around, as Eton took a crystal vase out of the cupboard and headed to the kitchen.

"Mother is upstairs at her friend Valiya's," Eton called out over the sound of water running. "Said she'll be back in an hour." He reappeared from the kitchen and put the flowers into the vase. "Grandfather is at the banquet in the Palace of Congresses. He should be home by ten o'clock. Varvara Patrovna left home an hour ago... Sit down, please." He looked at Jack uncertainly as if unsure what he was supposed to do next. "Would you like something to drink?"

Jack sat down on the sofa and grinned at him. "Nah, it's okay. I'll wait for everybody... Your friends are coming too, right?"

"Anya and Gosha will come over soon." Eton sat down on a chair by the table. "They are at Anya's place. She lives in the next entrance way. Seva will come over later, around ten maybe. And Lara—she called you, didn't she?"

"She did, yesterday. Said she would be back from the banquet before eleven. Is it the same banquet your grandfather's at? In the Kremlin?"

"Yes, it is. Her father takes her along for receptions all the time."

"That's how I met her—at the July 4th reception her father brought her to. I'm enormously grateful to Deputy Minister Novikov for that. And to Lara, for inviting me to a certain student concert at the MGU," Jack added, smiling softly at him.

Eton gazed at Jack thoughtfully for a few moments, then blurted out, "I like it more when you're unshaven."

"Is that so?" Jack grinned, feeling both awkward and ridiculously pleased.

"Yes. I, um, love to feel the uhm..." Eton quickly brushed the back of his fingers against his own cheek.

"Stubble?"

"Yes, I like to feel *it* on my skin."

Jack couldn't see it in the diffused light, but was pretty sure that the deep shade on Eton's face was not all from the flickering, multicolor lights adorning the fir tree. He sighed and shook his head. "I'm flattered, Eton. Really. But let's talk about something else, bud, alright?... So tell me, in layman's language, what's your post grad research about?"

Eton was still trying to explain to Jack the difference between nuclear fission and nuclear fusion when Anya and Gosha arrived. Ten minutes later Eton's mother returned from her friend's. After the exchange of greetings and heartfelt thankyous—Jack for the invitation and Eton's mother for the flowers and presents—the women headed to the kitchen and started laying out the New Year's Eve fare on the table. Gosha immediately turned on the

TV and took a strategic position at the table right across from the TV set. A show called *Goluboy Ogonyok*, the Little Blue Light, featuring the most popular singers, actors and comedians, was about to start on Channel One. It was the traditional New Year's Eve music and talk show that the entire country watched and Gosha didn't want to miss a second of it.

They started leisurely with the dinner while watching the show, exchanging comments and asking Jack about American shows and actors. He told them about his recent favorite, "Late Night with David Letterman", even mimicking some of Letterman's guests, which brought Gosha to tears, he was laughing so hard. Even Vera Mikhailovna and Anya were chuckling softly, both looking at Jack with expressions of quiet, friendly admiration. Almost the same expression with which, he had noticed, they looked at Eton.

When Seva and Grisha showed up at around nine thirty, a chilled bottle of Stolichnaya appeared on the table and the drinking went up a notch—among the boys at least. Eton's mother and Anya sipped at their sweet, fortified wine, smiling at them, looking contented. After the third toast, to Soviet-American friendship, Eton asked Jack if he was driving. When Jack said not today, he nodded, looking pleased, and said he would drive him home later and stopped drinking.

Prof. Volkonsky came home from the banquet shortly after ten o'clock. After a hearty handshake he told Jack that Lara sent her apologies for not showing up at the time she'd promised she would—her father had insisted on her staying with him till the end of the function—but she hoped Jack would wait for her. Volkonsky looked at Jack with poorly hidden sympathy as he passed on the message. As did others, Jack noticed. All except Eton, who stared at his plate, his face dull but his eyes blazing.

Around eleven, Dr. Arceniev with his wife dropped by to wish Prof. Volkonsky's family and Jack a happy new year. Anya's father was already loose-tongued and a little too flirty and it rather obviously displeased her mother. Jack noticed a hint of unfriendliness in Mrs. Arcenieva's expression as she watched her husband out of the corner of her eye as he was talking to Eton's mother. It looked like the couple's visit made half the people in the room uncomfortable and Jack wondered why.

The vodka glasses were filled and Arceniev said an elaborate toast, which was followed by hugs, kisses, handshakes and backslapping. There was an awkward moment, then Vera asked in a perfunctory tone if the couple wanted to join everybody at the table.

Mrs. Arcenieva gave a tight smile. "Thanks, but—"

"But of course we will!" countered her husband and sat right down on the spare chair next to Jack.

Seva jumped up, offered his chair to Mrs. Arcenieva and went to fetch another one. Vera asked Eton to help her bring new plates and more food.

The conversation around the table didn't flow as effortlessly as before and in a few minutes Grisha waved Seva out for a smoke. Jack excused himself and went looking for the restroom. Whatever the problem was between these people, he didn't really want to witness what was going to happen next. But mostly, he didn't care to see the pained and apologetic look on Eton's face whenever he caught Jack's eye. He hoped Anya's parents would leave soon so that the atmosphere could revert to what it had been before they'd come.

Jack lingered as long as he could. When he sensed it was about to seem strange to be missing for so long, he pulled the flush, walked out and stepped into the bathroom next to the toilet. He had just started soaping his hands when the door opened quickly. Eton slipped in and locked the door quietly behind him.

He met Eton's eyes in the mirror over the sink, anxiousness unfurling in his stomach. "Eton, we shouldn't...," he whispered.

"Shh... It's alright." He wrapped his arms around Jack, aligning his body with Jack's, head to toe, and pressed his lips into the nape of Jack's neck.

Jack sighed, closed his eyes and leaned back.

They stood like that for a minute, Eton rocking him ever so slightly. Then he placed another gentle kiss at the back of Jack's head. "I love you."

It was faint as a breath but Jack heard it all the same. He froze, his eyes flying open, his heart about to burst out of his chest, his mind screaming.

No, no, no, that's not right! Don't do this, Eton! You can't do this, friend! You can't do this to me!!

Their eyes met in the mirror. At the sight of the distress in Jack's, Eton's face shut down at once. He let go of Jack, opened the door, stepped out and closed quietly it behind him without a single word.

When Jack had regained his composure, pasted back on his usual affable expression and emerged to rejoin the party, Grisha and Seva were back at the table. The Arceniev elders were still there. Eton wasn't.

Jack didn't sit down. Instead, he reached for the new bottle of vodka on the table, refilled everybody's glasses and, smiling with exaggerated cheerfulness, proposed a toast "to the fair ladies behind all men of significance".

The rest of the men stood up to join him and all gulped down their brimming shot glasses. Five minutes later, Jack asked if he could make another toast and proposed one "to the eternal beauty of Russian women". He didn't have to make another one—the Russians took over, as if on a cue, and half an hour the vodka bottle was consumed.

Eton returned to the table after the third toast and was immediately made to take a penalty shot. He took one, but refused to drink any more, explaining he had to drive later.

Jack laughed and said, "Don't worry, my friend, I'll take a taxi. You can't *not* drink on New Year's, can you?"

Eton didn't say anything, just threw him a quick, enigmatic look. He didn't join the others when another bottle of vodka was opened, however.

Lara called half an hour before midnight. Eton's mother, who answered the phone, called Jack out into the corridor and passed the receiver to him, her smile sympathetic.

As he took the phone, Lara launched into a long, breathless apology, explaining that her father hadn't let her go, so now she was not able to get home by the countdown and she was so sorry that she made Jack wait for her and she promised to make it up to him later. She sounded tipsy.

Jack accepted her apologies with a loud sigh, declared he missed her and wished her the most beautiful things in the coming New Year. After he hung up, Jack locked himself in the toilet, sat down on the seat and pressed his fingers against his temples. He closed his eyes and wished fervently that he could get drunk enough not to remember... anything! But he couldn't get drunk, not here, not now.

He sat there until Vera knocked on the door and asked if he was alright. She peered into Jack's eyes as he stepped out, patted on his arm and said, "Everything will be alright. She's a good girl. Just a little too lighthearted sometimes." Her eyes were kind, her tone caring.

Back in the living room, everybody tried, discreetly they thought, to cheer Jack up by toasting him, offering him food, telling blonde jokes. He laughed dutifully, accepted all the toasts and food and tried to appear his usual cheerful self when his gaze happened to drift in Eton's direction.

Eton's face was inscrutable again, his smile tightlipped and obviously forced. But apparently everyone was used to his moods and paid him little heed. Except Anya: she tried surreptitiously to cheer her friend up by leaning his way sometimes and whispering something to him under her breath. Eventually it made him smile a fraction wider and drape his arm across the back of her chair.

Jack brushed aside the irrational desire to strangle Anya, stood up and proposed another toast—to friendship between all the people in the world and a world without nuclear wars. Then the New Year finally arrived, greeted with yet another toast and everybody wishing one another a happy New Year and Jack wishing the moment would come when he could excuse himself and leave. He desperately needed to be alone. To try to forget this evening, regain his composure and move on.

His moment came when Anya's mother stood up some ten minutes into the New Year and prepared to leave. Jack took the opportunity to announce that he should go home as well. He didn't manage to make Eton stay home though, and fifteen minutes later they were in his car, heading toward Jack's part of town.

The night was bight, the snowflakes floating in an endless roundelay in the crisp air. They were silent for a long time, pretending to be listening to a wordless tune on the radio. Jack felt he was going to explode any minute, with all the things boiling in his head. In his chest. He bit hard on the inside of his cheeks, fighting to keep his turmoil to himself.

Finally, he caved in. "I thought we talked about it, Eton! Why would you go and say..." The words got stuck in his throat.

But Eton continued his thought like he was reading Jack's mind, "That I love you? Because I do." He looked straight ahead of him, his voice low, unyielding.

"But Eton—"

"And you don't have to say or do anything about it, Jack. It is just one of those things. It happens."

"Eton, I—"

"Don't!... It's fine, Jack." He finally turned his head to look at Jack and smiled a little. "It's just me. Don't worry about it... Okay?"

He quickly brushed the back of his fingers along Jack's jaw line, still smiling, but Jack could see a world of loneliness in his eyes, even in the dark. Then Eton turned back to the road, reached to turn up the volume of the radio.

The vaguely familiar, haunting instrumental filled the confined space of the car, making Jack cringe. Who in their right mind play such fucking sad music on New Year's eve? Weren't people supposed to celebrate, to be happy, to laugh, to tell each other that they—

Fuck, fuck, fuck!!

Eton dropped Jack off three blocks from his house, said, "See you later", his tone steady, not even a hint of reproach or bitterness in it. Or anything at all for that matter. Just a normal, everyday tone.

"Yeah, see you later." Jack smiled at him, knowing that his smile would look fake to himself if he could see it.

The car took off the second Jack shut the door, the wheels flinging up fresh snow in Jack's face. There were a few people walking on the street—some drunk, some just having lots of fun. Within a hundred meters, the booze caught up with him. Jack dashed to the nearest tree and threw up the contents of his stomach onto the pristine white of the new snow. He retched, trying as well to get rid of the heavy lump lodged just below his solar plexus. Nothing came out but bile and stinging moisture that burned his eyes like acid.

Joe had said that boys like them don't cry and Jack didn't. Wouldn't! Agent Jack Smith code-name SAL... Fuck, no, TRISTAN! That's right, *case officer* TRISTAN... He could do that, no problem, sir. It was just all the bloody vodka he had consumed that was making him drunk.

He laughed and threw a happy-new-year back at a high-as-kites group of young people passing by, turning down the girls' invitation to join them, and staggered back to his apartment block. He wished a happy New Year to the *militsia* guard, who obviously had had some too and was amiable, then rode the smelly elevator up to his floor, leaning back against its flimsy wall, with his eyes closed.

In his apartment, Jack shrugged off his heavy overcoat and fur hat, kicked off the boots. He left everything lying on the floor and went straight to the cupboard in the sitting room. He took out a new bottle of Jack Daniels, broke the seal and downed a quarter of it in several big gulps. The fiery liquid kicked the tears out of Jack's eyes but that was fine, as long as it helped him to get rid of the brick in his chest. He set the open bottle down on the coffee table and staggered into the bedroom.

He collapsed across the bed, fully clothed, closed his eyes and started counting, waiting for the booze to knock him out cold. He didn't have to wait very long. Then, as he was spiraling down into the cotton-thick, black, bottomless hole, his last thought was fuck Joe... And fuck the boys who don't cry...

Chapter 38

January 1, Wednesday. 11:15 p.m.

I have screwed up, haven't I? Ruined our friendship. Driven you away. I am the completest idiot: I knew you didn't want to hear it. Yet I went ahead and said it aloud. Couldn't keep my damn mouth shut.

Will you ever forgive me, Jack?

But then, even if you will not, it doesn't change anything: I love you. So very much. Maybe for the rest of my life.

Happy New Year, cowboy!

January 2, Thursday. 10 minutes to midnight.

Dear Jack,

They have just transmitted your President Reagan's speech addressing the Soviet people on TV. He started by saying "Good evening. This is Ronald Reagan, President of the United States of America." So informal. He ended by wishing everybody "chistoye nebo". In Russian. "A clear sky". Not a very typical New Year wish. Don't think it's an American thing, either. What did he mean? I wonder if he knows about the NW effects after a nuclear war—a smoke covered sky, for months. He also said he hoped the talks about nuclear arms reduction between our countries will be speedier in 1986. Maybe he knows.

Then they transmitted Gorbachev's speech to Americans. He said he hope there would be less of mistrust between ~~us~~ our countries.

I trust you, Jack. I hope you trust me, too.

Your friend,

E.

January 8, Wednesday. 10:00 p.m.

Dear Jack,

I have gone through the catalogs at the MGU's and Lenin libraries and haven't been able to find Grandfather's original study. Only references to it in some later works on NW, including Grandfather's recent research. In both libraries they said all copies were on loan. This is not uncommon, esp. for a not widely circulated research paper.

Then they asked if I wanted to leave my name and they would call me when it's available. Normally I would do that. But I recalled your reservations and suspicions about everything and everyone. It must be hard to live in the environment you can't trust anyone. I didn't leave my name. Don't want you to worry about it when I tell you about the results of my search.

If you still want to talk to me.

I will take back what I said, Jack, if you don't want any of it. I will keep it all to myself. I have done it before; I can do it again. No big deal. Your friendship is all I want.

Your friend always,

E.

The last thing is not true. That's not all I want. But it doesn't matter. I just want you back, cowboy. In whatever way you want to be associated with me.

E.

January 15, Wednesday. 1:37a.m.

Dear Jack,

Just come back from the 1st Moscow Rock Festival. Yes, it was still an "underground" event. Even though they have been organizing semi-opened rock labs in Leningrad and Tallinn for three years now. Still, it's a progress, isn't it? My favorite is still Nautilus, from Sverdlovsk. Slava, the lead singer, is seriously talented. Beautiful too. Almost as beautiful as you. Artyom also thinks that he will go far.

Don't know if my band is ready. Perhaps we should record a few songs and give them to Artyom for vetting. Not the songs in English though. Your songs. Don't know if I will ever be ready to play them to others. Least of all to you.

E.

January 18, Saturday. Midnight.

Called you but you weren't home. You don't want anything to do with me anymore, do you? Or maybe you are out of the country again?

I wish I could stop thinking about you.

Maybe I am condemned to you. For life. Maybe even from the day I was born.

E.

January 19.

Don't know what time it is. Could be the next day. Who cares!

So I'm drunk. So what? You don't care, anyway. I'm nothing to you but a great fuck.

Fuck. That's how you called what we did.

No. I don't believe it. You made love to me. We made love. Right? Fucking can't feel that way. I know how "fucking" feels. And I know you didn't feel that way either when you were with me. I saw it in your eyes. I saw something! Something...

So dizzyingly blue

cornflowers were

last summer in the meadow,

like tattered fragments of the sky,

unraveled story of my life.

I must have imagined that "something". Otherwise you would have called by now.

Fuck you, Jack! Why can't you just call and lie to me? Tell me you want to be my friend. Lie to me! I will even take that. That's how low I have fallen.

I hate you!

I hate myself!

I love you.

January 26, Sunday. 10p.m.

Dear Jack,

I am sorry. I got my shit together. I'm sober now, and for the last 3 days.

Sevka came and dragged my ass out; disposed of the bottles before Anya came over, helped to clean up. I'm a bastard for treating them like I do. I should either marry Anya or let Sevka marry her. But I keep leading them on. Because it's convenient. And safe. And everybody thinks that is the way it should be.

Will I ever be able to be who I want to be? With whom I want to be?

Impossible dreams. Just like my parents'. They never came true.

E.

February 1, Saturday. 11:45 p.m.

Dear Jack,

We played 2 songs for Artyom today. He liked them, esp. my "Atomic Twilight" (it's not really a song, more like a theme and variation, with a bit of recitative). He gave us some good advice, too. Said we are ready to register for the rock lab.

It has been warm today, around zero, and raining with snow since afternoon. I was restless and decided to walk from the University. It took me 85 minutes to get home. Got soaked. Came up with a new song. For you. Even if you don't want any of this, it's for you.

> I want to kiss away the sadness from your lashes
> I want to empty all my life into your arms
> I want to hope into your dreams
> I want to glow under your skin
> And I want to drown in the bluest of the blue —
> the color of your eyes.
> So, burn up the scores,
> turn off the stage lights
> and lock up all guitars—
> the only melody
> I celebrate tonight
> is the music of your heart.

Where are you, cowboy? I wish you peace in everything you do.

Your friend,

E.

* * *

Jack took the last drag on his cigarette and shivered. It was chilly in the doorway at the end of the carriage, but he wasn't in a hurry to return to his well-heated first-class compartment. His new friend Jim Grover, the political officer at the US Embassy in East Berlin, and his wife Ellie were having yet another round of tea. Jack checked the time again. Another hour and a half before they reached Berlin Ostbahnhof, East Berlin's main train station. He liked the couple but felt he could use a break after the two and a half days of old Jim's philosophical deliberations and Ellie's smothering patronage.

Ok, so he was a jerk—they genuinely liked him, treated him like a son, even though they had known him for less than three weeks. But he desperately needed a moment alone and if freezing in the drafty, noisy end of carriage was the price, so be it.

It was getting dark, although it was not yet five o'clock in the afternoon, and snowing. Again.

Since he arrived in East Berlin three weeks ago it had rained or snowed continuously. In fact, it had been raining or snowing everywhere after the night Eto... since he'd gotten his instructions to go to Paris. *Everywhere*—Moscow, Paris, Frankfurt, Berlin, both East and West, and Dresden from where they were now returning. And it would still be raining *and* snowing in Berlin when they got there. Fucking weather! Made him feel like he would never see the sun again.

On top of weeks of lousy weather, and that other thing he tried hard not to think about, nothing seemed to work out as Joe Coburn had planned...

* * *

Late afternoon on New Year's Day, as Jack was nursing a hangover from the night before, he received a call from the commo room. It was the third time the phone rang in the space of ten minutes, so he gave in. Sounding annoyed, the officer on duty informed Jack that he was to come over to pick up his high priority cable.

It was from William, who instructed Jack to pack his bag and leave to Paris. But not before he had applied for a business visa to East Germany: Jack was being seconded to the Embassy in East Berlin for a month to help with a student exchange program.

So that was it, the special assignment that he'd been prepped for in Garmisch. And the Paris leg was probably for the pre-op briefing. Probably by the Chief of Ops himself, given the "sensitive" nature of the assignment, Jack figured, feeling resentful.

It was by Joe Coburn indeed, at a safe house at the fringes of Paris. To Jack's relief, his boss was preoccupied and all business the whole time. No wonder, considering what Jack learned during their briefing.

By December 31st, the Company had lost six Soviet agents in seven months. Not counting the two who had managed to come in from the cold, two non-human assets and other agencies' busted officers. It was either technical or human penetration, and the prime suspect was Moscow Station.

As a result, their Division Chief had introduced new procedures for handling Soviet agents until the leak was plugged. All reporting on agents was to be in person on this side of the Iron Curtain. No sensitive briefings in the Tank, no cable communication about potential agents, the main targets of operation GTTALION included. All other communications between Langley and the field were to be double encrypted. Until further notice.

So much for the Moscow situation.

In East Berlin, conditions were somewhat different. The key difference was that it was virtually impossible to recruit agents in the Democratic Republic of Germany. The Ministerium fur Staatssicherheit, infamously known as the Stasi, had such a tight grip on its people that virtually no one dared to spy for anybody but the Stasi itself. For the latter work, there were quite a few willing parties. As a result, the handful of agents whom East Berlin Station had been able to recruit since the erection of the Berlin Wall in 1961 had all turned out to be double agents.

The situation had somewhat changed two years earlier, with the arrival of a new Chief of Station, Florence Neumann, a rising star of the European Division. Within a year, the Station was running an agent. True, he was a low level, active duty surveillance officer, but a Stasi officer nonetheless. It was a breakthrough and overnight the tiny East Berlin Station had turned from a backwater post into a place where "real business" was carried out.

By this time, the Four Power Berlin Agreement of 1971 had started working for real, and as a result there was a small but steady flow of East Germans coming for day work in West Berlin. Nobody had any doubts that those cleared for crossing to the Western sector included Stasi officers and their agents. But it helped to warm up the relationship between the two blocs as well as life in blockaded West Berlin, thus was accepted as inevitable.

Over the last few months, the Deputy COS had held a few meetings in different hotels around West Berlin with the agent they called Baldie, who had revealed everything he knew about Stasi surveillance and the officers in his unit. Now it was time for the second target.

Florence Neumann had spotted him by chance in a small bar in West Berlin. She recognized him immediately: he was one of the senior officers in Baldie's unit whose pictures he had shared with his handlers. She pretended not to notice him, but requested additional info from Baldie on all senior officers of his unit. At the same time, the picture of the man, now nicknamed Blondie, was circulated to the West Berlin Station together with a request to cover the bar. Sure enough, Blondie turned up twice more, on the same day of the week. That and Baldie's report on the man had raised hopes that he might be recruitable. Now they needed to decide what pitch should be used on him.

And so Jack's task on this assignment was to frequent the bar, amongst others in the vicinity, assess the target and, if opportune, make contact.

However, that wasn't the only assignment Jack had in East Berlin: he was to start out his secondment by flirting with all women at the Embassy, but gradually to "set his eyes" on Florence Neumann. By the end of his stay, the two of them had to project the image of a couple smitten with each other.

Seeing Jack's pressed together lips, Joe patiently explained that it was primarily for the sake of the unmarried East Berlin COS who had been pitched by the Sovs a few months ago.

One of her Hungarian contacts had invited her to a quiet restaurant in East Berlin, but never showed up. While waiting for him, she had been approached by a KGB officer. The Russian showed her a video production of "This is Your Life" on a portable video cassette player. It had obviously been taken by concealed cameras through pinholes in her apartment. The "story" was that Neumann might be involved with one of her female East Berlin officers—something she would certainly not want Langley to know.

The East Berlin chief thanked the man for the entertainment and told him he could go sell it to someone else, and that she would report the incident to Washington. The next morning her report on the attempted recruitment was on the desks of SE Division's chief and his Head of Ops.

It meant the Sovs were using that tactic again. Had they barked up the wrong tree, Jack wondered, or did the woman simply have nerve? He didn't ask Joe if the KGB was right and why the Agency hadn't grabbed the opportunity to place Florence Neumann as a dangle. Joe had said he was the best of the pack, the most adaptable. Yeah, right, he was probably the only one stupid enough to participate in Joe Coburn's obscure schemes.

After the briefing, Jack spent another two days playing a tourist in Paris. Then on the second Wednesday of January, he took the train to Frankfurt, got his East German visa on Thursday and on Friday landed at Berlin Schönefeld Airport. He checked in at Unter den Linden Hotel on the corner of Friedrichstrasse in downtown East Berlin, then crossed over to West Berlin and hit the bars. On his third night out in town, he "bumped" into Florence Neumann at one of the bars.

She looked younger than her thirty-eight years of age and was more uptight than in the picture Joe had shown him in Paris. Jack figured maybe she liked the idea of them playing the dating game as much as he did. Anyway, it was part of their jobs, so they started "running into each other" often after that.

By the end of his first week, Jack was on first name terms with most of the staff at the Embassy and spending most of his lunches in female company. Every evening he would cross Checkpoint Charlie to West Berlin and spend his time and the Company's money at bars and restaurants around his "target ground".

He spotted Blondie on Thursday of his second week, one of the two days of the week the man reportedly showed up at this bar. It was a strange place, featuring a mélange of regular straights folks, macho types in leather, gays, prostitutes of all denominations and even a couple of cross-dressers. No wonder Neumann's assessment of Blondie was that he was either gay or had some other, "unorthodox sexual interest".

Jack wondered what she had been doing at that bar in the first place. He couldn't tell whether she was a lesbian or not. He figured out two things though: that she tried very hard to project an image of a party girl she wasn't and that he was not her type. Neither of them implicated her as not being straight though.

The thing Jack was more or less certain about was that Blondie wasn't queer: after an hour of sitting in a dark corner nursing a beer, Blondie picked up the drunkest, most unsightly prostitute and left with her. So he was probably into "other unorthodox sexual interests". But that wasn't Jack's job anymore—he'd done his bit.

What baffled him was that Joe had gone to such lengths to bring him over for what seemed like a simple job. If Florence couldn't be seen covering the target, surely one of the West Berlin Station's case officers could have done it, right? All they had to do was to hang out long enough at this place.

Unless playing a cover boyfriend for Florence Neumann was in fact his primary assignment.

Or was it she who was intended to be his "beard", in Joe Coburn's grand scheme of things? Jesus, this was all so fucking twisted, he didn't know what he was doing and for what purpose any more.

The following week at the bar, Jack created a little accident while Blondie was waiting for his drink. He bumped into the leather-clad slender youth with lined eyes who was standing right behind Blondie, causing him to spill his whole glass of beer over the Stasi's jacket and pants. The poisonous glare the man gave the youth convinced Jack that if their target was queer, he was so deeply closeted that he didn't even realize it himself.

What he also noticed was a flicker of recognition in the man's eyes when they met Jack's. The German dropped his gaze, put his beer down and headed to the gents, then left the bar shortly after. Jack figured the Stasi knew that he worked at the US Embassy in East Berlin— after all, the man was from the surveillance unit that covered the Embassy. The fact that he didn't engage with Jack but fled when Jack tried to strike up a conversation indicated that he might not be there on "official" business.

That was the last time Jack saw Blondie. He didn't know what happened to him afterwards, but it wasn't his job anyway—pitching Stasi officers was the prerogative of East Berlin Station.

The assignment with Florence Neumann had produced no better results. They went out every other day and managed to look love-struck. Jack slept over at her place three times and every time they had raucous sex—for the Stasi's records. However, there was no real chemistry between them and it put a strain on both of them. So by the time they were supposed to spend a romantic weekend in Dresden before Jack's departure, Florence announced she was summoned to Bonn and, after a staged stormy night at her apartment, left town. Jack went ahead with the trip and spent the weekend in Dresden with the Grovers instead.

* * *

He lit another cigarette and leaned against the cold plastic wall of the corridor. Another five minutes and he would be fine… If only he could get rid of the guilty feeling that he hadn't called…

Never mind…

* * *

He liked Dresden, in no small part due to Jim and Ellie. They knew the city and its history inside out and were happy to share their enthusiasm with Jack. It was Jim's third posting in East Germany and the couple truly appreciated the country and empathized with its people.

They dragged him around town on trams, then on foot, in the rain, to show him the Zwinger, the bridge over the Elbe called the Blue Wonder, the ruins of the Frauenkirche. The highlight of the trip was the performance of Wagner's Lohengrin at Semperoper. Jack wasn't really an opera fan, but the night at the magnificent, newly rebuilt theater left him in quiet awe.

In the end, Jack had managed to enjoy his bonus trip to Dresden, despite the stifling Stasi coverage put on them the moment they left Berlin. However, the Stasi wasn't the only security organ that took an interest in Jack's escapades in East Germany: he was under no illusions about Volodya, a short and scrawny Russian with thin, straw-colored hair and dark circles under the pale gray eyes.

Jack had singled the man out the moment he sighted him chasing the departing Berlin - Dresden fast train and jumping into their first-class car reserved primarily for foreigners. Volodya hadn't approached them that time, but was all over Jack when they had miraculously found themselves in the adjacent seats in Semperoper.

Volodya rejoiced when he'd learned that Jack was visiting the GDR but actually was based in Moscow—where Volodya was from, too. They ordered Champagne during the intermission, for acquaintance's sake, then spent the rest of the night after the performance in the restaurant of the hotel where Jack and the Grovers stayed. To the displeasure of the older couple, who were truly worried about Jack and wouldn't leave him alone with the suspicious Russian type. Jack ordered a bottle of Stolichnaya and German cold cuts and they talked about life in Moscow and Dresden, mostly Jack again, peppering his German with Russian words, leaning into his new friend Volodya, until the restaurant closed up at midnight. They kissed three times in the old Russian tradition and Volodya left. But not before vowing to be in touch and to call Jack when he was back in Moscow.

* * *

So finally, they were making a move on him. Joe should be happy—his plan was working. Well, sort of, as it seemed they wouldn't need to resort to SEABROOK to set him up as a dangle. Jack prayed they wouldn't use it at all. And definitely not in relation to Eton… Shit, he should have called him before leaving Moscow in a hurry. But things had been so hectic before his departure that he hadn't had a chance…

Yeah, right. Ok, so he'd been confused and reeling from… the night at the Volkonskys' and wasn't ready to talk to *him* yet. So now, he just had to live with the guilt that had been festering in him ever since he had left Moscow…

Jack exhaled sharply, crushed the cigarette butt against the sole of his boot, and dropped it in the small cast-iron ashtray on the wall. If you can't mend it, you'll just have to stand it, as his old man used to say. Old bastard, why did he get to be right most of the time?

Or did he?

He wrenched opened the door to the passenger section and closed it firmly behind him with the determination he didn't feel.

Chapter 39

It was about -20C and snowing again when Jack returned to Moscow in the first week of February. During the day, the wind swirled the falling snow in a never-ending roundelay; at night, myriads of snowflakes floated in the air, muffling all sounds, blanketing everything in primeval white, transforming the city into a fairytale setting. Somehow, as soon as he exited from Sheremetyevo Airport, Jack's restlessness evaporated. He felt oddly at home.

New security rules and arrangements aside, his usual Embassy crowd and Stella greeted him like a prodigal son, throwing a welcome-back party for him at the Marines Club. The next day was his birthday, so he organized his own celebration at Uncle Sam's, then moving to the Marines Club and ending at the Seabees' joint after midnight. Around one in the morning, he hauled up drunken and giggling Stella, called a taxi and took her home. She was pretty much wasted but wouldn't let go of him, so he suggested that they have another drink—part of his plan, anyway. When he poured out two shots of whiskey in two tumblers, she happily gulped down hers and passed out on the couch.

Jack put his down, lifted her up, like a huge rag doll, and took her to the bedroom where he carefully put her on the bed, unclothed her and tucked her in with her red and black comforter. Then he undressed down to his boxers and t-shirt, climbed in on the other side and pulled a corner of the comforter over him.

He closed his eyes and kept very still. He knew he wouldn't be able to sleep—he'd actually had only four drinks the whole evening, not enough to dissolve the adrenaline coursing through his veins. But he needed some rest in order to get himself into the op run state of alertness. If he was going to do this. Today. This morning.

The thought had cropped up on the train from Dresden. At first, Jack discarded the idea as a totally stupid thing to do: if the KGB didn't get him, then the Company would definitely fire him, should they learn about his antics. But the idea wouldn't go away, and by the time he landed in Moscow, Jack had a full operational plan in his head.

He had to do this, right? He'd been an asshole and now had to let Eton know that he was sorry. But he suspected that if he called, Eton wouldn't want to talk to him—not after he'd disappeared without a word for a month yet again. He couldn't bear the thought of Eton hanging up on him. So he would do this and if Eton threw him out *then*, so be it. He deserved it. At least he would say he was sorry while looking straight into his friend's eyes, like a man.

Jack opened his eyes and looked at his wristwatch. It was ten minutes to 5:00a.m. He felt calm and in control, like at the start of an operation.

He got up quietly, picked up his clothes and tiptoed to the bathroom where he took a quiet shower, drying himself off with a hand towel. Then he brushed his teeth with a folding toothbrush he had brought with him and placed it in the glass together with Stella's. Once dressed, he scribbled "Baby, thank you for the wonderful evening & night. Didn't want to wake you up. See you later, J." on a yellow Post-IT, stuck it on the door of the fridge, took his shoulder bag and left, carefully pulling the door behind him till he heard the lock click.

Jack prepared a sheepish smile and a chatty greeting for the *militsia* guard in the booth in front of the compound, but nobody was there when he stepped out. He knew his departure would be recorded on the hidden cameras though, wherever they were. To hell with them, so they would eventually figure out that he had been missing for a few hours, big deal. He would come up with a story later if necessary.

If they didn't put a tail on him now that is.

It was 5:15 a.m., forty-five minutes before the Metro opened and the trains started running. Jack turned up the collar of his winter coat and commenced his improvised surveillance detection run, on foot—first to the west, towards Gorky Park, then three blocks south, then four blocks east, gradually moving south-west towards the district where Eton lived. By the time the Metro opened, Jack was only one station away from Metro Oktyabrskaya, the nearest one to Stella's place. And freezing. He'd checked the thermometer on Stella's kitchen window before he left: minus 22 Celsius. As if he could do anything about it— tough luck.

Jack took the Metro's gray line going south, instead of Eton's orange one. He alighted at Station Kakhovskaya, almost due west from Station Belyaevo, the nearest to Eton's place, and started walking again. By 7:00 a.m. Jack was pretty sure he was free of surveillance. And hoped that Eton didn't have to go anywhere early today.

And that he was alone.

He called from the phone booth one block from Eton's apartment building. Eton answered on the sixth ring, his voice brusque, alarmed. "*Allo?*"

"*Privet*, Etah—" his voice cracked, and he pretended to cough. "Sorry, it's me... Have I, um, woken you up?"

There was a short pause before Eton answered, "No, I've got up already... *Privet*." He was obviously at loss for words.

"Listen, um, I just thought... We need to talk, Eton... Can I come up?"

"Now?"

"I'm half a block from your place."

"You are *where*? But of course, come up. Yes, please!"

"Alright, thanks. Will be there in five minutes."

Jack hung up, took a final, covert look around and scurried towards the familiar apartment block. He took the elevator to the fourth floor, walked up the rest. The door opened as soon as he came up to it and Jack ducked inside.

The only light in the apartment was coming from the kitchen on the right, and the bedside light from the bedroom on the left.

"Hi again... God, it's cold outside," Jack said in English, feeling self-conscious, not sure where to start. "Sorry that I'm so early. I—"

"It's okay. Take your coat off and come in. I'll make you a hot tea... Or coffee?" He sounded awkward and avoided looking at Jack.

So he was still mad at Jack then. Served him right.

"A coffee please, if you have it..."

For Christ's sake, hasn't he just offered it?

"Sure. Come on into the living room. You can turn on the light there." He hesitated but said nothing more, turned around and went to the kitchen.

Jack thought he heard Eton stifle a sigh.

Right, this was going to be short.

He dropped his shoulder bag on the floor, hung up his coat, took off his boots and walked to the living room in his socks. In the doorways, he reached for the switch on the wall on the right—the same place as in his apartment. When the pale orange glow flooded the room, Jack look around.

He hadn't really seen it the last time he was there—they'd never got as far as the living room. Now he took his time, taking in little details about Eton's habitat that might be all he would have to hang on to for the foreseeable future. He hoped not though.

The room was of a standard size for a two-bedroom apartment, around 30 square meters, cramped with a complete set of furniture and furnishings. A mahogany-colored four-seat dinner table; a wall-length cupboard filled with books and a medium sized TV on the lowest shelf; a couch opposite the cupboard and a cozy chair with two cushions near the balcony; a floor lamp with a shade the same gold-brown color as the bedside lamp Jack remembered seeing in the bedroom. The floor-length curtains at the tiny balcony had the same motif as the carpet on the wall, the tablecloth and the lampshades—gold, deep reds and browns. There was a faint smell of cigarettes and coffee about the place, and also of burnt solder and… burnt paper? Jack inhaled deeply, taking in a lungful of those masculine scents, trying to commit them to memory.

As he sat down on the sofa, Jack noticed a book with a faux-leather cover on the seat of the armchair. He picked it up and only then realized that it wasn't a book, but an expensive looking diary in a fancy binding. It fell open in the middle where a ballpoint pen was snapped in.

Eton had said he used to write a diary when he was kid, to his imaginary friend Jack… And when Jack teased him about him thinking of Jack as his childhood pen pal in the flesh, Eton hadn't denied it…

Suddenly sweat broke around Jack's hairline and under his arms.

No, he can't be doing this. Not here. You can't do this, Eton, you can't!!

He quickly leafed through the diary. Some of the pages were missing, torn out; there were verses written on others.

"I want to kiss the sorrow off your lashes…"

A postcard fell out from between the pages, a reproduction of a painting of a dark-haired ranch boy wearing an old straw hat and red kerchief around his neck, and with it, two pressed-dry cornflowers on one stem.

Jack bent down, picked them up swiftly, put them back in between the pages and closed the diary. When he raised his head, Eton was standing at the door with a steaming cup of coffee, staring at him, startled.

Fuck!

"I'm sorry. I thought it was a book… But Eton, have you been—"

"No." Eton shook his head firmly.

"But it's a diary, isn't it? You still keep a diary? And you write about…?"

Oh, God, this was not happening! How could he be so stupid, this boy?!

"Jack, listen to me. Please." Eton put the cup of coffee on the table and took a few quick steps towards him. "I don't *keep* a diary. Okay?"

"You don't? But this is *your* diary. Isn't it?" Jack thrust the notebook towards him.

"Yes. But look, there's nothing in it." Eton grabbed the diary from his hand, opened it and fanned the pages open to show Jack that most of them were blank. "Only a few songs… There's nothing in here about you. See? You don't need to worry, Jack."

Eton smiled weakly at him and Jack realized that he looked embarrassed and contrite.

"I don't *keep* a diary," he repeated and shook his head slowly.

"What does *that* mean? Do you write in your diary?"

"Yes." Eton sighed. "But as I said, I don't *keep* what I write. Except for the songs."

"What do you do with the rest?" Jack was confused now.

"I burn them. As soon as I finish writing… Nobody's ever seen them, Jack. Please, don't worry… Please?"

Jack peered at him, still baffled. "But if you burn it, why write it?"

Eton dropped his eyes, stuffed his hands in his jeans' pockets and shuffled his feet. Then he raised his head to meet Jack's eyes and shrugged awkwardly, the color creeping up his cheeks and forehead. "Just need to talk sometimes… to someone… To you," he finished under his breath and looked away.

There was a long pause as Jack tried to swallow down a lump the size of an apple in his throat. God, give him the strength to… He didn't know what he wanted do about this unbelievable man.

Clearly disturbed by the silence, Eton ventured to look at him again. He met Jack's eyes and whispered, "I'm sorry."

Jack bridged the distance between them in two large steps and stopped, unsure what he should do next—forgive Eton or seek his forgiveness? He put his hands on his shoulders, gazed into his troubled eyes, then rested his forehead against Eton's and closed his eyes.

Eton gently slipped his arms around Jack's waist, leaned in and brushed his lips against Jack's. The touch was feather-light, as if he was seeking permission.

Jack swallowed, pressed his mouth into the side of Eton's face and whispered brokenly, "I'm sorry. I was a prick… I should've called…"

Eton's embrace tightened immediately. "Shh, it's alright… Forget what I said… that night. It doesn't matter." He leaned back a little and peered into his eyes. "We're still friends, right?"

"Right," Jack nodded, trying to ignore the dart of pain in his chest.

Hadn't he wanted Eton to take back *the words*? He had just done it. So what was the problem?

Eton leaned in again, his lips a hair's breadth from Jack's, but not touching, waiting for Jack to show him what he wanted. Jack took a shaky breath, covered Eton's mouth with his for a moment and let go. Then he began to slowly plant soft, open-mouth kisses on Eton's lips, his eyes, his forehead, his chin.

"Christ, Eton... D'you have... any idea... whatcha do... t' me? If they find out... 'bout us..."

Eton caught Jack's face between his hands, waited until Jack opened his eyes and said solemnly, "Jack, do what you have to do. Don't worry about me. Just know this: whatever you do, I will still... you will still be my friend. Always."

Jack laughed helplessly, overcome with tenderness that he had always thought of as a momentary weakness. "C'mere, *friend*. I'll show you what I gotta do... now."

He pulled Eton's face close and started kissing him anew, slowly inching down his neck, his collarbone, his chest, Jack's chapped fingers clearing the path for his soft lips and hot, wet tongue. He had already figured out what could drive this man delirious, and he intended to take him there again, right here on the couch in his living room, right this frigging minute.

Eton's legs started buckling, so Jack pushed him gently towards the couch, laid him down, knelt by his side and began unzipping his jeans.

"You don't have to," Eton protested weakly, his eyes already glazed over.

Jack stopped and cocked an eyebrow. "Tell me you don't like it and I'll quit."

Eton's face flushed red. "No! Uh, I like it, but—"

"Then shut up and enjoy."

It didn't take him long to bring Eton to climax, but that was alright—it was only seven-thirty, so he had another hour and thirty minutes before all conscientious Soviet citizens would be having their morning teas and coffees at work and he could make a discreet exit from Eton's apartment and building.

When Eton came back to his senses, he got up, pulled up his jeans without zipping them, took Jack's hand and wordlessly led him to the bedroom. He pushed Jack gently toward the bed, then turned around and left the room again.

He returned half a minute later, a pack of condoms in his hand. Jack was standing by the bed wearing nothing but socks, his clothes scattered on the floor. Eton's eyes immediately zeroed in on his proudly erect cock, jutting out of the nest of dark hair.

"Like what you see?" Jack smiled sheepishly and swallowed, trying to control his heart.

Eton closed in on him quickly and put the pack on the bedside table without looking. The next thing Jack knew, both of Eton's hands were on him. "Yesss." He kissed Jack on the lips and knelt down.

Jack shuddered as the wet hotness enveloped the head of his achingly hard dick. "Etohnn, I won't lassst," he hissed.

Eton let go of him and stood up, pushed Jack down on the bed and undressed quickly. "Condom?" he asked solemnly, sitting down next to Jack and reaching for the condom pack. "It's my turn."

He pushed Jack firmly onto his back and straddled him. Then, without further ado, he tore the foil and rolled the condom onto Jack. After generously coating Jack's erection and his fingers with saliva, he pulled at Jack's hand and placed the fingers at his opening.

"Help me."

"Yeah."

Eton sucked in his breath and closed his eye, as Jack breached him, his head thrown back, his thighs flexing. "Two now," he grated out impatiently, taking deep breaths.

Jack didn't think Eton was ready for that yet, but did as he'd been told. He pushed the second finger into his lover, stretching him, his other hand wrapped tight around Eton's shaft. He thought he could come just by looking at what his hands were doing to Eton.

In a moment, he opened his eyes, pushed Jack's hands away with visible effort, and repositioned himself over Jack's erection.

"Too soon, Eton. It'll hurt." Jack was barely able to resist the urge to thrust, the pressure on the tip of his cock so maddeningly sweet.

"It's worth it." He met Jack's eyes and his lips curled up a little. "*You* are. I want you."

"Slowly then… Or I'll shoot… Oh, *Christ!*"

He didn't stand a chance. The pleasure was too intense as Eton eased ever so slowly down onto him. Then, almost as soon as he started riding, Jack climaxed and exploded in a thousand brilliant little suns.

He knew he was dreaming and in his dream, he was running late. So late that Nurimbekoff and William had sent out the entire Moscow Station to look for him. And cabled Joe, too, to request a search and rescue squad. The problem was, he couldn't open his eyes. Couldn't wrench himself free of the iron hold that someone had put on him, from behind. Couldn't, because it was so incredibly gentle, at the same time so hard, so firm. Made him feel safe. Made him feel lo… truly cared for. How would he ever be able to feel like this again if he left now?… And, God help him, he was so late…

He jerked, startled, and opened his eyes.

The bedside lamp under the golden brown shade cast a warm, soft light on everything. The alarm clock next to it showed 8:13 a.m. The heavy curtains on the window were tightly drawn but Jack knew it was still dark outside and would stay dark for another hour at least.

Eton stirred behind him. "It's still early," he murmured, pulling Jack closer and pressing his face into Jack's neck.

"How do you know, smarty-pants?" Jack hummed, trying to hold back his out-of-control grin.

"You worry too much."

"Just enough for the two of us."

"You don't need to worry about me, Jack. Really." His tone softened, and he kissed the back of Jack's head.

"Someone has to." Jack turned around in his arms to face him, draping his arm over Eton's hip. "We have thirty minutes. What you wanna do? Wanna talk?" He smiled encouragingly at his friend.

Eton's ears and cheeks flushed. "Okay." He smiled back a little, but Jack saw doubt in his eyes.

"But?"

"Well, um... You only, um, came once." The color on his face deepened. "It's not fair."

Christ, this man was incorrigible!

Jack grinned happily. "You wanna give me a birthday present?"

"Birthday present? When is your birthday?"

"Yesterday, actually."

"Yesterday?" Eton raised himself on an elbow, looking both surprised and distraught. "Why didn't you..." He trailed off, his face clouded.

"I just got back a couple of days ago, bud... Thought I needed *this* birthday present," Jack slid his arm around Eton's waist and pulled him close.

"I haven't prepared anything special for—"

"You have *everything* special that I want... for a present," Jack whispered and pushed a knee in between his legs.

You are my present, baby...

"Okay... What do you want me to do?" Eton was still raised up on his elbow, gazing down on Jack, concerned.

"Nothing. Just be yourself... with me..." He buried his face into Eton's chest.

Just hold me...

As if he had read Jack's thoughts, Eton put one arm around his shoulders, and cradled Jack's head against his chest with the other. He pressed his mouth and nose into Jack's hair. "God, Jack," he said with a quiet, sad chuckle, "Who else could I be myself with, if not you?"

They remained nestled in their embrace for a few moments. Then Eton began to kiss Jack, first his forehead, his cheeks, his eyes, stopping to savor his mouth, then shifting so he could nibble and suck his neck and collarbone, as Jack had done for him on the couch. Slowly and deliberately, he kissed his way down his chest, smiling to hear Jack's stifled moans. When Eton reached his quivering stomach, Jack pushed him back, rolled Eton on his side and wrapped himself around his back, their bodies fitting together perfectly.

"You okay with this?" he murmured as he reached down and dragged his fingers along Eton's crack, probing.

"Yes," Eton breathed. "You can... fuck me." There was a hint of a smile in his voice.

Jack reached for a condom on the bedside table, quickly prepped himself, then snaked his arm under Eton and pulled his hips up. Eton pushed back the moment Jack pressed himself against his opening.

"I wanna make love to you," Jack whispered fiercely, and slid into him with one smooth stroke.

They did it unhurriedly this time, Jack spooning behind Eton, holding him tight, trying his best to rein in the unbearable desire to race to the finish line. He tried to focus on each sensation Eton elicited with his caresses, on his movements, memorizing each moan, each sigh, tried to give all he had in him to the one person who accepted him the way he was, flawed and unsure, the one person who gave him what he had been yearning for all these years, just like that, without asking anything in return.

Chapter 40

When they came down to earth from their euphoric heights, Eton tried to insist on driving Jack home again. Or at least to the Metro downtown where he could take the direct line home. This time Jack stood his ground: he had to do a half-decent SDR to come in from the black and there was no way of doing it with Eton around. The organs were probably already on the lookout for him: by the time he emerged at his compound, he would have been "unaccounted for" for at least 5 hours. He had no doubt they wouldn't let him go unpunished and prayed it would be something simple so that he could come up with a plausible story for his bosses too.

He was glad that the morning was cold and murky, and it was snowing heavily again, so that he could turn down his fur hat that covered half of his face. He kept his head down and walked fast toward Metro Belyaevo, then turned right and scurried toward the massive concrete bunker of a complex that was Pushkin Institute of Russian Language and Literature—just a student running late for his morning class. At the bus station in front of its entrance, he jumped onto the first one that turned up and alighted at Metro Station Yugo-Zapadnaya.

As he was descending the stairs to the underground pass, Jack slipped, landing awkwardly on the ice-slicked steps covered with a new layer of snow that neither the *babushkas* nor city authorities were able to keep up with clearing lately. And it occurred to him then what his story for being late to work would be.

In short, Jack took a dive on the ice near his Metro station. He didn't bother going home: flagged down a taxi and, holding his injured hand, and went straight to the Embassy's doctor. Jack entertained Dr. Callaway ("You can call me Martha," she smiled,) with the account of his unfortunate accident, while she fussed over his wrist and thumb. In the end, she prescribed him three full days of rest at home.

Jack's punishment came the next day when his Mustang, parked inside the guarded compound, had the side window smashed, the cassette player ripped off and the cassettes cleared out of the side box. If that weren't enough, the driver's door was bashed and a front tyre punctured.

The drawback was that it left Jack without a car. The general services unit was so overwhelmed with the implementation of the new security measures that those who lived outside were instructed not to bring their cars into the Embassy compound without security's approval. The other alternative was the garage that belonged to the UPDK, the omnipresent diplomatic services office of the Ministry of Foreign Affairs that everybody knew run by the KGB. Jack settled for waiting for his turn at the Embassy's mechanics workshop.

But that was not all: the following day he was put under a comprehensive coverage, which by the end of the month was still going strong. Jack didn't think they suspected him of being involved in espionage activities, though—his shadowing was too much in your face, as if they wanted to make sure Jack had no illusions about being watched.

February 8, Saturday. 12:25 a.m.

Dear Jack,

I am stupidly drunk-happy: one, you've come back; and two, we made love. That was what you said you wanted—to make love to me. And then you did. My God! I will die if it gets any better than that: my heart will not be able to contain all that I feel and will simply explode.

I won't tell you about it. I have learned my lesson. And this is fine. I am certain you saw it in my eyes, anyway. And I know you liked making love with me, too.

Still cannot believe you found out about me ~~keeping~~ writing a diary to you. For a moment, I thought you would kill me. Come on, Jack! I know I am idealistic and act like a child. Sometimes. But I am not naïve. As I said, you worry too much, cowboy.

Now you know how much I need you in my life. Ha, you have been part of it since I was nine. You are part of me. You will be part of me for the rest of my life.

I wish I could be part of yours. But it doesn't matter.

Don't remember who said "If you truly love someone, let them go free."

You just do what you need to do, my blue cornflower, moy vasi'liok.

I love you.

E.

February 11, Tuesday. 11:08p.m.

Dear Jack,

I still haven't come up with any idea of a birthday present to you. Everything seems so insignificant and materialistic compared to what you have given me. The only thing that might somehow convey my gratitude is the last song I have written, The Music of Your Heart.

Have just written the lyrics on a postcard. Thinking of giving it to you when we meet at the Lenin Library. I will sing it to you next time you come to my place. Hope you will like it.

You know what? I will sing this song at the rock fest. Don't care if they only allow songs in Russian (it is a Russian rock festival). I am a Russian too, even though some of my songs are in English. It shouldn't matter which language we sing. Our hearts speak the same language, regardless of who we are.

I will do it for you, cowboy. Will you come to see me perform?

Yours always,

E.

February 14, Friday. 1:15 a.m.

Dear Jack,

Just got back from Artyom's place. I went to see him about the song—to "show" it to him and ask him to help us to enter it in the festival. He is very influential in the rock community. So I played it to him. He liked it and promised to help. With a condition: I have to translate or write part of it in Russian. I can do that. Now I need to practice it with my guys.

We were still talking when a group of Artyom's friends arrived. From Leningrad. I couldn't believe my eyes: it was Viktor Tsoi, the band leader of Kino, with his guitarist and his drummer. And Yura's (the guitarist) girl who is a rock singer too. Her name is Joanna, and she is from California, too. I had heard about her before. Sometimes she performs with Boris Grebenshchikov. Yes, with The B.G. that every Soviet rock fan knows.

Artyom introduced us, told them I have a band too and we are going to play in Leningrad in March. They will too as guests. Can't believe we are going to play on the same stage in the same performance as guys like Kino and Nautilus.

Then we drank tea and vodka and talked in the kitchen. Joanna has been smuggling home-made records of Kino, B.G.'s Aquarium and 2 other rock bands to California. They are going to release an album this summer in America, called "Red Wave". This is truly amazing!

And Joanna and Yura are going to get married later this year.

~~I wonder if you or I were a girl, would you...~~ Never mind.

Then Joanna told us about the release of A. Shcharansky in West Berlin 2 days ago, in exchange for Soviet bloc's spies. He is a refusnik and has been in gulag for nearly 10 years now for "anti-government activities". Grandfather says he is a talented mathematician. Our newspapers haven't mentioned his release, but western newspapers have. Joanna brought one with her for Artyom, The Washington Post.

I've read the article and can't forget what Shcharansky said at his trial:

"I am happy that I lived honestly and in peace with my conscience, and I never lied even when I was threatened with death."

Jack, I wish I were able to say this too. I wish both of us could.

Will we ever be?

E.

February 15, Saturday. 12:25a.m.

Dear Jack,

My band is falling apart.

Told my guys that we're going to sing my Engl. language song at the rock festival. They said okay, and I gave them the score and the text. We started practicing. Sevka was floundering and could not seem to get in the right mood. I told him off. He snapped back. I told him to focus if he wanted to participate in the festival. He said he didn't anymore and walked out. I ran after him ready to fight him. Caught him at the door. He told me to get lost, together with "my Natasha", to leave Anya alone and not to come near him. He looked at me with such anger and accusation that I didn't find anything to say. So he left. That was the end of the practice. And perhaps of the band, too. Now we can forget about the festival.

Natasha is a girl we met at the conservatory. She is taking vocal classes on the same days Sevka and I are taking ours. She has huge baby-blue eyes. And she seems to ~~like me~~ have a crush on me. I had a coffee with her a couple of days ago and drove her home afterwards.

I thought I had to justify somehow the lyrics of the song if I was to sing it to people. Unfortunately, none of girls I'm close friends with has blue eyes like you. But they must not know that the song is for you, right? So I thought let them think it is about Natasha. Now it is backfiring.

I know Sevka cares for Anya deeply. Just did not expect that it could ruin our friendship. And the band. But I can't blame him. If I were him, I would have done the same.

And I still HAVE TO sing this damned song at the festival. Because it is for you. It is a present to you, cowboy.

So if I am a traitor, like Sevka said, I will go ahead and be an ultimate traitor: I will ask Artyom to find us a drummer, even for the rock fest only. He offered to do it last year. Hope it is not too late.

E.

February 17, Monday. 8:13p.m.

I don't know what is going on, Jack, why everything seems to be falling apart.

I had an unpleasant conversation with Grisha today. As a result, I have fallen out with him, too. He told me now that our exchange project is complete I should stop meeting and hanging out with you. Because "people" have started talking that I am hanging out with an American from the Embassy. He said it is good for neither me, nor my family. I told him I can hang out with whom I want to. And my family can take care of itself, too. He then said that I better think about when Grandfather cannot protect us anymore because he is not eternal. I told him to get lost. He looked at me sadly and said he will then better stay away because he doesn't want to betray me as I am his friend.

Is this the price I have to pay for being friends with you? Will I lose all of my friends, one by one?

There's a ballad in "Juno and Avos" with this verse: "There's no other fair price for Love/Only one's life is enough, only life is enough...".

What price am I willing to pay for a chance of being with you? I would not think twice if it is my life only. But what if I had to pay with lives of others? My family, my friends?

I don't know, cowboy. I don't want to think about it. I hope it will never come to it.

I hope my life alone will be enough. It is yours anyway.

Your friend,

E

* * *

Just as Joe Cohen had warned him in Paris, the new security rules in Moscow didn't stop at those imposed by the Company on its Station. For one thing, when he returned from his secondment in East Berlin, Jack found his manual typewriter "removed". Apparently, the visiting State Department's security team from Washington had determined that the KGB listening post across the ten-lane avenue could pick up the sound made by manual typewriters and decipher the text being typed. Besides typewriters, the Embassy's security office had also been busy testing everybody's cars and some apartments for spy dust, putting new cipher locks on all office doors and cabinets, and issuing written instructions on how to dispose of documents and stationary that had been used to prepare classified documents. Even things like used correction tape now had to be treated similarly to classified documents.

However, the biggest change was the major reassignment of offices, which resulted in all Embassy's local staff being moved to the auxiliary buildings in the courtyard. All Americans and temporaries of other "western" nationalities had been moved to the fifth and sixth floors of the commissary building. As a result, the CAO's local team assistant, Tanya, was moved to the outer office and Todd, the youngest of the CAO's staff, was moved up from the ground floor to share the office with Glenn and Jack. With the three of them crammed into a tiny office, the partitions between the desks were removed and it became rather tricky for Jack to do his "non-cultural" type of reporting.

In addition, the security office had introduced multicolored ID badges with photos, which staff were to wear at all times in the main office building: blue for staff with clearances, white for those without, white with a black "V" for contractors, nannies and teachers, and pink for the local staff, even though they were no longer allowed into the main offices.

It meant that the charwomen, usually chaperoned by the marines while doing the cleaning inside the building, were banned too, leaving the foreign secretaries and other junior staff with the additional task of cleaning their own and their bosses' offices. The marines were also put in charge of changing the light bulbs and of other small manual tasks until the State Department figured out how to handle the staffing of low-level jobs previously performed by locals.

The one good thing about the tightened security rules, as far as Jack was concerned, was that the reporting became minimal. All Moscow Station's sensitive reporting was now delivered in person by senior officers, either in Washington or at another secure location on the other side of the Iron Curtain. And there was no more briefing on classified matters in the Tank, nor via cable communication with HQ. As a result, Jack didn't have to discuss his every action with the COS or William, and his "sensitive" reporting was reduced to a few handwritten notes and requests that were quickly and wordlessly reviewed and approved by William in his office.

Toward the end of February, Jack noticed some irregular activities on the part of some Moscow Station's case officers. William had been staying in the office late, sometimes very late, but delegated most of his responsibilities as the CAO to Glenn and Jack. On a few occasions, as Jack was leaving Uncle Sam's late at night, he noted the cars belonging to his boss and two other case officers on the Embassy grounds. Usually folks who didn't live in the commissary building parked their cars on the streets nearby. He guessed that Moscow Station was preparing for an operation.

His deduction was affirmed two days before the International Women's Day, which the Russians called the Day of 8 March. William called him to his office first thing in the morning and told him that he was being tasked to assist Tanya to shop for presents for the wives and daughters of their Soviet counterparts on the occasion of Women's Day. And since Jack's car was still grounded, he could use William's Ford for a couple of days. The sheet of paper that the CAO had slid in front of Jack instructed him to run the car around town the whole day during those two days. And do what was asked of him without questions.

It was probably a bren, Jack figured, a brief meeting with an agent, if the Station chief was pulling all available hands on deck. He wondered who was going to meet with the agent and why William's car was to be "flashed" to the KGB. He doubted it was William — the man barely spoke any Russian, and the Company didn't usually assign case officers who didn't speak the agents' language to run them. Unless the agents spoke good English, like the KGB and diplomatic staff stationed in America. Or like MEDIAN, an official at the Moscow-based Institute of the USA and Canada, a Soviet think-tank specializing in research on everything American and Canadian.

Early the next day, Saturday, Jack collected William's car from the Embassy and went for a shopping spree at a handful of duty free shops around town. By noon, he'd managed to spend a small fortune on more gifts and flowers than strictly necessary, not only for his Russian contacts, friends and colleagues, but also for Stella, the wife of Uncle Sam's owner, Doctor Martha and a few other women he socialized with at the Embassy. In the afternoon, he started calling the recipients of the gifts and delivering them in person. Neither Lara, nor Vera Mikhailovna were home when Jack called, so he left the flowers and chocolates with their housekeepers and a note for Lara, asking her if she would like to go out the next day.

It was almost nine o'clock when he returned home. As he was turning into the driveway of his compound, Jack noted a cream-colored Lada as it passed behind. It had been on his tail since morning, alternating with a red one, neither of them trying to be discreet about their presence.

Great, he'd gotten their attention. Just what his bosses had wanted.

The next morning, he called Lara to see if she wanted to go out for lunch and a movie. His car was still grounded, he explained apologetically, and he'd have to return the one he'd borrowed before 5:00 p.m. It wasn't exactly accurate, but four hours was all he was prepared to spend with her.

She happily accepted his invitation, and at noon sharp, Jack picked her up in front of her apartment building. They went to the restaurant at Hotel Rossiya and picked the same table by the large window overlooking St. Basil's domes. Over lunch, Lara told him about her plans to join LenKom Theater where she would perform in the rock opera "Juno and Avos" opposite the leading man Nikolai Karachentsov, and in Russian classical dramas directed by no less than Nikita Mikhalkov himself. She seemed to have little doubt that that was exactly what she was going to do in a year's time. In the meantime, she would be playing the leading role in the new musical Karelin was staging especially for her, as her graduation project.

"This one is very special. But I can't tell you more just yet." She looked at once thrilled and conspiratorial. "Only that Eton has agreed to write some rock songs for it."

"Has he?" The news rubbed Jack the wrong way. Why hadn't Eton mentioned anything about it? And he'd thought the boy didn't like Karelin.

"Unbelievable, *da*? I think it's because of *Krylia*. Sad, isn't it?"

"Sad? What do you mean? Why?"

"You don't know?" She stared at him. "Hasn't Eton told you?"

"Told me what?" Suddenly, Jack felt anxious.

Lara pulled her lips in between her teeth for a second. "Maybe not... Alright, but don't tell him that I told you, *kharasho*? So, Eton and Seva have fallen out and... Well, I think *Krylia* are no anymore."

"What?! I thought you said they were childhood friends. What happened?" And what about Eton's plans for *Krylia* to take part in the rock festival in Leningrad? He wanted to ask Lara about it, but wasn't sure he was supposed to know.

Lara picked at her chocolate cake, then raised her eyes and sighed. "I think it's something to do with Anya," she said, then added hastily, "Poor girl, she's has been trying to reconcile them. Not sure it's working, though."

Shit, he had told Eton to go out with Anya, for appearances sake. Was it backfiring? Eton hadn't said anything about it when they talked on the phone a week ago. He had to talk to his friend to find out what was going on. He didn't know if he could help, probably not, but he had to know.

Jack said he had no doubt the three of them would reconcile soon and changed the subject.

After lunch, they went to see the rerun of "Tootsie" in the cinema theater on the ground floor of the hotel. Once again, Lara held on to his hand through the film but didn't attempt anything more than that. When Jack dropped her off, they exchanged a friendly goodbye kiss and agreed to do it again soon.

On his way to the Embassy, Jack pondered over the fact that he had yet to see the two Ladas that had been tailing him the past couple of days. Maybe they'd decided that Jack was a harmless gadabout. Or maybe they figured that Moscow Station's ops run had already transpired the day before and they could have a break. The KGB always knew when something was up at Moscow Station. The trick for its case officers was to pull that "something" off without being caught.

As Jack was parking, he noticed that there were more cars on the street near the Embassy than usual for a Sunday afternoon. More uniformed *militsia* and plain-clothed characters positioned noticeably around the perimeter of the compound. He tried to ignore the chill down the spine as he strolled nonchalantly to the entrance. The *militsia* man standing by the side of the gate gave him a hard stare, didn't return the nod.

"Hey, Frank. What's up? Are we having a party today?" Jack flashed his ID at the young marine in the booth inside the gate.

"Jack. You're late for the main show, man. Not sure you'll like it, though." Frank's expression was an odd mixture of alarm, curiosity and suspicion.

No! It can't be. Not again!

"Yeah? Surprise me!" He grinned widely, playing up excitement.

"Your boss was detained last night. By the KGB."

Chapter 41

"*What*?! You kidding me, right?"

Frank shrugged, his tone grim. "Told you, you wouldn't like it."

"But he's a fucking CAO, for Christ's sake! Why would the KGB detain him?" Jack exclaimed loudly, knowing he would be heard from the street.

"You askin' me? He's *your* boss, man, not mine." The marine's expression turned suspicious again. "You sure the CAO's all he was?"

"Jesus, who knows anything here anymore!" Jack threw his hands in the air, his bewilderment and frustration real. "I'd better go 'n find out. Thanks for warning me."

"No problem, man... See you later at the club?" Frank called after him.

"Maybe," Jack tossed back without slowing down.

He spent a few hours at Uncle Sam's where he was the center of the attention. Each new person to arrive asked him if he knew anything about William Osbourne III that could have gotten him in trouble with the Sovs. Like spying, for instance. Because everybody knew that had it been something else, like women or illegal currency exchange, they would have merely raised a scandal. Instead, they had taken him to Lubianka, the prison at the KGB headquarters.

By 9:00 p.m. and the fifth round of consolation beers, Jack was beat. He wished he could go home, down a double shot of whiskey and crash. He excused himself, said he would be back and headed to the main building.

Grant and Charlie at the metal door on the ninth floor were a little more sympathetic. He chatted with them for a couple of minutes before descending to his office. Leaving the door ajar and without turning on the light, he sat at his desk for a long while, collecting his thoughts.

With William Osbourne burned, the count was seven in nine months. And the rolled-up agent this time was probably the English-speaking civilian who worked—had worked!—at the Institute of America and Canada. Seven lost agents in nine months and two ambushed case officers. Again, not counting the two agents that had managed to come in and two busted non-human assets. Worse still, this time it was his direct boss. Jack had little doubt he would have to shoulder some of the consequences. He just didn't know what they'd be. He prayed that his deep cover would remain intact. Not that Eton and his friends would know; but still, Jack didn't want anyone else in Moscow, besides the chief, to know about his real occupation.

He sighed, reached for the phone and dialed an internal number.

"Speaking." The man's voice was deceptively calm and leisurely, as if nothing out of the ordinary had happened.

Jack pitched his voice low and said hesitantly, "Good evening, sir. This is Redmond. I'm calling to confirm our meeting tomorrow."

"Redmond? Oh, yes. Thanks for calling. In fact, I was thinking maybe we should catch up today. Are you calling on the internal line?"

"Yes, sir."

"Good. I'll see you in fifteen minutes. Your place?"

"Yes, sir."

"Excellent. See you in a bit."

The line went dead.

Jack put down the receiver and opened the right bottom drawer of his desk. He fumbled inside, pulled out a small flashlight and went to the door. He locked the door, switched on the torch, pointing it at the floor, and returned to his desk to wait for the COS.

Fifteen minutes later, there was a light tap on the door. Nurimbekoff didn't come in when Jack opened it, instead cocked his head towards William's office. He unlocked the door, then locked it securely behind them before proceeding to the little dark room at the back, with Jack's point light charting the way.

"Come in here," Nurimbekoff whispered. "And keep it down." He closed the door tightly and only then turned on the light. "It's relatively secure in here. Sit down, Jack. It's good that you called."

"I've brought back *his* car and... just learned..." Jack wasn't sure what else to say.

"Good. I'm flying back to HQ tomorrow night and need you to put everything on hold in the meantime. I mean *everything*."

"Yes, sir."

"There'll be several staff briefings tomorrow. You and the rest of the USIA staff will be under a lot of pressure. Play dumb. And loud. Unfortunately, we have neither the time nor facilities to go work out details. I trust you know what to do. You've been doing a good job."

"Thank you, sir."

"Marat."

"Thanks, Marat... What if my contacts ask about *him*?"

"Hopefully they won't. It won't be officially announced for a few days. Then you make yourself scarce. At least until I'm back."

"Yesss, alright... What about the NW exchange program? And the parties to it?"

"We'll have to do some damage control. But that's not for you to worry about. The USIA will send a new CAO. Don't think we can use this slot from now on. We'll need to decide how to manage you. In any case, we'll have a clearer picture in a week's time. In the meantime, here's Mark Morris's number, for code red situations." Nurimbekoff produced a scrap of paper from his pocket and handed to Jack.

Mark Morris was the new Deputy COS who had arrived last September.

Jack took the slip of paper. "Does he know about me?"

"He knows the Station's headcount, not you personally. But he will know when, *if* you call."

Jack nodded, trying not to let his relief show. "Code word?"

"Redmond... Now, the car. You'll be asked about it tomorrow. Make some noise. Look for *him*, try to return the keys. Complain when you can't. Give it to the security office in a couple of days. Alright? Good... Anything else?"

"May I ask... what happened?"

"Ambush." Nurimbekoff stifled a sigh.

"On an op run?"

"Yes."

"When is he leaving?"

"In two days."

"What do I do when I see him?"

"You won't. Not here. Don't stay late in the office though."

"Yesss... Okay."

"The number." Nurimbekoff indicated the slip of paper with the phone number in Jack's hand.

"Oh, right."

Jack ran through the number twice, then closed his eyes trying to memorize it. In a minute, he opened his eyes and handed the scrap back to the COS.

"Good. Now you can go and spend some *quality time* at the Marines Club," Nurimbekoff said softly, but his eyes were serious. He wasn't joking.

As expected, Monday started with a series of briefings at Spaso House. Given the large number of staff, visiting missions and other American citizens who happened to be in town, the briefings continued through Tuesday.

Ambassador Hart summoned Jack and his USIA colleagues just before lunch and briefed them on the state of affairs with William Osbourne, how they should behave and answer questions about their ex-boss. He reminded them of the policy of no fraternization with locals and added that social involvements should not lead to emotional ones. The Ambassador looked as though he knew his little speech was excessive but was something he had to do.

They all nodded and mumbled, "Yes, sir", and Jack asked warily if that was what had actually happened—William had become emotionally involved with someone? He thanked God that the anxiousness he felt looked appropriate and that others couldn't see the cold sweat broken out under his arms.

The Ambassador gave him an evasive, long-winded answer, then let them go quickly before more questions could be asked.

Jack was also summoned to Don Steward's office, where the head of security asked him about William's car and what Jack had been doing during the past two days. Jack played dumb and loud as he handed over his boss's car key to Don. The man gave him another no-fraternization-with-locals sermon before letting him go.

William Osbourne's detention was not the only spy-related news that shook the day. On

Monday, the front pages of the American newspapers carried the Reagan administration's announcement of its decision to cut one third of the Soviet contingent at the United Nations - part of its anti-espionage program. The general reader might not have linked the two episodes together, since the Soviet version of William Osbourne's detention didn't go public until Thursday, but Moscow Station and the Embassy's senior diplomatic staff did.

As a result, Jack and his USIA colleagues were in the center of attention for most of the week and had to endure a steady flow of nosy questions every time they turned up in public. For Jack it meant every day before work, during lunchtime and after work until midnight. The topic folks were keen to discuss with him the most, and which he hated the most, was why William had lent him his car. He managed to play an active part in the speculations on the subject of his ex-boss. However, by Thursday evening, when the Sovs finally announced the incident on the national news program *Vremya*, Jack had used up all of his reserve of patience and good-natured banter and felt sapped dry.

On Friday morning, all Soviet and foreign dailies quoted TASS's official statement, which announced that the Cultural Affairs Officer, William Osbourne, had been detained in Moscow on Monday while conducting a clandestine meeting with a Soviet citizen recruited by U.S. intelligence. The evidence found by the security organs fully implicated him in activities incompatible with his official status and Osbourne was ordered to leave the Soviet Union by March 16th.

Jack braced himself for another wave of interest in the William Osbourne affair. He prayed for the day to end soon, so that he could have a few drinks at the club, then maybe a couple more at home. Then he'd disconnect his phone and sleep for the whole weekend. Nurimbekoff was expected to return on Monday and Jack hoped the COS would bring back *some* news if not good news.

At half past four, Heather the librarian called him and asked if he could come down—she had news that she wanted to share with him. Christ, what else now, he thought, but said, "Coming, sweetie-pie" with forced enthusiasm. It turned out that, due to the shortage of space at the commissary, the library was being dismantled and all the books were now free for the taking. As Jack was one of her best friends at the Embassy, Heather wanted to share the news with him first in case he was interested in any particular books, she said, smiling shyly at him.

Jack spent an hour in the tiny library in the basement room of the commissary building, trying to guess which books Eton might want to have. In the end, he decided that the forty-volume set of Encyclopedia Britannica, which included five volumes on science, would probably be it.

Nurimbekoff returned on Monday, but Jack wasn't summoned for a briefing until Wednesday night, this time in the dark and empty room in the basement that had once housed the Embassy's library. When Jack asked why not the Tank, he was told that the safe room was being checked for security breaches. Which could only mean it had been bugged too. Jack recalled all the meetings he'd had with William and the COS in the Tank in the course of the past year. Jesus Christ! But it wasn't like he could do a damn thing about it, except hold his breath and pray.

Nurimbekoff briefed him in a hushed tone and Jack had to strain to hear what Moscow

Station chief was saying. It was more or less the same story he had told Jack before: as it had been decided to keep his cover intact—for now—Jack was to report directly to the COS and to keep *all* activities down, until a new structure and communication channels were in place. He would continue his work with the Soviet Nuclear Winter team within the USIA's exchange project, including preparations for the Soviet scientists' trip to America in April. Jack would accompany them and would stay back for his "annual leave". By that time, the dust would have settled and the Station's case officers, including Jack, would be able to resume their work.

Then Nurimbekoff instructed Jack on *their* version of William Osbourne's expulsion: an affair with a local woman. On their last rendezvous, William had been ambushed by the KGB. They tried to blackmail him into working for them. When William refused, they had taken him to Lubianka, forcibly stuffed compromising material into his briefcase and accused him of spying.

Of course, there would be no official position about this, but rumors about William's extracurricular activities already started circulating. Jack would hear them fairly soon from the regulars at Uncle Sam's and, once again, was to actively participate in the discussions. He could then communicate this version, which implied that the Soviet version of the events was a hoax, to his contacts. Most Russians loathed the KGB, so his local contacts were more likely to believe the American version. This would keep William from being linked to the Company and Jack too, by association with his ex-boss.

Right. That explains where the little sermon about "no fraternization, no emotional involvements with locals" was coming from and why Ambassador Hart looked uneasy preaching it.

"When are you meeting with your local exchange team?" Nurimbekoff asked when he had finished his instructions.

"I'm supposed to call them sometime next week."

"Make sure you've done a few rounds on the topic with your pals here before talking to the Russians. It'll give you some practice. Sorry, we can't talk through the details. You'll have to play it by ear."

"I will... I think I still need to see them socially from time to time. It might look strange if I suddenly start avoiding."

"Fine. But let the dust settle for a week or two. And don't try to pull anything with them. You'll have plenty of time later. Stick to regular socializing."

"I got some books... from this library. The Encyclopedia Britannica. I want to give it to them... As a present." Jack hoped he sounded businesslike enough.

The COS peered at him for a long moment, deliberating, then nodded. "Can't see why not? In fact, it might be a good idea. Let me know if you need any paperwork in relation to the books." He patted Jack on the shoulder and smiled at him encouragingly. "You're doing a good job, son."

"Thank you." Jack nodded solemnly, fighting to suppress a sigh of relief—he was cleared to see his friends, to see Eton, without having to file reports on everything he did.

He could hardly wait until Saturday when he could call Eton to propose that they meet somewhere in town. He had little doubt that by now all his Russian contacts had either heard or read about William's detention and declaration as *persona non grata*. He wanted to tell him the American side of the story in person, even if he knew it was a lie.

He needed to see Eton, to put his friend's mind at rest.

He needed to hear the familiar voice rumbling "Don't worry", the voice that could stir up a cloud of butterflies in his stomach just by him remembering it.

On Saturday morning, he got up early, put on his running gear and left the apartment. He made a big loop to the south and east before stopping to make a phone call.

"*Allo*?"

Eton's voice was sleep clogged, as if he was talking into his pillow, and it made Jack smile. "*Privet*, Eton. It's me. Sorry to call so early, but I need to see you."

Eton awakened at once. "You coming up?"

"No. I'm near my place. Jogging."

"Ah, alright. When?"

"At nine?"

"Where?"

"Metro Station Oktyabrskaya, circle line. On the platform by the end of the train to Park Kultury Station."

"I will be there."

"Alright. Thank you... *friend*." Jack couldn't hold back a smile as he hung up.

Moscow's Metro. It had to be the most beautiful example of modern architecture Jack had ever seen. Could easily rival any museum in Washington D.C., if Jack was asked. In the first few months upon arrival, he had spent many weekends learning his way around the city by riding the Metro, wandering along its columned, frescos or mosaic-embellished stations, taking pictures, playing an awe-struck newcomer. He hadn't needed to play up—he had truly been in awe. And still was.

Sometimes he wished his compatriots back home could see it, along with many other things he had discovered in this country and about its people. Maybe if Americans knew more about them, things would have been different. Easier, friendlier, more accepting. On both sides...

He took the most direct route to Oktyabrskaya Station. For whoever was watching him today, it was intended to be a quick catch-up with a local friend on the way to the Embassy.

He spotted Eton on the other end of the platform as soon as he alighted from the train. The young man was leaning against the marble wall, facing Jack's way. When he noticed Jack hurrying toward him, his face didn't light up like the last few times they'd met. Jack couldn't recall when he'd last seen Eton wearing his usual impassive mask. But maybe it was a good thing too, so that nobody could see the way Eton May Volkonsky smiled at him—like Jack Smith was the best thing ever. Jack would have given anything to see that smile again, but this was neither the time nor the place for it.

"Hey, sorry I'm late. Have you been waiting long?" he asked as they were shaking hands.

"*Privet*. I've just arrived."

"I've brought you some tapes here." Jack took the tapes briefly out of the used plastic bag he'd been carrying—in case somebody was watching. "A couple of new movies." He put the tapes back in the bag and handed it to Eton.

"Thanks." Eton took the bag, looking at him quizzically. "We need to talk?"

"Yes."

"About your boss."

"Yes, that too. But let's get somewhere quiet first."

"How much time do you have?" He asked matter-of-factly, but Jack noticed he had bitten the inside of his lip.

"Not much. Sorry. I have to be at the Embassy by eleven."

Eton nodded weakly. "How about breakfast? There's a *blynnaya* shop not far from the Metro station."

It wasn't exactly what Jack had planned—it hadn't yet been a couple of weeks he had been told to wait. "Alright. Let's go."

They headed toward the escalator.

Jack turned around to face Eton, who was standing on a lower step behind him. "Did you call me?"

"Yes. But you weren't home."

"I thought you would. Sorry, I couldn't call you earlier. It's been a crazy couple of weeks."

"You've called." Eton's face softened, easing into the familiar little smile.

They reached the top of the escalator and exited onto the street. It was still early for a Saturday and there weren't many people out and about, braving the still wintery morning.

"I wanted to ask you something," Jack said.

"Yes?"

"I took Lara out on the March Eighth Day and she told me that Seva had left *Krylia*. What happened? I thought you guys were planning to perform at the rock festival in Leningrad."

Eton stopped to light a cigarette, shielding the tiny flame with his body and hands. He inhaled on it deeply and puffed out a cloud of while smoke. "We've quarreled."

"I see… Listen, I might not be the best person to help. In fact, I might even be the worst person to help. But if you need to talk…" He felt responsible for his friend's falling out. After all, it was he who had advised Eton to date Anya.

"Sevka thought I was cheating on Anya with, um, some other girl," Eton blurted out in his usual manner and sat off walking again.

"Right." The resentment that flared in his gut caught Jack by surprise. "Are you?"

Oh, c'mon! This is not about you!

Eton cut him a worried glance. "I'm not cheating on… on anyone! I just wanted us, *Krylia*, to perform *that* song in Leningrad. The one I gave you. I wanted people to think it was about some girl with, um, blue eyes." Color started spreading over his ear and forehead. "So I invited Natasha for a coffee and, um, drove her home… That's all." He peered into Jack's eyes. "Sevka bought it… He cares for Anya."

The song Eton had given him as a birthday present... "And I want to drown in the bluest of the blue, the color of your eyes."

Jesus.

"Eton, you should be more careful, bud. You can't—"

"It's part of your birthday present."

"Yes, I know." Jack stopped and reached for Eton's cigarette, briefly pressing his fingers into Eton's. "I'm touched. I truly am, but—"

"I'm going to sing it at the festival," Eton said, low and unyielding. "Artyom, um, a friend, has already found us a new drummer. A professional percussionist."

"So you're still going for the festival?" Jack handed the cigarette back, unsure if he should feel relieved or worried for his friend.

"Yes. You have to do at least *something* you want... Right?"

"Right." They walked in silence for a minute, then Jack asked again, "What about Anya and Seva?"

Eton took a last deep pull on the remains of the cigarette and flicked it in the trashcan they were passing by. "They'll be fine. *Better* without me." His tone was forceful as if he was trying to convince himself about it.

"What about you?" He felt hopeless, useless, not being able to help or advise his friend in any way—his best friend, the only person for whom he truly cared.

Whose life he wasn't a part of. Whose life he'd been screwing up slowly and surely.

Eton looked at him and smiled, his eyes tired. "I'm fine, Jack. Really. Please don't worry about me."

"Alright, then," Jack conceded, fully aware that it wasn't as alright as they both were trying to sound.

There was only a taxi driver in the cafeteria and an old couple who looked like out-of-towners. They took two trays, waited for their pancakes to be made on a large stove with a black metal sheet over it, got their hot chocolate drinks and sat down at the far corner by the window.

"Grandfather was called to the dean's office," Eton broke the silence as soon as they sat down. "He was questioned about your boss's connections to the exchange program. Grandfather says they're going to request an official statement from your Embassy."

"I'll call his office on Monday and arrange for a meeting... I'm sorry about all this, Eton."

"Not your fault, is it?... What about you? Have you been questioned about him?"

"Yes, all of us were... They told us we mustn't fraternize with locals... mustn't get *involved* with locals. I suppose now I'm being watched more closely by your *organs*, as well," Jack concluded grimly.

"What has it to do with 'fraternizing with locals'?" Eton furrowed his brows.

"They say William had an affair with a local woman. That he was caught by the *organs* at her place. When he refused to cooperate, they accused him of espionage."

Eton paled, the oh-shit expression on his face made Jack want to kick himself hard. But then, that could happen to him, too, right? *If* they had caught him. Except that when blackmailed he was supposed to "cooperate" with them. And what would happen to Eton then? Jack didn't want to think about it. No, it couldn't come to that. *He* had to make sure it wouldn't happen.

"Are you saying that the story told by *our* newspapers is not true? He is not a spy?"

"I'm just telling you what people at the Embassy are talking about and what we've been told not to do."

"If that's true, why didn't your Embassy issue a protest against such a crude lie?"

"I'm sure they did. They always do in such cases. Even when it isn't a lie." He shrugged awkwardly. "It's all politics."

Eton watched him intently, frowning in concentration. "What about you?"

Jack's heart skipped a beat. "*What* about me?" he asked carefully, arching his eyebrows.

"What do you think? Was he a spy or just having an affair?"

Jack sighed, playing up exasperation. "It doesn't matter what I think, Eton—it doesn't change a damn thing. Fact is, this incident has added a pile of crap on our plate, friend, and we'll have to deal with it. It means that I won't be able to visit your place. Too dangerous."

"I understand." Eton nodded. "As I said before, you do what you need to do, Jack. It doesn't change, uh… *anything* for me."

He didn't smile but his eyes were so soft that Jack had to look away for a moment.

"But we'll stay in touch, alright? Meet *socially*, once in a while." Jack tried to smile encouragingly, but it turned out cheerless.

Eton didn't answer. He picked up his fork and started eating. Jack attacked his plate. But in the end they left half of their pancakes and didn't talk much either.

Eton insisted on walking Jack back to the Metro and rode the escalator down with him, looking at his feet most of the time. But just as the train was arriving in the station, preceded by a low, thunder-like rumble, a gust of cool air, then loud metallic screeching, he looked up at Jack and asked urgently, "Will you come to Leningrad to see our performance?"

"I will, Eton. I promise."

Jack squeezed his hand in a bone-crushing handshake, hoping his smile conveyed the confidence both of them needed but had been running low on.

Chapter 42

March 23, Sunday. 11:25p.m.

Dear Jack,

Thank you for telling me what happened to your boss. I admit: before our meeting ~~I had been~~ my mind had been conjuring up theories. I even started speculating about you. I am sorry, but you are a cultural attaché like him. What was I supposed to think? Now I understand that your people are right: he must have had an affair with a local woman. Got caught. Blackmailed. Kicked out.

I am sure you know they do it to us, too. They can easily do it to Gosha, for example—force him to report on other students. Gosha is an easy victim: he has no protection. They will break him if they decide to use him. If he does as they tell him to, he'll get some privileges: a good job, an apartment in Moscow. But he'll have to live with the fact that he has betrayed his friends' trust.

Gosha is a good boy. But I don't know if he is strong enough to stand against them.

No, it cannot happen to you, cowboy. No way. I understand your precautions and your worries. I also know that you worry more about me than about yourself. Because I am reckless. I know that too. I have been safe behind Grandfather's back for too long. I ought to start thinking that it will not last forever—my Grandfather will not last forever. Once again, Grisha was right. He doesn't come around anymore. I only see him when we have lab sessions.

Before I met you, I had a general idea of where I was heading. It made sense. Now it doesn't anymore. Because how can it make any sense if all that matters nowadays is you?

I can't tell you how grateful I am to you for caring about me. I love you.

E.

March 30, Sunday. 11:47 p.m.

Dear Jack,

I ran into Anya today. Haven't seen her for almost 2 months. She said she and Sevka are going to get married after her graduation next year and will move to Leningrad. She looked like an older woman. Sadder. Severe. I feel like the last bastard. But what can I do? I will ruin her if I marry her. I don't want her to become bitter like her mother. Although it looks like she is heading that way already. I hope Sevka will make her happy.

She asked about William, said her father told her that he was your boss. Told me I should stay away from you; that you might be a spy, too, and I would get myself in trouble. I told her I heard from Grandfather that William had had an affair with a local woman and got caught. Apparently, she had heard that from her father too, but said she believed our newspapers, not rumors spread by who knows whom; besides, if that story were true, Lara would not have been dating you. Then she asked if I was dating anyone. I said I'm dating Natasha. She suddenly recalled she was late for a meeting, wished me luck and hurried away.

I am dating Natasha, Jack. You said I should, right? She is a nice girl. Kind, cheerful, with big light-blue eyes. Smiles a lot. She reminds me of you sometimes. Except she is a redhead. A good jazz singer too. Don't know what she is planning to do with that though—jazz is not very popular here. Ha, that's Russians for you: we are impractical; we do what we feel we have to, without thinking to what end. Or about consequences.

What consequences? They never stop us from pursuing what we yearn for.

Yours always,

E.

April 7, Monday. 0:30 a.m.

Dear Jack,

We have been practicing for the festival at Karelin's studio (I have written a few pieces for his new opera; he lets us use his studio in exchange). Artyom came to see us playing; said we are doing well.

After the practice, I ran into Karelin in the corridor. He has been looking unwell lately. Lara mentioned some time ago that he was having problems at the Institute. Maybe with the organs too: he is too outspoken, doesn't even hide his true self. I admire him for that. He makes me wonder if I would ever have the courage to do it.

Anyway, we talk and the conversation led to Lara, then to you. He said Lara had told him that we were friends. He gave me a strange look as if I was a mathematical problem he was trying to solve. I said Lara had introduced all of us to you and that you were the coordinator for Grandfather's exchange project. He seemed satisfied with that, but then suddenly said that you are a gorgeous looking man. I would have knocked him out if someone hadn't called him away at that moment.

How can a person be so admirable and so infuriating at the same time? God, please give me strength to stand him! Because he is a very decent man at heart.

E.

April 13, Sunday. 15 minutes to midnight.

Dear Jack,

It has been over 3 weeks since we talked. How are you? I told you to do what you need to do and do not worry about me, but I still wish you called. I just want to hear your voice.

No, it isn't the only thing

After midnight.

I was so glad you called. Then don't know what happened. Were you upset with me? I am sorry, cowboy. Maybe I shouldn't have mentioned Karelin and his questions about you. But you shouldn't worry about that. Honest! He's not my friend, but I know he's not a stukach—he wouldn't report on anyone. Everybody who knows him knows that. He defies the organs openly and they haven't been able to do anything to him. So far. But it is taking toll on him. And you may be right: he might be on drugs. But even so, he will not report on either you or me or anyone. And he doesn't know ANYTHING about you and me.

All right, he had been making allusions toward me even before I met you. But I am sure he doesn't know about me. It is just his style—he makes advances on anyone he likes, regardless of whether they are like ~~that~~ him or not.

He was asking me to write music for his shows forever. I only agreed recently. Wrote a few pieces for his new rock opera. It's different. It's brilliant. And inspiring. And makes you want to be part of it.

Jack, you don't have to worry about Karelin. I'll tell you more about him when we meet. Perhaps before you take Grandfather to America. I hope so.

Yours always,

E.

April 15, Tuesday. 10:15p.m.

Ran into Gosha today at the cafeteria in our central building. I haven't seen him since our project ended. We don't hang out anymore since my fall-out with Sevka and Anya. And Grisha. Lara is the only person I talk to nowadays.

Gosha behaved strangely as if he wanted to avoid talking to me. In short, he had been called up to the dean's office and asked about us (me specifically) hanging out and inviting Americans (you) to their homes. He was told that if he wants to graduate with honors and get a job in Moscow, he should let the dean know what is going on with me and Grandfather, who we see and what we talk about. Then the dean said that Gosha was on the list of the army conscripts to be reviewed in a few months.

Just like Grisha had predicted.

You don't want to be conscripted in the Soviet Army. My friends and I have been able to evade it so far. But we never know if we can avoid it all together.

I didn't ask him how he had answered. I could see it on his face—he can't lie at all. In truth, what could he do about it? He has no one to protect him but himself.

I'll talk to Grandfather. Maybe he can do something for Gosha.

E.

April 20, Sunday. Midnight.

Dear Jack,

You will be leaving to America in 8 days. You said you'll be there for a few weeks.

I haven't told you, but you will miss my birthday—May 9. Yes, I was born on the day the Sov. Union won the WWII 19 years before. We usually have a big Victory

Day-birthday dinner at Grandfather's place every year. Don't know if Grandfather will be back by that time. Don't know who of my friends will come this year. Perhaps I shouldn't be there either.

Maybe I will celebrate it at my place, with you. Like we celebrated yours three and a half months ago—in my bed. Even without you in person, you will still be there in my dreams. In my heart.

Will I see you before you leave? It has been 4 weeks since we met last. I need to see you.

Yours always,

E.

* * *

For a month after the deportation of their ex-boss, Jack and the rest of the USIA team found their lives in a state of flux. They underwent numerous briefings by various security officers during the office hours; after work, they speculated endlessly. During the last week of March their deputy head of department flew in from Washington to brief them and make interim arrangements—until the new CAO was in place.

Glenn was appointed acting CAO and Jack inherited William Osbourne's projects—he had been running most of them for William, anyway. As it happened, William's main project was the implementation of the Cultural Exchange Agreement between America and the Soviet Union, and the first activity on the list was the tour of America by the Kirov Ballet from Leningrad later that year. Naturally, the job required trips to Leningrad to meet with its management.

It took all Jack's willpower not to call Eton immediately to tell him that he was coming to see him play at the rock festival for certain. The William Osbourne affair hadn't been forgotten yet, and his friend didn't need extra attention from the *organs*. Besides, the KGB had ramped up their surveillance of Jack since the arrival of their Washington boss.

As a result, he didn't call Eton until the second week of April. And in the end didn't manage to tell him about his assignment in Leningrad: at one point in his story about rehearsals with his band, Eton mentioned Karelin's name and somehow the conversation went downhill from there. They didn't fight, but each knew that the other was wound up and frustrated because he couldn't say freely what he wanted say on the phone.

Afterwards, Jack tried to reconstruct what exactly had happened and why it had affected him in that way. He didn't trust Karelin, he told himself. Eton seemed to think differently: he had insisted that he didn't like the man either, but had protected him when Jack said he was probably a *stukach*—a snitch.

Yeah, that was it: he didn't like that Eton protected him. Not one bit. Didn't like it because he still remembered how the scrawny director had looked at Eton the first time they met at MGU. Like a cat at a bowl of sour cream. And now Eton was practicing with his band at this man's studio…

Wait a minute: are you jealous?

No, I'm not! But this Russian drives me… Am I?

What do you think?

No, he didn't want to think about it. Had no time to think about it...

Most of the following week Jack spent in Leningrad working with the administration office of the Kirov Ballet Theater. By the end of his four-day visit, he was on a first name basis with all leading dancers as well as administrators of the theater, and even got admirers, both women and men. All of them enthusiastically offered to show him around Leningrad and its suburbs if he decided to stay over the weekend.

He did stay for the weekend, and spent the whole of Saturday wandering around town with one of the prima ballerinas, the only Asian dancer, from Kazakhstan. Petite and willowy, with soulful black eyes, she didn't quite fit into the troupe. Somehow, they found each other's company comforting and unobtrusive.

Jack made her walk him along all major and side streets in the central part of the town, trying to memorize his way around. Just in case. He didn't know where Eton's rock festival would take place, where his friend would stay and what they would be doing afterwards, but wanted to be prepared.

He yearned to call Eton, to let him know that he was making plans to be at his concert, but the surveillance on him had been so tight that he decided against it. Instead, he called Lara and told her that he was in Leningrad on business. He hoped that at least she was still talking to Eton.

The KGB continued tailing him in Moscow though not as closely. Still, Jack didn't think another stunt, like the last time when he had visited Eton's place, was a good idea. And he had to see him before his departure for America—he'd be away for a month.

By Friday night, Jack had given up hope that his minders would give him a breather. He called Eton around eleven o'clock on his way home from the marines' bar. Eton was home, and they talked for a few minutes. Jack asked if he could drop by the next evening around nine o'clock for half an hour—to bring Eton a few books.

"I'm sorry, friend. I can't do more. *Neudobno*." The Russian word for "inconvenient" had multiple meanings, and he hoped Eton would understand what he really meant.

There was a moment of silence, then Eton sighed. "I understand".

Jack called off shortly after and headed home, noticing a beige Lada dropping off someone a few hundred yards behind him.

The next day was the first practice of the American softball team after the long Russian winter. Jack spent the morning and early afternoon playing shortstop, a position that nobody else wanted, and by the end of it, was beat. He returned to the Embassy with others, most of them Marines and Seabees who lived on the Embassy's grounds, had lunch and a few beers with them and returned to his apartment at around four.

He stood under a hot shower for a long time, running the details of various scenarios in his head over and again.

He was going for an open game and prayed they wouldn't decide to make the move on him today—he would be visiting a friend's home, they'd seen him doing that before, so it shouldn't be a big deal. He just hoped he'd have enough willpower to stand firm in the face of temptation whose name was Eton...

Shit, he got hard just by thinking about resisting the temptation. And he had thought he had worn himself out good playing softball.

Jack turned off the hot water and stood under the freezing shower until his skin started going numb and his teeth chattering. Then he climbed out, rubbed himself down with a towel and walked barefoot into the bedroom where he climbed under the comforter. Having found a comfortable position, he sighed and closed his eyes. And ordered himself not to think why visits to his best friend and lover (yeah, might as well say it!) had to be operational runs, with the KGB close on his heels.

At 7:30 p.m., he was ready to roll. The weather had been unseasonably warm for the last two days, so he put on his tennis shoes, the jean jacket over a denim shirt, picked up his backpack loaded with three volumes of science extras of the Encyclopedia Britannica and a large plastic bag with the remaining two tomes and went out.

As planned, the plastic bag burst right outside of the *militsia* guard's booth and the two thick books fell to the ground. The guard watched Jack bitching with an amused smirk, but didn't move from his post. Jack took his time inspecting the books for damage. Once satisfied, he jammed them into his backpack, opening it wide enough for the guard to see its contents. Then he smiled sheepishly at the Russian, stuffed the torn plastic bag into the overflowing dustbin by the booth and left the compound.

On the street, he didn't take any of the first four cars that stopped for him, haggling over the fare and bitching spiritedly. The fifth one was a private car with out-of-town plates. Jack took it and went straight to Eton's place. He alighted a block from his friend's apartment building and surreptitiously looked around him. It looked like he was clear, but he couldn't trust it as he hadn't done the SDR. But at least he had prepared a story, a plausible one he thought, just in case.

As he was nearing Eton's place, it occurred to him that perhaps he was being overly paranoid. Why would the KGB make a move on him now? They didn't know that he was a case officer, he was pretty sure of it by now. They had to be aware that Eton lived here, therefore Jack wasn't visiting a woman and they couldn't catch them having an affair and blackmail him into spying. Not a soul here knew that either he or Eton was gay. So what could they accuse him and Eton of, really? That they were pals, and he was visiting his friend before going home for a month? Hardly something that justified organizing an ambush. So what was the worst that could happen to them? His visit would be logged and they would keep it for using against them later when opportune.

Later, not now. For now, he could relax and…

Jack smiled to himself, impatience rolling in waves in his stomach as he quickened his steps into inner courtyard of the building.

The door opened three seconds after the ring.

"*Privet*. Come in, please."

The door immediately closed behind him and Jack heard the metallic click of the chain falling into place. He turned to Eton who still stood by the door.

"I'm sorry, I couldn't call earlier. I—"

"It's okay. I understand," Eton responded in English. He finally smiled a little and took a tentative step closer to Jack.

Jack dropped his loaded backpack, which landed in on the floor with a soft thud, caught Eton by his biceps and pulled him into his arms. Eton yielded to the embrace easily, circling his arms around Jack's waist. He buried his face in the base of Jack's neck and let out a shuddering exhale.

"God, Eton, I..." Jack choked on the words and bit on his lip.

Eton pulled back a little and gazed deep into Jack's eyes, his smile widening as he said quietly but clearly, "I know. Me too." He leaned in and covered Jack's lips with his for a moment, then pulled back again. "How much time do we have?" he asked without a smile.

Not enough.

"An hour... And a half." Jack planted a soft kiss on his lips and let go of him. "I've brought something for you here."

He hauled up his backpack from the floor, toed his runners off and proceeded into the sitting room.

Eton was close on his heels. "You shouldn't have, Jack. Really."

Jack opened his bag, pulled out two gold embossed black leather tomes and put them on the table without a word.

"What is it?" Eton picked one book up and read the title aloud, "Encyclopedia Britannica. Science and Future. Volume five." He watched wide-eyed as Jack unloaded the rest of the contents of his backpack on the table.

"I have thirty-five more at home. Our library was shut down, and they were up for the taking... Thought you might find it, um, useful."

Eton looked up at him, still lost for words. "Thirty... forty volumes! All for me?"

"It's your birthday present." Jack grinned.

"Thank you very much. But it's not my birthday yet."

"It will be eventually, right? You may even have the whole collection by then."

"Yes. It's on May 9th, actually."

"May 9th. Oh..."

Shit, he'd be in America.

"Yes. This is a... an enormous gift. No, it's true!" he insisted when Jack tried to object. "Nobody has ever given me anything like this for a present. Thank you so much... But you know, I'd rather just have you... as my birthday present." He stepped up and put his arms around Jack's waist.

At first, they just stood like that, leaning into each other, holding each other softly, breathing in the other's scent. But as seconds ticked away, their embrace tightened, their mouths came together, and then they were clinging to one another, frantic and desperate, like they were sinking and the other was his lifebuoy. Then, without breaking the kiss, Eton began to walk Jack backwards slowly toward the couch, one hand holding him by the neck while the other one fumbled with his belt buckle. He pushed Jack down so that he was sitting on the couch, knelt down on the floor between his knees and unbuttoned his jeans.

He had just pushed Jack's t-shirt all the way up, his hands worshiping Jack's quivering abs, when the phone shrieked. They froze, turned their heads slowly toward the red telephone set on the small table by the couch, their hearts accelerating to a sprint.

Eton swallowed. "We're not home," he mumbled through his teeth.

"Answer it, Eton. They have seen me coming here," Jack said quietly but firmly and pulled his t-shirt down.

Eton looked up at him, his expression a mixture of skepticism and disappointment. "Are you sure?"

"Yes. Answer the phone. Please."

Eton sprung up, adjusted himself and picked up the phone. He took a deep breath. "*Allo?*"

No, please God, no! Let it not be *them*!

"Oh, how are you?... I'm good, thanks. How's mama?" Eton looked at Jack, gave him an encouraging half smile and mouthed, "Grandfather". The next moment his smile waned, and he was frowning. "Yes, I have. Why? What happened?... How can they do this? Your trip was planned months ago!... *What*?!" There was a longer pause as Eton's grandfather explained what had happened. "Is this the one that—" He was apparently interrupted. "Damn, that'll ruin all his plans... Are you going to call him now?" He stared at Jack with strange expression on his face.

Jack was watching Eton closely as he talked on the phone. He pointed at his own chest and mouthed, "Me?"

Eton nodded distractedly and dropped his gaze. "Alright, I'll call him later... It's Saturday night, Grandpa. He's probably out... with his girlfriend." He turned his face away, but Jack still saw his ear pinked. "What should I tell him?... *Kharasho*... He'll be very upset. You know he has been working so hard on this project with us... Alright, Grandpa. I will tell him... Tell mama I will drop by tomorrow afternoon. Good night."

Eton sat still for a few moments after hanging up, then raised his eyes to meet Jack's. His face was clouded with concern.

"What did he say?" Jack asked, acutely aware that he sounded abrupt. Business-like.

"He asked for your home phone number. Said he needed to call you urgently." Eton looked as if he was still trying to digest what he had just heard.

"What happened?"

"He wants to personally let you know and apologize that he can't go to America the day after tomorrow." He sounded apologetic, like it was his fault.

"What?! But why? C'mon, Eton, spit it out already!"

Eton held Jack's eyes for a second, then said unhurriedly, as if he was weighing every word he was uttering, "There is an urgent, unforeseen matter that Grandfather has been asked by the Government to help with. He is flying out to Kiev tomorrow morning. He is calling you now. His lab will call you again tomorrow. And he has asked me to call you, too. Tonight if possible. He said he is extremely sorry for ruining your plans."

"Did he say what happened?"

Again, Eton hesitated, chewing on the inside of his lip. "Don't think I'm supposed to tell you... Oh, to hell with it! There was an accident at a power station not far from Kiev.

Sounds like it is very serious. He's been asked to join a group of specialists to look at the effects and consequences."

"What has your grandfather to do with power stations? He's an atmospheric physicist… Isn't he?" Jack asked suspiciously, trying frantically to figure what kind of game the Sovs were trying to play this time.

Eton nodded solemnly. "He is. But he's also a nuclear physicist, remember?" He sighed, conceding the rest of the story. "It's a nuclear power station. At a place call Chernobyl."

Chapter 43

They didn't talk after Eton's grandfather's call, both fully aware that Jack had to leave soon. They sat on the couch, thighs pressed together, Jack's arm wrapped around Eton's shoulders, Eton's hand on Jack's thigh. Then Eton asked if he wanted coffee and Jack nodded. They untangled themselves and trudged to the kitchen where Eton made two cups of strong instant coffee. They sat down across from each other at the kitchen table, sipping the bitter-sweet liquid in silence, sharing a cigarette, their legs touching and occasionally fingers.

Jack swallowed the last of his coffee and put down the empty cup. "I still don't understand. Don't they have other qualified specialists who could give advice on this matter? Don't get me wrong, I have the highest regards for your grandfather. But surely he's not the one and only nuclear physicist in this country."

"No. But he is not simply a qualified specialist," Eton said distractedly, still deep in thought.

"No? Who is he, then?"

Eton sighed, then chuckled sadly, eyeing the mug he was turning round in his fingers. "Life is so strange. The history repeats itself. Don't know if he realizes this." He raised his head and met Jack's eyes. "Do you know anything about, um, R-B-M-K reactors?"

Jack shook his head. "No. What are they?"

"They are our high-power, channel type nuclear reactors. They are only used here, in the Soviet Union. Grandfather with two of his colleagues came up with the idea to use the same principles and design of plutonium production to produce electricity. They first experimented with it in the fifties. Then in the sixties, they had the first industrial production tests."

"I didn't know that."

How come Prof. Volkonsky's file didn't have any of this? And he'd thought they'd had complete information on all participants of the nuclear winter project.

"Few people remember it today."

"Why?"

"His name was removed from all the work related to the RBMK reactors... He disagreed with the design. Thought it was not safe enough for industrial production."

"So they kicked him out?"

"He left. Started working on atmospheric physics instead. One of his, um, hobbies."

Jack cocked his head. "I didn't know it was possible to walk out on a State project, just like that."

"Perhaps that was why he agreed to lead the nuclear winter project instead." Eton chuckled sadly again. "With which *I* disagree."

"So why have they called on him now?"

Eton shrugged. "Maybe they have realized that he was right. From what I know, they did listen to him to some extent. The second generation reactors have been improved to lower the void coefficient of reactivity and increase its O-R-M." Seeing a blank expression on Jack's face, he hastened to explain, "It means they are safer than the previous model. They even invited grandfather to the opening ceremony of new power plants a few times."

"At this, eh, Churnovabill place?"

"Chernobyl Atomic Electro Station, yes. He took me there with him once, long time ago. But he said it's still not enough… He was right."

Jack lit up a new cigarette. "So… where else do they use these reactors?"

"At most atomic electro stations. In Leningrad, Kursk, Smolensk, Chernobyl. Then there's a new, big station in Litva."

"Lithuania."

"Lithuania." Eton repeated and smiled gratefully. "It has the largest RBMK reactor. One thousand five hundred megawatt. From what I know, it's the largest reactor in the world."

Jack studied his friend intently for a moment. "How come you know all this? Are you planning to be an engineer at an RBMK nuclear power plant?" he asked flippantly.

"No. I have read about it. Grandfather receives lots of scientific magazines… I want to drop the university."

"*What*?!" Jack stared at him.

"I want to be a musician. Play with my band. Write music… Maybe I can come to perform in America once day. Visit you maybe," Eton joked and smiled a little, then shrugged awkwardly when he saw Jack's reaction.

"Oh-kay," Jack intoned, trying to collect his thoughts. "What are your folks saying about that? Have you told them?"

"No!" Eton shook his head. "They would kill me. Or would die of heart attacks… Or both." He sighed and looked away. "Don't think I can do this till… while they are… with me. No, nobody knows about it. Only you."

A powerful, warm wave rolled over Jack. He reached for Eton's hand on top of the table, stood up, took a step aside and pulled at his hand. "C'mere." He gathered his friend in a tight, affectionate embrace, rocked him a little, like Eton had done to him a few times. "Maybe you will, bud… Maybe you will one day."

They remained in each other's arms for a minute, reveling in the other's scent and warmth, Jack trying to commit to memory the feeling of his lover's lean, young body in his arms. Then he loosened his hold and carefully extracted himself from Eton's embrace.

"I have to go, bud… So you can call and tell me about your grandfather," he joked humorlessly.

Eton distanced himself further from him, leaving Jack with a void where warmth had just been. They trudged to the door.

"What will happen to your trip now? Will you go anyway?" Eton asked.

Jack was lacing up his shoes. He looked up, only to catch his friend dropping his gaze to stare at his feet. "I don't know. I have to report it first. Then we'll see." Jack straightened up, lifting his shoulder bag from the floor. "Your grandfather didn't say anything about Dr. Arceniev, did he?"

"He didn't. Maybe he will still go. I'll find out."

"Okay." Jack looked at his watch. "It's five past ten. Call me around eleven. I should be home by then. I'll call you tomorrow night, alright?"

Eton only nodded in response, his face grim, looking anywhere but at Jack.

Shit, why was it so hard every time he had to go? They should have gotten used to it by now, shouldn't they? But there was an air of finality every time they parted that Jack couldn't shake off and it bothered him long after the goodbyes were said.

They shook hands, embraced for the last time, then Jack wrenched the door opened and closed it firmly behind him, before Eton could step out. On the street, he waved down a private car right in front of his friend's apartment block and went straight home.

Eton called at 11:05 p.m. and told him, his tone formal, that his grandfather was unable to go to America because of an urgent matter at the Academy of Sciences. Jack feigned disappointment and asked Eton to tell Prof. Volkonsky's lab to send an official notice the next day. He didn't care if tomorrow was Sunday, he added sulkily for good measure. His little act seemed to baffle Eton: he was quiet for a few seconds before saying apologetically that he would convey Jack's request to the department.

He rang off, then dialed Glenn's home number. The news elicited the same reaction from his colleague, who was acting as the head of CAO office until their new boss arrived. Except Glenn's whining was genuine. As Jack had expected, Glenn told him to go to the Embassy right away and send an urgent cable to HQ. Jack protested for a minute or two before grudgingly giving in.

He had to go to the Embassy anyway, to report on the unexpected change in his planned activities to his other superiors. Nurimbekoff was out of the country, so it was Mark Morris whom he had to call. The Deputy COS would at last meet the deep cover case officer of Moscow Station, whom he probably knew only by his code name, TRISTAN.

It was just before midnight when Jack reached the Embassy. He headed straight to the communications room and sent a cable to the USIA's HQ in Washington. He chatted for a few minutes with the officer on duty before heading to Uncle Sam's where he ordered a whiskey and coke and joined two contractors at the bar. Five minutes later, he excused himself and headed for the public phone in the corner near the restrooms.

A woman's voice answered. "Hello?"

Jack pitched his voice low, almost whispered, "Good evening, m'am. May I talk to Mr. Morris, please?"

"Hold a minute, please. I'll call him." Obviously an old hand, Mrs. Morris didn't ask who he was or why he was calling her husband after midnight.

There was a long pause, then Mark Morris's voice came on the line, brusque and impatient. "Yes, speaking."

Jack pictured in his mind the short, cocky New Yorker who had played on the opposing team at their softball game earlier that day: his powerful and wicked strikeouts had compensated in full for the man's lack of stature. Jack had stayed away from him, as he did with other case officers, except William.

"Good evening, sir. This is *Redmond*." He paused, waiting for a reaction on the other end.

"Yes. I'm listening," the voice replied neutrally.

Jack couldn't tell if the name had registered with the man. "I need to see you, sir. Now, if possible."

Mark Morris didn't falter. "You know my office. I'll be there in a quarter of an hour."

So he knew the name after all.

"I'll be there."

Exactly fifteen minutes later Jack was knocking softly on the door on the fifth floor.

The door opened and Morris waved Jack through with one hand while pointing down at the threshold with the other—the floor of the room was two fingers higher than that of the corridor. As Jack stepped in, he swiftly shut the door behind him.

The office was small and dark except for a shaded lamp on the virtually empty desk on the right. A bookcase took up most of the wall on the left and a large fireproof safe was tucked to the side. In the corner, a chair was overflowing with books and magazines. And there was not a file in sight. Mark Morris obviously followed the no-file-left-unlocked-overnight rule to the letter.

"Good evening... sir," Jack said as they shook hands. "Sorry for calling so late." He was unsure whether to behave casually or formally with the deputy chief who was only about six or seven years older than he was. In addition, they had played softball together on a few occasions. The man must have excelled on his last posting to be assigned at his comparatively young age as the deputy chief to the Agency's most important station, in the heart of the Main Enemy.

"It's alright, Jack," said Morris.

Jack tensed up. Moscow Station believed that the building on the other side of the ten-lane street had powerful listening devices aimed at the commissary building day and night. Jack hadn't been told that his deep cover would be breached that night to anyone but the deputy COS.

His anxiety didn't escape the other man, who smirked and pointed at the chairs at the heavy desk. "Relax, man. Take a seat. This room has been soundproofed. It's almost as secure as the Tank."

Now Jack noticed that in addition to the raised floor, the room's walls were covered with thick panels and the ceiling was lower than in other offices.

"So, the famous Jack from the CAO office." Mark Morris inspected Jack with interest, then chuckled. "Good job, man."

"Thank you, sir." Jack didn't like his patronizing smile, so he kept it formal.

"It's Mark. Or Morris. Your pick... And for fuck's sake, skip the 'sir'!"

"'Kay."

"Good. Tell me."

"Right. According to one of our exchange programs, I was supposed to accompany two Soviet scientists to Berkeley and New York. We were to leave on Monday. An hour and a half ago I got a call from the grandson of one of them. The boy's also part of the exchange team. He said his grandfather had been asked to join an extremely urgent mission. So he wasn't going to America... Apparently, there was a major accident at a nuclear power plant near Kiev. A place called Chernobyl. Serious enough for the government to ask leading scientists to fly there immediately."

"And the guy told you all this on the phone?" the deputy chief asked, raising his eyebrows in exaggerated disbelief.

"No, in person... It's part of an op," Jack explained when Mark Morris continued to stare at him quizzically. "It would be better if Nurimbekoff briefs you about it. When he's back." He hadn't been told whether he could talk about Operation TALION with the deputy chief.

"The op that Joe Coburn runs himself?" Morris asked. "I thought William was... Alright, I'll talk to Marat. So what are you saying here? The Sovs had an accident at one of their power plants and your contact reported to you about it. Besides, you're not going home on Monday. Correct?"

"Correct." He hesitated, then said firmly, "I think this accident is of somewhat extraordinary proportions. Otherwise they wouldn't have called upon my contact. He specializes in the effects of major nuclear wars. Or in this particular case, maybe of a nuclear catastrophe."

The deputy COS studied Jack for a few seconds, then nodded. "Sounds plausible. Where did you say that plant was?"

"A place called Chernobyl. Somewhere near Kiev."

"Let's have a look at the map."

From the bookcase, Morris produced a folded map the size of a magazine which he opened out and spread on the desktop.

They tried to find Chernobyl on the large map of the Soviet Union, but eventually gave up. They agreed that Morris would send a coded cable to HQ informing their Chief of Ops of a major accident at a nuclear power facility near Kiev and that Jack and his contact were not coming to America as planned. And they would reconvene in this office on Tuesday night. By that time, Nurimbekoff should be back and maybe even with some information on the accident, courtesy of the NSA.

Knowing how closed up the Soviet State was, Jack didn't expect any news about the accident in the press. Still, his job included, among other things, close monitoring of the local newspapers and TV so that was what he did for the next few days.

On Sunday, before anything came to light in the Soviet Union, first Sweden, then Finland and Denmark reported detecting abnormal levels of radioactivity on their territories. The source was believed to be in the Soviet Union. The international news wire service picked up the report, and the news began to spread across the globe like wildfire.

The surprise came on Monday evening when the State news agency TASS issued an unprecedented statement about the accident, which was read in the news program *Vremya* at 9:00 p.m.

"An accident has occurred at the Chernobyl atomic power station and one of the reactors was damaged," the female anchor read from the text on the desk in front of her, her tone emotionless. "Measures have been undertaken to eliminate the consequences of the accident. Aid is being given to those affected. A government commission has been set up."

The uncharacteristic disclosure, for all its brevity, left the world worrying that it could be a major accident and Jack swamped with unease. It then transpired that the Soviet official statement had been released *after* the Swedish Embassy had contacted the Soviet officialdom to ask about the leak and been told that they knew nothing about any nuclear accident.

On Tuesday, international news were full of speculation about events at the Soviet nuclear power plant sixty miles south of Kiev. Major newspapers and TV programs carried special interviews with and opinions by renowned physicists, nuclear engineers familiar with Soviet reactors and officials of the International Atomic Energy Agency. Several newspapers quickly labeled it the worst disaster in the history of nuclear power. But as yet, there was no meaningful clarification offered locally.

The consensus appeared to be that the accident involved a non-nuclear explosion caused by the loss of reactor coolant and possibly the meltdown of the reactor core. The experts suggested that most of the radiation should have been released within the first few hours, and that additional radioactive materials were not likely to escape in significant quantities. They believed that because of intense radiation, it would be impossible to get into the immediate damaged area. Therefore, the Soviets might have no choice but to allow the fire to burn itself out and it could continue for days.

On Tuesday night, Nurimbekoff, who had returned the previous day, confirmed the fact about the raging fires—together with major activities around the damaged reactor, they were clearly visible on the shots taken from the space by NSA's satellites. The COS also told Jack to prepare to go back to America as planned whether the Soviet scientists were going or not—he'd been in the country for over a year now and it was time for a short break. And before his departure, he was to catch up with his Soviet contacts.

Jack noticed that Nurimbekoff had mentioned not a single name during the entire meeting. He figured Mark Morris hadn't been cleared for TALION after all. Which was odd since he was the second in command at Moscow Station.

The Soviet authorities continued trickling out information about Chernobyl, leaving the world guessing. The international scrutiny of the Soviet Union intensified toward May 1st, the day the Government and Soviet people celebrated International Labor Day with a military parade and displays on Red Square, as well as in every city, town and village across the country. The cancelation of the celebrations on Red Square would be a signal that Chernobyl was indeed the catastrophe some scientists suspected.

But on Thursday, the Soviets held their customary grandiose May Day event, complete with a parade on the Red Square and large public concerts across the city. Similar festive walks, parades and public concerts in the open air were held in Kiev, Chernigov, Zhytomir and other towns within a hundred kilometer radius from the damaged power station.

Jack called Eton on Friday night to let him know he was leaving for the US on Monday and to ask if they could meet.

They met on Sunday afternoon in front of the Izmailov Park and spent nearly four hours hanging out, first around the flea market, then in the park. As they sauntered deep into the park grounds, Eton explained the potential effects of the Chernobyl station's reactor meltdown: they were as chilling as the air on that sunny but cold afternoon. Then they talked about Soviet underground music and Eton's new rocker friends, about Jack's friends during his university days, and about Karelin's new musical, in which Lara played the leading role and for which Eton had written a few songs. Then they watched in silence the silver, blue and mauve sunset over the park's largest pond, shivering from the night chill that arose from the dark water, sharing a cigarette to warm up, refusing to give up and go home.

It was late when Eton dropped him off a few blocks from his place. Jack lingered for a few more minutes, struggling to come up with something to break the uneasy silence that had descended on them like a suffocating blanket as soon as they climbed into the car.

Eton stared straight ahead of him, his long fingers wrapped around the steering wheel in a death grip. "You'll be back... Won't you?" he muttered finally, cutting a side-glance Jack's way.

It was the first time for the entire afternoon and evening that he had mentioned Jack's departure. And Jack realized that he wasn't the only one who felt like they were seeing each other for the last time every time they said goodbyes.

He put his hand on Eton's knee and squeezed it. "Of course I will, Eton. Don't you go around doubting it for a second! I'll be back in time for your concert. I promise... Are we good?" He leaned forward a little, trying to look into Eton's eyes, smiling at him reassuringly.

Eton nodded. "Yes... I'll wait." He offered Jack his hand and tried to smile too.

Jack swallowed, grabbed his hand and squeezed it with all his might, trying to convey to his friend all that he felt but couldn't put into words. Then he yanked his hand back, wrenched the door open and shut it resolutely behind him.

No, there could be no words for *this*, simply couldn't. Because, realistically, what could he tell Eton? What, when they both knew so goddamn well that *all this*—whatever it was that held them in such a tight grip—would have to end one day?

Chapter 44

Jack flew out of Moscow on Monday evening. PanAm had resumed direct flights between the US and Moscow the previous week, after ten years, and the State Department encouraged all Embassy staff to travel with the airline. Jack was glad he didn't have to pay for his travel, because at the whopping $2,700 for an economy class ticket, the airfare was nearly twice the price of a British Airways' flight via London. As it was, his Monday flight was the only non-stop flight PanAm offered—once a week to New York, on Boeing's new 747.

When Jack showed up at the USIA's HQ, the team assistant handed him two notes from a Ms. Joan Redmond asking him to call her back as soon as he could on the number she had left. He grinned sheepishly at the woman, a heavyset, bleached blonde in her mid-forties, who grumbled that she wasn't there to deliver messages from his girlfriends, and promised that it was the last time she'd heard from Joan.

Joan Redmond, huh? Jack wondered what could have happened since he left Moscow that Joe had him summoned with a code red alert and before Friday as it had been planned.

Friday, May 9th, the day the Soviet people celebrate their victory in World War II, which they call the Great Patriotic War for the Motherland.

May 9th, Eton's birthday.

Knowing that birthdays were a big deal for Russians, he had tried to delay his return to America. However, even the excuse that he shouldn't be leaving Moscow when his new USIA boss had just arrived didn't work. Nurimbekoff told him to leave on or before May 5th. He hadn't been given any explanation about why he was being ordered out of the country, but figured the Station must have something going on and they wanted to keep him completely out of the picture.

Jack called the number left in the note and a female voice told him that he had reached the operator of Starlight Technologies and asked how she could help him. He asked for Joan Redmond and was put through to the assistant of the SE Department's chief of ops who told him that Mr. Coburn wanted to see him in his office at 10:00 a.m. the next day.

On Thursday, Jack arrived an hour early and headed straight to the cafeteria on the UG level. To catch up on HQ's gossip to give himself head-ups before the meeting with Joe Coburn.

The Agency's compartmentalized security system extended all the way down to its cafeterias. There were two of them for staff at Langley—one on the top floor for general and overt employees and the other, on the UG level, for covert staff and field officers. The latter was smaller and more exclusive, but it was as efficient a grapevine as the upper one: having bonded at the Farm and shared some harsh field experience, case officers told each other about other people's assignments and gossiped about theirs and others' operations.

Jack saw a couple of familiar faces in the far corner, but the two men were engrossed in a quiet discussion. They nodded to him in greeting and went back to their conversation. Jack picked a sandwich, a coke and a coffee and asked permission of two women to join them at the table opposite the door.

The older one, Jane, was from the East German desk. Jack had met her before at a few functions. The younger one, Savannah, was a rookie, fresh out of the Farm, currently rotating through the Far East desk. She had a strong Texas drawl, a smile rivaling Jack's and a pair of huge, slightly sad brown eyes. Later he learned that the only work experience Savannah had was a year and half as a kindergarten teacher and two years with the Peace Corps in South East Asia. How she had ended up with the Company was beyond Jack.

Jane was sharing the latest agency gossip with her friend when Jack sat down at their table. She started over for his sake and Jack almost choked on his sandwich: a case officer had just been arrested in Moscow the previous night, on a bren with his agent—yet another one.

He didn't mention to the women that he was from Moscow Station, only said that he was just back from the field and waiting for a debrief.

When he came up to Joe Coburn's office, he was told that the chief of ops had been summoned for an urgent meeting with the DCI, together with the Head of SE Division. The assistant didn't know when he would be back or whether Mr. Coburn would have time for him then. Jack chatted with her for a few minutes, but didn't learn anything new about the latest Moscow roll-up case. So he left and went back to the USIA office.

On Friday, when Jack got back from lunch, there was a note on his desk, asking him to call a Daisy Fernandez at the number provided. He stared at the note, an edgy feeling settling in his gut. He didn't know anyone by the name of Daisy Fernandez and Joe's assistant was Donna.

He made his call from a public phone a block away from the USIA building, just in case. It was Starlight Technologies again, and the operator put him through him to Daisy Fernandez without questions.

"Hello?" a surly female voice answered and Jack had to remind himself that he wasn't in Moscow and in fact she was speaking English to him.

"Good afternoon. This is Jack Smith. I've been asked to call Ms. Daisy Fernandez at this number."

"Ah, yes, Mr. Smith. 'preciate your calling back. Can you talk?" She was obviously asking if he could be overheard.

"Yes, I'm on the street."

"I'm from the Office of Security. You're scheduled for a polygraph test on Monday. Eleven a.m. Room 1011E. I trust you know where our office is."

A chill ran down Jack's spine. "A, um, test?" He swallowed the word. "Are you sure?"

"Are you IO Jack Smith?" she asked irritably.

"Yes, that's me."

"And have you just returned from the field?" It sounded more like an accusation than a question. "I hope you know the procedure, Mr. Smith: a debriefing and a polygraph test are to be scheduled within ten working days from the date of return to the office. My record says you returned on Monday."

"That's correct."

"D'ya have any more questions, Mr. Smith?"

"Don't think I have."

"Very well, then. It's 11:00 a.m., room 1011E. And please don't be late," she instructed before hanging up.

Jack stared at the receiver in his hand, sweat breaking out under his arm, then put it back carefully in its cradle and walked out into the busy street drenched in balmy, early summer sunshine.

Shit! How in the hell was he gonna do this? How would he ever be able to pass a polygraph test when *every* mention of Moscow triggered the image of... of his target in his mind? When he went all weak inside just hearing his future agent's name? When he got hard just by imagining him smiling his crooked little smile at him? God help him, he was so fucked!

And why was it that he'd been scheduled in for a polygraph test? Hadn't Joe told him that he'd be exempt from it if he agreed to play a part—the *main* part—of operation SEABROOK? What the fuck had happened to that?

Nah, he wasn't gonna take it, thank you very much. Joe had dragged him into this shit, let Joe sort this shit out. He'd just let this op go bust—he'd tell them all about it and walk. He'd had enough of this spy crap, for the rest of his life!

Is that right? You gonna walk, huh? Gutsy, aren't we? And what about Eton? Your friend Eton, remember? The one who's waiting for you, 'cause you said you'd be back? What about him, Smith?

Shit. Shit!! I'm sorry, Eton! So sorry, baby...

He stopped abruptly in the middle of the street and shut his eyes tight for half a second, ignoring people bumping into him and growling their displeasure at him. Then he shook his head vigorously, took a deep breath and started walking resolutely toward Federal Center Metro Station, looking for another pay phone.

He called Joe's office and asked if he could come to see Mr. Coburn today—as it had originally been scheduled. But Donna told him that Mr. Coburn was fully booked today and his earliest availability was Tuesday at 4:00 p.m. Jack said Tuesday would do, asked her to book him in and rang off.

No, Tuesday wouldn't do and that was a fact.

He bent his head, pressed the edges of his palms into his eyes and froze.

Think, Smith. Think! It's only ten numbers and you already know three of them—two-oh-two. Only seven left. You did better than that at the Farm, didn't ya?

A long forgotten number. An unlisted, private number in Joe's office that he had given Jack a few years ago, before Jack joined the Company. He had never used it—had never planned on using it. That was why he was wracking his brain trying to recall it now.

He got it right only on the fifth attempt.

"Speaking." Joe's tone was abrupt. And tired.

Jack let out a shuddering breath and blurted out, "Joe. It's Jack."

There was a pause, then Joe said cautiously, "Yes?"

"It's Jack." It occurred to him that maybe he wasn't the only Jack his mentor knew, close and personal. "Jack from—"

"Yes, speaking." Joe's tone was a fraction softer this time and Jack realized that he might not be alone.

"I need to see you."

"I'm busy right now. Can it wait till Monday?"

"I'm afraid not." He was way out of line, but he didn't care. "It's urgent."

Joe hesitated. "Can you call me again in two hours?"

"Of course! I will… Thank you," he added and hung up, feeling almost apologetic.

But it was Joe who'd dragged him into all this, hadn't he? Without telling him what this shit was all about. Right? So he shouldn't feel apologetic about it. Joe Coburn had put him on the spot; Joe Coburn would have to get him out of it, period.

Two hours later Jack called from another payphone.

Joe answered on the second ring. "Speaking." He sounded resigned. Or maybe dead tired.

"It's me again. I need to talk to you, Joe. As I said, it's urgent."

"I got it. Where are you?"

"Downtown."

Never give away your exact location—that was what he'd been taught.

Joe chuckled. "Alright… I'll see you at eight, 35th and M Streets. A joint called Joe's. I'll be in the back… Are you alright?"

"I don't know." His jaw muscles flexed. "I'm hoping you'll tell me… See you at eight. Thanks again." He hung up quickly and walked out of the phone booth.

Joe's was a small, semi-dark place with a low ceiling and the ambience of the Prohibition times. The bearded bartender nodded to Jack ambivalently and turned to the small TV set at the end of the bar.

Joe Coburn was smoking in a small cubicle in the corner at the back, an empty tumbler in front of him. He looked rumpled with his jacket off, his tie loosened. Jack had never seen his mentor drinking hard liquor before, only wine, and as far as he knew Joe didn't smoke either. The chief of ops had aged more in the last year than in the previous five.

Must be all those rolled-up Soviet agents that were taking a toll on him—six or seven of them by now. Yeah, it was the foreign agents that Joe Coburn was always so protective about, not case officers, his compatriots. *Never* case officers. Foreign agents risked their lives for America, he said. Which implied that case officers didn't. Why, they all had diplomatic immunity, didn't they? The worst that could happen to a case officer in a foreign country was that he or she got caught, was declared *persona non grata* and sent home. Case officers were replaceable. Disposable. They were just pawns in Joe Coburn's grand games. Now Jack understood why some of them resented the SE Division's head of ops.

And why had he thought that Joe would help *him*? Because he had been Joe's… He'd been nothing to Joe! Or because he was the case officer in Joe Coburn's special op? But then again, he never gave a shit about his case officers.

"Jack, good to see you. Have a seat." Joe waved at the chair across the table. "A drink? Do you drink?"

He was already loose-tongued. And he didn't offer Jack his hand.

"Good evening, Joe. Thanks for agreeing to see me at such a short notice." Jack sat down, ignoring his mentor's provocative question, trying to figure how he should start, with Joe being in his out-of-the-office mood.

"Always a pleasure to see you, Jack." He smirked amiably.

Jack cringed inside, but tried to keep his expression agreeable. "Thanks," he mumbled.

"I'm going to have a bite. Will you join me?"

Any other time Jack would have probably found some excuse not to, but today wasn't that other time. He nodded. "Yeah. Thank you."

"Good." Joe smiled, looking pleased, and waved at the man behind the bar.

They placed their orders, then the waitress brought Jack his beer and Joe another double scotch and left.

"So, what's the urgency?"

"I need your help." Jack hated to admit it, but didn't really have a choice.

"Oh? Thought you didn't want any help from me." There was an uncomfortable pause, as Joe Coburn watched Jack tauntingly, then he sighed and asked, serious now, "What happened?"

Jack wanted to snarl at him, "You and your fucking SEABROOK happened", but bit his tongue. Instead, he said, "I'm booked for a polygraph test on Monday morning." He stared back at his mentor, who was looking at him quizzically now, and stated flatly, "I can't do that."

Not a muscle on Joe's face moved, only the playful shine in his eyes dimmed. "Why?"

The question took Jack aback. "Because of SEABROOK... And because you said I would be exempt if I'd accept to run it... the target."

Joe reflected on it for a few seconds. "What happened?" This time it was the Head of Ops asking, staid and in control.

"I made another move on him."

"When?"

"Over a week ago. When I reported on the power plant incident." Joe Coburn didn't say anything, just kept staring at him expectantly, so Jack continued, trying to steel himself, to reign in his voice and facial expression, "I was at his place. Brought him a birthday present before my departure. We had a few drinks, for his birthday. So I, um, took the opportunity and, um, made a move." He shrugged awkwardly and took a deep breath, trying to loosen the tight knot in his gut.

"Did you...?" Joe raised his eyebrows.

"No. Just gave him a, um..." he mouthed "blowjob" and clamped his teeth on the inside of his cheeks, disgusted with himself.

But Joe was not done questioning him yet. "Was he aware?"

"I think he was."

"You think?"

"He was."

"And? What did he say afterwards?"

"Nothing. Hasn't said a word about it since... Anyway, his grandfather called while I was there. Asked him for my home number so that he could call me to cancel the trip to America. He'd been asked to join the commission formed in relation to the power plant incident. I told the boy to call me at home. Then I reported the accident to Mark right after."

Joe flinched at the name and Jack froze. Mark Morris?!

"Was it Mark?... I was at the cafeteria the other day and heard that—"

"Fucking useless place!" Joe bristled. "Doesn't anybody know what 'classified' means anymore?"

Jack gazed at him silently, feeling sorry for his mentor. Must be hard losing those you care about... No, he didn't want to think about it. Not right now.

Joe took his silence as a question. He sighed and rubbed a hand over his face. "Another ambush... I knew this fucker would screw up again," he spat out and turned to wave at the bartender who had been ignoring them since their drinks had been served.

The waitress delivered their food order and asked if they wanted anything else. Joe said 'not now' and she left.

"Was it EASTBOUND?" Jack asked quietly after a while. They must have hardly any agents left in Moscow by now.

Joe didn't respond, continued chewing on his food, his eyes locked with Jack's.

Shit, it was the last of the three civilian agents they had had—a scientific source working at a research institute east of Moscow. He hadn't even been very active if Jack remembered correctly from his pre-assignment read-in.

"Has the leak been found?" He wasn't cleared for this information, but asked anyway.

Again, Joe didn't answer, instead turned to beckon for another bourbon coke. So, the answer was probably negative, Jack figured, his spirit sinking.

When Joe's drink was delivered, they ate in silence for a couple of minutes, each deep in his own thoughts.

"You said 'again'," Jack said cautiously.

Joe looked up from his plate, a lost expression on his face.

"You said, 'He screwed up again'."

Joe's eyes narrowed. "Didn't they tell you about it at the cafeteria?" he asked sarcastically. He put down his knife and fork, sighed again and shook his head in disbelief. "Son of a bitch was on a night run last month. Got disoriented. Was drunk, probably. Took a wrong turn and ended up—you won't believe this..." He paused for effect. "At the gate of HQ of the First fucking Directorate!"

Jack stared at him, his jaw hanging. HQ of the KGB's First Chief Directorate in the southern suburb of Moscow? Was he serious??

"That's right. Un-fucking-believable!" Joe swore under his breath.

"What happened then?"

"He was detained for a few minutes, questioned, then released. Or so he reported... And I have to believe this?... Fucking amateurs!" He picked up his fork and attacked his lamb shank.

Jack had never heard Joe bitching so bitterly before. He wished he had known what to say. "Do you *have* to?" he asked quietly.

Joe's head jerked up at that. "Don't have a choice. He's an offspring of one of the DCI's old buddies. Hope the old man knows now that being a shrewd Wall Street operator doesn't necessarily make someone a good field officer."

So Mark Morrison had once been an investment banker then. Now Jack understood where the arrogance was coming from—an investment banker from Wall Street. Christ, what were all these people doing at the Agency—investment bankers, lawyers, Peace Corp volunteers, God knew who else? No wonder the place was leaking like a sieve.

They worked on their food in silence for a few minutes, then Jack said cautiously, "About my test on Monday... Can you do something about it?"

Joe didn't respond right away. He took a sip of water from his glass, peering at Jack thoughtfully. "With all the shit going on over there, *everybody* coming back has to take the test." He sounded unconvincing, like he doubted the validity of his own words.

"I won't be able to pass it if they ask whether I'm hiding anything. I'll have to tell them... about SEABROOK." Jack held the eyes of the chief of ops, his jaw clenched.

Joe frowned. "You will, won't you?"

"You're not leaving me a choice, Joe. I can't be caught lying. And I can't be thrown out... Like that guy Howard." He shook his head stubbornly. "I can't, Joe. I can't." Not when he *had* to go back to Moscow.

There was a long pause, by the end of which Jack thought he was going to explode any moment now.

Finally, Joe sighed, picked up his fork again. "Let's finish the dinner and we'll see."

Jack got back to his rented studio just off DuPont Circle shortly after 11:00 p.m. with a bottle of cheap whiskey, two slices of carrot cake and a candle from a convenience store nearby. He put the cakes on two saucers and set them on the low coffee table. Then he lit the candle, poured two fingers of the whiskey into two teacups each and placed them by the cakes. Having set the table, he lowered himself on the tiny couch and took one cup.

"Happy birthday, Eton," he whispered and downed the content of the cup in one gulp, the way the Russians did it. He put the cup carefully back on the table, sat staring at the candle flame for a minute, then reached for the other cup. "And I *will* be back, don't you doubt it for a minute, friend," he said, louder this time, and knocked down the second drink.

For the next two days, except for a short outing for snacks, coke and cigarettes, Jack stayed put in his tiny apartment, waiting for Joe's call. But the chief of ops didn't call the next day, or the following day. So by midnight Sunday, Jack had a script in his head of what he was going to say at the test. He didn't intend to tell them everything, just that he was running a special, deep cover op in Moscow, reporting directly to the SE Division's

Head of Operations. As such, he could give no answer whatsoever to some of the test questions because they were directly linked to the op. And if they needed to know more, they could go talk to Joe Coburn. He couldn't say anything else.

With that, he took a mouthful of whiskey on an empty stomach, straight from the bottle, brushed his teeth and went to bed.

On Monday morning, Jack showed up at the Office of the Security for his polygraph test five minutes before eleven. Feeling drained and exhausted from lack of sleep, for once he didn't bother with small talk with the surly team assistant who logged him in and left him to wait at an empty desk outside the interview room.

At 11:10 a.m., the assistant brought him a glass of water and told him that his interviewer was running a little late, that he should be there in ten or fifteen minutes, and left.

At 11:25 a.m., she reappeared with a mug of tea this time, looking both annoyed and apologetic. She told Jack that his interviewer had been called in for an urgent meeting and asked Jack to wait for another twenty minutes. Here was some tea, and yes, he could smoke here if he wished.

When the woman returned at 11:50 a.m., she looked like she was going to kill someone. She made an effort to smile at Jack though, apologized to him and told him that his test had been postponed and he would be advised of a new date shortly.

Jack rolled his eyes and smiled at her, picked up his shoulder bag, said, "See you again soon" and left.

He headed down to the cafeteria, bought a ham and cheese sandwich, a coffee, and sat down in the far corner with his back to the room. He didn't manage to finish his lunch: halfway through he stood up abruptly, rushed to the rest room and threw up into the nearest toilet.

On Thursday when the call from the Company finally came through, it was Donna, Joe's assistant. Jack was scheduled to meet with the SE Division's chief and the chief of ops on Monday, at 12:00 p.m. And he was to bring along his report on the latest development of his operation, which he would write first thing on Monday morning in Joe Coburn's office.

Chapter 45

May 5, Monday. 11:43 p.m.

Dear Jack,

You are in the air right now, heading home. Your home. I thought of your apartment on Proletarskaya as your home. But of course it isn't. Your home is a distant place where I am not and will never be.

You said you will be back that I mustn't go around doubting it. I don't doubt you, cowboy. Not you. It is ~~life fate~~ chance that I doubt—I have already been given a chance; there might not be another. What will I do then?

I shouldn't think that way. I said I'll wait, so I should. It's only 22 days. I didn't see you for longer before, more than a month, twice. You were out of the country too. So why this heavy feeling now as if I'll never see you again?

Perhaps it is because of all the things happening lately. Too many unfortunate things. I have a premonition that things will change dramatically. Forever. Don't know what, don't know when, just feel that they will. And I admit: I dread it, whatever it is.

E.

May 6, Tuesday. 9:37pm

Dear Jack,

I found Grandfather's original paper on NW. I have read it. It isn't

Mother has just called. Grandfather returned from Ch. yesterday, but spent the whole day in Kremlin for meetings and just come home. Mother said he is not well. Asked me to come over. I'm going now. Will tell you about the NW study when you come back. If you are still interested in it.

E.

May 10, Saturday. Midnight.

Don't know where to start. So I will start from the beginning.

I went to Grandfather's place right after Mother's distressed call on Tue. It was close to 11pm by the time I got there. Mother started crying the moment I walked in. Said that Grandpa was sick, not eaten anything since the day before and chain smoking. He never smoked before.

I went to his room. He was sitting at his large desk, writing something, a burning cigarette in the ashtray full of cigarette butts. It was dark in the room. The only light was coming from the desk lamp. But even with that lighting I noticed that he looked different. At first, I couldn't understand what it was. Then realized that he looked tanned. I asked him how it was at Ch. and if it was very warm there. He looked at me without understanding at first, then laughed sadly and said, "It is hot, E, too hot". And I realized then that the tan was from the radiation he had received. That's why he is sick and can't eat. And he is smoking to kill the taste of metal in his mouth—that's what it tastes when you get a high dose of nuclear radiation.

God almighty, this isn't just an accident. It is a catastrophe of mass proportions! And it isn't resolved yet: the reactor's core is still burning and a solution how to extinguish it hasn't been found yet. Grandpa is going back there tomorrow, together with Legasov,.

Legasov is the head of the emergency committee. It is him who called Grandpa and asked him to join the committee. Perhaps he remembered that Grandpa had opposed the current design of the stations that house RBMK reactors. Or perhaps he remembered that Grandpa is heading an international project on the consequences of a nuclear catastrophe. Either way, Grandpa is the one who can tell them the truth.

In the beginning, Grandpa wouldn't tell us anything. But yesterday, after he returned from his medical checkup, he told me about it. And asked me not to tell anybody else, not even Mother.

I'm lost for words. It is horrifying. Reactor No. 4 is completely destroyed by explosion, its core is exposed to the air. Grandpa thinks it is a core meltdown, but there is no way of verifying it. Tons of uranium dioxide fuel and fission products were released into the air. And of course, the burning radiation contaminated the graphite. Grandpa says radiation dosimeters go off scale the moment they come near the site. As a result, they simply don't know what the radiation levels are. Perhaps hundreds of times above the acceptable levels. Grandpa thinks more. But no one knows for sure.

No one has ever imagined this can happen to us. No one was prepared. They have evacuated everybody from P., the small town near the station. More than 60,000 people. The core and the graphite are still burning and they are afraid it can trigger another explosion at No. 3. Then they will have to evacuate settlements within 100km radius, not 30km like now. Grandpa says firefighters and miners are trying to contain the burning graphite by pumping liquid nitrogen into reactor through a tunnel they have dug under the reactor room. They can only stay there for a minute at a time, the radiation levels are so high.

And even with that, I think he is not telling all.

How terrifyingly ironic: we have been modeling and debating over climatic consequences of a nuclear war. And here it is: people are dying even without a nuclear winter; all that was needed was an accident at an electro station. I know they are dying: it is inevitable at that level of radiation. And Legasov and Grandpa have to ask all those people—firefighters, soldiers—to go there to clean up the mess. That's what Grandpa is not telling. That's what has been keeping him sleepless since he got back a week ago. That's why L. has returned to Ch. on Wednesday and Grandpa is going back next Monday.

I wish I could do something to help. I asked Grandpa to take me with him. Of course, he said no, that I shouldn't even think of it. I feel so useless sitting here, doing nothing, speculating, while Grandpa and all those people are dying, fighting to keep all of us safe.

I promised Grandpa not to tell anybody. But I will keep this entry. We need to remember what we do to ourselves. And that all that happens to us is of our own device.

May 14, Wednesday. 11:07p.m.

Have just come back from Mother's place. Stayed there with her since Grandpa left. She hasn't been well lately—gets tired easily, sleeps a lot, but doesn't seem to be getting enough sleep. Maybe she works too much. She has finished her book about the history of our family, the Volkonskys and the Rezanovs. Not sure when she will be able to publish it. It is her own initiative, not any agency's order. She will need to find a publishing house that will agree to publish the book and pay her some money.

I have started cutting out and collecting news clips about Chernobyl. Maybe Grandpa will write a book about it someday. Or maybe I will write it myself.

This is the summary of what has been happening here since the explosion.

• April 26, around 1am: explosion at reactor No. 4. Apparently, the politburo was informed right away, because they called L. and told him to form a scientific committee on the same day to look at the consequences. L. left to Ch. after calling Grandpa. Grandpa called me to ask for J's phone number. I called J to tell him that Grandpa was not going to Am.

• April 27: Grandpa's account: he arrived at Ch. In the afternoon, he and L. managed to persuade the local authorities to start evacuating people from Priapyat, the town closest to Ch. Soldiers and helicopters arrived.

• April 28: the official announcement about Ch. was made on the evening news program on TV. It was published in newspapers the next day: exactly 22 words. Twenty-two damned words!

• April 29: Izvestia is the only newspaper carrying news about Ch. It said 2 persons died at explosion, thousands evacuated (Grandpa said over 60,000), but "situation is stable and medical assistance is being administered to those in need". They mentioned the scientific commission led by a former head of construction for oil and gas industry to investigate the cause of the accident. How about L. and Grandpa who are killing themselves trying to find a solution to their fucking problem??!!

• April 30: No news on Ch.

• May 1: they admitted that 197 people were injured and 2 died and the damaged reactor was "shut down". What the hell does that mean?? Grandfather said that they were still trying to bury the reactor with tons of lead, boron, dolomite, sand and clay that were being dropped down from helicopters. And despite all, they went ahead and held festivities and parades on Red Square and in Kiev on the occasion of May 1 Day. Why am I even surprised? I'm old enough to know that they don't care.

• May 2: nothing in our newspapers or TV. But I ran into Grisha at MGU who said "a friend" had been listening to a "foreign radio". They reported that B. Yeltsin, the Secretary of the CP of Moscow, on his visit in Hamburg, gave an interview to foreign press and said that 49,000 people had been evacuated, 200 are ill, 25 are critically ill. He also said that the rescuers were trying to extinguish the fire by helicopters dropping wet sand, lead and boron on the reactor, but it's still smoldering. He's a brave man. Nothing like this has been reported here. I wonder what will happen to him when his returns from overseas?

• May 3: nothing in the news again. Grandpa said several politburo members with a small entourage arrived in Ch. on Sat. They left the same day.

• May 5: L. and Grandpa returned to Moscow to report to the politburo. Also to Hans Blix, the chairman of International Atomic Energy Agency who arrived with a small group of scientists. Finally, Pravda published a longer article. Perhaps in relation to H.B.'s arrival. They admitted the fire was still burning, and the situation was very difficult. They said firemen were fighting the blaze on top of the ruined building, their boots got stuck in melted bitumen because the temperature was so high. They were courageous men, it said. What they didn't say was that those courageous men were clueless of what they were facing and will die, if haven't yet. There is no way one can survive after a few minutes near the exposed core of a nuclear reactor.

• May 6: a politburo member held a news conference with journalists. The text was then published and televised. Finally they admitted that 49,000 people were evacuated ON THE 2ND DAY after explosion!! 204 hospitalized, 18 in bad condition.

• May 7+8: news on TV, then in newspapers next day. The cleaning up continues, including building up the banks of Priapyat River to protect it from potential radioactive contamination. American and Israeli doctors are helping with bone marrow transplant. They say it is the only remedy from acute radiation.

• May 9: Pravda published the interview with academician Velikhov. He is a nuclear and plasma physicist, no. 2 at the Academy of Sciences. He indicated that the core may be melting that the situation is grave; that they are digging a tunnel under the reactor. Then he said that regrettably, the struggle is not finished and there are thousands of people fighting to contain it every day. Grandpa finally told me about what is going on there. Perhaps as a birthday present: to show me that he thinks of me as a grown up person whom he can trust. I sincerely hope so.

• May 10: the Council of Min. issued its 6th statement since the accident, fourteen days ago. It says the reactor core is cooling down and radiation levels around Ch. are dropping sharply. Good news, just a little too late. Several newspapers mentioned the news conference the IAEA delegation gave journalists upon their return from Ch. Morris Rosen, the director of safety of the IAEA, said they had flown a helicopter near the reactor and seen a light gray smoke, which indicated that the fire was extinguished. He also said (or at least our newspapers quoted him as saying) that "relatively little" radiation is escaping from the reactor now and there are no hot spots inside the core. That's not what Grandpa said. So who's lying—an IAEA representative (an Am.), or our newspapers? Three pieces of positive news: (1) No. 3 is intact and has been shutdown; (2) our side has agreed to provide radiation readings around Ch. to the IAEA every day; (3) they are going to build a sarcophagus over the reactor. But how? It's still smoldering.

• May 11: Grandpa went back to Ch. Mother was very upset, spent the whole day in her room. I stayed with her. News on TV showed another interview with academician Velikhov, from Kiev. And a short documentary taken from a moving car in the danger zone: abandoned streets, traffic patrol in masks, people in white coats and masks working in a building inside the zone. Velikhov said Ch. could have been a catastrophe, but the worse is over and Ch. will go down in history as the worst nuclear accident in the world's history. Could have been??

• May 12: the 7th official statement since the accident. Pravda, then the news channel said 6 people died and 35 in grave conditions. I assume in addition to the previous 2 + 18. The true effects of the radiation are starting to show. Unfortunately, this isn't the last time we'll hear bad news. They also said that 3 local party officials were disciplined for late evacuation and failing to give timely information about the accident. To whom? The politburo knew about it within hours: they ordered a scientific commission to be formed, headed by Legasov, didn't they?

• May 13: Pradva published a statement about the number of people died and in critical condition by now: 6 and 35 in all. It also quoted acad. Velikhov as saying that the scientist averted the catastrophe by pumping the water (from the cooling reservoir under the reactor) and drilling holes (also under the reactor) to draw the heat out. Soviet Rossiya quoted him saying that 5 people, including a deputy director of national atomic energy agency, volunteered to dive into radioactive water in the reservoir in an attempt to drain it from under the reactor. He said their effort succeeded. He didn't say if those additional 4 deaths and 17 critically ill are those who worked under the burning reactor.

• May 14: Gorbachev finally appeared on evening news just now. He talked about half an hour, admitted that the accident was of a magnitude never experienced in the history of mankind, conveyed his deepest condolences to families of those who died and suffered. The toll is 9 deaths and 299 hospitalized with radiation sickness. Over 92,000 evacuated. He also proposed to set up an international system for early warning and disclosure of nuclear accidents and a system of rapid mutual assistance. He mentioned 2 Am. doctors, helping with bone marrow transplant for those who received heavy doses of radiation. He thanked the Am. doctors working here and countries that offered help, but condemned America and Germany for their "mountains of lies" about thousands of casualties and desolate Kiev. He obviously reads what we don't have access to. Perhaps I should also listen to VOA or Radio Europe—maybe I can get more information from them. Besides Gorbachev's appearance, several newspapers published: interviews with firefighters, who said 4 of their friends died 15 days after fighting fire on top of the reactor building; that head of foreign diplomatic missions in Moscow are invited to visit areas around Ch.; that Intourist continues providing its touristic services to more than 1,300 foreign tourist currently in Kiev; that Ukraine has pulled all milk-based products from shops and markets.

I will continue this diary in a few days.

May 15, Thursday. 8:47p.m.

Dear Jack,

Where are you now? I wish you were here. But I am also glad that you are not. This thing with Am. diplomats caught spying continues: they announced another arrest yesterday. The third in less than a year.

Last night I was busy writing up the summary of Ch. events and missed it on the news. Today I opened a newspaper and found it: Mark Morris, a Defense Dept. attaché from Am. Embassy, was arrested last week and declared "persona non grata". The article says he was meeting with a Soviet citizen identified as an agent of Am. intelligence services and that he carried documents that proved his activities incompatible with his diplomatic status.

That is exactly what they said in your boss's case too, isn't it? Not even 3 months have passed since William was caught and expelled "for spying". You said he had been having an affair with a local woman. What about this Mark Morris? Has he also been having an affair with a local woman? How many Am. diplomats are having affairs with local women here? And then there is J, who is ~~having an affair~~ loved by a local guy.

I am sorry, cowboy. I don't know what to think anymore. Too many things have transpired lately. I feel like I am drowning under the weight of events that keep happening—to me, to others because of me. To all of us in this country because of who we are and what we did. Or didn't do and let this happen. Now I keep thinking: what could we have done differently and why didn't we do it? What can I do not to let it happen again?

I wish you were here in my arms. I am grateful that you are here in my thoughts. And I will keep you safe in my heart. Forever.

E.

May 18, Sunday. 10:40 p.m.

Dear Jack,

I have been re-reading the news clippings about Ch., thinking about what Grandpa said, thinking about our NW project and Grandpa's original study; about why he did what he did; about me and what I am doing with myself.

Some things Gorbachev said on TV have stuck in my head. He said: "For the first time we encountered such a tremendous force going out of control." And: "The accident at Chernobyl showed again what an abyss will open if nuclear war befalls mankind."

Chernobyl is nothing—NOTHING!!—compared to detonating one modern nuclear bomb. Yet, the radiation level in Ch. is perhaps hundreds of times higher than in Hiroshima and Nagasaki combined. You were so right, my love, when you asked what would happen to all the people in case of a major nuclear war. This is what will happen: we will all die slow and painful death. And the few of us who survive, sick and injured, will then have to endure the nuclear winter.

I think Grandpa blames himself for not standing his ground back in the 60s when he opposed the design of the RBKM reactors. Perhaps he feels he should have fought them back then. Or at least should have tried to steer them to a safer solution. Then Ch. might not have happened. But he is not an engineer, not sure what he could have done. Now he is trying to redeem himself by putting himself on the frontline, trying to help in any way he humanly can.

And this has led me to ask myself: what the hell am I doing? I can do more than just drag my feet to and from Grandpa's lab, toying with the idea of quitting physics and joining the ranks of wild, defiant rock musicians. I have been given skills and knowledge to do what not too many others can: try to make the application of nuclear physics safer. Maybe I won't achieve much in my lifetime, but at least I'll be able to say with clear consciousness at the end of my life that I have done my best to contribute to this. Something that Grandpa pains over now. Poor Grandpa.

I told you that I wanted to quit studying and play music. But now I have decided I should complete my studies and do something useful. Perhaps I should start taking engineering courses in addition to nuclear physics. I will talk to Grandpa about this when he returns.

You may think that I am just a fickle little boy. I sincerely hope you will not. No, I KNOW you will support me when I explain to you why I want to do this. I think I know you well by now. I can always write and play music in my free time, right? I can do both. I will, Jack. I will play for you. I think you like me playing music.

By the way, Artyom called yesterday, said he and Alla Pugacheva are organizing a big concert for Chernobyl on May 30th. He asked if we want to perform there too. If we do, he will put us first on the list, so that we can do our number and catch the night train to Leningrad. I said yes. I am sure the boys will be happy to do it too. We will be late for the opening of the rock festival, but it doesn't matter. We have to do this: it is for Chernobyl, for all the people whose life it has ruined.

Will you be back by then? Will you come to Leningrad?

So many things I want to tell you. And most of all that I love you. Very much. Yours always.

E.

Chapter 46

When Jack woke up on Friday morning, later than usual, crystal strings of sunlight were stealing through the thick, heavy curtains. He rolled over and closed his eyes again. He didn't have to go anywhere: for the USIA, he was on leave; for the Company, he wasn't expected at the office till Monday morning. He had three full days to do whatever he wanted, go wherever he wished and didn't have to report his whereabouts to anyone. He was home and for once could be just another guy on the street.

He tried to get back to sleep, but couldn't shake off the restlessness that had suddenly come over him. So he got up, put on a pair of old, faded jeans, a plain white t-shirt and canvas shoes, and went out in search of a hearty American breakfast. He strolled toward Georgetown, looking for the first place that would appeal to him.

As he was crossing 27th Street, a flash of blue in a shop window caught his eye. It was a small coffee shop with white cream cupcakes arranged in a basket in its window. The topmost cupcake was crowned with three bright blue cornflowers. Jack pushed the door and stepped inside.

The shop was empty, except for a long-haired, pimply youth behind the counter. Jack asked for a mug of coffee, a raspberry and two blueberry cupcakes, fished out an issue of the Washington Post from the newsstand and sat down at the tiny table by the window. Then, as if the thought had just occurred to him, he pointed at the cornflower cake and said he wanted it too.

The boy gave him a blank stare at first, then shrugged and went to retrieve it from the shop window.

Jack took a bite of a raspberry cake, unfolded the newspaper and scanned the front page.

"House OKs Budget with Defense Cuts."

"Reagan to See Jewish Leaders, Push Saudi Sales."

"State Dept. Employee Fired for Leaking Data to Media."

Interesting.

"The official, identified only as an official with a civil service ranking of GS-15, leaked information involving U.S. diplomatic relations, said department spokesman Charles E. Piedmont."

Oh, Christ! Here too...

"More Chernobyl Deaths 'Unavoidable': But L.A. Doctor Says U.S.-Soviet Team May Save Many."

A thought occurred to him that Prof. Volkonsky was probably still there, in the midst of the action. From the little interaction he had had with the academician, Jack thought he wasn't a man who'd worry about his safety in the face of the calamity.

He fumbled with the newspaper, looking for the article.

"MOSCOW... Dr. Robert P. Gale, a UCLA bone marrow specialist, said 28 people with radiation illness are in the worst condition, adding, "We hope that a substantial number of these patients will survive." Seven others already have died from the effects of radiation..."

Shit.

Eyeing the three blue cornflowers, he wondered what Eton was reading about the accident back in Moscow. Chernobyl had been a major item in the news every day since he got back. On the other hand, there had hardly been anything about it in the Soviet press the few days before Jack's departure and he suspected very little had been published by the Soviets since. He wished he could share what he had read with Eton, maybe talk about it with him or just listen to Eton's rumbling voice telling him about nuclear fusion, or fission. Or Soviet rock bands. Or whatever he wanted to tell Jack, he didn't mind one bit, as long as his friend was talking.

By the time he reached the classifieds section, Jack was on the second mug of coffee and there was only the cornflower cupcake left on the plate in front of him. He pulled the flowers out carefully, licked the cream off their short stubby stems and put them by the plate. Then he bit off a piece of the cake and idly scanned the ads.

His interest rekindled as he got to the real estate column and noticed a couple of ads for farmland. One of them was for a "secluded mountain horse farm in Highland county VA. 25 acres w/300sf 1.5 story cabin; 10-horse stable, incl. horses; small barn; mountain-top open pasture and meadow; 25% wooded; fenced perimeter; spring, creek."

A small, secluded horse farm for 10 horses; a cabin; mountains, woods and a creek.

C'mon, this is Virginia, not California. You don't want to be near this place... When it's time to quit.

It is just the right size, sounds like the right place...

You don't have the money, remember?

So what? Haven't seen a ranch... a farm with horses for...

Since last summer when Eton had taken him to the Russian village by the river to see horses. What were they? Oh yeah, Orlov trotters. Then the next day he had taken Jack to that fairytale place. A cornflower heaven...

And he had said he wanted to visit Jack's ranch one day...

By the time he took his rented Chevy out of town the next day, Jack knew most of what he needed about the little horse farm on a mountain near the West Virginia border. He even had a story for Mrs. Sutton, the recently widowed owner of the property, hoping that she would let him wander around the farm and horses after his admission that he didn't have money to buy it yet, even at the rock-bottom price it was selling for.

It was a beautiful spring day. The sun shon radiantly on the fresh green grass and a gentle breeze caressed the white and pink blossoms of apple, cherry and plum trees. Jack wished he could share all this with Eton, just as his friend had done for him in the Russian countryside. Maybe one day...

Fifteen miles after Monterey he turned left onto the country road that led up the mountain. The simple, wooden gate to the farm was open. A carved wooden plaque over the entrance read "Welcome to Hillside Creek Farm" and on the right post was a small "For Sale" sign.

As he drove slowly in, at first Jack saw no one around the log building to the left that looked like the stable. Then he noticed a man in dark blue denims and a white Stetson at the far end of the stable. He was saddling a bay mare, with his back to the path leading onto the farm. Something in his bearing disturbed Jack, but he couldn't immediately figure what it was. Then, probably hearing the sound of the approaching car, the man turned around.

Jack's heart leaped to his throat. He stopped the car, took a couple of deep breaths, got out and headed toward the man.

Who was young, tall and lithe. And blond. Someone Jack didn't know.

Someone who could be Eton. For the man looked amazingly like Eton in cowboy wear.

The cowboy watched him with amiable expectation as Jack strolled up to him.

"Hello. Sorry for intruding without an appointment. I was passing though Monterey and heard that your farm is up for sale. So I thought I'd swing by. My name's Jack Smith." He thrust his hand out, his smile wide and apologetic.

The young man returned the smile and shook Jack's hand firmly. "No problem. Tom Cole. It's my aunt's ranch, um, farm. And yes, she's selling." He had a heavy Texas drawl and his hand was large, rough and callused like Jack's. A cowboy's hand, not a musician's.

Tom turned out to be from San Angelo, Texas. He had come up there with his mother, Mrs. Sutton's sister, to help his recently widowed aunt Rose to sell the farm and move to Texas where she was originally from. Jack said he was of ranching stock too, from Wyoming, now working in Washington, and missing ranch life. They chatted for while and Tom offered to show him around, even after Jack's admission that he couldn't afford a ranch right now. The young man brought another horse out of the stable and they set out for a ride.

They went up to the lush meadow with the stunning view of rolling mountains all around, rode down the mountain and along the lazy creek, the namesake of the place. When they returned, Jack brushed down his mount, then met with Mrs. Sutton and her sister, Mrs. Cole, who insisted he have tea with them. Afterwards, Tom saw him to his car, shook his hand cordially and slipped a scrap of paper into Jack's hand, saying if he ever wanted to buy a ranch down Texas, he knew whom he should call.

It was nearly midnight when Jack got back to his apartment. He couldn't fall asleep for a long time, trying and failing to push away the absurd thought that had been inundating him ever since he left Hillside Creek Farm: that it could be his ranch. And it probably would be one day. But why couldn't it be Eton riding it with him—on his ranch, *their* ranch? Why?

On Sunday, the edginess returned with vengeance. Jack briefly entertained the idea of catching up with a couple of colleagues from the USIA, but couldn't muster the energy to put himself in an appropriate mood. He had breakfast on his own again, flipping through newspapers, looking for the news from the Soviet Union, feeling like he *must* find something important there.

When he was done with his breakfast, but not with his craving for more Russian news, Jack resolved to visit a place he knew he could find what his mind needed—Hillwood Estate.

Jack had found it a few years ago, when he was only exploring Washington D.C. He had visited its private museum a few times, honing his knowledge of Russian culture on its large collection of Russian decorative art, paintings and Faberge.

He spent an hour wandering around the mansion and the gardens. But it wasn't till he got to the little wooden *dacha* tucked in a far corner of the large estate that Jack realized what it was that he felt: he missed *everything* he had left behind in Moscow.

He was home, in his America, living his personal American dream. But instead of hanging out, playing sports, or drinking beer and shooting shit with his American friends, he was moping around, feeling blue, missing Russia... And Russians.

Whom he would leave behind in the near future not to see again. Ever.

It didn't make any sense.

He left the museum shortly after, returned to Georgetown and spent the rest of the day hanging around with strangers at the downtown bars.

It was nearly midnight when Jack got back to his flat. He sat staring at the telephone for a long time before picking it up and dialing a number ingrained in his mind. His ho... his *father's* home number.

The first time Jack had called home was a year to the day since he had run away to join the army. The old man had hung up on him the moment he said, "Hi, Dad. This is Jack". He tried three more times after that first call. The first two went unanswered; the last time was on the eve of his departure to Moscow. His father answered, but he was drunk as a skunk and Jack doubted the following morning the old man remembered whom he had talked to the previous night.

"Hello?" a woman's voice answered.

She sounded young. And maybe a tiny bit tipsy.

It caught Jack by surprise: a woman in his father's house. But then why not? His mother had passed many years ago and he couldn't expect a man to live alone for the rest of his life, could he? Even an old bastard like his father.

"Good evening, ma'am. Can I talk to, um, Mr. Smith, please?"

"Waittaminute, please." She didn't take the phone too far away from her face as she called out in a sing-song voice, "Johnny, someone here fer you."

Johnny?? Whatever...

She probably held the receiver out to the old man because his voice reached Jack loud and clear. "Who's that?" He wasn't drunk yet, but already surly.

"Ah don't know, darlin'," she answered patiently. Probably had some experience.

"Then ask, woman!"

"Alright, darlin', alright."

Jack automatically made an effort not to cringe as if she could see his expression.

"Who's asking him, please?"

"It's his son, Jack."

There was a pause, like she was digesting the news. "Ah, okay. Please hold, honey... John, it's your son," she said, then in a loud whisper, "You didn't tell me you had a son." She sounded like she had suddenly sobered up.

There was another pause, followed by a downpour of obscenities. "Ain't got no fucking son! Not that piece a shit! Tell that fucking pansy never to call here again!"

Apparently, the woman pressed the phone to her body, because the sound was suddenly muted. Then after a moment she came back on the line, sounding a little rushed. "Listen, Jack. I'm sorry, but John, your father, isn't feeling very well at the moment. Maybe he'll be better in the morning. Is there a number he can call you back?"

Jack suppressed a sigh. "Thank you, ma'am. It's very kind of you. But I don't think he's gonna call me tomorrow. Or ever. Not this fucking pansy." He chucked bitterly.

"I'm really sorry, honey." She was whispering now. "But he hasn't been in a good disposition lately."

Yeah, right, since he was born probably.

"Don't worry about it. I understand... Anyway, I wish you all the best. You sound like a kindhearted person. Don't let the old bastard kill that kindness in you. And please tell him I won't bother him ever again. Goodbye." He hung up before she could say anything else.

He was home.

On Monday morning, Jack arrived at HQ early and headed down to the cafeteria. He took his coffee and croissants, sat down at a table in the far corner and opened the newspaper he had bought on the street.

He skimmed the front-page headlines quickly.

"Officials Identify Three Victims of Air Crashes Near Van Nuys Airport."

"Britain, 3 Other Nations Alert for Channel Terror."

"Inquiry Set Up on Day of Blast, Soviet Declares."

Yes! Here it is.

He quickly turned the page.

"May 19, 1986. Associated Press. MOSCOW—A Soviet nuclear power expert said today that the Kremlin named a panel to investigate the Chernobyl accident on the day the disaster occurred. His statement appeared to contradict assertions that Moscow was without reliable reports on the accident for two days.

Ivan Yemelyanov, first deputy director of the Soviet state institute that designed the Chernobyl reactor, said the investigating commission looking into the disaster was at work "on the very day of the accident, April 26."

Of course, it had been set up on the very first day, Jack knew it for certain—his best friend's grandfather had been asked to join that "investigating commission" on the same day he was—

"Hi, Jack. Mind if I join you?"

He raised his eyes to meet Savannah's toothy smile.

"Hey, Savannah. Not at all." He matched her smile with his grin and folded his newspaper.

She put her tray down. "Thanks. And you can call me Sevan."

"Alright, Sevan... So, how was your weekend?"

"A friend and I went to the opening of 'Top Gun'. A Tom Cruise and Val Kilmer movie.

And Kelly McGillis. Do you like Kelly McGillis?"

They chatted about movies and actors, then, when the topic was exhausted, she suddenly said, "You didn't mention that you were from Moscow Station."

Jack blinked. They were not supposed to talk about their postings.

"Thought you'd know eventually... *If* you needed to know." He peered at her through squinted eyes.

"I asked around," she said bluntly. "Seems like you're quite popular." She was gazing at him with open interest.

"Really? I didn't know. So what do they say about me?"

"Lemme see... They say that you're—"

"Excuse the intrusion." A solidly built, military type in his early thirties was standing at their table. "Jones, Bob is looking for you. Something urgent 's come up." He turned to Jack. "Sorry, mate."

Savannah's smile shrunk. "Thanks. I'll be upstairs in a minute." Her smitten little girl's tone was gone too.

"It's urgent," the man insisted.

"I heard you the first time, O'Leary." She gave him a hard stare. "I'll be up there in a minute."

Muttering an oath under his breath, the man turned on his heel and left.

Savannah rolled her eyes and smiled apologetically. "I don't understand why we recruit ex-military types as case officers. He's from my cohort. Do you think he'll ever be able to keep his cover? Unless they plan to place him as a mercenary." She let out a giggle and took a sip of her latte.

"I guess we need mercenaries too," Jack said tentatively.

In addition to shape-shifters like you, sweet pea.

"Anyway, I have to run, Jack. Let's catch up again so that you can tell me all about Moscow."

"Sure. Let's do it."

"Here's my number." Savannah scribbled on a napkin and pushed it toward him. "See you around, Jack. And don't wait too long." She flashed her teeth at him and flitted away.

Pretty and friendly Savannah Jones. Jack wondered if it was her real name. If he wasn't the only one recruited for Joe Coburn's type of special ops...

He went up to Joe Coburn's office at 9:00 a.m. sharp and was taken into a small office with a computer, two cubicles away. Joe dropped in just as Jack was starting to type his report and instructed him to write down the details of operation TALION *only*. He held Jack's eyes until he nodded his understanding, then added that he would be asked to report "the rest" verbally.

Jack spent two and a half hours writing his progress report, cross checking the dates of his recollections with the calendar on the desk. By noon, he had written eight and a half pages.

The meeting with the Head of SE Division lasted forty-five minutes and went quite well, as Jack concluded afterwards. Burt Gabber was known to shout or scream at his subordinates sometimes, but with Jack, he was almost friendly. They went through some details of the Moscow operation, like who had approved Jack's contacts with his targets and when, and where those discussions had usually taken place. He was particularly interested in Jack's interaction with William Osbourne and Mark Morris. The Division head seemed satisfied with Jack's responses; although Jack couldn't figure what conclusion the man had drawn from their interview. And the whole time he gave no indication whatsoever that he knew about SEABROOK op.

Joe sat opposite Jack next to the SE Division head, silent and impassive. But when Gabber asked Jack to run by him again how and where he had been when he learned about Chernobyl, Jack could feel Joe's eyes burning into him as he answered.

Later, when he reran the episode in his head, Jack couldn't decide what Joe's subtle reaction had meant. Did he doubt Jack's account about his visit to Eton's place? Or did the fact that Eton told Jack about Chernobyl mean that in Joe Coburn's mind the Russian had crossed the line: he was no longer just a potential target but an agent. A foreign agent—the kind Joe cared about the most.

After a short debrief with Joe in his office, Jack left HQ around five o'clock, feeling heady with relief. Joe had confirmed that he wouldn't have to take a polygraph test—"this time", he had added, but that was fine by Jack. He told Jack that Moscow Station's secure room was being rebuilt with materials flown over from America but it wasn't ready yet, so operational reporting remained minimal, and, finally, that he could continue developing Eton Volkonsky. Slowly. "Consider him a long term investment," he said.

So maybe Joe considered Eton a newly recruited agent now, even if he hadn't signed the papers yet. Which meant that from now on, Eton May Volkonsky, codename GTSALT, was under special protection of SE Division's Chief of Clandestine Operations. It meant that if at any time Joe Coburn learned that SALT's life was in danger, he'd do everything in his power to make sure that the agent remained alive. Even pull him out of the Soviet Union. And then—

Don't even think it, Smith!

I'm not thinking anything! I've been instructed to develop him and I'm gonna do it.

Do it. Just don't kid yourself with stupid ideas. You *know* it's impossible.

Right...

If he was to develop Eton, he would need to make sure that his friend had a way out. Namely Joe Coburn. For that, Eton must continue to be of special interest to the Company. That is, continue to be a promising nuclear physicist, eventually working at some important, preferably "closed", State research institution. Rock musicians were of no interest to the Agency, no matter how talented they were. It meant that, to keep Eton safe, Jack would have to persuade him to give up his dream, to continue with his studies and go to work for some nuclear research institute. Which was exactly the path Eton had been on when Jack had met him the previous July.

These thoughts plagued Jack's mind for the rest of the week. His annual leave was pretty much ruined: there were only five days left before he had to return to Moscow and then go to Leningrad for Eton's show. *And* he had to show up for the last briefing with Joe Coburn before his departure.

On Wednesday, Jack drove on impulse to Highland, Virginia. Only to find the gates to the farm closed, with SOLD pasted over the FOR SALE sign. He turned around and drove directly back. He got to his apartment eight hours later, feeling drained and disturbed. He didn't believe in signs, but somehow could neither explain nor rid himself of the startling disappointment brought on by his futile visit to Hillside Creek Farm.

On Friday, the scheduled two-hour briefing with Joe turned into an eight-hour operational planning session with Joe Coburn and Marat Nurimbekoff, who had gotten back to HQ a few days before. It turned out Moscow Station needed to pick up two status update signals from the remaining two active Soviet agents, one in Moscow, the other in Leningrad. It had been decided that Jack was the one to do both runs. The signal in Moscow was to be sighted and reported on only, in the afternoon of May 29th. The one in Leningrad was to be picked up and confirmed with a similar signal, a chalk sign at a different site, before midnight on 31st of May.

He had promised Eton he'd be in Leningrad for his performance on May 30th, no matter what. So before leaving for America, he'd applied for a travel permit and left instructions with the team assistant to buy him an overnight train ticket to Leningrad on May 29th. Of course, he had also informed Nurimbekoff about his trip and its purpose. That probably explained why they had decided that Jack was to do the run in Leningrad, instead of one of the three case officers at the Leningrad Station.

It was just before nine o'clock when Jack got back to town. He found a payphone near DuPont Circle and called Savannah, praying that she wasn't home. She wasn't. So he left a message on her answering machine, apologizing for not calling earlier, bidding her goodbye in case he couldn't get hold of her before returning to the field.

He bought a take away burger and coke and went back to his apartment.

Next morning, he went out to buy himself a few things at the only western wear shop he knew in Georgetown, between N and O Streets. He was on his way out when the cowboy hats on the rack to the left of the door caught his eye. When he left the shop fifteen minutes later, a cream-colored Stetson with a braided leather band was nestling between denim shirts, jeans and woolen socks in the shopping bag.

He couldn't recall seeing Eton wearing hats, nor was he sure if cowboy hats were considered a good present in Russia. But he had his old black Stetson with him in Moscow, which he wore occasionally, and somehow it made the ranch idea seem like—

Like a totally stupid idea! What have you been smoking lately, Smith?!

He didn't have an answer to that, so he just brushed the question away and tried not to think about it.

On Sunday, when Jack boarded the direct PanAm flight to Moscow, a third of his suitcase was occupied by presents: cosmetics for the girls at the Embassy, women's magazines for Lara and perfume for her mother, silk shawls for Vera Mikhailovna and Anya, music video cassettes for *Krylia* boys, a pair of Wrangler jeans for Gosha. And in his carry-on bag, carefully wrapped in cornflower-blue gift paper, were a vinyl record, The Best of The Eagles, and a cowboy hat.

Chapter 47

May 25, Sunday. 11:47p.m.

Dear Jack,

You said today is the day when you leave New York to return to Moscow. You should arrive tomorrow afternoon.

Grandpa returned from Ch. on Friday morning. He looks tanner than last time and exhausted. He is in the Kremlin's hospital for a comprehensive test, will be checked out for the meeting with the Politburo tomorrow morning. Maybe they will let him come home. But whatever they decide, the hospital has already warned us that the test results will not be available to relatives. Maybe Grandpa has told them not to give us. He wants to go back there next week. He will kill himself there, but doesn't listen to us. Says it is his responsibility. I wish I could do something to help. How did you say it? "I feel so fucking useless". That's how I feel.

About the Chernobyl concert that Artyom and Alla Pugacheva are organizing: Artyom says she got the permission to organize it at the Olympic Stadium. It is the largest place in the city. This woman is amazing! She can pull off anything.

Artyom says we should play my Nuclear Twilight. It would be an honor. At least some contribution from us. We will be taking the overnight train to Leningrad right after the concert. It means that we will miss the opening of the festival and perhaps the first few performances.

Are you taking the train or the airplane? Hope to hear from you soon.

Yours,

E.

May 27, Tuesday. Midnight.

Dear Jack,

You should be back by now. Hope you will call soon and we can meet up before Leningrad. I need want to talk to you.

Have you been following the developments at Ch.? I wonder if your newspapers say the same thing as Radio Liberty. They broadcast rumors every day because there is so little information about what is really going on there. And yes, I have been listening to RL, first with Mother at her place, then at home. Never thought she was listening to western broadcasts. She always seemed such a proper Soviet citizen, so "politically right" to me. I've realized how little I know her. She is my mother, supposed to be the closest person I have, isn't she? I wonder if what she knows about me. I hope she doesn't know about me very well. It will only break her heart.

Grandpa is home. He looks a little better than when he got back last week, but still doesn't eat much and smokes a lot. Yesterday I told him about my decision to take some engineering courses. He understood. Shook my hand, hugged me. Told me he will teach me everything he knows. And that I can use his library and journals, whatever I need.

Then he told me about Ch. Said it is frighteningly similar to our very first battle in the WWII, the battle for the city of Brest: now, like then, we were completely unprepared, unarmed, uninformed, and helpless in the face of the deadly force; yet every single person was fighting till his last breath for the motherland. I understand now why Grandpa insists on going back there: he is one of the few who understand what is going on; he can't just leave people who are clueless on their own, dying.

I wish he would let me go with him. I would do anything they need to help. As a nuclear physicist, I feel responsible too.

Hope you understand.

E.

May 29, Thursday. 10pm.

Dear Jack,

You will never know how relieved I was to hear your voice last night: you are back. And you said it felt like coming home. If by "home" you meant a place where there is always someone waiting for you, thinking of you, then yes, this is your home. And will be, for as long as I live.

So glad you are coming to Leningrad. As I said, Sevka will be waiting for you outside of the House of Culture. I will tell you later about what is up with him and me, but yes, he is coming to L. with us and so is Lara. Artyom has arranged a pass for you and them.

I must go to bed now. It is a big day for me and Krylia tomorrow. I need to be in good form.

See you in Leningrad. I will sing for you.

Your friend,

E.

May 30, Friday. 1:25am

Jack, this decision to continue with nuclear physics and take on engineering will perhaps result in me working for some closed research institute in 2-3 years. You will be gone by then. But it means that I will not be able to come visit you in America. Unless I achieve Grandpa's or Legasov's status, or like some of our other prominent scientists. I don't think I am that smart and dedicated. So it means "never". It breaks my heart every time I think about it. But it was meant to be that way from the moment we met, right? I was just a fool to think that if I stayed away from what I was meant to do, then maybe I would be able to change my destiny. Now I know what my destiny is: to do something useful for my people, to love you and never to see you again. I have grown up, cowboy.

Yours always,

E.

* * *

Jack returned to find the American community in Moscow pervaded by suspicious nervousness, just like last August when the spy dust had been announced. The medical staff sent in by the State Department had found traces of Iodine-131, an element associated with nuclear fission products, in samples of milk, reportedly "above the level of concern". Consequently, most American families of diplomats, journalists and businessmen were buying milk and vegetables brought in from Finland. As a result, the Embassy's procurement of food supplies from overseas had tripled overnight.

On the positive side, the information flow about the damaged reactor had doubled too. On the first Monday after Jack's return a news conference was broadcast on local TV, featuring a leading Soviet physicist and vice president of the Academy of Sciences, E. Velikhov. He raised the death toll to nineteen and warned of the "theoretical possibility" of further danger from the radioactive core of the reactor. He also revealed that the special commission had tentatively concluded that the accident had been caused by "a number of consecutive incorrect actions" of the plant's personnel, thus laying the blame on the technicians operating the reactor.

Jack managed to call Eton only two days after his return. And was startled all over again by the joy that enveloped him when the familiar baritone murmured, "*privet*, welcome back" in his ear. They talked for a long while, sharing the news of the past three weeks, trying to read between each other's words, laughing easily, feeling heady and carefree.

The signal collection run on Thursday went off without the slightest hiccup and by 8:30p.m. Jack was reporting to Nurimbekoff in the COS's soundproof inner office. He could still make it to the Leningrad Station in time to catch the midnight train that Lara and Seva were taking, but decided to stay back. He rolled his eyes at himself: maybe it was frickin' girly, but the thought that he and Eton were in the same city tonight gave him a warm, fuzzy feeling.

Jack landed at Pulkovo Airport before noon. Once out in the main hall, he headed to the last exit on the left. From afar, he noticed the man in a checkered cap through the glass door. The Russian leaned with his back against the glass, smoking, a colorful magazine rolled-up into a tube in his left hand. The transporter.

Jack came up to him with a cigarette and asked for light. Wordlessly, the man produced a bright red and blue plastic lighter from his pocket and handed it to Jack.

Jack lit his cigarette. "Are you available for a ride?" he asked, returning the lighter.

"I can only take you to Nevsky Prospect."

"That'll do. I'm staying there."

"Hotel Baltiyskaya?"

"*da*." It was the name of the hotel Jack was booked in.

"Via Arsenalnaya Embankment?"

"Yes, please."

Arsenal Embankment wasn't the straightest way to get to Nevsky Avenue from the airport. But that was where Jack was supposed to pick up the status signal in this drive through.

The Russian unglued himself from the wall he was leaning against and pointed with his head to the taxi line at the curb.

"*Nu poydyom*—let's go then."

Lara and Seva picked him up at his hotel at six o'clock. Half an hour later, they were standing in front of the gray monolith of Nevsky Palace of Culture that belonged to Nevsky Machine Building Plant. It was the home of semi-official Leningrad Rock Club, the organizer of the 4th Leningrad Rock Festival. The area surrounding the concrete, Soviet style building was swarming with young people, mostly guys, many of them bearded and many more long-haired. Jack also noticed several odd characters milling around, not blending very well into the crowd.

Seva left them waiting by the door and went to get the special guest pass for Jack. He returned ten minutes later with a tall, scraggy youth in an oversized, used-to-be white t-shirt that looked like he had been sleeping in it for at least a week. The young man cut a quick, skeptical glance at Lara in her trendy stonewashed denim outfit and turned all his attention to Jack. He introduced himself as Val and solemnly explained that he'd been instructed by Artyom to take care of Jack—take him around, introduce him to some of Leningrad's and the Soviet Union's best rock bands. Val shepherded them past a group of young, moody men guarding the entrance and led them straight to the backstage door.

"Joanna wants to meet with you," he told Jack.

"Joanna?"

"You don't know Joanna?" He gaped at Jack in disbelief.

Right at that moment a young woman in her mid-twenties came out of the door. She was wearing a leather vest over an oversized t-shirt with "Save the World" written on the front and a pair of big sunglasses. Her locks were short and dyed blond on the top, long and mousey brown at the back.

"Hi, I'm Joanna," she said in English, offering Jack her hand. "And you must be Jack. We were supposed to meet at Amanda's last year, but you didn't show." Her accent was Californian, her voice husky, and there was a whiff of alcohol in her breath. "Amanda was raving about you."

"She's too kind." Jack grinned at her. "I'm sorry I missed the dinner. But it's great to finally meet you now." He couldn't see her eyes behind the shades, but could feel her studying him. "Please meet my friends, Lara and Seva. They're from Moscow."

Joanna nodded to the Russians who were awe-struck, gazing at her wide-eyed.

Jack recalled Eton telling him about Russian bands he admired—Boris G. with his band Akvarium, Viktor Tsoi and Kino, a band from Sverdlovsk call Nautilus, few others. And Joanna, a singer from Los Angeles who'd come to Leningrad one day, met with Boris and his friends, and stayed to become a permanent feature of Soviet underground rock scene.

"Are you going to sing with Boris?" asked Lara who'd been uncharacteristically quiet, but now seemed to liven up in the presence of a rock star from America.

"We will, tomorrow." Joanna nodded and turned to Jack again. "Artyom and Boris are still in Moscow. At the Chernobyl concert. They'll only get here tomorrow morning. But don't worry. Val here will take care of you."

"Thank you. Much appreciated."

"Alright, I have to run now. Just wanted to say hi and welcome to Amanda's good friend." She took two steps towards the door. "By the way, are you joining our gathering tomorrow night?"

"Are we?" Jack looked at Seva. Seeing a wistful look on the young man's face, he turned to Joanna with an apologetic smile. "I'm here with my friends, a band called *Krylia*. Don't know what their plans are."

"You mean the student band Artyom is bringing from Moscow? They can join us too. Artyom says their front man is a cool kid and a good singer… See you later, then?" She waved her hand at them and disappeared behind the door.

The concert hall was dark during the show, with the only illumination coming from flashing, multicolor lights on the stage. Ear-splitting electric guitar chords and the thundering crash of drums and cymbals cascaded on wildly enthusiastic fans, many of whom looked as unkempt and stoned as the bands. Jack had never been to a rock concert at home, but suspected what he was seeing and hearing might not be too different from a similar show somewhere in America. Except for the songs. On this side of the Iron Curtain, they sounded defiant—calling for a change, calling for action. He hadn't expected to hear songs titled "Get Out of Control" and "We Want Changes" in a jam-packed thousand-seat concert hall in the second city of the Soviet Union.

From the vibes Jack caught during and after the shows, it seemed he wasn't the only one stunned by the novelty and audacity of the themes, the lyrics and the performance of well-known and new rock bands. *Krylia* were one of them.

Eton and his crew arrived on the second day of the festival and Jack didn't see or talk to him until the program resumed in early afternoon.

He was standing in the wide gallery that ran along the perimeter of the building, talking with Artyom and Joanna, with Lara close by his side, looking like she was miles away. Artyom was explaining to him the novel aspects of the current rock festival comparing to the past three and the trend emerging on the Soviet rock scene since Gorbachev had proclaimed glastnost.

"By the way, have you seen *Krylia*'s Nuclear Twilight?" Artyom asked when he had finished his monolog, which Jack suspected he had delivered not for the first time.

Jack looked at Lara who shook her head.

"No, not yet."

"Then prepare to be surprised. Yesterday they brought many people to tears at the concert in Moscow. This guy Eton is very talented," Artyom told Joanna. "You'll like him, Jo. He sings in perfect English, too."

"*Otlichno*, excellent!" Joanna nodded and added in heavily accented Russian. "Invite him to *tusovka* tonight."

Just then, Eton emerged at the end of the gallery, heading toward them, flanked by Seva and a young man Jack didn't know.

"There's Eton!" Lara exclaimed.

"Speak of the devil," Joanna clucked.

Artyom quickly introduced Eton and the young man, *Krylia*'s new drummer Kostia, to Joanna.

"I hear many good things about you, Eton," Joanna said as they shook hands, studying him with unhidden interest.

"Thank you." Eton muttered, barely looking at her. He nodded to Lara and offered his hand to Jack. "Thank you for coming."

Jack squeezed his hand in a firm handshake, trying to reign in his grin. "We've just heard a lot of good things about you guys. Artyom says you were quite a blast yesterday. Can't wait to see it myself."

Eton's ears pinked. "It's all thanks to him. He gave us a chance to perform in such an event... Actually, we were looking for you, Artyom."

"Anything happen?" Artyom asked suspiciously.

"Nothing... Just want to let you know that I'm going to sing in English tonight. The song I told you about."

Artyom threw his hands up in exasperation. "But Eton, didn't we talk about it? You guys will be disqualified. It's a—"

"A song in English?" Joanna chipped in. "You wrote it?"

"Yes."

She turned to Artyom. "Let him do it, Art. Boris and I will sing one song in English, too." Seeing her friend's shocked expression, she grinned at him conciliatory. "We want to make a surprise. Hey, I know you like good surprise!" She punched him on the shoulder and turned to Eton. "Do it as you think right. Not listen to nobody," she said in faulty Russian, smiling wickedly.

"We won't. Thank you, Joanna. So we'll go to prepare for it now... See you all later?"

Eton looked over at everybody before his eyes locked with Jack's for a fleeting moment. He nodded a silent goodbye to all and quickly retreated, with Kostia the drummer close on his heels.

Krylia's entry wasn't until after five, by which time Jack thought he'd had enough of Soviet rock for the next few years. Besides, he'd had heavy surveillance on him in the morning and decided to wait until evening to do his op run. So now, all he had was seven hours before the midnight deadline. He would have to leave right after Eton's performance, make his way to the Palace Bridge over Big Neva River where he was to leave a chalk sign at a specific place on the wrought-iron railing of the bridge.

When the MC finally announced *Krylia*, Jack was as wound up as he thought Eton and his band might be. He was sitting near the right end of the third row, Lara and Seva on his left, and Artyom and Val on his right. Joanna and her friends, members of several Leningrad rock bands, were in the first two rows in front of them. They started clapping enthusiastically as soon as *Krylia* stepped out on the stage. Joanna's friends joined in, followed by the whole audience.

All five members of the band wore black t-shirts with torn off sleeves and faded, frayed jeans with cuts and holes. Their hair looked wet and unkempt, and they all wore striking make-up: huge blackened eyes and crimson red mouths on powder-white faces. After a few minutes of tuning of their instruments, Eton nodded to someone in the wings and stage lights were extinguished, except for the spots.

The music they played was an extravagant collage of hard rock, pop rock and fragments of classical music. Eton's usual cool, emotionless façade was now furiously expressive as he read and chanted verses of poetry, intermingling them with recitations of the principles of nuclear reaction, a list of major nuclear accidents and war, ending it with Chernobyl. His passion drove his band to play with breathtaking intensity. Then came the finale: a prolonged incantation, in total darkness, with only the faint *ting* of a triangle as accompaniment—"Listen to the sound of the light dying."

The utter silence that followed the triangle's last, crystal chime was deafening. When the lights suddenly flared up, Artyom and Joanna leapt up from their seats, clapping and cheering, followed by their rockers friends in the two front rows. Then the rest of the audience erupted in a thunderous standing ovation.

Jack was flooded with such pride for his friend that he added an Indian war cry to the cheers. Seva picked it up, then Joanna and her rockers, then the rest of the concert hall, and the ovation turned riotous.

Even with his unsmiling mask up again, Eton looked stunned. He stood in the bright spotlight, shuffling his feet, holding his guitar in front of his chest like a shield. His band members came back to their senses quickly. They started smiling and waving to the audience, exchanging happy grins and handshakes with each other. It wasn't until Alex, the bass guitarist, came up to Eton, shook hands and exchanged a few words with him, that the young man relaxed, nodded faintly and gave the audience his tight-lipped smile. Then he stepped up to the microphone.

"Um, thank you. We're glad you liked our performance… And now, we'd like to dedicate the following number to someone, um, lots of you know. Our good friend from America." He stretched his hand, indicating the spot where Jack was sitting.

Jack went rigid, his stomach falling.

No, Eton, no! What are you—

Right then Joanna sprung up from her seat in front of him, waving enthusiastically at the stage, then at the audience which started cheering again and chanting 'Joanna! Joanna!'

"Thank you!" Joanna called out, beaming at the stage. "In English, Eton! Sing in English!"

Eton smiled in her direction and nodded. Then his eyes locked with Jack's and Jack saw his friend's smile widen.

The lights dimmed and *Krylia* commenced their next number. It started as a quiet ballad, almost like a lullaby, Eton murmuring the words into the microphone over the haunting sounds of violins that the keyboardist was making on his electric organ. Then gradually the music grew, guitars joined, then drums and soon Eton was pouring his heart out, singing with such passion that for a moment Jack forgot to breathe. When the refrain was about to start for the third time, Joanna jumped up on the stage and joined Eton at the microphone, rendering her throaty voice to the chorus. Some young people in the back rows picked it up too and soon the whole audience was standing, singing along, swaying to the poignant melody.

It was close to six o'clock when the MC announced a break. Jack stood up, suppressing a sigh of relief. He really had to go: his op run deadline was only six hours away.

"Do you guys want to have a quick bite with us before the next section?" Artyom asked Jack. "I'm sure your friends would like to join, too," he added, pointing at the backstage with his head when he saw Jack's hesitation.

"You *must* come with us, Jack," Joanna butted in, talking to him in English. "We have to make a good showing on this occasion, compatriot!"

"What is the occasion?" Jack asked cautiously.

"The Soviet rock reaching America this month. In the form of a double album called Red Wave." She beamed, then turned to the Russians. "I tell Jack he must come celebrate Red Wave with us today."

"It would never happen, if not for Joanna here," Artyom said, putting his arm around her shoulders.

"And Amanda," Joanna added.

"Amanda?" Jack was surprised.

"*Da!*" Joanna nodded with a smug smile. "She is not here anymore, so we can tell everybody. She helped us get the records *out*." She arched her eyebrows emphatically.

"She smuggled them out?" Seva asked, incredulous.

"*Da!* She helped with record studio, too. Very good woman with *connections*… We going? I will tell more at dinner."

"I'm afraid I can't join you now." Jack said, apologetic. "I have a meeting I can't miss."

"I'll walk with you to the Metro," Lara chimed in suddenly, looking at Jack with pleading eyes. "I need to go, too. But I'll come back later," she explained to others.

"Will you come to the *tusovka* tonight?" Joanna asked Jack in English. "You may not have another chance like this—to meet with *all* Leningrad's leading rock bands and their friends."

"Please come," said Artyom.

"Thank you. I will. I just might be running a little late."

"Don't worry, we won't be done till morning," Joanna laughed and turned to her friend. "Art, give him the address."

As Artyom was writing the address on a piece of paper, Eton and his band arrived. They all looked a little high with excitement, even their tightlipped bandleader.

"Boys, you come with us to dinner now," Joanna announced to the newcomers. "We must celebrate your debut."

There was a chorus of thanks, then the two guitarists, Alex and Vadim, squeezed in between the rows of chairs to chat to Seva.

Eton watched warily as Artyom handed Jack the scrap of paper. "Are we all going?" he asked, not addressing anyone in particular.

"Jack and Lara are going away. They will come back later," Joanna said.

"I have to go back to the hotel. For a meeting." Jack brushed away the desire to slap her.

"But I'll come to the *tusovka* later. Got the address here." He waved the piece of paper, like it was the proof that he'd come. "Lara might come before me, though. Right, Lara?"

"I'll wait for you... To make sure you won't go missing," she added, seeing Jack's expression.

"You don't have to. I'm not sure what time I'll be free."

What's wrong with you people today?

"We can talk about it on the way to Metro. Let's go. We'll see you all later!" Lara said, waving at everybody.

Jack suppressed a sigh, shook hands all around, smiling wide, repeating again and again 'see you tonight'. When he turned to shake hands with Eton, his friend didn't return the smile. He looked through Jack, his face impassive, his eyes full of shadows.

"Eton," Jack said quietly while others were chatting about the dinner and *tusovka*.

Eton's gaze focused, but he didn't say anything.

"Thank you, bud," Jack whispered in English, then added louder in Russian, "See you later. *Tonight*."

Chapter 48

As they were walking out of the hulking concrete edifice that was the palace of culture, Jack noticed a young couple hurrying through its grand entrance.

He had noted them earlier, shortly after his arrival. The couple didn't quite blend in with the deliberately uncombed crowd of young people, many of whom looked as though they'd been drinking for days. Both blond and dressed neatly in clean jeans and white t-shirts, the pair seemed alert and more interested in each other than in the show, constantly whispering and touching. And they had been hanging around within a dozen yards of Jack most of the time.

"So, where are you going?" Jack asked as they were strolling towards the main street.

Lara shrugged. "I don't care. I just needed to get out of there... I've had enough rock to last me a year." She smiled, looking both relieved and a little sad. She hadn't been her usual vibrant and confident self—pensive most of the time, with faint shadows under her eyes.

Jack stopped, caught her by her arm and pulled her to face him, and so that he could see the alleyway leading to the palace of culture. "Are you alright?"

The tidy couple was closing in on them, arm in arm, the woman giggling at something the man was whispering in her ear.

"I'm fine. Just a bit tired."

The couple passed by without a glance at them.

"Are you sure? You haven't been yourself for the last two days. You hardly talk anymore... But of course you don't have to tell me if you don't want to."

She snaked her arm through his. "It's nothing serious, really... Just some issues with... um, a friend. He hasn't been doing well lately. I'm trying to help."

The blond couple reached the main street and stopped, deep in a quiet conversation.

"I see... Can I help?"

She stared at Jack with a strange expression on her face, then burst out laughing. "No, don't think you can in this case. Anyway, let's go or you'll be late for your meeting." She pulled at his arm.

The man and woman were heading off to the right where the bus station was. There was a trolleybus stop and a tram station thirty meters to the left too, all of them going in the same direction, to Alexander Nevsky Square Metro Station. Jack turned right.

"Let's get to the Metro. I'll take you to wherever you're going, then will go back for the meeting."

"*Kharasho*, alright. I'll think of where to go by the time we get there."

When the bus arrived, Jack positioned them at the back door behind two matronly women with plastic shopping bags. The neat couple stood at the front door behind an elderly man. As the doors opened, Jack gave a hand to the women getting onto the bus. When Lara mounted, he put one foot on the lowest step and halted. Just as the door was about to close, he stepped back down, yanking Lara out of the bus.

"Are you crazy?! What are you doing?" Lara looked both perplexed and annoyed.

Jack stepped back onto the pavement, pulling her with him, and grinned sheepishly. "Actually, I don't have any meeting. I just needed to get out of there, too. Guess I'm not a rock fan either."

She stared at him in disbelief, then her face eased into a tired smile. "You *are* crazy... So, what are we going to do now?"

A tram was approaching on the other side of road, heading in the opposite direction.

"Let's take the tram and ride around."

"*Kharasho*. Let's go then." She looked amused.

As they were about to board the tram, Jack tugged at her arm. "Lara, promise not to tell the guys. I mean, that I didn't have any meeting and you and I just needed some timeout. Promise? Please, Lara!"

She giggled, almost her old cheerful self, and took his hand, interlinking their fingers. "I promise."

They rode the tram to the end of the long avenue, then changed to another one going in the opposite direction. When their screeching and clanging tram crossed Alexander Nevsky Bridge to the other side of the river, they alighted and took another one going in the direction of Vasilievsky Island. They sat side by side, watching the streets and buildings drifting by the window, holding hands occasionally, pointing at and discussing various architectural attractions, parks and embankments.

It was nearly eight when they finally got out a few blocks away from the Palace Bridge, Jack's ultimate destination. They bought ice cream and strolled along the embankment in the direction of the bridge.

Two hours into the improvised SDR, and they had no surveillance. Well, unless he was wrong about Lara and she was the surveillance today, and the neat couple at the palace of culture had been a decoy. In which case, he was taking them straight to the signal site. But then, it might be a perfect chance to let them catch and recruit him. Wasn't it what Joe & Co. expected of him? Now he only needed to figure how to leave the chalk sign on top of one of the cast-iron posts of the bridge.

They were nearing the head of Palace Bridge when Jack noticed a small, overflowing trashcan at the corner of the yellow building with white columns across the street. He quickly finished his ice cream and rolled its paper wrap into a ball.

"Are you done?"

She finished the last mouthful of the ice cream and gave Jack the wrapping. Jack dodged through a gap between the cars. A minute later he crossed back over, smiling enigmatically, his right hand curled into a fist.

"What is it?" Lara asked suspiciously.

"Look what I found." He uncurled his fingers to reveal three pieces of chalk on his palm—white, yellow and light blue. "We're going to play this little game folks usually play in San Francisco on Golden Gate Bridge." He didn't know if anyone played any game on Golden Gate Bridge, least of all the one he had in mind, but then he was willing to bet that Lara didn't know that either.

"What game?" Her face lit up, curious.

"Well, it's a kind of wishing game. It goes like this: as we walk across the bridge, we each write a wish on every other post between the bridge railing sections. For example, you write on the first post, I write on the second, you on the third, I on the fourth and so on."

"One wish on each post?"

"No, one or two words at a time till you've written the whole wish. Then we go back and each reads what the other person has written, but in reverse."

"Oh... So you'll read what I've written." She furrowed her delicately lined eyebrows.

"You can draw a picture or a sign, if you don't want me to know what your wish is."

"No, it's fine. You can read my wish." She took his hand and swung it softly. "I'm just trying to understand the game... Alright. So, who'll go first?"

"You first." He offered her the bits of chalk.

There were people strolling on the bridge, enjoying the evening sun and cool air, so they tried to be discreet about writing on the bridge posts, hanging around them longer than needed. Ten minutes later, they were walking back, reading aloud what the other had written.

Jack's wish was less altruistic than Lara's—to remain with his friends forever. But that was fine. The main thing was that he'd accomplished his mission: the symbol for infinity written with yellow chalk was left on the dark green top of the post, the one between the tenth and eleventh sections of the railing, on the right from the island side.

It took Lara ten posts to write her wish, one word each: that everything would come together well for someone whose name she had coded to look like a butterfly turned upside down.

"It's very kind of you, Lara," Jack said when they got back to the head of the bridge. "I feel so selfish now."

"I'm not that selfless. He just needs it badly... Never mind." She forced a smile at him. "I'm hungry."

"Me too." Jack looked at his watch. It was quarter to nine, yet the sun was still high. "Sorry, I completely lost track of time."

"Let's go have a snack before the *tusovka*. I don't think there'll be much to eat there... Unless you like vodka with boiled ham for dinner."

Their "snack" was a four-course dinner in a vast restaurant called Neva. Claiming she was starving, Lara ordered all house specialties recommended by the waiter: Leningrad salad, Neva-style cabbage *stchi* soup, fried fillet white fish and wild strawberry ice cream for dessert. She sagged again after ordering the food, fingering the corner of the napkin while Jack talked about the rock festival, about the latest gossip about American actors, then asked her about the new play she had told him she was rehearsing. She shrugged and said halfheartedly that everybody was on summer holidays and rehearsals wouldn't resume before October.

There was a long pause as they concentrated on their soups, then Jack put down his spoon and asked lightly, "So what's up with your friend then? Bad grades?"

Lara looked up, her face blank. "Which friend?"

"The one for whom you wrote the wish on the bridge. The butterfly."

She straightened in her chair, looked away for a moment, then sighed. "Ah... Troubles... with authorities."

"With authorities? You mean with *militsia*?"

"Them too."

"What did he do? Smashed someone's window playing football? Drunk driving?" Jack asked, masking his insistence with nonchalance. He needed to know that it wasn't anyone he knew.

"No, he's just... stubborn like a mule!" Lara said with sudden heat.

...

"I'm going to sing in English tonight."

"But Eton, we've talked about it!"

...

"You just do what you need to do, Jack. Don't worry about me."

...

"Oh... Anyone I know?"

She hesitated, bit on her lip.

Not Eton, please!

"You've met him... A few times."

"Have I?" Suddenly, Jack felt lightheaded. He coughed twice, covering up the wave of relief.

Lara sighed. "It's Viktor. He's been having trouble because of, um, his experimental plays."

Jack recalled his conversation with Amanda the previous year. Stubborn like a mule, she had said, didn't even try to be discreet about who he was. And it dawned on him that the upside down butterfly on the bridge post was actually two stylized back-to-back letters "B" which were Russian "V"—for Viktor. And the color of the chalk she had chosen was light blue: *goluboy*, gay.

Because of his plays, huh?

"Sorry to hear... And you still want to act in his plays?"

"Of course, I do," she prickled. "It's an honor to be in one of his plays. We all want to."

Her last statement wasn't as emphatic as the first and Jack figured maybe not all of her friends shared her sentiments.

The waiter brought their mains and took the soup plates away.

"So what is it that he is being stubborn about?"

"Everything has to be, uh, the way he thinks is *right*. Or true. Even if it's detrimental to him."

"And you're trying to help him."

"I've tried. But he wouldn't listen to me. I just give up!" She glared at her plate, pouting and for the rest of the evening she just pushed her food around with her fork.

Jack let her be. He felt a stir of sympathy for Karelin, but the Russian director wasn't any of his business. He only wished that Lara hadn't been so wounded about her failure to help her teacher.

By the time the taxi dropped them off at the address Artyom had given him, it was nearly eleven o'clock and night was just beginning to fall. In front of them was a short alleyway leading to an iron gate, behind which stood a three-story red-brick building that looked like an old factory. To the left, facing the street was another 19th century, two-story house, with a large sign on top: "Abrasive Factory Ilyich". On the right was a tiny square with a statue of Lenin on a tall granite stand, a flowerbed and a neat line of fir trees surrounding it. Everything else behind and to the right of the statue was hidden by the thicket of trees that extended all the way down the street.

"I think this is it," Jack said. "Let's go in?" He took a couple of steps toward the gate, but realized that Lara wasn't with him. "Lara? What is it?"

"Let's not go in just yet." She sounded wary.

"Thought you liked parties."

"I do. But not right now. I've got a headache and need a bit of a fresh air... Let's walk a little along the street."

"We're late, Lara. They must be wondering where we are." He wasn't sure about others, but suspected that Eton was and it made him both impatient and anxious—he'd been missing for too long. And with Lara, too.

"Just for ten minutes. Please!" She pulled at his arm.

Jack had never heard her pleading and it did him in. "Alright. Let's have a quick walk. I hope our friends won't kill us for being so late."

"Don't worry. They're probably all drunk by now and all forgotten about us. Let's go."

They returned to the street and strolled past the little square, then along the low, wrought-iron fence from the same era as the factory building, overgrown bushes and tall trees rising just inside it. The two-lane street they were walking along was deserted.

Lara clung to his arm like he were her life vest. Jack thought he'd let her be for a while—they were going to plunge into a wild party of strangers in a few minutes, and in her current mood she was probably not ready for it.

A couple were necking against a tree a few meters from the fence, oblivious to the world. The guy pushed his girlfriend flat against the rough bark of the old tree, his hands under her t-shirt, lifting it to her chest, exposing her flesh. The girl giggled and said something unintelligible. She was drunk.

"Some people are lucky," Lara remarked when they had passed the couple.

"You mean that girl? What is so lucky about being drunk and used on the street?"

"But she's getting what she wants."

Jack gaped at her. "What do *you* want that you haven't got yet?"

- 352 -

She didn't answer right away, but when she did, she craned her neck to see his face. "You."

That brought Jack to a halt. "Lara, sweetheart, we've talked about it, haven't we?" he exclaimed, his tone contrite.

"We have. I remember." She started walking again, pulling him with her.

"I'm sorry, Lara, but—"

"You know what Viktor said about you?"

The question took him aback. "What did he say?"

"Once I was telling him about you and how I would marry you one day and leave for America." She let out a sad giggle when Jack stopped in his tracks again. "Don't worry. I was just trying to make him jealous. He looked at me with an amused expression. Then he said that it would probably be another... a mistake. Because you might be *goluboy*, gay."

Jack stumbled, his stomach dropped like a stone. "*What*?!"

"That's what he said." Lara shrugged. "But then he says that about others, too."

Fuck! What does *that* mean? Oh, fuck!!

He swallowed hard and made a titanic effort to keep his tone low and level. "Lara, are you trying to offend me or to challenge me?"

She mulled it over for two seconds, watching him closely with a curious little smile. "Maybe both." She turned around and began walking back.

Jack faltered before setting off after her. When he caught up with her, he exhaled sharply. "I told you, Lara: I'm a dip—"

"I know, Jack. And I know that it doesn't mean a damn if you *really* like someone... You don't really like me, do you?" She cut him a sideway glance.

"But I do like you. Honestly, I do!"

"Alright, but not like... like a man liking a woman."

"I do like you like that, too. But—"

"But you're not in love with me. Yes, I know that. But then you don't *have* to be in love to want a woman, do you? I know that, too." She sighed. "You are just not attracted to me at all, Jack. Most men I like are. Except you... And Viktor."

"But you can't label a man gay, Lara, just because he doesn't try to get under the skirt of a pretty woman," he objected heatedly, throwing his hands up.

She put her hand on his arm in a pacifying gesture and smiled sadly at him. "Alright, Jack, alright. Maybe not you..." She turned away.

"Are you saying that Viktor is... um, *goluboy*?" Jack asked cautiously.

Now Lara stopped in her tracks. She stared at him, her eyes wide in surprise. "Are you saying you didn't know?"

"Well, I've heard rumors, but..."

"*Everybody* knows, Jack. He doesn't even try to be discreet about it!" There was a note of desperation in her voice and something else...

Like pain, maybe?

They walked in silence for a minute or two.

"You really care for him, don't you?" Jack asked quietly.

There was an even longer pause before she replied. "I'll do anything for him."

The determination in Lara's voice startled Jack. He hadn't suspected such depth of feeling in this privileged daughter of a Soviet high ranking government official. Somehow, it reminded him of the pampered, aristocratic wives and girlfriends of the Decembrists who had left behind their lavish lives and followed their exiled men deep into the frozen expanses of Siberia.

"You love him… don't you?" Jack gazed at her in wonder.

She glanced at him, then shrugged and turned away. "It doesn't matter. He's gay, remember?" There was no resentment in her voice, just sadness.

Jack caught her by her arm, pulled her to a stop and into his arms. "Come here, you silly thing." He held her loosely in his arms for a while, kissed her softly on top of her head, feeling sorry for her.

Her arms sneaked around his waist and she pressed her cheek into his chest. "I wish I could love *you*, Jack. I thought it would be so easy: you're so chivalrous, so handsome. And a good friend, too."

Jack choked out a laugh. "You don't want to do that, Lara! I'm a foreigner, remember? I'll leave this place one day."

"It doesn't matter. I still wish I could love you." She rose up on her toes, put her arms around his neck and pulled his head down to hers. "Maybe I still can?" she whispered and pressed her mouth against Jack's.

His first impulse was to push her away, but her words echoed back at him, condemning— "Viktor said you might be gay", "Maybe not you". He fought the urge and held her body tight to him, plundering her mouth with his tongue.

I'll show you gay, you silly little girl.

In a minute, she pushed his head back softly, gasping for air. "My God, Jack! Let's take a taxi and go to my… to the place we're staying."

Jack loosened his hold, raised his head and… froze.

Eton was standing in the middle of the pavement a dozen meters from them, a cigarette dangling from the corner of his mouth, his hand with the lighter in it stopped in midair. His face was a mask of distress.

Lara caught the sudden change in Jack and turned her head, following his gaze. "Eton! Are you looking for us?" She disentangled herself from Jack's arms and took a step away. "We're about to come in. Is there anything left for us in there?"

Eton dropped his gaze the moment she turned around. He took the cigarette out of his mouth slowly and raised his eyes: his usual impassive façade was back in place.

"There's still plenty of booze, if you hurry up," he mumbled. His fingers flexed and the cigarette snapped in two.

Right at that moment Seva and Alex stepped out on the pavement from behind the trees where the iron fence square-angled into the park ground.

"Jack, Lara!" Seva exclaimed, sounding buzzed. "Where the hell have you been? Everybody's been waiting for you!"

"*Privet*, guys," Jack mumbled. "Sorry, we've—"

"We've just arrived," Lara interrupted him and breezed on. "Jack's meeting took longer than anticipated. I was waiting for him forever!" She grasped Jacks arm and pulled him towards the guys. "So, have you been sent out as an honorary escort for us?"

"*Nyet*," Seva laughed. "We were going to have a smoke here. Care to have one with us?" he asked Jack.

"Sure." Jack nodded eagerly.

He fumbled in the front pockets of his jean jacket, pulled out his cigarettes and offered them to the guys, who had huddled in a chummy group—Seva in the middle, his arm around Eton's shoulders, Alex's hand on Seva's shoulder.

Lara waited patiently while the men smoked, never leaving Jack's side. Seva did most of the talking, about the gathering and who was present there, with Jack asking question to keep him going.

It turned out that the *tusovka* was taking place in the wooden building behind the thicket of trees that separated it from the road. A friend of Kino's bandleader, who worked at the factory as a night guard and wrote poetry and lyrics for rock bands, had gotten permission from the administration to hold his "birthday" party on the premises. Most of Leningrad's rock bands, a few bands from Moscow and Ural and their close friends had come; some of them had just arrived, and all of them with booze and snacks. So Jack and Lara hadn't missed anything as the jam session was only starting, now that the rockers had had enough alcohol in them to set them "flying", said Seva laughing.

As they were finishing their smoke, a bleached blond pixie of a girl scuttled out on the sidewalk. "Eton, guys! Come in now! We're starting."

Jack recalled her singing with one of the bands during the festival. The band, Bravo, had stood out from the rest thanks to their sleek, dandyish outfits—jackets, ties and dress shoes—and their music that sounded more rock-n-roll.

The girl came straight up to Eton, giggling, obviously tipsy, and took his hand. Only then she noticed Lara and Jack.

They were introduced and Zhanna immediately declared to the newly arrived that *Krylia* was her new favorite rock band and Eton her favorite singer. She held on to his hand during the conversation and then as they followed the narrow path towards the clubhouse.

She hardly left Eton's side for most of the night, drank as much as he did, whispered in his ear from time to time, leaning into him, her lips occasionally touching the side of his face.

Jack sat on the opposite side of the packed room, across from Eton and the pixie. He was sandwiched between Joanna and Lara, both of whom were getting increasingly drunk as the night progressed. He tried not to look Eton's way, talked to either one of the girls, or to everybody during the breaks when another band was preparing to play. But sometimes he couldn't resist stealing a quick glance at Eton; some other times he felt he was being watched, but Eton dropped his eyes the moment he caught Jack looking his way. His face was more relaxed than when they first came in and he even gifted the pixie with his tight-lip smile occasionally, in response to her whispers.

It was past 1:00 a.m. when Artyom called on Eton and his band. The boys moved up to the front of the tight ring and picked up their guitars. Kostya sat down in front of the only drum they had, and since there was no keyboard, Vadim was given a pair of maracas. They played a fragment from Nuclear Twilight, improvising, Eton droning over the wild guitar riff. Then Joanna demanded his new ballad, so he did that as well. He played it differently, though, his eyes fixed on his fingers as they caressed the guitar strings. He sang quietly and softly the entire time, but everyone could sense the gut-wrenching melancholy underneath his composed delivery.

When the last guitar note died and the clubhouse erupted in cheers, Eton stood up, smiled awkwardly, and said he needed a smoke break. He squeezed through the crowd, which parted just enough to let him through, and walked out of the room.

The gathering took the break as an opening for the next round of vodka. Jack waited five minutes, then stood up and excused himself. Lara rose and said she was going to the ladies too. She was unsteady, so Jack held her arm. In front of the rest rooms she waved at him, said "see you later", giggling, and disappeared behind the door. Jack went into the men's room, quickly washed his hands and walked out, quietly closing the door behind him.

There were three guys smoking on the porch, two of them sitting on the bench against the wall, their legs touching. The third was leaning back against the railing. Jack mumbled he needed a walk and staggered down the steps, faking an unsteady walk. He tottered into the thicket to the left of the house, stopped after a dozen steps and leaned against a tree. When he was sure that nobody was following him, nor watching, Jack slipped behind the tree and stole deeper into the park.

He found his friend at the very end of the park, where the trees receded to a narrow opening in front of a tall brick wall. Eton was leaning against the wall, looking up at the sky, a burning cigarette butt between his fingers. The street lamp at the end of the wall cast a golden glow on his hair and face.

"Here you are." Jack stepped out of the trees and stopped right in front of him. "I was looking for you."

Eton lowered his gaze, stared at him for a long, tense moment, then smirked. "What for?" His tone was sad, not accusing.

Jack sighed, made two steps and leaned against the wall next to Eton, their shoulders touching. "You know what for." He reached for Eton's hand, took the cigarette butt from his fingers and crushed it against the wall. "We need to talk."

"No, we *don't* need to talk." Eton pushed away from the wall. "I know what you're going to say."

"You do."

"Yes."

"You *sure*?" Jack started to lose his cool.

"Very sure."

"Then what is the fucking *matter* with you, Eton May Volkonsky?" he exploded. His frustration at not being able to hold Eton in his arms and say he was so fucking sorry, his desperation at seeing things go from bad to worse no matter how hard he tried to keep everything in balance, and then all the shit he had been weathering lately, all created havoc in his mind. "You *know* that I have to do this! You *know* that I have no choice, if I want to see you. You stupid, reckless shithead!" He took a quick step toward Eton and pushed his shoulders hard.

Eton froze, then lunged at Jack, grabbed him by his shoulders and slammed him into the wall. "Yes, I know I'm stupid," he hissed, his breath reeking of alcohol and cigarettes. "For loving you. But I don't care, you hear? You're mine and *will* be mine, no matter what you do! You bastard!" He crushed his lips against Jack's mouth, pushing himself flat against Jack's body.

It took him forever to react, the exquisite feel of Eton's body against his, the sweet taste of him were so intoxicating they robbed him of all rational thought. But the moment his mind focused, he shoved Eton back. "Are you out of your fucking mind, Eton?! There're people—"

"What's going on here?"

Chapter 49

Lara wobbled out and stopped by a big tree at the edge of the clearing, swaying, peering at them. "You boysss fiiighting?" she slurred.

They gaped at her for what seemed like an eternity. But before either of them could manage a reply, Lara slumped against the tree and sank to the ground. She was completely wasted.

They carried her back to the clubhouse, where Joanna and one other girl took her to the ladies. After a brief discussion with the *Krylia* boys, they agreed that Eton, who along with Seva was staying in the same apartment as Lara, would help Jack bring her there. Seva and the rest of the band would stay at the *tusovka* until it wound down, most likely sometime in the early morning.

Eton went out to find a taxi and returned with a private Lada fifteen minutes later. Jack picked up Lara, who was passed out on the old, smelly couch at the back of the wooden house, and carried her to the car.

Seva, who went to see the three of them off, offered Jack to take his place at the apartment. "Save you a trip back to the hotel," he said, shaking hands with Jack.

"What about you?"

"I'll stay with the guys at Kostya's relatives."

"Alright, thanks. We'll see how it goes."

In ten minutes, they got out in front of an old building on a narrow street near Vytebsky Train Station. Lara was still out cold, so Jack carried her up to the third floor like a big rag doll. While they were climbing the stairs, Eton told Jack in a loud whisper that the owners of the place were old friends of Lara's parents, currently in Bulgaria, and that they had left the keys so that their friends had a place to stay when they visited Leningrad.

The apartment was spacious, with a high ceiling and expensive furniture and fittings. It obviously belonged to a *nomenclatura* family. But unlike Prof. Volkonsky's home, with its well-used antique furniture and paintings, this one reminded Jack of Lara's apartment—expensive wallpaper in beige and gold colors, imported furniture, thick oriental rugs on the floor and walls.

Having toed off their shoes by the door, Eton showed Jack to the room at the end of the wide corridor, opened the door and turned on the light. The spacious master bedroom featured a king-size bed—a rarity given the Soviet Union's standard box-sized apartments—, a ceiling-height wardrobe along one wall, a dressing table and a settee—all brand spanking new.

Jack put Lara down on the bed, carefully peeled the denim jacket and the shoes off her, rolled her on her side and tucked the blanket around her. Eton stood in the doorway watching him, pensive but alert, as if he hadn't been drinking steadily just an hour ago.

Jack came up to him and put a hand on his shoulder. "We need to talk, friend."

"I know." Eton nodded, his expression contrite. "I'm sorry."

Jack pushed him gently out of the doorway, turned off the light and closed the bedroom door behind him.

"Can we smoke in the kitchen?"

"Yes."

In the kitchen, as Eton opened the top section of the large window, Jack pulled out his cigarettes, lit one and offered it to his friend. Eton inhaled it deeply and returned it to him. They parked themselves at the windowsill, blowing smoke out of the opened window.

"It's about Lara."

"Jack, don't worry about Lara. She won't remember anything in the morning."

"How do you know she won't?"

"It's not the first time." Seeing an air of doubt on Jack's face, he explained, "When she gets too drunk, she just passes out and then doesn't remember what happened the night before. Don't worry, okay?"

Jack studied his face for a second, then nodded. "Alright, if you say so. But that's not what I wanted to tell you about Lara."

"No? Then what?" Eton frowned.

Jack pulled on his cigarette and blew a smoke ring. "Someone has suggested to Lara that I might be gay." He kept his tone light, not wanting to freak Eton out.

"*What*?! Who?"

"You friend Karelin."

"He's *not* my friend... But why did he say that? How do you know?"

"Lara told me. Apparently, he said that when Lara tried to make him jealous by saying she was going to marry me."

"She tried to make Karelin jealous?? But he is gay. She knows that. Everybody knows... Why did she tell you all this?" He squinted at Jack suspiciously.

Jack sighed. He wished he had had more time to figure out about how to best put this bizarre story across to Eton. "I noticed that she'd been down these last two days, so I asked her about it. She said that a friend of hers was having trouble with authorities. When I pressed her for details, she admitted it was Karelin. The way she talked about him, I figured she cared for him." Seeing a blank look on Eton's face, he explained, "She's in love with him."

"She is *what*??" Eton stared at him like he'd suddenly grown horns. "She told you *that*, too?"

"Well, not *exactly* that. But she didn't deny it when I asked her if she loved him... Anyway, apparently she tried to provoke Karelin by saying that she'd marry me. And he responded that she'd be making a big mistake as I might be gay."

Eton studied his face, gnawing on his lip, understanding slowly dawning on his face. "When I saw you two on the street... You were trying, um, to prove they were wrong about you... Right?"

Jack smirked sadly. "Not that I had much choice." He looked sadly at the burnt out cigarette in his hand, crushed it against the top of the cigarette pack and stuck the butt back in it.

Eton seized his hand and pressed it to his stomach. "Forgive me," he whispered.

"That's alright." Jack squeezed his hand briefly, let go of it and detached himself from the windowsill. "Let's go to the sitting room." It was dark outside and he didn't want to stand for too long in the illuminated window.

In the guestroom, as Eton reached to turn on the light, Jack caught his hand, and pulled him into his arms. Eton yielded to his embrace eagerly, closing his arms around Jack's waist, and pressing his face into the side of Jack's neck.

"Jaaack," he sighed.

They stood holding each other for a long time, and Jack thought that if it was all they could share today, that was enough too.

"You don't seem too worried about what Karelin said about me," he said finally, nuzzling Eton's neck.

"I *am* worried," Eton leaned back to look into his eyes. "But not too much... Sometimes he, um, goes after regular, after straight guys, too."

"He does? I noticed how he looked at *you*."

Jack's serious tone seemed to disturbed Eton. He fidgeted. "Don't pay attention to him. He does that to many people."

"I'll break his arms if he tries anything with you," Jack said through gritted teeth, yanking Eton back into a tight embrace.

"Don't worry. I'll break his arms before you," Eton mumbled into Jack's neck, an echo of a smile in his voice, then rubbed his lips against Jack's two-day old stubble. "Hmmm... I like this." He ground his groin against Jack, setting off fireworks in Jack's stomach.

Jack distanced his rapidly growing erection away from Eton's crotch. "We can't, bud. Not here... I'm sorry."

Eton gazed into his eyes, smiled sadly and nodded. Jack kissed him quickly on the lips and let go of him. Eton leaned against the wall near the door, hand stuck in the pockets of his jeans.

"So, what're we gonna do about Karelin?" Jack asked. "I need your help with this. You know him better than me."

"We don't need to do anything."

"We don't? But he told Lara. He can tell anyone."

"I don't believe he'll tell anyone else. Maybe he just wanted her to be careful with, um, foreigners... Or maybe he was jealous indeed." Seeing a quizzical look on Jack's face, he explained, "He's very protective of Lara. Otherwise, he usually minds his own business."

"He told me all about *you* on the very first day we met," Jack pointed out. "That you were a very talented person and could do anything you wanted, if you put your mind to it."

"I mean he won't say anything that can harm another person."

"Why are you defending him?"

"I'm not defending him. I'm just telling you what everybody knows. Karelin will never report on any one, Jack. That's why he's having problems with authorities."

"And what if they break him?" Jack was fully aware that there was nothing they could do about it. He just didn't like Eton standing up for the scrawny director, even if the man was a saint.

"Very unlikely. They haven't been able to do it since he was a student." Eton pushed off the wall, came up close and put his arms around Jack's waist. "Jack, you don't need to worry about Karelin. Or about me..." He covered Jack's lips with his for a second. "With anyone... And you're right: you should make sure Lara doesn't have any, um, *wrong ideas* about you."

Jack closed his eyes and leaned his forehead against Eton's. "I'm sorry."

"You have no choice, right? And I promise not to kiss you when there are people around anymore. But please let me do it now... Jack?"

His voice was full of such longing that Jack's guts melted into one big aching knot. He opened his eyes and let out a resigned chuckle. "Christ, Eton! What should I do with you, huh? You'll be the death of me one day."

"I told you. I'll die with you," Eton whispered against Jack's lips, then grabbed his head and kissed him hard and long.

It was more than Jack's resolve could stand. As if his hands had a mind of their own, they slipped down Eton's back, pressing the lean hard body to his groin. They groaned in unison as Eton began to grind against him.

With great effort, Jack eased Eton's hips away from him. "Not here, Etahnn," he gasped, trying to catch his breath.

Eton opened his eyes, his expression dazed, and desperate. "*Please*, Jack..."

"Bathroom," Jack whispered and pushed him gently toward the door.

"Oh... *Yes!*"

Once the bathroom door was locked, Jack turned on the tap over the sink to let the water running and quickly undid his belt. Eton got the idea instantly, started pulling his jersey off.

Jack caught him by his arm. "This has to be real quick, okay?"

"Right."

"Alright, then lose these." He tugged at the band of Eton's jeans.

Eton didn't waste any more time: he unzipped and pushed his jeans down, letting his fully erect cock spring free, then swiftly peeled off his undershirt and socks.

Jack stripped his clothes off in less than thirty seconds, dropped them all on the tile floor next to Eton's and climbed into the big cast-iron bathtub.

"Get in here." He held his other hand out for Eton.

Eton didn't need a second invitation. He sat down in between Jack's legs, circling his own around Jack's waist and closed his fingers around Jack's shaft.

"Lemme." He pushed down slowly.

"Wait!" Jack gasped and seized his wrist. "Not like this."

He shunted forward until their crotches touched, slicked Eton's palms with saliva, and wrapped them around both of them. Eton whimpered and closed his eyes. Jack put his hands over Eton's and began to pump. He tried to keep it slow, but soon Eton was going full throttle, plowing through and sending them over the edge into searing, blinding pleasure.

"Oh God... Jack..." Eton groaned and leaned forward, burying his face into the curve between Jack's neck and his shoulder.

Jack pressed his lips into his lover's shoulder for a moment and let out a long, contented sigh. "Know what?" he whispered through a smile. "I couldn't get back here fast enough... Read *every* news article about Russia in *every* fucking newspaper I could lay my hands on... " He tittered. "So how have you been, Eton?"

When Jack got to his hotel at half past five in the morning, having walked the whole way back, he undressed and quickly climbed into the narrow bed. With Eton's scent still on his skin, he just wanted to cocoon in his little secret world to revel in the memory of the fleeting moments of joy they had shared, drawing out for as long as he could the giddiness he still felt from Eton's touches. It felt like home again.

* * *

June 2, Monday. 23:50p.m.

Dear Jack,

You don't know how much it meant to me that you came to see me performing. The special prize we received for our Nuclear Twilight cannot compare to it. Your presence was my Grand Prix. Especially for the song I wrote and sang to you, in English. I am glad everybody liked it too. Joanna said she wants both pieces recorded for the next Soviet rock album she is planning to produce in Am. next year. Never thought my music was going to be played in America. I wish I could tell Mother and Grandpa about it. Maybe I will.

Jack, the truth is that I am more worried about what Karelin told Lara than I let you see. But I couldn't see, still don't, what could be done about it. All I could think of doing was to try and put your mind at ease about Karelin. I have no idea why he said that to Lara. He is usually careful about what he says in order not to harm others.

So I guess what you are doing with Lara is the best thing that can be done in this situation. I hate to think about it, but you are right. As always. I am sorry for nearly screwing it up again. Don't even know why you want to be with someone so stupid and reckless. Yet, you let this stupid reckless me love you. I am grateful for it, Jack. And I will do my best to be careful. I promise.

Yours always,

E.

June 6, Friday. 10:35 p.m.

Dear Jack,

They have just announced on Vremya that America carried out another nuclear test in Nevada. This is the 5th one this year. They also said that 2 days ago 149 people had been arrested and charged for holding a demonstration against nuclear tests there.

I don't understand it, Jack. I truly don't: with all the devastation and death that happened in Ch. and your Gov. still carries on with the arms race. I'm sure they know all about it in America. I know our authorities don't give us all information about what is going on, but at least they have stopped all nuclear tests. We are all humans, aren't we? How can we do this? How can we let this happen? I don't know what to say.

E.

P.S. Grandpa has returned from Ch. this morning. He will stay in the hospital for a few days for the tests. Mother and I are going to visit him tomorrow morning. I'll call you in the evening. Maybe we can meet up over the weekend somewhere. Maybe my place? I need to see you, Jack.

Your friend,

E.

June 7, Saturday. 10pm.

I didn't have time the last few weeks to keep the Ch. diary. Just finished cutting out news clips. Hope to talk to Grandpa about it when he gets back home. Here's some key news in the press:

• May 19: Pravda carried an article in which they virtually admitted that it had been a mistake to withhold the information from public for 3 days after the explosion. Amazing! Is this the effects of "glasnost"? I sincerely hope so.

• May 20: 13 deaths reported + 300 hospitalized with severe radiation sickness. Germany's Chancellor Helmut Kohl was reported to have asked the SU to pay compensation for the accident. Is he serious??

• May 27: 19 deaths, 35 in critical conditions, 300 with "significant" radiation exposure. They report about what happens on the territory of Ukraine only. What about Belorussia?

• May 30: the concert for Ch. victims at Olympics Stadium. Biggest rock bands turn out, incl. "unofficial" and "semi-official" ones. Krylia participated with Nuclear Twilight. Artyom said around 150,000 rubles was collected from the ticket sales only. The TV plans to produce and sell the records too.

• June 2: first mention of evacuation in Belarus (in Pravda), Gomel is mentioned but not the number of people. They talk about isolated "dirty spots" - radiation contaminated places beyond the 30km radius in Belorussia. Of course: if they detected increased levels radiation in Sweden and Radio Lib. says Poland and Germany have reported it too, how can Belorussia escape it?

• June 4: 60,000 children have been evacuated in Belorussia reported Pravda. No location mentioned.

• June 6: 20,000 more evacuated in Belorussia. It has been 42 days and they have only started evacuating people now?? 26 deaths, 10 in critical conditions, God knows how many still in hospitals. Grandfather returned from Ch. He is dead tired, aged 10 years. They have put him in the Kremlin hospital for checkups and "observation".

Grandpa said the report on what really happened will be made public. Really? I will believe when I see it.

June 9, Monday. 11am.

Dear Jack,

Just got back and have put your Eagles disk on. It is playing Hotel California now. Can't believe you still remember me singing it for you the first time we met. I think you also remember me saying once that I want to visit your ranch in Am. one day. This is what the cowboy hat means, right? You didn't say so, but I think I know. Thank you so much again, cowboy. They are the best presents I have ever got from anyone. Because they mean so much to me. I ~~hope~~ know they mean something to you, too.

Jack, I KNEW you would understand me when I told you that I want to continue my studies and take some extra courses. But you also understood that it means I'll never come visit you in Am. I know you did: you held me for a long time so that I couldn't see your face, and when you let me go your eyelashes were damp. I pretended not to notice. But I confess: it took me all my will not to cry, right then, in your arms. God, Jack, I know I'll miss you so much when you are gone that it tears my heart to pieces now, when you are still in my arms. I don't know how I will go on. Just know that I have to.

I am a heartless bastard, but I was glad that Grandpa was still in the hospital and Mother left to visit her sick friend when you came: I had you for myself for an hour. You would laugh if you knew, but I have brought the sheets and the pillowcase we slept on back to my place. They are on my bed here now. I will sleep in your arms tonight. I love you, my blue cornflower.
E.

June 13, Friday. Midnight.

Dear Jack,

I talked to Grandpa today. Asked his advice about extra courses I should take. He asked what I want to do when I finish my studies. I said "something useful". What else could I say? I don't know what I want to do, but I also could not say that I want to be a rock musician. Because it is not considered useful here.

Remember Pasha, the guy who let us organize the tusovka at the factory clubhouse in Leningrad? He is a microbiologist, but he wants to write poetry. He is a talented poet and lyricist. But because he didn't study literature, he can't find a job as a poet or writer. Also because he writes "unacceptable" poetry. So now he works as a night guard at the factory and writes lyrics for his rocker friends. They are the only ones who think highly of him. The rest think he is good for nothing.

Back to me. After talking to Grandpa, I have decided I will take computational mathematics, electronics and radio-physics. Maybe even join Gosha and Anya in their classes at the Math. Faculty. I will start reading up textbooks next week in preparation for the new academic year.

So. This means that I will have to tell my guys that I can't play with them as often as we agreed earlier. Before Chernobyl. They will be disappointed, esp. after the special prize we received in Leningrad. But I can't tell them why I am doing this. They will not understand. They will think that I am a stupid idealist. Maybe they are right.

I suspect you and Grandpa are and will be the only people who understand me in this. Maybe Mother will too when I tell her. But she and Grandpa will always stand by me, even when they don't understand me. They are my family. This is what we do in our family.

Jack, I hope you know that you can ALWAYS rely on me. I will do anything for you. As if you were my family. I wish I were your family. I don't know how, but this is just who you are to me: the brother, the best friend and ~~a lover~~ the beloved, all in one.

Is there such a thing? Like "husband and wife" but for 2 guys?

What is wrong about me loving you, anyway? You make me better. You make me feel special. You make me feel like I can do anything.

I love you.

E.

Chapter 50

The first week of June saw the culmination of another spy case, in which the score went to Americans: A Baltimore court handed down three life sentences to Ronald W. Pelton, a former NSA communications specialist, for passing secrets to the KGB. Pelton was one of the two spies reportedly sold to the CIA by Vitaly Yurchenko. The second mole, and defector, Edward Lee Howard, remained at large.

The Pelton trial was soon overshadowed by the Reagan administration's revelation that it intended to abandon the Strategic Arms Limitation Treaty, SALT 2, and to proceed with the "Star Wars" initiatives. The Soviet government immediately issued a warning that such a decision would effectively kill any plans for the summit between Reagan and Gorbachev, provisionally scheduled for later in the year.

That and the struggle to clean up Chernobyl, now reported on by the Soviet press with fatalistic regularity, were the subjects that dominated conversations at Uncle Sam's in June.

At night, different thoughts inundated Jack. They had emerged since the day Eton told him about his plans to continue his studies because he wanted "to do something useful for my people". Jack immediately understood why: Chernobyl. By now, he had learned enough about Russians to know that under their artless, bordering on boorish veneer and manners, they hid their guileless, idealistic hearts.

His friend's plans had given rise to an unsettling question: what did *he* want to do in his life? For some reason, his old dreams and plans didn't seem that motivating anymore—what, a small ranch in California, a horse and cow operation, a little wife and a couple of children, maybe? Everything that represented a regular American dream. Of course, it was alright to have a dream, but Jack couldn't remember the last time he had thought of doing something truly useful for *his* people?

He recalled the early days with the Company when they had tried to impress upon new recruits similarly idealistic ideas. "You're here to fight evil, to protect America and American people." He had believed them and tried to live by them at first. But that belief had gradually been eroded by things Jack learned, first at HQ, then in Moscow. How, for instance, was he supposed to "protect American people" with his "special" assignment to compromise one Eton May Volkonsky and then recruit him to work for the Company and the NSA? Eton, whose secret dream was to become the next Bon Jovi? And why? Just because some big shot at the NSA was still sore about his father's defection over twenty years ago? How was *that* going to protect American people?

On top of that, the image of the evil enemy the Company had tried to ingrain in them hadn't stuck. Even Jack's KGB shadows didn't seem as sinister as they were supposed to be—they were just doing their job, one that wasn't too different from his own. Or not. Their job might be even nobler: they were protecting *their* people from the likes of Jack with his snooping, snitching, and conniving. It felt more and more like a pointless, never-ending game and he was getting weary of playing it.

But then what other choice did he have? Especially now, when his friend had gotten into his stubborn, idealistic head that he had to do something useful for his people. Which meant that the chances of Eton agreeing to leave this country one day suddenly went from "possible" to "highly unlikely", or even "definitely not happening". So what was *he* supposed to do now, except to continue playing this senseless game that he had so stupidly let Joe drag him into?

Topping it all was the incident with Lara and Karelin's insinuation that Jack could be gay. After Leningrad, Jack spent a week deliberating whether he should send a code red alert to Joe Coburn. He figured he would be summoned for a debriefing again, and he was simply not ready for that. In the end, he resolved to wait for further development—after all, Joe Coburn & Co wanted him to be recruited by the Sovs along *these* lines, didn't they?

He called Lara twice to ask her out. She apologized both times, saying she had other arrangements. She sounded tired, like in Leningrad. Then one day, she called Jack herself. Only to tell him that she was leaving Moscow for 2 months and he mustn't think she was avoiding him.

Then, there was yet another complication: Stella. Apparently, she had not wasted her time during Jack's trip to America and as a result was now engaged to a car dealer from Atlanta whom she had met at Hotel Intourist's bar. She invited Jack over to her place "for old time's sake", but he refused, pretending to be all hurt and pissy, and then stayed away from to her until she left for America a month later.

But it meant that he needed to look for another official date. Lara was no good because she was Russian. Strictly speaking, they weren't even supposed to socialize with locals, let alone date them. And so Jack's thoughts drifted to Savannah. And to Joe's insistence that he should marry someone from the ops, or at least from the Agency. Now Jack understood why. In his circumstances, it was convenient; it was easy; it was just about doing their jobs, with no complications about having to build a true relationship.

He understood then that Joe had probably tried to give him a chance with Florence Neumann. It hadn't worked: there hadn't been even a hint of chemistry between them. It was different with Savannah, however: she was easy to be with, and Jack actually liked her. In a way, she reminded him of Lara—lighthearted and girly, with a similar hidden strength that one could only glimpse when she was under pressure. And she seemed to like him, too.

Alright, so maybe Savannah it was. Maybe he would tell Joe about it at their next op briefing. It would give him time to get accustomed to the idea before his next holiday home when he would see her again and start dating her. Then maybe another year before they got married. By that time, he would be out of Moscow. Out of Eton's life in Moscow. It was just something he had to do, somewhere else, not in Moscow, and his friend didn't need to know about it.

That night he got drunk and stayed overnight at the marines' quarters. Grant was on duty and let Jack sleep it off on his bunk bed.

As Jack was leaving in the early hours of the morning, he passed by the TV room. The door was ajar, and he caught a glimpse of a woman on the sofa. She ducked down quickly, hiding behind the settee's back, but Jack thought he recognized the girl. She was one of the junior staff in the visa section and had an unusual name for a Russian: Viola. He recalled having seen her chatting and flirting with the marines a few times, which by itself wasn't allowed. Her presence in the marines' quarters now was a major security breach.

Jack turned to the restroom, instead of the stairs. He needed a moment to think what he should do about the girl.

Grant was washing his hands at the sink. He turned to Jack as he walked in, his face startled. "Hey, Jack. Got up already?"

"Grant... Thanks for letting me crash on your bed."

"Anytime, man." The marine turned off the water and walked over to the towel rack near the door.

Jack went to the sink Grant had just used, put his hand on the tap handle, but didn't turn the water on. "Listen, it's none of my business of course, but the girl in the TV room —"

"Don't worry, man. We're leaving now." Grant's smile was as forced as his reassurances. "She just, eh, needed to use the bathroom." His face turned red when he saw Jack's arched eyebrows and he was suddenly in a hurry. "We're out of here. See you later, Jack." When he was one foot through the door, he stopped and looked at Jack over his shoulder. "Jack, you won't tell anyone, will you?"

Jack splashed some cold water on his face and mumbled into the sink, "Just get her out of here." He raised his eyes to give Grant a hard stare. "You're in *big* trouble, Grant, if anyone learns you hang out with the Sovs."

"Why always me?! Others —"

"Stop right there!" Jack snapped up and raised a hand. "I don't want to know it, alright? Just go, man... Just go."

The marine opened his mouth to object, then changed his mind, turned around and walked out, closing the door quietly behind him.

Jack agonized over the incident for two days. He hated to betray a buddy, knowing how restricted the marine guards were, confined to the tiny world of the Embassy. But then, the Embassy's security was part of his Agency's job, too and so it was his job to report on any breach he witnessed, or even suspected, to the security office.

In the end, he resolved to write a detailed report to Nurimbekoff. He figured that if the Station chief decided to notify the regional security officer about the incident, he would most probably withhold Jack's and Grant's names from his account in order to protect Jack's cover. The only name that would be revealed would probably be the girl's, and if they found out that something was going on between her and Grant, well, then there was nothing much Jack could do about it.

* * *

In May, Jack was assigned a new project by the USIA. Turner Broadcasting System was producing a 7-hour documentary about the Soviet Union as part of a series called "Portrait of the World" and some of it was planned to be shot on location. Jack was tasked with looking after the WTBS producer and his crew while they were working in the country.

As soon as his new project commenced, Jack got himself involved into a side project, the first Goodwill Games, a pet project of WTBS' owner, Ted Turner. The media mogul had dreamed it up as a response to the boycotting of the recent Olympic Games by countries on both sides of the Cold War divide. Because of his involvement with WTBS, Jack found himself sorting out local bureaucratic procedures for Ted, and sometimes for his wife Jane and their two children, during the games in Moscow.

One quirk about Turner that struck a chord with Jack was his obsession with the possibility of a nuclear war between the Soviet Union and America. One couldn't talk to him for more than five minutes without the topic coming up. And after two glasses of wine he would start talking about universal love.

"I love all people over the world," he would say. "And we better all start loving each other or we're going to blow each other to kingdom come." Once he turned to Jack. "Say, Jack, you have a Russian girlfriend? No? You should find one. What is there not to love about them? They are gorgeous, all of them. Don't you think?" Ted slapped him on the back. "Let's have this toast for love... 'Member what the Eagles sang? Love will keep us alive. Clever bastards!"

The day after the closing of the Games Turner invited a bizarre combination of guests on a boat tour along Moskva River. The group included American sportsmen, Soviet bureaucrats and journalists of various stripes.

Toward the end of the three-hour ride, Jack and Mike Demidoff wandered away from the crowd of journalists surrounding the tipsy media magnate. They sat down on the bench at the far end of the white river-cruise ship and nursed their bottles of Heineken, enjoying the sun and cool breeze. They chatted idly about the Games, then about the latest on Chernobyl. Jack told Mike about the international conference on Chernobyl to be held in Vienna in August, about which he had heard from the Embassy's environmental office.

Mike listened to him distractedly and gave him an odd look when Jack excused himself, promising to be back with fresh drinks. When he returned with two cold beers, the older man mumbled his thanks, peering at him thoughtfully. "Aren't you driving today?"

Jack grinned sheepishly. "It's just the second one. Then no more."

Mike threw a quick glance over his shoulder and took a big gulp from his bottle. "I'm thinking of asking you a favor, Jack."

"Sure, Mike. Fire away. You want me to get you more information on Chernobyl?" Jack lowered his voice conspiratorially. "I may even be able to get a firsthand account."

"That would be great... But that's not what I meant."

"No? What then?"

"I'd like to ask you to pass a small package to Don Steward."

"To Don?" Jack looked at him in surprise.

"Yes... Do you mind?"

"Not at all!" Jack shrugged demonstratively, his mind on full alert. "Will it be alright if I give it to him on Monday? Don't suppose he works weekend. Unless there's an emergency."

"That will be fine. I appreciate it, Jack." He hesitated. "Would you mind terribly coming by my office after this to pick up the package? It's just a ten minute drive from the pier."

He gave Jack an imploring half-smile.

"Alright." Jack nodded, eyeing the journalist expectantly. Surely, he didn't expect Jack to do him the favor without explaining what it was all about?

Mike took another big swig from his bottle. "Please keep it between us, okay?"

"Sure, Mike."

"I found this package on my desk yesterday," he said in half whisper, even though there wasn't a soul near them. "A note was stuck to it, saying 'For the attention of competent parties. Please pass on. Thank you.'"

"You mean you don't know who left it?"

"No idea. You know our office. It's like an open house. Especially on crazy days like this." He pointed at the crowd around Turner. "People just come and go. Our secretaries can't keep up with all the visitors."

Jack didn't buy Mike's story, but nodded nonetheless. "I see... So, have you opened it?"

"No! I don't want to know. And I'd rather not take it to the Embassy myself. Just in case... You know what I mean?"

"I think so... So you want *me* to give it to Don. What should I tell him?"

"Tell him I'll come see him Monday afternoon... Say, do you know Marat Nurimbekoff?" Mike asked suddenly. "Isn't he a counselor on regional affairs or something?"

Jack frowned, as if in concentration. "From the political section? I heard he's a specialist on Afghanistan. I talked to him a couple of times, but don't know him very well. Why?"

"I remember William mentioning that the man was interested in *unconventional* sources of information. Thought you might know him, too."

Mike was bullshitting again: there was no way William would discuss Chief of Moscow Station with anyone who didn't know who Nurimbekoff truly was.

"No, I don't. William never mentioned anything about him to me. I'd probably know him better had he hung out at Uncle Sam's or at the Marine's Bar." He snickered, then continued in loud whisper, "Say, Mike, is this the first time this kinda thing's happened to you? It's like a spy movie!"

"Yes. First time," Mike said quickly. Too quickly.

Right then the Los Angeles Times' resident correspondent rolled up to them and the conversation circled back to the international conference on Chernobyl in Vienna.

After the boat trip, Jack drove them to Mike's place. He left twenty minutes later with a large, brown envelope under his jacket, with something in it that felt like a soft-cover notebook. At the Embassy, he called Nurimbekoff from the public phone at Uncle Sam's. Half an hour later, he was in the Tank which had been re-constructed from parts flown in with a special cargo from the States, relaying the strange conversation with Mike Demidoff to the COS, the envelope on the conference table between them.

Nurimbekoff instructed Jack to lock the envelope in his drawer for now and take it to Don the first thing on Monday. "It'll come to us," the COS said, seeing Jack's surprised expression. He explained that this was the second occasion Mike had passed a package from some mysterious volunteer. The first time he had given it to William.

He let Jack go shortly after, having instructed him to stay away from the reporter.

After the boat trip, Jack's shadowing had intensified. The truth was, it had become quite systematic since he started his work with the WTBS team and then with Ted Turner and his entourage. So much so that for two months after Leningrad, he only managed to catch up with Eton twice: first when he brought his American presents to Prof. Volkonsky's house, then at Eton's place, on the last day of the World Cup finals in Mexico—the Moscow streets were virtually empty and he was surveillance free for the whole day. But after the incident with Mike, the shadowing became more comprehensive than ever before. Jack noted it in his reports to the COS, but otherwise, there really wasn't much he could do about it.

On the first Sunday of August, Jack returned to Moscow on the last flight from Volgograd where he'd spent three days herding the WTBS' production crew. As he was opening the door of his apartment, he heard the phone going off and his heart skipped a beat.

Eton!

It had been over a month since they had last talked. He kicked the door closed, dropped his duffel bag in the corridor and stormed into the sitting room. He took a deep breath, trying to control his heart and his smile, before answering, "Hello?"

"Hi, Jack. This is Joanna. Sorry for calling late." She let out a short, throaty laugh, sounding like she had a serious amount of alcohol in her.

Jack brushed away a flash of disappointment. "Oh. Hi, Joanna. That's alright. What are you doing in Moscow? Another festival?"

"Ah, no. For *pominki*. And for a wedding. Sometime soon. Hopefully." She chortled again. "Jack, can you help with your consular people please? They're so fucking unhelpful! 'Scuse the French. Oh, get away, Yura!" She bitched at someone in Russian, keeping the phone away from her face. "I talk to Jack here. You want him help us or not?… Sorry, Jack. Where were we? Oh, right, can we meet tomorrow? Please!"

It didn't seem wise to talk to Joanna right then—he risked getting stuck on the phone for half an hour. "Alright. Let's have lunch tomorrow. Where do you want to meet?"

They agreed to meet at noon the next day at a cafeteria at the beginning of Kalinin Avenue and Jack hung up. Had she said *pominki*, the wake that the Russians usually held on the third, ninth and fortieth days after the burial? He wondered who had died.

He spotted her the moment he walked into the self-service cafeteria. Joanna was at a table in the far corner, facing the door, along with a dark-haired man, young, as far as Jack could tell from his back. She was telling him something in a hushed tone, a besotted look on her glowing face. She saw Jack and waved at him.

"Hey, Jack. Thanks a bunch for coming to see us," she said in English as Jack came up their table, then switched to Russian. "You know Yura?" Her American accent was thick, and she sounded tipsy again.

"I do. You play guitar for Kino, don't you?"

He shook hands with Yura. The young man nodded and mumbled his greetings. He looked a little flushed too, and Jack caught a whiff of alcohol fumes. He sat down next to Joanna.

"So what can I do for you?"

"Let's go get some food first. We haven't had breakfast this morning," she said and sprung up from her chair.

Jack followed Joanna while Yura guarded their table. When they returned with trays full of typical Soviet lunch—fresh cabbage salad, *rassolnik* soup, stewed beef with mashed potatoes and dry fruits *kompot* drink—the rocker pair quickly devoured their salads and soups, and only then did Joanna put her spoon down and tell Jack what she wanted him to help with.

It turned out that she and Yura were in love and had decided to get married, but the consular section at the American Embassy was being pigheaded about her papers. Or rather about the lack of certain ones. Joanna croaked a laugh when Jack's gaze traveled from her to Yura, his eyes round with surprise.

"Yeah, I know, everybody thinks that I'm with Boris. Or with Artyom. But no, we're just very good friends. Yura is my Russian love." She reached over the table for the young man's hand.

Yura squeezed her fingers and quickly withdrew his hand, hiding them under the table. He looked embarrassed.

They discussed the consular section's requirements for a while, mostly Joanna bitching about her difficulties. She was afraid she wouldn't be able to get another Soviet visa if she went home for the useless papers that the stupid bureaucrats at the Embassy wanted. Her Russian love, who didn't speak English, chewed on his food silently, looking bored.

When they finished their lunch and Joanna had exhausted her topic, Jack took advantage of a momentary lull in the conversation and asked casually, "So, who's died?"

"Excuse me?"

"You said yesterday that you were here for a wedding and a wake."

"Ah, yes… It's a, uh, a friend, I guess. I met him a few times, but he was a good friend of Artyom's and Yura's band's. A theater director. Very talented, but quite a… an oddity in this country, I'd say." She dropped her voice to loud whisper. "He was openly gay."

No fucking way!

"Viktor Karelin?"

"You know him?" Now she stared at him in surprise.

"A little. He was a friend of Amanda's." And Lara's. And Eton's. No, not Eton's. "So, what happened? I saw him recently and thought he was fine."

"Reportedly a heart attack. But who knows? They say he collapsed and died right on the street near his house."

…

"Troubles… with authorities," Lara said reluctantly.

"With authorities? You mean with militsia?"

"With them, too… He's stubborn like a mule!… Everything has to be, um, the way he thinks is right. Or true. Even if it's detrimental to him."

…

- 372 -

"When was it?"

Did Lara know? That would break her heart. Poor girl…

"Ten days ago. Yesterday was the ninth day wake at the studio he ran."

"Was Lara there?"

"Lara? No, she wasn't… I heard she was his favorite. *Da*, Yura?" She smiled at her fiancé and reached for his hand over the table.

"*Shto?*" He smiled at her self-consciously, asking what she meant, and pulled his hand back.

"Lara was Karelin's favorite, *da*?" Joanna repeated in Russian.

"*Da*." Yura nodded. "She actually helped him quite a lot, with her connections. More than any other of his friends could. Because of her standing, you know."

"I know." Jack nodded thoughtfully. "She's a good friend… So, are you guys planning to move to America after your marriage?"

They talked about Joanna and Yura's plans for a while, then it was two o'clock, time for Jack to return to work. He promised to help the couple as much as he could and left.

In the evening, he stopped on the way home and called Lara from a *taxaphone*. Nobody answered. He replaced the receiver, then picked it up again and dialed Eton's number.

After three tones, the familiar baritone murmured in his ear, "Sorry, I'm away on construction work. I will be back the last week of August and will call you right away if you leave me a message. *Poka*."

Jack hung up, feeling like a piece of shit. The message had been left for him, of course. Because now he knew that regardless of what he did, or didn't do, Eton would do anything he could to make sure that Jack didn't have to worry about him.

Jack picked the handset up again and redialed the number he knew he wouldn't likely forget anytime soon. He waited till the end of Eton's message, then pitched his voice low, and said with a soft smile, as if Eton could see him, "*Privet*, it's me. Sorry, friend, I couldn't call earlier. It was *inconvenient*. I'll call again when you get back and we'll catch up… Somewhere. Alright?… Alright, I'll call later." He felt he had to say something else, something less impassive, something that would let Eton know that he cared. But he hesitated for too long and the tape on Eton's answering machine ran out, leaving him with jarring busy tone. He glared at the handset, then slammed it back on its hook. "Now, you take care of yourself, bud, you hear?" he whispered fiercely at the heavy, gray telephone set. "It means so fucking much to me!"

Chapter 51

On Thursday morning, Jack arrived at work twenty minutes late. He had been doing it frequently lately—a fine touch to his cover that Nurimbekoff approved before leaving home for vacation. July and August were slow months when more than half of the Embassy was on vacation. So were Glenn and Tim Lockwood, who replaced William as the Senior Cultural Affairs Officer, and Todd had returned to pursue his master's at home. As a result, Jack was enjoying his privacy in the cramped little office, which he had been sharing with Glenn and Todd since February.

He sat a big cappuccino from Uncle Sam's on the desk, made himself comfortable, and started with his first tasks of the day: scanning local newspapers for news that could be of interest to either of his lines of work. As a rule, he browsed through them in a particular order: *Pravda*, the mouthpiece of the Central Committee of the CPSU, then *Izvestia*, which conveyed the views of the Government, then *Moskovskaya Pravda* of the Moscow city authorities, then *Komsomolskaya Pravda* of the Soviet Youth, *Krasnaya Zvezda* of the Soviet armed forces, *Trud* of the Soviet Trade Unions and so on. He always saved for last the one he actually read—*Literaturnaya Gazetta*, a weekly cultural and political newspaper known to push the limits of permissible views and commentary.

Jack was about to toss the copy of *Izvestia* aside when the headline on a short article on the back page caught his eye. "Asylum Granted to American Citizen."

It was a TASS announcement about Edward Lee Howard's defection to the Soviet Union and his request for asylum. "Guided by humanitarian considerations", the Presidium of the Supreme Soviet, had granted Howard's request, the paper said. The article described him as a U.S. citizen and a former CIA officer, but didn't mention that he'd been accused of spying in America. Nor did the statement say when Howard had entered the Soviet Union or where he was now.

Jack recalled the rumors circulating at HQ that Howard had fled to South America. That had made his defection slightly less alarming since he was out of touch with his handlers as well. But a trained and read-in case officer, even if he was an ex, in the hands of the KGB for their full-time milking, it was a nightmare in the making. Now that he was in Moscow, Howard's handlers could show him pictures of all staff at the American Embassy — any case officer who hadn't yet been uncovered by the organs now certainly would be. For starters.

Jesus Christ! Now what?

Jack was pretty sure Howard didn't know him—the man had been fired around the time Jack had just begun his training at the Farm—which he couldn't say about other case officers.

After the expulsions of William Osbourne and Mark Morris, there were only five officers left in Moscow, including Jack, and two in Leningrad. And out of the agent network, as far as Jack knew, only two more or less active agents were remaining in the Soviet Union. And Eton, who was expected to be pitched at some point. Jack didn't know if other case officers had any "pre-recruitment material".

Three days later, Jack was summoned to Frankfurt. When he arrived at the hotel, the receptionist who checked him in handed him a message. It was an invitation for breakfast with Mr. Derek Malone at Steigenberger Frankfurter Hof the next day.

The breakfast itself and the subsequent two and a half hour debrief in Joe's hotel room were much less taxing than Jack had braced himself for. The chief of ops' looked tired and seemed preoccupied, most of his questions sounded perfunctory. But occasionally he would latch onto an aspect of the situation they were discussing once again the bulldog that Jack and other case officers knew so well.

Jack told him about the op run in Leningrad, which he had carried out with Lara on his arm, giving his boss the details not included in his post-op report submitted to Nurimbekoff.

Joe smirked appreciatively. "Good job. But try not to pull such tricks again."

Then Jack recounted his conversation with Lara concerning Karelin's implication that he might be gay. Joe didn't interrupt him, let Jack finish, then asked why he hadn't reported the incident immediately. Jack had come prepared for this. He had waited to be pitched after that strange conversation, he explained, ready to enact the original plan, even though it was Lara, not Eton, who had turned out to be with the KGB. But nothing had happened. Then Karelin had died of a heart attack, reportedly due to the constant pressure from the *organs* that he had been subjected to. Again, nobody had approached Jack. So maybe Lara wasn't with the KGB after all.

Joe toyed with his tumbler, swirling the ice cubes in his whiskey for nearly a minute. "Alright. So what are the next steps?" finally he asked.

They agreed that Jack would continue "engaging" with Lara and "give in" to her advances, if opportune. Which meant that Joe hadn't completely bought Jack's arguments that Lara wasn't with the KGB and still hoped that at some point Jack would enter the game as a dangle.

Then Joe briefed him on the Howard case, and then finally it was Eton Volkonsky's turn. Jack reported tersely that his target was now taking additional courses in math and engineering with the aim of joining some research institute after his studies. Joe mumbled "Good" and instructed Jack to hold back for now, until further notice. When Jack asked for clearance to continue "purely social interaction" with his Soviet contacts, Joe hesitated before saying "Fine" and his tone was noncommittal.

When all Jack's assignments had been covered and plans of action agreed, he decided that it might be the right time to broach the topic of Savannah.

"Joe, I think I'm ready for a, um, marriage," he said and nodded when Joe, who was refilling his tumbler, raised the bottle of Glenfiddich to Jack.

"The woman from the Embassy? Didn't you report that you'd split with her?"

It meant that Joe did read all his reports carefully — Jack had only mentioned it briefly, in one short sentence. Why had he even doubted it?

"We did. But it's not her."

"Oh." Joe raised his eyebrows, watching him with interest — Jack hadn't mentioned any new date in his last reports.

"It's someone from the Company... From the Ops."

"All-right."

"She's from the new cohort. We met in May, when I was at HQ... We didn't date or anything, just hung out twice," he explained when Joe continued scrutinizing him—field officers were expected to report about their personal relationships promptly, even on casual ones.

"Yet you're ready to *marry* her?"

"I suppose she needs a husband too. Doesn't she? Well, if she's going to be placed overseas through the State Department... But of course we'll have to date first. When we have a chance."

Joe took a sip from his tumbler. "Are you attempting to delay this *process*? And you think dating her while you're home would give you a sufficient cover to stay single in the field? Now, Jack, that's *not* a sound strategy."

"Well, I don't see how else it can be done, Joe. It's not like she can come to Moscow and move in with me next month. We haven't even dated yet!"

"We'll see what can be done about it. If you're ready, we will sort her out. What's her name?"

Shit, he should have kept his big mouth shut about her moving in with him in Moscow. Now it looked like he was stuck with his own idea.

"Savannah Jones."

"Which division?"

"She was rotating through the Far East desk in May."

"And you're ready to marry her. Love at first sight?" Joe smirked.

Jack didn't like Joe's tone but made an effort to keep it light. "We have good chemistry... I guess."

"Alright. We'll see."

Joe wrapped up the meeting shortly after, with instructions to put all agent development activities on ice for now—at least until things settled down after Howard's defection. When Jack asked how long he thought it would be, Joe shrugged and said that there might be complications. Then he let Jack go, telling him to take the next two days off and enjoy his stay in Frankfurt.

Jack could have called several acquaintances he knew from his Frankfurt posting days, but he didn't feel up to it. He spent three days wandering around the old part of the town, sitting in street cafes, watching people enjoying themselves in the sun, till the city began to light up. Then at night, he hung out at the bars, talking to strangers until late.

On Sunday, Jack arrived at the airport three hours before the flight. He bought a carton of Marlboros in the duty free shop, then at the news stand he picked up a selection of English language newspapers and also magazines that he knew Russians always appreciated. Having bought a coffee, he settled down and commenced browsing through newspapers, looking for Soviet-related news.

He recalled his trip home three months earlier when he had still been telling himself that this compulsive need to read everything about Russia was nothing but business. He'd stopped doing that and now knew that it was more than just work. It was personal.

Today the newspapers were crawling with the sort of news he craved when he was on *this* side of the Iron Curtain.

"Soviets Eager for A Pact: Kremlin Fears Arms Race Would Harm Economy. Washington — With the reopening of the Geneva arms control talks less than a month away, U.S. strategists have concluded that the Kremlin wants to reach an agreement to prevent a costly arms race that could frustrate Soviet leader Mikhail S. Gorbachev's plans for economic reform... 'It appears that Gorbachev has made the domestic economy his top priority,' one official said. 'Economic reform will make such demands on resources that they can ill afford a renewed arms race'..."

Yeah, right. They're probably spending millions on cleaning up after Chernobyl... Here it is...

"Chernobyl Design Flaws Made Accident Worse, Soviet Report Concedes. VIENNA — Human error was the overriding cause of the Chernobyl nuclear accident, but the reactor's design made it a difficult one to manage, according to nuclear safety experts who have read the Soviet Union's government report on the disaster..."

"Reminder of Hiroshima: Japanese Tourists Shun Europe After Chernobyl."

"Thatcher to Visit Moscow."

"FBI Holds Soviet U.N. Employee on Spy Charges."

Goddamn! It was probably the "complications" Joe had mentioned.

Jack quickly turned to the page featuring the full article.

"WASHINGTON — FBI agents arrested a Soviet diplomat working for the United Nations on Saturday as he sought to buy classified documents related to a U.S. Air Force jet engine from a young man on a New York subway platform...

Gennadiy Zakharov has had credentials as a scientific affairs officer assigned to the U.N. Secretariat. Because he has only limited diplomatic immunity, he will be prosecuted to the full extent of U.S. espionage laws... FBI spokesman Lane Bonner said.

... first approached the informant in December 1982... had numerous meetings with the informant and paid him, then a student, thousands of dollars for a wide range of valuable but unclassified data in the areas of computers and artificial intelligence. When the student graduated and got a job with the defense subcontractor... began "encouraging him in obtaining classified national defense documents..."

Jack folded the newspaper carefully, put it on top of the pile on the chair next to him and reached for his pack of Lucky Strikes. He lit a cigarette and made a couple of deep pulls, staring through the thick glass wall at the sunny afternoon outside.

This guy Zakharov had been doing what he was doing, hadn't he? And had been burnt by his contact... Could have been written about him and Eton. Except that he hadn't been encouraging Eton—

Is that right? What about his Grandfather's original work on nuclear winter?

Yeah, but it isn't "classified national defense" material, is it?

How do you know that? Isn't it why neither you nor Eton have been able to find it so far?

Fine! But it's my job, alright?

Alright, so he was an asshole who was trying to do his job, but Eton... Eton wasn't informing on him... Was he?

No, he was *not* going down that road again. He was a hundred and one percent certain that Eton wasn't on the KGB's payroll. And he knew that Eton cared for him. So he said and Jack believed him.

What about you?

What about what?

You know what.

Well, I... He is... There'll be no other one like him. No one. For me...

When Jack arrived at the office on Monday morning, he found a folded yellow sticker note between his pens. It said, "2100 Tank". It meant that Nurimbekoff had a key to their office too. Glenn wasn't due back from his annual leave for another week, so Jack had the office all to himself. He could have taken a week off and gone somewhere. Could have stayed in Frankfurt.

No, he couldn't, because Eton was returning from his construction work this week and Jack had to see him. And Lara too if only to tell her that he was awfully sorry about Karelin.

He was finishing his scanning of the pile of local newspapers from the previous week when his phone rang.

"Jack, there's Miss Plante down here who'd like to talk to you." It was one of the secretaries on the ground floor.

"Thank you, Sveta. Put her on, please."

Amanda? In Moscow? He thought she'd never—

"Hello, Jack. How are you?"

"Amanda! Good gracious God, how *are* you? What are you doing here? I mean when did you get in here?" He didn't need to act up that much, he was truly glad to hear from her.

"Hey, hey, slow down, would you?" She chuckled. "I'm glad to hear you, too. I just got here yesterday. I'm sorting out my papers here at the Embassy and thought I'd give you a call."

"You stay right there, Mandy. Don't go anywhere. I'll be right down."

They spent two hours at Uncle Sam's, having coffee, then lunch, then coffee again, and talking. Amanda was in Moscow to write a feature article for Vanity Fair about three contemporary Russian talents who had been suppressed by the authorities, or forced to create and perform semi-officially—artist Ilya Glazunov, rocker Boris Grebenshchikov and theater director Viktor Karelin. And yes, the main reason for her visit the memorial communion for Karelin on his fortieth day of passing that his friends were organizing. She told Jack that initially the memorial was supposed to be held at Danilovsky Monastery, the first monastery the authorities had allowed to reopen, three years ago. However, the monks had learned about Karelin's "unorthodox background" and refused to hold the service for him. So now, the *pominki* was going to be at playhouse of the Theater Institute, immediately before the showing of Karelin's last play.

It so happened that Mike's posting as the bureau chief of US News and World Report in the Soviet Union was coming to an end too and he was due to head home at the end of September. So Amanda was also here to pick up things she had left behind when she deserted Mike in haste the year before.

"Do you want to come for the play?" Amanda asked after pause in her story. "I don't think it will be staged again. Not anytime soon."

"Why? Something controversial again?"

Amanda snorted. "You tell me. It's a story about an exceptionally talented actress who's been put in a mental institution because she believes she is alternatively Michelangelo, Lord Byron and Tchaikovsky. And thus relives their individual love stories. With men," she concluded under her breath.

"Wow! And let me guess: Lara Novikova is playing this brilliant mental case... She said she was rehearsing for Karelin's latest play, but never mentioned what it was about."

"Are you still seeing her?"

"Well, to the extent possible for a foreign diplomat to see a local in this country." Jack shrugged.

"That's such bullshit, Jack! It has never been a stopper for those who are truly in love. Even for diplomats. You just aren't that interested, are you?... Alright, alright." She reached across the table and patted his hand when Jack tried to object. "It's none of my business, I know."

They agreed to meet up for lunch, or dinner, or drinks over the weekend and arrange to go to Karelin's event then.

In the evening, his meeting with Nurimbekoff in the Tank was brief. The COS more or less repeated Joe Coburn's instructions for Jack to put all agent-related activities on hold, in view of Howard's defection and Zakharov's arrest. Jack gave him a quick account of his conversation with Amanda and requested clearance for his meetings with his Soviet contacts—he couldn't be seen by his "friends" as shunning them under these unique circumstances. Nurimbekoff agreed, with the condition that all meetings would be purely social. And Jack was to report back immediately if there was anything out of the ordinary.

It meant that his bosses were expecting the spy war to continue. The Americans had just scored with the arrest of Zakharov, which was an obvious comeback to the announcement of Howard's asylum in Moscow. Not dissimilar to the DCI leaking information about Yurchenko's defection to the US on the heels of several roll-ups of American assets in Moscow. Or the heightened publicity around Pelton's trial for spying for the Soviets, following two expulsions of American diplomats for behavior "incompatible with their diplomatic status". The press had labeled 1985 the Year of the Spy. But if the trend continued like this, it remained to be seen which year, this or last, would end up being more devastating.

On the way home from work, Jack drove to GUM, the State Universal Department Store, on the eastern side of Red Square. Housed in a long, three-story 19th century building that combined elements of Russian medieval architecture with a beautiful glass roof, GUM was Moscow's most elegant shopping mall. And the largest, with four long aisles on each floor, but most importantly, it had thirteen entrances and as many corners with public phones on different floors of different aisles. A perfect place for shopping. Or getting lost and making calls privately.

As he parked his car and strolled in through one of GUM's entrances, Jack noticed the driver of the dark blue *Zhiguli* that had been on his tail since he left the Embassy rushing toward the next entrance. The man had parked twenty meters down the street, even though there was plenty of space right next to Jack's Mustang.

The moment Jack was inside and out of sight of his shadow, he dashed up the stairs to the right of the entrance, then quickly walked across a bridge to a different aisle. He had no doubt that his minder would find him soon, but wanted to make a couple of calls without company if he could help it.

"*Allo?*"

Was Jack imagining it or did his friend sound hopeful?

"It's me. *Privet*," he said, grinning at the gray, cast-iron casing of the public phone like it was the friendliest face he'd seen in his life.

"*Privet*. I just returned yesterday and got your message. Anything happen?"

"Have you heard about Viktor yet?"

There was a slight pause, then a sigh. "Yes. Lara called last night... She asked us to accompany the play they are staging after his memorial service."

"How is she keeping?"

"I haven't seen her yet. But she sounded like she was, um, keeping up."

"I'll call her later. How about you?"

"I'm fine. Really. It is all... distressing. Otherwise, everything is alright... When can we meet?"

"I'm not sure. I'll try my best to drop by your place sometime this week. If it's *convenient*. I mean, depends on *how it goes*, you know." He hoped his friend would understand what he meant.

"I understand. You can come *anytime* that's convenient."

"I will try to give you head-ups."

"If it's convenient. Otherwise, just come up. *Anytime*," Eton repeated, and Jack could hear a smile in his voice.

"Alright... And Eton?" He bit on his lip.

"I'm here."

"You take good care of yourself, you hear? It's very important... to me."

There was a moment of silence on the other end, then Eton's voice came back, low and steadfast, "I will. I promise."

"Alright. I'll see you soon. *Poka*." He hung up quickly, before Eton could respond, wondering if he had said too much on the phone.

For the next three days Jack's shadowing was so tight he couldn't find a breather for even a moment. He tried to pin point an event that could have triggered such a comprehensive coverage, but couldn't come up with anything in particular. And he started fearing that this would be his reality for the rest of his posting.

Then on Saturday, he suddenly found himself clear of surveillance. He spent most of the day running errands around town, trying to single out a tail. By late afternoon, he decided that there was probably none. At quarter to seven, he was about to head out, aiming to get to Eton's place by nine o'clock evening news time, when the phone rang.

Duh! I'm not here! I'm out!

He stood by the door for a few moments, hoping that whoever was calling would take the cue and give up. But the phone continued ringing.

He sighed and walked back into the sitting room. "Hello?"

"Jack. Don Steward here. How are you?"

"Hey, Don. Anything happened?" It had to be if the head of security office was calling him home on a Saturday night.

"We need to have a chat with you. It's kinda urgent. 'Preciate it if you could come down to the commissary."

"What, *now*? It's Saturday night, Don. Can't it wait till Monday?"

"Sorry, Jack. It's an emergency. We need you right now. It's the Ambassador's request."

"Alright." He sighed demonstratively into the phone. "I'll be on my way in ten. Hope nothing too serious."

"I hope so, too. Just get over here, alright? See you on the ninth floor."

Jack put the receiver down and sat staring at the phone, trying to figure what the emergency could be and why the regional security officer would call him in.

It could be the security breaches at the marines' quarters that he had reported to Nurimbekoff.

Or the content of Mike's package that he had dropped off at Don's over a month ago.

But then why had he said that Jack was being summoned at Ambassador Hart's request? Security breaches and information from defectors were not the Ambassador's direct concerns, were they?

On the other hand, he was ultimately responsible for his Embassy's staff—for their wellbeing as well as for their conduct, in accordance with the rules and procedures... Like the rule of "no fraternizing with locals", for instance, of which he had reminded them right after William Osbourne's arrest in March.

But from the little he knew about the man, Jack couldn't see Ambassador Hart pulling the rug from under someone like that on a Saturday night, through the RSO. It was just not his style. Besides, the last time Jack had seen him at his residence was three weeks earlier, when he arranged for the producer and two others members of the WTBS crew to interview him and Mrs. Hart. The Ambassador had been cordial and informal, and they had all been invited to stay for tea afterwards.

It couldn't be that Jack was spending too much time with his Russian contacts, could it? No, he didn't even want to think about it. They were *not* going to ask him to stop seeing his Soviet friends. Because if they were, he would get Nurimbekoff and Joe Coburn involved, his deep cover be damned!

Chapter 52

The traffic was light, typical of a weekend night in Moscow, and Jack got to the Embassy in less than half an hour.

"Hey, Frank! Everything alright?" He held his ID up and went through the tourniquet.

"Jack, how's it going, man? Comin' in for dinner?"

"Maybe. First need to fix something in the office I forgot, running around with those TV people." He lingered once inside. "Anything of interest happening?"

"Not sure. Maybe it's nothing. Ambassador came in an hour ago."

"On a Saturday?"

"Know who he's seeing?" Frank held his pause. "Your old flame. The Brit chick."

"Amanda? Meeting with Ambassador?" He was genuinely surprised.

"Yeah, that's her, Amanda. She looked rushed. You sure you aren't comin' in to see her?"

"If I wasn't, I am now for sure." Jack winked at the marine. "Thanks, man. Catch up later!"

He gave Frank a quick wave and hurried towards the commissary building. As he yanked the heavy door open, he found himself face to face with Amanda, reaching out to push it. She did look ruffled.

"Amanda! Hi! What are you doing here on a Saturday?"

"Jack! Didn't expect to see you here. But so glad I do." Her face lightened up a little. "I was meeting with Ambassador Hart."

"Oh yeah? An interview for Vanity Fair?"

"Mike has been kidnapped... Arrested."

"What?! By the KGB? Are you sure, Mandy?"

"I saw it with my own eyes," she said, still visibly shaken.

"You *saw* it? You mean you were physically there?"

"Less than fifty yards away."

"Jesus! I'm so sorry, Mandy... What did the Ambassador say?"

She rolled her eyes. "The usual. 'We'll take all possible measures, blah, blah, blah'... Do you have time, Jack? I'd really appreciate an hour of your company right now... I need a drink."

"Sure, Mandy. Can you wait for me? I need to do a couple of things upstairs. Tell you what: why don't you go to Uncle Sam's and have a drink. I'll be with you in twenty minutes, half an hour max."

"Alright." Her little smile was both weary and resigned.

"I'll be down as soon as I'm done, sweetie-pie." He hugged her, kissed her on top of her head and rushed to the lifts.

Don Steward was already waiting for him on the ninth floor. As they shook hands, the head of security apologized again, then ushered him into the Tank where he told Jack to wait. He returned in five minutes with Ambassador Hart and Nurimbekoff. Jack's heart sank at the sight of Moscow Station's chief, but he kept an expression of curiosity firmly in place.

When the Ambassador was done with greetings and apologies, Don said, "I'm sure you've met Mr. Nurimbekoff, Jack. He's regional affairs counselor in Political Section."

Jack smiled politely. "Yes, I have. Mr. Nurimbekoff, we talked at the Marines Ball last year. About Afghanistan."

"Good to catch up with you again, Jack," the COS said pleasantly as they shook hands. "Circumstances could be better, though."

Jack turned to the Ambassador. "Sir, is this about Mike Demidoff? I've just run into his ex-wife downstairs. She said he's been kidnapped. Or arrested."

Ambassador Hart confirmed what Amanda had said and explained that an official protest was going to be lodged with the authorities shortly. However, before that, the security office had to determine, to the extent possible, if there were any plausible grounds for Mike Demidoff's arrest. Mr. Nurimbekoff was very knowledgeable on the Soviet Union's political environment and had kindly agreed to give advice.

They asked Jack to run through once more his conversation with Mike on the Moskva River cruise and the favor he had asked of Jack. Then they asked whether by any chance Jack had "found out" or had an idea of what was in the envelope. He shook his head resolutely, said he hadn't had a chance, but he surely had been toying with ideas because it had all been so mysterious. In any case, he said, he was hoping to learn now what it had all been about and especially what had happened to Mike. Who was a friend; as was his ex-wife, Amanda.

Once Don Steward and Nurimbekoff had exhausted their questions, Ambassador Hart explained that they believed Mike's arrest was related to the recent arrest of a Soviet physicist in New York and that the State Department would do everything to secure Mike's expedient release. He let Jack go, but asked him to be discreet about the favor the journalist had asked him to do, as well as about this conversation.

Five minutes later, Jack was sitting across from Amanda, two gin and tonics in front of them, and she was telling him what she had witnessed.

She was supposed to come to Mike's place to pick up her belongings at noon. In the morning, she'd had a meeting with Artyom on Lenin Hills and had taken a trolleybus from there to the neighborhood where Mike lived. A few blocks from Lenin Avenue, she spotted Mike through the window. He was walking on the other side of the street, a white plastic bag in his hand. She got off at the next stop and started to cross the road, intending to wait for him. She was in the middle of the road, fifty yards away, when it happened: a black Volga and a white van stopped in front of and behind Mike, half a dozen men in civilian clothes spilled out into the street and surrounded him. Two of them grabbed and handcuffed him without even taking away the bag. They shoved him into the van and both cars sped off. All this had transpired in about thirty seconds, the time it took her to reach the pavement.

Twenty minutes later, Amanda was in Mike's office contacting the incoming bureau chief. By 2:00 p.m., she and Harold Treutlen had talked to the US News and World Report's editor, then to the head of security who had asked her to come to the Embassy at 5:00 p.m., and to Ambassador Hart who had assured her that he was taking this matter in his hands personally. All of them had insisted that the incident was undoubtedly linked to the recent arrest of Gennadiy Zakharov by the FBI.

At 3:00 p.m., the bureau and all other news agencies in town had received a cable from TASS announcing the arrest of Mike Demidoff. For spying activities.

At 4:00 p.m., Amanda had given an interview to correspondents of major western newspapers who had gathered in Mike's apartment.

Then she had spent two and a half hours at the Embassy, first talking with Don Steward and his people, then with the Ambassador, then filling in papers. Now, she desperately needed someone to help her to put things into perspective and have another drink with her.

"And you are *the* person to have a few drinks with." She reached across the table, took Jack's hand and gave him a tired smile.

"Anytime, Mandy. Let me get you another drink." He stood up.

"What about you?"

"I'm driving today. Actually, I can take you back to… wherever you're staying tonight. I mean when you're ready… I'll be right back."

When he returned with another gin and tonic and placed it in front of her, Amanda mumbled her thanks, watched him thoughtfully. "Jack, can I ask you a favor?"

"Sure, Mandy. Shoot." Something told him that he might not like it.

"I don't want to stay in a hotel room tonight. It would feel like a prison cell after all this crap. I also hate staying at Mike's alone. Who knows who might make an unwelcome visit the coming days?"

"You want me to stay there with you?"

"Could you?"

She smiled weakly, and Jack saw something like fear in her eyes, so unlike the Amanda he used to know.

Why are you here again, Mandy? And how can you do this shit without a diplomatic cover, you silly girl?

"I'd rather not show up at Mike's, Mandy… But you're welcome to crash at my place," he hastened to add, seeing disappointment blooming on her face. "For as long as you need."

"Sorry for ruining your Saturday night, Jack. But it's just for one night." Amanda looked both relieved and apologetic. "I'll get my shit together by tomorrow. I promise." She reached out again and put her hand on his side of the table.

"No worries." Jack took her hand and smiled at her reassuringly. "As I said, you can stay as long as you need. I don't envy you right now, Mandy. Not at all."

They agreed that he would take her back to Mike's place so that she could sort out her belongings, then Jack would call before coming back, closer to midnight, and would take her to his apartment.

It was half past nine when Jack dropped her off in front of the old, Stalin era brick building where Mike lived. Amanda leaned over, kissed him on the cheek, said "see you later, handsome", and sprung out of the car.

Jack sped off right away, heading southwest toward the district where Eton lived. A few blocks from the Eton's apartment building, he turned into a narrow street. He cruised along it until he found a secluded corner in the gap between two tall, gray, concrete cage buildings that housed foreign students studying Russian at the Moscow State Pedagogical Institute.

Compared to districts where local folks lived, the area was busy. Groups of young people hurried toward the sounds of music, laughing and chatting merrily: it was a typical discotheque night in the student quarters. Jack parked his car and got out. He lingered on the pavement for a minute, watching young people passing by, lit a cigarette and wandered in the direction of the main street.

On the way to the familiar building on Profsoyuznaya Street he stopped twice at public phones. The second time he actually made a call.

"*Allo?*"

Eton's tone *was* hopeful and Jack wondered at the warm, joyful feeling that swelled in his chest every time he heard his friend's voice.

"*Privet*. It's me. I'll be there in fifteen minutes."

"Alright."

"See you in a bit."

He hung up and strolled down the street. It was half past ten, and the street was deserted, but he made an effort to temper his pace and glance over the shoulder stealthily from time to time.

The door opened before the doorbell chime died, and Jack walked straight into Eton's embrace. They stood clinging to each other for a minute, Jack reveling in the feel of Eton's lithe body in his arms, breathing in his scent, wondrously smoky and fresh at the same time.

Finally, Eton let out a contented sigh and loosened his embrace. He kissed Jack softly on the lips and peered into his eyes. "Something happened? Besides Karelin."

Jack nuzzled his neck and let go of him. "Yeah. We need to talk. And I only have..." He glanced at his watch. "Thirty five minutes. I'm sorry."

"I understand." Eton nodded, tried to smile reassuringly, but didn't quite make it. "You want coffee?"

"Yes, please."

They plodded to the kitchen where Eton put on the kettle and Jack opened the top section of the window and lit a cigarette. After a deep drag, he handed it over to Eton and sat down on one of the kitchen stools. Eton sat down on the other side of the small table and stretched out his legs so that his knees crossed with Jack's.

"There was another arrest this morning. A journalist this time."

"Again?! For spying? I mean, according to *them*."

"Probably. I haven't heard anything about the charges yet. Anyway, it's Amanda's ex-husband, Mike."

"*What*?! No way!... Do you know she's here? Artyom told us she planned to come to Karelin's, uh, *pominki*. And the show."

"Yeah, I ran into her at the Embassy and took her home. Mike's home. I have to pick her up before midnight and, um, take her to my place. She's a bit distressed and needs someone to be with her, you know."

"Of course. I understand." Eton looked concerned. And sympathetic. "How is she?"

"I'd say pretty cool for someone who witnessed her husband's—ex-husband's—arrest a few hours ago."

"She saw it? My god! Where did it happen?"

Eton made them two cups of black instant coffee while Jack recounted Amanda's story of Mike's arrest, adding that it was thought to be linked to the arrest of a Soviet UN representative in the US. Then Jack told him about the various tit-for-tat expulsions between the Soviet Union, Great Britain and America since the previous year.

Eton hadn't known about half of them. He listened to Jack without interruption, toying with the matchbox on the table. "That Russian who was arrested in New York, what did he do?" he asked when Jack finished.

The question caught Jack by surprise. He extracted the matchbox from Eton's restless fingers and lit another cigarette. "Newspapers say he tried to get information from someone who was an FBI informant."

"Did they say what kind of information?"

Jack shrugged, trying to ward off the uneasiness that had descended on him with Eton's first question about Zakharov. "Some classified technology information. They say the informant worked for a defense contractor."

"I see." He reached for Jack's cigarette, deliberately brushing his fingers against Jack's in the process, and stuck it in between his lips. "What about Mike? Do you think he works for the CIA?"

Eton's question grated Jack's like sandpaper. "I don't think so. I think he's just collateral damage in the spy war between our countries."

"What about Zakharov? Is he also, uh, 'collateral damage'? Maybe not, knowing our *organs*. I think all our people posted in the West work for them."

Jack let out a noncommittal grunt. He took Eton's hand, leaned forward and took a drag on the cigarette in his fingers.

"Do you think this spy war will continue? Your, um, American side will do something in response?" Eton asked quietly after a while.

Jack withdrew his hand back to his end of the table. "I don't know. I hope not... But won't be surprised if it does."

Eton squashed the cigarette butt into the ashtray, stood up, took the empty cups to the sink and started washing them. For a moment the only sounds were of water hissing from the tap and clink of china and cutlery.

"How are your rehearsals for Karelin's play?" Jack asked when the silence started weighing heavy on them.

Eton stood with his back to Jack, putting the cups up on the drying rack. "It's alright. The guys are happy we're playing again... Will you come?"

"Don't know... It might be *inconvenient*, you know."

Shit, how could he explain to Eton that hanging around with Amanda would most probably put him right back under heavy surveillance? But she had practically begged for his company and he hadn't had the heart to turn her down.

Eton sat down on his stool but didn't stretch his legs out to cross them with Jack's this time. "Do you think Amanda will come? Artyom said she is writing an article about Karelin and will come to the memorial." He sounded resigned as if he already knew the answer to his question.

"Not sure it's a good idea. Amanda might have all the attention of the organs now since her interview with western press about Mike's arrest. You guys surely don't need to draw more attention to your special event. Right?"

Eton nodded, and Jack could see understanding sparring with hurt in his eyes. "I'm sorry, bud." He stretched his hand out, palm up, seeking truce. "I couldn't say no to her. She was a bit desperate."

Eton took Jack's hand with both of his, leaned over and pressed his lips onto Jack's fingers. Then he straightened up, and said with a sad half smile, "I understand. You're a very good friend, Jack... The best friend I've known."

By the time Jack brought Amanda to his apartment, it was close to one o'clock in the morning. He told her to feel at home and went to change the sheets on his bed for her to sleep in. However, she insisted on sleeping on the couch in the sitting room. So Jack brought her a set of bed linen, a pillow and a spare blanket, gave her a hug and retreated to the bedroom.

He woke up sometime during the night, startled by the feeling that he was being watched. Amanda was standing by his bed, holding her pillow and blanket to her chest, the dim light from the floor lamp in the sitting room casting dull yellow shadows on the corridor wall behind her.

"I'm sorry, Jack. I can't sleep. Can I stay here with you? I promise to behave," she hastened to add when a response hadn't come right away.

"Yeah. Okay." He stifled a sigh and shifted to one side of his double bed.

"Thank you thank you thank you!" she whispered, put her pillow down next to his and climbed up on top of his blanket. Then she leaned over and kissed him on the cheek. "Hmm. Don't you shave nowadays anymore? I like you more when you're well shaven and in a tux." She chuckled softly, then lay down with her back to Jack, wrapped herself in her blanket, curled up in a ball and whispered, half into her pillow, "Good night, handsome. Thanks so much for having me."

In the morning, she had a coffee Jack made her but refused the breakfast, then at the door, kissed Jack briefly on the lips, said "You're the best" and left.

By 9:00 a.m., a news war broke out.

As the first round, all major Soviet newspapers and the TV news service announced the arrest of Mike Demidoff, caught in the act of receiving classified documents from an unnamed local contact.

American and European newspapers with bureaus in Moscow quickly fired back the interview with Amanda, shedding a sinister light on the event. All of them linked Mike Demidoff's arrest with the arrest of Gennadiy Zakharov in New York the week before.

Next, the Embassy made an official protest, calling Demidoff's detention a crude provocation, and demanded his immediate release. In Washington, the US News and World Report denounced the Soviet action as a "frame-up".

Entered the heavy artillery: in his statement from Santa Barbara, California where he was on vacation, Reagan said, "We are making every effort to gain access to Demidoff and to secure his release from custody... Based on the information we have, it is clear that the grounds on which he has been detained are contrived."

On Monday, after visiting Mike at the KGB's detention center, Amanda gave another interview to foreign press, which quickly circulated worldwide.

For the whole following week, Demidoff's arrest featured extensively in all major newspapers and TV programs in the West with journalists rallying for one of their flock. This only heightened the tension between the two superpowers as they prepared for the summit. By September 8th, when the Soviet Union formally filed an espionage charge against Mike Demidoff, the White House had issued at least three strongly worded statements, including one that said the arrest could affect the summit. On the same day, TASS released a statement by Gorbachev in which he said there was no guarantee that he would meet Reagan later that year in any case.

Soon news emerged of possible negotiations about a swap of Mike Demidoff for Gennadiy Zakharov. Reagan first discarded the idea and sent a personal plea to Gorbachev to release Demidoff instead. The request went unanswered. Then on September 13th, both Demidoff and Zakharov were suddenly released into the custody of their respective Ambassadors while further negotiations between two countries ensued.

Things got complicated when on September 17th the Reagan administration issued an order expelling twenty-five UN-based Soviet diplomats. It, however, denied that the action was related to the spy charges against Mike Demidoff. Its statement said that it was a follow-up to a decision announced six months ago, to enforce cutbacks in the Soviets' U.N. presence. An unidentified source in the State Department stated, though, that all the diplomats were intelligence officers and that the effect of this action on the KGB operation in America was like "ripping its heart out".

Heavyweight negotiations behind closed doors ensued, headed by Secretary of State Shultz and Foreign Secretary Shevardnadze who had arrived to Washington to discuss prospects for a summit. They held the world riveted for a week. Occasionally, a word or two would be leaked out through unnamed sources in either the State Department or the Soviet Embassy, all of them daunting.

On September 27th, the White House rejected yet another Soviet proposal for settling the Demidoff case and also ruled out the relaxation of the expulsion order against twenty-five members of the Soviet mission to the UN. The Soviet Embassy threatened that the Soviet

Union would retaliate if the orders were not rescinded. To which Reagan responded, in his speech in Ft Meade, Maryland, that his administration would continue to root out spies and punish them severely.

Then, unexpectedly, on September 29th, Demidoff was released, whisked away to Sheremetyevo Airport and put on a PanAm flight to Frankfurt. In Washington, when the baffled press asked Reagan about the "spy swap" deal, he denied it was a trade-off for Zakharov, and told reporters that details of the arrangements would be announced tomorrow.

The climax came the next day as promised.

In a perfectly timed move, the two superpowers simultaneously issued surprise announcements: Reagan and Gorbachev would be meeting in Reykjavik on October 11th—in twelve days! At the same time, details were disclosed about deals to release Zakharov from the United States, where he faced spy charges, and for the Soviet Union to free imprisoned human rights leader, physicist Yuri Orlov.

The American administration continued denying any connection between Demidoff and Zakharov cases and claimed the journalist's release was part of "broader range of events" that included some relaxation of the expulsion orders for Soviet diplomats. Details about such a "relaxation" were not immediately available.

Jack woke up before his 6:45 a.m. alarm, feeling energized. He put on his jogging gear and went out.

It had been over a month since he talked to Eton, the day Mike had been arrested and Amanda had spent a night at his place. As he had expected, the KGB had put him under comprehensive, continuous surveillance, which seemed to have been scaled back with the resolution of Demidoff - Zakharov affair. As a result, in the last four days he had noticed a shadow only twice.

On the street, the cold drizzle of the last two days had finally stopped and the soggy autumn air had warmed up a little. Traffic was light, and the sidewalks were empty at this time on a Saturday morning, except for an occasional passerby scuttling to the nearest Metro station.

Jack did a full lap around the block before stopping at a *taxaphone* on the corner of a Stalin-era brick house.

"*Allo?*" Eton sounded a little out of breath. And smiling.

"*Privet.* It's me. Have I woken you up?"

"*Privet.* No. I'm, um, exercising… Are you jogging?"

Jack couldn't recall when he'd stopped being startled by Eton's near psychic questions— his friend seemed to remember what Jack usually did and where every time he called him.

"Yeah." Jack grinned. "Just a couple of laps around the block here."

"Thought you might call."

Now, that was downright spooky.

As if he was reading Jack's mind, Eton added, "After Mike's release, I thought things would calm down… Right?"

"Right. Yes, it seems so… Anyway, how are things?"

"Good. The academic year has started. I'm taking, um, some additional courses… as I told you."

"Yeah?… Alright. Good."

Eton had probably noted the change in his tone. "Sorry," he said quietly.

Oh, c'mon, Smith!

"It's alright, Eton. You don't have to apologize for anything, friend. You just do what you think you have to do. Alright?"

There was a sigh on the other end of the line. "Alright. Thank you—"

"So how's your grandfather?"

"Not too bad for someone who spent over a month *there*. He went to Vienna last month, for that conference on, um, the *accident*."

"Yes, I've read about it."

There was a pause while they were trying to come up with a neutral topic so that there was no need to talk in codes. Eton beat him to it.

"You know, there will be an art exhibition tomorrow at the New Tretyakov Gallery, opposite Gorky Park. They're exhibiting paintings from the avant-garde collection. For the first time. You want to go?"

"That would be good… Yes, let's go!"

"Do you want me to call Lara and ask her out with us?" Eton's tone was solemn, sincere. "She hasn't been going out much lately. Says she needs to focus on her final year."

Duh. With all the anxiety around Mike's arrest, he hadn't managed to call Lara. Come to think about it, he hadn't talked to her since June.

"I'll call her… You know what? I'll invite her and you with your guys to my place for dinner. But for tomorrow, let's not call anyone."

Chapter 53

October 5, Sunday. Midnight.

Dear Jack,

So glad you could come to the exhibition. Sorry I acted stupid in the beginning. Hadn't seen you for over a month. My brain just ceased functioning and all I could think was how someone's eyes could be THAT blue? And how could it be that this someone wants to be with me? Wants me. I still haven't got used to it. Guys talk about girls in these terms, not about other guys. Forgive me for saying this, but you are beautiful.

About the exhibition: it was good, wasn't it? Can't say I fully understand those paintings, especially Malevich. But it's great that they are finally being displayed. They are representation of the souls of the artists. Who deserve to be "heard".

Jack, this is perhaps the opening up that we didn't believe would ever come. If this process continues, maybe we will be able to see the light. Perhaps not tomorrow, but one day. It will come, right?

Your friend,

E.

October 7, Tuesday. 10:47pm.

Dear Jack,

Grisha and I were called to the office of the dean today. Grandfather was there too, and the deputy dean. And Prof. Belykh from the Nuclear Research Institute in Dubna. I met him last year when they offered me a research position. In short, Grisha and I got an offer for internship. They have a major research project and my diploma project folds neatly into it. All (except Grandfather) were surprised that I agreed so fast. Perhaps they thought I would say no again and they would have to persuade me. That's it. We will start working there in January.

Afterwards, Grisha and I went to lunch. He asked if I had seen you lately. I said sometimes. He said maybe I shouldn't anymore as we'd be starting our work at a closed institute soon. I didn't say anything. He was right.

This is it, Jack. This is what I wanted, isn't it? To do something useful. And this is what I dreaded, too—that I won't be able to see you again. I didn't expect it would happen so soon.

I pray it will be something truly useful for my people. It must be!

Remaining yours forever,

E.

October 10, Friday. Twelve minutes to midnight.

Jack,

Please don't worry that you can't invite us for dinner. I understand. Some other time, cowboy.

Although I'm not even sure about "some other time". Besides the internship in Dubna, the news about the arrest of Amanda's husband has also been bothering me. They reported he had been meeting with a student from Frunze, who gave him some secret documents and maps. Then I listened to Radio Liberty. They say what you told me: that it is the KGB's retaliation for the arrest of Zakharov. With all this going on, I don't know if seeing you is a good idea. For you, cowboy. I don't know what I'll do if something like that happens to you.

Do you think the summit tomorrow will change anything? I know it is silly, but I still hope it will.

Yours always,

E.

October 12, Sunday. 11:12pm.

They showed Gorbachev's news conference in Reykjavik on TV just now. It was long and ambiguous as usual. The commentators haven't provided the "interpretation" yet, but I guess the summit has failed. Otherwise, G. wouldn't say that R. is stubborn and cannot make decisions without his aides. That he does what the military-industrial complex tells him to do. Typical cold war statements.

Don't know what I hoped for. Not that the success of this summit would have resulted in any major change in our lives. But I feel disappointed nonetheless. Maybe because of the numerous ill-fated events this year that I hoped for a glimmer of hope. Of what I don't even know.

October 13, Monday. 9:55pm.

Had lunch with Grandfather today. He asked if I had seen you lately, told me now that the NW project had ended, perhaps I shouldn't anymore as it could affect my work in Dubna. I said, I know. He patted my hand and said unfortunately in this country we can't always choose who we want to be friends with.

When I got home, there were three women sitting on the bench in front of our entryway. They live in this building. One of them asked why my "new, handsome friend" has not come visit me lately and if he is an aspirant at MGU.

Damn!!

You are right, cowboy. Nowhere is safe. Nowhere in this damned country. I am so sorry.

E.

October 15, Wednesday. 2 minutes to midnight.

Jack,

I'm sorry for ~~saying~~ writing this. But I have to write it down or I'll go insane. I'll burn it afterwards anyway, so writing this down may make it go away.

I have been thinking about this for some time and these thoughts are poisoning my mind. It's about the recent cases of spies being caught, here and in America, diplomats expelled for something they may or may not have done. I know it's all politics; it's the cold war between our countries, etc. I never lost sleep about it before. Now it's different.

A thought has been sneaking into my mind time after time: what if? What if what our organs are saying is true? What if they were all spies? They were caught while meeting with their local contacts, right? They all had "local contacts".

OK, that wasn't the question I wanted to ask. The real question is: what if you are, too?

There, I have said it.

I am not feeling any better. And now have more questions: if you are, what are you after? What do you need? From me. I am just a student.

A nuclear physics student.

That guy in New York, whom Zakharov tried to recruit for the KGB, was a student in the beginning, too. Then he started working for a defense industry company.

No.

No and no! I don't believe it! You are not like them. You encouraged me to be a musician. Told me to do what I wanted to do—play music. It was I who decided that I want to be a physicist and do something useful for this goddamned country.

No, you cannot be like them! Because you are my best friend, my cowboy. My love.

Are you, Jack?

* * *

Jack didn't get the clearance to host a dinner for his Russian friends. Not only that, Nurimbekoff advised him to stay away from them. For now. Seeing Jack's disappointment, the COS patted him on the shoulder. "You're doing a good job, but let's wait until the dust settles."

On October 14th, back from Reykjavik, Ambassador Hart shared his impressions of the summit at a country team meeting. He tried to put a positive spin on it, but everyone had read the news: it had been a total failure and the heads of the two superpowers hadn't even tried to fake optimism.

The summit's outcome affected Jack in a strange way: he felt cheated. He didn't know what exactly he had been expecting from the summit. He had had a vague hope that something would change, and that something would trigger other changes that could affect him personally. But that was all nonsense of course. If anything were going to change, it wouldn't be in his lifetime.

Ambassador Hart didn't share any insight on how the Soviets might react to Washington's expulsion of twenty-five Soviet diplomats either. But speculations were rampant inside the Embassy and everybody braced for increased harassment from the *organs*.

The Soviets came back the following Monday. The first thing they learned upon arriving at work was that overnight four of the Embassy's staff plus one from the Consulate in Leningrad had been declared *personae non gratae* and ordered to leave the country.

It was a complete undoing of the Company's operation in the Soviet Union. Of the five PNG-ed diplomats, three were case officers—two from Moscow and one from Leningrad. Excluding the Station chief, his secretary and two communications officers, the hit left the Station with only three active case officers in Moscow, including Jack, and one in Leningrad. But then, they didn't have all that many agents left to run, anyway.

Jack stayed in the office late, unnerved by the escalation of events, waiting for an emergency briefing with Nurimbekoff. It never came. So by 8:00 p.m. he gave up and came down to Uncle Sam's for dinner. The place was uncharacteristically busy for a Monday night, vibrating with anxious anticipation. Groups of diplomats, contractors and visitors were discussing past events and speculating what would happen next. Jack joined the crowd at the bar and asked for a beer. He could've killed for a whiskey, but held back.

On the way home, he debated whether he should call Eton. His friend had probably heard about the expulsion of American diplomats by now. Jack had no doubt Eton had questions for him again. Questions were fine; he could handle those. What he didn't want was for Eton to worry about all this political shit.

He decided to wait. Till he heard from Nurimbekoff. Maybe he would manage to arrange for them to meet somewhere and talk at length.

Or maybe he should just go to Eton's place, like last time. Then he would report about it to Joe Coburn.

He went to bed feeling much better, the thought he would be seeing Eton soon shining like a little sun in his chest. His friend Eton.

His best friend Eton. His Eton...

On Tuesday, the news reached the Embassy in the early afternoon: the State Department had decided to reduce the maximum number of Soviet personnel with diplomatic status in the U.S. from 310 to 255. To meet this new ceiling, fifty-five Soviet diplomats were asked to leave, including five who were declared *personae non gratae*.

Work came to a halt at the Embassy. People were busy meeting, discussing, checking the newsroom and, generally, trying to figure what was going to happen next. Nobody had even a shadow of doubt that the Sovs would retaliate. The question was *how*. Would they expel an equivalent number of Americans from Moscow and Leningrad? Would they impose an even lower ceiling, which would force the State Department to lower theirs to keep the score even?

Late in the evening, Nurimbekoff summoned Jack to the Tank. The COS told him that the Company was expecting more people to be ousted. As the recent expulsions by the State Department had effectively crippled the KGB's *rezidentura* in Washington and San Francisco, there was little hope that case officers on the KGB's suspect list would remain unscathed. Nurimbekoff was positive though that Jack would be fine.

The retaliation came at 1:00 p.m. the next day. With no warning, the Soviets shut down the Embassy's direct telephone line with Washington. This had never happened before and it caught everyone unprepared.

At 3:00 p.m., TASS reported the execution of Adolf Tolkachev, a Soviet citizen who had spied for the United States, one of those whom Edward Lee Howard had exposed. In the evening, Gorbachev gave a speech on US-Soviet relations on the news program *Vremya*.

The Soviet leader unleashed a scathing attack on the Reagan administration, accusing it of "half-truths" and "pure deceit" at the summit. He blamed Reagan for distorting the summit and taking actions which "to a normal human simply look wild". Citing the expulsion of the Soviet officials, Gorbachev promised that the Soviet Union would take "reciprocal, very hard measures". He didn't say what they would be, but if anyone had been harboring any hope before, now no one doubted that more Americans would be ousted.

The Sovs let the other shoe drop the next day.

When Jack arrived at work, early for a change, the first thing he found on his desk was a copy of the statement by Soviet Foreign Ministry. It announced that, effective immediately, all 260 Soviet employees of the Embassy and the Consulate in Leningrad were being withdrawn—the team assistants, interpreters, drivers, Uncle Sam's kitchen staff, technicians, cleaners and other auxiliary staff. All of them.

Un-fucking-believable!

Five minutes later, his telephone rang. It was Ambassador Hart's assistant asking him to come up: the Ambassador wanted to talk to him.

Jack sat staring at the phone for a long while, dread like a giant, icy-cold hand squeezing his insides.

No, it couldn't be. Please, God, not him!

He expected to see Nurimbekoff with the Ambassador; instead, it was the new CAO. They sat down. After asking if Jack had read the announcement and receiving a gloomy "yes, sir", Ambassador Hart broke the news: in addition to withdrawing the local staff, the Soviets were expelling five diplomats as *personae non gratae*. *And* they were ordering out two more to bring the number of American diplomats to 255. The bad news was that Jack's name was on the list. However, the good news was that he was one of the two who were merely "recommended for downsizing".

"It means that you can return at a later date when there's an opening," the Ambassador said, trying to sound cheerful. "I'm awfully sorry to lose such a capable officer like you, Jack. But as I'm sure you understand, these are complex and sensitive times. You can call me or write to me if you ever need a reference. I'll be happy to give you an excellent testimonial."

Why me?! Jack was screaming inside, but he nodded grimly and said, "I understand, sir. Thank you for your support."

He left the Ambassador's office shortly, trying to hold himself together.

So they had given him and the other downsized diplomat a month for winding down before their departure. A month. He could do with a month. He would come to Eton's place and explain to him that he had been transferred. He would need to think of a way they could stay in touch. Yeah, he could do with a month. It was just the hazard of the job, right? There was nothing he could do about it, and there was no point in wallowing in it.

By noon, TASS had broadcasted the announcement about the latest round of expulsions, complete with the names of five PNG-ed diplomats—four from Moscow and one from Leningrad. Two others were briefly mentioned, but not named. And there was no mention of the withdrawal of all the Soviet staff from the Embassy and the Consulate. By that time, however, the Soviet sanction was breaking news on all America's major TV stations.

By 10:00 p.m., when he went to see Nurimbekoff in the Tank, Jack had had two meetings with Tim Lockwood and the rest of the USIA team, and they'd all had final drinks at Uncle Sam's, which Luigi was shutting down now that all his Russian staff was gone.

Nurimbekoff looked calm and composed, despite the fact that the operation he was in charge of had effectively been shut down. He didn't waste time on commiserations and started the briefing as soon as they'd sat down. First, the fact that Jack was given a month to wind down probably meant that the organs didn't associate him with Moscow Station. Which was good news. But since the expelled case officers were departing on Saturday, and Nurimbekoff himself was leaving on Sunday, with no definite return date, Jack would be left with neither support nor communication channels. Therefore, he was to fly out on Tuesday. That would give him time to make a final communication with Eton Volkonsky and Lara Novikova to tell them that he would try to keep in touch. However, he could see them *only* if he was free of surveillance. Since his name hadn't been released by the Sovs—and Nurimbekoff didn't believe it would be—Jack could tell his Russian friends that he had to go back home for urgent family reasons. In his follow up communication in a few months' time, he would tell them that he had been reassigned. Finally, Nurimbekoff told Jack it was his last briefing in Moscow, and that he would receive further instructions upon his return to HQ.

The meeting lasted less than fifteen minutes, then Jack was on his own: for the next few days, he'd have no one to clear his actions with, no one to report to. Problem was, now he had only five days.

Five days to come up with something. Five days to tell Eton about... Fuck, what was he supposed to tell Eton about his sudden departure? Five days wasn't enough to come up with... a plan, a story, a something!!

Get a grip, Smith! Focus. You're going to see him. To tell him you're leaving. You MUST see him, surveillance or not!

By Friday evening, Jack had completed his handover, cleaned up his desk and left the office for the last time, all his belongings in one large plastic bag. On the way out, he picked up a pizza at the new cafeteria set up on old Uncle Sam's premises, promised his marine buddies that he would come on Saturday for a farewell bash, and drove home.

He was shadowed. And the next day too, as he drove his Mustang to the Embassy and back, then cruised around a couple of major stores downtown, buying Russian souvenirs and making phone calls from public phones. Not that he had family or many friends to buy presents for, but he had a plan, and as a rule, shopping was a good way to do one's SDR.

At 7:00 p.m. on Saturday, Jack put his raincoat on over a military jacket, the type foreign students and trendy Russians favored, and drove to the Embassy. Night was falling, and it was raining and cold—a perfect weather for what he had in mind. A beige Lada picked up with him less than a hundred yards from his compound, but that was alright. He still had time. He had promised to have a couple of rounds with his buddies tonight, anyway.

When he left the Embassy by the back gate just after 10:00 p.m., it was drizzling. He pulled the hood of the raincoat over his head and darted toward Metro Station Krasnopresnenskaya. He lingered outside, leaning against one of the fluted columns of the station's entrance and lit a cigarette.

The traffic was light, but steady, and there was only one car parked at the curb twenty yards down the street—an old, red *Zhiguli*. A group of four young people bounced by, then a couple of bickering drunkards, followed by a woman with a broken umbrella, lugging a tatty, bulging plastic bag. The owner of the *Zhiguli* rushed out from behind station, got into his car and drove away.

He seemed to be clear of surveillance, probably thanks to the foul weather. Still, Jack didn't want to risk it. Not on his last trip to... his last days in this goddamn city. He had figured he wouldn't have time to do a proper SDR, so his plan was to use the safe passage house.

It was an old apartment block in the western part of the city, with a concealed passage through the basement to the street on the other side of the building. The Station had two or three such sites, to be used only in emergency situations—when the surveillance had to be shaken off, period. Once used, a site was considered compromised and abandoned. Jack decided that tonight was such a situation.

He dropped the cigarette in the trashcan, flagged down a private car and asked to be taken to Malaya Filyovskaya Street. Half an hour later, with the raincoat now neatly tucked under the military jacket, he was riding in another private car, heading south. He alighted four blocks from Eton's apartment building and found a phone booth.

He glanced at his watch. 11:25pm. He quickly dialed the number.

Eton answered when Jack was about to hang up. "*Allo?*"

"*Privet*. It's me."

"*Privet*." He sounded gruff.

"I'm not far from your place... Can I, um, come up?"

There was a slight hesitation before a terse "yes". It didn't sound right. It didn't sound like Eton. *His* Eton.

"Everything's alright?" Jack asked cautiously.

There came a heavy sigh, and then the Eton he wanted to hear was on the line. "Yes. Don't worry. Come up, please."

"Alright. Ten minutes."

It was a good thing that the rain had picked up again because now his mad dash to Eton's place didn't look too suspicious—just someone braving the rain, hurrying home from the metro station. He reached the tall brick building in less than seven minutes. In the semi-dark entryway, he shook off the rainwater and tiptoed up the stairs.

The door was ajar, and the hallway was dark. Jack walked in swiftly, put the door chain on and turned around. Eton was standing in the small corridor that led to the kitchen, leaning against the wall, hands jammed into the jeans' pockets. The yellow light behind him gilded his blond curls and left his face in shadow.

"Hey... Lemme take these off." Jack peeled off his jacket and toed off his shoes. "It's pissing rain outside... God, I'm soaked." He chuckled, trying to fill the awkward silence.

Eton pushed off the wall and disappeared in the bathroom. A moment later, he came out with a large towel and handed it to Jack without a word.

Jack thought he caught a whiff of alcohol. He peered into Eton's face, trying to read his eyes in the semi-darkness. "Thank you." He dried his face and smiled weakly, unsure of what to say next.

"I'll get you a pair of dry socks." He walked past Jack, keeping a meter of space between them. A minute later, he returned with the socks and a pair of neatly folded jeans.

"Take these, too. They should fit. You can change in there," he said, pointing to the sitting room. "I'll make tea."

When Eton emerged in the doorway with a mug of steaming tea, Jack had changed and was pacing the narrow stretch of the open space between the tiny balcony and the dinner table—four steps to, then four steps fro. He stopped midway, watched warily as his friend sat the mug down on the table, stuffed his hands in his jeans' pockets again and raised his head. He did look tired, his eyes bloodshot.

They stood there, gazing at each other for a long, awkward moment, then Eton asked quietly, "It's about these recent events, um, evictions, isn't it?"

"Yeah." Jack drew his cheeks in and bit on them.

Eton dropped his gaze, chewed on his lower lip, then looked up again. "They've told you not to meet with, um, us anymore?"

"Yes... No, but... It's more than that." Jack's well-rehearsed little speech had deserted his brain the moment he walked through the door and now he was scrambling for words. He stuck his hands deep in his pockets and hunched his shoulders.

"More than that? What do you mean?"

Shit, there wasn't an easy way of putting it, was there?

"I'm leaving, Eton. On Tuesday."

"Leaving? For how long?" He took a step toward Jack, face firing up with alarm.

"For um... They've expelled me."

"They *what*?! But... but your name is *not* on the list... *Right*?"

"Right. I'm one of the other two."

Eton took another step closer, his anxiousness almost palpable. "But... How could it happen? *Why*?! Is it because of...?" He froze, staring at Jack, wild-eyed.

"I have, um..." Jack was about to say he had no idea why, but the look on Eton' face made him bite his tongue.

There was a long moment of silence, then Eton asked quietly, his tone and expression serene, "Jack. Are you a spy?"

Fuck!!

Jack swallowed, pulled his hands out of his pockets and raked his fingers through his hair. "Listen, Et—"

"No. Just tell me. The truth. *Are* you?"

I'm sorry, so fucking sorry! I wish to God I wasn't... No, but then we wouldn't have met, right? No, I'm not sorry!

"I'm sorry," he whispered and rubbed his hands over his face.

Eton's eyes were fixed on the floor, his stoic façade crumbling, distress slipping through. "So it means *all this* has been a—"

"No, Eton! No. Not all. Not this... between us." He took a step forward.

"No. Stay away." Eton held up his hand, palm out as though it were his shield. His face was contorted, anger battling with anguish.

"Eton, please! Let me explain." Jack took another, larger step, thinking that if he could just touch Eton, his friend would understand that not everything had been lies, not what he felt. "This *thing* between us, it's—"

Jack never finished his plea. The next moment he found himself sprawled on the floor, blinded and stunned by a lightning punch in the face.

"I warned you," Eton grated out through his teeth.

The throbbing pain on his cheekbone began to spread, but it was nothing compared to the one twisting his insides into a thousand knots, making Jack want to puke. He lay back down on the floor, holding his face, pressing his fingers into his eyes, as if trying to push the tears back.

He felt rather than heard Eton kneeling down on the floor next to him.

"You ok?" His voice was gruff, tormented. "Let me see... Jack?" He pulled tentatively at Jack's wrist.

Jack yielded reluctantly, brushing away the dampness in the process, but kept his eyes tightly shut. He felt Eton's cool fingers on his face, his warm breath, laced with cigarettes and alcohol, then heard his broken whisper, "I'm sorry", a quick brush of the lips on his temple, just above his busted cheek. He opened his eyes and saw the same anguish he felt on Eton's face, as if he was looking at himself in the mirror. He reached out, put a hand on his friend's neck and pulled him gently down.

Next thing he knew they were both on the floor, Eton's body heavy on top of him, his hands clasping Jack's head, kissing and biting his lips like he was trying to suck the life out of him. Jack reached down, tugged Eton's pullover and undershirt up and slid his hands underneath. Eton groaned into his mouth, ground against him, then sat up abruptly, straddling Jack. He started undoing both his and Jack's belts furiously, his hands trembling with impatience. But when Jack reached down to help him, he caught Jack's hand, then the other, and pinned them on the floor on both sides of Jack's body.

"No. *I* will do it," he rasped. He opened Jack's jeans, peeled them off his body and yanked them down. Then he jumped to his feet and pushed his own jeans and his boxers down in one swift movement, kicking them aside. He dropped on his knees, fisted Jack's length firmly, leaned forward and took him in his mouth.

Jack hissed and bucked involuntarily, making Eton gag. He pulled back, grabbed Jack's hand and wrapped it at the base of his own cock. "Hold it," he whispered through gritted teeth. Then he straddled Jack quickly and positioned himself over him.

"Eton, don't do... Oh, *Christ!*" he choked out as Eton impaled himself on him. The dry friction caused more pain than pleasure and Jack began to lose his erection.

Eton sagged over him, his eyes closed, biting his lips viciously, his breathing erratic, his cock going limp. He held still for a moment, leaning on his arms, his palms flat on Jack's chest, then made a weak attempt at riding.

"Don't... Shhh..." Jack stroked his lover's thighs, coaxing him to rise and let him go. Then he sat up, lowering Eton on the floor and pulled him close. Eton's long legs folded, closing around him. Jack rested his forehead against Eton's and sighed. "I'm so sorry, Eton. So fucking sorry. You have no idea!"

Eton's eyes were closed, his eyelashes damp, his lips pressed together in a thin, woeful line. But he didn't move away. Instead, his hands wandered blindly up Jack's shoulders and settled there, his thumbs kneading them forcefully, as though he was trying to rub all lies and half-truths off Jack.

Finally, he let out a long, rugged exhale. "D'you remember..." His voice flaked. He cleared his throat and started over. "Remember what I said? On the New Year's Eve."

"Yes, Eton. I do."

I will always remember it, baby. Always!

"Ten months. Right? Almost... You know what has changed since then?"

What has changed? God... Chernobyl. Lara. Karelin. Now you know that I'm a fucking spy. That I've lied...

"Everything? I'm sor—"

"Nothing." Eton tilted his head back and opened his eyes. They were dry and full of shadows. "For me - nothing. Please remember that... sometimes." He swallowed hard and looked away.

Jack tugged at his lover's hand, pressed it firmly over his heart, and pulled him into a tight embrace. "You know what?" he whispered fervently, "I'm *not* sorry. Not for one fucking second, friend."

Jack got back to his apartment after five o'clock in the morning, having walked most of the twenty roundabout kilometers from Eton's place in the freezing rain. He dropped his jacket and raincoat on the floor by the door, toed off the waterlogged runners and trudged to the bathroom in Eton's socks, leaving a trail of wet footsteps on the parquet. In the bathroom, he started the hot shower and, biting his lips to keep his teeth from chattering, began to undress. When his shaking hands had finally won the battle with the buttons and the zipper, he dropped his dry sweater and shirt on the floor, on top of Eton's soaked-through jeans, climbed into the bathtub and closed his eyes.

He sat under the gushing shower for a long time, clasping his knees to his chest, unable to tell what brought more relief—the piss that he could finally release, the scalding water or the tears. When his skin couldn't take it anymore, Jack got out and toweled himself dry. Then he turned around and braced his hands on the sink, his head bowed.

So this was it. His mission, his contacts, his friends. His life in Moscow. Over.

His *life*? What life? It was all a sham, a pretense of a regular life. But the incredible thing was that it had actually felt real. For once, he had felt like he belonged—to this place, to these people...

Okay, he had only two days left in this goddamn country, might as well admit it: it felt like he belonged with *him*, this impossible man with an unusual and beautiful name: Eton.

...

"You know what has changed since then?" Eton says, his tone steadfast.

...

Jack raised his head, swept a hand across the mirror and stared at the face looking back at him. Two-day-old stubble, lips bitten raw, angry bruise spreading over the cheekbone. Blue eyes full of shadows—the same shadows that he'd seen in Eton's eyes when he was leaving...

As usual, Eton had insisted on taking him home. But he had shaken his head, choked out a bitter laugh. "You can't."

God, how couldn't he see, one so smart, so understanding, that the place Jack returning to wasn't his home? The person he was leaving behind was...

...

"For me - nothing."

...

Problem was, it had changed everything for Jack. *He* had changed it, one Eton May Volkonsky. Every-fucking-thing!

PART III - RENEGADES

Chapter 54

"I'm sorry, Eton. So sorry, you have no idea!"

"Remember what I said?" Eton's eyes are sad, not accusing.

"Don't go, please! I need to tell you—"

"Nothing has changed." He shakes his head, turns around and walks away...

Jack woke up with a start, heart pounding, mouth dry. And the spot on the pillow under his cheek was wet. He opened his eyes. The electronic clock on the bedside table showed five thirty-seven. Fifty-three minutes to his wake-up call. He sighed and closed his eyes again.

Sometimes he wished he had stopped having these dreams. But the next moment he would berate himself, fearing that his wish might come true. No, he'd rather have these disturbing dreams about Eton than no dreams at all. Like during those sixteen months when he hadn't "seen" Eton's face, not once, and was terrified that he was forgetting him. Betraying him yet again. He had promised to always remember him. OK, so he hadn't told Eton *that*, but it didn't matter. What did matter was that he had sworn to himself he wouldn't, then not even two months later he'd stopped having dreams of him, and then thought he'd do anything to have his dreams back. Anything!

What had brought Eton back was a massive explosion outside Islamabad that had wiped out their entire ammo dump at Ojhri Camp. Ten thousand tons of rockets, mortars, small-arms ammunition, plastic explosives and Stingers—all blown to hell in one go. That night Eton came back to him and stayed put. In his dreams. Then, not all his dreams about Eton ended with heartbreak. There were also dizzying nights when he didn't want to get up in the morning...

* * *

The expulsion of the last four case officers and the de facto shutdown of the CIA operation in the Soviet Union in October 1986 were in the end overshadowed by other events, which took the Company and the press by storm.

The first was the Iran Contra affair instigated by Reagan's admission that America had been secretly selling arms to Iran. Next was Director Casey's rapidly deteriorating health, leading to his resignation. Finally, in December 1986, the "marines secrets-for-sex" scandal broke out, set off by the confession of a marine guard at the US Embassy in Moscow, Clayton Lonetree, that he might have been manipulated by the KGB. An oddball of a loner was Clayton, whose only friend and confidant was Grant Whittaker, one of Jack's marine buddies. These events, and particularly the latter, triggered a major reshuffling in the Company.

As a result, in early December 1986, Joe Coburn was reassigned to Islamabad as Chief of Station and Head of Afghan Task Force's field operation to manage the Company's growing support to Afghan mujahedin. In January, he started pulling together his field ops team.

Jack was one of the *firsts* transferred to Joe Coburn's special unit. It wasn't exactly what he had planned on doing after his return from Moscow. Furthermore, it effectively meant that operations TALION and SEABROOK were put on hold.

The debriefing with Joe Coburn and the Director of Operations on SEABROOK took place a week after Jack's return to HQ. He repeated what he had written in his report: he came out to Eton May Volkonsky as a CIA officer and pitched him. The young man reacted violently at first, but Jack managed to appease him, and he agreed to be "in touch" with Jack. However, he turned down Jack's suggestion that someone else would contact him—it had to be Jack, or nobody. The boy still needed a lot of handholding before he was ready to deliver, Jack conceded, but they had time. The important thing was that he was now working at the nuclear institute in Dubna. What Jack couldn't confirm was whether the boy was a homosexual.

The DO shook his hand and said that his achievement would be taken into account for his annual performance review. But it would be best for Jack, both professionally and for security reasons, if he continued reporting to Joe Coburn.

Jack received his reassignment to the Afghan Task Force in mid-December. A week before the New Year of 1987, he resigned from his cover job with the US Information Agency and enrolled in a journalism course at George Washington University. Thus began his new, "official" career as a freelance reporter.

In addition, Jack took a crash course in Pashtun and specialized training on unconventional warfare at the Farm. For four and a half months, he went through the motions, sleeping five, sometimes four hours a night, his mind switching off the moment his head hit the pillow. Which was good as it left him no time to think about anything else. No time to do anything else, either. Least of all to date Savannah like he'd planned.

Savannah Jones was part of Jack's plan to return to Moscow. He knew it might take him three - four years, but he didn't allow himself to doubt that eventually he would get there. He was fairly certain he would be the one to continue TALION, considering what he had reported about Eton. Unlike other Moscow Station officers, he hadn't been declared a persona non grata by Russians, therefore could return when the dust had settled. Hence, all he had to do was make himself eligible for the next Moscow posting through the State Department. It meant that he must get married.

Things changed when Jack got a new cover. As a freelance reporter, he didn't need to have a wife to be posted overseas. In fact, it wasn't a good idea to have a wife waiting at home when you were assigned to a place like Afghanistan. But to have a gorgeous date in Washington DC—who was also a fellow case officer—was convenient. And even more so since they seemed to be on the same page as far as their relationship went.

Savanna was rotating through the Near East Division when Jack returned to Washington, working as back office support for active projects in Israel. Since Israel was handling the arms procurement for the Pakistanis, who acted as the front for Afghan mujahedin, she knew enough about Joe Coburn's recruitment for the Afghan field ops. At a staff meeting, she confided to Jack that she had applied for the opening but was turned down, despite her decent Farsi and excellent recommendations.

By March, the snowballing marine sex-for-secret scandal prompted a congressional inquiry about security breaches at the Embassy in Moscow. The most serious one concerned the allegation that Lonetree had escorted KGB agents into sensitive spaces within the Embassy, including the Communication Processing Unit, aka the Tank, and let them stay there for unspecified amount of time. The entire marine dispatch was recalled.

In the second week of March, Grant Whitaker and another marine, Arnold Bracy, who admitted to have been seeing Russian women, were charged with espionage and arrested. Later, it was revealed that several people at the Embassy knew about the marines' relationships with local women.

In April, Jack was summoned for questioning about his friendship with the marines and his verbal report to the Regional Security Officer. His written report to Nurimbekoff about him witnessing a Russian staff at the marines' quarters wasn't mentioned, and Jack figured the Company had swept it under the carpet.

In May, as a contract reporter for the Associated Press, Jack arrived in Islamabad. He took up a tiny two-room apartment in a colonial building a mile and a half away from the security tight compound where Joe and the field task force lived.

With the Iran Contra affair still snowballing, the CIA was paranoid about its direct support to the mujahedin being noticed. In this respect, Jack's journalistic job was a win-win deal: the AP got reports and pictures from the ground; the Company got a great cover for one of its officers to come and go across the border and keep an eye on the traffic of the weapons supplied to the mujahedin through the Pakistani military and security forces.

Jack's first border crossing occurred 3 weeks after his arrival. He was to join the entourage of Charlie Wilson, a congressman from Texas and ardent supporter of the Afghan program, on his visit to a mujahedin camp on the other side of the Pakistan-Afghanistan border. Coincidentally or not, his visit happened at the same time with the delivery of Stinger missiles to the mujahedin. Having heard stories about Charlie Wilson's "Angels", Jack was only mildly surprised to see the congressman's "staff member", Annalisa, dazzling in her ornate cowgirl outfit, joining their otherwise all-male Afghan expedition. What did raise his eyebrows was Joe Coburn's instruction on the eve of the three-day trip: Jack was to see to it that the congressional delegate got all he wanted, even if it was firing a Stinger at the Soviet choppers.

"He pays all his and our bills five times over." Joe shrugged, seeing Jack's quizzical expression.

It didn't come to that, to the obvious relief of the head of the Pakistani security unit that accompanied the congressman. The Texan toyed with a Stinger, had a few pictures taken with the Afghan commander and his guerrilla fighters, and returned the handheld missile.

The second time Jack followed a party comprising several doctors and volunteer-nurses from Doctors Without Borders. They visited an Afghan refugee camp near the Pakistani border, one of many where around two and a half million refugees from around the country had congregated. Even with his dirt poor, redneck background Jack was keenly aware that he had been better off than most of those he saw: his family had a house, six acres of land, three horses, a dozen of cows and a piece of shit of a truck. These people had nothing. Stuck in a feudal time warp, they had no home, no life, no future. And worst of all, there was nothing they could do to change their lot.

On the fourth crossing, he was caught in a Soviet air raid on a village in Konar Valley. The fast-flowing Konar River cut through a range of spectacular gorges, snaked its way through valleys dotted with kishlaks of mudstone houses and blanketed with crimson, pink and white *poppy fields. Most of the valleys were flanked by soaring walls of rock that rose thousands of feet to end in pine-covered plateaus. Jack accompanied a party of three Pakistani paramilitary instructors and a group of mujahedin transporting a shipment of mortars and Kalashnikovs to their camp further up north. It was then that he truly understood the meaning of a phrase he'd heard more than once before: "Our gold, their blood". What had once been a poor but idyllic village on the river with cherry and apricot trees lining its banks, in less than half an hour, had been reduced to a pile of smoking, blood-smeared rubble.*

On his next trip, Jack found out that when the mujahedin didn't fight the Sovs, they fought each other, raiding and savaging villages and villagers with the same ruthlessness they fought the invaders. It wasn't all about the struggle for independence; more often than not, it was the fight for domination—a medieval, centuries old war for power and land. And Jack couldn't quite figure out what exactly he and his colleagues were doing there, in the name of security of America and the American people.

What particularly disturbed him was the neglect and abuse that Afghan children and women suffered at the hands of their men. But that was in accordance with the laws of Islam, he was told by a redheaded French surgeon from Doctors Without Borders as she was assaulting his belt buckle at the back of a cave that served as the operating room.

"You're a good man, Jack," she said as they were parting. "But try not to meddle with the local traditions and mores. It's a strange place. Kindness here is like an elastic band: it stretches from right to wrong, and often you don't even notice how one end morphs into the other."

It wasn't until a few months later that he understood what she had meant.

Jack had noticed from his first interactions with the mujahedin that the entourages of Afghan commanders' often included one or two boys between the ages of ten and fifteen. They didn't look like guerrilla fighters. He assumed they were close relatives of the commanders since everybody treated them with strange deference so atypical of these brutish men of zealous faith. Farooq, the AP's Pakistani associate whom Jack had befriended, shrugged when asked about the boys, and said they were "chai boys", commanders' personal servants. Usually eager to explain any local convention, this time the Pakistani was unwilling to talk, so Jack didn't press. But the vagueness of Farooq's answer left him wondering.

He found his answer a few months later when he and a Pakistani security team of four accompanied a delivery of Stingers to a mujahedin camp northeast of Khost. After the demonstration of the weapons, they were invited to the commander's home in a large village nearby owned by the man's family.

* * *

The guest room *hujra* was a typical rectangular chamber, unfurnished, carpeted wall to wall with thick but well-worn rugs. Oil lamps on the floor and on the walls cast a dim light on the gathering of two dozen bearded men sitting on the floor. In the center, a white cloth was laid out, covered with large plates overflowing with grilled meat *kebabs*, *naan* bread, *palau* rice, dry fruits and nuts—an abundance of food Jack hadn't seen on this side of the border. Hash pipes and tea were served by four boys, aged eleven to sixteen, all dressed in traditional *shalwar kameez*, but in bright colors atypical for Afghans—crimson, pink, pale blue and mauve.

The host, Jalil Haq, invited Jack and the Pakistanis to sit next to him. As they settled down on the cushions, a boy approached Jack with a copper bowl and an elaborate ceramic pot. His crimson *kameez* heightened the fairness of his skin, and his eyes under thick, jet-black lashes were light, vivid green. The boy dropped his gaze when he saw Jack eyeing him and turned to the guest sitting next to him, offering him to wash his hands.

As the dinner progressed, and the guests got looser from hash, Jack noticed that the men were paying more attention to the boys—looked at them sideways, whispering and giggling. He smothered a surge of distaste, wishing for the dinner to end soon. An hour had passed before the village elders praised God, thanked the host and prepared to leave. Jack stood up, said his thanks, turning down the invitation to stay, and followed the elders out.

In the mud brick guesthouse across the yard where he was to spend the night, Jack pulled out his lightweight sleeping bag, rolled it out along the wall and lay down on top of it. It was one of the nights when he felt restless, struggling to keep his mind from venturing back to the time and place he tried not to think of too often. Especially not on trips like this where there was no alcohol to ease him to sleep.

Faint sounds of music reached him: someone was singing, accompanied by a *dutar*, a local two-string lute. When the song ended, and the singer started a new tune, Jack got up, put on his jacket and stepped out into the courtyard.

The autumn night was clear and crisp, the moon just off its fullest. Jack lit a cigarette, breathed in a lungful of cigarette smoke, fresh mountain air laced with smells of goats, manure and dry earth, and leaned against the mud wall. There was not a sound around, except for the singing, clearer now, coming from the *hujra* in the main house. Its small window into the courtyard was open a crack, a string of light slipping through the drawn curtains.

Jack strained to listen.

"His body's so soft, his lips so tender... Oh boy, you set your lover on fire," a young voice sang.

Did he get it right? No, it couldn't be. Women were the lowliest class of citizens here, no more than domestic slaves. These people didn't even have brothels.

He crossed the courtyard in a dozen quiet steps and peeked in through the thin gap between the curtains.

The guests who had stayed back were still sitting around the perimeter of the room, but the white centerpiece had been cleared. A slender figure wearing a short jacket trimmed in gold tassels over a bright orange dress was swirling in the middle of the room. A darker orange silk scarf covered the face and neck, little bells around the cuffs and ankles jingling to the rhythm of the song.

A woman?! How in the hell could it be?

Right then, the dancer made one final swirl to the music, dropped gracefully to her knees, facing the window, and brushed the scarf off her face with a flirtatious sweep of a hand.

Jack gulped.

It was the boy with piercing green eyes, Omar. Wearing a dress, eye shadow and lipstick, he looked like a girl. A man sitting right under the window rose, took a couple of steps toward the boy, and squatted down next to him. Jalil. The *mujahedin* commander pulled the white cloth off his shoulder and patted the sweat off the boy's face. Then he stroked his face and murmured something to him. Omar smiled weakly and dropped his gaze bashfully. The men around the room made guttural approving sounds, one even clapped.

Jack stepped back, took the last, gut-deep drag on his half-burnt cigarette and returned to his room. It was downright creepy, but he could see why. As dictated by their religion, men couldn't have women joining them at their gatherings, so they had boys dressed up like girls instead.

Dancing girls…

No, he didn't care to know more. He had his orders: whatever happened amongst locals, if it wasn't a threat to the United States' security, it was none of their business. Jack turned the kerosene lamp low, climbed into the sleeping bag, closed his eyes, and willed himself to sleep.

He was awakened by voices arguing somewhere nearby. In the courtyard, he figured, shrugging off shreds of uneasy sleep. The argument was about… who was taking someone home tonight. The going rate appeared to be two goats, a brand new Egyptian AK folding rifle and one hundred American dollars; the arbiter was the host. And then someone dropped the name of the barter: Omar.

Jack shivered in disgust, sickened to the core. Were these people for fucking real?! Wasn't this a place where the Holy Koran ruled? This couldn't be! But then the little show in the house hadn't looked like it had all been dreamt up by Jalil Haq: the boys who served them at the dinner had looked like they'd been doing it all their lives, and Omar, he'd definitely been trained to dance.

This is sick!

And why the fuck had they never been briefed about *this*, neither at the Farm, nor in Islamabad? Surely *they* must know about this revolting shit going on here. Joe Coburn definitely should. And what had he told Jack instead? Not to interfere in any dispute between the locals because it was none of their business.

Yeah, right… Fuck you, Joe! Fuck you all, you sonsuvbitches!!

He ripped his sleeping bag open in one furious sweep, jumped up, and stormed out into the courtyard in his socks.

"Five hundred American dollars!" he growled, barely reigning in the contempt he felt.

The men turned to stare at him in stunned silence. The host recovered first, and launched into an elaborate speech: the rules of hospitality dictated that the boy must be given as a gift to the esteemed guest, if Jack wished to have the boy for the night. He pushed Omar towards Jack. But then, the man continued, if the guest insisted, he couldn't possibly refuse the five hundred dollars—a generous gift from the honorable guest of the house.

Jack insisted. It was more than half of the "travel money" he had on him, but it didn't matter. What mattered was that the boy was freed from these dirty old men tonight. And he'd figure later what to do next.

Jack waved Omar into his quarters, flicked his lighter up, and waited patiently for the boy to take off his plastic sandals before stepping in gingerly. Then he walked in, turned up the storm-light and closed the door.

- 410 -

There were muted sounds of an agitated conversation in the courtyard as Jalil Haq tried to appease his other guests. Then the flimsy wooden gate in the mud wall creaked open, praises to God and to the host were said, and everything went quiet.

Jack pointed to the stack of blankets and pillows piled up high against the wall and told Omar to turn the lamp down when he was ready to sleep. Then he dragged his sleeping bag to the door, placed it right next to it, and climbed in.

"Am I not going to sleep with *burra sahib* tonight?" the boy asked timidly, calling Jack "big, important man".

Jack groaned inside. "No, Omar. You will sleep there and I sleep here."

There was a long pause, then Omar whispered, "Am I not pleasing to *burra sahib*?" He sounded upset. "I'm the best dancer in the province. I look good... do I not?"

Jack blew out an exasperated sigh and sat up. "Listen, Omar. It is not about you. Yes, you are a great dancer, and I like you. But I don't sleep with boys." Not with underage boys that was for sure! "It is not right. You must... go to school, not do this..." Jack bit his tongue. Easy for him to preach, but the poor kid had no say in what happened to him in this life. Like most everybody in this goddamn country.

"I plan to, when I'm eighteen and have lots of money... But now I'm in big trouble." Omar said flatly, and lay down, pulling the blanket up to his chin.

"Why? What happen?"

"Everybody wanted me to go home with them, but *burra sahib* asked for me as a gift. They will be angry now. Nobody will want to have me anymore." Seeing Jack's puzzled expression, the boy explained, "They will think I slept with... eh, an infidel. Please forgive me for saying, *burra sahib*... They may even kill me when you have gone."

"You are joking!" The boy was clearly not joking.

"No, I'm not joking. I'm sad."

Shit. What now?

Jack got up, stepped up the place where Omar was lying by the pile of blankets and pillows, wrapped in an old, heavy quilt.

The boy raised his head. "*Burra sahib* is going to get me?"

Jack clenched his jaw. "No, Omar. I take blankets, my bed and sleep outside by the door. And *nobody* thinks that you slept with infidel."

"But *burra sahib* can't sleep outside the door like a dog!" Omar sprang up, sounding worried now. "*Agah sahib* will kill me when he learns!"

"Nobody kills you, Omar. *Nobody*. I promise. You go to sleep, boy." Jack stepped out with two armfuls of bedding and shut the door firmly behind him.

The next day, for one of Jack's two cameras and three hundred dollars, leaving him with just fifty bucks for the way back, Jalil Haq let Omar go with him. He didn't have a plan, but couldn't leave the boy behind after what he'd heard and seen. And definitely not after what Omar had confided to him in quiet, emotionless voice of what was awaiting him after Jack was gone.

However, he had to leave the boy at a refugee camp near the Pakistani border. Omar had no papers, and Jack didn't have enough money left to bribe his way through. He promised to come back with papers for Omar and put him up in Islamabad at one of the NGO-run centers for Afghan refugees. The green-eyed boy smiled at him, said he would wait and pray for *burra sahib* every day, because *burra sahib* was the best owner he'd ever had, and he wanted to serve *burra sahib* even after he turned eighteen and grew a beard. And he would do anything for *burra sahib*, anything he wanted.

When Jack returned with papers three weeks later, Omar was gone. He was told that the boy's uncle had come and taken him home up north. When Jack pressed for the uncle's name, he was told that his name was Rahim Ershadi. Jack thanked the head of the camp, apologized for all the trouble, and left, feeling deeply disappointed, furious and helpless at the same time.

Rahim Ershadi was the name of Jalil Haq's second in command.

* * *

All Jack's attempts to find Omar were futile. He never heard about the green-eyed boy again. And why should he? The boy was just one of thousands of Afghan dancing boys just like him.

Instead, he learned a lot about Afghanistan's centuries old tradition of bacha bazi— "playing with kids". Or dancing boys, as Westerners prudishly called them. It turned out, quite a few foreigners knew about the practice. One connoisseur of Afghan culture explained to Jack that dancing boys were a status symbol, and that there was always rivalry between mujahedin commanders about who had the best and prettiest dancing boys. Then Joe reminded him that it wasn't their business to change the local customs, no matter how repulsive they might be.

"The Chinese eat cats, and the Vietnamese eat dogs," he shrugged and patted Jack's knee, "Chill, Jack. You're doing a great job. Just don't overdo it."

Jack nodded, his jaw clenched. But after that incident, the sympathy for Afghan men that he still had simply evaporated.

Jack spent three weeks of the winter holidays of 1987 in Washington, two of them with Savannah. They started out by eating out every day, then spent the entire weekend going around museums during the day and seeing movies in the evening. Afterwards Jack stayed at her tiny apartment in Georgetown, and they had sex, followed by a cozy breakfast in bed the next morning, and more sex.

He stayed at her place for the rest of his home leave.

The night before his departure to Pakistan, Savannah rolled off him, and said, "Jack, let's get married."

"What?"

"You need a wife for your overseas postings, don't you? Maybe not now, but after your Afghan assignment," she reasoned. "And I need a husband for mine, too." Seeing Jack's expression, she added with a quick laugh, "Don't worry, honey-pie. It's all business. You'll still have your life and I'll keep mine. And we'll cover each other's back... A deal?"

It wasn't a bad deal at all and fell squarely into Jack's plans. They agreed to discuss their marriage with their respective units' heads and arrange a wedding over the summer. They settled on a small and simple affair. Savannah didn't want to invite any of her relatives to her arranged wedding, not even her mother, and Jack had no relatives, except his father who didn't want to know him.

Contrary to his expectations, Jack's wedding plans did not enthuse Joe Coburn. He listened to Jack without interruption, his expression neutral, then said that he would get back to him on that issue. Since Jack wasn't really in a hurry to wed, he agreed to wait.

Joe still hadn't come back to him by the end of March. Then on April 10th, the ammunition depot at Ojhri Camp blew up, wiping out thousands of tons of weapons and killing over thirteen hundred people. Jack had been visiting a local contact who lived near the camp and left his house fifteen minutes before the explosion.

Jack didn't go to bed that night. He spent the night at the cordoned-off zone of destruction, scavenging for news and photos. Then he stayed up until dawn, drinking with a group of paramilitary types at the Agency's compound. He got home around seven in the morning, showered and changed, took a couple of "go pills", of which there was always a ready supply from the Station, and headed out hunting for news again. By the time he got back to his apartment again, it was far past midnight, and he was dead on his feet.

That night, after nearly sixteen months of absence, Eton came back to him. And had stayed in his dreams ever since.

* * *

Eton had said that last time they were together that nothing changed for him, even after he had learned the truth about Jack. It had been two and a half years since that night in Moscow. In another life, in a different world. A lifetime ago. But sometimes Jack felt like it had been just yesterday. When he closed his eyes, he could still recall how Eton's young, hard body filled his arms, the warmth of Eton's lips on his, and the serene feeling of completeness and peace that came over him only when he was with Eton.

He had thought that things would change that the longing would fade with time. But maybe Eton was right: some things in life don't change.

Chapter 55

Jack was making himself the second round of morning coffee when the phone rang.

"Hi, Jack. It's Helen. Your office said you're working from home today."

"Good morning, sweetie-pie. Yeah, need some peace and quiet to finish my articles... But what are you still doing here? Thought you had headed back home for the summer."

"We are. On Monday."

"That's right. I've lost track of what day it is today. In any case, I promise to look after Paul while you're away." He chuckled. Helen, her husband Paul Millard, the Sunday Times' correspondent in East Berlin, and their two young kids occupied the apartment below Jack's.

"I know you two. You'll probably live on beer and junk food for the whole month."

Jack pictured her rolling her eyes and hastened to assure her, "We'll have dinners sometimes. You approve the food at Metzer Eck, don't you?"

Helen sighed theatrically. "I hope Barbel will look after you two, scruffy urchins. In the meantime," she continued over Jack's feeble protests, "We'll be having a going away dinner on Saturday. I've booked you in. Don't you dare stand me up this time, Jack Smith. Lizzie and I will never forgive you." Helen tried to sound stern, but Jack could hear notes of amusement in her tone of voice.

Three-year-old Lizzie was the spitting image of her petite, blonde, gray-eyed mum. She considered Jack her personal playmate and refused to leave his side whenever she saw him.

"Not this time. I swear!"

"All right, Jack. I take your word for that... By the way, you can drop by for dinner tonight, too. If you want." Helen had a strange compulsion to try to feed Jack every time she talked to him.

"Thanks, hon. But I'm fixed for tonight. I'll see you on Saturday, okay? And please tell Lizzie I won't miss her farewell party for love nor money."

Jack returned to his coffee, lit a cigarette and sat down with a steaming mug by the opened window. The chestnut and lime trees in the small park across the street were still young, and he could see the top floors of decrepit buildings on the other side of the park over their crowns. One of those buildings, largely abandoned, contained East Berlin Station's safe house reserved as his safe haven.

Jack had been there twice to put on the disguise for his support ops. He was impressed how painstakingly the concealed basement space was equipped: there were a Sig P226, a Beretta M9 and an MPi-KMS, the East German version of AKM, ammunition enough to start a small war, cash enough to buy a rescue helicopter, several sets of passports and local IDs, communication equipment and other cloak and dagger paraphernalia. The place also had everything two people on the run needed to live comfortably for a month. It felt good to have such a fallback, although Jack thought at the level of activities East Berlin

Station operated, he wouldn't need most of what was there. After the head-spinning series of disastrous events in Moscow, then his Afghan experience, all human misery, guns and testosterone, the assignment in East Berlin was downright boring. The ordinariness of his existence here, even with new friends on both sides of the Wall and the exuberant nightlife in West Berlin, made time drag. It felt like this interim period of his life would never end. But there was nothing he could do to speed things up, was there? So he just had to take a deep breath, grit his teeth and wait. Because after this, Jack hoped—no, he was *certain* that after this shit hole his next stop would be Moscow.

* * *

Although Jack's field assignment was effectively over by May 1988, when the Soviets began withdrawing from Afghanistan, he remained in Islamabad for another six months. He still covered action on the ground for the AP, but now focused on the human side of the war. It was during these last months of the posting that his stories and photographs, most of them about the Afghan refugee camps, started to appear in American newspapers under his own name.

Joe Coburn returned to Washington at the end of September to take over as Head of the SE Division. Jack came back in early November, just around the time promotions were announced, including his. His cover job with the AP was assessed as "effective", and Joe in his new role decided to stress test it on the other side of the Iron Curtain, starting with East Germany. Thus, shortly after his return, Jack began to prepare for his next posting as an AP reporter based in East Berlin. The understanding was that his next stop would be Moscow.

Jack also resumed dating Savannah. But since he wasn't going to be posted through the State Department this time, there was little pressure to get married right away. And with Savannah leaving in January for her first overseas posting, they agreed to postpone their wedding plans for a year, maybe two.

He ran their plan by Joe, and the division chief conceded that for Jack to operate without a diplomatic cover, a wife with one would be a great backup in Moscow. However, for now, they should just get going with their respective postings.

In March 1989, Jack arrived in East Berlin as one of AP's two full time reporters. He took up a refurbished apartment on the top floor of a turn of the century building three miles east of the Berlin Wall.

He was flying high. It wasn't Moscow yet, but this was as close as he could get to it for now— just over 1,600 kilometers, less than a three hour flight away. He was told that the security in East Berlin was more stringent for the diplomatic staff than in Moscow, but as he wasn't one of them now, he thought it was possibly more lax. Or maybe the Stasi was more confident in the discipline of fear they had instituted in Democratic Republic of Germany. In any case, Jack didn't mind at all that his coverage here was as light as in his Moscow days. So much so that he struck up friendships with a few locals in less than five months. It felt almost like "home": conversations held in whispers in the kitchen with taps running and the TV on, anyone who approached you on the street or in a bar could be a Stasi or at least an informer. Like in Russia, friendship mattered the most. Or maybe even more, because the methodical ruthlessness of the East German security organs was said to be greater, too. Something Jack didn't care to find out without a diplomatic cover. The nearness to West Berlin and the relative ease of the border crossing procedure were probably the reasons why Joe Coburn had decided to test this type of cover, which the Agency hadn't used for a very long time, in East Germany.

* * *

After his morning coffee, Jack started typing his two pieces after his trip to Hamburg where he'd interviewed three East German soccer players who'd defected in Sweden. The trio had told Jack that they'd regularly been given performance-enhancing drugs in the months prior to major international competitions. The story fell neatly into his recent series on this topic.

It had begun a month earlier when, through his German contacts, he did an exclusive interview with two other defectors—veterans of East German sport. They had impeccable credentials: one was a four-time world champion ski jumper and a gold-medal winner in the 1976 Winter Olympics, and the other a former chairman of the East German judo federation, the highest-ranking East German sports official ever to defect. In their account about their lives in the communist Germany, they claimed that virtually all medal-winning East German athletes were force-fed anabolic steroids, beginning as early as age thirteen, including figure skating, gymnastics and swimming. A week later, Jack corroborated the story with two other East German medal-winning athletes who now lived in Vienna and Hamburg.

His first report had set off a wave of outrage in the international press. Two weeks later the DTSB, East Germany's central sports organization, had to acknowledge for the first time that there was indeed a drug problem in amongst its athletes. It denied, however, that the sportsmen were administered endurance enhancing drugs forcibly on regular basis.

Jack's exposé reports had not endeared him to the East German authorities, but the fact that the AP had circulated the interviews before Reuters and West German *Bild* got to the sources had firmed up Jack's reputation in the trade. It also played neatly into East Berlin Station's hands: thanks to Jack's legitimate romping around scavenging for news, the Station had made a recruitment, adding a prized Stasi officer to the Company's disappointingly shortlist of East German agents.

* * *

For decades, the Agency's spy games in East Germany had been pathetic. The local security service, Ministerium für Staatssicherheit, or Stasi for short, had so successfully instilled fear in the East German population that hardly anybody dared play for the other side. Then in the mid '80s, the then chief of East Berlin Station, Florence Neumann, had succeeded in recruiting three agents in the space of two years, of whom two were Stasi officers from the surveillance division. However, shortly after, one of them provided the Station with proof that the other two were in fact double agents. Nevertheless, it was progress.

Soon, the Station had a complete list of names of the MfS surveillance unit that covered East Berlin Station and military attachés at the Embassy, along with their photos and photos of their cars. Before long, all case officers at the Station knew the Stasi surveillance team and their cars by sight. The only thing they didn't have was their home addresses.

Then one day, while taking a casual date home, Jack noticed the car of a Stasi from the surveillance team near her building. It belonged to a tall rake of a man nicknamed Hawk by the Station for his distinct aquiline nose. A few days later, disguised as a local worker, Jack turned up at the bus stop across the street from the building where he thought the man lived. He mingled with a small crowd of commuters waiting to catch an early morning bus to work, and sure enough, at exactly half past seven Hawk drove his car out into the street and headed toward the city center.

An operation was quickly pulled together. One morning two weeks later, a letter was planted in Hawk's car. It contained a generous offer of money in exchange for working for the Company. To convince Hawk it wasn't a ruse by his superiors to test his loyalty, the previous East Berlin Station chief whom Hawk had known as a CIA officer was posted across the street. The letter asked him to leave a sign if he agreed to the proposal.

* * *

And so two days ago, Jack had picked up the sign. Of course, the German was still to be interviewed and tested, but it was a good start, nonetheless.

Jack finished his articles just before noon. He went to the kitchen, made himself a sandwich and sat down with a can of coke and a pile of newspapers by his plate. He put aside the local *Neues Deutscheland* and the Soviet *Pravda*, which he had read with his morning coffee, and spread the Washington Post over one end of the kitchen table. As was his habit, he scanned the front page looking for Soviet news.

When he returned from Moscow, at first Jack had closely followed the news in the Soviet Union through Soviet newspapers he could read at HQ's library. However, soon the preps and training for the new field assignment took up all his waking hours, and Jack gradually gave up making an effort to seek out Russian news. He managed to get access and thumb through Moscow Station's files before his departure to Pakistan, but found no updates on any of the operations in the Soviet Union. Of course, not. What had he expected? He was the case officer for TALION and without him there, who else would report on developments with his local contacts?

The eighteen months in Pakistan were light on Russian news, most coming from American or British newspapers and TV newscasts. Following the signing of the Geneva Accord and the beginning of the Soviet troop withdrawal from Afghanistan, Soviet news coverage peaked. But even that didn't satisfy Jack's need.

It became easier to placate this craving when Jack returned from Pakistan. And when he was reassigned to East Berlin, it felt like coming home from a long voyage as updates from Moscow were always in the local media.

What seemed almost surreal was their content. Two years ago, even in his wildest dreams, Jack couldn't have imagined that he'd be reading *this* kind of news about Russia, less so that Soviet newspapers would be carrying it. He often wondered what Prof. Volkonsky, and more importantly, what Eton would have said about all that was going on in Russia.

"Three Thousand Soviet Miners End Strike With Unprecedented Gains". It was the first major labor strike in the Soviet Union, and it could never have happened a few years ago, maybe even a year ago.

What about this one: "Ex-Soviet Army Marshal to Testify"? The former chief of staff of the Soviet Army was to testify before the House's Armed Services Committee. A Soviet Marshal questioned by Americans about arms control and Soviet military budget? Totally out of this world! And on the progress of the arms reduction talks—"Soviets Welcome NATO Proposals to Cut Forces".

He had missed the turning point when the Sovs started accepting American proposals, Even now, at this advanced stage, their willingness to go along was mindboggling. And he wasn't alone: the agreement on the proposals was two months ahead of schedule, making one veteran negotiator describe the pace as "almost breathtaking".

Jack wondered if things had changed for Eton and his friends. What was Eton doing now? Probably had completed his *aspirantura* by this time and got his Candidate of Science degree, the equivalent of a Ph.D. in the West. That boy could have had a seriously bright future with his brains had he lived in America. But since things seemed to have been changing in the right direction lately, maybe he would have one in Russia, too...

If Jack Smith and the Company wouldn't screw it up for him.

He put away the Los Angeles Times and picked up the last publication in the pile, the June issue of *Wohin in Berlin?*, a thick periodical featuring notices and reviews of cultural events in and around East Berlin. He leafed idly through the first few pages, paused on the Theater section. Then as he turned the page, his heart leaped to his throat.

Gazing at him from a full-page theatrical poster was Lara, her face half turned into the profile of an older man, her eyes both hopeful and sad.

Jack's eyes devoured the text the moment his mind started functioning again.

"July 1st - July 15th. Metropol Theater. Guest performance by Moscow LenKom Theater's Experimental Studio. Presenting Rock Operas "Juno and Avos" and "The Rise and Fall of the Artist". Director Viktor Karelin (posthumous). Music A. Rybnikov, E. Volkonsky. Lyrics A. Voznesensky, V. Karelin, E. Volkonsky. Lead vocals: Larisa Novikova-Volkonskaya, Evgheniy Belykh, Vyacheslav Lanskoy."

July 15th. Tomorrow.

Shit! Why didn't you read the damn magazine earlier, idiot? It has been in the pile forever!

Lara in Juno and Avos. She's made it. They have made it, she and Karelin both. It's all your effort, isn't it, Lara? Well done, girl!

Volkonskaya... She's made it here too. But how? They weren't... didn't... Right?

Or maybe they *had* been and had him framed. Maybe it had all been one big Russian spectacle for one gullible shithead like Jack Smith. They were both great actors, weren't they? He had seen them on the stage—they were terrific, especially *the boy*... So why he was even surprised now?

So. Does it mean that...?

No, he wasn't going to speculate. What he was going to do was to get off his ass and try to get a ticket for this last show of hers tomorrow and then try to see her afterwards.

Right, tomorrow, Saturday... Saturday?!

Fuck. He couldn't stand up Helen and her little daughter once again. That would be the third time since he'd known them. But then he *must* see Lara, too. *Must* talk to her. To find out if he had been compromised after all. By his friends.

By Eton.

He got a ticket for the show that night by the late afternoon, procured through his local friends who frequented Metzer Eck, a corner bar not far from his apartment block. In the beginning Barbel, the jovial owner of the bar, was upset that he wasn't coming for their regular Friday night gathering, the fourth one in a row he wouldn't be joining. But she was mollified when Jack confided that he used to know the leading lady well and had even gone out with her a few times when he worked in Moscow. It turned out that Barbel and her partner, Axel, had seen both operas a week earlier and left impressed, especially with Karelin's The Rise and Fall of the Artist.

"It is *quite* non-traditional for a Russian play. Seems more like western directing. I'm surprised they've been allowed to put it on stage."

"By the way, I knew the director, too. He wasn't in favor back then. So I'm surprised too."

"How fascinating! Now you must come on Saturday to tell us about your Russian friends," Barbel insisted. She and her friends were all well-connected in the arts world and avid theater-goers.

"Sorry, Barbel, I can't do this Saturday, either. But I'll come on Sunday. I promise."

"All right. Sunday night it is, then. I'll tell everybody. Dinner and beers are on the house. In the meantime, enjoy the show, dear."

Jack didn't know if he was going to enjoy it. He dreaded he might not. But even if Lara was going to wipe out all his hopes and everything he had been longing for, he still had to know.

Chapter 56

The Rise And Fall Of The Artist was a big hit with German theater-goers. The cast received a standing ovation and the lead vocalists, Lara and her counterpart Vyacheslav Lanskoy, graciously performed an encore of the play's main ballad, "Will You Remember Me When I'm Gone?" The show's pamphlet stated only that the composers were A. Rybnikov and E. Volkonsky, but Jack thought he had recognized the familiar pattern of Eton's songs he had heard before: slow and haunting start, ending with explosive, gut-wrenchingly passionate chorus lines. Which Lara and this other guy, Vyacheslav, had delivered convincingly.

The cast was still taking curtain calls when Jack made his way out, then along the corridor to the backstage. Before the show, he had found out where Lara's dressing room was and had ordered a basket of crimson roses to be delivered by the finale. Knowing German punctuality, he was sure she would find it in her room when she returned, along with a note that said, "With love and admiration, Jack S. P.S. I'm here, outside." He hoped she still remembered who Jack S. was. But most importantly that she would check out right away the flowers and notes that probably filled her room.

There were a few reporters loitering in the corridor near Lara's and the leading men's dressing rooms. Jack put on his press tag and joined them. By the time the actors returned, more than a dozen people were crowding backstage, with two guards blocking the passage to the actors' changing rooms.

When Lara appeared at the other end of the corridor, followed by the leading man and a woman in her forties with her arms full of costumes, the gathering bunched up, clamoring and calling out to the them, trying to get closer. The guards pushed back, their faces deadpan. Lara smiled languidly at the host of admirers, gave her colleague a wave of a hand and disappeared behind the door of her room.

Jack pressed his back to the wall, preparing to hold out the siege and be the last man standing here, if necessary.

A vaguely familiar, dark-haired man in his late twenties with a large bouquet of pale yellow roses unceremoniously pushed his way through the crowd.

"*Fraulein* Volkonskaya is waiting for me," he announced and was let through, obviously recognized by the guards. He tapped on the door and was let in by Lara's assistant.

"Matthias Hoffman," said the tall rake of a girl standing next to Jack. She wore a loose, fatigue-colored t-shirt and baggy trousers of the same color. Her bleached blond hair was crop-cut and spiky.

"Sorry, I'm rather new here." Jack grinned sheepishly at her.

"He's an actor. Some say he's our own Patrick Swayze." She responded with a quick smile and resumed scanning the corridor.

"Alright. But you are not here for him, right? Let me guess. Vyacheslav Lanskoy?"

"No. I'm here for *her*." She tipped her chin at Lara's dressing room. "She's the sexiest woman I've ever seen," the girl declared with a thin, challenging smile, staring Jack down.

"I see... And I must say I agree with you." He held her stare, but his smile was tightlipped. He had enough on his plate tonight and didn't want to spend time pondering if this was a Stasi probe or not.

The door swung open and Lara's assistant appeared in the doorway. "Which of you are *Dzhehk Smeet?*" she asked in Russian, addressing the crowd.

"I'm Jack Smith." Jack pushed off the wall and started carefully boring his way through the crowd of people, who all turned to look at him. He heard the tall girl groaning behind his back.

"I'm Jack Smith," he repeated, smiling wide, when he was standing in front of the Russian woman.

She glared at him, then nodded solemnly. "She is right. Amazing color of the eyes. Come in, please." She stepped aside to let Jack through the door.

The changing room was unexpectedly large, perhaps intended to be shared by at least three people. Besides a dressing table along the far wall, brightly lit by a dozen or so lightbulbs framing the large mirror, the room featured a suite of antique furniture—a bureau, a recliner, two balloon-back chairs, a curved-legged table and a screen divider.

Lara was sitting at the dresser with her back to the door, facing her visitor. The German actor was sitting on the recliner, straight-backed, his face tight.

"... Matthias, but I can't. I know I said I *might* be available tonight. But now it looks like I'm not." She didn't bother to give him any reason why not, instead turned to Jack. "Hello, Jack. Will you give me a minute? Let me see my good friend Matthias off first. Make yourself comfortable in the meantime." She turned and smiled sweetly at Matthias and offered him her hand without standing up. "See you at the reception on Sunday?"

Matthias stood up and shook her hand, trying rather unsuccessfully to cover his disappointment with nonchalance. "Yes, of course," he said in accented Russian. "See you on Sunday, Lara." He nodded to Jack icily and walked out.

When the door closed behind the German, Lara stood up and made a step toward Jack who was standing near the door. Her hair was still plastered down by a net, but most of the heavy makeup was gone, making her look like a tomboy—a younger and more vulnerable version of the sexless characters she had portrayed in the play.

"Lara, it's so good to see you." Jack approached her gingerly, unsure which way their encounter would go. "Look at you! You've made it big time, haven't you? Congratulations!"

"Thank you, Jack. Good to see you, too." She smiled weakly, eyeing Jack's press tag, obviously puzzled and undecided how to behave. She turned to her assistant, who was sorting a pile of costumes thrown over the screen divider. "Raisa Petrovna, leave it till tomorrow morning. They won't run away. Go join others for drinks now."

The woman looked suspiciously at Lara, then at Jack. "You sure you don't need me to help with anything? With the reporters?" She glared at the tag hanging from the chain around Jack's neck.

"Jack here is an old friend," Lara explained. "He used to work in Moscow and... He'll protect me from other reporters out there. *da*, Jack?" Her smile still didn't match her playful tone.

"Of course I will. Don't you worry, Raisa Petrovna. I promise to bring Lara back to the hotel safe and sound."

They stood waiting patiently for the woman to change into her street shoes and collect her bag behind the screen, mumbling something inaudible. Already in the doorway, she turned and said over her shoulder to Lara, "Don't stay out too late", then nodded ambivalently to Jack and left.

As soon as the door closed behind the older woman, Lara asked urgently, as if the question had been burning her tongue and she needed to spit it out, "So you're not a diplomat anymore? Since when?"

"Since I left Moscow. Became a reporter instead… As you see." He shrugged.

She bit on her lip, furrowed her heavily kohled eyebrows. "Did they fire you?"

And suddenly Jack was looking at the Lara he'd known back in Moscow—a kind, feisty girl who didn't know how to take no for an answer.

"No, I resigned. It didn't really work for me."

"Is it true that you were expelled because you were friends with us? With me?" she added quietly, her tone concerned, and made another step toward Jack.

The question surprised him, made him falter with what he had planned to say. "Um, I don't know, Lara. They didn't tell why, just asked me to leave… Did you receive my postcard?"

"Yes, I did. As did everybody else." She took the final few steps and threw her arms up around his neck. "Oh, Jack, you should have been a journalist from the beginning. They wouldn't have done it to you, I'm sure. I know two girls who are married to Western journalists," she muttered into his chest.

Jack gave her a quick hug and carefully extracted himself from her arms. "Then I might not have met you all… But I'm glad for you: you've got what you wanted, right? Larisa Novikova-Volkonskaya in Juno and Avos. You've made it, Lara. Well done!" He hoped the bitterness he felt hadn't seeped through his tone.

"Thank you." Her smile was bright and contented this time. "Let me finish taking off my makeup, then we will go somewhere to have a drink for our reunion. *Kharasho*?" She returned to the dressing table without waiting for his response and took the net off her hair.

"Alright." Jack sat down on the nearest chair, counted to ten and asked casually, "So, how's Eton?"

"He's fine, thanks. He's…" She started breezily, then trailed off and turned slowly around to face him with one of her hands in midair. "Jack, it's not exactly like what you think," she said quietly.

"It isn't? And what *exactly* do you think I'm thinking?" he asked, trying to mask the challenge in his tone with overstated surprise.

"About me. And Eton. It's, eh… No, let me finish this first." She turned abruptly to the mirror. "I'll tell you later, *kharasho*?"

It wasn't like he could force her to talk, so Jack gave her the approved version of his life after Moscow instead, while she was taking off the rest of her makeup and changing. Then she left him in the room and went to let her colleagues know she wasn't returning to the hotel with them. When she returned, they fought their way through the crowd of admirers and photo reporters in the corridor, and Jack led her to the back of the theater where he had left his car.

As he was holding the door of his old, dusty Volkswagen Golf for Lara, Jack recalled that the last time he had driven her around he owned a flashy Mustang. But she didn't bat an eye, settled into his car gracefully as though it were a limo.

"So where do you want to go?"

Lara mulled it over for a moment. "My hotel is one block from here. But we'd better not talk there. Let's find another place. Do you know any?"

"We can drive around for a bit if you want to talk. Then we can drop by a place I know. What do you want to do?"

"Let's drive around."

What Lara told him in the next half hour shook Jack to the core. Later on when he wrote up his report and tried to analyze it, he found the story too devastating to be a ploy.

* * *

Karelin's death and Jack's expulsion marked the beginning of a long, unlucky spell for Eton. In February 1987, his mother, Vera Mikhailovna, died within a month of being diagnosed with brain tumor. She was forty-three. Prof. Volkonsky took his daughter's passing badly, and in April gave in to the second heart attack, leaving Eton all on his own.

True, Eton still had relatives on both of his grandfather's and grandmother's sides, but few people were aware that most members of Volkonsky and Rezanov families had fled the country during the October Revolution and in the early 1920s. Given such a background, it was a miracle that Prof. Volkonsky had achieved the status he enjoyed in Soviet Russia. Or maybe he had just been lucky, chosen by the state to showcase the fairness of the Soviet system.

After his death however, the system came to its usual senses and less than a week later Eton received notice from the personnel department of the Academy of Science. It announced that the apartment where Prof. Volkonsky and his family had been living in since 1947 was being requisitioned, along with the dacha in Peredelkino. Eton was given a month to clear out and hand over the keys to the personnel department. Oh, and by the way, Mikhail Alexandrovich's papers and diaries were also becoming property of the Academy.

It was then that Lara told Eton they should get married. For the first time. Her father could help Eton to keep Volkonsky family's property, but to do that both the apartment and the dacha must get registered under Lara's name.

Naturally, Eton refused—what else did you think he would do? Oh, those Russian men, don't feed them, just let them revel in suffering and drink themselves to death! Too proud to let a silly woman rescue them.

So with the help of Anya, Seva and Varvara Petrovna, Volkonsky's family housekeeper, Eton cleaned out both places in a week and handed in the keys. After that he dropped out of the University and nose-dived into a drinking bout, hardly leaving his apartment for almost a month. Then he got into a fight, nearly killed someone, was jailed and put up in a cell with criminals. Lara was only able to bail him out three days later. By that time, he had gotten into another fight, this time with his cellmates. It landed him in the prison's infirmary with two busted ribs and knife scars on his back. His three cellmates fared a little better—one broken nose, a broken arm and a busted face.

Then came August and Eton received a conscription letter with an assignment to a motor rifle division in Turkmenistan. It meant that his next stop, after the three-month compulsory training, would be Afghanistan. In an attempt to rescue her friend, Lara proposed again that they get married, so that her father could arrange a transfer for Eton to somewhere near Moscow. Eton refused. He left for Ashkhabad in September and disappeared.

Lara tracked him down only in March. And arranged to receive regular updates on his status and whereabouts. By then, he had been fighting in Afghanistan for three months. No, of course he hadn't known about her initiatives back then, but had appreciated it afterwards. Because that was how she learned about him being wounded and recovering in a military hospital in Tashkent. Together with Anya and Varvara Petrovna, she flew to Tashkent to visit him. They were shocked to see Eton's condition. The wound? It had probably been a light wound to start with—a bullet had hit him below the right shoulder and had broken a rib. Which wasn't too bad as far as bullet wounds went. However, because it had happened somewhere deep inside Afghanistan, by the time they brought him back to the hospital in Kabul, his splintered rib had pierced his lung, causing it to collapse.

Eton fully recovered from his physical wounds in two months—first in a military hospital in Tashkent, then in one of the best Moscow hospitals, thanks again to Lara's effort. However, mentally he remained a complete wreck. Tormented by nightmares, he couldn't sleep without hashish, pills or booze, or some combination of the three. He chain-smoked, did not eat much, and it was nearly impossible to get a word out of him at times. On the other hand, he had been writing songs and become popular amongst Afghan war veterans.

Appalled at his state, Lara finally put her foot down: enough was enough; he must marry her. She told Eton that it was only for the sake of his transfer from the Afghanistan-based division. Otherwise, they would each remain free to go out with whoever they wanted. The latter was particularly important for Lara: she wanted a husband who would let her do what she wanted to do when she wanted to do it. Only then, Eton reluctantly agreed. The wedding was arranged in August, and in September, Eton was transferred to another army unit.

* * *

They sat in the car parked in the deep shadow of a wall of lilac bushes at the end of a narrow street, windows down, both smoking. The only sound that reminded them that they were in the city and there was life around was the distant rumble of the late traffic on the main avenue nearby.

Lara tossed her cigarette butt out and sighed. "He's getting better now. Although sometimes it still feels like he is living in a parallel world that he wouldn't let anyone into."

Jack's guts had wrapped in one huge, painful knot ever since Lara had started telling him Eton's story. So much so that he had had to stop the car and take a smoke halfway through, hoping that Lara wouldn't notice his shaking hands.

He took the last drag on his cigarette, covering up a shaky exhale of relief, flicked the butt outside, and took her hand. "And how have *you* been, Lara?" He squeezed her slender fingers affectionately.

"I'm fine. Graduated two years ago, and they took me into LenKom's experimental studio. Not exactly what I had planned. I want to be a movie actress. But I need to do this first."

"Do what? Play in Juno and Avos opposite Nicolai Karachentsov?"

"Play in The Rise and Fall with whoever dares to do it with me. It took me a while to persuade them, and my father too, to stage Viktor's plays. This is its premier, you know. We haven't even performed it in Moscow yet." She turned in her seat to face him and took his hand with both of hers. "Jack, I'm so glad we've found each other again. It must be fate, *da*?"

"It must be. And I'm glad too that I've found you here, Lara." He pulled his hand back carefully, started the car and reversed it into the road.

"Eton will be glad, too," Lara said thoughtfully.

The faint note of uncertainty in her tone stung Jack. "You think so?"

"I know he will," she said, firmer this time. "You're his *best* friend after all." She cut him a sideways glance.

"I'm proud to be considered one of you, his old friends."

"That's not what I mean. I mean you're more of a friend to him than any of us, his old friends." Jack felt her eyes piercing him. "Maybe even more than *all* of us together. Hope he's such a friend to you too," she added sternly.

Sheesh, girl! Aren't you being overprotective?

He smiled at her, seeking truce. "Eton was, *is* one of the best friends I've ever had. Along with you, dear Lara. And you guys will always be my best friends... You know what? I'll write to him. Is that alright?"

Lara didn't answer, just gazed at him with a strange little smile on her lips.

"Lara? Will you take my letter back to him?"

Her mysterious smile blossomed into a big, satisfied grin. "Actually, he's here in Germany."

Chapter 57

Jack was changing gear. His foot jerked, releasing the pedal too soon, and the gearbox protested noisily. "Damn! Sorry... What did you say?"

"He's about twenty minutes from here." Lara shrugged, watching him out of the corner of her eye.

"So he's here with you," Jack muttered, his mind working ten miles a minute.

He's here too. So it's a trap... Isn't it? Didn't she say he was in the army? Or maybe—

"Not *with* me. But yes, he's here." She looked smug. "His regiment is in Bernau bei Berlin, fifteen kilometers from here."

He's in the Sov's Western Group of Forces!

"I see. And you planned on not telling me *that*?"

"Not if I saw that our friendship no longer meant anything to you," Lara stated flatly. "And by the way, Jack, shave off your beard, would you? It makes you look old."

Suddenly Jack felt drained. His eyes were scratchy as if they were full of sand, his throat parched. He wanted to strangle this obnoxious little Russian princess. He wanted to give her the biggest hug he could for being so protective about the person who meant more than anybody else to him. He needed a timeout. But more importantly, he needed a drink.

"Maybe we should stop for a snack and a drink. What do you say?"

"It's eleven thirty, Jack. Don't they all close at midnight?"

"Not all. I know a place. We can talk there too. If you have more to tell me."

"*Kharasho.* Let's go there."

He parked near his apartment building, and they walked a few blocks to Metze Eck. It was one of a handful of old restaurants in East Berlin that had survived the nationalization. Barbel's family had owned the place since 1913 and, luckily, it remained in her hands.

The weekly game of *Skat* was in full swing when they arrived. As Jack had expected, they were met by affable Barbel and quickly introduced to Metzer Eck's regulars.

Jack knew them all, and they considered him part of their tightknit group. Barbel's cynical but good-natured partner Axel, the heart of the congregation; Bernard, a classical musician, and his wife Ursel, with her insatiable appetite for the latest western fashion clothes; Kurt, an aging music-hall singer; Manfred, an obese man in his early thirties who lived on disability subsidy and by selling copies of disco tapes smuggled in from West Berlin; Jurgen, a stage designer who had a secret crush on Jack that everybody knew about; and Fritz who ran a hostel for print workers and paid lip service to the communist party because he had to "belong" to hold his job.

Barbel went out of her way to extend her compliments to Lara in her rusty, high school Russian. When she couldn't find enough Russian words, she asked Jack to translate to Lara that she wasn't the only celebrity who had visited her restaurant: in 1986, when Sergio Leone was in East Berlin for the premier of his film, Once Upon A time in America, he had come for a dinner with his friends at Metzer Eck. Lara grinned happily and said it must be a sign that she would make it because she planned to become a movie actress.

After a few minutes of pleasantries, Jack told them that he and Lara needed to catch up and asked to be seated somewhere they could talk. Barbel escorted them to the back of the restaurant, took their order and left them alone in the semi-private corner table.

"So, what else haven't you told me yet?" Jack asked.

"Eton is coming up to Berlin to see me tomorrow," Lara said in a loud whisper, her eyes shining.

God, give him strength not to smack her!

"When?"

"Some time in the afternoon."

"Oh, come on, Lara! Just spit it out!"

She grinned at him, looking thoroughly pleased. "I don't know exactly when. He said his leave of absence would start from midday tomorrow. So he will come to the hotel in the afternoon and will stay until our departure for home on Tuesday morning."

Two and a half, almost three days. He *had* to see him to… just to see him. That would be enough.

"I'd like to see him."

"I thought you might. I think he would like to see you too. But I need to ask him first… He's not the Eton you used to know, Jack." Her face clouded again.

"I understand. I will call you tomorrow night. Is it alright?"

"*Kharasho*. I'll have to break the news about you to him gently. Otherwise he will…" She sighed. "Don't even know how he will behave. He is even more unpredictable than before… Jack, I'm asking you: please be patient with him."

It was long past midnight when Jack got home. He knew he wouldn't be able to sleep but didn't want to toss and turn all night either, thinking about how he was going to report on the unexpected reconnection with his Russian targets. So he took two double shots of whiskey before going to bed and forced himself to read Gorky Park, a crime novel set in the Soviet Union that he had bought at a flea market in DC but never found time to read it.

He allowed himself to start planning the call with his chiefs while making coffee the next morning.

Since he was promoted after the Afghan assignment, he had no longer needed to pre-clear all his operational activities. However, this case was different. His contact with Lara Novikova and especially with Eton Volkonsky could potentially reactivate an operation that had been put on ice after Jack's departure from the Soviet Union. Another complication was, while Jack was officially mapped to East Berlin Station, its chief, David Rolston, didn't know about Moscow Station's operations. What the COS did know was that Jack was part of a special op, reporting directly to the Division Head through a separate channel.

Jack had first met David Rolston at HQ, a month before his East Berlin posting. They started off on a good note, despite Rolston's learning of Jack's direct access to the Division Head. They spent three days with Joe Coburn, working out the procedure for his deep cover activities and the reporting lines. In short, to protect his cover, Jack could only meet his COS outside of East Germany, and preferably outside of West Germany too, which was infested with KGB moles.

Unless there was an emergency and Jack needed support or advice urgently. Like now. He could contact the COS through a special number at the US Mission Berlin, redirected via a secured line to East Berlin Station. All he needed to do was to call the Mission from any payphone in West Berlin.

Alternatively, he could call the dedicated "help line" at the Hill Station, the giant NSA-run listening facility, also in West Berlin. His call would be redirected to the com-room at HQ, then on to the Division Head.

He decided to call the East Berlin COS: he was the person who would be arranging help for Jack, maybe even exfiltration if he ever needed it on this assignment, so he'd better keep David Rolston in the loop of all he did where possible.

At 1:00 p.m., he called the Mission from a McDonald's off Ku'damm and asked for an emergency call with David Rolston in an hour. One hour and twenty minutes later he was conditionally cleared for the reactivation of operation TALION, pending confirmation and further instructions from HQ, which he could collect at his dedicated "mail box" in 48 hours.

He returned to his apartment just before five o'clock and spent the next two hours planning for his reengagement with his agent under development, GTSALT. As a rule, he had to map out in detail at least two plans, A and B. However, it looked like he needed to think through more options, because a) as Lara suggested, Eton might not want to see him; b) Eton might agree to see him, but would behave as if nothing had happened between them back in Moscow; or c) Eton might agree to see him and... nothing had changed.

For God's sake! Too much has changed since Moscow. Too much for him... Are you going to recruit him, like you told Joe you had? How can you do it to him after what you have learned?

If I don't, how can I see him again?... Be with him again?

You are a selfish bastard, Smith! All you can think of is yourself. What about him, the man you call your best friend? Hasn't he had enough?

If not me, it would be someone else. I'll protect him better than anybody else.

What was wrong with him?! Why was he kidding himself? By recruiting Eton, he would only fix him for his downfall. Wasn't that what had happened to all their agents in Russia in '85-'86? They had all been caught. Except for the two who had managed to come in from the cold. Jack had helped one who was exfiltrated by the Brits in '85, Colonel Oleg Gordievsky. But he wouldn't be able to exfiltrate Eton May Volkonsky—he wasn't in the Soviet Union now and God only knew if and when they would let him return. So yeah, the best thing Jack Smith could do for the one person he cared about the most was to let him go.

Someone said if you care for someone set them free... Let go, Smith. You can't do anything good for him. Lara will take the best care of him. Considering the circumstances, she has been doing a terrific job already, hasn't she? Let him be. Let be...

Jack went down to Helen and Paul's for the farewell dinner flying high in a state of nervous euphoria that he couldn't shake off, not even with a triple whiskey shot. It took him a titanic effort to take part in the conversation around the table and not to steal glances at the clock on the wall. And he was grateful to little Lizzie who kept him distracted from his restless anticipation with her incessant chatter. By nine, after reading a bedtime story to Lizzie and bidding her and her five-year-old brother Oliver goodbyes and sweet dreams, Jack was nearly at the end of his tether. But he made himself stay for a brandy with Paul and his two colleagues and a chat about western sports and politics. They deliberately avoided discussing the Socialist block events that had been on front pages of newspapers for days: Solidarity Party's victory in the Polish elections, the continuing repressions in China following the Tiananmen Square massacre, the mounting hostilities between the Soviet republics of Armenia and Azerbaijan over Nagorny Karabakh, and between Tajikistan and Kirgizia over sources of water.

By ten thirty, Jack was a nervous wreck and for once was grateful for his training—he was pretty sure nobody had noticed anything out of the ordinary about him tonight. He figured Lara should be back at the hotel by now and, as they had agreed, expecting his call. He headed towards Hotel Unter den Linden, taking dark side streets, looking out for a secluded phone booth.

He found one off Linienstrasse, called the hotel and asked for Lara's room. When the receptionist asked for his name, he said "Matthias Hoffman" and was immediately put through. The phone rang twice, clicked and the achingly familiar voice rumbled, "*Allo?*"

Jack's heart missed a beat.

Shit, now what? He had planned to talk to Lara first, to agree what he was supposed to know about Eton and what he wasn't, and now—

"Good evening," he said in Russian, pitching his voice low. "Could I talk to Lara, please?" Silence followed at the other end. "*Allo?*"

Jack thought he heard a shaky intake of air, then the voice said cautiously, "It's me, Eton."

"*Privet*, Eton."

Damn, Lara! What do you want me to do, huh?

"Lara's out. With her colleagues…" Eton was obviously not terribly well prepared for this conversation either.

"I see… Did she tell you that I'd call?"

"Yes."

And?

"I'm glad you have… that you're calling… Are you nearby?"

"Yes, less than a fifteen-minute walk from your hotel… Do you want to… to have a drink somewhere?"

"Alright. Where?"

"Just walk out of the hotel on to Friedrichstrasse and head north toward the river. Keep to the right. I'll meet you halfway… Then we'll find a place for drinks."

"Alright." Eton hung up as soon as the word was out of his mouth.

Jack stared at the telephone's handset, trying to collect his thoughts. Then he blew out a long breath, put it carefully back in its cradle and walked out into the street.

There were few pedestrians on the streets, and Jack spotted from afar the tall, familiar figure walking along the bridge. He scanned both sides of the street in front and behind Eton, trying to determine if he was followed. It didn't seem so. Maybe Soviet soldiers weren't high on the Stasi's list of subjects to be shadowed.

Until they found out that *this* Soviet soldier was meeting with an American journalist. So maybe it wasn't a good idea for Eton to be meeting with him.

Jack stopped at the corner of a building at the intersection, away from the murky pools of lights streaming down from the street lamps, and leaned his shoulder against the wall. Eton didn't notice him. He walked quickly by, head held high, looking straight ahead. He was wearing a dark windbreaker, jeans and runners, and only the crew cut and his rigid gait suggested his military affiliation.

"Eton," Jack called softly when the young man had passed him and reached the curb, ready to cross the street.

Eton whipped around, his elbows pressed tightly to his sides as if he was pointing a rifle at the source of the noise.

Jack's chest constricted. "It's me," he said in Russian and stepped out into the dim circle of light. "Sorry I've startled you."

Eton stuffed his hands into the pockets of his jacket, made a few strides towards Jack but stopped short of getting up close. "Sorry. I was... Didn't expect you'd be here."

Jack covered the last few steps and stretched his hand out, smiling but uncertain. "*Privet*, Eton."

"*Privet*." Eton shook his hand guardedly and didn't return the smile.

Right.

"Let's take a walk this way. There's a place twenty minutes from here. We can have a drink... and talk there... If you want."

"Yes. Let's go." Eton nodded and took a hurried step away in the direction Jack had just pointed.

Okay... Maybe it's better this way.

They walked in silence for a few minutes, half a meter of space between them. Jack cut a few side-glances at Eton, trying to decide what he could let Eton know what Lara had told him. But the young man's face was the impassive mask Jack remembered from their very first few meetings. Except that with his hairline receding at the sides and deep lines at the corners of his mouth, Eton looked five or six years older than he was—they looked the same age now.

Jack swallowed down the lump in his throat and inched closer. "Lara's told me about your mother and grandfather. I'm so sorry, Eton, I don't even know what to say."

"Thank you. No need to say anything. It is life... I suppose."

"So how long how you been here?"

"Almost a year."

- 430 -

Seven to eight months in Afghanistan and a year here. He's due for demobilization soon.

As if reading Jack's thoughts, Eton nodded. "Less than four months left... What about you? How long have you been here?"

"Since March."

Suddenly Jack realized that it had been exactly four years since he had first met Eton at a student concert at the MGU. And it was March too when he had first arrived in Moscow.

"You must have a lot of new friends here."

Has he just sounded resentful?

Jack groaned mentally and stopped.

When he realized he was walking alone, Eton stopped too and turned around.

Jack walked up to him, into his personal space. "I do have new friends and acquaintances here, Eton," he said in English, quietly but firmly. "But you're still my *best friend. That* hasn't changed."

Eton nodded, met Jack's eyes for a fleeting moment, his lips pressed together, and started walking again. Jack caught up with him and they walked side by side in silence for a few minutes.

"Lara said you're not a diplomat anymore," Eton said in Russian, ignoring Jack's attempt to reinstate their old private habit of chatting in English when they were alone.

"That's right. I resigned after... I left Moscow. Became a correspondent, started working for the Associated Press."

"What about your other... *work*?" Eton asked after a while.

What is this? This can't be a pitch. He can't be... Can he?

Jack stopped again and caught Eton by his arm. "Eton, it's not something I can talk about, you know... Unless..."

"Unless I'm... *working* with you?"

Shit. It didn't sound good at all... Or maybe it did—for Joe Coburn: it seemed like his scheme was beginning to work...

Except why would the KGB go after him *now* when he was no longer a diplomat and didn't have access to sensitive information? Unless they had known that he was a case officer all this while... But then why wait until now? Why expel him from Moscow when they could have just pitched him there and then? With what had been going on between him and Eton, it would have been a piece of cake.

"You know what? Let's take a walk in the park. It's a couple of blocks from here. It's better to talk in the park than in a restaurant. We can have drinks later... What do you say?"

"Alright."

Jack furtively scanned the surroundings while they were crossing the street and entering a little city park. The street was empty, except for a *Trabant* or two rushing by now and then, and a group of youngsters on the bench at the corner of the nearest building. They found their way in the deep shadows under the trees, with occasional puddles of dim yellow light cast by a few park lamps, till they found a bench and sat down. Jack pulled out his cigarettes and offered the pack to Eton. The young man took one, produced a lighter and gave Jack the flame first.

You're not gonna like this. But sorry, friend, you've started it.

"Eton, do you realize that by knowing about me and not reporting it you make yourself a collaborator?"

Did you or did you not report on me, Eton Volkonsky?

"Isn't it what you wanted? Or you were after Grandpa? You were particularly interested in his Nuclear Winter Theory... weren't you?"

The bitterness in Eton's tone grazed at Jack's insides like a rusty knife. "I'm sorry, but it was my fucking job, alright?" he bristled, catching himself off guard.

Fuck! You just ousted yourself lock, stock and barrel, Smith!

If Eton had had any lingering doubt about what Jack had been after, he probably had none now. It baffled Jack how easily this man could make him lose control of his mouth when even the roughest of tests at the Farm and the real life crap never could.

He reached a hand out cautiously to touch Eton's. "I'm truly sorry I had to do it, Eton... But I'm not sorry for the rest. Never for what we had! You've been the best... *friend* I ever had."

The best thing that ever happened to me, baby. Even if you're going to pitch me now.

Eton didn't pull back his hand, but didn't respond to Jack's touch, either. Jack sighed, clasped his friend's hand briefly and retracted.

Lara had been right when she said he wasn't the same Eton he'd known two years ago.

"If you're still doing... *that job*, I shouldn't meet with you... Should I?" Eton finally said in English, his eyes fixed on tall, dark silhouettes of the trees in front of them.

Jack lit a new cigarette, made a couple of hard pulls and handed it to Eton. "Better not... I guess."

This time Eton was silent for much longer, smoking, elbows resting on his knees, head hung low. Then he straightened up and gave the cigarette back to Jack. "You know, I found Grandfather's original work on nuclear winter. Soon after Chernobyl. Didn't have a chance to tell you... back then."

No, Eton! Please, don't!

"When Grandfather died, I also found his notebooks. There are things in them people should know. I think,.. But they will never publish it back home. Even with *glasnost*."

Lara had said the Academy of Science wanted those papers. Had they gotten them? If so, had they been "doctored"? Had they been through the organs too?

"Why are you telling me this now, Eton?"

"Who else can I tell?"

The artlessness of the question and the infinite sadness in his tone almost broke Jack's heart.

Eton turned to face him and, for the first time since they had reunited, looked Jack straight in the eyes. His own were steady and full of shadows. It was the same Eton he remembered from their last meeting in Moscow. The man he could neither forget nor forgive himself for leaving the way he had.

Nothing has changed. For me, nothing.

Chapter 58

They sat on the park bench for a long time, talking and smoking. Eton was still holding back, even after admitting that Jack was the only person he could tell what was on his mind. His answers to Jack were short and terse, and he didn't volunteer anything himself. It felt like they had gone back to the beginning, with mostly Jack talking, telling his newfound friend about his life elsewhere, and Eton trying not to be overwhelmed by the warm enthusiasm Jack was showering on him.

Truth was Jack had to play it up a little. Otherwise, he wasn't sure he could make his cover story sound believable—his resignation from the State Department in December '86, his journalism course at George Washington University, his job as a freelance reporter on regional conflicts between India and Pakistan, Iran and Iraq, and on the war in Afghanistan. Then Jack briefly described his life in Islamabad and his travels in the region. Not about his trips into Afghanistan, though, nor about the Ojhri Camp explosion he had narrowly escaped. Somehow, he felt that Eton wasn't ready to hear those things yet. *They* were not ready.

It was nearly midnight when Eton recalled he had promised Lara to be waiting for her at the hotel and stood up. Jack rose and pulled him into a rough, friendly hug.

"God, Eton! So good to see you again. I never thought I'd see you here... So soon," he added in whisper, breathing in the familiar yet somewhat new scent of the man he used to know intimately.

Eton froze for a second, then put his arms around Jack's waist and back, squeezed him mightily and let go. He stepped back, gave Jack's face a critical look over and smiled faintly. "You look... different."

Jack's first impulse was to shoot "You like it?" at him. But he thought his friend wasn't ready for their old playfulness either. He palmed his beard and chuckled. "You need a beard to blend in... in the Middle East. I just never got down to shaving it off after my return. I will. When I find the right motivation."

Eton nodded, stuffed his hand in his the pockets of his windbreaker and looked away. "Let's go."

"Okay, let's roll then."

Right... Lara was right.

They strode in awkward silence for a few minutes. The night air was chilly, loaded with moisture straining to burst into rain. The streets were half-dark and empty, with hardly a car passing by, and if not for an occasional motorbike, it could have passed for Moscow.

As usual, Jack caved in first. "So, you and Lara... doing anything tomorrow?" he asked, faking nonchalance.

"No. She has two performances tomorrow, at two and at seven. Perhaps a reception afterwards."

"Are you going?"

"No. I've seen her performing many times. And I don't like banquets."

"She's good, isn't she?"

"Yes." He hesitated before adding quietly, his tone resigned, "I'm indebted to her. For everything... For this too." He took a step sideways, closer, and brushed Jack's hand with the back of his own.

A jubilant wave surged in Jack's chest. He bumped his shoulder into Eton's and briefly squeezed his hand. "Me, too." He puffed out a deep, contented exhale. "I'll be indebted to her till the day I die."

Sleep eluded Jack again, but this time he didn't care. He spent half of the night re-running their conversation in his head, rehearsing what he would tell Eton the next time they met—tomorrow, as they had agreed. Jack didn't look forward to Eton's pointed questions and was wary of his friend's powers of deduction. They made him feel like they were playing chess and Eton could guess where Jack would go three moves ahead. But the most daunting was the thought that he would have to lie to Eton. Yet again. Because there were things, Jack simply couldn't tell him about. Like Operation SEABROOK. He prayed that Eton would never ask.

He fell asleep in the early hours of the morning and when he woke up, unusually late, the sheets were still damp from his joyous dreams.

In the bathroom, he stared at himself in the mirror for a full minute. Then he rummaged in the medicine cabinet for his beard scissors and clipped his full beard down to short scruff, almost stubble. Eton used to like him that way...

Oh, for Christ's sake! It doesn't matter anymore what he liked or didn't like. You gonna let him go, right?... Right?!

What if he wants to stay?

With you?? Where? Where are you going to "stay" with him, dimwit?

Fuck you!

He hurled the towel at his own reflection in the mirror, sending the toothbrush and the shaving kit clattering down the sink. He put them back in their places and clumped morosely to the bedroom.

After a mug of instant coffee and a slice of *Schlackwurst* on a roll, he collected the pile of newspapers he had dumped by the door the day before, and tramped into the sitting room. Ten minutes later, he gave up turning pages, unable to concentrate on what he was doing. He tried to jot down a few ideas for his next piece on East German sportsmen, but couldn't muster enough enthusiasm for that either. So he went back to the bedroom and started rummaging in the top drawer of his wardrobe. When he found what he was looking for, he returned to the sitting room, fumbled with his CD player deck, then sprawled out on the couch and closed his eyes.

He didn't notice when he dozed off, but when he jolted awake, his lashes were damp. The disk had started over and the Eagles were playing Desperado again.

He managed to occupy himself, if not his mind, until four o'clock in the afternoon by cleaning his poorly renovated apartment to the state of spotless shine, going out to buy milk, bread and *Leberwurst* for breakfast, then jogging and washing his running gear afterwards.

At 4:10 p.m. he called Lara's hotel, said he was Matthias Hoffman and was put through.

Eton answered the phone on the second ring. He said Lara should be back from the matinee in half an hour, and that she had instructed him to ask Jack if he wanted to have a quick lunch with them at the place Jack had taken her to before. Jack said of course, he'd be waiting for them in front of the hotel at quarter to five. Eton mumbled, "Thank you. See you," and hung up.

Jack stared at the handset in his hand and shook his head. It was the weirdest phone call between them ever, and he started doubting if he should have "the talk" with Eton this time.

He turned up at the hotel at 4:45 p.m. sharp. Only to end up waiting for nearly fifteen minutes till Eton and Lara came down—he visibly fuming, she with not even a hint of remorse for being late. After holding the taxi door open for Lara and exchanging a handshake with Eton, Jack got into the front seat and asked the driver to take them to corner of Prenzlauer and Metzer Strasse.

As the car steered out into the wide avenue, Lara said, "Jack, turn around again, please?"

He turned in his seat to look at her. "Yes?"

"You look *much* better now, *daragusha*." She smiled at him sweetly. "But I still prefer it when you're clean shaven."

Eton, in the left-hand seat, turned away to stare out of the window, but Jack noticed that the side of his face and his ear pinked.

They had an early dinner at Metze Eck with Lara and Jack doing most of the talking. Eton listened to their banter absentmindedly, an occasional, almost-smile haunting the corners of his mouth, his nervous fingers rolling bread balls on the table.

At one point, Lara reached for Eton's and Jack's hands on the table and exclaimed, "Jack, Eton, you can't imagine how glad I am that we've met again!" She laughed, sounding high. "Let's never be out of touch again. What do you say, Jack?" She let go of Eton's hand, but held on to Jack's.

He squeezed her hand and mumbled, "Yes, let's," watching Eton out of the corner of his eye, then pulled his hand back.

Eton stood up, his jaw tight. "I'll be back," he said and headed towards the restroom.

Jack watched the tall lankly figure disappear behind the door, then reach out and covered Lara's hand. "Lara, I don't think he likes your idea. Let's not push him."

"But Jack, he doesn't know himself what—"

"Please, Lara! Let him be."

She peered into Jack's eyes, the corner of her mouth dropping, and sighed dejectedly. "I don't know what else to do, Jack. I'm afraid he'll drink himself to death when he is demobilized in a few months. I knew several Afghan vets who ended badly when they came home."

"Maybe he'll return to the MGU and finish his *aspirantura*."

"He won't. He has become completely disinterested in physics. In everything! He'll stay home and write his songs about war... And will die from vodka and drugs."

"So what do you want to do?"

Lara bit on her lip, a hint of desperation in her gaze, obviously trying to decide if she should tell Jack whatever was on her mind or not. She sighed again. "Not now. Eton will be back any minute... How about you take me out shopping tomorrow morning? I have a free day tomorrow. Then we can talk. *Kharasho*?"

It wasn't particularly alright since he had planned to go to Potsdam and then to finish his article about East German sportsmen defecting to the West. In fact, it was due today, but he had been too distracted to do anything sensible this morning.

"Alright."

"Excellent! How about ten? And please, Jack, not *one word* to Eton that I want to talk to you about him. Promise?"

Jack studied her for a moment, then nodded tentatively. "What are you going to tell Eton?"

"Tell him about what?"

"About me taking you shopping."

"That you're taking me out shopping. He doesn't like doing it so I've asked you." She shrugged dismissively. "Besides you know Berlin better than him *and* speak the language."

Jack had nothing to say to that. He just hoped Eton would understand... Like he used to say he had, regardless of what Jack had done or said.

When Eton returned to the table, Lara announced to him that Jack was taking her shopping the next day. Jack raised his shoulders, smiled apologetically when Eton cut him an inscrutable glance. Eton shrugged and mumbled "Alright," his face noncommittal.

At six, Lara said she needed to return to the theater to prepare for the evening show. She insisted that Jack and Eton stay back and continue their dinner, but Eton said quietly, with a note of finality in his tone, "I'm taking you back."

When they dropped her off at Metropol Theater, Lara said she wouldn't be back till midnight, maybe even later. "So please don't wait up for me," she told Eton, then turned to Jack. "You *promised* me, Jack." She gave him an emphatic stare. "That you'll come to see me off at the train station... *Da*?"

When Lara had disappeared inside the theater, Jack asked the taxi driver to take them to Treptower Park. During the fifteen-minute ride, he ran his mouth, chatting to the driver and giving Eton touristic information about the landmarks they were passing. Eton responded with guttural sounds, didn't say a full sentence once.

When they alighted at the entrance, the weather, ambivalent and dull since morning, had finally decided it was the time for a rain. So as they strolled in, they found themselves walking against a steady stream of people hurrying out, aiming to get under a roof before the downpour started in earnest.

"Do you mind getting wet?" Jack stopped.

"No. We need to talk... Right?"

"Right. And it's better we talk in the open air."

"Let's go visit the Russian Soldier." Eton allowed himself a half smile and headed toward the central part of the park.

Jack was still figuring how to start with what he wanted to say when Eton asked, "Is it about Grandfather's papers?"

"Yeah... Sorry, Eton, but since you mentioned it, I have to ask... You said yesterday that people should learn about them. What did you mean?"

They had made half a dozen steps before Eton responded, choosing his words carefully, "I'm not an expert on, um, intelligence matters, but I don't think they will be of significant importance for... your *organization*. Or any other one similar to it."

"Right... Then who should learn about them?"

"Scientists. People. Those who care about what can happen to our world. People with decency... I don't know..." he trailed off, then added morosely under his breath, "I'm an idiot who never grows up. Nobody gives a damn!"

Jack gripped at his shoulder and shook him up softly. "I do. A lot."

"For your work."

"No! Not only... You know that, right? Eton?"

"Do I?" Eton gave him a sideway glare.

The drizzle was picking up strength, the raindrops unexpectedly cold. Jack shivered and zipped up his jacket. "There's a veranda over there, near the pond." He pointed to the range of trees on the right. "Let's run?"

Eton nodded, and they took off toward the pond.

Apparently, people had noted the weather forecast, and the park ground near the small lake called Karpfenteich, usually popular with locals, was deserted. They dashed into the little shelter—a raised wooden platform under a conical roof, simple wooden planks for railing and a narrow bench along the perimeter. Having brushed the raindrops from their faces and hair, they sat down next to each other.

Jack pulled out his pack of Marlboros, lit up two and handed one to Eton. "Listen, Eton. I know it is hard for you to trust me again. But I'm asking you to try. If you decide not to, it will be the last time... I won't bother you ever again." It took a huge effort to keep his voice steady saying the last words.

Eton turned to him, his brows furrowed, lips pressed together in a thin, long-suffering line.

"This is difficult for me too, because I'm trained to suspect *every* Soviet to be a KGB. Or at least an informer... But you already knew that, didn't you? You asked me to trust you and I did..."

The fuck you did!

"Well, most of the time." Jack sighed and rubbed his face with his hand.

Eton continued watching him silently, smoking, and there was no reproach in his sad, brown eyes.

"I'm not supposed to tell you what I'm about to. And if anyone ever finds out, I will be screwed in so many ways, I don't even want to think about it... But I'm gonna tell you, anyway. Because based on it, you need to decide, Eton, what you want to do from now on... Alright?" Eton didn't respond in any way, so Jack continued, "Alright, so... I reported to my bosses when I returned from Moscow that I had recruited you as an agent."

"*What*?! Why did you do that?"

"Because that was what they wanted to hear. And it gave me a reason to request to be assigned to Moscow again, someday... I told them you wanted no one but me to run, um, to work with you."

Eton digested it for a moment, furrowing his brows. "What about Grandfather? Weren't you after him?"

"His work, yes. But not him personally. Personally, it was you that I... they have been after."

There was another moment of silence, then Eton asked quietly, "Why me? I am... was just a student. "

Why did you even bother hoping that he wouldn't ask this question? And you're *not* gonna lie to him now, you're not! You're screwed anyway if he tells anybody about all this.

Jack stood up, dropped his cigarette butt in the small litter box attached to the railing near the stairs, then turned to face Eton. He raked his hair with both his hands, let out a sharp exhale. "It's complicated. But essentially, it's because of your father."

"My father? What it has to do with my father?" Eton stared at him, confused.

"Do you know what he did before he came to live in the Soviet Union? And why he came there?"

"Are you saying he was a spy too? For whom?"

"Not exactly a spy, but close. He was a defector. Used to work for the NSA. That's our largest intelligence agency," Jack explained, seeing his friend's blank stare. "They're very low profile... So, yeah, one day, your father decided that what the agency was doing was wrong and defected to the Soviet Union... Ok, it was not *that* simple, but that's the gist of it... It was a big scandal back in the sixties."

Eton gazed at him for at least a minute, chewing on his lips, and Jack could almost see his brain churning. Then he blew out a breath and said, his tone dripping bitter sarcasm, "So he joined the KGB."

"Well, I don't think he actually *joined* them. But I suspect he provided them with a load of sensitive information."

"So... am I supposed to be some sort of revenge?"

God, he is fast!

"Sort of... Yes."

"And you are not with the CIA?"

Jack didn't respond to the question directly, instead said, "The NSA doesn't have capacity for humint, um, to run agents." He shrugged, despising himself for not being able to give a straight answer to a simple question.

"Why are you telling me this? Isn't it a state secret?" Eton looked at him from under his brows.

"What is?"

"That this N-S-A doesn't have capacity to run agents."

"No, not really. Let me put it this way: those who are interested can find out about it in publicly available materials."

Eton nodded, pulled out his cigarettes and lit one up without offering Jack. They sat like that for a long time, each deep in his own deliberations, a meter of empty space between them. The downpour outside was easing, but the sky didn't lighten up, the gray mass of the rainy clouds hung low, stuck in the pinnacles of tall pines and poplars that framed the alley of the World War II memorial.

Eton crushed the cigarette butt against the undersize of the bench and flipped it toward the litter box. It landed squarely in the target. "So what do I have to decide based on what you have just told me?"

Jack straightened up. "Right."

The pitch, now.

"If you want me to do something with your grandfather's work… If you want me to come back to Moscow to, um, *work* with you… Or if you ever want to come to live…"

Let go, Smith. He won't make it. Let him go!

"Or I can make it… *us* go away, and you'll forget about what I've told you and never hear from us *ever* again."

There was a long pause as Eton gazed into Jack's eyes, searching for answers. "How?"

"How what?"

"How are you going to make them go away and leave me alone? You're just a, um, person. One man. They are a large organization. *Two* large organizations. A system, just like ours. They make stupid decisions that make no goddamn sense and let us clean up the shit. Pay for their fucking political games with our lives!"

Jack listened to his friend wide-eyed. He had never heard Eton bitching so viciously or swearing before. When he finished, Jack gripped his shoulder, shook it lightly. "Don't worry. I can do it." He snorted bitterly. "It'll probably be one of the easier things I've done."

"You're not going to tell me."

"No. You don't need to know this shit." Joe Coburn would hate it, but fuck Joe Coburn! He had dragged Jack into this shit; he would have to face the music.

"And you know what? If you want any of your grandfather's papers to be published in the West, I'll do it. Me personally, not through the agency." Jack let out a curt laugh. "Christ, if Amanda could smuggle your friends' records to be published in Los Angeles, I certainly can do it, too."

"You'll do that?"

"I will. You want people to know, right? So they will know."

"Why?" He didn't sound suspicious this time. It was as if Eton knew what Jack was thinking but wanted to hear him saying it aloud.

"Because you're my friend, Eton, and it's the least I can do to make up for not being able… not being truthful with you."

"And you want to, um, fuck up your life by making your… agencies leave me alone?"

"Something like that." Jack chuckled sadly. "But it doesn't matter. As you said, they all make stupid decisions and make us mop their shit with our fucking lives. I'm through with it, anyway."

I just needed to return to Moscow… to see you, baby.

Eton stood up and turned to gaze toward the memorial alley for the Soviet soldiers. He hesitated, then took a step to where Jack sat, their knees touching, and rested his hand on Jack's shoulder. "Thank you, Jack," he mumbled, sounding almost like his old self. "It means a lot to me."

Chapter 59

They sat side by side in the little pavilion, watching the rain, talking and sharing a cigarette. Jack told Eton about his job as a reporter, what he had seen travelling in the socialist bloc countries: things seemed to be changing, people getting restless, raising their voices and standing up for what they wanted. Then he asked Eton if he was going to carry on with his postgraduate studies at the MGU when he returned to Moscow.

Eton jerked a shoulder and turned away. "Don't think so," he said at long last.

"Why not?"

Eton gave him a duh look.

"I'm sorry." It was the answer Jack had expected, but hoped he was wrong.

"Not your fault... Never wanted to be a physicist, anyway."

Jack lit a new cigarette and gave it to Eton. "What are you going to do then?"

"Don't know. Play music in restaurants maybe... If they take me."

"How about the other *Krylia* guys? What are they doing?"

"Sevka is a researcher at a micro-biology laboratory in Moscow. He and Anya have a daughter, Tanechka. One and a half years old. Alex and Kostia have formed a new band, Danger Zone. Vadim immigrated to Israel last year. And Yura is on his archeological trips all the time. Somewhere in Turkmenistan nowadays."

"And they haven't been conscripted?"

"They escaped it."

"And you didn't... Lara told me you had turned her down on—"

"I was a fool," Eton spat out, then continued, tight and low, "I wanted to die. In the war... Until I saw it with my own eyes. I understood then that I had been an idiot."

Jack felt like he would explode any minute now. He knew he had been a source of Eton's distress, adding to his anguish over the death of his loved ones: he had made his friend promise to look after himself, knowing full well what he and his Company were doing to Eton.

He put a hand on Eton's knee and squeezed it briefly. "Eton, I don't know what to say except that I'm sorry... Thing is, I'm also *not* sorry. Because if not for, um, my job, I wouldn't have met you."

Goddamn it, Smith! You're thinking about yourself again!

"Maybe we shouldn't have met," he muttered gloomily.

Eton didn't comfort him this time. He stood up and took a step away, toward the exit. "What is done can't be undone. You have to live with what you've been given... Anyway, let's find a place where we can have a drink." He offered Jack his crooked little smile. "We have to celebrated, um, us meeting again, don't we?"

The rain had stopped, and the dusk was creeping down over the tall, rustling poplars along the path. They meandered around the puddles of rainwater, big and small in the cracked asphalt, heading toward the park's exit.

"I need to use the restroom," Jack said, pointing at the low concrete structure behind the big lilac bushes by the gate.

Eton nodded and followed him.

There was only one bare light bulb burning inside, but the toilet's tiled floor, the walls and partitions looked clean, and it reeked of bleach, not urine.

His chin tucked in, Eton headed straight into one of the four stalls. He pulled the door shut with a small bang and came out only when Jack had finished washing his hands and turned off the water. He rubbed his hands under the cold water longer than necessary, his face severe, eyes fixed on his own little action. Finally, he turned off the tap, dried his hands against his jeans-clad thighs and headed towards the door—all without even a glance at Jack.

When he walked past Jack and reached out for the door handle, Jack caught him by his shoulder. "Eton."

Eton froze, a hand in midair. His shoulders went up like he was preparing himself for a blow. Jack closed the space between them and put the other hand on his friend's other shoulder. He pressed his nose and mouth into the back of Eton's head, closed his eyes and inhaled deeply.

"Etahhn..."

He wasn't sure what had happened, but the next thing he knew he was squashed against the wall, Eton's body hard and flat against his, Eton's mouth on his, kissing and biting his lips furiously. He caught Eton's head, trying to hold him still, but Eton seized his wrists and pinned them against the wall on both sides of his head. Then he buried his face in the hollow between Jack's neck and his shoulder, and started thrusting against his groin, hissing something through his teeth. Jack insides warped into an aching knot when he figured what Eton was mumbling in Russian: "You want *this*, huh? You want *this*?"

The assault didn't last long. After a few thrusts, Eton shuddered, let out a groan and sagged against Jack. He let go of Jack's wrists, his fingers clawed at Jack's biceps instead. "I'm sorry... I'm sorry," he whispered into Jack's neck, sounding close to tears.

Jack put his arms around him, held him close with one, softly rubbing his back with the other.

"I didn't... I haven't... Oh, God, I'm so sorry!"

"Shhh... It's alright, Eton... It's alright, bud."

They stood like that for a few minutes—Eton clinging to Jack, his breath erratic, Jack holding him, stroking his back, his closely cropped head—then Eton let out a shuddering exhale and stepped back, out of Jack's embrace.

He met Jack's eyes for an instant, then fixed his gaze on the floor at the far end of the room. "Please forgive me." His tone was glum. "You must know, I... I'm not the same as before."

"It doesn't matter, bud." Jack reached out to stroke his face, and his throat constricted when Eton flinched at the caress. "We have all changed. Afghanistan would change anybody."

- 443 -

"You were there, too?"

"Yes. On the other side. I'll tell you about it later, okay? Tomorrow, maybe. Now let me see you back to the hotel. We both need to wind down a bit right now... Alright?"

They flagged down a taxi at the park's gate and rode in silence most of the way to the hotel, their knees touching and occasionally their fingers. They shook hands, holding on for a heartbeat longer than usual, and Eton even tried to smile at Jack. "See you tomorrow?" he asked, before getting out of the car.

"Yes. See you tomorrow, friend."

Jack got only four hours sleep, but by 9:00 a.m., his article had been faxed to Bonn, and he got a day off in exchange for a trip to Leipzig on Wednesday. By ten o'clock, he was sitting in the lobby of Hotel Unter den Linden.

Lara was only five minutes late this time and was all pouty. Right after a curt greeting, she started complaining that Eton had been rushing her since half-past nine, and ranted as they drove to the *Centrum*, the largest department store in East Berlin. Then she clammed up, her expression wary, and didn't utter a word, until Jack parked on a side street.

"Why have we stopped?"

"You wanted to go shopping, didn't you? Let's go then."

"Let's talk first... Let's drive around." For all her commanding tone, she seemed hesitant, uncertain.

"Alright."

Lara pulled out the cigarettes from her purse and rolled down the window. They drove in silence for a few minutes, then she sighed and turned to Jack. "I've been thinking... Jack, you're the only person I know who can help."

"Of course, Lara. If I can, I will."

"Jack, I've been trying to find a way to contact Eton's relatives in France. I told you that Eton had relatives there, didn't I?"

"You did," Jack said cautiously, trying to figure where this was all heading.

"It is more difficult than I thought." She let out a sad chuckle.

"Eton wants to find his relatives?"

"No, Eton knows *nothing* about this... And you've promised not to tell him! *Da*?"

"All-right... Can I ask what you're planning to do when you find them?"

Lara studied him, thoughtful. "I want them to help Eton to get out of the Soviet Union," she said, her tone low and firm.

"You want *what*?!" Jack dropped a gear and steered the car closer to the sidewalk.

"He needs to get out of the Soviet Union, Jack."

"Why? It's his home, isn't it? He has never lived anywhere else."

"No, it is not. He has never really considered the Soviet Union his home, even though he was born and raised there... He has always dreamed about California. The faraway fairytale place he has never been," she intoned. "That's where his father was from. Moscow was his home only because the people he loved lived there—his family. Now he has no one

- 444 -

left there... I'm not his family as you know," she said flatly at Jack's raised eyebrows. "I'm his friend who is trying to help."

"If California is the place he wants to be, why are you looking for his distant relatives in France? Why not his father's family?" Jack cut her a puzzled glance.

Lara made a face like he had asked something stupid. "Because they are Russians. They *will* take care of him, no question about it... I'm not so sure about his father's family." She rolled her eyes at Jack's skeptical stare. "Look, I know almost nothing about his father. Only that his name was Emil May, and he was from California. That's all. Eton doesn't talk about him."

"But he told you about California."

"Of course not!" Seeing that Jack wasn't going to let her off the hook, she surrendered. "I stumbled upon Vera Mikhailovna's diary in Eton's bed once, when he was home after the hospital... I read just a couple of pages." She raised her shoulders and shook her head, looking all young and naïve. "It was all about Eton."

"What else did you read there?"

"Nothing much. Just what I've told you," Lara said breezily and shrugged again.

She was lying.

"That was all?" Jack gave her a hard stare.

"Well... She also thought that you were a good friend to Eton."

He didn't like the way Lara said it and the way she looked at him from under her eyebrows, her pretty lips pressed together, so he changed the subject. "Why do you think Eton wants to leave? He knows no one outside of the Soviet Union, not even his relatives. Has no friends..."

He knows you, dickhead! *You* are his friend.

But it's not what she's trying to do... Right?

Are you sure?

She wants to find his relatives in France, not America, doesn't she?... She's bluffing... Shit! She can't know... can she?

He made an effort to refocus on what Lara was saying.

"... In the beginning. But if we care for him, we have to persuade him."

"*We?*"

"Yes, Jack. He may not listen to me, but he will listen to you. I *know* he will."

"Wait a minute, Lara. First, you said you wanted me to help to locate his relatives in France. Now you're saying I have to persuade him to leave the country where he was born and has lived all his life... What are you trying to do, girl? Huh?"

"Jaack, Jaaack!" she exclaimed, exasperated. "He'll fall apart there, the state he is in now. He will just rot away. He is *not* going to recover in Moscow... You see, things have been changing fast at home, opening up with *glasnost*. They have let us stage one of the most controversial of Viktor's plays, as you can see. Rock bands are getting out from the underground and are playing on TV nowadays. Moscow will host an international hard rock festival next month. All his idols are coming—Bon Jovi, Ozzie Osborne, Scorpions. They have even published Solzhenitsyn. Can you believe it? And Eton? He notices none of this! But then none of the Afghan veterans I know do. It is as if they live in a separate world: they get together to get drunk, or high, and to talk about Afghanistan. They are all just wasting away, all in their twenties... And a handful who understood they didn't fit at home, they went back to Afghanistan. To die there... Please, Jack, I can't have him dying on me, too!" She grabbed Jack's arm, almost hysterical.

Jack turned into a narrow side street and parked at the entrance to a small city park.

"Calm down, sweetheart, will you?" He took her hand in both of his and smiled at her encouragingly. "I saw and talked to Eton these last two evenings. Yes, he has changed a little. But you might be exaggerating things a bit, don't you think?"

Lara gazed at him sadly and pulled her hand back. "That's because he hasn't taken a drop of alcohol since he has come up to Berlin. Because he knew he would be meeting with *you*."

She fumbled in her purse, lit up another cigarette and offered her lighter to Jack when he pulled out his pack.

"What are you trying to tell me, Lara?"

"Jack, I already told you. You were not listening." She sighed dramatically. "You're the *only* person I trust enough to ask this favor, knowing that this will not end up in some dossier on Lubianka. Same with Eton—he trusts you. He looks up to you. He listens to you. You are our *friend*, Jack. And it means a lot where we're coming from... I thought you knew that?"

God, girl, you have not the slightest idea!

Or have you?

He watched her warily, then sighed. "Alright, Lara. I'll see what I can find out. But it won't be fast. Like you, I'd like to keep this discreet... Alright?"

"Of course, Jack! Thank you so much. I knew you'd agree to help um, me!" She leaned over, snaked her arm around his neck and planted a kiss on his jaw. "Hmm, you always smell so good. Too bad I have a date here already." She winked at him.

Jack took her back to the shopping center and spent the next two and a half hours following her around while she shopped at *Centrum*, then at a more exclusive *Exquit* shop nearby which sold locally made fashionable clothing and accessories not widely available or affordable for the average salaried citizen of the *DDR*. When he brought her back to her hotel, she needed his help to get all her purchases up to her room.

Eton opened the door and seemed startled by the sight of Jack, laden with Lara's shopping bags. He was unshaven and barefoot, in a pair of old, washed out jeans and a dark blue t-shirt, looking both rugged and vulnerable at the same time.

"*Privet*," Lara said, breezing past him. "Have you had lunch already? No?" She dumped her bags on the double bed in the middle of the room and gestured to Jack to do the same. She then turned to Eton who was still standing near the door. "Let's have a quick bite with Jack downstairs. Then I will have to get ready. Matthias will come to fetch me at six... Eton, don't just stand there, please! Put your shoes on if you're coming with us."

Eton glared at her, mumbled "yes, madam" and went to put on his shoes. When they were out in the corridor, following Lara to the lifts, he shot Jack a sideways glance and mumbled, "Women", a corner of his mouth curled up in a mocking half-smile that Jack remembered so well.

They had a quick lunch of sausage soup, cold cuts with sauerkraut and dark rye bread, and Lara told Jack about her plans for that night.

She was invited by her friend Matthias Hoffman to the party he and his crew were throwing to celebrate their film getting approval for public screening. The state censor's office had held it up longer than usual, and for several months they had feared that it wouldn't be approved. Then a few days ago, they had been told that the film was being released. With only minor cuts.

"What is it about?" Lara raised her eyes at Jack's question, then resumed buttering a slice of bread. "About love and... *relationships*... Interestingly, the title is in English. It's called Coming Out. Matthias plays the leading role, of a school teacher," she explained without looking up from her plate. "By the way, Jack, I'll come to Berlin again in September, for the Berlin Festival of Drama and Music. I should be part of the LenKom's main company by then. We will get together again, *da*? Maybe I will even get a visa to West Berlin. You'll take me there, won't you, Jack? People here are raving about shops on Ku'damm. I'm sure you know them all. *Da*?"

Lara carried on chattering for another half hour, with Jack chipping in from time to time. Finally, she dropped her napkin on the plate and said she had to go upstairs to get ready for the party. She would be back before midnight as she would like to have at least a three-hour sleep before the trip back to Moscow. And she hoped that Jack would come to the railway station to see her off — would he?

When she left, Jack settled the bill. They crossed over to the tree-lined alley that separated the two-way Unter den Linden and sat down on a bench. Jack pulled out his cigarettes, and they sat smoking in silence for a while.

"So what do you want to do?" Jack asked in Russian, aware that around major hotels, even the park benches were bugged.

Eton mulled over it, knitting his brows, then smirked. "Let's hit the bars. It's my last day of leave of absence. A good reason to get drunk."

"Alright." Jack looked at his wristwatch. "It's still early, but I'm sure we can find a place where we can start."

They strolled along Friedrichstrasse towards the train station. It was the rush hour, and the street was busy with both traffic and pedestrians hurrying to do their shopping before heading home. They picked up their pace so as not to stand out from the crowd.

Because of its proximity to Berlin's main station the stuffy little restaurant-bar called Zur Nolle was doing a brisk business, despite the early hour on a Monday afternoon. They ordered two beers and two shots of *Wodka Gorbatschow* at the bar, then found a free table well away from the windows. They downed their shots, and Jack ordered another round.

"You haven't asked me anything about... Lara and me," Eton said, his eyes fixed on the shot glass he was swirling in his fingers.

"Lara told me."

"Of course." Eton chuckled humorlessly. "She was supposed to be with you, right?"

Jack took a swig of his beer and put the mug back on the coaster. "No. With neither of us... Don't worry about it Eton. I understand."

Eton looked up, the corners of his mouth curling up slightly. "I used to say that. Now you're telling me."

"Good. We understand each other well then, right?" He smiled at Eton, hoping he came across convincing, then flashed a grin at the waitress who had brought them their second round of vodkas. "*Danke*."

Eton nodded and gulped down his shot without waiting for Jack, chasing it with a long swill of beer.

"Don't worry about—"

"We can't go to your place, can we?" Eton muttered, not meeting Jack's eyes.

"M... *my* place? You want to..."

Duh! What's wrong with you, Smith?!

"I'm sorry, bud. It's not a good idea."

Eton nodded gloomily. "I don't know *any* place here," he said under his breath, the color spreading from his neck to his face.

"Alright, alright. Let me think... I should know, right? Just give me a minute, friend. I'll come up with something."

Chapter 60

It wasn't meant to be.

He walked Eton for over an hour through the labyrinth of side streets and back alleys to the war-marked shell of a building in Prenzlauer Berg district. He had used a tiny cloistered room on the top floor to don his disguise during a recent op. He prayed that vagrants had not lifted the dirty bedroll with a matching set of outfit he had left behind.

They never had a chance to find out. A dozen punks were getting high on grass on the ground floor, singing along to Queen's "We Are The Champions", undaunted by the screeching noises made by their old cassette player. There was no way they could get to the staircase unnoticed, so after an exchange of disappointed glances, and Eton shaking his head, Jack aborted the attempt.

They found a bar opposite Kollwitzplatz and spent the rest of the evening there, knocking back vodka and beer, silent and brooding. After four shots and three beers, horny as hell, Jack resolved to take Eton to his safe house. Fuck Joe Coburn and the Company! After all, it was reserved for his use mostly, right? But apparently alcohol had the opposite effect on Eton: when Jack leaned in and whispered, "I have another place", he shook his head morosely and downed half of his fourth beer in one go.

In the end, they shared a few desperate kisses in a public toilet on their way back to the hotel and quick hand-jobs. And as Jack's shudders were subsiding, he choked into Eton's neck, "Missed you so bad."

He dreamt of fields of cornflowers that night, and of Eton who smiled at him wide and bright, and said, "I've never felt so true, so... just me."

Jack arrived at Hauptbahnhof just before 6:00 a.m. and rushed to Platform 8A where the Moskva Express was waiting—dark green sleeping cars, cozy white curtains on the windows, train attendants in bluish-gray uniforms, all of which he still remembered so well.

The LenKom's company occupied the sleeper coach number 5 and the commotion and chatter in front of it was energetic and loud. Actors and their friends congregated in small groups on the platform, some with fluted tea glasses in hand and bottles of Stolichnaya, others with flowers and boxes of chocolates in plastic bags, all talking and laughing. The largest party comprised seven or eight men and Jack guessed Lara was in the middle. He didn't see Eton amongst them.

As he was closing in on the group, a short, skinny Russian with thinning blond hair jumped down from the coach further down the platform and hastened toward them. He elbowed his way through the circle of men, most of them at least half a head taller than him, and somehow they just let him through.

Jack stopped and turned away from the train, but kept the group in his peripheral vision. He fumbled for a cigarette and flicked his lighter. He knew the man.

In a minute or two, the shorty re-emerged from the group and Jack heard Lara's voice calling after him, "Send it to me by post, Volodya. I'll be waiting."

The Russian slowed down and called back over his shoulder, "Of course, Lara. Till we meet again in September!"

It was Volodya from Dresden.

From the first moment they met on his trip to Dresden with Jim and Ellie Grover in January '87, Jack had been convinced that the man was KGB. Later, East Berlin Station had confirmed his gut feel. And he was here again. More importantly, he knew Lara, and obviously well enough to be on an informal first name basis with her.

What about Eton? And where the fuck was Eton?

Volodya walked past right behind Jack's back, picking up his pace. But after half a dozen steps he slowed down, like he had forgotten something, then he stopped and swirled around.

Jack barely managed to turn his back on him. He strolled up to the trashcan under the lamppost in the middle of the platform, dropped his cigarette in it and headed over to join the group of admirers around Lara. He felt the other man's eyes on his back, but there was little he could do—he could neither pretend he was seeing off someone else, nor walk away.

"Jack, *daragusha*! Thought you wouldn't come." Lara snaked her arm through his.

She introduced her fans to him: two attachés from the Soviet Embassy, three reporters of Russian and German newspapers, a young LenKom actor, the deputy director of the Metropole Theater and Lara's "very good friend" Matthias Hoffman.

Jack shook hands with the men and joined their conversation about Berlin Festivals of Drama and Music. Soon, Eton appeared and parked himself quietly behind the two Soviet attachés who were standing in the circle across from him and Lara. He caught Jack's eye and smiled faintly, then fixed his gaze on Lara, who gave him a little wave of her hand and continued chatting with her admirers.

A few minutes later the loudspeaker announced the departure of Moskva Express in five minutes, and the attendants started herding the passengers onto the train and their friends off it. Lara offered her hand benevolently to each man, except for Jack and Matthias with whom she exchanged three kisses, Russian style.

"Not a word to Eton. You promised, Jack!" she whispered as she kissed him.

"Don't worry. Safe journey!" He smiled, looking intently into her eyes, trying to figure out what game she was playing—*they* were playing... Right?

She pressed her palm in the middle of his chest, grinned happily, then pivoted around and flitted to Eton.

Jack dropped his gaze, fumbled in his pocket for his cigarette pack. He didn't want to see them putting on an act of a happily married couple—it was so not in Eton's style...

Is that so? Or maybe you don't want to see them kissing? Stings, doesn't it?

Go to hell!

Now he knew what Eton must have felt when he caught him with his tongue down Lara's throat in that dark alley in Leningrad.

When he raised his eyes, Lara was inside the coach, smiling through the glass at her men on the platform. Then she looked down at Eton who stood by her window, a small duffel bag at his feet, and mouthed, "Remember what I said". Eton nodded and raised his hand in a parting gesture as the train jerked and screeched and started rolling. The sendoff crowd made a few steps along with it, but was quickly left behind as the locomotive gained speed and in a minute disappeared around the bend.

Those left on the platform bade each other goodbyes and hurriedly took their leave.

"Have you had breakfast?" Jack asked as they were strolling along the rapidly clearing platform, slowing their pace, as they got closer to the station hall.

"No."

"Care to join me?"

Eton nodded.

A few minutes later, they were buying pastries and coffee in the busy cafeteria inside Hauptbahnhof's newly renovated main hall. They chose a table at the far end from the exit and sat down. They ate in silence for a few minutes.

"Eton, can I ask you something?"

"Yes." Eton raised his eyes.

"There was a guy named Volodya on the platform. He left before you returned. Do you know him?... Is he Lara's friend?"

"He's not a friend. Just an admirer of hers."

"How long have you known him?"

Eton shrugged. "We first met him at the LenKom's premier over two weeks ago. Lara said he'd been coming to the theater every two or three days. Why? Do *you* know him?"

Jack grimaced. "He's with... the *organs*."

Eton expression didn't change. He took a sip from his mug. "How do you know?"

"I know. I *accidentally* ran into him twice, three years ago in Dresden. Too accidentally... So I checked up on him."

"I see... Felix and Chengiz are probably with them too. In fact, I wouldn't be surprised if all the staff at our embassies overseas are with the organs. Just one of those things they do," he mumbled and took a bite of his cake.

"Aren't you concerned about Lara... and him?"

What about you and him, Eton?

"Do I have a choice?"

The challenge in Eton's tone made Jack wince mentally and bite his tongue. They finished their cakes and coffees in silence.

"Can I ask you something else?" Jack said, putting his empty coffee mug down on the table.

"Of course." Eton nodded, obviously trying to sound amiable.

"Does Lara know... about you?... And me?"

- 451 -

"Why? What did she tell you?" Eton furrowed his brows.

She knows!

"Nothing specifically, but she kept alluding... What does she know?"

"She knows nothing about you. Nothing," Eton repeated, firm and low, then continued in a less assured tone. "She may suspect about me."

"God, Eton, she was suspicious about me back in Moscow, remember? Your, *her* friend Karelin told her that I might be... So now if she suspects that you are too, how difficult it is to put two and two together?" He knew he sounded exasperated but couldn't help it—this was getting totally out of control.

"She doesn't know for sure," Eton said, a stubborn note in his tone. "And even if she knew, she wouldn't tell anyone."

"How do you know?"

"I know. She would have done it already if she wanted, wouldn't she? She is too much sometime. Most of the times even. But I trust her. She's a good friend. Loyal." He flicked out a cigarette from the pack and squinted at Jack. "But if you suspect both her *and* me, then I don't have anything else to say."

Fuck! Fuck...

"I'm sorry, Eton. I didn't..." He wanted to say that he didn't mean it, but of course he did and knew that Eton knew it too. He sighed in resignation and mumbled, "I'm sorry."

"Me too." Eton's tone and expression softened. "I wish I could do something to make you trust me. But I know I can't... It's all because of your job..."

Jack nodded dejectedly. He reached out, pulled Eton's cigarette out of his fingers and took a deep drag on it. Then he bought another round of coffees and they sat there for a long time, sometimes chatting, sometimes in companionable silence.

When it was time for Eton to go, Jack saw him off to the platform. As the train pulled in, the swarm of passengers around them surged nearer to the edge of the platform. They stepped back instead and embraced, and Jack stealthily slipped a scrap of paper into Eton's pocket.

"It's Metze Eck's address and phone. You can leave a message for me with Barbel. Or send a postcard. For Johann. She will pass it to me... You can trust her," he added, smiling sadly.

"Alright. I may come up next month. Will try to send a postcard beforehand... And Jack?" He looked squarely into Jack's eyes, squeezing his hand in a firm handshake. "I believe you."

Eton's gaze was both steady and sad, and Jack knew he had been given one more chance.

That night in West Berlin Jack put through an urgent request for a full debrief with the COS. David Rolston would notify Joe Coburn, and it was possible that the Division Head would summon both of them for a meeting at one of NATO's military bases in Europe. In the meantime, Jack would have to write up a report on the three days he had spent with the young Volkonsky couple. But before he started, he had to decide what was going into his report and the subsequent debrief and what wasn't. Not just yet.

Jack knew his apartment had been searched as soon as he stepped through the doorway: the umbrella that he had placed to look like it had fallen from the stand by the door had been moved.

His apartment had been searched twice since he had arrived in East Berlin. The place was bugged like any foreigner's accommodation in this part of the world, but it had seemed that after the first two months of intensive coverage the Stasi had decided to keep him under "observation light". And now this, three days after his encounter with Volodya from Dresden. Jack had no doubt that Volodya had recognized him. Actually, he had been surprised that the Russian hadn't come up to resume their acquaintance right then and there.

Jack kicked off his shoes, dropped his duffel bag on the floor and walked straight to the cupboard in the sitting room. He fiddled noisily with the bottle of whiskey and a tumbler, poured himself a drink, took a gulp, let out a loud, contented sigh and flopped onto the nearest armchair. Only then did he inspect the room.

Whoever searched the place had done a great job of being discreet—a layman probably wouldn't even notice anything out of ordinary. But Steve McCurry's photobook on the coffee table that Jack had left opened to page twenty seven was now opened to page twenty five. The lighter on the bookshelf was supposed to angle at exactly forty-five degrees to the row of the odd assortment of books, its end touching the letter M of Fodor's guidebook "Germany, West and East". It was now virtually parallel to it, starting at the letter Y.

Jack stood up, fetched his duffel bag by the door and tromped into the bedroom. Once there, he sat the tumbler on the bedside table, flopped the bag on the bed and unzipped it in one sweeping stroke. Then he turned around and stepped up to the wardrobe. Squatting down, he opened the bottom drawer where he kept things that… he shouldn't have kept. A couple of the Eagles audio cassettes and one of Bon Jovi, his picture cut from a magazine and stuck under the cassette case cover—blond, long-haired and unsmiling, a guitar upside down under one arm. A couple of Playboy magazines—the rangy playmate featured in one of them had big, soulful brown eyes. A sheet from a copy of July's New York Times used as the drawer's bottom cover, the back page carrying a 380-word piece from the AP: the New York Supreme Court gave family status to a gay couple in an inheritance lawsuit. Of course, other pages of the newspaper went as bottom covers into the other three drawers of his wardrobe. And he also kept random stuff in the bottom drawer—a battered Walkman with the headset cable wrapped around it, a pack of new socks, a couple of new and used writing pads, half a block of new Kodak film.

Sure enough, the contents of the drawers had been checked too, including the Playboy magazines—a hair he had meticulously placed between pages 9 and 10 of one of them had disappeared. The newspaper had been moved, but probably not taken out completely. The tapes were stacked just a tad too neatly.

Jack pushed the drawer closed, went back to the bed and sat down. He'd better get rid of the newspaper and... of all other things which might give away even the slightest hint at what could be on his mind. He lay back on the bed and closed his eyes.

He had promised Eton to make himself and his people scarce. Now he had to get rid of even the allusion of what his friend meant to him. What would he have left after that?

He reached for the tumbler and downed the smoky liquid on two big gulps.

* * *

A week later, Jack flew to Munich with David for a debrief with Joe Coburn over the satellite phone at the US Army Garrison in Garmisch. It lasted for 3 hours and by the end, Jack was drained and dying for a drink.

What he reported to his superiors was that after the death of his mother and grandfather, and especially after Afghanistan, Eton May Volkonsky was pretty much done for. It was unlikely that he would return to complete his postgrad and even more unlikely that he would be taken back into the nuclear physics research program in Dubna. Even his status as Minister of Culture Novikov's son-in-law might not help—the man was wrecked. Why had the pair married? It looked like it had been the girl's initiative. From a provincial background, she got an old Russian aristocratic name and lineage in exchange for the protection her highly positioned family could give Volkonsky. That was how he had been transferred from Afghanistan to East Germany.

The more noteworthy news was that Novikova-Volkonskaya was linked to a KGB operative whom Jack had met three years back. In fact, their acquaintance had looked informal and friendly, out in the open. So either Lara and Volodya were indeed just acquaintances, or the KGB was using a tactic similar to the SE Division's: what was blatantly in your face couldn't possibly be covert.

The Volkonsky pair insisted that they wanted to stay in contact with Jack, both while Eton was still in Germany and after his demobilization. The young man still considered Jack his friend and the woman, well, she seemed as ready to hit on anything with a dick as she had ever been.

Other news was that after two and a half months of light coverage, the surveillance on Jack had picked up after his encounter with Volodya at the train station. His apartment had been thoroughly searched and he wouldn't be surprised if they'd planted a camera too. It was possible that now he had both the Stasi and the KGB breathing down his neck.

Finally, with Lara coming to East Berlin for a music and drama festival in September, he would be seeing the Russians again and he wouldn't be surprised if either she or her friend Volodya from Dresden, or both of them, would try to pitch him.

And no, he didn't think Eton Volkonsky was with the KGB—the man was unmanageable now. Unstable.

It was past 9:00 p.m. when Jack got back to Munich. He hit the bar closest to his hotel and spent the rest of the evening shooting beers and talking about politics and sports with strangers.

That night he dreamed of Eton again. His friend was in the Soviet army uniform, flanked by Lara, Volodya from Dresden, Jack's Moscow shadows whom he used to refer to as Vova and Petya, and some other suspicious characters he couldn't place. Jack watched warily as the Russians closed ranks behind Eton, and asked him, "Are you with them?"

Eton glanced over his shoulder, then met Jack's gaze, his eyes weary and sad. "Do I have a choice?"

Jack jerked awake, disoriented and sweating, and it took him a long time to get back to sleep.

Chapter 61

Jack was the last to board the Lufthansa flight to West Berlin. He crammed into his window seat and opened the first newspaper in his pack, the Washington Post. Half way down the headlines, one caught his eye: "High Level Career Diplomat Suspected as a Soviet Spy."

"...Director of the State Department's Bureau of European and Canadian Affairs... Rose steadily over a 30-year career to become the United States' second-ranking official in Austria... Suspected of spying for the Soviet Union... Sources said was videotaped giving a briefcase of materials to a Soviet agent..."

He recalled an operation in Brussels, three months ago.

It had been classified "Substandard", the prefix denoting that it was carried out without the host country being notified. For this reason, the local Station could not run the op and the Company had to fly in case officers from other countries. The objective was to photograph the meeting between the target and an alien thought to be a KGB deep cover operative. The target was a senior State Department official in President Bush's entourage on his European visit.

And now here he was, Felix Bloch, a State Department Director, staring at Jack from the top of the page, his identity and the revelation that he had been under the FBI's investigation for the last two months brought to light.

"A source close to the investigation said the videotape of Bloch was not made by the FBI but by another investigative agency, which he would not identify. The source would not say whether the CIA has participated in the probe...."

Thank God they hadn't dug up about the Company's little "substandard" op in Brussels. It was also reassuring that the article said videotape, not photographs. It meant that the FBI, which had requested his Agency to help in the first place, had managed to keep the CIA's involvement under wraps.

USA TODAY carried a piece on another Soviet spy convicted of espionage two days earlier—one James W. Hall III. The man had served as a signals intelligence analyst at an Army Security outfit on the West German-Czechoslovakian border in early 80s and for years been selling code secrets to East Germans *and* the Sovs. Since his arrest several months ago, Hall's name had become a sinister household name thanks to in-depth coverage of his case by the press.

Bloch and Hall were not the only spy cases that held American public's attention that summer. In early August, another West Germany-based serviceman was apprehended, and this time the US Air Force was in the limelight. The detainee was Capt. John Hirsch, an electrical engineer at Tempelhof Airport in West Berlin, suspected of having sold secret documents to the Russians.

August of 1989 saw other events that kept political analysts riveted, along with everyone who had been following the developments in the socialist block since Gorbachev announced *perestroika*.

The Soviet Union was falling apart. In addition to the unprecedented and widespread coal miners strikes, there were violent clashes between Tajiks and Kyrgyz over the water sources, an out-and-out war between Armenia and Azerbaijan for the district of Nagorny Karabach, and between Georgia and the autonomous district of Abkhazia, which demanded independence. The bloody ethnic conflicts between former brotherly Soviet republics left administrative offices, businesses and factories closed, dusk to dawn curfews imposed in major towns. For the first time in decades, travel permits were reintroduced in the Caucasus region.

In its wrenching effort to reform the crumbling economy, the Supreme Soviet granted wide-ranging economic autonomy to Estonia and Lithuania, and it was understood that Latvia would soon follow.

Closer to the West, the move by Hungary to take down the wire fences along its border had triggered a tide of East Germans arriving "for holidays", only to slip across into Austria. The number of applicants for West German visas ballooned overnight. So much so that on the second week of August, West Germany had to shut down its diplomatic mission in East Berlin—"until further notice"—to stem the flood of people seeking exit visas. However, while the Soviet Union, Poland and Hungary were adopting more liberal policies, East Germany was aggravating the situation by continuing its policy of repression. Thus, from June to August alone around 2,500 East Germans were reportedly jailed for trying to escape to the West.

Meanwhile, on August 23rd, Hungary removed border restrictions with Austria. The next day in Poland, Tadeusz Mazowiecki of the opposition Solidarity movement was elected Prime Minister.

* * *

His shadowing intensified when Jack returned from Munich. Instead of his regular escort, now there were at least two others following him around, including a petite, mousy woman. By the end of the third week, when he had resigned to what it seemed his life would be from now on, the stalking suddenly slackened, and Jack started breathing freer again.

Early Sunday evening he returned from the Austrian-Hungarian border, where he had been covering a large peace demonstration nicknamed the Pan-European Picnic. He dropped his bag by the bedroom door, quickly changed and headed out to Metzer Eck. He had been away for nearly a week and all that time been praying that he hadn't missed anything.

He hadn't. The moment Jack walked in, Barbel waved him to the backroom and handed a postcard. "A new *friend*?" She winked at him. "Bring them here."

Written in German, in Eton's clear, almost block handwriting, the message read, "Dear Johann. Arriving on 26, at 09:35. Coffee at the station? N."

"En" as in Eton. Jack chuckled and shook his head, feeling exuberant. Why not? If he was Johann, then Eton could be N.

And the 26th was next Saturday.

As usual, the cozy little restaurant was not particularly busy on a Sunday night. Only half of its dozen tables were occupied, and one of them, at the back, by Barbel's friends.

Jack ordered his dinner and joined the table where Axel, Bernard the musician and his big-haired, fashionable wife Ursel were talking quietly over beers. He listened distractedly to the conversation at first, his mind a million miles away. but, the moment the words "holiday" and "Hungary" caught his attention, Jack was all ears.

It turned out, Bernard and his wife had finally got their visas, for which they had applied three months ago, and were leaving the following week for their holiday. On Lake Balaton. Ursel was thrilled and didn't even try to hide it. Her bespectacled, balding hubby, the leading cellist of the Berlin Radio Symphony Orchestra, was subdued and edgy. The pair didn't have children, so Ursel channeled her bottomless reservoir of energy and care onto her soft-spoken husband and on procuring the latest Western fashion.

When Jack said he had just returned from Austrian-Hungarian border, Ursel and Barbel fired a barrage of questions at him, demanding to know in minute detail about the situation there and whether it was true, that one could walk across the border, just like that. And although nobody mentioned it explicitly during the entire conversation, everyone understood, that the lucky pair didn't plan to return from their holiday.

Towards the end of the dinner, Ursel turned uncharacteristically quiet. When Jack stood up, preparing to leave, she hooked her arm through his and pulled him unceremoniously to the backroom. "Jack, I'd like to ask you a big favor, *Bitte*," she said low, a pleading expression on her face.

It wasn't the first time that she had asked Jack a favor. Ursel had a cousin in West Berlin who had also been her best friend before the Wall came up in 1961 when both were just twelve. They had remained as close as the Wall permitted them to be, and Gretchen had been sending Ursel trendy clothes from the West now and then. Jack had acted as their courier three times since they became friends, and Ursel had no reservations about asking him for favors.

"You need this season's swimsuit for your trip to Balaton?" Jack teased.

She giggled nervously. "*Nein*! But it's a bit... unusual a request this time I'm afraid... Jack, I'd like to ask you to take a suitcase with my stuff to Gretchen. Nothing illegal, I promise," she hastened to assure when Jack squinted his eyes. "It's just mementos and... little things I want her to keep for me."

"I see... Alright. I'll help you. This is the last time, isn't it?" Jack winked.

"Oh, Jack! *Danke, Danke, Danke*!" She threw herself at him and kissed him on both cheeks. "And, yes, I *hope* it's the last time." She let out an excited little laugh. "I'll leave the suitcase with Barbel. You can collect it when it's convenient for you. And I'll owe you a *big* dinner and a bottle of wine when I... see you next time." She winked back at him and turned around to head back to the dining room, pulling Jack along by his arm.

He held her back. "Ursel, can I ask you a favor in return?"

She swerved back to him. "Of course, Jack. Anything... What is it?" she prompted, seeing as he was just standing there, chewing on the corner of his lip.

"I have a friend who's coming up to Berlin next weekend. For a couple of days... Um, she can't stay at my place... If you know what I mean." He shrugged, looking apologetic.

"She needs a place to stay, is that it?"

"Yes."

"Your friend is welcome to stay at our place, Jack. I'll prepare the bedroom for her and leave the key with Barbel, too. And she can use anything she'll find in the fridge." She grinned at Jack, thrilled that she could return him a favor. Then she stepped up and threw her arms around Jack again. "Don't know when we'll see each other again. But we will, I'm sure. You can always check with Gretchen for news about me."

When they returned to the table, Jack shook hands with everyone and left, feeling high with a sense of accomplishment. Now he had "a place". Of course, he still needed to check it out before taking Eton there, but at least it would be a proper home with a proper bed, not a dirty mattress on the broken floor of a war-gutted carcass of a building, where Jack had taken him to last time. His friend deserved more than that. And surely didn't need to be reminded of what bombs and bullets left behind when he was in the arms of someone who cared.

The next day Jack drove to Leipzig to check out a rumor that lately, Monday evening services at the Nicolaikirche, an old church downtown Leipzig, had been more than just peace prayers for dissenting churchgoers. He spent three days talking to pastors, "peace prayers" and random folks on the street, pleased that his counter surveillance skills turned out quite handy for his overt job too. By Thursday night, he had submitted six news reports and a feature article co-written with his senior colleague from the AP's East Berlin office. Terry Kellerman preferred covering major political events and let Jack do the rest. Jack was happy to leave the politics and politicians to good old Terry, content that people he met with and talked to were regular folks with their everyday problems and joys.

On Friday night, he picked up the key to Ursel's apartment. The next day, he got up at 6:00 a.m. and went out jogging. The morning was grim and gusty, threatening to explode into a heavy rain any moment, just the kind of weather that Jack liked when he needed no shadowing.

The rundown building where Ursel and Bernard lived was a dozen blocks from Jack's place and only two streets away from the Wall. Stealthily, Jack ran up the tired but spotless staircase to the fifth and last floor, noiselessly opened and then closed the ancient hardwood door behind him.

Despite the telltale signs of decades of use without major refurbishment, the apartment looked well looked after. The commode with curved legs in the hallway was obviously an antique item as were the matching dressing table and the chest of drawers in the bedroom. Everything else bore the stamp of socialist mass production—the wall-size cupboard and the coffee table made of pressed wood, the RFT Colorlux television set, the sand-colored couch and armchairs, the standing lamp under a pale yellow shade. Above all, the apartment was a classic example of what the rest of the world called "the German neatness".

A large window and a narrow door opening onto a tiny balcony took up most of the wall opposite the bedroom door. The balcony was curtained by a waterfall of grapevines overgrowing from the roof. The double bed in the middle of the room was covered with an over-sized spread, a mass-produced imitation of ancient tapestry. A set of clean towels was stacked neatly on the edge of the bed. The dressing table boasted neat rows of small boxes and containers with toiletries, combs and brushes, dress jewelry, half-used bottles of perfumes and eau-de-cologne.

The tiny room next to the bedroom was obviously Bernard's study. There were countless neat stacks of sheet music, music-related magazines and books everywhere—on the shelves of the narrow bookcase, on the desk, on a chair in one corner. A timeworn cello was perched on a stand by the desk, its old case leaning against the chair.

The small kitchen was sparkling clean and orderly, too. The fridge and kitchen cabinets were well stocked with everything needed by a household of two. And, as anywhere else in the apartment, nothing in the kitchen indicated that its owners had left for good.

Ten minutes of close inspection left Jack satisfied. It was unlikely that the place was bugged—Ursel and Bernard were just an ordinary couple, leading a conventional life of ordinary citizens of the *DDR*. The old building's partitions were thick enough not to transmit sounds from the apartments on the other side of the wall, above or below.

Yeah, he could safely bring Eton to this place. Maybe even stay here for the night with him… If that was something Eton wanted too.

He returned from his jogging an hour later, soaking wet from the violent outburst of a cold rain that had caught him a hundred meters from his apartment block. He showered and changed, had breakfast with his morning newspapers while waiting for the rain to cease. Just before ten o'clock, he was at Checkpoint Charlie. The pretty border guard, whom the foreign community in East Berlin called Lovely Rita, scanned his passport and waved him past the barrier with an almost friendly smile. At noon, a coded cable went out of the US West Berlin Mission, addressed to Chief of the SE Division, saying that Jack's scheduled trip back home was delayed due to a request for meeting by an op contact. He also placed a call with David Rolston to let him know about the change of his travel plans.

He got home just before midnight and needed an extra shot of whiskey to get himself settled down for the night. His sleep was heavy and dreamless, but when he got up in the morning and saw a square of clear blue sky out of his bedroom window, he told himself that today would be the day when all his dreams of the last few years would finally come true.

At 9:30 a.m. sharp on Saturday Jack was in the busy cafeteria in new central building of Hauptbahnhof, parked at the same little plastic-top table where he and Eton had sat after seeing Lara off. In front of him were an empty cup of coffee, a ham sandwich that he had barely touched and folded copies of Neues Deutschland and Berliner Zeitung that he hadn't even opened. He watched travelers hustling by as he ran through his mind the two bits of news he thought might interest Eton—the debut of his idol, Soviet rocker Boris Grebenschikov in Los Angeles the week before, and the upcoming international hard rock festival in Moscow where another of Eton's old heart-throbs, Bon Jovi, was taking part. Lara had said that after his return from Afghanistan, Eton had lost all his old interests, but Jack hoped his friend would turn around.

He saw him as soon as the young man walked through the door. Their eyes met, and a corner of Eton's mouth pulled up in response to Jack's face-splitting grin. He was wearing jeans and the dark blue windbreaker Jack remembered from the last time, a small black and red rucksack over his shoulder.

Jack stood up, and they shook hands.

"*Privet*, Eton."

"*Privet*. Have you been waiting long?"

"No." He glanced down at his watch and grinned at his friend again. "Only twenty three and a half minutes."

"I'm sorry. I waited till the others went into town."

"No worries… Breakfast?" Eton shook his head and sat down. "How about a coffee?"

"Yes, thanks."

"I'll be right back."

In a minute, Jack returned with a tray with two cups of steaming coffee. "How long are you staying this time?"

"Till Monday. I have an appointment at the embassy on Monday morning. Have to be back to the garrison by noon."

Two days. Two fucking days!

"So what's the plan?"

Eton shrugged awkwardly. "I have no plans. Just free time… I have to return to the consulate's guest house by eleven tonight. With the other guys."

"Right."

Eton nodded, apologetic, and pulled out his cigarettes.

"Anywhere else you need to go today?"

"No. Why?"

"Because I've found a place where we can crash," Jack said in a loud whisper, barely able to contain his excitement. "It's a friend's place," he explained, seeing Eton's suspicious glance. His enthusiasm deflated a little when Eton didn't say anything, just sat there smoking, eyes fixed on the tip of his burning cigarette. "Is that alright?"

Eton looked up briefly, his expression wary. "Yes… Can we talk there too?"

"Of course we can. My friends are vacationing in Hungary and have given me the key to their apartment. We have the whole day today if you don't have any other plans."

"Except the meeting at the embassy, I have no other plans for today or tomorrow." He finally met Jack's eyes and smiled shyly. "I've come to see you."

Chapter 62

They stopped by a grocery store outside the train station to buy bread, cold cuts, apples and vodka, then strolled casually up north, taking side streets where Jack could pick out a tail, in case they were shadowed. An hour later, they were standing in front of the building where Ulrika and Bernard lived. Jack scanned the street, stalling until an elderly couple disappeared behind the corner, and only then pulled open the entrance door. He held it for Eton, crowded him in. God must have heard his prayers because they didn't run into anyone walking up the stairs. A minute later, they were in the apartment with the door securely chained from the inside.

Jack lowered his shoulder bag on the floor, toed off his runners and hung his jacket on the rack. Eton draped his jacket over Jack's and turned around. They stood motionless, gazing at each other, then Jack stepped up, cupped Eton's face with both of his hands and planted a soft, lingering kiss on his lips.

"God, I've been dying to do this since I laid my eyes on you this morning," he muttered, smiling happily.

When he made a step back, Eton caught him by his arm, yanked him back and attacked Jack's mouth, holding Jack's head firmly with his hands. Jack wrapped his arms around him and pressed his whole body against Eton's lanky frame. When Eton's mouth slipped to the side of his neck just below his ear, Jack's head fell back, his legs about to buckle under him.

"Bedroom?" he whispered.

Eton nodded, looking dazed.

Clinging to one another, they stumbled down the corridor and into the bedroom. Eton shoved him onto the bed and climbed on top of him, his mouth latching onto Jack's neck again.

"Etaahnn, wait." Jack pushed him up gently. Eton opened his eyes, disoriented. "Don't you want to undress?"

Eton's gaze focused at once. He sat up and started unbuttoning his shirt slowly, his eyes averted. By the time Jack had shed his clothes and climbed under the bed covers, he was sitting on the edge of the bed, still wearing boxers and a sleeveless undershirt, staring down at his clasped hands.

"Eton, everything alright?"

Without looking at him, Eton lifted a corner of the bedspread and climbed in. He rolled onto Jack, buried his face in the hollow between his neck and shoulder, and held still. Jack could feel his friend's heart racing against his side and that he had lost half of his earlier erection. He didn't understand what had happened, but didn't ask, just let him be, holding him, stroking his back gently.

In a while, Eton started kissing him again, his hands roaming all over Jack's body. However, when Jack slipped a hand under the waistband of his boxers, Eton froze again.

Jack dragged his palm further down and came upon a thin, long cord of hardened flesh where he remembered none.

A scar.

His heart squeezed. He rolled them over and started planting soft little kisses on Eton's face, his neck, his shoulders, murmuring soothingly, "It's alright, baby. It's alright." Then he slid down, pushed the hem of Eton's undershirt up, and let his mouth linger over the taut, quivering belly, leaving a cool, wet mark wherever his lips touched, stroking him through the thin material of his boxers. When he knew Eton was ready, he gently lifted the waistband and pulled it down, releasing Eton's straining cock.

"Jaaack... Come here." He pulled at Jack's arm.

Jack lay down on top of him, aligning their bodies in the perfect fit that he remembered so well. Eton covered his lips with his own and prodded his hardness into him. Jack got the clue and started rocking his hips, slowly and deliberately at first, then gaining speed, almost frantic, until both exploded, one after the other, in a blinding white bliss.

When Jack came to his senses and opened his eyes, the first thing he saw was Eton. His friend was lying on his side, watching him, a soft half smile haunting his face. As he realized he was staring straight into Jack's eyes, Eton shifted uneasily, color creeping up his cheeks.

"Hey..." Jack grinned at him. "You alright?"

"Yes." Eton's smile widened a fraction, but only for a second. Then his face clouded, and he mumbled, "I'm sorry. For the... earlier."

"Don't worry about it." Jack shifted closer and draped his arm over Eton's waist. "It doesn't matter. I mean the scar." He kissed Eton softly on his lips.

Eton closed his eyes, his jaw muscles rolling. Then he sat up, quickly shed his undershirt and his boxers, climbed back in bed and quickly pulled the coverlet up to his chin. But not quick enough for Jack to miss a dimpled, reddish-brown scar just below his right collarbone.

A bullet wound.

"It has been too long." Eton smiled weakly. "Too many things happened... I need to... get used to you again." He reached out and touched Jack's face, and Jack had to close his eyes to will the surging moisture back. "To your face... Your lips... Your eyes..." Eton murmured, dragging his fingertips over the parts of Jack's body he was naming. "Your neck... Your shoulders... Your chest..."

Without opening his eyes, Jack caught his hand, pulled it down, and placed it over his cock. Eton's fingers closed around him.

"This too... I missed it." Eton shuffled closer and pressed his erection into Jack's hip.

"You want me in you?" Jack whispered.

It was the wrong thing to say. Eton froze, his eyes taking on a disturbed look.

Jack sighed mentally, pulled at Eton's hand and planted a wet kiss on his palm. "We don't have to... Or if you want, you can fuck me." He couldn't believe he had said that. He had only bottomed three times in his life and they hadn't been the best of his sexual experiences.

But his offer distressed Eton even more. He peered anxiously at Jack, then rolled onto his back and covered his eyes with his forearm. "No."

Something was clearly not right. Jack was pretty sure his friend wanted it. He reached down and palmed Eton's throbbing length. "Why not? You want it, don't you?"

Eton pushed his hand away, sat up and wrapped his arms around his folded legs. He cut Jack a quick glance, his eyes full of shadows, and turned away. "I can't."

The hurt and longing in his tone bewildered Jack. "You mean you won't have sex with me?"

"*No*!! Not that. But I can't... *fuck* you," he mumbled, grimacing, like it was a wrong thing to say. He met Jack's eyes and shook his head sadly. "And you shouldn't *give* yourself to me if you don't..." His voice broke, and he ended in a raspy whisper, "love me."

Jack thought his heart was going to burst through his chest and he knew this time he wouldn't be able to hide the tears. But he didn't care. He yanked Eton into his arms, held his head to his chest, pressing hot kisses into Eton's hair, his forehead, his cheeks, his lips.

"Oh, Jesus, Eton. I'm sorry, baby... I'm so fucking sorry! *Of course* I love you... I love you so much... it hurts... Can't even start telling you... what you mean to me... I missed you so bad..."

Eton's frame began heaving in Jack's arms as he broke down in quiet sobs. He clung to Jack, hiding his wet face in the crook of his shoulder and Jack had to strain to hear what he was choking out under his breath.

"Nothing left... only you... Jaaack... love you... I love you so..."

Jack laid them both down and pulled the sheet over them. He held his lover for a long time, stroking Eton's back, his arm, his shoulder, his face, aware of the growing wet spot on the pillow under his cheek.

He didn't know when they had dozed off, drained by their sudden outburst, but when he awoke, Eton was still asleep. He was lying on his back, his face half turned to Jack's side, looking youthful and at peace. Jack watched him for a few moments, propped up on one elbow, then leaned down and brushed his lips over the scar on Eton's shoulder.

Now that he had said the word aloud, it turned out to be so easy to also admit to himself that the reason he had been constantly thinking about Eton, ever since they had met, wasn't because he was his target, his star agent, or even his best friend ever. Although he was all of those things to him, too. No, it was because he, Jack Smith, was in love with this man of amazing beauty inside and out. And the most incredible thing was that this unbelievable man loved him too and continued loving Jack even after his admission of who he was and what he did. No, it must be something larger than love, from the very first day... It must have been fate. Like that girl, Eton's friend at the Moscow Festival, had said... And he had been a fool, trying to justify his feelings with any crap he could come up with. To protect himself from hurting again. It still hurt, for other reasons, but it also felt... amazingly good.

Mind-blowing is the word, dimwit.

Jack chuckled to himself and slipped out of bed.

When he returned from the bathroom with a towel, Eton met him with a shy little smile. "Sorry, I was a mess," he muttered.

"That makes two of us." Jack smiled back as he sat down on the bed. "Lemme clean you up while the towel's still hot." He threw the sheet off Eton and started wiping the traces of their love off his body. Then he turned the towel around and rubbed Eton down with the dry end.

When he finished, Eton examined his own front, sat up and said with a straight face, "Thank you. Now I am good to go to the bathroom."

"Gah! You could have told me, Eton. I wouldn't have bothered."

"Why? I like it when you look after me... Like a mother hen," Eton shot Jack a wicked smirk, and proceeded to the door.

"Dumbass!" Jack launched the balled-up towel after his friend, grinning happily.

Eton's reaction was instantaneous: he swung around and caught the towel, and sauntered out, looking smug.

As he neared the door, his bare back was in full view and Jack's grin slipped, his guts rolled into a tight ball.

There were actually two scars on his back, not one, each about fifty centimeters long. The thinner and paler one ran from under his left arm half way down his back, across and down to his waist on the right. The other, deep pink and protruded, picked up from the end of the first, ran down and across his right buttock, ending at the lower half of the left buttock. Both cuts had probably been inflicted with the same sharp instrument, a knife or maybe broken glass, but the lower back scar hadn't healed as well as the other one.

He recalled Lara saying that Eton had been jailed for a drunken fight and put in a cell with criminals, fought again, with his cellmates, and was released three weeks later with scars on his back. From the little Jack knew about Soviet prisons, sexual abuse was a commonplace initiation for new prisoners. Especially those who came from an intelligentsia background and hadn't had prior criminal records. That was why he'd fought in prison, hadn't he? And probably that was why he'd been so anxious about bottoming for Jack... No, it was *not* possible! They wouldn't have cut him up, had they managed to get to him. Right? Eton was a fighter; he had fought them. That was why they had branded him with those scars.

Jack's chest constricted. He felt like he was going to break down again. He pressed the tips of his fingers against his eyelids and let out a shaky exhale.

What would someone do to keep the ones they loved safe? What would *he* do?

When Eton came back to bed, they made love, Jack straddling him, trying not to be overwhelmed by sensations he hadn't known existed. Eton's face was a mixture of bliss and anxious concentration. He reached for Jack's hands, interlaced their fingers and smiled, his smile wide and joyful.

"Jaack... I love you."

It was all they needed to set them off. Jack closed his eyes and started riding.

They didn't need much. In a few moments, Eton cried out his release and soon Jack followed suit, pressing their joined hands into his core. He collapsed on Eton, carried away by rolling waves of undiluted pleasure and something else. And this time Jack knew what it was that he felt: love.

When they woke up again, it was after half-past two. Filtering through the swaying leaves of the grapevines over the balcony, the afternoon sun dappled the bedroom walls, the floor and their bodies with flickering shadows. They padded barefoot to the bathroom and showered together, crowding each other in the narrow bathtub, exchanging occasional touches and kisses. Then they ate their lunch of cold cuts and bread, washing it down with instant coffee from Ursel's cupboard, and returned to the bedroom.

As Jack cracked open the balcony door, Eton sprawled out on the bedspread and lit a cigarette. As Jack propped himself up on the pillow wedged against the headboard, Eton shunted up to rest against him, his head on Jack's right shoulder.

Jack wrapped his arm around his chest, reached for Eton's cigarette with his other hand and took a deep, contented puff. "I could die just for *this*."

"For a cigarette?" Eton asked innocently.

"Dumbass!" Jack pressed a happy grin into his temple.

"I dream about *this*... sometimes..." Eton mumbled.

Tell him, Smith. Tell him, for god's sake!

Jack closed his eyes and whispered, "I didn't... in the beginning... It upset me no end."

"Then what happened?" Eton asked quietly after a while.

"Then? Ojhri Camp happened. You know about it?"

"Ojhri? The American weapon storage in Pakistan? The one that exploded? It was a joint KGB-KHAD operation, we were told... What about it?"

"I was visiting a colleague who lived nearby. Left the place fifteen minutes before the explosion. When it went off, I was driving back to Islamabad... A flying missile hit a car twenty meters behind me. Blew it clean off the road." He felt it as Eton's breath caught, and his heart accelerated under his hand. "Good thing was you came back to me... in my dreams." He chuckled awkwardly and took a few quick puffs on the cigarette.

There was a long moment of silence as they relived their memories of the times past, Jack drawing little circles on Eton's chest, occasionally brushing the scar on his shoulder.

"Will you tell me about *this*? Someday?" he asked quietly, touching the lacerated flesh with his fingertips.

"Of course I'll tell you. What do you want to know?"

"Everything? When, where, how..."

Eton made the last draw on their cigarette and crushed it in the ashtray on the nightstand. He shifted uncomfortably and sighed. "When? It was the day the withdrawal from Afghanistan began. May 15th, 1988." And he told Jack about his last combat operation in Afghanistan—"the last war", he called it.

Eton's company had received orders to secure two heights along the highway to ensure safe passage of Soviet and Afghan government armed columns from Khost to Kabul. They didn't encounter resistance at first as if the *dukhi* had all abandoned the area. So they baked under the blazing sun on their barren ridge the whole day, watching longingly the row of tall, mighty poplars by the small *kishlak* in the valley below.

The first attack came with the dawn, followed by three more before noon, all of which they managed to fend off. After the last assault, his platoon was ordered to finish off the retreating *mujahedin*. They chased them down to the *kishlak* in the valley and found it completely deserted as if the glimpses of villagers and the smoke over their dwellings they saw the day before had been mirages. The soldiers split into teams of two or three to check the low mud-brick houses behind wattle fences. They were all empty, with only a goat, a chicken or a dog here and there, wandering, bewildered and lost.

Then, in a tiny courtyard, Eton and his comrade Pasha came across one live human soul: a boy standing in the doorway of the mud house, watching them, his face impassive. He shook his head when Pasha asked, "Mujahedin?" He inched aside when Pasha peered into the house, but remained standing there, half hidden by the door. Eton checked the covered enclosure where livestock and cattle were kept. Nothing. Pasha waved at the boy, and they turned their backs on him to head out.

It was Eton's boxer reaction that had saved his life. He whipped around and fired his AKM the moment he heard the metallic click. He still caught a bullet which broke his rib. Nothing too serious though. However, by the time they brought him in an armored carrier to the hospital in Kabul, the broken rib had pierced his lung, and the lung collapsed. Pashka wasn't as lucky: got four bullets in his back and neck and died on the spot. Or maybe he *was* lucky, God only knew...

Eton carefully extracted himself from Jack's arms. "I'll be back." He slid out of bed.

Jack lit a cigarette. His nerves were string tight, guts rolled into a tense ball. He took a couple of deep, shaky breaths trying to relax.

In a minute Eton returned with the opened vodka bottle and two glasses. "Now it's about the right time to have a drink." He smirked ruefully, handing Jack a glass. He sat down with his legs crossed on top of the bed and poured two fingers of the clear liquid into both of them. "To those who didn't return," he said, raising up and quickly knocking back his glass.

When Jack had downed his, Eton refilled their glasses. He sat the bottle on the floor, leaned back against the headboard next to Jack. He took Jack's hand, kissed the edge of his palm before inhaling deeply on the cigarette in Jack's fingers.

Jack pulled at his hand and pressed it onto his stomach. "You said you were brought to the hospital in an armored carrier. Didn't they use helicopters for medevac... for evacuation? From what I know the Sov, um, they operated a huge fleet of MI-8 helicopters... Didn't they?"

Eton entwined their fingers and shrugged. "They did. Before my time. But then the *mujaheds* got Stingers from the uh... And that was the end of all evacuations by helicopters."

Jack closed his eyes and bit hard on the inside of his lip. God forgive him! Because he himself might not...

"And you know what was the strangest thing? I should have hated that boy, right? For killing Pashka. For shooting me... But I didn't. I felt so sorry for him I wanted to cry... Couldn't tell anyone about it either..." He drew a lungful of cigarette smoke and breathed out shakily. "I can still see him sometimes. Right in front of my eyes... Fourteen, fifteen at most. Green-eyes, fair skin. Almost like a pretty girl in his white *kameez*. He should have held some musical instrument, not a machine gun... And then bullet holes bloomed like poppy flowers on his chest... where I planted them." He gulped down the content of the glass he had been clutching in his other hand.

"Where was it?" Jack asked after a moment of heavy silence, his voice raspy with dread. He felt lightheaded as if his lungs were not getting enough air.

No, please God, no! It could not be!

"South-east of Gardez."

"Jalil Haq's territory?"

"Yes. You know the place?" Eton leaned away from Jack to look him in the eyes, his lips pressed together in a tight, thin line. "Have you been there?"

"Yeah…" He closed his eyes and swallowed over a lump in his throat. "October '87."

"What did you…?"

"I had no fucking idea… I'm so sorry, Eton." What else could he say? "Was busy saving green-eyed boys from a bunch of dirty old man to whom I had first delivered Stingers, baby"?

Eton slipped down in bed and lay flat on this back. He covered his eyes with his forearm, his jaw muscles rolling. On the inside of his bicep, Jack noticed a small tattoo of a stylized Coptic cross that looked like a flower.

"Eton…" He touched the cross with his fingertips and whispered, "I'm so fucking sorry, baby, you have no idea. I wish I'd known…" But as he was saying it Jack knew that even if he *had* known, there was devastatingly little he could have done to change… anything at all.

Eton jerked his arm down at Jack's touch and opened his eyes. He looked drained but his eyes were soft. "It's not your fault… Right?" He forced a little smile. "And it still changes nothing… Let's drink to that." He sat up, reached for the bottle and quickly refilled his glass. "To things that remain with us, *in* us no matter what."

Then Eton poured yet another round, and they drank "to those our thoughts of whom have got us through". Then they lay down facing each other, tangled their arms and legs, and swapped their Afghan stories, getting up sometimes to light a cigarette or to pour a drink. They agreed that Afghanistan was the Soviet Union's Vietnam, except that their countries had been on the "wrong" sides this time. Then Jack told Eton how he had once spent a night at an improvised hospital in the mountains near Khost run by a Kabul-born surgeon and every night when everyone was asleep, the soft spoken doctor with dead-tired eyes shot his mortally wounded patients because he didn't have enough medical supplies to spend on terminal cases. Then Eton told Jack how his company had suffered an airstrike by its own MIGs ordered to wipe out the settlement where Jalil Haq was reportedly hiding. The *mujahedin* commander escaped while Eton's unit lost two thirds of its soldiers. All survivors were awarded Medals for Battle Merit. But when Eton returned home, Lara told him to keep quiet about it, because decorated *Afghantsy* weren't held in high regard in the *intelligencia* circles at home.

"Coming home was… strange," Eton said, after a long moment of silence. "I couldn't sleep at first, everything was too still. Like before a raid… And when I walked in the hospital's park, I kept checking around, for the signs of *dukhi* behind the trees. Or looking for a vantage point where I can dig in. Just in case…" He crushed another butt into the full ashtray. "Then once, Lara came to visit with Sevka and Anya, and brought a photo camera. When it was my turn to take a picture of the three of them, I was caught by surprise: the camera made a loud click, but there was no recoil. It was weird…"

Jack could find no words to reply. He hugged Eton close to his heart, trying to hold back the surging tears.

When night fell, they went out, found a public phone and Eton called the consulate's guesthouse to let his comrades know he was staying out for the night. The person on the other end seemed to object, but Eton closed the conversation with a quiet but firm "I'll be there tomorrow night", and hung up.

They had a quick dinner at a cafeteria a few blocks away. The only other customers were six shaven-headed young men dressed similarly in black and brown, talking and laughing noisily.

When they returned to Ursel's apartment, they showered quickly and got back in bed.

"By the way," said Jack, leaning back into Eton's embrace. "Do you know that Jon Bon Jovi and Ozzy Osbourne are performing in Moscow today?"

"I know. My guys are probably watching it on TV at the guest house right now."

"Don't *you* want to see it?"

"I do. But it doesn't matter." Eton tightened his arms around Jack. "I'd rather be here," he whispered and pressed his lips into the back of Jack's head.

A mighty wave of warmth swept over Jack, melting his insides. He stroked the arm across his chest. "Hope your absence won't get you into too much trouble, bud."

"Don't worry. They won't do anything that they haven't already done before."

"Like what?"

"Make me work in the kitchen for a few days. Or clean the toilets. Or refuse to give me a leave of absence." Eton shrugged. "I'm going to be demobilized soon anyway, so it doesn't matter." His last words didn't sound very confident as if their implication had sunk in with him as he was uttering them.

There was a moment of silence, then Jack asked quietly, "When?"

Eton shifted uncomfortably. "End of November, early December."

We still have time. Three months…

What for? Haven't you done enough harm already?

It's not my fault, alright? How in the fucking hell could I know?!

Alright! But you've promised him, remember? Let him be!

"Will I see you before… *that*?" Jack muttered, his mouth suddenly dry.

Eton's embrace tightened, and he buried his face into the hollow between Jack's neck and his shoulder. "Of course," he breathed. "I will come to see you again."

They held each other until sleep overtook them, but even when they drifted apart in their restless slumber, their hands, arms or legs were still touching, clinging, not letting go. Jack jolted awake during the night, disoriented, his heart racing, his chest tight with the sense of foreboding, and he couldn't get back to sleep for a long time.

The next time he woke up, it was dawn and the room was filled with hazy, milky light. Eton was sleeping peacefully on his back, his face half turned into the crook of his left arm, raised and folded over his head. Jack looked at him for a long time while, propped up on one elbow, trying to commit to memory every minute detail of Eton's face and body. The angular curve of his jawline, the bold stroke of his eyebrow, the mole under the cheekbone, the lips relaxed and slightly opened in the sleep, the prominent muscle on the side of his neck, a wisp of soft blond hair under his arm, the muted power in the arch of his biceps. The tattoo of the Coptic cross that looked like a flower...

A Coptic cross. Eton hadn't had it before, *that* Jack remembered very well. So maybe he had it tattooed when he needed something to hold on to, something to give him strength in the time of calamity. Like faith, for example... But why a Coptic cross? Shouldn't it be an Orthodox cross that the blue-blooded Russians still secretly held on to—three horizontal crossbeams over a longer vertical one?

A blue cross that looked like a flower... A blue flower... When Jack touched it earlier with his fingertips, Eton had jerked his armed down quickly, color rising on his cheeks...

And it suddenly dawned on him that the tattoo wasn't a cross at all. It was a stylized cornflower disguised to look like a cross. A blue cornflower on the inside of his left bicep, hidden, close to his heart. And when they were drinking earlier, Eton had raised a toast "To those our thoughts of whom have got us through"...

Jack lay back down and closed his eyes, his throat constricted, his lashes damp. He prayed to God to give him strength, because how could he take so much love given to him just like that, with nothing asked in return?

They were both subdued that whole day. After Jack returned from his quick outing to buy food, cigarettes and another bottle of vodka, they had a quick breakfast, then moved to Bernard's studio. They sat side by side on the floor, smoking, carried away by the haunting sounds of Bach's Suits for Cello from the vinyl record player flooding the confined space. Afterwards, they ushered each other to the bedroom and made love, unhurried and sweet, then slept, and made love again, passionate, almost aggressive this time. Then Jack made a lunch of omelet with tomatoes, mushrooms and onions, and Wiener Würstchen on the side, and they washed it down with half a bottle of vodka and two rounds of coffee, while the Bon Jovi tape that Jack had brought for Eton was playing in the sitting room.

At five, they started cleaning up the apartment, scrubbing it of all signs of their two enchanted days there. Together, they washed the bed linen and towels in the bathtub, aired the bedroom and cleaned the kitchen to its original state of spotless German orderliness.

Jack was hanging up the still damp sheets and towels on the clotheslines in the bathroom when Eton came quietly up to him. He put his arms around Jack and pressed his body into his back. Jack closed his eyes and leaned back. Eton started planting soft kisses on the back of his neck, his shoulders and the sides of his face. Then Jack turned around and covered Eton's lips with his mouth, reveling in the sound of little moans at the back of his lover's throat, and it was the most joyful thing to do in the world to whisper in his ear "I love you, baby".

After a while, Eton pushed lightly on his shoulders and peered into his eyes, smiling softly, his expression both determined and serene. "You said you will make your people all go away. Including yourself."

Jack's smile froze and started slipping from his face. "I did." He swallowed and cleared his throat. "I've promised and I'll do it, Eton. Don't you worry about it." He willed himself to hold the remnants of the smile firmly in place and prayed that Eton wouldn't notice that his heart was breaking into pieces.

"I'm not worried. I just... I don't *want* you to go away, Jack." His smile widened a fraction, his eyes imploring. "You go ahead and do whatever you need to do... about me. I will return to complete my *aspirantura* at MGU."

Chapter 63

Jack's first reaction was "It's a trap! He's a dangle." But Eton's eyes were soft and full of pain, as though he were reading Jack's thoughts and they were cutting him all up inside. Then he recalled the cornflower tattoo on Eton's bicep.

You're such a fucking asshole, Smith!

I am. I know. I'm sorry, baby.

"God, Eton, you have no idea what you're getting yourself into, friend."

He tried to dissuade Eton, describing the initial assessment process to him. The Company would ask him to "produce" the best information he could obtain, and fast—okay, so his grandfather's original nuclear winter study might just do it—and they wouldn't be satisfied until the information was corroborated. Then a senior officer would come out with an assessment team, and they would interview him and polygraph him, looking for signs of deception, half-truths, or uncertainties. They would ask Eton questions he wouldn't be able to answer without exposing his secret; they would ask him how he was doing with his case officer and they would know immediately that the two of them were "involved".

Then he told Eton about the rolled-up agents in Moscow back in '85 - '86.

"It was the worst year and a half in the Agency's history. We lost... almost all of them... You know, the average life of an agent in the Soviet Union is around two years. Two fucking years, Eton, do you understand?" He wrestled the cigarettes out of the jeans pocket, all riled up, hands shaking.

Eton stood up from behind the kitchen table, cracked opened the window. He returned to his seat, pulled at Jack's hand and took a drag on his cigarette, watching Jack nervously through the cloud of smoke. "And no one managed to, uhm, get out?"

"Less than a hand full... You must have produced exceptionally valuable information and then be in a life-threatening danger for the Agency to decide to exfiltrate... to get you out."

This time Eton was silent for longer, head bowed, eyes fixed on his hands clasping and unclasping on the tabletop. Finally, he looked up. "How much I will need to *produce* to be able to buy a small ranch... in California?"

Jack turned to stare out of the window for a moment, glad it was getting dark outside and they hadn't turned on the light.

"It's not worth it, bud," he said softly and took both of Eton's hands in his, trying to read his eyes in the twilight. "It's your life that'll be at stake."

"So what? Can't lose you again," Eton muttered, shaking his head stubbornly. He reached over the table, gripped Jack by the neck and leaned his forehead into Jack's. "You are the only fam... one I have left."

And what was he supposed to say to *that*, especially when it was exactly how he felt too?

But even then Jack didn't stop trying. He told Eton about Lara's request to help find Eton's relatives in France and her intention to ask them to sponsor Eton out—he thought that was a good chance. Eton smirked ruefully, said that Vadim and his parents had waited nearly ten years for their permits to leave. And they'd been sponsored by Vadim's uncle, *and* Vadim had neither been in the army nor in Afghanistan. With his background, Eton didn't believe he would ever be let out of the country. Certainly not after his service time with an air-defense missile regiment in Germany.

Jack went cold. He told Eton they should be very careful with their meetings because they surely didn't need any attention from any-fucking-one.

In the end, they agreed that Jack would report Eton's firm recruitment and that he was ready to hand over his grandfather's original work on nuclear winter to the Agency upon his return to Moscow.

Jack brushed aside his lover's reservations about the relevance of the study for intelligence purposes. "You don't know about it and I haven't seen it. So let's agree that we just don't know what it's worth. Don't mention anything to anyone about your doubts."

Then Jack told him that there were elements of the operation that he couldn't disclose and that Eton would just have to trust him and do exactly as he said. He took Eton's hand, interlinked their fingers and said, low and steadfast, "I'll do everything I can to get you out safely, Eton. I promise".

Eton looked at him solemnly, pressed his lips into their joined fingers, and said quietly, "I trust you, Jack."

* * *

Jack was torn. On one hand, he was flying high with the newfound awareness of his true feelings for Eton and the knowledge that Eton felt the same about him, if not more. On the other hand, now that his protective shield of self-delusion had fallen away, Jack suddenly found himself neck-deep in shit.

Back in Moscow, he had been content telling himself that what he had felt was temporary infatuation with the target he had been tasked to recruit through seduction. Now he had no choice but admit to himself that he had crossed the line with Eton May Volkonsky. Which was an absolute no-no, totally unacceptable, plain violation of the key rule for a case officer with his agent. Worse still, he had crossed this line a long time ago and never reported it.

He had few qualms about not telling Joe Coburn the whole truth about the level of his sexual involvement with Eton—hiding things related to his true identity had been a self-preservation mechanism he had mastered ever since he realized, at the age of fourteen, that he was different from his redneck buddies. Sometimes he thought it was precisely because of his ability to easily and continually live a lie that Joe Coburn had recruited him in the first place. Bah, if anyone should understand how this kind of things went, it was Joe. And once they had meticulously trained and endlessly coached Jack to lie, to sneak, to steal and to deceive others, even if they labeled those others "the Main Enemy", how could Joe and the Company seriously expect him to tell them *everything*, to tell them *the* truth and *only* the truth? It was the biggest fucking joke he had ever heard!

Nonetheless, he still had a job to do. And even if over the years he had become increasingly unconvinced about things he was told to do or not to do, it was still a job to be done, following its basic rules. And the rule in this situation was that the case officer must not—repeat, MUST NOT—become emotionally and physically involved with his agent. Okay, so he got a license to breach it under the special engagement rules of this Director's case op because that was how this op had been designed. But the emotional involvement, *that* was like the ultimate killer. And he had dived head first into a deep pool of shit, on his first assignment. Maybe his father had been right after all—that he was just a fuck-up who couldn't do anything right.

Shit.

In any case, now he had to figure out how to deliver the news of his gravest blunder ever to Joe Coburn—*if* he decided to report on himself, that is. The good news for Joe and Co. was that he had secured his Moscow recruitment and now GTSALT was committed and ready to return to complete his doctoral studies in nuclear physics and make himself eligible to work in closed research institutes.

Jack flew back to the States on Tuesday. What he had thought would be a regular debriefing with the Division chief on his special op turned into the design and approval process of a new project for SALT. In East Germany.

Jack was summoned to Joe Coburn's office the very day he arrived in Washington. Also awaiting him there were East Berlin Station's chief David Rolston, the Division's chief of operations Stan Werner, and counterintelligence chief Jesse Reilly. Each man had a thin file in front of him and Jack was given one too when he sat down at the long conference table. It contained his last three operational reports on his interaction with his Soviet contacts in East Berlin.

The four men ran Jack through some minute details of his reports for two hours. CI chief Reilly had the most questions and Jack couldn't blame him: a man volunteering to spy for the US while his wife seemed to be associated with the KGB sounded more than suspicious. Then he asked Jack what he thought of his recruit's sudden eagerness to cooperate. Jack explained that the young man had become utterly disillusioned with the system when he was abruptly left alone to fend for himself. And after the Afghanistan experience, he now felt more attuned to his father's origins and his dream was to live in California. But he didn't believe the Sovs would ever let him out.

Jack felt Joe Coburn's eyes burning holes into him as he spoke. He willed himself to look straight into the Division chief's eyes, to keep his expression businesslike, nothing more—after all, they had trained him well, and Joe himself had said more than once that Jack was a good student.

The chiefs couldn't agree on how to proceed with SALT. Rolston wanted to test him while he was still in serving East Germany, at a missile division. Chief Werner thought it was too early. CI chief Reilly suggested wryly that they should prepare a parallel plan—for handling a double agent—because that was what SALT could turn out to be. Joe Coburn offered no opinion but said he would have a separate session with Jack right after the meeting.

When he and Joe were alone, Jack went through his account again, but this time with details classified under the SEABROOK part of the op. In short, Eton Volkonsky had let Jack put his hands on him when he was blind drunk, but the next day the target had not acknowledged in any way that he remembered what had happened the night before.

Since Russian men were more tactile amongst buddies and when drunk sometime crossed the line of "good behavior", it was hard to tell if the incident had meant anything for the Russian. So there was a possibility that he was a latent homosexual, but if so, the man seemed in total denial. Jack recommended therefore that they skip this issue altogether when SALT was polygraphed—if they didn't want to see him bolt.

There was also a small complication: SALT seemed to have developed a weak spot for Jack, perhaps because of Jack's "legend" of being from California, where his father was from. On one hand, it was an effective agent control mechanism, given the heightened sense of personal loyalty typical to Russians. On the other hand, such loyalty might not be transferable should anyone else be assigned to handle SALT later.

"What about you, Jack? Is there a weak spot in you?" asked Joe after a long pause.

Jack allowed himself to sigh. "The poor bastard's been in bad shape for too long. Lost all the family he's got in the span of two months, got himself thrown in prison, then nearly died in Afghanistan. I hope he'll recover quickly, now that he's seen a glimmer of possibility of something better." The Division chief was still watching him intently, so Jack hastened to add, "Don't worry, it'll be all good by the time we start production in Moscow. The recruitment euphoria will subside and it'll be all business."

Joe leaned forward ever so slightly and squinted at Jack. "*Will* be all business?" he asked gently.

Watch out, Smith! Don't shoot from the hip!

"I was just thinking… Maybe we shouldn't hurry? He's too fragile—"

"If you're aiming to put it on the back burner, don't even think about it, Jack. It's out of the question. I'll put someone else on the case if you tell me I should… But not now. He's not ready for a handover. You get him up to speed and start producing, and I'll see what can be done about transferring him to someone else if that's what you want."

Jack hoped the sigh he didn't quite stifle sounded like one of resignation and not of relief that he felt. "It's alright, Joe, I'll do it. He just needs some time to get used to the idea of working for us… Of being handled by someone he has considered to be a close friend… with no strings attached."

Joe sat back again, watching him intently. "You think we shouldn't get him started producing while he's in Germany?"

Jack's heart sank. Joe liked to pose this kind of question when he wanted something done, but knew that the implementer might not like it.

"It's too soon. He's neither trained nor in the right state of mind to do anything right now. And we don't have much time either—he'll be demobilized in early November." Eton had said early December, but a month was nothing when an agent wasn't ready, was it?

"Then *get* him ready. We might not get another access point to the Soviet air defense systems any time soon. Especially with the reduction of their troops in East Germany… Besides, East Berlin Station hasn't had any collection agent worth mentioning for a while. David will owe you big time, take my word for it… It's your chance, Jack," he added, seeing little enthusiasm on Jack's side. "Remember, your recruitment track record is a bit lackluster for your grade. You need a good, robust case to polish it up."

"It's not my fault, is it?" Jack mumbled, looking at the Division chief from under his eyebrows. "I'd be happy to run normal ops, instead of... *pilots*." He had almost spat out "pointless ops".

"Director's case pilots are given to the best of our best, Jack. You know that, don't you? You're doing well, boy. All I'm saying is that you need to speed up with SALT. You've been developing him since '85. He should finally start producing."

"I didn't choose to target him," Jack countered stubbornly, fully aware that he was crossing the line. But Joe Coburn looked like he was in a good mood, so Jack pushed his luck. "It was you and the NSA who wanted him honey-trapped... *That* didn't work. And he is still not ready. He isn't—"

"Jack, I don't want to hear about it anymore. Between you, David and Stan's team, you'll prepare the field project outline for an operation with SALT in East Germany. By 2100 Thursday. I'll make sure it's approved by the time you're back in the field. Then you and East Berlin Station will make SALT ready and start producing. *Before* his departure home." Joe stood up. "We'll have the ops plan briefing before you head back to Berlin. Donna will call you with the time."

Jack spent the next two and a half days preparing his project documents for approval. He tried his best to cover his wariness and heavy heart with continual rants to all who would listen about how his long-deserved home leave had been ruined by an unexpected new op he was to process for approval.

By the time he boarded the Lufthansa flight back to East Berlin, operation BROOM, an extension of operation TALION, had gone up the chain of command for approval. The plan was that the next time SALT came down to East Berlin, Jack was to persuade him to start working towards his dream of acquiring a ranch in California while still in Germany. Once agreed, Jack would arrange for an interview with the East Berlin COS. Since there was too little time for a full assessment of him in Germany, Joe Coburn's Deputy, Pat Richmond, in charge of the USSR operations, would fly out for the interview. Once he passed that, SALT would be briefed on his objectives and given a crash course on tradecraft. And Jack was of course the one to train him. With the goal of getting *tangible* results by the end of November.

It meant they had only three months. Three bloody months! Jack wished he had persisted and convinced Eton to let him make the Company go away and leave him alone. Now what was he gonna do? Eton was totally unprepared for this shit. CI chief Reilly hadn't been convinced that GTSALT wasn't a KGB double agent, but Jack was pretty damn sure: his straight as an arrow friend wasn't with the KGB. Couldn't be.

What if there was a way of exfiltrating Eton from Germany *before* he returned to Moscow? What if Eton signaled that he was in mortal danger and asked to be exfilled? Would the Company agree to get him out? What danger would that have to be for the Division Chief to agree to get Eton out?

Jack thought he might find the answer to that. Joe Coburn would hate it, but fuck Joe Coburn! He was tired of being Joe Coburn's bellboy. There wasn't much difference between him and Omar, Jalil Haq's dancing boy, was there, and never mind the education he had managed to obtain, the highflying job he'd then landed, and the dreams he might actually be able to realize one day. Even with all the accomplishments that he had never imagined himself capable of twenty years ago, he had been nothing more than Joe Coburn's dancing boy all this time. And now he was about to do his final act and put Eton in harm's way. Because how different was it what he was going to do from what the green-eyed boy had done that had nearly killed his Eton?

Eton, who continued trusting Jack even after he learned that Jack had been lying to him. Eton who loved Jack despite who he was and what he did. Eton May Volkonsky who was inevitably going to be Jack Smith's downfall.

So what you gonna do, huh, Smith? What you gonna do?

Chapter 64

Operation BROOM was not the only op Jack had brought back with him. The other case he was expected to develop with East Berlin Station was Operation PIPER in which the target was Volodya from Dresden.

It turned out that the Company had a surprisingly meaningful file on the man, despite virtual inaccessibility of both the local security services and their Soviet counterpart in East Germany.

His full name and designation was Vladimir Vasilievich Bunin, scientific and cultural attaché, posted at the Soviet Consulate General in Dresden since May 1985; actively covered and engaged students at Dresden Polytechnic Institute; married, wife Lyubov Konstantinovna, nee Shubina, informally known as Lyuba; two daughters aged four and three, all residing at number 101 Raderbergerstrasse, in apartment 10.

The assessment section sounded like observations of a layman. "Calculative and highly suspicious. Patient and composed outside, reportedly abusive but never in the presence of outsiders. Likes to be seen as a generous spender. Weakness for beautiful young women". Some of the comments came across like secondhand information, and the man's wife Lyuba was mentioned a fair bit, so Jack guessed the source was one of Lyuba's girlfriends. Which was an impressive development work, and he wondered why he hadn't been briefed about this agent working for the Sovs in East Germany. Until he figured out during the op planning meeting that the source belonged to the "friendly services", most probably the West German BND.

The operation was built on two premises proven effective in a number of other cases. The first was that the KGB's focus overseas, especially in East Germany, was recruitment of people who traveled to the West often—journalists, scientists, artists, singers, actors and the like. And the second was that having had a taste of a better life overseas, even if it was only in other Soviet bloc countries, KGB operatives at the end of their posting were substantially easier targets. With this in mind, Jack's task was to make contact with Volodya, PIPER-1, develop the relationship and let Volodya recruit him as a bridge agent, a courier. At the same time, Jack was to assess him for recruitment. If PIPER-1 turned out to be recruitable, another case officer would come in and do the pitching.

PIPER-2, Larissa "Lara" Novikova-Volkonskaya, would be the conduit for Jack's access to PIPER-1. Unless, like four years back, the man would "accidentally" run into Jack again. With the scarcity of noteworthy recruitable material in a backwater like Dresden, the Division's chiefs believed that the Sovs couldn't ignore such a target as an American reporter.

* * *

Jack got a postcard from Eton on Thursday, the week he had returned from America.

Barbel winked at him as she handed it over. "The date from out of town? You can bring her here."

"Thank you, Barbel. But I'm not sure she would... It's complicated."

He scanned the postcard, folded it and stuck it in the inside pocket of his jacket. It said in German "This Saturday 11 for some Hours. Bar opposite the Station. N."

"I see." Barbel nodded, then asked with the typical German directness, "If you need a place, I can give you the keys to Ursel's apartment again."

Jack grinned sheepishly at her. "Thank you, Barbel. It's the last time, I promise!"

It was the last time indeed: from now on, they were going to use a different mode of communication since Jack was to keep in touch with his agent regularly under the new op. Jack was of two minds about returning to Ursel and Bernard's place without a sweep of the place for bugs. But they needed a place where they could have a conversation and he hadn't had time to prepare such a place... Of course, he could always brief Eton in the open air—on a walk in a park, for example. However, briefing Eton was not the only thing he wanted to do.

Yeah, right. Thinking about ourselves again, aren't we?

Go to hell! He needs it too, alright?

You sure?

He loves me... And I love him too!

Alright then, you do need a place.

On Saturday, he got up at 5:00 a.m., washed down a leftover pastry with a lukewarm coffee and left his place before his shadows turned up—at exactly 8:00 a.m. as a rule. Or *when* they did turn up that was, which hadn't been too often lately. However, with the new operation on, Jack didn't want to risk being accidentally caught up with the Stasi's routine checking on him.

He took off jogging, keeping within the radius of one mile from his apartment block. After half an hour of circling the area, he ducked into the abandoned building where his safe haven was, changed into nondescript clothes and shoes, and slipped onto another street through a glassless window on the ground floor. He walked the streets, then rode the U-Bahn, until one hour before he was to meet Eton in the restaurant-bar across the street from the train station on Friedrichstrasse. He got off at Marx-Engels-Platz station and took side streets, weaving his way back to the terminal.

The weather was warm and balmy, and the autumn sun lavished its soft golden light on the yellow, red and deep green foliage of the trees. Jack parked himself in a secluded doorway from where he could observe both the station's exit and the restaurant on the other side of the little square bound by two narrow one-way streets. He was clear of surveillance, but wanted to make sure that Eton was clear too before approaching him.

He almost missed him when Eton emerged from around the corner, a few minutes before eleven, and strolled casually toward the restaurant. Jack scanned both sides of the street for signs of shadowing and noted nothing suspicious. He waited as Eton disappeared inside, then another ten minutes, his stomach hollow with anticipation. Then he sauntered across the street and passed by the restaurant before abruptly turning back and pushing quickly through the restaurant's door.

Eton was sitting in the far corner on the left, half turned to the entrance.

"Privet." Jack exhaled, grinning happily and held Eton's hand for half a second longer than he should. "Do you mind switching to this seat?" He waited for Eton to move to the opposite chair and sat down facing the door.

For a moment they just sat there eyeing one another, each wordlessly trying to tell the other "I missed you".

"So how long do we have?" asked Jack after the waitress had brought their coffees.

"I need to be back before six," Eton said, apologetic.

"That means back at the station by five. So we have around five hours." Minus two to three hours to get to and from the place where they could talk in private. "Do you want to have a walk in the park or... to go somewhere?"

"To that apartment?"

"No. I'm sorry. We can't go there this time."

"You have another place?" Eton asked awkwardly.

"Yes. But we need to walk there. Separately. It will take about an hour and a half."

Eton peered into his eyes, as if he were trying to read Jack's mind, then nodded. "I understand... Alright."

"Great." Jack produced a folded scrap of paper from the inner pocket of his jacket and slipped it across the table towards Eton. "These are the directions. See if you understand." Written in Russian, the instruction named no streets, only counting them off till the next left or right turn. "It starts from outside of this place and ends at the building which you should reach in about ninety minutes, walking at a leisurely pace."

Eton perused the paper for half a minute, then raised his head. "It's clear. And I'll see you there?"

"Yes. I'll be covering your back... Just in case. You were clear when you came," he added and smiled reassuringly, seeing his friend worrying his eyebrows.

"Like in a sp... a movie." Eton smiled weakly.

Jack chuckled humorlessly in response. "Welcome to my world."

They reached the place in seventy minutes instead of ninety according to Jack's well-intended plan. After a quick scrutiny of the street, Jack waved Eton through the tunnel-like gateway of the derelict, turn-of-the-century building, half of which still bore the open wounds from the war. With Jack leading the way, they ascended the broken staircase with its beautiful ironwork mostly intact. On the fifth floor, they turned right, followed the short corridor toward the door at the end.

The place had been mercilessly plundered, but traces remained of its old elegant comfort. Most of the valances and some heavy curtains were still in place, covered in decades of dust. There was a neo-classical settee in the largest room, its velvet cover threadbare, and a lopsided cupboard with the smashed mirror. A tatty mattress lay on the floor along the wall of what used to be a bedroom, and in the third, smallest room featured a broken child's bed and a red rocking horse, startlingly intact. Most of the parquet in the sitting room was gone, burnt in the crumbling fireplace by someone who had taken shelter there before them. Everything smelled of dust, mold and the passage of time.

Jack stood in the doorway of the room with the cupboard, waiting patiently for Eton to finish his inspection, then caught him by his arm and pulled him into an embrace. "Sorry I haven't managed to arrange a better place." He covered Eton's lips with his.

"Doesn't matter," Eton murmured, pulling back for a second. "As long as you're with me."

"We can't do much here either. There's no running water."

"I can hold you... Can't I?" He ran his hands under Jack's sweatshirt, his palms flat on Jack's back, dragged them up then down.

"Yeah..." Jack closed his eyes and stopped worrying about what they didn't have right now. But when Eton's hands started tugging at his belt, he caught them and opened his eyes. "We need to talk first... I'm sorry."

Eton nuzzled the side of his face. "It doesn't matter."

"What doesn't matter?"

"What you need to tell me."

Jack pulled back a little and peered into his lover's flushed face. "You don't know what I'm going to tell you."

Eton straightened up and opened his eyes. "They're not going expel you again, are they?"

"No! Not that I know of."

"Then it doesn't matter." His lips curled up in a gentle little smile. Then seeing Jack's anxious face, he sighed and asked quietly, "They want me to start spying now?"

The question caught Jack's off guard. "Why do you say that?" he asked cautiously.

"I thought they would." Eton let go of Jack and shrugged. "If you told them that I'm in the anti-air missile division."

"I'm sorry, but I had no choice. They had already known that you were stationed in Bernau."

"I understand. They could find out anyway, right?"

Jack puffed out a sharp breath and raked all ten fingers through his hair. "I tried to delay this till Moscow. I swear I did! But they—"

"It's alright, Jack. I know you did... So... you want me to start now?" Eton's face was now solemn, lips pressed together in a thin, determined line and his eyes...

Christ, how can you look him in the eyes and do this, Smith? How you gonna do that?

No, he can't do it. He mustn't!

"You don't have to do it."

"I'll do it. I don't owe them, my government, anything."

"Fuck *them*! It's about *you*. You *cannot* be doing this shit, Eton... I can't let you."

"What I can't do is lose you again." Eton shook his head stubbornly. "You have to let me do this, Jack."

Jack pulled out a pack of Lucky Strikes and a lighter from his pocket, sat down on the floor and leaned back against the wall. He lit a cigarette, inhaled and handed it over to

Eton. "What if I can get you out?"

Eton took the cigarette and sat down against the wall next to Jack, their shoulders touching. "How?"

"I'll come up with a plan. Just give me some time. Till the next time we meet. When Lara comes over. End of the month, isn't it?"

"Yes." Eton took a few drags on the cigarette and handed it back. "What about your... bosses? What will they say?"

Jack shrugged, puffing out a big cloud of smoke. "They don't need to know."

"You're going to..."

"Lie to them?" He barked out a sardonic laugh. "Christ, Eton, that's what they've taught me to do! That's what I do for a living." He craned his neck to look into his friend's eyes. "You don't seriously think that I've told them everything about us, do you?"

"No, but... this is different. This is too... big."

"Same shit. Don't worry about it."

There was a long moment of silence. Eton reached for Jack's hand and squeezed it. "What will happen to you afterwards?"

"I'll quit... Will find something else to do."

Eton gnawed on his lips for a long while, then asked quietly, "What about your ranch?"

"My ranch?"

It took a moment for the question to sink in with Jack and he realized he hadn't been thinking about his dream ranch in California for some time now. He tugged at his lover's hand and pressed his lips into the weathered knuckles of Eton's long, slender fingers. "I'll have a ranch, bud... We'll make it, one way or the other."

He got up, went to the cupboard and started rummaging in it. He first pulled out a ragged bedroll that looked like it belonged to a tramp and threw it over the mattress on the floor. Then out came a beaten up thermos and a big, reused plastic bottle of water, bread, boiled eggs, cucumbers and apples.

"Like a student picnic back home," Eton chuckled as he helped Jack to arrange the food on an old towel spread on top of the blanket.

They took off their shoes and got settled on the mattress. Then, while they were eating, Jack explained his plan on how they should deal with the Agency's request for a meeting with its senior officers and for immediate start of production.

The next day, Jack said, he would report that Eton had agreed to meet with the Deputy Division Head and the Chief of East Berlin Station. The meeting would be arranged around the time Lara came over for the Berlin Music and Drama Festival. It shouldn't take more than two hours, Jack assured when he saw Eton's doubtful look, and Jack would be there as well. The main purpose of the meeting was to verify Eton's *bona fide* personally. Jack explained what kind of questions Eton should expect, including uncomfortable or intimate ones, then they discussed in detail what kinds of answers Eton would give.

But first, Jack needed from Eton some basic information about his division so that he could report on the progress with the new agent. This would give him time to come up with an exfiltration plan and start the preparations. He would also need to know the exact date of Eton's departure home. Then, Jack ran Eton through the basic routine for new agents—modes of communication and signaling, fundamentals of counter-surveillance, emergency calls for meeting. He wrote down an East Berlin phone number for Eton to use in emergency situations and told him to learn it by heart before they leave.

"It will be redirected to an untraceable number in West Berlin. You can leave a message for either Uncle Hans or Auntie Bertha with the day and time you will be at one of the two respective meeting places. Next Saturday will mean this Friday, the following Sunday is next Saturday and so on. I'll get the message within two hours. But so will the Chief of Station here—before me. So if it's super-urgent, leave the message for Auntie Bertha and I'll come out two hours *before* the time you have indicated. If for any reason we miss each other, I'll come to look for you here. Do you remember how to get here from the station? Good. Now let's go through it all again."

He made Eton repeat four times all instructions, signals, meeting places, text of two types of messages and an address to send his postcards, the phone number and the emergency meetings routine.

"Eton, from the moment you walk out of here, you must be *extremely* careful. Do not take or keep anything sensitive. Do not even snoop in the areas where classified information might be kept. In short, do not even try playing a spy. And most important, do not do *anything* you haven't normally done until now. You understand?" He knew he sounded ridiculous, but didn't care—all he could think of was that Eton wasn't ready for any of this. Never would be. And now he also understood why the rules prescribed that emotionally compromised case officers were to be removed immediately from the case they were handling.

"Don't worry. I'll be fine."

"No, that's not good enough. Agents die because they are careless," Jack grated out, his tone unyielding, and Eton lost his amused half smile. "I need you to follow the routine to the letter. Can you do it for me?"

"Yes, Jack. I'll do it."

Jack's expression softened. He leaned over and took Eton's hand. "It's not a game, bud… I can't get you caught up in this."

Eton pulled at his hand and rubbed his cheek against Jack's fingers. "What about you?"

"I'll be fine, don't worry," he said and grinned goofily, realizing he had just repeated Eton's line.

"But you are not a diplomat anymore. You don't have diplomatic immunity. They can arrest you, like Amanda's husband, can't they?"

"They won't… And if they do, the embassy will get me out." It wasn't exactly that simple, but Eton didn't need to know about it.

It was nearly four o'clock when Jack was finally satisfied with the results of his briefing.

"Alright." He put aside the notepad and the pencil, sprawled out on the makeshift bed, finally allowing himself an easy smile. "I think you're set for a while… Provided you strictly follow what we've agreed."

"Yes, sir. Provided you let me kiss you now." Eton stretched out next to him and wrapped an arm over Jack's chest, pressing himself into Jack's side.

"We don't have time, Eton. I'm sorry, but you have to go, like in five minutes." He kissed him softly on the lips.

"We have an hour at least. My train is at five thirty and I can get to the station in thirty minutes."

Eton shifted up on him and pressed his lips into Jack's neck just below his jawline. Jack's arms sneaked around his waist, his legs parted, letting Eton settle snuggly against him.

"Your train is… ah, at five twenty five," he mumbled, his voice catching. "And you need an hour to walk casually, uh, and discreetly from here to the station."

"You said I shouldn't do anything I don't usually do." Eton pulled back a little to gaze into his eyes. "So I'm going to run. That's what I normally do." He smiled wickedly, his hand fumbling with Jack's belt buckle.

"God, Eton, you're the worst agent the Company's ever recruited." Jack laughed breathlessly. "And you make me the worst handler, too." He lifted himself to let Eton pulled his jeans down.

"Then we're just right for each other." Eton peeled the boxers off Jack's body.

"Ushhh, yeah… Okay, you win. Twenty minutes."

"Thirty." Eton gave him his enigmatic little smile, eyes imploring, and opened his own jeans with his free hand.

"You are incorrigible, Eton May Volkonsky!" Jack rolled his eyes, trying but failing to hold back a happy grin. He pushed Eton softly off his body, sat up and tugged at his shirt. "Alright, lose this, then."

They shed their clothes and fell back into each other's arms, Eton on top of Jack, in between his thighs, one of Jack's legs hooked up over the back of Eton's knees. They kissed and caressed each other's bodies unhurriedly, gazing at each other's faces, and Jack saw in his lover's eyes the same wonder he felt: how could it be that this man from the other side of this irrational, nonsensical world was the *only* one who made him feel whole and his life complete?

Then Eton started rocking gently against him, slowly building up the desire that always smoldered under the surface whenever they were within each other's reach. They held back for as long as they could, reveling in the maddeningly sweet sensation that kept unfurling, engulfing them, until the pleasure was unbearable, and they were chasing each other over the cliff and into free fall.

Chapter 65

Once again, Jack was torn and teetering. On one hand, he loathed the necessity to report to HQ the intel he had gathered from Eton, worried sick that his friend's life was at stake should the Sovs get a whiff of his deeds. On the other hand, as a meticulously trained operations officer, weary and disillusioned though he may be, he was proud of his agent's progress. Which again left him totally disgusted with himself.

Eton had described so thoroughly and methodically his division in general and his regiment in particular that Jack had to stop him, saying that he'd better keep some of the details for later meetings. The one piece of info that Jack thought could be a killer concerned the long- range ground-to-air missile system at Eton's base called S-300. According to him, it had been covertly transported to the base recently, installed under heavy camouflage and kept top secret.

After Eton left, Jack cleared all traces of their visit in the abandoned apartment and descended to the safe house in the basement. Once there, he jotted down notes in a regular, half-used reporter notepad, writing with invisible ink, trying to recall every word Eton had said, then censoring out the info they had agreed to hold back until next time.

That night he struggled to put the vexing thoughts out of his mind—that his report would reach HQ in less than twenty-four hours and the little men with rolled-up sleeves in windowless offices would start digging. They would want to know what Eton May Volkonsky's motivation was, what his current and his potential access was, what he wanted in return, how much it would cost the Company, and most importantly they would want to validate his *bona fide*, and they would not be satisfied until the information Eton had provided was corroborated.

And he had to pass the polygraph test.

Jack turned in bed for the umpteenth time, tossed the thin summer blanket aside, his neck and chest damp with perspiration.

He didn't believe his friend could pass the test. Especially not the part about his case officer. Even Jack wasn't at all confident he could pass it if asked about his agent. And he had years of experience of smuggling his sexual identity past the goddamn machine, code named LCFLUTTER. So now what he needed, and fast, was a tactic to delay his friend's "fluttering" until Moscow, and then make damn sure that Moscow never happens to Eton again.

Coming up with a plan to exfiltrate Eton from East to West Berlin wasn't particularly difficult. He did not look too Slavic, spoke perfect English, with only a hint of an accent, so he could easily pass for a first generation American of Northern European origin. Procuring identification and travel documents and designing a legend for Eton would take a month and a half at most. Preparing him for crossing the border would take three meetings over three weekends. That would take them until the end of October. Then Jack would need to choose a date for crossing—the C-Day. Checkpoint Charlie was a no brainer as the crossover point—most foreigners entered and left East Berlin through this site. Besides,

Jack knew all Grenzpolizeien, the border guards, at this crossing. At least by their faces and their habits if not by their names. So the best days would be those when either the female guard, Lovely Rita, was on duty, or the easygoing bear of a man whom foreign correspondents called Yogi Bear. He should be able to determine their days on duty by the end of September when he and Eton would have to sit down to fix the C-Day—a day towards the end of November, just before Eton's repatriation. Yes, they were running a very high risk, especially with no additional support he could call upon, but it was all doable, Jack thought. And he was confident that Eton would be able to pull it off—he was a damn good actor, for God's sake, Jack had seen it with his own eyes!

Then came the thorny part: once in West Berlin, what would Eton do? Sure, Jack could buy him an air ticket to West Germany, to France, to America, or anywhere else Eton wanted—the passport he was going to procure for his lover would stand that. But what would he do there, in France, America or wherever else, knowing not a soul, with nowhere to go and not the slightest idea of how to survive in the West, all on his own? For no matter how smart and talented the man was, Jack had no illusions about him: Eton May Volkonsky was the ultimate romantic, a dreamer who had led a charmed, sheltered existence for most of his life. That is until two years ago when fortune had dealt him a series of cruel blows and rudely jerked him out of his dreamland and into the harsh reality that life was. And even then he had been mostly taken care of by others—by Lara and his other friends, by the state through the Soviet Army, probably by others that Jack didn't know. So now, if Jack wanted to wrestle him out of his caretakers' hands, he would need to arrange for his best friend and lover to be taken care of, at least initially, by someone else. Because no matter how much he wanted to do it himself, Jack knew he couldn't—not right away, and maybe not for a long time.

Jack's first idea about this part of the plan had been that he and Eton would disappear together. But he had quickly discarded it because he knew that eventually the Company would find them, he had no illusions about that. Besides, he couldn't stand the thought of Eton escaping the Soviet Union only to end up on the run for the rest of his life.

Then Jack figured that the best party to "place" Eton with a new life and identity was probably the Company itself. He didn't believe that Joe Coburn would ever agree to exfil Eton before he had produced something significant, and even then his life would have to be in real danger. So his options were either to blackmail old Joe into doing it or present him with a done deal. But knowing his mentor, Jack had no doubt that Joe would make it damn sure that Jack would never see Eton again. Ever. He couldn't risk such a possibility—no way, no how! So, the only option left was to find someone else who would help Eton to settle in the West.

Like his relatives in France, for example. Whom Lara had asked him to help find. Right, that would probably be the best. Then, they would have to stay out of touch for a while, until Jack was done with the Company and was positive that he was out of its sight and attention after the "mysterious disappearance" of his star agent.

Jack suspected Eton would object to his plan though: the last time they talked, his friend had been adamant about not losing contact ever again. It meant that he would have to do his best to convince Eton that if they wanted to be... (what, together? Yeah, together, somehow, someday, somewhere), they would need to be apart for some time. He didn't know for how long, but it was still better than "never", right? He prayed Eton would agree.

On Sunday night, Paul Millard dropped by to ask if Jack cared to go out for a drink. He raised his eyebrows emphatically and pointed at the staircase with his chin: he wanted to talk. On the way to Metzer Eck, he asked Jack if he had been following the developing story in Leipzig.

Since the early 80s, Friedensgebet, Prayers for Peace, on Mondays had been a regular weekly event at one of Leipzig's main churches, Nikolaikirche, and every East Germany-based foreign reporter had covered them at least once. However, the word out was that after the previous Monday prayers around a thousand people had held a peaceful demonstration on the square in front of the church. Paul had also heard that the coming Monday expected to draw an even larger crowd.

They agreed to drive to Leipzig the next day.

It was still early for the evening prayers when they arrived in Leipzig. They left Jack's car on Ritterstrasse, opposite the park, and went looking for a place where they could mingle with locals, try to gauge public sentiments over a stein of beer.

"Hey, Paul, can I ask you a favor?" Jack said as they were strolling unhurriedly in the general direction of the church.

"Sure. What's up?"

"I have a couple of friends in Moscow and they've asked me to help to locate their distant relatives in France. Discreetly. Like in 'very discreetly', if you know what I mean."

Jack peered at the Englishman until he nodded. A year ago Paul had been seconded to Moscow for a few months and he knew how these things were.

"So I thought maybe it'd be even better if someone three times removed would do the inquiring. You said your first boss has recently moved to Paris. Do you think you could ask him?"

Paul reflected on it for three seconds. "Can't see why not... Who are your friends?"

"You might have heard the name. Volkonsky."

Paul cut Jack a glance, furrowing his brows. "As in 'Prince Volkonsky'? The Decembrist?"

"That's the family." He hoped Paul didn't know Professor Volkonsky and his immediate family though.

"Wait a minute... Is your friend Larisa Volkonskaya, the leading lady of the LenKom's experimental studio? They were here last month, weren't they?"

So he knew. But maybe not about Eton. "Yes, that's her."

"I wanted to go see one of their shows. But first Oliver got the flu, then Helen, then I was in Hungary. We never made it. I heard they were good. Did you manage...? Of course, you did, lucky bastard... I seem to recall there was another Volkonsky on the bill. Either the composer or the lyricist, I forgot which. Her sibling?"

"Both the composer and the lyricist. Her husband."

Paul gave him a long, thoughtful look. "I see... Let me guess. It's the lady who wants you to *discreetly* find her husband's blue-blooded relatives overseas. Am I wrong?"

Jack shook his head, then seeing Paul's emphatically arched eyebrow, he shrugged and grinned, acting up a little. "We're just good friends. That's all!"

It worked. Paul smirked and said innocently, "I'm not saying anything… Just don't let Helen know about it. Your reputation will be ruined, in her eyes."

The demonstration was peaceful, but the mood was somber, even brooding. A small group of young people in the middle of the crowd held placards declaring *Glasnost in Staat und Kirche*. Glasnost in State and church. *Keine Gewalt!* No violence! And *Wir sind das VOLK!* We are the PEOPLE! There were no speeches, or slogans shouted, just a large gathering of people amassed in a quiet protest. When the dusk fell, candles were lit, points of light flickering like giant fireflies. And the whole time the congregation was watched by throngs of *Volkspolizei*, who stood around stacks of riot shields, waiting for orders. In the end, the orders never came.

Afterwards, the two of them drove past the Soviet base on the outskirt of the city, looking for signs of imminent mobilization.

"If the tanks roll, like in 1953, they'd be from here, wouldn't they?" asked Paul.

Jack nodded. "Probably."

They didn't notice any extraordinary activities around the base, or anywhere else for that matter, all the way back to Berlin. What Jack did take note of, but his English friend didn't, was that they had been shadowed, and it wasn't one of his usual Stasi tails.

On Wednesday morning, Jack was to drive to Dresden for a few meetings at the Technical University as part of his AP job. He was also hoping that his Volkswagen Rabbit with distinctive blue plates that identified him as a foreign journalist would attract the attention of other "interested parties" besides the Stasi and hopefully would bring him to Volodya PIPER1. For this reason he started early in the morning, planning to wander around the University's campus, which he knew was one of the KGB's favored agents recruiting grounds.

It was nearing quarter to eight when he left his apartment, ready to hit the road. The main avenue two blocks away was already busy, but the narrow street he lived on was still quiet and four of the five Trabbies that usually provided his old Volkswagen company at night were still lining the curbs, plus a white *Wartburg*. Paul's red VW Polo with blue correspondent plates was also there, three cars down behind Jack's.

He climbed into his car, turned to drop the backpack on the passenger seat when he saw a large brown envelope on the floor under the glove compartment. Jack sat motionless for a few seconds, staring at it, then quickly scanned his surroundings.

A woman with a big sack plodding toward the main street, away from Jack. A middle-aged man with a mailbag approaching from the other end. The *Wartburg* on the other side of the street was a stranger—Jack didn't recognize the plate number. But it was empty.

He watched the street for another minute, then quickly stuffed the envelope in his shoulder bag, got out and hurried back, up to his apartment.

It was probably not the best of ideas to take the envelope to his place—it could be a Stasi provocation and God knew what could happen next. But the AP office, a converted three-room apartment in a nineteenth-century building, was seven streets away, and his cubicle was open to the whole world to see. Besides, he had little doubt that their three local staffers—Gertrude, the middle-aged, matronly administrator, the petite and pretty Elsa the secretary with translucent pale-blue eyes, and the handsome and athletic Rosamund the cleaner—were all Inoffizielle Mitarbeiter, Stasi's informants.

In his apartment, Jack put the security chain on the door, turned on his CD player, fired up the kettle and carefully teased the envelope open with the kitchen knife. Inside, there was another brown envelope, folded in double, and a note written in block letters: *BITTE HELFEN SIE, DEN ADRESSATEN ZU LIEFERN*—Please help to deliver to the addressee.

Jack unfolded the second envelope and went cold. It was addressed to Herr David Rolston, *Botschaft der Vereinigten Staaten in der DDR*, the US Embassy in the GDR.

He stared at the address for what felt like an eternity, sweat breaking out under his collar and on his upper lip.

Shit!! He was fucked, his cover blown!

…Wasn't he? If this was a provocation — and that was exactly how it looked — the Stasi were going to storm into his apartment any minute now. Weren't they? He would be totally fucked with the incriminating evidence in his hands and he wasn't at all confident that the Company would be able to get him out anytime soon.

Unless he managed to burn it before they got in here.

He sprung up from the kitchen stool, took a quick step towards the burning gas stove and… faltered.

It would probably take them a few minutes to ram through his security chain, so he still had time… Right? It wouldn't take too long to open the second envelope and read whatever was in it. A minute was all he needed.

Jack swiftly picked up the knife and opened the second brown envelope. There was a third, elongated white envelope inside. He opened it hurriedly, trying to make as little noise as possible, his hands shaking slightly with the adrenalin rush.

Inside were four folded half-sheets of A4-size paper. The top one was a typed note, stating in German that the author had access to "materials on the persons who were sources, targets and collaborators of a local intelligence agency". The author offered information about the "materials" and their location for ten thousand American dollars. The answer in the form of a postcard addressed to Hilda Fromm should be sent to a postbox in Potsdam. A contact mode would then be communicated.

The other three sheets were hand-copied samples of what looked like index file cards. The first contained basic personal information on an agent, codename Paul, the date of his recruitment and a registration number. The second sheet was apparently the first page of another file and contained the beginning of a detailed account of an operation carried out in January 1983 in West Germany. The card had the same registration number as the first one. And so did the third sheet which contained the true name of the agent—James William Hall, Warrant Officer, the NSA Station, Teufelsberg, Berlin.

Holy fucking shit!!

Jack remembered that case of James W. Hall III, but it was one of those rare occasions when he hadn't followed an espionage trial to the end. And the reason was that the last days of the trial had fallen on the week when Eton came back into his life. But he had read enough to remember that Hall had been an officer in the Army's G2 intelligence section, specialized in electronic warfare and involved in "voice intercepts and cryptanalysis" which in layman's language meant electronic eavesdropping. During the trial, Hall had admitted that he had been selling the US Army secrets for money to the East Germans *and* the Soviets at the same time. Now someone from the other side was offering to sell the proof of Hall's treason, as well as others' like him.

For ten fucking grand! This fucking game would never end, would it? So there, Smith: it is now your 24/7 job to get Eton out of this shit. A-S-A-P. Unharmed. Which means that you cannot get busted now. Repeat, cannot! Everything else is *not* important.

He stood by the gas stove and tried to commit to memory the content and the look of the four sheets of paper. It took him longer than usual because half of his brain and other senses were on guard, ready to catch any unfriendly sound at the door, to thrust the paper in the fire at a slightest notion of danger. But everything was quiet, except for an occasional muted rush of a car passing by on the street below. He closed his eyes, reciting the letter and copies of file cards in his mind. He then held the letter over the fire for a second, dropped it in the sink and watched the flame devouring it. When there was nothing left but a little mound of black ashes, he turned the tap and waited for the water to wash them clean down the drain.

David Rolston wouldn't be pleased to hear about the loss of intel material, especially one addressed to him, but damned if Jack cared. He had other priorities. First and foremost, he must keep himself safe. For Eton. And maybe, just maybe, for *them*.

Chapter 66

Jack drove to Dresden as planned since his itinerary had been fixed beforehand and he didn't want anyone questioning his last minute changes. And all the way there and back he mulled over one question: what should he report about the envelope?

He knew he had to report the incident. It could always be a test by the Company. Farfetched? Yes, but possible, given that for some time now he had been partially exempted from the polygraph, and when he had to take it, he was given a set of questions constructed to go around Operation SEABROOK. You couldn't be too careful when you had something cooking that you wanted your chiefs never to find out, right? So, he *would* report the envelope. The question was whether he should disclose the content of the letter or say that he had burnt it without opening.

By the time Jack got to West Berlin, it was nearly 7:00 p.m. and he had made up his mind to report the content of letter as well. He reasoned that if it wasn't the Company's test, they would keep him in East Berlin to wait for further developments. And he *had* to stay in East Berlin — until Eton was safely on the other side of the Iron Curtain. He figured that even if HQ decided it was getting too hot and he should be pulled out, David Rolston would fight to keep him. Because for now Jack was the only link that could lead Rolston to the ultimate prize of his posting as East Berlin COS, the Stasi's agent files.

That the letter had contained copies of the Stasi's agents files Jack had little doubt. It was possible that it was the Stasi testing him, a common ploy used as part of the regular sweep out of foreign journalists accredited in East Berlin. But then they could have flaunted other, lesser sources, couldn't they? Could have offered one source—why put the entire file system as bait? No, it was too big to be a test. Besides, the way the letter was dropped on him resembled the KGB's attempt to frame Mike Demidoff in Moscow back in 1986.

Jack did an hour-long SDR, before leaving his car near Zoo Bahnhof and taking back streets to the safe house. Once there, he made himself a mug of strong and sweet instant coffee and sat down at the kitchen table to jot down the content of the letter from memory. When he finished, he dialed a special number and asked for an urgent meeting with David Rolston at the safe house at eight o'clock the next morning. Then he locked his report in the safe and left.

On the street, he flagged down a taxi a mile away from the safe house. He picked up a smartly dressed up woman at a bar on Ku'damm, treated her to a late night dinner and one too many drinks, and after midnight took her to her home in a quiet neighborhood in Charlottenburg. When he slipped out of the spacious and tastefully decorated apartment the next morning, the woman was still fast asleep.

David was already at the safe house when Jack arrived. And had read the report. Jack ran the COS through the details again. If Rolston was annoyed about the destruction of the letter, he hid it well. The only indication of his disapproval was his remark at the end of their debriefing.

"Thank you, Jack. Good job... But it would be even better if you make an effort to secure the original material next time."

"Sure, David." Jack nodded, knowing well that he wouldn't do it next time either, and there was nothing the COS could do about it.

Rolston instructed him to return to the safe house the next day to pick up a passport and credit cards before taking the earliest flight to Munich. A car would be waiting for him at the airport to drive to Garmisch. Jack reckoned the meetings with whoever came out for the new op planning shouldn't take more than two days, so by Monday morning he should be back in East Berlin.

That wasn't, however, the way things went.

When Jack landed at Munich International Airport on Friday morning, he was met by a courier with an instruction to follow him to the NATO base. From there Jack boarded a Lockheed C5B Galaxy airlifter, together with a small group of paratroopers returning to their home base, and by 3:45 p.m. DC time, he was riding the elevator to the sixth floor, heading for one of the meeting rooms he had been directed to the moment he signed in.

Apparently, HQ had taken the letter more seriously than had Jack or even David Rolston. The first briefing was with Joe Coburn and his heads of Counter Intelligence and Ops. The meeting lasted thirty minutes and by the end of it, Jack's life for the next two days had been scheduled down to the minute.

Since it was critical that Jack's absence in East Germany went unnoticed, he was to show up on the other side of the Wall on Monday night at the latest. As a result, his full debrief and the new op planning was to start as soon as he had checked in at a safe house a few miles from HQ.

He started off with a senior analyst from the Division Chief's office, Fred Lewis. Besides the exhaustive debrief on the content, the layout and the wording of the letter, his job was to profile all Jack's local contacts and everybody else he had come across in East Germany—Russians, Brits, diplomats, scholars, statesmen, sportsmen, as well as the Americans he had met in East Berlin.

Fred documented profiles of each of Jack's contacts based on his description and every detail Jack could recall from his conversations and interactions with them, even the most trivial and inconsequential. By midday Saturday, the list Fred had been typing on a portable computer consisted of two hundred and fifty nine entries, of which a hundred and six had more information that just a name and occupation. During the following two-hour session with David Rolston and a deputy from CI, the four of them managed to narrow down the list to seventeen people who could either be the author of the letter or the courier.

The seller offered the Stasi agents files, so logically it pointed to a Stasi officer. But the prime suspect on Jack's list was Volodya from Dresden. He had no proof that it was the KGB, just a hunch.

Fred the analyst was skeptical. The CI deputy chief said he would like to see more evidence that the seller was KGB, besides the similarities to the Moscow cases. Of which, by the way, the Stasi could have learnt from their big brother easily. David Rolston didn't care one way or the other who the seller was and was ready to dish out ten grand to learn more.

The next day, the limited planning session with David and someone from the Ops that Jack had expected turned out to be a full-blown operational planning exercise. Present were the Deputy Head of CI, the Deputy Head of Ops, but more surprising was the presence of Pat Richmond, Joe Coburn's Deputy in charge of the Soviet ops. So maybe Joe too thought that the seller could be KGB.

The views were once again divided. Pat Richmond, who'd had nearly all his case officers busted and expulsed from Moscow in '85 - '86, thought that Jack was at risk without a diplomatic cover and should be brought in immediately. David Rolston disagreed. Finally, his Station had secured a couple of very promising leads, both tied with the same case officer. He couldn't afford to let go of him.

During the session, Jack also learned that the intel provided by Eton was a hit too, although it was still being corroborated.

Richmond gave Jack a pat on his back during one of the breaks. "Great job, son. You take good care of your source."

"Thank you, sir. I surely will." Jack nodded solemnly, trying to block the hot surge of passion in his chest from slipping through.

By 5:00 p.m. Sunday, the plan was drawn, a new field project outline drafted, ready to go for approval the next day. The key point was that Jack was staying in the field. A girlfriend with diplomatic cover would be placed at East Berlin Station ASAP and Jack would move in with her. In the meantime, he would not engage in any collection activity, would try to have company wherever he went, preferably foreigners, and would check in every three days. A support team would be brought in to provide him counter surveillance cover for a few weeks until the COS was satisfied with his security situation. And finally, Jack would set up a meeting for Pat Richmond with SALT. Who would also be polygraphed as soon as a specialist with the equipment were transported into East Berlin.

Shit! He'd been hoping that they would leave the interview till Eton was back in Moscow. And the polygraph? No way would Eton pass it. Now what? Shadowed by his own people and paired off with a Company-sponsored girlfriend, now that they had only eleven weeks left till the C-Day? He should have planned better! And why hadn't he asked for Eton's picture earlier? Why hadn't he agreed with Eton on a way he could contact him in case of emergency? He should have known that the Company would... He shouldn't have reported the content of the goddamn envelope! But what he *really* shouldn't have done was get Eton neck-deep in this shit together with himself!

It was nearly 6:00 p.m. when the last person had left the safe house.

As Jack sprawled out on the bed, fully dressed and completely drained, the phone rang. It was Joe Coburn's secretary, Donna. She instructed him to show at a Mediterranean restaurant in Arlington at 8:00 p.m., said that a taxi would pick him up at 4:00 a.m. the next day, wished him a good trip back and hung up.

The dinner was a typical Joe Coburn affair—private and casual, great food and booze, strictly no business at first. When the waitress had brought their coffees and drinks, and left, Joe produced his cigarettes, offered them to Jack and sat back. Jack steeled himself for business talk—again from his experience, *tête-à-tête* with Joe Coburn meant he might not like it.

"How are things with the EMV kid?" Joe finally asked.

Jack slammed down the resentment, nodded and said unhurriedly, "Good, considering his, um, fragile condition. It's in my reports… But that's not what you're asking, is it?"

"No. I'm interested in the progress of SEABROOK."

Hold his eyes… Two, three… Don't swallow. "There's nothing new since my last report. I didn't see him." No water, not just yet. "Why? Anything happened?" Jack allowed himself to raise his eyebrows.

Joe watched him closely for a few seconds, then took a sip from his tumbler. "Yes. We're closing the case."

"What do you mean?"

"Our joint venture partner has closed and archived it. We might as well do it and run the other part of the op on its own."

Shit, what's going on?!

"What happened?" Jack hoped he came across sufficiently concerned, but not too eager.

"The mastermind of the JV has retired last month. His successor has other priorities and *your* case apparently isn't one of them."

"Sooo, what does it mean… for me?" This time he didn't need to play act his uncertainty.

"Nothing much will change. You'll continue developing him. Except that we don't need to *establish* anything. Nor to develop the 'seabrook' angle anymore. And you don't have to process the closing memo. I'll put someone else on it… Happy?" Joe smirked and took another sip of his bourbon and coke.

Jack sat looking at him for a few moments, knitting his eyebrows, then said quietly, "It has been a waste of time, since you ask, Joe. Both ops. The man's useless. Probably the worst of them. Unstable, total lack of discipline, no sense of purpose whatsoever." He shook his head, grimacing as if in disgust, and took a long swig of beer.

Joe stared at him, his eyes narrowed, dubious. "Why have you recruited him, then?"

"Joe, you don't recruit the Sovs, they recruit themselves, remember? That's what we've been taught. And it's actually true. I just reported what had happened and gave my assessment. A negative one, by the way. It wasn't me who decided to operationalize him in EG… It's all in my reports." He let out a long sigh of exasperation.

"That decision has paid off, by the way," Joe said after a moment of silence. "The info he's produced is first-class."

"Which part?"

"On the mechanical installations."

The S-300 missiles at his base. Shit, if someone gets a whiff about this…

"Has it been corroborated? Pat said the other day that we were still working on it."

"Yes, the confirmation came in this morning… From the Brits," he added in response to the silent question in Jack's eyes.

"What's so special about these *installations*?"

The Division Chief hesitated before answering, kept his voice low. "It's a new class. We knew they had it, but not that they had them so close… I would say for the time being his production is adequate... Don't discard him just yet, Jack. Who knows, he may come around and you'll have a long-term asset in your portfolio."

Jack held his mentor's gaze for three seconds, then asked tentatively, "What if he goes along with, um, *seabrook*? What do I do then?"

Joe straightened up. "Is there anything you didn't tell me?"

"There *is* something. I didn't have a chance to tell."

"What is it?"

Forgive me, baby! I have to do this.

"He caught me unawares, pinned me to the wall, got off. Then apologized profusely. He was very contrite. And scared."

"When was it?"

"Four weeks ago. The last time I met him."

"Had you two been drinking again?"

"Yes, as usual. Maybe it's getting to him... So what do I do if it turns out that he's finally decided he likes it? With SEABROOK off the table, what do I do with all this shit, Joe?"

The Division Chief gazed at him, stone-faced.

Haven't expected this, have you? Now suck it up, buddy.

Jack hesitated, then continued, lowering his voice to almost a whisper, "So I think 'fluttering' him right now might not be such a good idea."

There was a long, pregnant pause before Joe Coburn spoke up, "We'll see... Maybe we can arrange the case transfer... But don't keep your expectations high, Jack. It may not happen before he returns home. For now, I need you to get him to produce more of what he has, taking advantage of his current location." Joe waved at the waitress, signaling for the bill.

Shit, it meant that he could forget about an assignment in Moscow. Which in turn meant that it was now, while Eton was in East Germany, or never. He really needed to hurry up with the preparations. The passport should be—

"Do you have a girlfriend?"

"Pardon me? No, not presently."

"What do you do for sex?" It wasn't personal and the Division Chief made it clear enough.

"I go to West Berlin."

Joe's eyes narrowed. "I hope you're being careful in *West Berlin*."

"I am always careful. You don't have to worry about that."

"Good. It makes the planning easier... I hope your marital plans with that chick from Near East Department, whatshername, are still on."

"Savannah Jones?" He didn't buy for a second that Joe Coburn had forgotten her name.

"Yes, that's the one. I'll see if we can have her moved to East Berlin and you two can start making your wedding plans."

"Thanks for the good news, Joe." He hoped the pleasantly surprised expression he put on looked half-genuine. "I haven't heard from her for a while, but hope she and I are still on the same page... When do you think she'll be transferred?"

Joe studied his face intently, then his lips twitched in a thin smirk. "Soon. Don't worry, Jack, we're covering your back. Just make sure it doesn't interfere with your ops."

Yeah, right. And how the fuck he was supposed to juggle this one? The last person he needed in East Berlin now was Savannah. He prayed to all gods he didn't believe in that the "soon" Joe had promised didn't happen till Eton was on the right side of the Wall.

He returned to East Berlin late on Monday, minutes before Checkpoint Charlie closed for the night. The next day, he found himself being comprehensively shadowed. He noticed a couple of faces of his regular Stasi tails, then thought he recognized the man at the bar in Hotel Stadt Berlin, deep in conversation with a platinum blonde with punk style hairdo— Jack had seen him passing by his car the morning before. Over the following days, he spotted at least two others he had never seen before, but couldn't tell if they were Stasi, KGB or the counter surveillance support afforded him by the Company.

Jack called the post office where Eton was supposed to send a postcard whenever he needed to contact him. Nothing. There were no phone messages left for him at the Company's emergency number either.

Paul was away on a trip, so on Wednesday Jack dropped by Panorama Bar at Hotel Stadt Berlin after work again. There were always a few Western tourists and business people watering there before and after the dinner hour. At seven, he left the bar with a couple of students from Leeds on their last night out in East Germany. He took them to Metzer Eck for a "thoroughly local dinner".

As soon as they had placed their orders, Barbel beckoned him to the back. She handed him a postcard that read, "Dear Johann, I will come on Sunday Morning after the Parade. See you at the Coffee Place at Noon. N."

The parade. Eton probably meant the military parade on the occasion of the 40th anniversary of the German Democratic Republic, three weeks away. He was glad that his stubborn ass of a friend didn't use the Company's channel. But somehow he knew that this message was in line with their agreed procedure: the third Sunday meant the second Saturday from now; meeting at noon meant meeting 10:00 a.m.

Jack knew the train schedule from Bernau by heart: the earliest one arrived at Berlin Hauptbahnhof at 9:29am; the next one stopped at Bahnhof Friedrichstrasse at 9:58am. Eton said "the coffee place", not "the bar" which would be Zur Nolle just outside of Bahnhof on Friedrichstrasse. It meant Eton would arrive at Hauptbahnhof and the coffee place was the cafeteria inside the station's main hall. A meeting at 10:00 a.m. would give Jack two to three hours to disguise and do his surveillance detection routine before he got to the station.

And he would figure out later if he was going to report on his agent's request for a meeting. His smart ass of a friend had given him this choice.

On Friday, Jack had finally located a "cobbler" in West Berlin and place an order for a "clean" passport of a male, twenty-five to thirty-five years of age, from an English speaking country, preferably Australia, New Zealand or South Africa. The passport would have to be legal for at least six months and not reported stolen immediately upon its "acquisition", and it would have to be "adjusted" to carry an East German tourist visa and an entry stamp at the Checkpoint Charlie border crossing. The picture of its new owner would be provided within two to three weeks, together with the date of his entry into the *DDR*.

The passport together with other arrangements had taken a quarter of Jack's savings, but it didn't matter—he was planning to set up a bank account with most of the rest for Eton, anyway. He knew he would have a hard time convincing his friend to accept it but hoped that telling him it was a loan he expected Eton to repay later would do the trick.

Oh, c'mon, who was he kidding? He wanted it to be a loan because he knew that his straight as an arrow Eton would make damn sure that the debt was repaid and if possible in person. And that was all Jack wanted—to see him again, sometime, no matter when...

Paul returned from London the following week and brought back information about the Volkonsky clan. According to the findings of Paul's contact, there were at least two Volkonsky families currently living in France. The first was Prince Andrei Volkonsky, a composer of classical music, who lived in Aix-en-Provence, reportedly alone. The second family had adopted a westernized version of their name—Wolkonsky. The living patriarch was Prince Alexandre Wolkonsky who had two children, a son and a daughter—Prince Cyril and his wife lived in Toulouse with their three offspring, and Princess Marina, her husband and two children resided near Bordeaux. A separate sheet of paper contained four addresses.

Then there was another page with names, which Paul thought might also be of interest to Jack's friends. Andrei and Maria Wolkonsky had immigrated to the US in the seventies, and their sister Olga had married an Argentinian and moved to Buenos Aires. Paul's colleague didn't check on their whereabouts in the States, but Paul said he'd be happy to help out, if Jack's friends were interested in finding their American relatives.

That night Jack drove to West Berlin and left the folder containing the addresses in a paid locker at Zoo Bahnhof. He didn't think that going to America right after the crossing was a sensible thing for Eton to do. But the idea that his friend *could* do so if he wanted to, sometime in the future, made Jack feel weak at the knees.

Chapter 67

It was still dark when Jack snuck out of his apartment block and cut through backyards and alleys to the abandoned workers' dorm in Prenzlauer Berg. When he left an hour later, it was daylight and drizzling, and he was unrecognizable. The gray wig and full beard, thick black-rimmed glasses and the stooping gait aged him by decades; the long, well-worn overcoat disguised his height. He spent two hours shuffling around, ducking in and out of food stores and cafeterias within a mile radius of the Hauptbahnhof.

At 9:15 a.m., he was standing at the head of the platform opposite the one where Eton's train would be arriving, a copy of Neues Deutschland in his hands, covertly observing the surroundings over the top of the opened newspaper. He noted two loitering characters who he thought might be plainclothes, but when Eton appeared from the train and headed towards the main hall, they didn't follow him. Jack waited for another five minutes. Still nothing. He folded his newspaper and waddled off in the direction in which Eton had disappeared.

The cafeteria was busier than the last time they had met. Perhaps because of the approaching 40th anniversary of the GDR there were more travelers, more people waiting for their family or friends, or seeing them off, and therefore more watchers. Or maybe because there was something brewing. Jack had felt it each time he visited Leipzig and Dresden in the last two months.

Eton was sitting at the table to the left of the door, a cup of steaming tea in front of him. There were a couple of empty tables at the back of the room, but not where Eton sat. Jack bought a coffee at the counter and hobbled with his tray toward his friend. As he was passing by, the newspapers he was carrying slipped from under his arm and scattered at Eton's feet.

Jack stopped, shuffling his feet awkwardly. "*Verzeihen Sie mir,*" he mumbled the apology and sat his tray on the table, intending to reach down for his newspapers.

Eton leaned over and pick them up first. "*Bitte hier.*" He handed Jack the newspapers, his expression polite, obviously not recognizing Jack in his disguise.

"It's me, Eton," Jack whispered in Russian, then said louder, "*Vielen Dank.* Do you mind if I sit here?" He pointed at the seat across Eton's and smiled encouragingly at his friend's startled expression.

"*Bitte...*"

"*Danke schön*, young man! I promise not to bother you." He picked up his cup of coffee, brought it up to his mouth and muttered, his lips barely moving, "Toilet across the hall. Ten minutes."

Soon Eton got up, nodded politely and left. Jack took his time finishing his coffee, then collected his newspapers and headed out too after depositing his tray and the empty cup on a used tableware rack.

There was a steady flow of visitors to the men's room, but Jack still managed to catch a half a minute when there was no one at the stalls to stealthily deposit into Eton's pocket a piece of paper crumpled into a tight ball. "Directions. From the main entrance," he said under his breath. "In ten minutes. And don't rush. I'll cover you."

Eton cut him a quick glance from under his brows, his lips pressed together. He nodded curtly. In ten minutes, he exited through the station's main doorway as instructed, turned left and strolled casually down the street. Jack was trailing a dozen steps behind him.

They got to the safe house in Prenzlauer Berg in an hour, having changed buses twice and walked for a couple of miles. Up in the crumbling, top-floor apartment that had at one time been a safe house, Jack peeled off his wig and beard, dropped them on top of his shabby overcoat on the floor and turned to Eton. Who had been watching him without a word, leaning against the decaying wall.

"Sorry for that. I've been shadowed rather intensively lately. Thought you didn't need any of that."

Eton stepped up and pulled him into an embrace. "You worry too much, Jack," he mumbled into Jack's neck, just below his ear, and inhaled deeply.

Jack held still for a moment, his eyes closed. Then he kissed his lover softly on the lips and pulled back. "Just enough for the two of us... How much time have we got today? We have a lot to cover."

"I have to be back before five."

"Shit. Only three hours. Let's get started then."

He shucked off his thoroughly worn loafers and sat down cross-legged on the ratty old mattress on the floor. Eton followed him without further ado.

In the next hour, Jack ran Eton through his exfiltration plan, complete with backup arrangements in case things didn't go according to Plan A. The only part that he held back was the names of the people involved and the addresses. It wasn't because he didn't trust Eton, but he decided it would be safer if he gave them to him just before the C-day.

The gist of the plan was that the crossing would happen on Eton's leave of absence in Berlin, a week or two before his departure back to Moscow. He would have to slip out on his comrades and come to a safe house, sometime between 7:00 and 9:00 p.m. Jack would be there waiting and everything would be ready for him—a passport, clothes and a bag with appropriate pocket litter, like money in various currencies, West Berlin bus tickets, hotel and restaurant receipts etc. Eton would become a citizen of an English speaking country—which one would depend on the passport Jack would have been able to procure by then. At 10:00 p.m., they would meet with a group of two or three foreign students who would be waiting for them at one of the bars downtown. They would cross to West Berlin through Checkpoint Charlie between 11:30 p.m. and midnight, with Eton and one of the students acting drunk. On the other side, Eton would stay overnight at a hotel in town, then board a plane and leave West Berlin the next day.

Jack told Eton about the two Volkonsky families in France whose addresses he had obtained. And about the other two families in America. However, he thought Eton should go to France and stay there for a while. Then in a few years, when the dust would have settled, and the Agency forgotten about him, he could move to America. Well, if that was the place Eton wanted to live, of course.

Eton listened to him without interruptions with an expression of somber concentration on his face. He asked few questions, and when Jack finished, he was silent for a long moment, staring down at his hands. "You're not going then." He stole a quick glance at Jack, barely hiding the disappointment in his tone and eyes.

Jack sighed and reached for his hand. "You know I want to, don't you? Eton? I wish I could drop everything and go with you. But I can't. Not right away, bud. We can't let the Agency know that I helped you to cross over." The Agency was primarily Joe Coburn, but Eton didn't need to know it for now. Jack wasn't sure when he would tell him about Joe, but definitely not now. "They may suspect of course, but they mustn't know for sure. That's why it's better if you stay in France... Just for a few years," he added seeing Eton's pressed together lips and his rolling jaw muscles. "I'll set up a bank account so that you have—it'll be a *loan*, okay?" He cut Eton off when his friend tried to object. "You can pay it back to me when you come to America... Okay?"

As he had expected, it worked. Eton thought it over for a few seconds before nodding. "I will find you and pay you back," he stated, squeezing Jack's fingers.

"I know you will." Jack grinned, relieved, and tugged at his hand. "Come here."

They necked for a few minutes, then Jack pushed his friend gently back and made him repeat the plan in as many details as he could recall. It was crucial that Eton bought into the plan, made it his own, took charge and made it happen. An agent who didn't believe in a plan was a disaster in waiting, or so they'd been taught and Jack wasn't about to put it to a test. Then they thrashed out how Eton was going to split from his comrades when they were on their LOA in Berlin, discussing scenarios of how things could pan out.

Eton still didn't have a confirmed departure date, only knew that it would be the end of November or the first week of December at the latest. However, he thought he would be able to come to Berlin during Lara's tour for the Music and Drama Festival—he had already applied for his LOA during October 7th and 8th and from October 13th to 16th when Lara's troupe would be leaving.

"I'll have to tell her about this," Eton said, puffing out a swirl of cigarette smoke.

Jack, who had been slouching against the wall, jolted up. "No. It's out of the question." He searched Eton's eyes, his face hard. "You're not telling anyone. *No one*, you hear me?"

"Yes, I hear you, Jack." Eton straightened up too and forcefully crushed the half-finished cigarette on the defaced floor. "But I can't just... drop her like that. It's not decent. After all she has done for me. We wouldn't be here today if it hadn't been for her."

"Don't get me wrong, I'm grateful to her too. And will be till the day I die. But you cannot tell her *now*... You can write to her once you're in France. She will understand. That's what she wants anyway, right? For you to get out of the Soviet Union. She was the one who asked me to find your relatives in France in the first place, remember?"

"She will worry herself to death if I don't return with everybody. I need to tell her..." Eton's tone lost most of the stubborn notes, but he wasn't giving up on his idea just yet.

"Eton, she hangs out with KGB operatives. She talks too much." He ignored Eton's look-who's-talking face. "She may spill—"

"She will not tell anyone. She can keep secrets."

There was a loaded pause, before Jack asking warily, "What secrets are we talking about?... Eton? What does she know?"

Eton fumbled in his jacket pocket and pulled out his Marlboros. "I think she knows about me." He blew a small milky cloud to one side. "But she doesn't tell even me that she knows. And *what* she knows."

Jack groaned mentally. He wanted to ask how Eton had found out and when, but what did it matter if he couldn't do shit about it?

"So she knows about us... Right? Fucking great! Christ, Eton, do you even understand how this fucks everything up?"

"Life *is* fucked up, Jack. I'm sure you know all about it. Guess we have no choice but try our best to cope." When Jack didn't say anything in response, he continued, softer, "You can trust her, Jack. I do."

Jack rubbed his face with both of his hands and reached for Eton's cigarette. He inhaled a lungful and gave it back. "Aright. I'll think about how to *cope* with it later. Now about the plan. Even if you trust her a hundred and one percent, Eton, do *not* tell her. You will spare her having to cover it up for you. If she doesn't know, she won't need to make an effort to keep it secret. She won't need to be extra cautious talking about you and your upcoming discharge when the topic comes up... I know she is an excellent actress, but there's gonna be lots of partying while she's here, right? And Lara *can* get carried away a little when she parties. We both know that, don't we?"

In the end, Eton reluctantly agreed not to tell Lara, but send her a message from France instead. He didn't move from his place, smoking, while Jack pulled two bottles of milk, two packs of biscuits and two big apples out of the used plastic bag he'd been carrying around and put them on the mattress. He waited until Jack sat down, reached inside his inner jacket pocket and produced an envelope folded in two.

"Passport pictures," he said to Jack's raised eyebrows. His chest heaved in a stifled sigh.

"Everything alright?"

"It makes me a defector, like my father, doesn't it?" Eton smirked humorlessly. "And you know what? He was gay too... I think."

Jack hadn't quite believed what he had read about Emil May and Richard Hamilton in the files, but now that Eton was saying that too...

"How do you know?" His hand covered Eton's for a second as he handed him one of the bottles of milk.

"From Mother's diaries. She didn't write it directly, but I guessed reading between the lines... Perhaps that was why she figured it out about me, too. Said I was exactly like Father."

"Sounds like your father was a very decent man, defector or not."

Eton shrugged awkwardly, suddenly very busy opening his milk bottle. "She never stopped loving him," he mumbled as if to himself. "Even after she'd understood that he, um, preferred someone else... His friend Rich... I think."

"The two of them worked in the NSA and defected together. It was a big case back then," Jack said over a bite of biscuit and took a swig from the bottle of milk.

"I met him once when he came from Leningrad to visit my father... It seems to me now that Father made Rich stay away from him. Then he missed him, talked about him a lot. Told me stories about the time they both lived in California... No idea what happened between them to make Father treat him like that."

There was a long pause, then Jack asked cautiously, "Does Lara know about your father?"

Eton's head went up at that. "No." He searched Jack's eyes, putting two and two together. "This was not in the diary she found. That one concerned only me... Mostly."

"And me... Right?"

"Yes. But not what you think."

"Eton, I need to know what Lara knows. To be able to deal with this little *situation* we're having here."

Eton nodded, not looking at Jack. "Mother suspected, uh, figured out that I thought of you as my childhood imaginary friend Jack. No, she didn't suspect anything about you. Just thought you were a good person. She wrote that she hoped you would be a good friend to me... Even after you find out about me..." He trailed off, clearly not telling all there was.

"Is that all?"

"I think that is all you need to know to *cope* with the *situation*." Eton sounded a little uncertain in spite of his definite answer.

"And you're not going to tell me the rest?"

"Are you sure you want to know?"

"In my line of business, Eton, knowing more is *always* better than knowing less," he said cautiously, not sure where this all was heading.

"It's not business. It's personal." Eton shrugged, sucked in a nervous breath, his eyes everywhere but on Jack. "Alright. You've asked for it... So, she wrote that she hoped I wasn't like her. And grandpa. Wasn't... *odnolyub*."

"Monogamous?"

"Can love only one person." Eton raised his head and met Jack's eyes. "For life... But we don't have any choice in this, right?" He chuckled, trying to make it sound lighthearted. "It is like being born blond. Or homosexual... Or with the bluest eyes that no one else has."

They didn't talk much during the rest of their lunch, followed by a cigarette they shared, sitting side-by-side, their shoulders and legs touching, their fingers entwined. Then Jack resumed his instructions, preparing Eton for the interview with a chief who would fly in from Washington on either October 14th or 15th, as they had agreed. He ran his friend through all possible questions, gave him tips on how to hold himself and how to reply, recalling how Joe had coached him like this, a long time ago, how it had worked for him and why.

The most difficult part of the interview was the polygraph but Jack hoped it would be delayed until Moscow—the security was much tighter in East Berlin and the Agency had little time and local resources to arrange such an operation. Still, he was nervous about the questions he knew Eton would be asked—about him as Eton's case officer and how they got along. He drilled Eton again and again, asking thorny personal questions and nitpicking at Eton's answers, so much so that at some point Eton had had enough.

"You're worrying too much, Jack. I'll be fine." He sprawled on the dirty mattress, folded his arms under his head.

"It's not a game, Eton. They are pros. They will crack you in three seconds if you are not focused. I've done this before and I'm telling you: it's virtually impossible to beat the system."

"But you have been doing it for many years, haven't you? I will manage, too. Don't worry." He glanced quickly at his watch and tugged at Jack's sleeve. "We have only twenty minutes left. Can we do something else?"

"For Christ's sake, Eton! Can you *not* think about sex for a second? This is exactly what I'm scared shitless of. If anyone from the Company is around us, anyone at all, and you even *think* about it, we're done. We'll be totally done for, Eton. Do you understand it?"

"Yes, I understand... Can I ask you something?" He sat up, his face impassive, the stubborn notes back in his quiet voice.

Jack rolled his eyes and sighed in resignation. "Yes, you can."

"Back Moscow when did you realize that I, um, wanted you?"

"When?" Jack frowned. "Umm... the night on the river, in the countryside? Why?"

"Because I was dying to kiss you since the first day we met. You never noticed?"

His friend actually had a point there. Jack wouldn't have believed if someone had told him earlier on that Eton liked him. Until that mesmerizing night on the moonlit river.

"No, I didn't. I thought you didn't like me. It upset me no end. So your coming on to me that night caught me by total friggin' surprise." He chucked softly at the reminiscence. "I see your point, bud. Nevertheless, they are pros. It's not as easy to fool them as you think."

"You're a pro too."

"I'm biased. I can be blinded-sided... That's why they take case officers off the cases if they get emotionally involved with their agents."

Now it was Eton's turn to sigh and roll his eyes in frustration. "Jack. I was hiding from friends and teachers that I knew English since I was seven. Because my father told me, I would be better off if they didn't know. Then, when I was fifteen, I also started hiding who I truly was. And nobody, except Mother, ever suspected anything about me. Not even you. No, let me finish, please... The only *reason* you see me as I am, without my armor, is because I *want* you to know who I truly am. Because I know you accept me the way I am. Only you, cowboy..." He took Jack's hand and pressed a kiss onto of his fingers. "That's why I believe I can take this honesty test from your bosses... And no, I'm not with the KGB, in case this makes you suspicious again. And the only reason I have agreed to work along with your CIA is because of *you*, Jack. Because I don't want you to go away... So please stop worrying so much about me. I shall be very careful, okay? For you, cowboy." He leaned forward, gripping at Jack's neck, and whispered against his lips, "For us."

What else could Jack do or say to that? He closed his eyes and gave in to the sweetest of sensations that always engulfed him, drowning out everything around, every time this frustratingly hardheaded yet incredibly loving man took him into his arms.

Chapter 68

The next morning Jack drove to a safe house near Zoo Bahnhof to write a report on his meeting with SALT. He ended it with a notice that the agent would be ready for an interview in East Berlin on either October 14th or 15th. Jack would need to know the location of the meeting by October 8th at the latest to be able to inform and instruct SALT appropriately.

It was gray and foggy when he left the safe house, and the Sunday morning traffic was light. He bought a stack of newspapers at a newsstand, picked a small cafe on the corner of Kantstrasse and Savignyplatz and sat down at the corner table by the window. While waiting for his breakfast, he started on his daily fix of world news.

"4,000 East Germans Victoriously Leaving Czechoslovakia, Poland," screamed the headline on front page of the newspaper on the top of the stack, *Bild am Sonntag*.

It went on reporting that following a surprise agreement between the governments involved, late Saturday, the East German refugees who had been camping at West German embassies in Czechoslovakia and Poland began leaving the missions.

At the same time, the East German news agency ADN announced that East Berlin had agreed to "expel" the refugees aboard a special train that will carry them to the West through East German territory.

Damn! He was so friggin' behind on this rapidly evolving story.

It wasn't the first time since July when Eton had come back into his life that Jack was missing out on breaking news. He had even gotten a reminder from his senior colleague about his late submissions the month before. Between his AP job, his covert job and clandestine meetings with Eton, Jack was scrambling to find enough hours in a day to keep everybody happy. Including himself. He'd have to make sure he joined Paul next Monday on one of his trips to Leipzig. Paul had mentioned last time that the gathering following the Monday prayer after the 40th anniversary of the GDR was going to be huge.

Paul's The Sunday Times carried an article on the difficult progress of the Soviet *perestroika* reforms.

"Ukraine a Stumbling Block for Reforms, Gorbachev Warns. MOSCOW — President Mikhail S. Gorbachev warned Saturday that his reform program will falter across the country if it stumbles in the Ukraine, the Soviet Union's second-largest republic, which recently has been racked by nationalist, labor and religious unrest..."

As Jack turned the page, an AP wire service's blurb caught his eye.

"11 Gay Couples Married in Denmark. COPENHAGEN — Hundreds of people cheered and threw rice as 11 homosexual couples got married on the day the law allowing such unions came into effect... Denmark became the first country to give homosexual couples legal status when its Parliament approved a gay rights bill in May..."

I'll be damned!

He knew it was totally silly, but the occasional news about gay rights in Europe had always drawn him, and inevitably left him stirred and yearning. For what, he wasn't sure, because he was certain that if *this* ever happened in America, it wouldn't be in his lifetime. Not in the least because he didn't have anyone... *like that* who wanted to be with him. Except maybe Savannah, for the wrong reasons. But that was before. Now he had Eton— impossible, stubborn, idealistic, irresistible Eton. Who had said he would do anything for Jack. "For us," he'd said. And even though Jack knew that the "us" wasn't happening anytime soon, maybe even not ever, somehow it sounded... real.

Maybe it *was* real and possible?

Why not, if the Washington Post and USA Today featured opinions like this nowadays: "Gorbachev's Success Is In The US Interest", by a former diplomat who had also been a CIA official. Or how about this article written by two Americans and a Russian from the US-Soviet Task Force on Terrorism, "The CIA and KGB Come Together To Combat The Threat of Terrorism"? Jack had never imagined that he would be reading such things a year ago. So what if Eton's "us" was possible, too? Someday...

But of course first he'd have to make damn sure that Eton was delivered safely to the other side of the Wall in eight weeks' time.

On Monday, it turned out that Paul was out of the country, so Jack drove to Prague instead to see if he could catch the tail of the exodus of East German refugees. There he caught another drama.

Having learned about the trains full of their compatriots allowed to leave to the West, crowds of young East Germans had taken off in their *Trabants*, heading to Czechoslovakia and Poland. By the time Jack got to Bonn's mission in Prague, at least two hundred East Germans were camped inside the embassy and a hundred more outside. Despite the agreement with the GDR not to take in any more refugees, Bonn decided to admit this new batch. The prospect of another deal with East Berlin, however, looked bleak.

When an embassy official made an announcement at the gate that the wait for a visa could be up to six weeks, a young male nurse from Dresden turned to Jack and said, with an enthusiastic smile, "Better six weeks on the street here than six years at home."

By Monday evening, the crowd in front of the embassy had grown to several thousand. Attempts by the police to disperse it and to cordon off the embassy area did not yield any visible results and by nightfall, the Czech authorities had given up.

Jack spent half the night chatting to a group of students who huddled together a dozen steps from the police guard's booth. The night was cold and wet, but the excited young people refused to give in when the freedom they craved was so close at hand.

It was nearly three o'clock in the morning when he got back to his car on a side street nearby to try to get some sleep. He returned at nine with a plastic bag full of sweet buns and half a dozen bottles of milk for his new friends. They hadn't moved an inch from the spot where he'd left them and met him with boisterous cheers.

By midday, their fate was announced: East Germany had agreed that those who were in Prague already could travel to West Germany. But it also slammed the door shut on any further departures by suspending unrestricted travel to Czechoslovakia.

Jack saw the young people off at Prague's main train station, kissed the girls goodbye, shook hands with the boys and left them in the company of several thousand of their compatriots to wait for their train to freedom.

It was nearly nine o'clock and pouring when Jack returned to East Berlin. After a hot shower, a bowl of canned tomato soup with a stale roll, and a double shot of whiskey he sat down at his portable typewriter and by midnight had churned out two news articles and a feature story about the events and people he had met in the last two days.

He went to bed feeling a bit better—at least one of his jobs was done, so tomorrow he could spend the day working on Eton's escape. Working "for us". His plan was to drive to Freie Universität Berlin, known also as FU Berlin, to look for people who would agree to help an escapee.

Founded in 1948 as the counterweight to pro-communist Humboldt University, FU Berlin in West Berlin had been notorious in the early days of the Wall as a stronghold of the student movement that helped young East Germans defect to the West. The wave had subsided a few years later, but from what Jack had heard, it had never really died away completely.

Jack's plan was to find those people and ask them to help on the C-Day.

The following morning, when he came down to his car, another large brown envelope was waiting for him, wedged against the back wall under the glove compartment.

Fuck. He had hoped it wouldn't happen again. Not to him and definitely not now.

The thing was, after long debates at HQ, the chiefs had decided *not* to respond to the first letter to test if it was a Stasi provocation. Pat Richmond, who had been running the Soviet ops for over a decade, insisted that a genuine volunteer wouldn't stop trying after the first failed attempt. Especially not the Sovs—if it was indeed Volodya from Dresden as Jack suspected.

"He'll try it again," the Deputy Division Chief had said. "*Then* you would take the letter to the Embassy. And we will respond accordingly."

Jack sighed and stealthily read his surroundings.

The previous night's downpour had dwindled into an irksome drizzle, and the street was virtually empty except for the light but steady flow of traffic on the main street at one end. As far as Jack could see, there were no strange cars parked either in front or behind him. Of course, it didn't mean that he wasn't being watched. Maybe even from his own apartment building. It only meant that he might not be ambushed this time.

Jack had been almost sure that it wasn't a Stasi trap and Pat Richmond had agreed with him on this point. So now he had two options: he could drive to the Embassy which was twelve minutes away with no traffic; or he could leave the envelope where it was, go up to his apartment, call the Embassy and ask for the security officer who was supposed to have been briefed about Jack's potential call. However, there was no telling how long it would take for the man to come over to retrieve the envelope. Then he would probably want Jack to come with him to the Embassy to file a report, and to tell him all about—

No, he didn't have time for all that. Besides, if those who had planted the letter in his car were watching him, it would be a good idea to prove them right about him being just an innocent letterman.

Jack started the car and headed to Neustradtische Kirchstrasse, trying to stay calm and driving as fast as he could without attracting attention. Fifteen minutes later, he left the envelope at the reception, saying he would return before the closing. In an hour, he was in the middle of Ku'damm, calling a special number to leave David Rolston a message to pick up the delivery and meet him at a safe house at 9:00p.m.

He spent most of the day at FU Berlin, supposedly interviewing students for a feature article he was writing. By late afternoon, he finally tracked down one of the people he had been looking for. He barely made it back to the Embassy to report the incident with the letter to the security officer, then returned to West Berlin.

The COS was already at the safe house when Jack arrived. It turned out the second letter was the exact copy of the first one, except that this time the author also wrote that it was his last attempt at a contact and if he did not receive a response at the indicated postbox by October 15th, the deal was off the table. Jack related to the COS how he had found the letter in his car, his activities ever since and what he had told the security officer at the Embassy. What he left out of his account was his visit to FU Berlin.

David listened to him attentively, asking only a couple of questions. When Jack finished, he nodded, satisfied. "Thanks you, Jack. Great job... I'm flying home tomorrow. In case we need an urgent briefing with you, be prepared to fly out to Ramstein on short notice. Maybe even over this weekend."

No! Not this weekend, please!

"Is it possible to have the briefing next Tuesday?" Jack asked cagily.

"Why? Anything the matter?"

"My AP job, David. I have to stay here to cover the 40th anniversary of the *DDR*. Then I have to go to Leipzig on Monday. Rumor is there will be a big event there. I *have* to be there... Besides, PIPER 2 is supposed to be arriving in town with her troupe on Friday, too. She may be looking for me."

"And her husband?"

"Yes, he'll probably come up to spend the weekend with her... And if we're lucky, PIPER1 might show too for the Festival."

"Alright. We'll target next Tuesday then."

By Thursday night, Jack had found out that during the festival the Russian LenKom troupe would be staying at Newa Hotel near the sealed off Nordbahnhof station. It was just a fifteen-minute walk to both Jack's place and his safe house. He left a note with his phone number for Lara at the reception: he'd love to see her this evening and she could leave a message for him with time and place on his answering machine in case he was not home, and he hoped to see her soon.

By 6:00 p.m. Friday, he still hadn't heard from her. He called the hotel at seven, gave his name and was put through her room. Nobody answered. At ten, he called again, and she still wasn't there. Nor at eleven thirty. This time the hotel suggested he leaves a message. Instead, he called at eight the next morning from a payphone not far from the hotel.

Lara answered at long last, sounding tired. She apologized for not calling the day before, started to explain why, but then stopped abruptly and asked if they could instead have breakfast together—yes, now.

Forty minutes later, they were sitting in a cafeteria two streets away from the hotel. Her buttery blond hair Jack remembered from the last time was now back to her original color, sandy, but with a little highlighting, it looked rich and warm. She looked lovely and Jack didn't waste his time in telling her about it.

"Thank you, *daragusha!*" She smiled and arched her eyebrows. "We must look good together, mustn't we? A shame we can't be together."

Jack nodded ambivalently and quickly changed the subject.

At first, they were the only ones in the small, brightly lit place. However, as soon as they got their orders, a long-haired man in trendy stone-washed jeans and a black leather jacket with a stack of newspapers under his arm walked in. He bought a coffee at the counter and took a table near the door. It was one of the three new shadows Jack had acquired in the last few days—more precisely, since he'd found the second letter in his car—and he couldn't tell whether the man was Stasi, KGB or his counter-surveillance support.

When Lara remained silent, Jack smiled encouragingly at her. "So, tell me, what happened? And how have you been, anyway?" he asked.

"Did you see the man by the door?" she whispered, leaning forward, smiling and looking straight into Jack's eyes as though telling him something intimate. "Don't turn around."

"Yes, I noticed him. Why?" he whispered back.

"I saw him standing at the hotel door when we left. Now he's here. I think he has been following us."

Right. Whoever he was, the man wasn't doing a very good job if a civilian had noticed him... Unless it was done on purpose... Or was she no longer an innocent civilian?

"Maybe." Jack threw a quick glance at the man. "I'm followed around all the time. So much so that I don't pay attention to it anymore."

Lara bit her lip, studying his face. "I was asked about you yesterday," she blurted out in a loud whisper.

"What do you mean? By whom?"

"A security service man from the embassy." She reached over, took Jack's hand on the table and continued in a low voice, a lovey-dovey smile on her face as if they were flirting. "As soon as we arrived, they gathered us all together and gave a lecture about interacting with foreigners during the festival. That we need to be very careful and report any suspicious, and even innocent, questions and requests made by any foreigner. Even from the socialist countries. Usually they only do it before we leave Moscow. This time they did it twice... After the briefing, Felix from the embassy called me aside—you met him at the train station last time, remember? He asked if you were in contact with me. And with Eton."

Shit! This was not good.

"He remembered me? I'm flattered," he said and patted her hand. "So what did you say?"

"I pointed out that I couldn't have seen to you yet since we'd just arrived. But I told him that I planned to see you because you were going to take me to West Berlin. I got a visa this time, Jack!" She beamed. "You'll take me to Ku'damm, *da?*"

"Yes, of course. But what else did Felix tell you?"

He could almost see Lara wince mentally.

"He wanted me to invite you to one of our banquets. He also asked if I knew what you liked—drinking, women, and such... I said yes, you do everything men usually do." She shrugged at Jack's expression. "Am I wrong?"

"Of course not, *daragusha*." Jack pulled at her hand and briefly pressed his lips to the back of her fingers. "That's all he wanted from you? To arrange for me to come to your banquet?"

Lara giggled, sounding relieved. "That's all."

"But he isn't the only one with the *organs*, is he?"

"Of course not. They all are... You know that, don't you?"

"Yes, I know about *them*... What about *you*, Lara? Are you with them, too? I've been sitting here and wondering why you're telling me all this... You're not supposed to, right?"

The playful expression on Lara's face slowly evaporated, but she didn't take her hand back. "Because you're my friend, Jack. No matter what I do and who I'm with... I thought you knew what friendship means for us Russians."

"I see... So are you with them?"

She pulled her hand back, looking cagy. "I'm not *with* them... But sometimes favors you do get you favors back, you know."

"And what will you get for arranging for Felix a chance meeting with me?"

"Nothing now. But I need to do this favor, Jack. For later... It's nothing serious! *Da?*"

"Essentially, what you're doing, Lara, is you're selling me to them."

"It's not like *that*!" She was getting exasperated and Jack had to indicate with his eyes the man by the door to make her lower her voice again. "I've just told you about it, haven't I? I know you can handle it. I'm sure they tried it with you before. They try it with all foreigners, especially from embassies and with journalists. You'll be fine, *da*, Jack? I know you will." It sounded like she was trying to convince herself more than she was trying to convince Jack.

Either she was buying his trust with this twisted ploy or she was really in a hot spot and forced to do it—she, a little Soviet princess, the daughter of a Minister, a candidate for the Politburo. What could have possibly happened? In any case, it looked like the KGB had finally taken an interest in Jack. Maybe it could even be treated as an indication that the letters had come from the KGB, not the Stasi. Pat Richmond and the CI Chief would definitely like this.

Jack let out an exaggerated sigh. "Alright, Lara. I'll come to your banquet and let your Felix get me a drink or two. But you will owe me a favor for this, too. Alright?"

"Of course, Jack! Thank you, *daragusha*!" She beamed at him and took a sip of her cold tea.

Jack toyed with his pastry. "So, what else did Felix say about Eton? It might not do him any good if they knew he's hanging out with... um, a foreigner."

"No, he didn't ask anything else."

"Is he coming up to see you this weekend?" Jack asked, faking nonchalance.

"He can't come this time." Lara shook her head, a faintly troubled expression clouding her face again.

"Why?"

Because he's been spending all his LOAs on you, asshole!

"They haven't given him a leave this time. But I'll see what I can do, so that they let him go next weekend… And you know what, I think you're right, Jack. Maybe it would be better if you don't see Eton while he's here in Germany."

Chapter 69

Saturday, October 7th was the 40th anniversary of the GDR.

Jack spent most of the day on the streets of East Berlin. In the morning, he joined Terry and two other AP colleagues from the Bonn office for the military parade on Karl-Marx-Allee. The whole event took around an hour and Jack thought it was too somber despite the upbeat marching music performed continuously by a triple-sized military orchestra. He wasn't the only one left unimpressed: the unsmiling locals observing the display of the *DDR's* military might around him also looked bored. Jack recalled the parades on Red Square: never less than two hour long, they usually culminated with a jubilant procession of the people's representatives from all over the Soviet Union, their fervent enthusiasm and profound sense of pride contagious, lingering long after.

Or maybe it was something to do with Russians and their love for... whatever, whoever they loved...

At noon, having submitted his write-ups at the office, Jack headed out again. Around 2:00 p.m., a crowd started building up under the TV tower on Alexanderplatz. At first, there was only a few dozen people milling around, most of them young, some trendy in stonewashed jeans and short bomber jackets, some with punk hairdos. By four, the crowd numbered in the hundreds and there were several groups holding tempered discussions about changes they would like to see. At 5:00 p.m., a dozen of covered trucks with *Volkspolizei* in ceremonial uniforms and several sedan cars with plain-clothes began to line up on the streets leading to Alexanderplatz. That didn't deter the crowd which continued to grow bigger and louder.

As the night fell and the dim lights on the square were turned on, someone with a megaphone urged everyone to go to Palast der Republik where a reception was being given for foreign leaders who attended the *"40 Jahre DDR"*. A hum of approval rolled over the plaza. The mass of people swayed, started trickling, then pouring into the wide Karl-Liebknecht-Strasse. Someone shouted "Freedom! Freedom!" Another young voice yelled "Gorby! Gorby!", but the assembly didn't pick it up. Most people were content just to talk quietly while striding towards Marx-Engles-Platz in the middle of Museum Island.

Jack walked in the midst of the procession, taking pictures and striking up conversations with demonstrators. People gladly shared their views when they heard his accented German and saw his foreign correspondent tag.

The crackdown came without warning. Within minutes, the column of demonstrators was rounded up by throngs of *Volkspolizei* linking arms, cutting off both ends of the wide avenue. Then police trucks moved in, some of them with oversized mesh screens in front painted in red and white chevrons—to herd crowds out of the way, as it turned out later. Troops of uniformed police barged into the procession, driving it against the buildings on one side of the street. Plain-clothed men began grabbing and pulling those walking at the front towards the trucks with now opened tailgates. The crowd first pushed back, shouting *"Vopos out! Stasi out!"*, then fought back, and before long, the street erupted in violence.

Jack dodged the first wave of *Vopos* and started retreating towards Marienkirche, the shutter of his camera firing like a machine gun. It wasn't probably such a good idea, because when he reached the old church, three young men in black leather jackets stepped out of the dark. They look no different from the young demonstrators Jack had talked to earlier, but he recognized one of them. Black haired and mustached, he was one of Jack's regular tails in Leipzig and Dresden. He was carrying a baton.

Jack stopped and raised his hands, palms forward, smiling amiably. "*Kameraden*, I'm a foreign journalist," he said in German and raised his correspondent tag. "Here's my ID."

The three plain-clothes continue closing in on him silently, spanning out, surrounding him as they got nearer.

Shit, this was not good. You didn't want to be caught alone in this sort of situation, every reporter knew that. Now he regretted not accepting Paul's invitation to join him and his friend from The Daily Telegraph.

"I'm an American journalist, guys," he said in English, then repeated it louder, in German, glancing quickly around. There was no one else nearby. He began backing off toward the main street. "Guys, guys, let's be civilized, okay? I give you my camera and we part ways amiably. Okay?" Jack took the camera off his neck and offered it to the Stasis.

His Leipzig minder reached him first. Without preamble, he struck at the camera with the baton, kicking it out of Jack's hands, smashing it to pieces. Another one grabbed at Jack's tag, snatched it and hurled it into the melee on the street.

The attack threw Jack completely off guard. He had assumed they had seen him shooting the crackdown and were after his camera, that they would only frisk him, rough him up a little. But not this. This was totally—

The blow would have caught Jack on the side of his head, hadn't his trained instincts kicked in. He ducked, raised both arms to cover his head, and the baton struck his shoulder. "Ow! What are you doing?!" he yelled. "You have no right! I'm an American citizen and I didn't break any law!"

They had obviously known that already. Two of the attackers grabbed Jack by the arms, holding him in place, while the third relieved him of his wallet, his swatch, his backpack and sent them flying into the middle of the crowd that was scuffling with the police. Now Jack had nothing on him to prove he was an American journalist.

They began to hit him.

He could easily wrestle out of their hands and even rough the three of them up in return. But by doing so he would have revealed his combat skills and raise questions about him. So he let them topple him to the ground, trying his best to protect his head and front from their vicious blows. However, when they lifted him up and manhandled him towards the truck, Jack panicked.

Fuck, no! They could beat him all they wanted but they mustn't detain him! Even if they didn't know he was a CIA officer, if he spent even an hour at the Stasi's quarters, the Company would recall him and God knew how long the post-arrest debrief at HQ would last. He couldn't let it happen. Not now!

Jack wrenched off the hands of the two Stasis holding him, shoved them aside and set off towards the river. But he hadn't made half a dozen steps when something hit him on the back. He blacked out for a second, then fell heavily on the ground, stunned and disoriented, all his muscles contracting wildly.

The next thing he knew he was being shoved into the back of a police truck together with several demonstrators. The Germans watched him sprawling on the bed of the truck, their eyes sympathetic, but nobody dared to help. Jack dragged himself up and slumped at the end of the bench near the tailgate, his hands and legs still shaking uncontrollably. "How could this happen? How could you let this happen, Smith?!" was all his brain could muster up.

As the truck took off along Spandauer Strasse, Jack caught the eyes of a man under a street lamp behind the police cordon. He was smartly dressed, his hair neatly combed and shining, as though heading to Palast of Republik for the party. His mind still hazy, Jack mechanically registered that the man held his eyes and nodded to him furtively. When he came to his senses from what he suspected had been an electroshock, he prayed to all gods that the man was his SD support.

He probably was, because at three o'clock in the morning, Terry Kellerman and the consular officer on duty came to get him out of the Stasi prison. The commandant apologized, said it had been a mistake, that Jack had been drunk and violent at the demonstration and hadn't had any papers on him. Jack said it was all bullshit and that his papers and the foreign correspondent tag had been taken from him by the men who had arrested him. The consular officer said the embassy would issue a note of protest to the ministry of foreign affairs the first thing in the morning and they left.

Jack spent the rest of the night in the Embassy's tiny medical office. When Tony McGuire, the Embassy's security officer, came in the morning, Jack gave him a detailed account of his arrest and the four and a half hours he had spent in detention. After tape-recording Jack's report, McGuire patted him on the back and told him to try not to get himself in yet another spy affair in East Germany.

Back in his apartment, Jack shed his clothes that stank of sweat, fear and prison damp, opened a new bottle of JD and trudged wearily to the bathroom. He turned on the hot water and climbed into the narrow bathtub without waiting for it to fill up. Having gulped down three mouthfuls straight from the bottle, he leaned back and closed his eyes.

He had been prepped for such situations, taught how to behave, how to hold himself together in the enemy's prison. He had been trained to withstand the enemy's "aggressive interrogation techniques". He'd read first and second hand accounts about communist regimes' prisons and gulags. But he hadn't been prepared to witness what he had seen there, let alone be one of thousands of detainees—all lined up in the courtyard the size of a football field, hands behind their heads, glaring projector lights piercing through the dark, air thick with cold autumn drizzle. It was like in a World War II movie which title he couldn't recall, and Jack wondered how different it was from the Nazi's prisons fifty years back. Then he thought of Eton and the three weeks his friend had spent in a Moscow prison. With criminals, Lara had said... And he asked himself if he was ready to spend twenty years in an American prison so that the man he loved could go free...

No, he didn't want to think about that. What he must think about was what's going to happen to him now, once he was back at HQ. Eight weeks before Eton was supposed to go... No, not "supposed to", but "*would*" go free. He would make damn sure it happened!

He sat in the bathtub until the steaming water went cold and the whiskey in the bottle was three fingers less than when he had started. Then he got out and went to bed.

When he woke up, Jack hurried to Terry's place that doubled as the AP's East Berlin office. He told his senior colleague he needed a week off. Then he asked Terry to repeat the story about how he had learned of Jack's arrest.

Terry had received a phone call shortly after midnight and the anonymous caller said that Jack had been arrested. No, the caller hadn't mentioned Jack's name, but said "your tall colleague with blue eyes" and yes, he'd spoken perfect German. As soon as the caller hung up, Terry phoned the Embassy, then drove up there to join the consular officer who was dispatched get Jack back from Hohenschönhausen Detention Center, the Stasi's main prison near its HQ in Karlhost.

"I've shot off a piece about your arrest and how we got you out. But what *you* should do, Jack, is write a feature. Not too many of us can boast that they've been inside a Stasi prison *and* got out that fast," Terry said with a laugh and poured Jack a generous portion of whiskey. "The only other person I know is Mike Demidoff who did a stint in the KGB prison. You've been in Moscow, you know him, don't you?"

Jack said he would think about the story, thanked the older man again for getting him out and left. He cruised around the city, trying to gauge if he was shadowed. He stopped by *Centrum* shopping center, had a late lunch at a bar on Unter den Linden. Nothing.

As the night fell, he packed his bags and drove to the safe house in West Berlin. Sure enough, there was a note from David waiting for him, together with a Lufthansa ticket to Frankfurt under his name early next morning and an American Airlines ticket from Frankfurt to Washington under a name Jack used often to get out of West Germany unnoticed.

Jack fetched a bottle of Johnny Walker and a bag of chips from the cupboard and spent most of the night writing his report on the arrest, then a feature story about people he had met at the demonstration in East Berlin. He knew an exhaustive debrief and polygraphing awaited him at HQ—he could take that. He just prayed that they would let him go back to East Berlin in a few days. He could even cope with a couple of weeks away. He recalled how the busted case officers who spent a few hours in the KGB prison in Moscow had been grilled afterwards—for at least a month, some even longer.

Yeah, but I have neither been busted nor expelled. They don't even bother to shadow me, for Christ's sake.

Exactly! They let you go, just like that. Why? You think chief Reilly and his boys won't be wondering?

Yeah, right, but had I been doubled up, wouldn't the Stasi have put on a show of covering me, maybe even kicking me out of the country for added authenticity? Nah, they did it to teach me a lesson... Right?

Maybe they knew that we'd be thinking along those lines. So they've let you go to compromise you in the Company's eyes and make the CI guys suspicious and ground you because you've been on their list for some time and so you'll be playing into their hands...

Whose list? Whose hands? This is so fucking twisted!

No shit... So just man up, Smith. You're taking the polygraph this time. You make damn sure it's squeaky clean. Eton's life depends on your lying skills.

Early next morning Jack flew to Frankfurt and from there to Washington DC.

The debrief took nearly twenty hours. He went through his account of the events on October 7th as well as the day before and after three times with three different sets of interviewers. After the first session, Jack was told that he would be polygraphed the following day. Jack responded that he was stressed and tired and had been drinking too. So while he was prepared to be "fluttered" any time, he thought in his state he would probably blow it even without lying.

He told Joe Coburn the same at their one-on-one meeting in his office that night.

The Division Chief studied him in silence for a long moment, then shook his head and said, "Just prepare yourself well." He let Jack go shortly after.

He was polygraphed on the morning of the third day. The session lasted for ninety minutes and the questions were strictly on his detention and his possible recruitment by the Stasi or the KGB. No personal questions, or questions about the agents he ran, or had run, were asked. At the end of the session, the polygraph operator, a soft-spoken man in his mid-fifties, shook Jack's hand and told him that he'd be advised about the results by his direct superior.

After fluttering, Jack was told to go to the infirmary for a medical checkup, then "go home" and have some rest.

He didn't have a home, so he spent a day and a half at the hotel doing what he'd been told: resting, sleeping, drinking beer, watching football on TV, eating junk food, then sleeping some more. And trying not to think. Not even about Eton.

Especially not about Eton.

Joe Coburn's secretary called in the early afternoon on Thursday and said the chief wanted to see him in an hour. Forty-five minutes later Jack was waiting in his front office.

Joe patted his back, said, "Well done," and that Jack was cleared. He also said that a decision had been made to respond to the anonymous letter offering access to the Stasi files. The planning was scheduled for Friday morning and after that Jack was to fly back to the field immediately.

After the meeting with Joe, Jack spent two hours with two seniors from the Directorate of Intel—the analytics people. Their questions revolved around the situation in East Germany. They didn't want to hear hard facts—they had all the facts they wanted at their disposal already. What they wanted to know was intangible things, like what people thought, what they looked forward to, what little changes were happening day to day. Jack tried his best to describe people's mood, their increasing weariness that he'd seen lately, and their impatience that felt close to boiling over.

"Something's bound to happen in that place, sooner or later," he concluded and raked all ten fingers through his hair. "It's just a matter of time."

"Like what?" the older of the two analysts, Tom, asked.

"I don't know. People are already demonstrating, right? From what I've heard, the one in Leipzig three days ago gathered over seventy thousand people. How far is that from a revolution?"

Tom smiled politely and started collecting his papers. "You really think so? After what happened to you and all those demonstrators last week?... Anyway, thank you for your time, Jack. We appreciate your input."

They stood up, shook hands with Jack and left.

Yeah, right, they probably thought he was off his rocker after a night in the Stasi's prison. Alright, so he'd been a bit stressed out and had had one too many in the last five days. But he also knew what he'd seen with his own eyes, as opposed to what they could see from their tiny windowless rooms in the middle of the capital of all fucking politics.

When Jack arrived at the meeting room for the op planning the next morning, he was met by David Rolston, the deputy heads of CI and Ops and—surprise, surprise!—Savannah Jones.

She gave Jack a firm handshake, a quick hug and whispered, "We'll talk later."

Jack nodded, not caring whether she noticed the surge of weariness that engulfed him at her pleased little smile.

He was told right away that, in view of the recent developments, it had been decided to accelerate the planned enhancement of Jack's security support—in the form of a girlfriend with a diplomatic cover. Officer Jones had been selected for this assignment and would start her new posting as a PR and communications assistant at the Embassy in East Berlin on November 1st. Furthermore, to protect both Jack and the assets in his portfolio, he would be gradually handing over SALT, PIPER1 and PIPER2 to case officer Jones. The handover process would begin as soon as Savannah re-located to East Berlin, preferably before SALT's return to Moscow.

Great! Just fucking great! Getting saddled with Savannah right now was *just* what he needed, with only six weeks before the C-Day.

But that wasn't all. Savannah had also been assigned to the security detail covering Pat Richmond's planned meeting with SALT in East Berlin. For that purpose, a five-day diplomatic visa had been obtained for her—officially, for a pre-assignment trip before her upcoming posting. However, due to security concerns in relation to Jack's recent detention, the Deputy Division Chief's trip had been canceled and SALT's assessment interview postponed till Moscow. Nevertheless, it had been decided that Savannah was still coming out and would be accompanying Jack to the banquet that Lara had invited him to at the instigation of a KGB operative.

It took Jack a major effort to ward off anxious thoughts about how he was going to introduce Savannah to Eton and Lara and concentrate on the briefing. Suddenly his pal Savannah with her easygoing ways and big friendly grin was a great big liability. Even an outright threat. The only benefit he and Eton gained from all this was that Eton's assessment and fluttering was now put on hold.

The next briefing session was on Jack and Savannah's legend—on how to position her with Jack's agents, targets and friends—as well as on their joint objectives and targets in

East Germany. They were told that "upstairs" had decided that, given his current unique situation, SALT would be expected to deliver as much as possible while he was still in East Germany—*before* the interview and polygraphing, as it happened. The target info was the operational manuals of the new missile system at his base. Then they discussed the potential ops dates and alternative dates, modes of contacts, communication channels, operational and counter surveillance support, tools and other tradecraft issues. Savannah was asked to prepare the ops brief for approval.

Thus, the case handover promised by Joe had officially commenced.

By the time the case planning was done, it was nearly 2:00 p.m. They all grabbed a quick bite in the cafeteria, then Jack and Savannah went to prepare for their departures to West Berlin that night—with different airlines.

He didn't sleep at all during the flight back, imagining various scenarios of Savannah's first meeting with Lara and Eton. The thought of introducing her as his ex-girlfriend, and then pretending that he was getting back together with her, made him feel sick. Worst of all, he couldn't tell Eton that Savannah was also with the Company, that their relationship was only a cover. Not right away. He had already broken every single rule by keeping secret his involvement with his agent, as well as by telling his lover plenty of things he shouldn't have, but blowing Savannah's cover even before she arrived at the duty station? It was the worst thing that could befall a case officer and Jack could not do that to her. It wasn't her fault he was head over heels in love with his agent. Who was, by the way, a guy. The smartest, most gorgeous and loving guy—person!—Jack had ever met. He felt trapped in an impossible situation.

God, why did his life have to be so fucked up all the time?

Jack got home on Saturday morning and found seven messages waiting for him on his answering machine. Three of them were from Lara and one from Savannah.

"*Privet*, Jack. It's me. Please call me back. I need to talk to you. About the reception. *Poka, daragusha!*"

"*Privet*, Jack. It's me again. Where have you disappeared? Call me please. The reception is this Saturday after the show. And I have four tickets for you for Saturday night, too. For you and your friends. Please call."

"Jack, this is Lara. If you don't call me before five today, don't bother calling me ever again. *Poka.*"

"Hello Jack, it's me, Sevan. I'm in West Berlin, staying at Savigny hotel, near Ku'damm. I was on the flight here with your buddy Peter and he gave me your phone number. It would be totally awesome to catch up, Jackie! I haven't seen you for ages! Hope you've shaven off your ugly beard. (Giggle). Anyway, call me at 8813001, room 51. Or better still, come for diner. Or breakfast. Or both, if you want. (Giggle). I'll be here till next Monday. Isn't that great? Ciaaao, baby!"

Yeah, right... He regretted the day he had told Joe that he wanted to marry Savannah.

Of course, the Savannah who'd left a message on his answering machine was only a cover. Not too dissimilar to his own, in fact. Still, he didn't need it, didn't need her here right now and definitely not as his girlfriend.

Okay, so eventually Eton would learn that she was with the Company—when Jack handed the case over to her. *Then* he would tell Eton that Savannah with her diplomatic passport was only his cover, his security support. *Then* Eton would hopefully understand that this was just something Jack had to do—like he and Lara, right? But for now, for this coming weekend...

For the first time since Eton had come back to him, or maybe for the first time ever, Jack didn't look forward to seeing him.

Chapter 70

The first thing Jack did after opening his suitcase was call Lara. He apologized profusely for not returning her call right away, said he'd had some problems with local police and had taken a few days off, out of the country. Naturally, he wouldn't dream of missing her gala show and was it possible to bring his friends to the banquet, too? She answered sulkily at first, but her tone softened when she heard about Jack's problems. Yes, of course, Jack could bring his friends to the reception that would be taking place at the theater after the show. He desperately wanted to ask if Eton got his LOA, but knew he shouldn't talk about him on the phone. So he was both disappointed and glad that Lara didn't mention him either.

By noon, Jack was in the lobby of the Savigny hotel. In a few minutes, Savannah stormed down and gave him a breathless greeting, as if they were high school sweethearts who hadn't seen each other for decades. Jack had to make a major effort to match her enthusiasm. Once they had "reacquainted", he gave Savannah a short tour of Ku'damm, followed by a lunch at a cozy little restaurant near Kaiser Wilhelm Gedachtniskirche. Having picked up Savannah's evening dress at her hotel, they crossed over to East Berlin where Jack brought her to his apartment.

The moment the door closed behind them, they launched into a steamy sex session. It was part of their meticulously worked out plan—for the benefit of the eavesdropping Stasi. Somehow, Jack felt that it wasn't just work for Savannah. The way she clung to him, and that dazed expression on her face as he thrust into her, it was like it meant something to her. Suddenly it made him feel guilty and disappointed with himself.

Oh, c'mon, it was just a fuck, the good old cover, for his job and more importantly for his identity, right? He had done this many times before, so why should he feel this way now? Surely, Eton and Lara had sex too. They were husband and wife, for God's sake! Lara had a voracious appetite for sex, and Eton... Eton was always horny... Just like him. So of course they...

Shit, he'd been doing quite well not thinking about *that*. Why now all of a sudden? Damn you, Savannah!

At quarter to seven, Paul, Helen, Savannah and Jack were standing in the foyer of the Metropol Theater, the women in little black dresses and pearls, the men with flowers intended for the leading lady of the night, Larissa Novikova-Volkonskaya. For their gala evening show, the LenKom company was playing the original version of "Juno and Avos" with the original leading actor, Nikolai Karachentsov, hence neither Karelin's nor Eton's names featured on the posters. There was no sign of Eton in the theater either. Jack hadn't managed to get hold of Lara before the show started and didn't know if Eton was coming up to see her.

But perhaps it was better that way. Because when Jack and his friends got to their seats in the first row of the dress circle, they found themselves in the company of at least a dozen Soviet diplomats. Jack immediately ticked off those he'd met or knew through their files at HQ: the *rezidents*, heads of the KGB's East Berlin and Dresden *rezidenturas*, Felix and Chengiz from the Soviet Embassy, Volodya from Dresden and a few others who Jack figured were KGB too, all accompanied by their wives.

Felix "recognized" Jack immediately. He jumped up from his seat and thrust his hand in Jack's over the heads of his colleagues. They stood up too and shook hands with Savannah, Helen and Paul. Volodya slapped Jack on his arm as though they were old friends who hadn't seen each other in years. Jack pretended he was trying to recall which year it was that they had first met.

"January eighty six," Volodya prompted with a tight-lipped smile that looked like a grimace, his pale blue eyes skimming over Savannah.

"Savannah, this is Volodya. He's just reminded me that we met back in '86. Savannah doesn't speak Russian," Jack said while the Russian was shaking hands with her. "But she'll be coming to work in Berlin soon."

"*Ich lerne Deutsch zu sprechen.*" Savannah beamed at the short, skinny Russian who was still holding her hand, then turned to his wife, a plump, dyed blonde with tired eyes who was trying hard to look indifferent. "I'm Savannah. So pleased to meet you."

"Lyuba." The woman gave Savannah a limp handshake, her lips twitching weakly.

The wives of the other Soviet diplomats were a little more enthusiastic and their smiles were a touch friendlier, but mostly they were busily assessing their Western counterparts' evening attires.

When everybody had settled in their places, Savannah leaned in, her lips brushing Jack's ear, and whispered, "Am I a lucky girl or what? Off the plane and right into the lions' den." She nuzzled Jack's cheek.

"Don't overdo it, please," Jack whispered back, wearily forcing a grin.

Savannah giggled and slapped his arm playfully. "Bad boy!"

Jack caught Helen's bemused glance and Peter's cheeky smirk and silently thanked God that Eton hadn't got his leave after all.

The closing reception was held at the cafe on the lower lobby of the theater. A long table was laid out in the middle, overflowing with banquet-style food—canapés, cold cuts, fruits and chocolate cakes. And booze, lots of it. The only difference from banquets Jack had seen in Moscow was that the thin line of Stolichnaya and Soviet Champagne was far outnumbered by the battery of schnapps and Wodka Gorbatschow that Germans favored.

The reception crowd consisted of actors, musicians, journalists and diplomats, mostly Soviet and German, but also a few Czechs, Bulgarians, and Yugoslavs.

In fifteen minutes, Helen and Paul excused themselves and left, followed by Volodya's and Felix's wives soon after, leaving Jack and Savannah in the company of Soviet diplomats most of whom, they both knew, were KGB. As usual, Jack was doing the heavy lifting in the conversation, acting as Savannah's translator at the same time. He told the Russians about his encounter with the Stasi at the demonstration, which explained the fading bruise on the left side of his face. Jack skipped the few hours he had spent at the Stasi's detention center though, figuring whoever wanted to know more would eventually find out, but he shouldn't incense the Stasi more that he apparently had already.

Lara showed up half an hour into the party, on the arm of the leading man, Nicolai Karachentsov. The actor's annoyed expression was replaced by a broad, charitable grin of a star as soon as the guests turned to the pair with congratulations on another successful tour. Lara's eyes found Jack, registered his presence and his company, then she returned her attention to the Soviet Consul General who was toasting her and her companion.

A few minutes later, she made her way to their group, which by now had dwindled down to Savannah, Jack, Felix and Volodya. The three men kissed Lara's hand gallantly and congratulated her yet again, then Jack introduced Savannah to her. Lara's grand smile never faltered as she offered her fingers to the excitedly grinning American woman, but her eyes narrowed almost imperceptibly. After a minute of pleasantries, she asked Jack to step aside with her.

They stopped in the alcove near the staircase.

"So, is that your new girlfriend?" Lara asked pointedly and took a sip of her Champagne.

Jack resigned mentally and shrugged. "No, not really. We've known each other for a long time. She was a colleague at the USIA in Washington. *Before* my Moscow posting."

"What does it mean, 'not really'? *Is* she your girlfriend or *isn't* she?"

"Lara, I just reconnected with her yesterday. I haven't seen her for ages!"

"Ah, she *was* your girlfriend then... So you like her more than me." She looked both curious and indignant. "May I ask why? She's all bones and her mouth is too big. Is she, oh sorry, *was* she good in bed?"

"Oh, come on, Lara!" Jack rolled his eyes.

"So you are not going to tell me why her and not me then?"

"It was a long time ago, for God's sake!"

"What was long time ago? Her or me?"

"Lara, please! You *know* I couldn't. I was a diplomat. We weren't supposed to—"

"Give me a break, Jack! We do many things we aren't supposed to when we want them badly enough... Don't we?" She peered into Jack's eyes, pressing her lips together, then sighed dramatically. "Alright, I forgive you this time. You had your reasons, and I had... other options. *Da?*"

Jack bowed his head. "I'm sorry."

"Anyway, it wasn't what I was looking for you for. Eton is here... No, not *here*. At the hotel. He hates banquets. I wanted to ask if you want... will have time to have lunch with us tomorrow."

"Yes, of course, Lara. When, where?"

"Call me in the morning. Around eight o'clock... Is *she* staying with you?"

Jack ignored the jibe. "No, she's staying in West Berlin. But even if she'd stayed with me, it wouldn't mean I had to take her everywhere."

Not yet. Hopefully, not ever.

Lara studied him for a moment, then nodded. "*Ladno*, alright. We'll be having a night cap before we break for the night. Just a small circle of... friends. Please join." It sounded like more than just an invitation and she glared at him emphatically for good measure.

Jack nodded obediently. "Alright. I will join you. But I'll need to leave at eleven. I have to take Savannah back to West Berlin and return before checkpoints close for the night."

"Alright... And tell your *not-really-girlfriend* she's invited to join us, too."

By the time the group of "friends" Lara mentioned had gathered around the buffet table for a round of last drinks, most of them were high. Or at least faking it—Jack had little doubt about that. The latter included Savannah, their new KGB "friends" Volodya and Felix and himself. Laughing loudly and repeating that she was with Jack, Savannah parried Volodya's flagrant courting in Russian, peppered with English words he knew. She also put on an animated show of fighting Volodya's attempts to get her drunk.

Felix caught Jack in the restroom and advised him to be vigilant with Volodya or he would steal his girlfriend. "Our Volodya is known for, um, *adopting* things that belong to others," he said, slurring his words a little, and laughed.

Jack confided that Savannah was his ex-girlfriend, and he had only met her again the day before after a long time. Standing in the corridor, they bantered for a while about Savannah, Lara, Western and Russian women in general. Before returning to the table, Felix said they should get together for a drink, maybe at Stadt Hotel's bar where there were always great girls and music—well, if Jack liked all that too. Of course Jack did, so they shook hands on that, patting each other's shoulders.

At 11:00 p.m., Jack announced that he had to take Savannah back to West Berlin and started shaking hands with their new friends, slapping backs and kissing goodbye the Russian way.

Lara whispered in his ear, "Call me tomorrow morning."

Felix said under his breath, shaking hands with Jack, "Remember what I said: be careful with him," and screwed his eyes at Volodya.

The latter insisted on seeing Savannah off to the taxi. He helped her into her coat, offered his arm and led her up the staircase to the lobby on the ground floor.

Jack was held back for a minute by Felix who insisted on exchanging phone numbers, so when he caught up with Savannah and Volodya, they were already standing on the pavement in front of the entrance.

Savannah was either acting very well or really tipsy, holding on to Volodya's arm, laughing and talking loudly. "Volodya, you are a bad boy!... No! I can't!"

Volodya, at least three inches shorter than Savannah in her high heels, leaned into her and said something.

She giggled drunkenly. "*Nein*, Volodya, ahm with Jack. *Ich bin, ah, mit Jack.*" She was slurring badly. "We gonna, um, get married. Meh-rid, you understand, you silly thing? Like you and Lyuba. *Ahm mit* Jack."

Jack came up and took her under the other arm. "Come on, Savannah. Let's get you back to the hotel. You've had enough for today, girl." He smiled tightly at Volodya, displaying thinly veiled displeasure. "Thank you for taking care of my girlfriend," he said in Russian.

"You should really look after such a beauty better." The Russian who barely came up to Jack's nose slapped him on the back, but his exaggeratedly friendly smile did not reach his pale eyes. "Even when she becomes your wife. There are always people around who wouldn't hesitate to take care of what's not well looked after." He turned to Savannah again, took her hand and kissed it gallantly. "I'll see you around, beautiful."

Jack helped tottering Savannah into a taxi at the curb and walked around the back of the vehicle to the other side. As he was opening the door to climb in, he caught sight of a tall, lanky figure not twenty yards from the entrance. The man was walking away in the opposite direction, hands in his jacket pockets, shoulders hunched like he was expecting a blow in his back.

Jack almost groaned aloud. It was Eton.

* * *

He called Lara's hotel at 8:00 a.m. sharp the next morning, praying that she would answer the phone, not Eton. She did and their conversation was short: she confirmed the meeting and told him to meet her by the fountain on Alexanderplatz at 12:00 p.m., the *Centrum* side. Or inside the department store, near the door if it rained.

She paused before asking, "Will you come alone?"

"Of course, Lara. I told you."

"Alright. *Poka*." She hung up before Jack could respond.

By the time he installed himself under the concrete staircase in front of *Centrum* department store, Jack had been to West Berlin for a breakfast with Savannah, run a few errands in West and then East Berlin, both as part of his cover. Then he had done a surveillance detection routine before heading to the meeting place—mostly because of Eton. He expected them to take the U-Bahn, which meant they would have to pass the external staircase on their way to the fountain. He thought he wasn't followed—he had been covered only sporadically since his arrest. But he knew he should never be too confident, especially about his counter surveillance support.

As he had expected, they entered the plaza from the side of Alexanderplatz U-Bahn station. Lara stormed past Jack, pretty lips pouted, eyes blazing. Eton was strolling behind her, his shoulders up, head down, hands in the jacket pockets.

"Eton," Jack called softly as his friend was passing the staircase.

Eton whipped around, his shoulders and hands instantly falling into a defensive boxer's position: left shoulder forward, fists up, covering the chin, eyes wild, unseeing.

Jack's chest constricted. "Eton, it's me." He stepped out from behind the concrete flight of the stairs, not sure if he should come any closer.

Eton's eyes focused. He straightened up, took a step back and stuffed his hands back in his pockets. "Sorry," he mumbled, turning to look after his wife. "Lara!"

Lara was nearing the entrance of the department store. She whirled around. "What now?" she snapped, but brightened at the sight of Jack. "Jack, *privet*! Are you waiting for us here? Excellent! We're going into *Centrum*." She took a step closer to the doorway, stopped and threw a quick glance over her shoulder to see if the men were following her. "Come on, boys! Don't just stand there like statues. Let's go inside."

Eton followed her without even a side-glance at Jack. He wore his old impenetrable mask and Jack prayed uncharitably that Lara was the cause of his friend's surliness, not him.

"Everything alright?" Jack asked quietly, bumping into him as both were passing through the glass door. He caught a whiff of alcohol fumes laced with the fresh, strong smell of tobacco.

Eton didn't answer, just shrugged, eyes fixed on Lara who breezed across the atrium towards a restaurant at the back of the building, not a glimmer of doubt that both men were close on her heels.

Unlike the busy cafeteria near the entrance, the rather Spartan-looking but spacious and neat restaurant was virtually empty. They chose a table against the wall and sat down.

A short, plump waitress with dyed jet-black hair brought them the menus.

"Vodka Gorbachov two hundred grams, cold cuts, pickles and bread," Eton said in fairly good German, without even opening the menu.

"Eton!" Lara hissed.

"You can go now, if you want," Eton said flatly. He pulled out his cigarettes and turned to the waitress again. "And an ashtray please."

The girl didn't bat an eye, said, "In a moment", and disappeared.

"Guys, guys, don't quarrel, I beg you," Jack admonished his friends cautiously. He had never seen them fighting and wasn't sure what he should say or do.

Lara stopped glaring at Eton and turned to him. "Jack, I have to leave shortly."

"Oh... Something happened?" Jack threw a worried glance at Eton.

"I've promised a friend I'll come visit his studio. And today is my last day in Berlin, as you know," she said matter-of-factly, not the least bit apologetic. "He'll come to pick me up in fifteen or twenty minutes."

Jack looked at her wide-eyed. "I see... Are you leaving, too?" he asked Eton.

"No. I don't have any *boyfriend* whom I've promised to visit today," Eton spat out, his tone dripping sarcasm.

Jesus! What the fuck, Eton?!

"Oh, shut up, Eton, will you?!" Lara exclaimed. "We have an agreement, haven't we? Haven't we? What is the matter with you today?!... Sorry, Jack." She looked both pissed off and resigned.

Eton stood up abruptly, almost toppling the chair, and headed toward the door.

"Where are you going now? Eton!" Lara called after him, her tone exasperated.

"Toilet," he threw over his shoulder without stopping and disappeared in the corridor outside.

Lara sat back and closed her eyes. "I'm sorry for this, Jack. He has been impossible since last night. I think he's having a relapse. Oh, dear God! He was doing so well since... lately. And now this again!"

"Can you tell me what happened, Lara?" He thought he knew what had happened, but prayed that he was wrong.

"I don't know... I got back to the hotel last night and found him drunk. He has been drinking and smoking the whole night, refused to go to bed, and I… I just don't know what to do with him anymore, Jack." She sounded like a little lost girl.

"Maybe he doesn't like you going out with other guys?"

You're such an asshole, Smith! It is because of you that he is like this today. Give her a break!

He reached across and took her hand. "I'm sorry, sweetie… Tell me what I can do for you."

"I was thinking maybe you can talk sense into him, Jack. He listens to you. I know he does," she insisted when Jack tried to object. "Maybe not right away today, but eventually he will. *Kharasho*, alright? Please, Jack!"

"Alright, I'll try." He needed to talk to Eton anyway, right?

"Oh, thank you, Jack!" She squeezed his hand with both of hers. "Thank you so much!… You know, I'd better go before he returns. I think I'm annoying him terribly today for some reason. He usually doesn't mind me, um, *going out*; even teases me about it. But today… I don't know what fly has bitten him. You don't mind me leaving him with you in such a, uh, unmanageable state, do you, Jack? I think he'll calm down with you. Honestly!" She smiled sweetly at Jack, stood up and picked up her handbag. "I'll be back in three, three and a half hours at most, alright?" She leaned in and kissed him on the cheek. "Thank you, *daragusha*! You are the best friend!"

The next moment she was gone.

The waitress had brought out vodka, cold cuts and an ashtray and left. Jack was starting to get worried when Eton finally returned to the table. His crew cut hair was damp and when his eyes locked with Jack's for a moment, Jack noticed that they were bloodshot. He looked dead tired, so unlike the last couple of times they had met.

"She's gone, hasn't she?" His voice was gruff and tired too.

"Yes, she has. She said she would be back in three hours and a half… Eton, listen. We need to talk."

Eton barked out a laugh, his expression was one of exaggerated disbelief. "To talk?! You said 'to talk'? I've heard *that* before… No, Jack, we *don't* need to talk. This is not Leningrad for you and I am not twenty-one. Not anymore."

Chapter 71

Jack winced. "You were at the theater last night, weren't you?"

He didn't sound guilty, did he? Why should he be? He'd just been doing his job... Right?

"Yes, I was. I was stupid for—" Eton choked out a bitter laugh. "I can't believe we're having this conversation again. Everything has changed. *We* have changed. Yet, here we are, in Berlin, having the same conversation we had three and a half years ago. This is just so... *fucking* unbelievable!" He poured himself a shot glass full of vodka, knocked it back and lit a cigarette. His hands were shaking.

Shit!

Jack swallowed, then cleared his throat. "Eton, I'm truly sorry for making it sound old, but we *have* to talk, bud... It isn't what you think."

"And what do you think I think?" There was a challenge in his question, but not his tone. He sounded resigned as though his outburst and the vodka had doused all the anger that had been burning inside him.

"It's about the woman you saw last night, isn't it? It is *not* what it seems, Eton. Why don't we finish with the lunch and go somewhere we can talk... What do you say?"

Eton stopped inspecting the burning tip of his cigarette and raised his eyes. "You're going to tell me that you have to do it, right? That it's like me and Lara?"

Goddamn! How did he do it, reading Jack's mind like it was an open book?

"*Please*, Eton." What else could he say? He hoped that Eton wouldn't make him beg because—

No, Eton wouldn't do such a thing to him. Not his Eton.

Eton exhaled deeply, blowing out all the air in his lungs, and closed his eyes. When he opened them again and met Jack's, he looked drained, but his eyes were soft and unbearably sad. "Alright. Let's go to a place where we can talk."

They took U-Bahn to Rosenthaler Platz station, then sprinted under the rain in the general direction of the derelict building two streets away from Jack's apartment block. It housed Jack's safe haven in its concealed basement, as well as a regular safe house on the top floor where Jack had taken Eton to once before. What could have been a five-minute jog from the station took them half an hour of darting in and out of entranceways of apartment buildings, groceries stores and bookshops. He could see that Eton was ticked off by this routine, but Jack couldn't afford to take any more risks than he already had—dashing around together for thirty minutes didn't even closely qualify as a counter-surveillance run.

It was quarter to two when they finally got into the empty, rundown apartment on the fourth floor. Now they only had an hour for the talk.

Jack locked the door behind them and took off his jacket. "Sorry, I haven't prepared anything today," he said as he shook the rainwater off on the defaced floor. "Didn't think we would be coming here."

"It's fine. We have to go back in an hour anyway, right?" Eton gave his black bomber jacket a couple good shakes and dropped it on the floor. He turned to Jack. "So, what did you want to tell me?"

Right. Savannah.

No, you can't do that!

He took a deep breath. "The woman you saw last night. Her name is Savannah…"

Eton watched him solemnly, like he'd already made up his mind that he'd accept whatever Jack was going to tell him.

"She's, um, my colleague. My security support. Because she's got a diplomatic passport."

You are so fucked, Smith!

"And she'll be taking you… your case over. She'll be your handler."

"What?! Why?" Eton's air of resignation had evaporated and suddenly he was all concerned.

"I was detained by Stasi last Saturday when I was covering a demonstration. It was nothing," he quickly added, seeing Eton's face firing up with alarm. "They just roughed me up a little for taking pictures of the anti-government protest. The embassy got me out a couple of hours later."

"Are you alright? Did they, um, beat you?" Eton closed in on him, peering anxiously into his face.

"Nothing to worry about. Just a few bruises that's all." He would tell Eton about what he'd seen in the detention center later. One day…

Eton yanked him into his arms and pressed his lips into the side of Jack's face. They stood like that for a long moment, clenched in a tight embrace, breathing in each other's scent, then Eton extracted himself carefully from Jack's arms and took a step back. "So why is this wo… your colleague is, uh, 'taking me over', if you're okay?"

Jack shrugged. "Well… I guess they're wary that I might have been, um, compromised in the detention center."

"You mean they don't trust you anymore? Because you were arrested?"

"It comes with the job. You have to suspect everybody for everything." He shrugged again. "Good thing is they've let me come back… With Savannah and her diplomatic passport as my security backup."

Eton shuffled his feet, his eyes fixed on something over Jack's shoulder. "Are you going to marry her?"

So he had heard Savannah's jabber, too. Jack puffed out a breath and raised his hands. "It doesn't mean anything." He shook his head emphatically. "It's just part of the job."

"Do you, um, sleep with her?"

"For God's sake, Eton! I *have* to, alight? You do know this whole country is bugged, don't you? If I'm introducing a woman around as my girlfriend, do you think the Stasi will buy it if I don't sleep with her? It means *nothing*! It's just like you and Lara, okay?"

"No, it's not."

"What do you mean 'it's not'?" Jack stared at him. "You mean you and Lara... You don't...?"

"No." Eton ears and forehead went pink. "Only once. We were both drunk... It won't happen again."

So they don't have sex... Wait a minute, is he expecting me *not* to have sex even with women? That's ridiculous!

"But it's just me. May be different for you." Eton picked up his jacket from the floor, fished out the cigarettes, lit one and walked stiffly past Jack toward the smaller room at the back.

Jack followed Eton into the used-to-be bedroom and found him sitting on the ragged mattress on the floor, leaning back against the wall, smoking. He sat down next to him, put a hand on his thigh and rubbed it softly. "I don't know what to say."

"Don't have to say anything. I just needed to know." He took a couple of quick puffs on the cigarette before offering it to Jack. "It's easier for me to... cope if I know for sure. Easier than to keep wondering."

"Sorry, bud, but I have no choice. I *have* to do it, for my work and... in general. I have to be... like everybody in my line of work. You understand, don't you?... Eton?"

Eton nodded distractedly. He reached out and took the cigarette back from Jack's fingers.

Dammit, Eton! Say something!

But Eton continued smoking without a word, staring at the wall in front of them.

Jack changed the subject. "Can I ask where Lara's gone? And what was going on with you two back there?"

That got Eton's attention: he cut Jack a quick glance. "You think it's related to the organs... Right?" When Jack didn't respond he shrugged. "It's not. She is... she's having affairs."

"Affairs?? As in 'many'?"

Eton rolled his eyes at Jack's quizzical look. "You know Lara. One at a time is not enough for her... She is having an affair with her leading man, Nikolai. Who's married. And is the jealous type. She told him she would be with me. So that she can go visit her German *friend* Matthias... Sometimes I just don't understand her." He crushed the spent cigarette onto the floor and lit a new one.

Jack reached for it and took a deep drag. He didn't like it that Eton was taking Lara's shenanigans *that* much to heart—you're only jealous when you... "Are you jealous or what?" he asked, trying to keep his tone light.

Eton's head went up again. "What?! No, it's not *that*..." He retrieved the cigarette from Jack fingers and stuck it in between his lips. "It's just... I shouldn't have come to the theater last night... I wanted to see you," he muttered and blew a big cloud of smoke.

"I'm sorry," Jack whispered.

"You were doing your job, right? Nor is it Lara's fault... By the way, this morning she didn't tell me that you had brought that girl to the banquet. Not a word. And she usually likes gossiping as you know." He gave Jack an emphatic look. "You can trust her, Jack. She knows when to be discreet and how to keep a secret."

Once again, Jack didn't know what to say. And he had thought he knew the Russians well. Or maybe it was just these two. His friends. His *best* friends. From the wrong side of the world.

When Jack had digested what he'd learned about his friends and the business-minded part of his brain had resumed its churning, he briefed Eton on what the Agency was expecting of him before his departure back to Moscow: a photocopy of the operating manual of the missile system at his base. However, he noted, Eton's drinking last night, and this morning was actually turning out rather opportune. He would report back to HQ that his agent was having a relapse, proving to be unstable, thus couldn't be trusted with intel collection and tradecraft equipment. So it wouldn't be a bad idea at all if Eton continued drinking for another couple of days, and the more visible his *zapoy* was the better. He just hoped that Eton wouldn't get into too much trouble when he returned to his unit intoxicated.

Eton smirked. "That's not a problem. Not something the base hasn't seen before."

Then Jack told him about his preparations for the crossing. Eton's new ID and supporting documents were all ready and waiting to be smuggled into East Berlin; a support group of two American students and one West German was on standby; a detailed plan of the crossing had been worked out, including a backup plan with an alternate crossing point. Now all they needed was a three-hour meeting, or better two meetings, for Jack to run Eton through all the details. With six weeks to go until the end of November, they needed to fix the C-Day as soon as possible so that Jack could start working out the shifts at the two selected checkpoints. And Eton would need to arrange two leaves of absence to come up to Berlin.

Eton was distracted and edgy during Jack's briefing, chain smoking, nervously bouncing one of his stretched out legs. Jack thought it was all the alcohol he had consumed since last night, so he decided to leave the details till the next time.

When their hour had run out, Jack said it would be better if Eton went back and waited for Lara alone. "We should avoid being seen together in the open, unless it's absolutely necessary. Alright?" He stood up from the floor.

Eton nodded and got up too, his eyes firmly fixed on the broken floor.

"You can go straight to the U-Bahn station. Fifteen minutes and you're at *Centrum*... Do you remember how to get here from the station? For the next time."

"Yes."

"Good... And please tell Lara I'm sorry I won't be able to come to see her off tomorrow. I have to take Savannah to the airport. I'll call her tonight. But you let her know, too. Okay?"

"Okay."

They walked in silence to the door where Eton picked up his jacket from the floor and put it on. All without even a glance in Jack's direction.

Jack sighed. He didn't like his friend's alcohol-induced mood swings when he needed all his attention and concentration. "Eton, what's wrong? If it's about Savannah, don't you—"

"They are sending us home earlier than planned. The whole division." Eton was finally looking at Jack, biting on his bottom lip, his eyes full of anguish. "I'm leaving on November tenth."

"*What*?! Goddamn it, Eton! Why didn't you tell me earlier?" Jack threw his hands up in the air. He was mad and beginning to panic, and the fear made him even angrier. "We have just wasted one fucking hour, now that we don't have time to lose!!"

Eton stepped up and put his arms around Jack's waist. "I'm sorry, cowboy, I should have told you earlier... I don't think this will work. I want to do this very much, please believe me. But as you said, we don't have time. I have to go back to Moscow."

Jack wrestled out of his arms. "No! You can't go back!" He took a deep breath, willing himself to wind down. "It *will* work, Eton. Don't you doubt it." He grabbed Eton by the shoulders, peering into his eyes. "We can make it, bud. All you need to do is to come to Berlin. Only once. Three hours. Three hours of your time is all I need to prepare you for the crossing... Can you do it, Eton? For me?"

Jack saw hope fighting doubt and despair on his lover's face and losing. Eton fumbled for his cigarettes, pulled one out and stuck it in the corner of his mouth. Then he changed his mind, pushed it back in the pack, then the pack into his jacket pocket.

Finally, he looked up and heaved a sigh. "I will try, Jack. But I need to be mentally prepared that I may *have* to return... I'll wait for you to come back to Moscow."

Shit, it was a disaster in the making. He shouldn't be thinking like this. He'd never make it if he got too comfortable falling back on the idea that he would return to Moscow and Jack would eventually follow him there.

"With all the shit that happened last week I don't think they'll let me go back to Moscow. That's why Savannah is taking you over here and now. I don't know when... or *if* I'll be able to come."

Don't give up on me, baby!

"Eton, listen. If you're giving up on me... on *us*, tell me now. I can't pull it off if you're not with me hundred percent... I'll come and find you in the West, bud, as soon as I can. But I can't promise that I'll come to Moscow." Of course, he would, no matter what, even to Moscow, Jack knew it by now. But he had to give Eton the last push.

It worked. Jack could see on Eton's face that he had made up his mind.

"Of course I'm with you, Jack. Please never doubt it. I will come to Berlin."

As there were only three weekends left until Friday, November 10th, they agreed that Eton would come up on Saturday, October 28th. Eton said that demobilizing soldiers were usually allowed to do their last shopping in Berlin before departure, so they decided that the C-Day would be either Saturday, November 4th or Sunday, November 5th—depending when Eton was granted his last LOA.

Jack gave him the phone number of a local bar he had been frequenting lately and said he'd be there every Monday, Wednesday and Friday between 8:00pm and 9:00pm—in case there was something urgent and Eton needed to let him know. If Jack wasn't there on those days, Eton was to call on the following due day.

When it was time for Eton to leave, they clenched in a full-bodied embrace, their lips locked in a bruising kiss. Jack could feel that his lover was desperately trying not to be overwhelmed by his doubts and fears, not unlike Jack himself, and he whispered fiercely in his ear, "We'll make it, Eton. I swear."

On Tuesday in West Berlin Jack debriefed with David Rolston about the reception at the theater and the attempts of the KGB operatives to befriend him and Savannah. Jack reasoned it wasn't a coincidence that Felix and Volodya were suddenly interested in him *now*, shortly after he had started receiving anonymous letters. He had been extensively out and about in East Germany for eight months already and his cover appeared to be holding well thus far. So one of the two was probably related to the letters, and if so, it had to be Volodya: he had been serving at Dresden *rezidentura* since 1985 and he was due to return home soon. As for Felix, it was the first year of his first posting abroad. As such, first, it was highly unlikely that he had access to the Stasi files, and second, he was still too new here to be thinking of anything else besides doing his highflying overseas job well.

Then Jack reported on his meeting with PIPER 2 and SALT and that it appeared that the man had been having a relapse—his wife had complained that he had been drinking all night; he had turned up to their lunch reunion with a hangover and ordered more booze the moment he sat down. When the wife shot off to see a German friend, Jack had taken him to one of the safe houses and tried to talk sense into him. No, he didn't believe it had had any lasting effect on the agent. As such, he recommended that they put operation BROOM together with SALT on hold. At least until he returned to Moscow. Which was going to happen soon: according to the agent, he was being repatriated in mid-November together with the entire tank division from his base at Bernau-bei-Berlin.

When Jack had finished his report, David told him that a reply to the anonymous letters had been sent to the post office box in Potsdam and the station was expecting the author to respond through a channel proposed by the Company. This should take Jack out of the equation, thus minimizing the risk of potential provocation or his exposure. The COS also told Jack that "friends" had confirmed that the hand-copied cards were identical to the index files used by the Stasi. Furthermore, the information on the agent codenamed Paul had also been corroborated—by the man himself: James W. Hall III had just begun serving his 40-year sentence on espionage charges at Fort Leavenworth, Kansas.

After sharing the good news, the COS asked Jack cautiously what he had told the smart-asses from the Directorate of Intel during his debrief at HQ. Apparently, whatever he had told them had now mutated into the Directors' inside joke that hotshots from Operations were coming home with reports of a revolution brewing in East Germany. Jack would have blown up, had David not anticipated it and told him that nobody at their directorate was taking the joke seriously. Jack recounted his conversation with the three analysts, adding grudgingly that next time he'd ask for someone from their division to be present when he talked to the DI folks.

When the COS left, he stayed for another hour at the safe house writing up his report. Then, after a round of bars on Ku'damm and a quick CS run, he dropped by the Zoo Bahnhoff to retrieve the file with addresses of the Volkonsky clan in France. He spent twenty minutes in the public toilet memorizing the names, addresses and phone numbers, which Paul Millard had obtained for him. Jack's plan was to take the coming Friday off and fly to Frankfurt where he would rent a car and drive across the border to Metz. From there he would fly down to Marseille, and then it was just a short drive to Aix-en-Provence where Prince Andrei Volkonsky, a classical music composer, resided—according to Paul's source, alone.

That night Jack couldn't settle down to sleep for a long time: even with all the beers he'd had on Ku'damm, his mind was churning a mile a minute with anticipation. It was long after midnight when he finally caved in, got up and poured himself a triple shot of whiskey. It was the last one for the next three weeks, he told himself. Because he needed to be in top form, collected and in control, to make this work for Eton.

For *them*.

Next morning, when Jack arrived at the office, Terry met him with a wire strip in his hands and a baffled expression on his face. "It's from ADN. Honecker has resigned."

Chapter 72

For the next two days Erich Honecker's resignation and the election of Egon Krenz, the youngest member of the Politburo, as the General Secretary of the Socialist Unity Party were the front, back and center news in all major, and even not so major, newspapers, radio and TV channels. The sentiment was one of breathless hope that Honecker's ousting might eventually lead to dramatic changes in what had been one of the most repressive regimes in the Socialist block.

These hopes were fueled by a parallel, no less dramatic event that took place on the same day in Budapest. There, in the glare of TV lights, broadcasted internationally, the Parliament declared Hungary a republic, thus marking the end of the communist regime and its return to a multi-party democracy. It was a proclamation of Hungary's independence from Moscow and the world took it for what it was.

If the August election of the anti-communist editor Tadeusz Mazowiecki as Prime Minister of Poland had been regarded as the chink in the Warsaw Pact, the events in East Germany and Hungary had brought about the realization that it might be a revolution after all.

The optimism was further fueled by a series of articles published in the next few days in Neues Deutschland, the East German communist party's official newspaper, calling for public debate to solve the country's mounting problems. "All important questions are up for discussion," the newspaper wrote, "including the reasons for the recent flight to the West of thousands of East German citizens... It is time to stop painting things in rosy colors." The articles were followed by East Berlin TV broadcasting the debates between the ruling politicians and the opposition activists who publicly demanded the formers' immediate resignation.

On October 23rd, Jack and Paul drove to Teltow, just outside East Berlin, to cover a meeting of several hundred workers from an electronics plant. During this meeting they witnessed the foundation of the *DDR*'s first independent labor union, named "Reform". After the meeting they barely made it to Leipzig, just in time for the massive pro-democracy rally where the opposition that had been steering the protests christened itself "New Forum".

The march in Leipzig wasn't the only rally that day: hundreds of thousands of protesters joined demonstration and walkouts in Berlin, Dresden, Halle and several other East German cities and towns. Toward the end of the day, in an apparent attempt to pacify the people, the government announced on State television that it was dropping the "Enemy of the State" charges against those who had fled the country via Hungary, Austria and Czechoslovakia.

On October 24th, the Parliament of GDR elected Egon Krenz as the President. For the first time in decades of Communist rule the empty ritual turned dramatic when 26 members of the Parliament voted against the appointment and 26 more abstained.

In his inaugural speech the newly elected President reaffirmed *DDR*'s allegiance to the

Communist cause and issued tough warnings against street demonstrations, saying that continued agitation could cause a "worsening of the situation."

A few hours after the Parliamentary vote, thousands of demonstrators marched through the center of East Berlin, chanting, "Egon Krenz, we are the opposition!" and "Parliament, Parliament, what a terrible thing to do!" Some placards proclaimed, "Egon, your election doesn't count, because the people didn't elect you."

This time Jack made sure he was covering the dramatic events in the company of four other reporters from three Western news agencies. Several units of fully armed police and plain-clothed Stasi stood by, watching, ready for another crackdown.

The orders never came.

On October 25th, the new head of state told a news conference that he would consider letting East Germans travel abroad more freely. However, when asked whether easier travel to the West would make the Berlin Wall obsolete, Krenz responded with a smile that stopped short of his eyes, "The wall has a very different meaning than what is implied in your question, doesn't it?"

Then, pushed for an answer, he made it very clear: the Wall was there to stay.

* * *

In the end Jack hadn't managed to get the long weekend off—both Terry Kellerman and David Rolston turned down his requests and told him he'd better be on top of the events. Which continued unfolding at a head-spinning pace.

On Sunday, Jack placed a call to Aix-en-Provence from the post office on the campus of FU Berlin. An elderly female voice told him in old-fashioned Russian that Andrey Mikhailovich was in Paris and wouldn't be back till Thursday. She refused to give him the phone number in Paris, however, or even the name of the hotel where the prince was staying.

Shit. Thursday was October 26th, only two days away from his meeting with Eton. They were to go over the details of the C-Op and Jack was to drill him on the process, including the days leading up to and after The Crossing. He'd decided for Eton that "after" meant France and had made Eton agree with his choice. And he wasn't ready with this part of the op.

You're useless, Smith! Just like your fa—

No! I'll fix it. It will all be sorted out by the C-Day.

You sure?

Yes. I swear, Eton, we *will* make it! We have to make it... Right?

On Wednesday night, Jack undertook the biggest risk in the whole operation, second only to the crossing itself: he smuggled the fake passport with Eton's picture and supporting documents into East Berlin. He timed it to just before the closing of Checkpoint Charlie for the night. The passport control and customs officers were about to turn down the lights and the border guards were retreating from the cold into the relative warmth of their concrete guard post. He grinned apologetically at Lovely Rita who glared at him and said sternly that he should try to return a little earlier next time. She peeked briefly into the trunk and the back seat of his car and let him through.

On Friday night, he called Andrey Volkonsky again.

A male voice answered in French. It sounded younger than the fifty-five the prince was supposed to be, according to Paul's file. Jack asked in Russian to speak to Andrey Mikhailovich. The man said, "*Bien sûr, un moment*," then Jack heard the muffled sound of him calling out, "*André, ceci est pour toi... Un Russe.*"

A minute later an older voice said into the phone in Russian, "I'm listening."

"Andrey Mikhailovich? Good evening. I'm calling on the account of a relative of yours. From the Soviet Union."

"You mean Peten'ka? What's happened with him?" the Prince asked quickly, sounding worried.

Jack didn't know who Peten'ka was and silently cursed himself for not having done better homework. "No, nothing's happened to him... I think. I actually meant your other relatives. From Moscow... Sergei Alexandrovich's family." He hoped Professor Volkonsky's name was known to the clan in the West—after all, he was an internationally renowned physicist.

There was a pause, then Volkonsky's voice came back, suspicious, "Who are you? You're not Russian."

Jack almost groaned aloud. It was what he was afraid of when he had realized he only had time for a phone call. He could easily persuade the man in person, but on the phone...

"No, I'm not. And I'm not asking for anything, except ten minutes of your time. Please let me explain. Don't hang up, please!"

He must have sounded desperate because after a moment's hesitation Volkonsky agreed to listen to what Jack had to say.

In the end, the prince agreed to help Eton when he came to Marseille. Jack told him that Eton would have some money to live on, until he found something to do, but he would need someone he could turn to for advice, especially in the beginning. He was hoping that once Prince Andrey Volkonsky got to know Eton better, he would be willing to help his young relative with more than just occasional advice, and better yet, without Eton asking. For now, the knowledge that his Eton had someone to turn to in France felt like a mountain taken off Jack's shoulders.

On Saturday, Jack was supposed to spend the whole day in West Berlin with Terry and another colleague from Bonn covering Dick Cheney's first visit to West Germany and West Berlin. He called Terry at quarter to seven in the morning to tell him that he had a nasty bug that had been keeping him on the can all night and that he'd be staying in for a day.

At 9:30 a.m. he was at the station, waiting for Eton's train to arrive at 10:38 a.m. When his friend walked swiftly into the main hall and headed to the toilets, Jack followed him, carefully keeping a distance, watching out for anything or anyone suspicious. In the men's room, catching a moment when there were only two of them at the sinks, Jack sneaked a couple of Mark notes and the scrap of paper with the address into the pocket of Eton's jacket.

"Take a private taxi," he said under his breath and walked out.

It was noon when they got to the safe house on the northernmost edge of Prenzlauer Berg, a gutted apartment on the second floor of a partially ruined building. They barricaded the doorway with the broken wooden door and, after a quick embrace, Jack led Eton inside of what used to be a two-bedroom apartment. In the smallest of the three rooms, its windows sealed and nailed up with cardboard, Jack fiddled with the battery powered storm lamp and it flooded the confined space with warm, sepia light.

They sat down on the threadbare mattress on the floor and stretched out their legs

"How much time do we have?" Jack asked, pulling out a notepad, two pencils, cigarettes, biscuits and a bottle of water from his backpack.

"Three hours. I have to be back by four thirty."

"Okay. I need all your attention and concentration today, Eton. Can you do it?"

"Yes. I can... I am ready, Jack. Don't worry."

"Alright. Let's get started then."

Jack's plan was simple and daring. And because it was so blatantly daring he believed it would work. In short, on November 4th, Saturday, the day when the demobilizing personnel of the Soviet military base at Bernau-bei-Berlin would be given a day in East Berlin to do their final shopping, Eton would slip away and come to the safe house near Jack's place. All the papers, clothes and everything else would be ready for him, and at around midnight he would just walk through the border through Checkpoint Charlie with a foreign passport.

According to the passport and other papers Jack had procured through the cobbler, Eton was a Canadian national, one Lukas Gregory Nielsen, born on May 10th, 1960, an assistant professor of information technology at the University of Western Ontario, currently residing in the city of London, Ontario. Besides the passport and the driver's license, there was a bankcard and a credit card, a hotel voucher and a key to room No. 9 at Hotel Elton in West Berlin, the declaration form of foreign currency importation, all in the name Greg Nielsen, who was supposed to have entered East Berlin through Checkpoint Charlie that morning.

The good news was that Eton wouldn't be crossing the border alone. At 10:30 p.m. the two of them would meet three students from FU Berlin at a bar on Unter den Linden, two Americans and a West German, and at around midnight Eton would follow them through Checkpoint Charlie, with one of the students and Eton acting drunk and wasted.

"In West Berlin, the guys will drop you off at Hotel Elton. There will be an air ticket to Marseille via Paris in the room's safe deposit box. Don't worry," Jack hastened to add, seeing Eton's worried expression, "I'll come to the hotel in the morning. But just in case, alright? The safe's four-digit code is the day and month of your birthday. The real one. There'll also be a suitcase with your clothes. They're all secondhand. Hope you don't mind... If I'm running late, a taxi will be waiting at eleven sharp to take you to the airport. Your flight to Paris is twelve fifty five."

"But you'll come, right?"

"Of course I will. But there always has to be a Plan B, bud. Just in case, okay?" He waited until Eton nodded, then continued, "In Marseille, take a taxi to the address that you'll find with the tickets. It's just a room, but it's near the area where lots of Russians live. The rent is paid for three months. The bankcard will last you for five, six months—it's a loan, Eton! Like we've agreed. You'll pay me back later, alright? Good... Okay, there is also a phone number in the package. It's one of your relatives', Prince Andrey Mikhailovich Volkonsky's. He lives thirty kilometers from Marseille. He knows you will be calling. He'll help you to—"

He never finished the sentence as Eton turned into him abruptly and covered his mouth with a fervent kiss. One of Jack's arms went around Eton's waist, as he cupped the nape of his lover's head gently with his free hand.

Eton heaved a breath. "I love you," he whispered and pressed his lips to Jack's once more. They were wet and salty.

"I love you, too, baby. Love you so much... I'm sorry it has to be this way. But I can't—"

"I know... Thank you, cowboy."

They held one another for a while, absorbing the other's warmth, saving it all up for later. When they had regained their composure, disentangled and sat back against the wall, Eton fired a cigarette and handed it to Jack. He took a few deep puffs and started his instruction on the Plan from the beginning, this time in minute details. Eton took notes of the things he needed to remember by heart. Then Jack made Eton repeat the Plan back to him three times, the last time without the notes.

When he was finally satisfied, Jack leaned back against the wall and let out a heavy sigh. "Now about Plan B."

"What do you mean Plan B? Haven't we covered everything already?"

"No, Eton. You always must have a Plan B, in case Plan A doesn't work out as you want. I mean in case you can't cross over on either November 4th or November 5th. For whatever reason." Jack sighed again and rubbed his face with both hands. "Unfortunately, with all the shit that has been happening these few weeks, I haven't managed to arrange a decent Plan B. So, the fallback plan is a bit, um, crude. And will remain 'work in progress' until it actually happens... In short, you'll stay in the safe house and I'll report to HQ that you've deserted and want to come in. And let them get you out."

Eton squinted at him suspiciously. "You said they don't *exfiltrate* agents unless they produced something very... big. I haven't done much yet. Why would they do it?"

"They will. I promise."

"And you are not going to tell me why."

"You don't need to know about it. You really don't. Trust me." And Jack swore to himself that his lover would never learn that he resorted to blackmailing his mentor to get him out and set him free.

Eton gazed at him thoughtfully. "Will I see you after... after *that*?"

Why had he kidded himself that Eton wouldn't ask this question? He hated this fallback plan too, but under the circumstances and the time pressure, he hadn't been able to come up with a better option.

He reached for Eton's hand and interlaced their fingers. "I promise I'll do everything in my power to find you, Eton. But it might not be soon... If we have to resort to Plan B, they'll put both of us through a rigorous debriefing, including polygraph tests... It means that they'll find out about us. And will most probably put you under, um, the special protection program." That was what Joe Cohen would do to make sure that Jack would never see Eton May Volkonsky again, ever. "It means that they'd give you a new identity and move you to an undisclosed location under a highly classified operation."

"I see."

Eton nodded, his jaw set firmly, and Jack knew that his man would do everything so that they wouldn't have to fall back on Plan B.

They discussed again the details of the plan, of the mode of communication and emergency contact procedure from now on, until it was time for Eton to go back. They stood clenched in a tight embrace for a long while, clinging to each other, unable to let go. It took all the resolve Jack could muster to push Eton's shoulders gently away.

"Time to get going, bud. I'll be waiting for your call on Thursday night. And Friday night as the backup. Eight to nine p.m."

"I will call."

He kissed Jack firmly on the lips, holding Jack's head with both of his hands, then broke the kiss abruptly, spun around and stormed out of the crumbling shell of a room.

On Sunday, the foreign press corps together with most of East Berlin witnessed the first public meeting with the newly formed opposition. Sponsored by East Berlin's major and attended by the city's communist party chief, the meeting eventually developed into an emotive exchange between the people and the communists. Many accused the leaders of misdeeds and excessive privileges; others charged the police with brutality against demonstrators on the 40th anniversary of the GDR. In an unprecedented move, East Berlin Police Chief apologized for the use of force. However, he insisted that police were correct in arresting some of the protesters, who, he said, had resorted to violence. The crowd of no less than twenty thousand jeered and whistled in response, Jack amongst them.

On Monday, another wave of demonstrations swept through East Germany. At least a quarter of a million people marched through Leipzig, calling for more democracy and that the communist leaders be accountable for the refugee crisis. Nearly a hundred thousand gathered in the northern city of Schwerin, holding candles in a silent protest as they carried banners demanding more freedom and urging the legalization of New Forum. Thousands more took to the streets in Karl Marx Stadt, Halle, Magdeburg, Cottbus and Poezneck, demanding civil rights and reforms.

The number of demonstrators countrywide was estimated to be the largest in East Germany since the workers' riots in 1953, when Soviet army tanks were deployed to restore order. This time, however, the protests were peaceful and not hindered by police. And, unprecedentedly, it was covered and reported on from the ground by the official news agency AND, an additional two dozen accredited reporters from Western news agencies.

On Tuesday morning, when Jack returned from Leipzig, there was a message from Savannah on his answering machine. She sounded dismayed and a little whiney.

"Hi, Jack, it's me. I'm calling to tell you that I'm not coming to East Berlin tomorrow.

These friggin' bureaucrats haven't processed my dip visa yet and refuse to give me a tourist visa in the meantime. And can you imagine? These id… they only told me about it this friggin' morning! I can't believe it, Jack. I am *so* disappointed! I've been looking forward to this so much. I've bought everything for our apartment. And now this. This is so frustrating!" A heave and a sniff, then she pulled herself together. "But I hope this delay is only for a couple of weeks. They said two to three weeks. Then we'll finally be together. Like we always wanted! Isn't it awesome, Jackie? I'm so excited! Be ready, sugar-babe, here I come!" She giggled, breathless. "Alright. So I just wanted to let you know. Even though it's costin' me almost five bucks a minute, I thought I'd give you a call, darlin'. You see? Everything's for you, Jackie! Alright. That's enough for today. I'll let you know in a few days when I'm coming. Bye, Jack. Love you!"

"Oh, no! Shit!" Jack exclaimed for the benefit of the Stasi, hoping his very pleased grin didn't percolate into his voice.

Things seemed to be falling into place neatly and it made Jack feel more confident that he and Eton would pull through just fine.

At midnight of the following day, the border with Czechoslovakia was suddenly reopened. By morning, thousands of East Germans were on the road again, heading for Prague. Paul called around noon to ask Jack if he wanted to join him and Colin again—they were leaving in two hours, heading to Geising, a little town on the border with Czechoslovakia, where most of the action was.

A two and a half hour drive to the border, maximum three. They would be there by five, have a few good stories by midnight, back in Berlin in the morning at the latest. He'd make it back for Eton's call in the evening. And he'd catch up on his sleep later, when Eton reached France safely.

Having passed Dresden, they found themselves in an exodus of busses, *Trabants*, *Wartburgs* and an occasional MZ motorcycle with a sidecar, all heading in the direction of the border. By midnight, the three of them had chronicled stories to last them for the next few issues of their newspapers and bulletins.

But it wasn't until after two o'clock on Thursday afternoon that Jack rolled into the AP's East Berlin office, tired, hungry and all wound up. He filed a couple of news blurbs and a short feature story, wolfed down a pack of biscuits, washing it down with a mug of instant coffee, and rushed home to change.

There was a message on his answering machine.

"Hello, Jack. This is Ben Stone, weekend editor from the Bonn office. Terry said you may have a good feature story cooking. I am in West Berlin and thought it would be good to catch up. How about drinks at six tonight? I'm staying at Am Zoo hotel."

Only it wasn't AP's weekend editor from Bonn but an emergency summons from David Rolston: Jack was to come to the Station's safe house in West Berlin, the one near Zoo Bahnhoff, tomorrow at 9:00 p.m.

Tomorrow, Friday. C-Day minus one. It meant that Eton *must* call today.

Please, Eton! Please!! I'm begging you! Please, call!

Jack waited in the little, stuffy bar in Prenzlauer Berg, two blocks away from the Wall, until long after the 9:00 p.m. cutoff time they had agreed.

Eton never called.

On Friday, he was at the bar half an hour early, both weary and restless, barely managing to keep his anxiousness from showing. He forced himself to swallow down a sausage and sauerkraut with a glass of beer—all the alcohol he could allow himself to drink before the C-Day.

At twenty to nine, Kurt the bartender waved him into the back room. "Boy, you owe me, Johann." He winked at Jack and closed the door behind him.

"Hello?"

"It's me."

"Yes. What happened? Why didn't you call yesterday?"

There was a deep sigh at the other end. "I couldn't get out... Listen, I... I'm sorry, but I can't come to Berlin tomorrow."

Chapter 73

Jack nearly dropped the receiver. "*What*?! No, En! Why??"

God, no! Please, not this!

"I'm really sorry... They've canceled all leave and trips to Berlin. Till the *departure* on Friday. There's something going on there. Something big."

"What time does the train leave?"

"Six thirty in the morning. We will be brought to the station by busses one hour before the departure."

Shit!... SHIT!!!

"En, you *must*—"

"Listen, um, *my wife* is coming to Berlin on Tuesday and is planning to go back with me."

Jack's stomach dropped like a brick. "Why?" he asked low and menacing.

No, she can't know it! Tell me you haven't told her, Eton!!

"It's *not* what you're thinking. I haven't told her. She doesn't know... She's coming for the debut of a film."

"A film? What are you talking about?"

"Remember, she told us about the film her friend Matthias is playing in? Called 'Coming Out'. They premier it on Thursday. It's about men who—"

"I know what 'coming out' means. But traveling so far only for *that*? And staying only for three days? You sure there's nothing else?"

The sharp exhale on the other side sounded exasperated this time. "Listen. It was *you* who told me that she loved Victor, remember?... Do you remember?"

"Yes, I remember."

"I didn't understand it back then. But later I understood. She has never stopped blaming herself for his death. She thinks she didn't do enough to help him... So this film, um, it's important to her."

Jack closed his eyes. God, these Russians were simply too much for him! The twentieth century was nearing the end, for Christ's sake, yet they persisted in living in the age of Turgenev, Lermontov and Dostoyevsky.

But then, wasn't it precisely *this*—this incredibly romantic and old-fashioned essence—that made his Eton the most special man he'd ever met?

"Alright. I see. It may even turn out to be a godsend. So maybe you can ask her—"

"Yes. I'll tell her I want to see the film. She'll be happy to arrange it."

"Okay, great. In that case, the whole *thing* is reset to... Thursday. Everything we talked about remains *exactly* the same. Including the calls two and one day before. Do you understand?"

"Yes. Fully."

"Good. And En, please wait for me once you get *there*. Things are going mad in this place and I'm running around like a headless chicken, trying to do ten jobs at the same time. So I might be, just might be, running late, okay? Please wait for me. I'll be there no matter what. You hear me?"

"Yes. I'll wait."

"Okay. Then we're all set." Jack allowed himself a soft smile that he hoped Eton could hear in his voice. "I'll see you, friend."

"*Do vstrechi, drug.*" And he hung up.

Till we meet, friend.

As soon as he crossed over to West Berlin, Jack called a special number and his call was redirected to the safe house. David Rolston was already there and impatient. Jack told him that he would be running late as he still needed to do his CS run. The COS said grudgingly, "Hurry up," and rang off.

It was after 10:00 p.m. when Jack got to the safe house. Rolston was talking on the phone in the study room and gestured for Jack to stay out and close the door. He came out of the study fifteen minutes later, not bothering to hide his annoyance.

It turned out the Station had reached an agreement with the author of the two letters dropped in Jack's car and as a result two ops had been scheduled—one was a cash drop-off and the other a collection.

Jack stared at the COS, struggling to hold back his incredulity. The Company didn't usually pay unknown sources whose identity together with the authenticity of the information hadn't been established. So how in the hell had the COS managed to get *this* approved?

Apparently, Rolston noticed Jack's surprise. He explained that the crux of the whole operation was the first part when the team would set up cameras around the drop-off site to record the identity of the cash collector. Who would be or at least would lead them to the author of the letters, and eventually to the source of the files. With the author's identity determined, the Station would be able to contact him directly and pitch him in the next op. That was the original plan which Savannah Jones had been assigned to as the lead case officer. However, the East Germans had delayed her diplomatic visa at the last moment, so now Rolston had to re-staff the op. The reason why Jack was summoned.

"When are the ops?" Jack asked all business like, fighting the urge to hold back his breath.

"The drop-off is on November seventh and the collection is on the ninth."

"In four days?" He swallowed, sweat breaking under his arms and his collar. "Isn't it too short a notice to re-staff an op?" he asked, fully aware that it wasn't like the Station had a choice.

"It is. That's why you're going to Frankfurt for a two-day op briefing tomorrow."

No! Not possible. He needed to fix the new C-Day protocol tomorrow. Everything had to be in place by November 7th when Eton would make his confirmation call.

"Can I go on Sunday? There's something big brewing in East Berlin tomorrow and I need to be there... It's my job too, David. History is in the making and I *must* be there. I'll be all set by Monday noon. You know me, David. I can do it."

Rolston watched him closely for a few moments, thoughtful, then nodded. "Alright. First flight to Frankfurt on Sunday. You can pick up your ticket at the airport three hours before the flight. In the name of Phillips... So, history in the making, you say?" Rolston smirked. "Do they say if they'll be taking down the Wall one of these days, too?"

"Who knows, David? With these mind-boggling events and changes spiraling out of control, the way I see it, it's totally possible." Jack didn't really think it was possible, at least not in the immediate future, but he wasn't prepared to discuss politics with the COS tonight.

"Right... Well, book me a front row seat while you're at it." David's tone was mocking, but not unkind.

Jack departed the safe house a few minutes later, leaving the COS to his next conference call with HQ.

The "big thing" the next day was a massive march in East Berlin organized by prominent artists and intellectuals officially sanctioned by Egon Krenz's new regime. It was the largest of all public demonstrations thus far, drawing nearly a million people to the streets of East Berlin and culminating with a series of speeches made by the party leaders as well as the opposition on Alexanderplatz. The crowd was surprisingly subdued despite Ergon Krenz's brow-raising announcement the previous day that he was retiring five older members of the Politburo and planning to implement political and economic reforms.

But what had blown Jack away was the appearance on the improvised stage of Marcus Wolf, the notorious Stasi's chief for more than 30 years before his retirement two years ago. And what did he say in his little speech? That over-reliance on security services should be done away with because it creates fear among the people.

Un-fucking-believable! If *that* wasn't a revolution, Jack didn't know what else was.

By the time Jack flew out to Frankfurt on Sunday, the new set of papers for Eton had been ordered, including the entry stamp in the passport, foreign currency exchange form, the hotel slip, all with the new crossing date stamped. The whole set was expected to be ready for collection by noon November 8th. The three students from FU Berlin—Stephen, Matt and Wolfgang—had been notified of the date change and were ready for what they considered a little smuggling job.

Everything seemed to be in order. The only thing left that Jack couldn't change was the collection operation on November 9th. His only hope was that it would be over by 8:00 p.m., and by 9:30 p.m. the latest he would be at the safe house where Eton would be waiting for him. He prayed that the op wouldn't be in Dresden... Nah, if it was indeed Volodya's deeds, he couldn't be so stupid as to pull his trick near the place he resided. It would probably be in East Berlin. Or in the worst case in Potsdam, which foreigners frequented... Yeah, Potsdam was fine. He could do Potsdam. He'd be back to East Berlin in under an hour. Okay, one hour and a half with a small CS run. They would make it for the meeting with Steven and his friends at 10:30 p.m. and then...

The op briefing with Rolston and two case officers from Bonn Station in a little cottage in the suburbs of Frankfurt took twenty six hours, including several coffee breaks and a longer one for sleep. Jack loathed every minute of it. Especially because he had to censor himself every second of those twenty six hours to prevent the disappointment and anxiety he felt from seeping out.

The op on November 7th was fine. He was to do a drop-off of a plastic bag with ten grand at 1400 on the train heading to Rostok, then alight at Wittstock and return to Berlin at around 1800. It was the collection op on November 9th at 1900 in Potsdam that he had a massive problem with. It would take up so much time, with two-hour counter surveillance runs before and after the collection. Which by the way was just a fucking decoy. The real collection would be taking place in Oranienburg. Even more infuriating, he'd have to return to East Berlin through the north end of the city, via Oranienburg itself. So he'd get to the safe house long after 10 p.m. if he did a proper CS routine before approaching it, as he should. It meant that he and Eton would have no time left for any errors or delays. If that wasn't a pain in the ass, he also needed to brief Eton, and Steve and his friends, about his time constrains. Except he couldn't. Because Eton wouldn't be able to come to East Berlin before the C-Day and… they were simply running out of fucking time, goddamn it!

He tried not to dwell on what would happen to him afterwards. The fact that his bosses had given him an easily identifiable role to play in these all-hands-on-board operation meant that they had decided to pierce his cover. So Jack would probably be repatriated shortly after. Or if the Company decided to let him stay on in East Berlin without a diplomatic cover, it was unlikely that they'd expect him to do recruitment and humint collection. Either way, it didn't really matter. The most important thing was that Eton would be on the other side by then and safe. Jack could live with whatever else that came his way.

As soon as he landed at Tegel Airport on Monday afternoon, Jack took a taxi and headed straight to the student village in Schlachtensee where Steven and Matt lived. He waited for them till 7:00 p.m., and in the end managed to brief them about the changes and possible delays. Now he only had to find a way to brief Eton about the same. Maybe he would mention it to him briefly on the phone, and would leave detailed written instructions in the package at the safe house…

Yeah, that's what he'd do.

He went to bed exhausted but content with himself. Confident again that they would pull it off.

The next day, while Jack and the entire East Berlin Station plus two case officers from Bonn were running the drop-off op, the East German government suffered another major setback: all forty-four members of the cabinet of ministers resigned.

The news spread like wildfire, followed by mounting rumors that at least eight Politburo members were to be retired in a day or two. So by the time Jack took his usual place at the bar preparing to wait for Eton's call, everybody around him was talking about the looming end of the communist regime and that in a year or two East Germany would be a different country.

Eton called shortly after eight and Kurt the bartender gave Jack the same wink and boy-you-owe-me line.

"*Allo*, it's me."

"Hey. How are you doing? Are we good for Thursday?"

"I think so. I've talked to, um, *my wife* this morning. She's here, making arrangements for me to come, uh, to see her. I should be there... perhaps by noon."

"This is great news! Listen, friend, there's a bit of a complication and I might be running late. But nothing to worry about, alright? Just wait for me *there*. I'll be there as soon as I can. Okay?"

"Yes... Anything the matter?" Eton sounded concerned.

Not good.

"No. Everything's fine. It's just that I might be delayed by work. That's all. Don't worry, alright?"

"Alright. You want the phone number where, um, my wife is staying?"

"Same place as last time? Or the previous time?"

"No. She's staying with her... local *friend*."

"Right. I'll get the number. Don't worry... So, it's Thursday then, right?"

"Yes. Thursday."

"Good. I'll be there, friend. No matter what."

"Alright. I'll see you."

Jack obtained Matthias Hoffman's phone number without much hassle and called it in the morning.

"Hallo."

"Good morning. I'm a friend of Lara's. Can I talk to her please?"

There was a pause, then the German asked acidly, "Is this Jack?"

"Yes, it is. Sorry for calling your home. But I need to talk to Lara, please."

"How did you get my number?"

"Lara's husband gave it to me... Can I talk to her?"

Matthias sighed, then Jack heard him calling out, "Lara, this is for you. Your American *friend* Jack."

Lara came on the line in under a minute, breathless, "Jack, *daragusha*! *Privet*! So good that you're calling. I need to talk to you. Can we meet for lunch?"

Jack opened his mouth to answer when he heard Matthias' voice, "Lara, we're having lunch with Gunter and Frank today."

"So what?" she countered, away from the phone. "He can join us, can't he? He can write a great article about your film for Western newspapers. Don't you want it?"

"Lara," Jack called. "I'm sorry, I can't do lunch today. How about dinner?"

"Dinner? Ah, no, I can't. I'm attending a farewell dinner tonight, at the consulate's compound... Wait a minute, but you know him. Volodya, remember? You met him a couple of times."

"Of course I know him. Is he leaving? When?"

"Tomorrow morning. He's driving his car home. But his wife with their two girls are leaving on the same train with us on Friday morning."

Fuck me!

"Last time we met him he didn't say anything about returning home. It seems everybody's leaving," Jack added grudgingly.

"Da, there're so many changes everywhere, my head is spinning. *Everything's* changing, Jack, and so fast! Isn't it wonderful? So, do you want to come to Volodya's farewell dinner tonight? I can call and tell him you're coming."

"No, thank you, sweetie. I don't want to impose. Besides, not sure if it's a good idea for me to show in the Soviet consulate's compound."

"*Ladno*, alright. How about lunch tomorrow? Eton should be here by noon I think. I can't do dinner," she added quickly. "We're going to attend the big release of Matthias' movie. It's about life and love of homosexuals, you know. It's called Coming Out."

"I've heard about it," Jack said noncommittally.

"Do you want to join us? Eton is going, too," she added cautiously.

Yes, she knows.

"I'm sorry, but I'll be tied up in the evening. It's a shame. I would have loved to join you... So, I'll see you all at the train station then? Departure is at six thirty, right?"

He could do six thirty before shooting to West Berlin to see Eton off. That was the least he could do for her before she leaves, a token of appreciation for taking care of his Eton.

"Yes, it's six thirty. Too bad we can't meet before the departure. God knows when we'll see each other again, Jack. So please do come to the station, *kharasho*?"

"I will, Lara. I promise."

"Alright. I have to go now. *Poka, daragusha*." She hung up without waiting for his goodbye.

As soon as he was off the phone with Lara, Jack called a special number and placed an urgent request for a meeting with David Rolston in West Berlin that night. He had no illusions that his info about Volodya—that a) he was in East Berlin, and b) he was leaving home the next morning—would change anything in the collection op. Jack knew that the COS and all viewed his insistent suggestions that the KGB operative from Dresden was the mastermind behind the letters as pure speculation. But he thought he should warn Rolston anyway and let the COS deduce for himself that there was a tiny possibility that they had been duped out of ten grand.

When Jack finished, Rolston was thoughtful for a few moments, then shook his head.

"I appreciate the info, of course. But his presence in East Berlin is no proof he's the author. Or the source."

"I know. But when I was at HQ last time, I filed a request to cross check with the *friends'* source if he had been in Dresden on the days the letters were dropped in my car. Do you know if we've heard back on this?"

"No, I don't. But even if we did, it still doesn't mean anything. Could be just coincidence."

"All three times?"

"We don't know about three times, do we? Jack, let's stop speculating about this Volodya from Dresden. Otherwise I'll think you have a fixation with the man."

"You're right. Let's drop it." Jack nodded, trying to sound agreeable and enthused. "Do we have any results from the drop-off yet?"

"Not yet. The films are still being processed."

Rolston's tone was a bit too forced and Jack figured they probably hadn't got any decent results. Which in turn probably meant that the cash had been wasted, just as Jack had speculated.

Unless he was totally wrong, of course, and they would hit the jackpot with the collection op. This was no doubt what the COS was hoping for. Before parting, he told Jack that he could call him at the safe house tomorrow, on the way back home from the op, and he would let Jack know if he was wrong. Jack said he'd be happy if he had been wrong and left.

He hung out on Ku'damm until late and returned to East Berlin just before the closing of the checkpoint. Hidden in the secret compartment in the trunk of his car were the newly stamped documents for Eton.

Chapter 74

At 1600 the next day Jack embarked on his decoy op, starting with an elaborate counter surveillance run in his car. By the time he reached the southern outskirts of Potsdam, he'd had a beer and three coffees with local patrons at two different cafeterias, jotted down a few pages of content for a feature story, and dropped by Sanssouci Park just before it closed down for the day. He made a few loops around the center of the town, before heading towards Templiner See where he was supposed to stop, get out of his car and loiter for a few minutes on the forest road. And for the entire duration, Jack had been shadowed by a team of three men and a woman in two cars: first a pale yellow *Trabant* had latched on his tail the moment he left Berlin, then halfway to Potsdam he had picked up a dark blue *Wartburg*, then they had rotated, covering him back and front, till it was time for him to return to Berlin.

It was twenty past eight when Jack was nearing the crossroad where according to his plan he was expected to turn left, make a stop in Oranienburg and call David Rolston who had been running both ops from West Berlin. The road ahead curved south east, then south to Pankow and East Berlin. There was something going on again: more cars were on the road than was customary for this time of the day or year, all of them coming from the direction of Oranienburg and heading toward the capital.

Jack took the left turn and sped up against the traffic flow into Oranienburg, trying to lose the *Wartburg* that had been shadowing him for the last thirty minutes. At the edge of the city, he saw a phone booth on the corner of an old apartment building and stopped the car a few dozen meters from it. The Warburg parked a street away.

Once inside the phone booth, he quickly dialed a special number in East Berlin and was redirected to the safe house on the other side of the Wall. He waited for almost a minute before hanging up.

Shit, what was going on? It had to be an emergency for the COS to leave the command post before the ops schedule expired. Or maybe they'd finished early, and all gone home?

He glanced at his watch. 8:38 p.m. An hour thirty-five minutes after the collection. Very unlikely, if it had been a hit... *If* it had been a hit. He doubted it.

But if it had been a miss, then obviously there was little else the team could do but close down and go home. If that was the case, he had to cross over to West Berlin to write up his report before midnight.

Damn it!

... Well, unless something extraordinary happened now that he could use as an excuse.

A group of five young people hustled out of the apartment block across the street and hurried to the solitary *Trabant* parked under the nearest street lamp. The two girls were squealing with excitement; the guys could barely contain their own.

"Hey, friends, what's going on?" Jack called out to them. "Where's everybody going so late? The road is jammed out there."

The young people stopped and stared at him as if he was an alien. "You don't know yet, friend?" one of the young men exclaimed and let out a nervous laugh. "They've just announced on TV that a free travel regime to the West is effective as of now. We're going to Bornholmerstrasse to check it out. Do you want to come with us?" Without waiting for an answer, they piled into the tiny car and shot off in the direction of the highway.

Jack gaped after the car until it disappeared behind the turn. What was this, a joke? But then all those cars he'd seen in the last twenty minutes, all heading in the same direction...

I'll be damned!

He dashed to his car, revved the engine and lurched after the *Trabant*.

As soon as he steered out into the main road, Jack turned on the radio. He tuned into RIAS, a West Berlin based radio station run by a group of Americans.

The agitated voice of one of the regular news anchors filled the close confines of the car. "... in essence means that the Wall that kept Germans apart for 28 years doesn't mean anything anymore. The spokesman of the communist party of East Germany said that anyone who wants to leave the country and go *anywhere* in the world at *any* time is free do so. Effective *immediately*! And anyone who wants to leave East Germany and travel to the West, but then return, would need a visa. But visas will be issued expediently at the police stations around the country."

Jack's brain short-circuited for a moment, and all he could think of was "I'll be damned! I'll be damned!" Then he accelerated and started overtaking the swelling flow of less spry local vehicles all heading in the direction of the city.

What under normal circumstances would be a twenty-minute drive took Jack all fifty, so by the time he reached the vicinity of the bridge on Bornholmerstrasse it was just before nine thirty. The area near the border crossing was swarming with people and cars, all swelling onto the bridge and against the barrier separating them from the other side of Berlin. He parked at the curb, watched the stream of people and cars passing by for a few minutes, then climbed in the car and started maneuvering out of the flow.

He was running late. And the blue *Wartburg* was still on his tail.

Jack had planned to return to his apartment after the op, wait until his minders decided that he was done for the day and left him alone, then to sneak out and take back streets to the safe house. However, with these astonishing events unfolding, there was no way in hell the Stasi would believe that he'd decided to go home to sleep.

He left his car on a side street a block away from Bornholmerstrasse and dived into the mushrooming crowd. He lost his shadow in ten minutes. However, even when he couldn't see his minder, the long-haired man in a blue bomber jacket, any more he couldn't risk heading straight to the safe house. So by the time he finally got there, it was quarter to eleven. He was truly and inexcusably late. And worst of all, he had no way of contacting either Stephen at the bar because he hadn't had enough time to set the meeting up properly, or Eton who was waiting for him at the safe house.

Jack rushed up the stairs, the white glow of his pen light just enough for him not to trip on the broken steps. Once inside the apartment, he quickly locked the door and whirled around, pointing his tiny beam into the dark.

"Eton!"

No answer, only the deeply muted, distant sound of activities somewhere out there.

He pointed the light to the right. The halogen storm lamp he had left for Eton sat by the door, but had obviously been moved. After a minute of roaming through all dilapidated chambers, Jack finally accepted with growing dread that Eton wasn't there.

He scurried to the bathroom.

The smells of dust and decay was laced very faintly with that of urine. He pushed away the broken ceramic wash basin, slid aside the fake brick section of the wall and directed the light beam into the hollow space the size of a small cabinet.

All the things he had prepared for Eton were still inside: backpack, clothes and shoes of American make, a clear plastic bag with receipts from restaurants, U-Bahn tickets, the foreign currency declaration form, a notebook, a pen, a pack of Marlboros and a Zippo lighter. A worn leather wallet with money inside. And the passport.

Everything was still there. But that wasn't all.

On top of the pile lay a six by nine inch parcel wrapped in an old, crumpled copy of Neues Deutschland held together by an oversized elastic band.

Jack went cold.

No, you didn't, Eton, you stubborn shithead! I told you, didn't I?!

He opened the package with shaking hands, holding the pen light in his mouth.

Inside was a book with its cover ripped off. The text in Russian on the front page read, "Ministry of Defense of the USSR. Strictly for service use. Copy number 817. Combat Machine S-300SP. Technical description and instruction for exploitation. Part II. Combat ammunition type 5V55R (nuclear)."

Jesus Christ, Eton! How can you be so fucking reckless?! What if you got caught? What would I do, huh? What would I do without you, you foolish, careless sonovabitch?!

He noticed the edge of a scrap of paper sticking out from between the pages and opened the book. It was a note scribbled in Eton's handwriting on a page torn out of the notebook: "I owe you DM300. EMV."

Jack quickly opened the wallet. The 250 Deutsche Mark and 50 Marks in banknotes of various denominations and loose change were gone.

But not the passport.

So, where is he gone now, without the passport? What will he do?... Oh, God, Eton, what have you done? You can't go back now... I'm so fucking sorry, baby, I've screwed up again. But please, please, please don't give up on me!

Hold your shit together, Smith! Think! Think, goddamn it!!

Right. So.

He had given Eton the address of Heifischer bar on Unter den Linden and Stephen's name. Stephen and his friends were supposed to meet him and Eton at the bar between 9:30 p.m. and 10:30 p.m. But the crossing wasn't supposed to happen till nearly midnight. So they might all be at the bar, waiting for him to show up.

The bar was two and a half miles from the safe house. With all the madness he'd seen on the streets coming here, Jack didn't think he'd be able to persuade someone to drive him in the direction opposite to the Wall. So flagging down a taxi or a private car wasn't an option. Sprinting to the bar would take him less than twenty minutes. But then it wasn't a good idea if you wanted to attract no attention whatsoever. A much safer option would be to return to his place and get the bicycle he'd left chained under the staircase. Jack had figured out soon after his arrival in East Berlin that cycling was a great way to lose a tail, as the Stasi didn't use bicycles, and he'd used this trick a few times since.

The rules dictated that Jack was to take the intel material down to the concealed basement and put it in the safe. But he didn't have time for that shit. He would return the next day, when Eton was safely on his way to France, and would do it then. *And* would figure out how to report the acquisition of the material to his bosses, too. Tomorrow, not now.

He took the passport and hid it in the secret compartment of his backpack. He knew it was reckless to say the least to run around town with a passport with Eton's picture on him, but Jack had no other option—he *had* to get the passport to Eton by any means. He hastily covered up the secret space with the fake fragment of the wall, rushed out of the apartment and down the stairs. At the entryway, he watched the street for only a few minutes before slipping out and walking swiftly to his apartment building.

Inside the hallway, as Jack was hurrying along the corridor to his bicycle under the staircase, he passed the rows of metal mailboxes on the walls. His was the last on the right. Despite the dim light, he thought he caught a glimpse of something peeking through the round holes right under the slit through which newspapers and letters were dropped in.

Jack jerked to a stop, took a step back.

No, it couldn't be from Eton. He didn't know where Jack lived.

He had already whirled around to dash to the bicycle, when a thought made him halt again, then walk back, his stomach hollow. He extracted the key chain and cautiously opened the moss-green mailbox.

Inside the box was a yellow envelope. A smaller one this time and unaddressed.

Oh, for Christ's sake, not again! Not now!!

Jack stared at the letter, his expression fierce, as if trying to will it to disappear. It didn't. And he couldn't just leave it in there without knowing what was inside. God only knew who could poke into his mailbox and find it.

Ten minutes. Go!

He stuffed the letter into the inside pocket of his jacket and dashed up the stairs, three steps at a time. Inside the apartment, he chained the door and walked fast into the kitchen. He didn't bother going through his usual routine of making noises like he was preparing the tea, just took the knife and slid the blade under the folded corner of the envelope.

The second, white envelope inside was addressed to Ms. Savannah Jones.

Fuck me!

Jack opened it without the slightest hesitation. Inside was a postcard with the view of a lake and a few words in block letters on the back: "DR. MEINRAD WAGNER. XV/5".

He faltered for a second, then slid the postcard back into the white envelope, stuffed it in the inner pocket of his jacket. It was just a name and whatever the author intended to convey to the recipient was not obvious to those who didn't know the whole background. He should be fine carrying it to the safe house. Later.

Unless it was a trap by the Stasi.

Jack didn't think it was. By now he was pretty certain that the author of the letters was Volodya from Dresden. Who had a little crush on Savannah. And who had apparently left East Germany this morning with the Company's ten grand in his pocket.

He was in the courtyard, mounting the bicycle, when it suddenly dawned on him. The title "DR." before the name wasn't "Doctor" at all. It was Dresden. And the letters X and V weren't letters, they were Latin number 15.

Meinrad Wagner from Department XV, Science and Technology, HVA, Section 5, Dresden. The source of Volodya's materials from the Stasi's agents files.

He had promised the "source of the intel" in his letters, not the intel itself, hadn't he? So, *this* was the source.

Holy shit! What now?

If he got caught with this shit on him, the three of them—the poor bastard Wagner, Savannah and Jack himself—would probably be done for. He should have burned the damn postcard while he was in the apartment. Now, it was... 11:24 p.m. and he *really* must get going, dammit!!

The street Jack could see through the gateway was uncharacteristically busy—it was just a narrow side street that was usually quiet even during the day. Now there were people and cars passing by, all in a big hurry.

Fuck it all, he couldn't go back! He'd take the risk.

Jack pushed off, driving hard on the pedals.

It took him under fifteen minutes to get to Heifischer by side streets and sometimes cutting through the stream of Trabies, and *Wartburgs*, all heading in the direction of city center. But by the time he walked through it door, it was *way* past eleven thirty when Eton and the students were supposed to start moving to Checkpoint Charlie. The bar crowd was thinning out, which was typical for this place where foreigners usually milled around at the end of their day visit to East Berlin.

Jack hastened to the bar where two waitresses were chatting with the bartender. Jack knew the younger one, Hanna, from his earlier visits here.

She beamed at him. "Hallo, Johann. You're late today. Have you been out there covering this incredible news?" She sounded breathless.

"Hallo, Hanna. It's a mad house out there." He hoped he wouldn't be fired by AP for missing the historical events transpiring out there.

"Have you been to any of the checkpoints yet?" the other waitress asked, looking no less fascinated.

"Not yet, but I'm going in a minute. I'm actually looking for my friends whom I was supposed to meet here. I'm so late. With all *this* going on."

The girls nodded understandingly.

"Two Americans and a West German. One with black-rimmed glasses; one red-headed. Were they here?"

"Yes. I served them," Hanna said. "The one with glasses said they were waiting for friends. They left about an hour ago."

"Damn!... What about—"

"Are you driving today, Johann?" Hanna was looking at him all impatient and hopeful.

"No, I'm on a bicycle. You can't get anywhere in a car tonight, you know. You need a lift?"

"Yes, Martha and I'll be off in fifteen minutes and we're heading to Ku'damm!" she squealed, unable to contain excitement.

"What do you mean?" Jack gaped at her, his head starting to spin.

Martha chipped in. "My brother has just called from West Berlin. He said they're letting people through Checkpoint Charlie and the crossing on Invalidenstrasse! We're going too, as soon as we close up!"

Holy fucking shit! It's happening!

And what are you still doing here, Smith?

"Can I ask something else, girls? Maybe you saw another friend of mine here: tall, blond man, in mid-twenties. A little moody, perhaps."

Please say yes! Please!!

"Yes, I remember him. He was quite handsome," said Martha and grinned. "American too, wasn't he? He came about an hour ago and sat quietly at the corner table, watching the door. He had only one beer."

"Did he talk to my other friends?"

"No, it didn't look like they knew each other... Did they?"

"I don't believe so... So they didn't leave together then?"

"No. I think the blond man was still here when your three friends left," Hanna butted in.

"What about the blond man? When did he leave?"

"I'm not sure." Martha hesitated. "My brother called, and I was talking to him in the office. When I returned, he was gone."

"What about you, Hanna?"

"No, I didn't see him leave either. But it couldn't have been more than half an hour ago. Sorry, Johann. But I'm sure your friends will forgive you when you explain that you were just doing your job out there. You can't be missing out on all these amazing events, can you?"

Christ, he *was* missing all the action. And it was *he* who would never forgive himself if he had failed the C-Op!

"I hope so, Hanna. Can I make a call in your office, please? It's very urgent."

He called Metzer Eck, recalling that Eton seemed to have preferred using it for their communication. The sensible and coolheaded Barbel was as breathless as the young girls in the bar and wanted to chat. Jack apologized, saying he had to run, and was only calling to ask if there were any messages for him. When Barbel said no, he apologized again and hung up.

On the street, he called from the nearest payphone to two operational numbers to check for messages. Nothing. He jumped on the bicycle and raced back to the safe house, against the swelling flow of cheering people and honking cars, all heading towards Brandenburger Tor.

God help him, but he was behind with every deadline and target there was—he wasn't out there collecting historical, once in a lifetime news; he was late to check in with the COS after his op and was carrying intel material on him; but worst of all, he was so goddamn late that he'd probably screwed it up for Eton.

Eton, who had entrusted him with his life. Eton, who had risked his life to get Jack what he thought Jack needed for his job.

You're so stupid, baby! I don't need all this shit. All I need is for you to be safe. I love you, Eton! Love you so much I'm losing my wits...

The only, lucky-chance relief was that it seemed the border crossing points were miraculously open, at this time of the night, for all to cross. But he hadn't the slightest idea how long this would remain the case. Thus, his most urgent, most imperative job for now was to find Eton and get him over to West Berlin. *Before* the little shithead decided to return to Moscow on the 6:30 a.m. train. And all his other jobs together with his numerous chiefs could go to burning hell!

He got to the safe house in record eight minutes. Everything was exactly the same as he'd left them. Eton hadn't returned.

Jack slipped out and sprinted to the nearest phone booth he knew, a block down the road. He dialed Matthias' number. He didn't think Lara and Matthias were home yet, but there was a chance that Eton might be there.

The answering machine kicked in after three rings. When the recording tone beeped, he said quietly, imploring, "*Lara*, this is Jack. Please pick up if you're there. I need to talk to you... Please!"

No response. Eton wasn't there or he would have answered. Right?

Think, Smith, think! Where could he go with the money but without the passport? Assuming he hasn't gone back to the Soviet consulate's guest house... No, you'll think about *that* scenario later. The last!

Maybe he went to one of the border crossing points where all East Berliners were heading tonight? He couldn't cross over without a passport, either foreign with proper visas or East German—Eton didn't have a civilian passport with him, or even a visa. So, if indeed he'd gone there, it would be just to witness this mind-boggling, breathtaking event unfolding.

The girls at the bar had said that Checkpoint Charlie and the one at Invalidenstrasse were open for crossing; of the two, Checkpoint Charlie was closer.

Jack jumped on his bicycle and raced down the street.

By now, most of the streets leading to the border crossing points on Friedrichstrasse were packed with traffic—cars and occasional minibuses full of people, a few motorbikes and bicycles, and people, tens of thousands of people, all talking and laughing loudly, agitated and overwhelmed. When Jack reached the intersection of Friedrichstrasse and Unter den Linden, he had to stop, to take in the view: eight neat lines of vehicles flooded the entire street in front of him, moving slowly but inevitably like lava in the direction of Brandenburg Gate.

A group of young people almost ran him over, laughing excitedly. "Don't stop, friend!" exclaimed the youth who had bumped into Jack. "Come with us, we're taking Brandenburger Tor!"

"Is it open too?" Jack called after them.

"We'll climb over it if it isn't!" the youth shouted and the group burst in cheers and catcalls.

Jack navigated across the flow of cars, jumped back on this bicycle and rushed down the road. The closer he got to Checkpoint Charlie, the denser was the traffic jam and louder the commotion. Eventually he had to abandon his cycle and continue on foot.

If he thought the crowds he'd seen so far were impressive, that was because he hadn't seen *this* yet: a live, thick wall of people, starting two blocks from the crossing point, heaving, swaying and pushing, and also cheering, laughing and singing with joy. And the most incredible thing was that it was moving, slowly but surely, toward the crossing point.

So it was all true then, what he'd heard—the border was open for all.

Jack squeezed past the mob of people inching through the border crossing. Three out of the four lanes leading to and from the passport and customs control were jam-packed with people—young, elderly, whole families with babies in push-chairs, some with dogs. The border guards looked bewildered and overwhelmed. Yogi Bear was amongst them, concerned and uncharacteristically sulky. They let people through, barely looking at their IDs.

Jack waved his passport with the foreign correspondent tag at Yogi Bear. "AP. Can I come through, please? I'm covering the event on both sides."

The big guard didn't even look at Jack's passport, shrugged at him gawkily and pointed with his head at the other side. "Go."

"Aren't you going to stamp it?" Jack was bummed.

"No time. Go!"

Jack strolled quickly across the notorious divide which was becoming obsolete with every passing second.

On the other side, he was met with an even more jubilant crowd, which cheered and applauded everybody coming through. Strangers patted Jack on the back and shoulders. Someone pressed a bottle of beer into his hand and clinked it with their own. It seemed like all Germany had dispensed with their reserve and crossed the line to come to West Berlin. And it was all becoming one big, uninhibited party: strangers hugged, people kissed as they crossed the line, some people cried in disbelief, while others on both sides of the road offered them bottles of beer and glasses of Champagne.

Jack veered to the right and pushed his way to Café Adler right on the corner overlooking the checkpoint. He needed to make a few phone calls. Normally he would never do such a thing, as everybody knew that half of the patrons in that cafeteria were intel folks — US, British, French, German, Russian and God knew who else. But today was different: nobody seemed to care who was going where or what they were doing.

The place was empty. Jack nodded to the beaming bartender who was standing at the door watching the sea of people and headed straight to the payphone in the corner.

First, he called Hotel Elton and asked if Mr. Greg Nielsen had checked in. He hadn't. Then Jack called Steven, knowing as he was dialing that he couldn't be home, not tonight. Then he tried Metzer Eck and Matthias' number again. Nothing.

Jack thanked the bartender and went out.

On the street, he stood watching the growing revelry for a minute. He saw several reporters he knew, from Reuters, the Washington Post and *Bild*, and some others he didn't — all working the crowd in a frenzy. A CNN's TV van pulled in, the technicians jumped out and began frantically unrolling cables.

And he was the only one who was missing out on all this.

Jack started walking against the swarms of West-Berliners with bottles of Champagne and beer flocking toward the gash in the Wall that Checkpoint Charlie had become. Consciously he knew he had to go back and find Eton, but something had blocked his rational thinking and for a moment all he could think of was that he had lost the momentum, had screwed up, that he was nowhere with anything right now.

Okay, so he needed a timeout, just a tiny little one. To comprehend what was going on. To sort out his priorities, justifications to provide his bosses, both covert and overt, for not doing what he was supposed to do, and explanations of what he had been doing. He needed to —

He was passing the BBC crew shooting the throng of East Berliners coming through the corridor made by their ecstatic Western compatriots. Something caught the attention of the camera man and he pointed his camera somewhere behind Jack. And it seemed like others were looking at it too, whatever it was.

Jack turned around.

The white beam of the TV light washed over two middle-aged men clinched in a tight embrace, one sobbing on the shoulder of the other, oblivious to the eyes of bystanders and the camera on them. Then they pulled apart, gazing into each other's eyes, the same enchanted look on their faces, and then, like in a slow motion sequence of a movie, their lips met in an open-mouthed kiss.

Jack gulped and turned away.

For fuck's sake, what is the matter with you, Smith? You need a timeout, huh? And what about Eton? What about Eton May Volkonsky, the man who loves you and would do anything for you? The man who needs you right fucking now. The man who YOU love, Smith, remember? More than anything in this fucking world, goddamn it!!

Right then, a thought crystalized in his mind that Eton had probably been the only one — the only thing! — that was real, genuine in his, Jack Smith's, world. Everything else was just shadows that he and his Company had been chasing after — the original Nuclear

Winter Theory, the KGB's true or imaginary informants, the Stasi ambiguous recruits and files, the so-called intel material that could be authentic or could just as well be a trap. All that had been just illusions of reality. Chimeras. Even his childhood dream of a ranch in California was just that, a dream which in the end might or might not come true. And then there was Eton...

Jack spun around and strode resolutely toward Checkpoint Charlie, elbowing his way through the dancing and cheering masses. But he had only taken a dozen steps when he stopped abruptly and froze—face to face with an American army policeman. Who was standing on the pavement, observing the exodus from East Berlin, not even trying to hide his amazement.

The GI looked closely at Jack, an expression of cautious alarm on his face. "Are you alright, sir?" When he saw Jack turning to look in the opposite direction from Checkpoint Charlie, grinning like a fool, the GI smiled understandingly. "Decided to head back to PanAm?" He nodded toward the American bar up the street where someone had just turned the sound system up full blast, the speakers facing the street through the open windows.

Jack flashed "The Smile" at the young soldier and puffed out a shuddering exhale, trying to slow down his racing heart. "Hell, yes! Can't miss the party, can I?"

"No need to hurry, sir. Funny, but the band has played that song three times in the past hour already. The singer's pretty darn good, though."

"You bet!" Jack waved at the soldier, elated, and hurried off, battling his way through the multitude of celebrating people and honking cars along Friedrichstrasse.

Up the street, the achingly familiar voice rose over the guitar riff, sending Hotel California's refrain spilling into the jubilant night, soaring up into Berlin's illuminated November sky.